By Michael Korda
QUEENIE
WORLDLY GOODS
CHARMED LIVES
SUCCESS!
POWER!
MALE CHAUVINISM

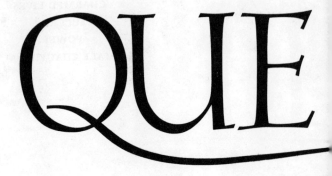

1985
LINDEN PRESS/SIMON & SCHUSTER

ENIE

Michael Korda

PUBLISHED BY LINDEN PRESS / SIMON & SCHUSTER
A DIVISION OF SIMON & SCHUSTER, INC.
SIMON & SCHUSTER BUILDING
ROCKEFELLER CENTER
1230 AVENUE OF THE AMERICAS
NEW YORK, NEW YORK 10020
LINDEN PRESS / SIMON & SCHUSTER AND COLOPHON ARE TRADEMARKS OF
    SIMON & SCHUSTER, INC.
DESIGNED BY EVE METZ
MANUFACTURED IN THE UNITED STATES OF AMERICA

The author is grateful for the permission to reprint lyrics from:
    LET'S DO IT by Cole Porter. © 1928 (Renewed) Warner Bros. Inc. All Rights
Reserved. Used By Permission
    HALF-CASTE WOMAN by Noel Coward. © 1931 (Renewed) Warner Bros. Inc.
All Rights Reserved. Used By Permission.
The author is also indebted to Eden Gray's A Complete Guide to the Tarot, Copyright © 1970 by Eden Gray, for much invaluable background to the history and practice of the Tarot.

10   9   8   7   6   5   4   3   2   1

LIBRARY OF CONGRESS CATALOGING IN PUBLICATION DATA
    KORDA, MICHAEL, DATE
        QUEENIE.

        I. TITLE.
PS3561.O6566Q4   1985   813'.54   84-25115
ISBN: 0-671-46668-2

This novel is a work of fiction. Names, characters, places and incidents are either the product of the author's imagination or are used fictitiously. Any resemblance to actual events or locales or persons, living or dead, is entirely coincidental.

FOR MARGARET, WITH ALL MY LOVE;

AND TO DICK AND JONI—
COLLEAGUES, COMRADES-IN-ARMS, FRIENDS.

"... *Half-caste woman,*
Living a life apart,
Where did your story begin?
Half-caste woman,
Have you a secret heart,
Waiting for someone to win?
Were you born of some queer magic,
In your shimmering gown?
Is there something strange or tragic,
Deep, deep down?"

NOEL COWARD

QUEENIE

THE CROWD OF REPORTERS outside the house in Bel Air parted to let the hearse through. It was white—in life she had always hated black.

An elderly servant, his features set in mourning, opened the wrought-iron gates and pointed toward the rear of the house, out of sight of the television cameras and photographers. He followed the car to the back door and silently led the funeral director up the back stairs.

In front of the bedroom door a young man waited for them. In his dark suit he might have been a funeral director himself, though something about his tanned good looks seemed out of place in the presence of death. "She's ready," he said.

They stepped into the big room. The concealed lighting was soft, almost dim. Billy Sofkin had designed it specially to flatter skin tones. Everything in the room was pink: the walls, the bed, the curtains, even the carpet. Everywhere there were flowers. The bed seemed in fact to be floating in them.

"So many flowers already, Mr. Tyrone?" the funeral director asked in a hushed voice.

"No," the young man said. "Mrs. Tyrone always had this many. Every day."

The funeral director stood at the foot of the bed and stared, awestruck, at the body, his hands clasped in front of him. It was not just that she was a star—he had buried stars before. It was the perfection of the face that astonished him. The eyes that had dazzled men and audiences for decades were closed, but the legendary cheekbones, the full lips, the gleaming black hair seemed untouched by time or illness. She was wearing a pink gown, and smiling.

"My God!" he exclaimed, "she's as beautiful as ever!"

Behind him his three assistants put down the aluminum shipping casket with a thump. "Perhaps you'd prefer not to see the—ah, removal," the funeral director said, but Tyrone showed no signs of leaving.

The funeral director tried to remember what he knew of the Tyrone marriage, though of course the most important thing to know was that everybody always referred to it as "Dawn Avalon's marriage," as if it wasn't worth knowing her husband's name. Years ago, she had staged a comeback with young Tyrone as her leading man, but it hadn't worked, at any rate for him. He remained known chiefly as her husband—the fifth or the sixth—most people found it hard to remember.

The picture did her own reputation no harm, of course. Nothing did. Women went to it to admire a woman who seemed to have beaten nature, fought age to a standstill.

There had been rumors from time to time over the years that the marriage was on the rocks, and the funeral director searched Tyrone's face for signs of grief, or the lack of it. But perhaps that had been the reason for Tyrone's failure as an actor—whatever his emotions were, they did not register on his face.

"Might I suggest—you remove the jewelry?"

Tyrone nodded. He bent over and removed the rings from Dawn's fingers. He had to work hard to pull them over the swollen joints. Toward the end, Dawn had always kept her hands hidden whenever possible. She could conceal much, but not the arthritic swellings in her fingers.

Tyrone's expression did not change. He seemed to be thinking about something. Then he made up his mind, took the rings out of his pocket and, with considerable effort, forced them back on her fingers again.

"She'd want to be buried with them," he explained. He stood up, nodded to the funeral director and walked out of the room with an unhurried calm.

The funeral director stood silently for a moment. He had seen a great deal in his career, but he had never seen a man kiss away a hundred thousand dollars' worth of diamonds. It was almost enough to make you believe in love, he thought. He clapped his hands at his assistants. "Zip 'er up!" he said briskly.

There would have to be a twenty-four-hour guard on the body, he told himself, or the rings would be gone long before she reached Forest Lawn.

"What *did* she die of?" Armand Silk asked.

Billy Sofkin shrugged. "Who knows? One face lift too many, I suppose?" His own had been lifted so many times that it was beginning to resemble a well-preserved crocodile handbag.

"How old was she?"

"Sixty, if she was a day. Maybe more. I remember doing the house for her when she married Charles Corsini."

They were lunching at the Polo Lounge, outdoors in the Loggia, under a flowered awning. Billy had decorated half the houses in Bel Air, Malibu and Cuernavaca, including Dawn Avalon's in all three places.

"She must have been richer than God," Billy said.

"Yes, indeedy! Timmy Tyrone is a lucky young man."

"He was devoted to her. So they *say*. What did she *really* die of, do you think?"

"Style and good taste. She held back old age as long as she could, but when her face finally started to go, she just gave up. You can't imagine Dawn in a wheelchair, or even looking like an old lady, can you? Neither could she. At her last fitting she told me she'd had the best out of life. She didn't see any point in waiting for the worst. The doctors gave her pills, you know. She wouldn't take them."

Armand Silk dressed most of the "old money" in Beverly Hills and Bel Air. He frowned as a young woman walked past in designer blue jeans and a silk blouse open to the navel. "Tacky," he whispered petulantly. Style was dead, along with Dawn Avalon. His clientele was getting so geriatric that he would soon be reduced to designing their funeral dresses.

Billy Sofkin leaned over, close to Silk's ear, his gold-and-lapis slave bracelet jingling. "What do you think they'll bury her in?" he asked.

Silk giggled. He had designed the gown she wore for her last public appearance, when the Academy of Motion Picture Arts and Sciences had awarded her a special Oscar. "If what they used to say about her is true," he whispered, "they should bury her in a sari."

There were so many people at Dawn Avalon's funeral service that it was by numbered invitation only. The Pinkertons turned away dozens of gate-crashers, and the ceremony was taped for the six o'clock news. Lord Beaumont, the greatest English actor of the century, read the eulogy, the majestic Shakespearean voice echoing over the loudspeakers above the dry rustle of the palm trees.

He had played his first great romantic screen role opposite Dawn over forty years ago, when he was a young man. Now, looking so old that he could have played Lear without makeup, he took off his thick reading glasses and stared blindly out at the audience, tears running down his cheeks.

He pushed away the microphone, closed his eyes and began to recite:

"Age cannot wither her, nor custom stale
Her infinite variety; other women cloy
The appetites they feed, but she makes hungry
Where most she satisfies."

"You got to hand it to Dickie," Aaron Diamond, Dawn's lawyer and agent for decades, whispered to his neighbor. "He's a class act."

The pallbearers included George Cukor, Cary Grant, Jimmy Stewart—even Frank Sinatra, who normally never did funerals for anyone. Two dozen white doves were released from cages as the pink flower-covered casket was lowered into the ground. There were so many flowers that Danny Zegrin had an asthma attack and had to be carried to his limousine.

That night Johnny Carson asked for a minute of silence, live on "The Tonight Show," in the number one segment. All over the world obituaries chronicled the life and marriages of Dawn Avalon. Dawn's childhood, as the beautiful daughter of wealthy English parents in the Raj, had been, as Polly Hammer reported in her Hollywood column, "that of a fairy-tale princess."

The next day, her will was read. Her estate was valued at over ten million dollars, not including the houses. She left the bulk of it in trust to the Corsini Foundation, for the acquisition of new works of art.

During her lifetime she had served as the chairperson of the board of directors, and had made it one of the most prestigious small museums in the world. Despite what was recognized by her fellow directors as a complete personal indifference to art, she had been the driving force behind the acquisition of the famous Wildner Caravaggio, outbidding the Metropolitan Museum, and setting a record auction price for an Old Master. When it was brought to her, she burst into tears.

"She was still carrying the torch for Charles Corsini," Aaron Diamond said, after reading the will. "Who can figure out women?"

To Timmy Tyrone, her last husband, she left a trust fund of five hundred thousand dollars and the silver Porsche Turbo she had bought him a year ago for his birthday. There were those who said Timmy turned white with rage when he heard the news.

When Diamond was asked about it, he replied, "She only loved one man all her life."

Then he sighed. He was old, very old, so old that he remembered Dawn Avalon in her early twenties when she first came to Hollywood—and there were people who said he had been old *then*.

"She never brought good luck to the men in her life," he added. "Look what happened to Charles Corsini . . ." He paused. "Why should it be any different for Timmy?"

Dawn also left her Van Gogh still life to the Corsini Foundation. Ever since anybody could remember, it had hung above her fireplace in the Malibu colony house, a small painting of a pair of blue gloves on a table, next to a bowl of flowers.

There was an engraved gold plaque on the frame which read: "To Dawn with love—David Konig, September 1, 1937." The museum curators unscrewed the plaque before putting the painting on exhibition and replaced it with one that simply read: "Bequest of Dawn Avalon."

"Who was Konig?" one of the assistant curators asked.

The older man beside him shrugged. "A producer. He discovered Dawn Avalon. Back in the days of black-and-white."

They looked at the painting. "He must have had good taste. Or a lot of money."

"Both. He was famous for it."

Lord Goldner was in a hurry, as usual. Despite his age and bulk, he was always in a hurry. One of his secretaries held his black overcoat so Goldner could slip his arms into it, another read his schedule aloud to him, a third was putting through a last-minute telephone call. Downstairs, the Rolls waited to take him to Heathrow for the Concorde to New York. An assistant was already in the car with a briefcase full of mail for Goldner to deal with on his way to the airport. Although well over eighty, he sometimes crossed the Atlantic both ways twice a week, with no sign of jet lag.

"Mr. Diamond on two, Lord Goldner," the third secretary said, punching the button on the Speakerphone.

"Aaron, dear boy," Goldner purred into space, as he stuck his arms into the overcoat. His glasses were twisted to one side, his black homburg was askew, he had a cigar clenched between his teeth, a big Montecruz Individuale #1—Goldner owned the plantation. He owned so many things that he had lost count of them. "What can I do for you?"

"It's something *I* can do for you."

"All the better."

"I meant to talk to you after the funeral, but I missed you."

"I left in a hurry. I didn't fancy standing around trading stories about poor Dawn with a crowd of geriatrics who didn't really *know* her. Besides, Danny Zegrin was holding his plane for me."

"I heard you bought a piece of Danny's company. You paid too much, you want my opinion."

Lord Goldner chuckled—an oily, knowing sound that had often been caricatured but never captured exactly. Diamond knew it was all the answer he was going to get. "*Mazel tov*," he said. "That's not why I called. Dawn left you something in her will."

Goldner took the cigar out of his mouth. He looked puzzled.

"She left you her share of some real estate. Some apartment building in London."

Goldner closed his eyes. "Curzon Tower, in Shepherd's Market," he said softly.

"Right. It's valued at five million pounds."

"It's worth a good deal more now. The Arabs all want a convenience flat in the West End. But of course Dawn wasn't thinking of the money. It's a sentimental gesture."

"What's sentimental about a piece of an *apartment* building, for chrissake? It's not even that old. I don't think Dawn ever lived there, did she?"

"No. She never lived there. But owning it meant a lot to her at one time." Goldner's secretaries were pointing at their watches frantically. He ignored them.

"I'll send you the papers. I don't understand these goddamned English deeds."

"Send them, send them, dear boy. My solicitors will take care of the whole thing."

"Will do," Diamond said. "Christ! I can't believe she's dead! She still looked beautiful last time I saw her. I knew Dawn a long, long time."

"Yes," Goldner said, drawing the word out slowly, so that the "s" sounded like a long, sad hiss. "So did I." And then, despite the fact that he was late and due in New York for a luncheon meeting, Lord Goldner sat down in his overcoat, his hat in his pudgy hand, and started to cry.

"Hello? Are you there?" Diamond asked from halfway around the world, but Goldner didn't reply. He was thinking about the day he had met her. She was the most beautiful girl he'd ever seen. Her beauty had never faded; he had come to think of her as immortal.

Now she was dead—and for the first time he felt his age. . . .

In Marrakech the sun was already hot. The roof of the villa was like the secret garden of a sultan, planted with trees, shrubs and flowers. The floor was tiled in the Arabic manner, in brilliant, swirling patterns. In the center of the roof garden was a Moorish fountain. Brightly colored birds flew in and out of the dwarf orange and lemon trees, their wings flashing against the blue sky and the white peaks of the Atlas Mountains.

Stretched out on a mat, a handsome young man was reading the Paris *Herald Tribune*. He was naked, his skin as bronzed and oily as that of a model in a suntan-lotion advertisement. He wore a thick gold bracelet on each wrist and a gold chain around his neck.

"Dominick!" he called. "Have you read the paper?"

At one end of the terraced roof there was a striped silk tent. From beneath its shade a deeper voice replied, "I can't be bothered. It's always two or three days late anyway."

"One has to keep *up*, dear—know what's going *on* in the world."

"I know what's going on in Marrakech. You didn't get home until three in the morning."

"Well, we can't all be expected to go to bed at ten. Some of us like a little bit of *excitement*, now and then."

"Some of us may find ourselves back in London teasing hair, if we're not careful."

"Let's not be bitchy. I didn't tease. I *cut*. Guess who died?"

"I haven't the foggiest. If there's one subject I don't want to hear about, it's death."

"It's your old friend Dawn Avalon, *that's* who! What do you think of that?"

Whatever the older man thought of it, he didn't say immediately. He lay back in his deck chair silently, wrapped head to foot in a bathrobe and towels, his face shaded by a broad straw hat, his eyes hidden by thick dark glasses. Only his hands were uncovered. They were pudgy, soft, dead white, sprinkled with the brown spots of age.

He unwrapped a peppermint lozenge and popped it into his mouth. He sucked on it with a greedy noise for a moment, then he laughed harshly.

"Jesus Christ!" he croaked triumphantly. "I *outlived* the bloody bitch!"

The room which had once been photographed in every architectural journal was now darkened, and it smelled faintly of age and sickness. One wall was made of tinted glass, overlooking the Pacific two hundred feet below. The far wall was of roughly dressed stone, with a fireplace large enough to roast an ox, though it seemed hardly out of proportion here, for the bedroom could easily have contained a normal house. The bed was huge, circular, raised on a carpeted dais. Above it, hanging from the raftered ceiling, was a circular mirror.

The man who had slept in that bed was famous. As a cinematographer, he had worked with some of the most beautiful women in the world—there were stars who would never allow anyone else to photograph them. As a director, he had become wealthy, with a string of box-office hits that were at once elegant and erotic. He had a gift for discovering beautiful young women and making them stars—it was in fact the gift for which he was most famous. They ran to type: each of them had long black hair, dark eyes, high cheekbones, perfect porcelain skin. It was rumored that he slept with all of them and that all of them had been in love with him, but he never married.

Now he slept alone—or rested uneasily, to be more exact—in a hospital bed, pulled close to the huge window so that he could look out to sea. He never spoke. The second stroke had left him paralyzed in all but the most basic bodily functions, and he was watched by a nurse round the clock, though there was seldom anything to do but to change the bottles of his IV unit. Glucose dripped into him from an IV stand at the head of the hospital bed. Urine dripped into a bottle at the foot of the bed. When the first bottle was empty or the second one was full, the nurse changed them, and asked the patient if he was all right, a ritual which never produced a reply, or even a flicker of recognition. He breathed. Sometimes he sighed. That was all.

The nurse sat by his bedside watching television, her arms folded.

Above the television set was a series of digital readings to monitor the old man's pulse and respiration. The set was placed so that he could look at it, for the doctors agreed that visual stimulation could do him no harm, might even keep his brain alive and functioning. So far, there had been no results worth recording. His eyes were open much of the time, but there was no sign that the sound or the picture was reaching his brain. He might have been staring at a blank wall.

The nurse clicked the remote control and switched to a rerun of Dawn Avalon's funeral. She watched it for a few minutes, until something caught her attention—a strange noise, as if something were wrong with the sound. She turned the sound down, but it continued. Then she realized, to her horror, that it was the patient. His mouth was open, his eyes were focused on the screen, his lips were moving. She thought for a moment that he must be dying, but the indicators on the monitors above the television set were all within normal parameters—for a basket case, anyway, she told herself.

She leaned over him, her ear close to his twisted mouth, trying to make sense out of the strangled, gargling noise that in no way resembled human speech. A little saliva ran down from the blue lips. She wiped it off with a Kleenex. It was just her luck that he would die on her shift, she thought.

"What's the matter, Mr. Chambrun?" she asked, not expecting a reply. It was a habit. You talked to patients even when they were vegetables. If you didn't, you stopped thinking of them as human beings, which was easy enough, but unprofessional.

He moved one trembling finger slightly toward the screen and made a harsh, croaking noise.

"I can't understand what you're saying."

The old man's finger shook with rage at his impotence. He closed his eyes as if he were trying to concentrate all his strength on what he wanted to say. "Queenie!" he whispered hoarsely.

"No, Mr. Chambrun. That's Dawn Avalon's funeral. The movie star. She died so soon after getting her Oscar, poor thing. . . ."

The old man opened his eyes; then he began to cry, tears running down his wrinkled cheeks, his breath coming in sobs. The digital readings above the television set flashed ominous warnings.

The nurse switched off the set and turned to prepare a hypodermic syringe, but the old man seemed even more disturbed than ever. Thinking he might be angry because she had turned off the set, she leaned over to calm him.

"It's for your own good, Mr. Chambrun," she said in her most sooth-ing bedside voice. "You were getting too excited watching it."

She plunged the hypodermic into his arm, but before the injection could take effect, he reached up with a clawlike hand and clutched her dress right below the bosom, holding on to the shiny white nylon of her uniform with surprising strength. "Queenie," the old man said clearly, "Queenie, I love you!"

Then he fell silent again as the injection hit his bloodstream. She watched his head fall back on the pillow and straightened his blanket.

She would have to call the doctor, she decided, to report this.

But she couldn't help wondering—who on earth was "Queenie"?

Part One

QUEENIE

CHAPTER 1

"QUEENIE, WHERE ARE YOU?"

The woman's voice echoed impatiently in the still, humid air. At eight in the morning, it was already over one hundred degrees. The cloudless sky was a lifeless gray, as if the heat had leached the color out of it. Outside the bungalow a tonga waited, the driver and his pony motionless despite the flies that buzzed around their eyes.

"*Queenie!*" the woman shouted again, banging the tip of her lace-edged parasol into the worn boards of the veranda for emphasis.

From behind the house the servants took up the cry more shrilly, their voices rising above the clatter of pots and pans in an unruly chorus. A pair of vultures, startled by the noise, rose from a tree across the way with a lazy flap of their dusty wings and soared over the house.

"Drat! Where *is* the child?" the woman said, opening the parasol with a sharp click as if she were trying to hide from the vultures.

"I'm here, Ma."

A girl appeared on the veranda. She wore a short starched white dress with a sash, white stockings to the knees and carried a child's solar topi with a pink ribbon for a band. Her face was a perfect heart-shaped oval, the eyes large and dark, framed in thick lashes; her long hair was gleaming black. She did not seem concerned about being late.

"We'll be late for chapel, you naughty girl. Wherever were you?"

"I didn't hear you, Ma."

The woman shook her head. In her long white dress she was an imposing, almost regal figure. She wore a hat of the kind favored by Queen Mary—a cylindrical velvet toque, decorated with a wisp of ostrich feathers and a veil.

"Put your topi on, child! How many times must I tell you? What does the sun do to the complexion?"

"It darkens it, Ma."

"Quite so, dear. And we don't want to get sunburned, do we?" the woman asked, though her own complexion was dark enough to be safe from any such risk—unlike that of the girl, whose skin was a pale, almost translucent color.

"It's ugly," the girl complained.

"Put it on, Queenie! Only the natives go hatless in the sun."

Glumly the child clapped the topi on her head. It was indeed ugly—and uncomfortable, too—and the pink ribbon merely emphasized its ugliness. At the sight of the ribbon, the woman stiffened in anger.

"What is that, girl?" she asked, waving the parasol in the general direction of the hat.

"A ribbon, Ma."

"Don't be cheeky! It's a *pink* ribbon, you bad girl! How dare you?" She folded the parasol, put it down against the railing, grabbed the topi from the girl's head and tore off the ribbon, holding it in her lace-gloved fingers as if it were soiled.

"Please, Ma, may I have it back?"

"You most certainly may not. How many times have I told you? We don't wear pink."

"I thought it was pretty."

"I'll give you pretty! Pink is vulgar. It's for common little chee-chees."

"But aren't we chee-chees, Ma?" the girl asked.

The woman dropped the ribbon and gave the child a slap on the cheek.

The sound woke the tonga driver, who stared at the woman and her daughter in amazement, then closed his eyes again to shut out the sight. Indians never hit children. It was unthinkable, but then the customs of these people, he told himself, were mysterious. They had no caste; they were neither Muslim nor Hindu. It was even said that they ate both beef *and* pork, thus offending the religious sensibilities of every community—though the old man could hardly bring himself to contemplate such an improbably complex sacrilege.

On the veranda there was a moment of silence; then the child began to cry.

"We are *not* chee-chees," the woman said. "We are Domiciled Europeans! Your grandfather was a pukka sahib, girl, and so was your poor father. I will not have you wearing pink like some cheap bar girl. Where on earth did you get it, Queenie?"

The girl stopped crying. Ma seldom put a hand to her, and it was shock more than pain that had caused the tears. "Uncle Morgan gave it to me," she said.

"*Did* he now?" And suddenly the woman gave up her ladylike tone and posture. Her voice rose, her accent took on a distinct singsong quality, more Indian than English, and with both hands on her ample hips she turned to face the door and shouted, "Morgan, you bad man, where are you?"

There was a movement from one of the windows, the noise of a rattan blind being raised, and a man's head appeared—a handsome face, the sallow complexion slightly darker than Queenie's, but nothing like as dark as the woman's, a small, gallant black mustache, contrasting rather oddly with a weak chin and full, self-indulgent lips. It was a face that women found attractive, but there was something soft and boyish about it, despite the mustache. The man's eyes were dark and, even from a distance, seemed to reflect a certain refined melancholy. He rubbed them now, then flattened one hand to shield them from the daylight. "What is it?" he asked. "Why are you waking me up like this when I need my sleep?"

"Why did you give Queenie a pink ribbon?"

"I brought the bloody thing home from the club. Somebody must have dropped it."

"Some dirty little tramp! You had no right to give it to our Queenie."

"Oh, what difference does it make, Vicky, for goodness sake? Stop making such a bloody row."

"I'll give you a row, my word! I won't have her wearing pink! Our Queenie will be a lady, I tell you *that!*"

The man looked at the little girl with her perfect profile, her huge, dark eyes, a few tears still clinging to the long, thick lashes, her slim legs. He laughed.

"What a bloody waste that will be!" he shouted. Then he pulled the blind down with a bang.

Morgan Jones turned away from the window and sighed. There was no point, he knew, in trying to go back to sleep. The heat was unbearable and would only get worse. Night would bring no relief—the sky above Calcutta would be hot and dark as an oven, so hot that even the natives were affected by it. They never seemed to go to bed, those who had a bed to go to. At two or three in the morning they were still squat-

ting in doorways by the Hooghly and on the pavements, glistening with
sweat as they fanned themselves, while all around them the night rever-
berated with the sounds of the East—chants, cries, bells, the endless
piercing sounds that were music to the native ear but just so much
meaningless noise to Westerners, a blend of horrible gongs, clanging,
tuneless, metallic strumming, ululating wails, endless repetitive drum-
ming, rising above the unmistakable smell of India, the rich, pungent
combination of open sewers, lush spices, overripe fruit and wood smoke
that brought tears to the eyes.

Here the nights were quieter, except for the guttural cry of the lame
watchman as he made his rounds. Admittedly, it wasn't like the neighborhoods where the sahibs lived and all the streets were paved, but at
least there were trees and gardens, however dusty and ill-tended. It's
not Home, of course, Morgan told himself—forgetting as usual that
he had never seen "Home," nor was he ever likely to.

His sister's outburst did not anger him. It was too hot for anger, to
begin with, but also he shared her feelings—or at least he understood
them. That she hated the color pink was perhaps foolish, but Morgan
knew, as she did, that it was by just such small things that their social
position was defined. It was easy to drop the unending struggle to keep
up standards, but the price was a quick, relentless descent. Calcutta was
full of families that had given up, allowed their daughters to marry
young men with darker skins, started to think of India as Home. In-
exorably the rot set in; before you knew it, the children, or the grand-
children, were living like natives—except that the natives would have
nothing to do with them and despised them as much as the English
did. It was easy enough to let go, as many did, but Morgan was determined to go home to the land his father had come from—and returned
to, leaving his family behind.

Even now, at the age of twenty-five, Morgan could hardly bring himself to think of that desertion. He knew that it was the custom, that
many Englishmen came out for ten or twelve years, lived with an Indian
woman, then went back to England to start a new family, or even resume family life where they had left off.

He also knew that it was not the custom of the pukka sahibs, with
their clubs, their wives, their regiments or senior government posts, to
do so. The Englishmen who took native wives were of the lower class—
railwaymen, telegraph workers, people who looked after canals, water-
works, electricity plants, jute mills, machinery. The women they lived
with were invariably of low caste, or no caste at all, for a woman of

caste would never give herself to a foreigner, Indians being as racially prejudiced as the English, if not more so.

Morgan's sister worshipped their father, whose faded photograph hung in an ornate frame on the parlor wall. It was hard to see much of the face, for the elder Jones wore a full, dark beard and his bushy eyebrows cast a shadow over his eyes, which were like those of an Old Testament prophet and which still caused Morgan to tremble.

His expression, even in the stiff, formal portrait, was curiously furtive, as if he was already considering the possibility of abandoning his family when he had it taken—indeed, Morgan suspected he might even have had the picture taken for the very purpose of leaving a memento of himself behind.

Over the years, Vicky had woven a gossamer web of legend around this grim, transient parent. As she told it, Jones had been a supervising railway surveyor, a man whose views on matters affecting the rails, roadbeds and bridges were sought after by superintendents and chief engineers—in short, a gentleman.

Morgan, who was six years younger than his sister, took most of this with a grain of salt, but saw no reason to argue over the matter with Vicky, to whom the whole subject was in any case sacred. *His* only memory of their father was of a short, angry, bearded man, smelling strongly of whiskey, coal dust and sweat, who demanded absolute obedience from his children and his wife—though whether he was actually married to their mother was open to question, in Morgan's opinion. The old lady herself did not seem to know or care, and Morgan thought it more likely that his father had simply made an arrangement with her parents, who would have been happy enough to get rid of a daughter without the expense of a dowry.

Morgan lit a cigarette, studied his face in the shaving mirror, then lathered it. There was no doubt that his eyes were the same as those of his father in the photograph, but somehow they failed to produce the same stern effect. His father's face was hard, demanding, self-righteous; in Morgan, the same features produced a face which was at once handsome and weak, as if the harsh planes and edges had been gently filed away. The dark, soulful eyes and brilliant teeth redeemed it, but Morgan knew that to many people this side of Suez they were the telltale signs of "wog blood." In England, he thought, he might have passed for Welsh.

He opened the door and shouted for hot water without producing a reply. In England, no doubt, you turned a tap and got all the hot water you wanted! But this was India, where nothing worked or was done easily.

He shouted again, louder, this time producing a commotion downstairs. From somewhere in the kitchen his mother screamed at the bath wallah in heavily accented English, while the cook and the ayah shouted at the unfortunate old man in Hindi, their voices rising as they cursed his laziness, his deafness, his low ancestry. The bath wallah shouted back, stoutly defending himself and his ancestors as he banged his brass and copper pitchers and pots to emphasize the difficulty and responsibility of his job.

From upstairs, several of Vicky's boarders shouted to demand quiet, while all around the bungalow the startled birds screamed and chattered, adding to the din.

Morgan groaned, not just because he was hung over, but because all this was so typically Anglo-Indian—the noise, the inefficiency, the fact that an Anglo-Indian had to shout to get an Indian to move, whereas a pukka sahib would not even have to raise his voice. He could hear his mother shouting still, having comfortably reverted to Hindi to continue her unflattering description of the bath wallah's forebears.

When Vicky was at home the old lady was obliged to speak English, which severely restricted her ability to hold a conversation, let alone curse a servant. She was no more comfortable with the English language than she was with the European clothes Vicky insisted she wear, for she had never mastered the mysteries of frocks, corsets, stockings and shoes. Her husband had been content to see her in a sari; now, at an age when she had every right to be left in peace, she was forced to wear flowered tea dresses, stockings which hung in folds on her legs, and shoes that hurt her feet, as a result of which she had taken up more or less permanent residence in the kitchen, where she could at least take off the shoes and gossip with cook and the ayah in whispered Hindi.

The room in which Morgan stood was small, bare, almost monastic. Such money as the family had to spare for decoration was spent on the parlor and the dining room, to impress visitors. The bedrooms were hardly more than cells, although Morgan had pinned to the walls a few pictures of English life torn from old periodicals—a sepia photograph of the Royal Enclosure at Ascot, a view of Piccadilly Circus, the young Prince of Wales leaning on his shooting stick at some sporting event.

Morgan's clothes hung from a pole at one end of the room, behind a flowered curtain. Along with his car, a battered Austin Bulldog, they were his most prized possessions: the evening dress which he wore to work every night, made up to order by S. Mohandas Brothers on Kali-

grat Road very reasonably, in the best Savile Row fashion, a white mess
jacket, three well-cared-for suits that could pass for London tailored, if
one didn't look too closely. Every night, he put his trousers under the
mattress to form a sharp crease and rinsed off his celluloid collar to prevent its turning yellow. He was the best-dressed man in the neighbor-
hood, which was only fitting, for he was no clerk or engine driver or
machinist, with fingernails stained dark from grease or ink. He was a
musician, an artist, a player of the saxophone in Calcutta's most elegant nightclub.

He glanced at the torn photograph pasted above his mirror. It was
the entrance to the Café de Paris on Piccadilly, the most expensive
nightclub in London. Outside its doorway, guarded by a majestic commissionaire, waited a row of chauffeurs and Rolls-Royce automobiles.

Morgan knew the details of the picture by heart. One day, he knew,
he would play there. It was a dream so sacred that he confided it to no
one except Queenie, whom he had pledged to secrecy.

He thought of the pink ribbon he had given his niece and smiled.
The child would be a great beauty when she grew up, you could see
that clear as the nose on your face, even though she was only eleven.
Then we'll have trouble; he told himself. This wasn't England, after
all. Girls bloomed fast in this climate—yes, and faded just as quickly,
too, he told himself grimly. Their opportunities lasted only as long as
their beauty.

Beauty would take a girl a long way, if she knew how to use it.
Anglo-Indian women with the right looks (and the right kind of pale
complexion) sometimes married Englishmen and went Home, where
they usually passed themselves off as the children of English parents in
India. The right kind of marriage might provide an escape for Queenie
one day, if she was lucky.

There was no such easy way out for Morgan. He patted his cheeks
with eau de cologne, smoothed the tips of his mustache with scented
wax, slipped on a white shirt and a pair of wide-bottomed white flannel
cricket trousers, and went down to eat breakfast, which he could already hear his mother and the cook arguing about shrilly.

Tea was Queenie's favorite meal. She was still smarting over the loss
of her ribbon—surely at the age of twelve, or *almost* twelve, she had
the right to put a ribbon on her topi—but the plates of cake and the
biscuits offered at least some consolation.

It was always served on the veranda, in the forlorn hope of catching a stray breeze. There were tins of Huntley & Palmer biscuits on the table, and Queenie liked the tins almost as much as the biscuits. They were painted with garish color pictures of London—the Changing of the Guard at Buckingham Palace, the Beefeaters at the Tower of London, Big Ben and the Thames. . . . She loved to look at the pictures and daydream about England, that fairy-tale land of green meadows, castles and cool forests that Ma and Morgan called Home. Ma had promised Queenie she would go Home one day, and Queenie longed to see it.

"This was always your Grandpa's favorite time of day," her mother said, buttering a slice of bread for Queenie. It was her rule that Queenie must eat a slice of bread and butter before she could have cake or biscuits—a rule which Grandma and the ayah found incomprehensible, since in their view the only point of having children was to spoil them.

"I can't think why," Morgan said. "It's beastly hot."

"Only if you *think* it is, dear," she said mildly. A fervent disciple of Mary Baker Eddy, she kept a copy of *Science and Life* beside her bed, along with her father's Bible. She did not believe in doctors, illness, stimulants or pain. Queenie had so far been lucky enough to avoid all four.

"My memory is that Pater preferred beer to tea, Vicky," Morgan said. "I must say I could do with a beer myself."

"Certainly not at teatime, Morgan!" she said decisively, and briskly poured a cup of tea for her brother. He accepted it with a sigh—there was no doubt, there never had been, that Victoria usually got her way. She enforced her own pukka standards by sheer willpower, not only over Morgan, but over everyone around her. Even the boarders lived in terror of Vicky. Only Magda, who had lived here the longest, ever dared to challenge Vicky, and indeed did so now, as she appeared through the hanging curtain that separated the living room from the veranda. In defiance of the strict custom of dressing for tea, she was wearing a flowered kimono.

"It's too hot to dress," Magda explained, without any effort to make it sound like an apology. Her accent was European, a throaty, guttural voice appropriate to some other, harsher, language. A lifetime of chain-smoking had lowered the pitch of Magda's voice to a husky growl, which some men found sexy, but which contrasted strangely with her fragile blond good looks—though these too were fading, like her voice.

To look at her was to know she had once been beautiful, but what remained of that beauty was merely an interesting ruin—high cheekbones, over which the pale skin was tightly drawn, a wide, sensuous mouth, large eyes as blue as the Thames on Queenie's biscuit tins. Beneath the eyes were deep purple hollows, signs of hard living, late nights, illness, suffering, or some combination of all of these. It was not a happy face; the bones were too close to the surface, so that in the harsh light the suggestion of a skull beneath the flesh was uncomfortably apparent.

"Tea?" Vicky asked brightly, glaring at the kimono.

"Tea, of course." Magda put three spoonfuls of sugar in her tea, then put an extra spoonful in Queenie's mug with a conspiratorial wink.

"Tea should be hot and sweet," Magda said, ignoring a dark look in her direction from Vicky. "In Russia, when I was there, we put a cube of sugar between our teeth, then drank the tea. Always from a glass, you understand. Ah, how good it was!"

"Tell us about the general, Magda," Queenie pleaded.

"The general? But, *ma petite*, you've heard about him a thousand times!"

"Leave poor Magda in peace, Queenie," Vicky said.

"No, no." Magda coughed—a deep, hacking cough that seemed to go on forever—then sipped her tea. "The general was a wonderful man, Queenie. Six feet tall—a giant, like a bear. When he laughed, it was like—thunder! He had a big, bushy beard, all silver."

"Like Ramdan Singh, the postman?"

"Not at all like Ramdan Singh! It was not a nasty little pointed Sikh beard; it was a *real* beard that came down to the general's chest and covered half his medals."

"Was he a very old man?"

"Not so old, *chérie*. Why?"

"You said his beard was silver."

Magda sighed and lit a cigarette, despite Vicky's evident disapproval of smoking at the tea table. "Well, I admit, he wasn't young. Generals never are."

"Did he live in a palace?"

"So many questions! He had a beautiful palace, Queenie, but I met him in the war, so I never saw it. I was playing in Kiev—my God, it was so cold on stage that I thought I would die!—and he came to my dressing room with a bottle of champagne, two glasses and a bucket of coal. You cannot imagine how much the coal mattered to me at that point. More than the champagne! In the morning, he sent a troika for me—a wonderful sleigh with three horses. His orderly gave me a fur-lined cape and a letter from the general inviting me to join him at his headquarters. The next four years we were never apart."

"He must have loved you very much," Queenie said enviously, her dark eyes fixed on Magda's face, ignoring the slice of raisin cake which her mother had placed on her plate now that the bread and butter was gone.

"Like life itself, little one. More than life itself, as things turned out. That's the only kind of love that matters, Queenie."

Magda blew a smoke ring into the windless heat and watched it hang there. "The rest is just—hot air."

Darkness fell abruptly. There was no twilight, no softening of the day. One moment it was bright and hot, the next it was pitch-black and hotter still.

"One misses the dusk," Magda said sadly. She shuffled the cards in front of her, sighing as they stuck to her fingers in the heat. Magda was never without a deck of cards. She told her own fortune endlessly, as if she were determined to find good news in the cards eventually.

The veranda was dimly lit by one lamp shining through the curtained door from the parlor. Electricity had reached them nearly a decade ago, but the power was not strong enough to allow more than a couple of rooms to be wired, and power failures were frequent—more the rule than the exception, in fact, now that Indians were beginning to replace the British and the Anglo-Indians as engineers in the Calcutta Power and Light Company. It was a subject of great concern to the Anglo-Indians, for their jobs were the whole reason for their existence as a separate community, and if natives were allowed to perform the same tasks, the Anglo-Indians' position as a specially protected minority was unlikely to survive for long.

There were those who supposed the British would never abandon a community of some two hundred thousand people with European blood—however little—and Queenie's mother was inevitably among these optimists. Morgan, whose work brought him into closer social contact with the British, thought otherwise, though in deference to his sister's patriotism he kept his thoughts to himself.

The war, he knew, had changed everything. The stern burra sahibs, who had remained almost as remote as the old Queen-Empress herself, were a vanishing breed by the early twenties. The young men who would have come out from England to replace them had died by the thousands in the mud of Flanders and the Somme. The English in India now danced to the music of jazz bands, the mem-sahibs wore bobbed hair, short skirts, rolled stockings and smoked cigarettes in public, giving great offense to Indians of every sect and caste.

He had cut a wide swath among them with his soulful eyes and his "sensitive" face, something that would have been unthinkable in the days before the Great War, when the mem-sahibs were as unapproachable for an Anglo-Indian as the sacred precincts of the Calcutta Turf Club. The Turf Club, of course, was still off-limits—not that there was a rule to that effect, it was simply "understood" like so much else in India. Morgan relished his reputation as a ladies' man, even exaggerated it, but it did not spare him from the occasional humiliation that was the lot of his community. There was no way he could pass for an Englishman here in Calcutta, and he had no desire for the companionship of his fellow Anglo-Indians, most of whom thought he was "stuck-up" and resented his success with Englishwomen, as well as the fact that he had escaped the tedium of a clerk's job on the railways.

Yet he was just as surely trapped as they were. There was no way to get ahead here. Painful as it was for every Anglo-Indian to accept, the British preferred the native Indians to people of mixed blood—perhaps because the very existence of the Anglo-Indian community was shameful proof that the British were no better than anyone else. It was the niggers who went to Oxford and came back as lawyers, Morgan told himself savagely, not people like him. He was under no illusions about the future. It would belong to men with better educations than his, however black. . . .

"Au travail," Magda said, pulling her kimono more tightly around her and slipping her cards into her pocket. "I must get to work. You, too, Morgan."

"Can I come with you?" Queenie asked.

"Of course you can't, dear," her mother said. "It will soon be bedtime."

"Besides," Magda added, standing up with a yawn, "you're too young. You'll have your fill of nightclubs when you're older."

"Can I go and watch Magda put her makeup on, Ma?" Queenie asked.

"Not tonight, dear," Vicky said, with a small sniff of disapproval. There was much that she disapproved of. She had always thought of herself as a respectable woman of the strictest moral standards, and it was true. She had stepped out of character only once, when she was swept off her feet at a Railway Institute dance by a smiling, black-haired Irishman named Tim "Tiger" Kelley, who had come out to India, via Australia, Tasmania and Singapore, as a jockey. Had she been anything but Anglo-Indian, she would have recognized Tiger as a rogue, but Tiger was white, and a white man was such a catch for an Anglo-Indian girl of her dark complexion that she asked no questions—which was just as well, since Tiger would have answered them with lies.

As it was, Vicky nevertheless treasured the memory of the five years she and Kelley had been married. Short as he was, Tiger was a wild man (hence his nickname), always ready for a drink or a party, generous with his own money—and, regrettably, with other people's as well, whenever he got the chance. His career on the Calcutta turf was abruptly terminated when the stewards accused him of betting against his own mounts, then holding them back, a charge which had been made against Tiger in other parts of the Empire, as it turned out, along with kiting bad checks, running up debts and bigamy. He fled from India, promising to send for Vicky and Queenie as soon as he could, and was never heard from again.

Life had not been easy for Vicky since, and not only because her own skin was too dark for comfort. Deserted by her dashing husband and crippled with his debts, she had been obliged to take in boarders "to make ends meet," and since she was unwilling to rent rooms to widowed train drivers or bachelor signalmen, coarse, dark-skinned Anglo-Indian fellows who only shaved once or twice a week and had grease under their fingernails, she found it more congenial to take in ladies. Needless to say, no Englishwoman would live in an Anglo-Indian household, but Calcutta was a cosmopolitan city, and, thanks to Morgan, she soon found European clients—women with unpronounceable names and sad eyes, who had made their way across much of Europe and Asia in the wake of war and revolution, and for whom Calcutta was often the last stop, unless they could save up enough money to go to Bombay, and from there by boat back to Europe.

Most of them worked as "dance hostesses" at Firpo's, or places like it, and if Vicky suspected that they earned their living in other, less reputable ways, she had always managed to conceal that suspicion from herself, though not from the neighbors. Indeed, she had reached her present situation as the owner of a lodging house for stray women of dubious morality by such small, inevitable steps that the moral issue had never occurred to her.

"Why can't I go and see Uncle Morgan playing?" Queenie asked, crumbling her piece of cake to pick out the raisins.

"It's not a place for children, Queenie. Eat the cake part, too, dear. You want to grow up strong and healthy, don't you?"

"What will I be when I grow up?"

Vicky stared at the child for a long moment. It was a question she often asked herself, and to which she had not yet found a satisfactory answer, if indeed there was one.

"You'll be a lady," she said.

"Do ladies go to nightclubs?"

"Certainly *not*."

"Not even with gentlemen?"

"Oh, how would I know? For goodness' sake, stop asking questions."

"Morgan says English ladies do."

Vicky gave an unpleasant glance in Morgan's direction, and he shrugged. He knew more about English ladies than she cared to have discussed at table, particularly in front of Queenie.

"It's true," he said, more for Vicky's benefit than Queenie's. "Still, when Queenie is grown-up, she can do as she pleases."

"We'll see," Vicky said with a sniff. "*If* she works hard at school"— she frowned in Queenie's direction to make it clear that this had not so far been the case—"and *if* she passes her exams, then she can have her pick of jobs. Look at Peggy D'Souza—*she* just got a job as typist for a big English firm on Connaught Street, right out of school. There she sits, in a really posh office, working for an Englishman. She doesn't have anything to do with the Indian clerks or babus. Mark my words, she'll end by marrying an English fellow, you'll see. And going Home with him, too!"

Morgan raised an eyebrow. Vicky's admiration for Peggy D'Souza was a familiar theme, though Morgan did not share her rosy view of Peggy's future. It was on the tip of his tongue to point out that Peggy had in fact *failed* her examination and had been hired for quite other reasons than her typing, but he remained silent. As for the D'Souzas, they had merely adopted their Portuguese surname two generations ago in the hope it would make it easier for them to pass as Europeans of Mediterranean coloring—a forlorn hope, since most of them, except for Peggy, were black as a boot.

"School is boring," Queenie said.

"Nonsense," Vicky replied automatically. "You have to study hard. Then you'll get a good job and go back to England to live like a real lady."

"I'd rather be an actress like Magda."

Vicky sighed. It was possible that Magda had once been an actress—certainly she sometimes talked of a theatrical past, though of what kind, and in what language, it was hard to say. She had a Gypsy's skill at tarot and fortunetelling, but Vicky viewed that as even less reputable than what she described as "actressing." In any event, the theater was hardly a suitable profession for Queenie, and she said so forcefully, sending the child off to the kitchen to bother Grandma and the ayah.

"You must not put silly ideas into Queenie's head," she said to Morgan, when they were alone.

"It's not any sillier than telling the child her father will send for her one day, Vicky."

"Well, he might."

"Vicky," Morgan said gently, "you know better than that. Tiger had a family in Tasmania and another one in South Africa—and those are the ones we *know* about. By now he's probably in Hong Kong, or Australia. Or more likely in jail."

"You didn't speak about him like that when he was here. Now, of course, he has a bad name."

"He was my friend," Morgan said quietly. "I *liked* Tiger. But he pulled his horses, Vicky, whatever you say. And he abandoned you and Queenie. He won't send for her. If Tiger Kelley went home to England, they'd be waiting for him at the dock with handcuffs."

She stared into the darkness. Everything Morgan said was no doubt true, but her whole being resisted it. She wanted the world for Queenie, including a proper father, though what she most wanted for the child was a chance to live in England—a chance that had never been in her own reach, and never would be.

In England Queenie would be free; nobody need ever know what she was or where she had come from. She was pale enough to be accepted as English, with perhaps just a touch of foreign blood, while in India she would always be at the mercy of a snide remark, a damaging rumor, a sideways glance, the mention of "a touch of the tar brush," or "a six-anna piece."

"Isn't it a pity," Vicky said, "that our children can only get ahead by leaving us?"

Morgan nodded. "Perhaps," he said gently, "it's not just the children who want to go."

Vicky rose and began to put the cups and plates on the tray. She threw the crumbs out over the railing into the garden for the birds.

Somewhere down the road a motorcycle popped and spluttered; from the kitchen came the sounds of Grandma and the ayah laughing, probably filling poor Queenie's head with nonsense. A locomotive whistled nearby—the railway was always close to the Anglo-Indian cantonment anywhere in India, for it was to run the trains that their grandfathers had come here, and to keep them running that their children had been bred. Trains were in the blood.

"Seven o'clock," Morgan said, listening to the mournful whistle and the crash of couplings. Even he, a saxophone player, knew the train schedules by heart and could tell the time by their whistles and signals so well that he didn't need a watch. "It's time to go."

"Yes, yes . . . Listen to that! Grandma and the ayah are chattering away to Queenie. They spoil the child. And they tell her these awful Indian stories . . ."

"It's part of her, too, Vicky. We all have a little bit of India in us. Not even such a little bit, let's face it."

He said this in a kindly tone, for Vicky's skin was darker than his by several shades, and this was a difference about which she was understandably sensitive.

Vicky picked up the tea tray. She seemed to have ignored her brother's remark, which was often the way she dealt with problems she didn't want to face—or perhaps couldn't.

She gave Morgan a quick nod, as if she was dismissing him to his world of nightclubs, jazz bands and mem-sahibs out for a night's slumming, and in a firm voice she said, "I'll not face it *ever*, Morgan!"

Queenie took her shoes off and sat down on the kitchen floor with a sigh. Ma hated the sight of bare feet and insisted on shoes. Worse still, she always bought them too small. Going barefoot, she believed, eventually gave a girl big feet. Natives had big, splayed feet; mem-sahibs had small, shapely feet. Ma was determined that Queenie should have the smallest, shapeliest feet imaginable, at whatever sacrifice in comfort.

Queenie liked the kitchen, and not only because it was forbidden territory, or because cook always had a few Indian sweetmeats—sticky, unhygienic concoctions of fruit, nuts and honey that Ma disapproved of almost as much as bare feet. Here there were no demands on her to "sit up straight," or to "behave like a lady," or to "mind your Ps and Qs." To Grandma and the servants she was "the little princess," and could behave as she pleased.

Queenie had seen pictures of English kitchens with linoleum floors and wood cabinets and a mysterious white box called a "fridge," but the kitchen was nothing like those. It was, in fact, a kind of shack, or lopsided lean-to, thrown up against the back of the house, with a galvanized tin roof and a dirt floor. There was no sink—the dishes were washed outside in the yard, in big copper tubs. Cook worked on a big cast-iron stove that shimmered like a mirage when it was lit, chewing betel nut to prevent herself from collapsing in the heat.

Grandma chewed betel nut, too, when she thought she could get away with it, and she scrubbed her teeth afterward with a roughened stick dipped in coarse salt to get rid of the telltale red stain. Sometimes she liked to weave flowers into Queenie's long hair, but they had to be removed before she left the kitchen, for that too was a "native" custom which Ma would never allow. The flowers grew outside, on the sides of the kitchen, and brightly colored birds occasionally flew through the open doorway or the ragged holes in the makeshift walls that passed for windows. It was, in every way, Queenie thought, a nicer place than the parlor.

Grandma and the ayah squatted, native-fashion, drinking tea. Both of them had brown faces, wrinkled and seamed with age, but the ayah's was happier, perhaps because she did not have to pretend to be anything but what she was—an elderly woman of no particular caste, as Indian as the hot, scented night outside. Also, Queenie could hardly help noticing, the ayah was considerably more comfortable—and more presentable—in her sari than Mrs. Jones was in her bedraggled frock, with half the hooks done up lopsided and the hem hanging down on one side.

From the doorway they could see down the long row of backyards during the day, each with a more or less identical kitchen, and comment on the "goings-on" of the entire street. At night they listened, like a pair of hawks.

"Shush!" Grandma whispered, leaning forward with a hand cupped around one ear. She listened for a moment, then nodded at the ayah. "The D'Souza girl is catching what-for from Mrs. D'Souza."

"Truly," the ayah said in Hindi, with satisfaction. Having spent a lifetime as a nanny, the ayah spoke Hindi and English more or less interchangeably, and was quite capable of beginning a sentence in one language and ending it in another. The ayah was far too old for any useful service, but like all Indian servants, she was a permanent fixture.

"Last night she came home late. Tonight she is going out again," Grandma reported, for the ayah was a little deaf.

Queenie could hear the noise of a quarrel from the house next door—voices rising to a high, singsong pitch, shouts as the other members of the family picked up the quarrel, tears. "I don't care, Ma, he's an Englishman!" she heard Peggy D'Souza shout above the din.

"She sleeps with an Englishman," Grandma said in Hindi.

The ayah nodded. "All the world knows. He brings her home in his car. They kissed each other in the street last night. This I saw with my own eyes."

Next door there was the sound of a slap, followed by crying. Mr. D'Souza, a dim figure in the darkness, came out of the house and lit his pipe—he was not allowed to smoke indoors—as he usually did when he wanted to escape from the problems of his womenfolk.

"Is it nice to kiss a man?" Queenie asked.

The two old ladies laughed, rocking back and forth on their heels. Even cook, who was usually silent, cackled and wheezed.

"Heh," the ayah said, chuckling as she spoke, "dost thou hear the little one? She is hardly weaned and already she asks about men!"

Grandma smiled. She leaned over and placed one hand under Queenie's chin, lifting the child's face so she could look into her eyes. "Our Queenie will have a bridegroom as handsome and strong as a prince!" Grandma said. "A burra sahib."

"Truly," the ayah said, nodding her head.

"But what will he actually *do*, Grandma?"

"This thou will discover with thy bridegroom, child. Thou shalt have a little pain—then much, much pleasure, and many babies."

"I don't want to have babies."

"When thou hast grown up, thou shalt want them, Queenie. A woman without babies has no honor in the eyes of the world."

"This is so," the ayah said, nodding.

Grandma looked at Queenie sternly. "Remember, though, that thou must never allow this to happen before marriage! Men do not prize what they get for nothing."

She pinched Queenie's cheek so hard that she almost burst into tears. "Thou must not talk to thy mother about this," Grandma warned. "About some things we know more than the British."

Quite who the "we" referred to was a subject of some confusion to Queenie. Grandma was clearly as Indian as the ayah, despite the Western clothes Ma had forced on her. Queenie had thought a good deal about this. Even by the most elementary rules of arithmetic, it meant that Ma and Morgan were half Indian, while she was one-quarter Indian—or three-quarters English, whichever way you chose to look at it.

It often seemed to Queenie that there might be something to be said for *being* Indian. Even to think such a thing, she knew, was a kind of treason, both to her own blood and to Ma. Yet she sometimes found herself wondering if Grandma was not perhaps wiser about life than Ma. Indians were by no means as stupid as Morgan made them out to be, she thought—and if "wogs," as he called them, were so awful, where did that leave them all? Morgan was half a wog himself, and it ran in Queenie's blood, too.

Besides, even though she was a child, Queenie had already learned that there was no such creature as an "Indian." This was a continent that uneasily contained high-caste Brahmins and untouchables, Hindus and Moslems, peaceful Bengali babus and warlike Sikhs, ferocious Pathans and pleasure-loving Kashmiris, Rajputs who were six feet tall and hill people who were almost Pygmies, none of them with much in common—not even a language, unless you included English—a land where women went veiled in purdah to temples where the walls were carved in a riot of forbidden sculptures, where a maharajah descended from a gold-plated Rolls-Royce to wash the feet of lepers and beggars, where children were allowed to die in the streets while the life of a cow was preserved with religious zeal. . . . All this was a part of her, and at the same time not a part.

Queenie wondered how she would look in a gold-brocaded silk sari, with heavy gold bracelets and necklaces, and one large pearl in her pierced nose. Surely she would be more beautiful than she was in her school uniform, and more free, too, for Indian women wore nothing under their saris, and giggled at the sight of the strange, uncomfortable undergarments of the feringhee mem-sahibs hanging on the cantonment washline.

It must be nice, Queenie thought, to be one thing or another, to know where you belonged. She snuggled close between the two old ladies, staring out into the night, where the only visible object was now the red glow from Mr. D'Souza's pipe.

"The baba is sleepy," the ayah said, making it into a kind of chant, as if a lullaby was her natural form of communication after a lifetime of crooning children to sleep.

"I'm not!" Queenie said, but she was. She struggled to keep awake, pinching her thighs from time to time because the pain made her open her eyes, though unless she was careful, it also made her cry. Ma claimed there was no such thing as pain, and while Queenie wanted to believe her, she had begun to wonder if Ma might just possibly be wrong. The thought made her feel guilty, and also a little frightened. If Ma was wrong about pain, what else might she be wrong about?

"Why is Mrs. D'Souza angry at Peggy?" she asked, more to keep herself awake and avoid the subject of going to bed than from any real curiosity.

"Peggy disobeyed her mother," Grandma said vaguely.

That made sense to Queenie, however sleepy she was. She wondered at what age you no longer had to obey your mother. Peggy seemed to her a grown-up, or almost so, so it must be a long way ahead, perhaps after you got married and began to obey your husband instead.

"If Peggy gets married will her husband take her Home?"

Grandma stared out at the night and sighed. "You'd better go to bed now," she said. "Before your Ma comes looking for you."

Then she put her hands gently on Queenie's face, the dark fingers stroking Queenie's fine, pale skin, and in a soft, sad voice she whispered, "This *is* home, Queenie."

CHAPTER 2

FOR THE DECADE he had worked here, Morgan had wondered why a nightclub presumably intended to take people's minds off the fact that they were in India should have been decorated with fake palm trees and Oriental arches.

In fact, the proprietor, Gaetano Firpo, had originally intended to base the decor on that of the Café de Paris in London, where he had once worked as a waiter before the Great War, but a fire during the construction, together with the threat of premature bankruptcy, forced him to buy up whatever was available in the way of local furnishings.

Gaudy chandeliers, none of them matching, hung from the striped, tented ceiling, small Benares brass tables were artfully arranged so that the unwary newcomer tripped over them on the way to the dance floor, everywhere there were artifacts of modern Oriental bad taste in its cheapest and most glittering form. Despite the fans clattering away lethargically between the chandeliers, the club was so hot and stuffy that even the most seasoned Calcutta residents sometimes fainted, but this was no disadvantage from Firpo's point of view. "The hotter it is, the more they drink," he said with satisfaction, whenever the subject was brought up.

By midnight, when the air was thick with cigarette smoke, the effect was that of a scene from hell as the red-faced, perspiring sahibs in evening dress crowded the dance floor with their wives or girlfriends, whose faces were equally flushed beneath disintegrating makeup.

No Indians were admitted; even the occasional maharajah came only if he was with a sahib's party, however welcome he might be in the nightclubs of London or Paris. It was not the kind of place where an Anglo-Indian man would be welcome, but of course *that* problem seldom arose. It was a question of class rather than color: few Anglo-

Indian men had either the inclination or the money to visit nightclubs, and most were strict Calvinists or Methodists as well. The Railway Institute represented the limit of their social ambitions—a further reason why Morgan despised his own people.

For young Anglo-Indian girls it was a different story. They were allowed in Firpo's, to the horror of their parents, the unspoken rule being that they must have pale complexions. Mostly they were brought by young Englishmen—the older generation would never have dreamed of doing it—but it was not unknown for Anglo-Indian girls "of the right sort," those who were bold enough, to come in pairs and sit at the bar, nursing a soft drink and trying to ignore the stares of the young sahibs and the undisguised hostility of the mem-sahibs of all ages. Invariably the girls wore pink dresses and danced better than the Englishwomen.

"It's in the blood," Morgan Jones said to himself, as he watched a young woman in pink dancing a tango during his break. Pink was Queenie's favorite color, too, he thought. Perhaps that was in the blood, too. . . . He thought about Queenie too much lately, he told himself. She was nearly fourteen—soon she would be old enough to be dancing here. The idea depressed him. He turned his attention to the girl in pink. She looked to him like Peggy D'Souza, but it was hard to tell in the dim, flickering light. Morgan waved toward her. She winked back, the flower in her hair bobbing as she danced by.

"Nice bint," the bass-fiddle player, an Australian named George Higgins, said admiringly. "I've had my eye on her all bloody evening," he added, with unintentional accuracy, for he had served in the Palestine campaign under General Allenby and had lost an eye as well as his front teeth in a fight with two lance corporals of the Royal Military Police in a Basra brothel. The teeth had been replaced by an Army dentist, with what appeared to be miniature lavatory tiles; the glass eye had a certain roguish, charming quality which the real one lacked— indeed, the glass one now seemed to be fixed cheerfully on Peggy D'Souza, while the good one stared lifelessly at Morgan.

"Not bad," Morgan agreed. His admiration for the English did not extend to Higgins. Morgan, whose class consciousness was intense and finely tuned, had never been able to fit Colonials into his scheme of things. He knew that he was in every way superior to Higgins, but an Australian ex-soldier, even one with one eye, still counted as a sahib. Higgins was unquestionably 100 percent white, and could therefore lord it over an Anglo-Indian.

To question this was to question the established order of things. Nevertheless, Morgan still despised Higgins, a feeling which he had so far managed to conceal, since Higgins was a man whose violent nature was all too apparent. Morgan feared physical violence. He had been bullied at school and beaten by his father. He had no stomach for fist fights, and he knew it. He suspected, to his humiliation, that Higgins knew it as well.

"Know her?" Higgins asked.

"No," Morgan lied. He was not about to introduce Higgins to Peggy D'Souza, if it was she.

"Bet you bloody do, cobber," Higgins said angrily. Even sober— which he was not—his temper was volatile and uncertain. "I saw her bloody wink at you, you know. She one of your people?"

Morgan smiled reflexively. Higgins's remark was not, on the face of things, an insult. Morgan made no secret of the fact that he was Anglo-Indian, which would in any case have been impossible to hide, and they were therefore undeniably "his" people, as the Australians were Higgins's, God help them. Is it an insult, Morgan wondered, to call a man what he is? But of course it *was* an insult, and Higgins's tone made it clear that it was intended as such.

"She might be," he answered, angry with himself for smiling.

Higgins nodded. "Too bloody right," he said. "You can see that just looking at her, mate. You don't see many Brit sheilas with a nice little ass like that—and not ashamed of shaking it about for all the world to see either. My word, I'll bet *she* knows what to do with a man— a real man, mind, not that pommy twit she's dancing with. Well, they learn early here, don't they?"

Morgan's attempt to explain that most Anglo-Indian girls were remarkably, even depressingly, virtuous, was hardly formed before Higgins interrupted him. "It's the heat," he said, leering at Morgan. "Stands to reason. Your half-breed's got stronger animal instincts, see? And the climate heats up the blood."

Higgins leaned over, his face close to Morgan's, as if they were conspirators. Morgan, who was standing next to the wall, was unable to back away. He had a close-up view of Higgins's bristly red mustache, the fine tracery of red veins on his nose and cheeks, the beads of sweat below his greased-back hair. Higgins's false teeth had tobacco stains on them; his glass eye seemed to have shifted so that the enamel pupil was focused at some far-distant point to his right, like that of a fish.

"Of course, you can't always tell," Higgins went on, the flat, nasal voice lowered to a whisper. "A lot of these girls can pass for white, right? Chap I know says you can always tell by looking at the cuticles, the gums—and the way they behave in bed." He laughed, a few flecks of spittle landing on Morgan's face. Morgan wiped his face with one hand.

"Hot in here," Higgins said sympathetically, noticing the gesture, as Peggy D'Souza, who had drifted close to them in the arms of her young Englishman, shouted, "Hello, Morgan."

"Hello, Peggy," Morgan said, aware even as he spoke that Higgins's good eye was fixed on him balefully, all comradeship gone.

"I thought you didn't bloody know her."

Morgan shrugged. "I wasn't sure it was Peggy."

"My ass! I thought we were mates. You think your bloody chee-chee bints are too good for an Aussie like Higgins, is that it, mate? You lot make me sick."

Higgins backed away with the instinct of an experienced barroom brawler—he was too close to Morgan to use his fists effectively and needed some distance to land the first punch. He feinted, cocking back his right arm, then aimed a vicious left undercut at Morgan's solar plexus, which stopped short because he had been grabbed from behind by old Firpo himself, who appeared, apparently from nowhere, at the mere hint of violence in his establishment.

"Not here!" he said. "I don't permit fighting among the help."

"It wasn't my fault, Mr. Firpo," Morgan said, unhappily aware that his voice had risen to a whine and taken on the singsong Anglo-Indian accent that the English made fun of. Still, he couldn't afford to lose his job—it was the one thing that made him different from the rest of his people.

"It wasn't *my* fault," Higgins mimicked ferociously. "I'll get you, you bastard!" He struggled briefly but uselessly. Higgins was no match for Firpo—he was merely a barroom fighter who liked using his fists when he'd had enough to drink and there was no woman immediately available. Firpo might be an old man, and monstrously fat, with the flat feet and ingratiating smile of a waiter, but he was a Sicilian. Violence did not shock or surprise him. When one of the Bengali dishwashers went berserk in the kitchen because of the heat, waving a cleaver in the air and howling incomprehensible curses, old Firpo had calmly walked over to the man, a smile on his face, and smashed his head in with a cast-iron skillet. The dishwasher fell to the tiled floor, his turban dripping blood, his eyes glazed as if he had died without even noticing the fact. "Back to work, everybody," Firpo had said,

smiling as if he had just given the dishwasher a raise. "We got customers to serve."

Firpo's nephew Alberto appeared silently, as he always did at the
first sign of trouble, his face impassive, his heavy beard disguised by a
thick coating of talcum powder which gave him a slightly clownish
appearance, unmatched by the dark, expressionless eyes.

"Trouble?" he asked.

Firpo shrugged. Alberto pushed Morgan to one side, stood in front
of Higgins, staring toward the far side of the room as if nothing he
saw here was of interest to him, and sharply brought his knee up into
Higgins's groin. Alberto's expression did not change; in fact, from a
distance of a few feet, it would have been impossible to see that anything had happened. Higgins gave a muffled groan—the old man was
holding his throat so tightly that he couldn't scream—then slumped
in pain, his hands clutched at his crotch, while old Firpo held him on
his feet.

"You go back to work," Alberto said calmly. "You play the fiddle.
You don't make no more trouble. If you do, I kill you. Unnerstan?"

Higgins nodded. He was drooling slightly, and his glass eye had
turned around so that only the white showed.

"That's good," Alberto said, patting the Australian on the cheek.
Alberto smiled, showing a row of gleaming gold teeth. "And Morgan,"
he said, "you forget all this happened, unnerstan? The customers want
to fight, okay, so long as they pay the damage. But not the help."

Morgan nodded, relieved that the blame had fallen on Higgins,
where it belonged. "Right-oh, Mr. Firpo," he said.

Alberto gave him a thuggish look from underneath his thick eyebrows, as if he thought Morgan was making fun of him. "Watch yourself," he said.

Morgan tried to smile cheerfully, sweat beginning to pour down his
face. He hoped he had not managed to give offense. "You can rely on
me," he said earnestly.

Alberto stared impassively past him at the dance floor, his hands
behind his back in the traditional posture of the maître d'. "I meant
watch out for Higgins," Alberto said coldly. "He ain't through with
you."

It was still dark when Morgan drove home from work, an hour or so
before dawn. It was the moment of his day he enjoyed most, except

on the nights when his ancient Baby Austin refused to start. It could not be said that it was cool, but it was as cool as Calcutta would get, and in the moving car, with the canvas top down, it was almost comfortable.

Morgan swerved violently to avoid a cow sleeping in the street, bounced over the deep ruts at the side of the road, prayed that he hadn't punctured a tire, and cursed India. In England, he told himself, there were no bloody cows sleeping in the streets, and no beggars sleeping there either. Unwary motorists in Calcutta frequently ran over beggars at night. If you did, it was unwise to stop. Within seconds you were surrounded by hundreds of screaming Indians, and when the police arrived, the victim would invariably claim that limbs missing since childhood had been torn off by the car.

Morgan sighed. This was 1931. If the advertisements he had seen in old copies of *The Saturday Evening Post* and *Collier's* were to be believed, Americans had washing machines, toasters, a radio in every home, skyscrapers, a car in every garage, sometimes even two, while here in India riots still broke out, in which thousands of people died, merely because the bloody Muslims led a bloody cow to the slaughterhouse past a bloody Hindu temple. In England, even the poor had indoor plumbing and enough to eat, while here there were four hundred million people who still wiped their asses with their fingers and performed their human needs in the streets, for all to see.

Morgan had worked at Firpo's for ten years, and England seemed as far away as ever. People said nice things about the way he played— his solos were much admired and applauded—but no talent scout had ever appeared to sign him up for an English band, and by now Morgan suspected none ever would. It was as hopeless as Ma's belief that Queenie's father would send for her one day.

He sat in the car and thought about Queenie for a moment, reluctant to go upstairs to bed. She was already beginning to present problems for her mother—predictably, in Morgan's opinion. She was no longer a child, after all. In this benighted country, girls of thirteen or fourteen were often married and already mothers. Granted, that was unthinkable these days among Anglo-Indians, but in one respect, at least, the loathsome Higgins had been right—Anglo-Indian girls did mature faster than the English. The rigid morality and stuffy conventions of the Anglo-Indian community were in part a defense against this inconvenient fact of life.

In Queenie's case, the problem was compounded by her beauty. Even in her school clothes she already showed the first signs of the body of a mature woman—long, finely formed legs, a slim waist, small, perfect breasts. Other fourteen-year-olds had good bodies, but it was Queenie's face that made her so special: the enormous dark eyes with their long, thick lashes, the high cheekbones, the lips so full and perfectly shaped that they seemed almost provocative on such a young girl. Even Queenie's movements were sensual—she had none of the gawkiness of adolescence. She performed the most ordinary tasks with a kind of natural physical grace, like a cat stretching. She had developed a remarkable gift for observing and imitating adults, as if she wanted to grow up overnight, but at other times she behaved just like a child.

Morgan found living at close quarters with such an early-blooming beauty a sore trial on his nerves. It was difficult to look at Queenie without thinking about sex. Sometimes it was impossible. It filled him with shame.

He turned off the motor, pulled on the parking brake and put the car keys into his pocket, stretching as he stood before the gate to the house. He started up the path, his patent-leather pumps clicking on the loose bricks, then stopped as he realized that something was out of place. Out of the corner of his eye he noticed a patch of white by the bushes to his left—something that didn't belong there, an unfamiliar object in a landscape that he knew by heart, even in the dark. For a fraction of a second he wondered if Vicky had left a towel or a napkin out to dry, but he knew perfectly well that this was unthinkable—the clothesline was behind the house, not out front where the neighbors would see it—and at the same instant he realized he was looking at a white shirt front, a familiar voice said, "Now you're going to get a lesson, you cheeky nigger bastard!"

Morgan stood rooted to the spot for a moment, not so much out of fear—though he *was* afraid, and could feel his scrotum tightening, his stomach knotting up—but more from anger at his own stupidity. He should have guessed that Higgins would ambush him—in fact, he *had* guessed and had managed to leave the club in the company of several other people in anticipation of just such an attack. Higgins had outsmarted him by waiting till he felt safe at home.

Higgins came crashing through the bush like a wild boar, grunted and landed a wild, arm-swinging punch on Morgan's cheek. The shock and the pain cleared Morgan's head. It was too late to apologize, and impossible to flee, for Higgins had already put his left arm around Morgan, pinning him close so he could use his right fist to jab Morgan in the kidneys. At any moment now, Higgins would knee him in the groin, Morgan knew that, and once he was down, Higgins would kick him unmercifully.

"Help!" Morgan cried, into the silent night, then his breath was cut off as Higgins gave him the expected knee in the balls, and Morgan, who knew the pain was only a foretaste of what he'd get from Higgins once he was on the ground, suddenly found himself reacting with the thoughtless fury of a panicked coward.

Gasping for breath, he drove his head into Higgins's face. Higgins gave a wild cry of surprise and pain, then lunged forward again, as Morgan feebly pummeled him, trying to protect himself with one hand while punching with the other, and wishing, not for the first time, that he had learned to box at school instead of getting out of it with one excuse after another.

He felt a terrible pain as his knuckles scraped against Higgins's false teeth, and wondered for an instant if he wouldn't have been better off not trying to resist the Australian in the first place.

Higgins landed a glancing blow on Morgan's nose, then closed in for the kill, tightening his arm around Morgan to force him to the ground, when Morgan saw something move behind them, a flash of white appearing from behind the bushes. Higgins may have noticed it, too—he turned his head suddenly at any rate, giving Morgan, who was on his knees, a chance to grab the big man's nose and one ear in his fingers; then there was a dull, loud thump and Higgins collapsed to the ground, his fingers twitching slightly. His glass eye had popped out and was staring up at the night sky lugubriously.

"Oh, my God," Queenie said. "I put his eye out! I'm going to be sick."

Morgan fought for his breath. He could see her now, quite clearly, standing over Higgins in her cotton nightgown, holding a brick. "It's all right," he said. "It's his glass eye. You haven't blinded him. Can you help me up?"

Queenie dropped the brick, leaned over and pulled Morgan to his feet. For a girl who hated gym and sports, she had unsuspected strength, he thought, and quickness of mind, too. He was surprised that he was able to notice, despite his pain, that one of the straps of her nightgown had broken, exposing a small, firm, perfectly shaped breast in the moonlight, as she leaned over him. The nipple was delicate and pointed, so close to Morgan's face that he was almost tempted to kiss it.

"You look awful," Queenie said. "Do you think your nose is broken?"

Morgan ran one hand over it, winced with the pain, but was unable to detect any movement of the cartilage. "I don't think so," he said thickly.

"Who is he?"

"A chap from the club. Higgins. A bloody-minded Australian. We had a fight about Peggy D'Souza of all things . . ." He stood up with difficulty. "Oh, my God, what are we to do with him? We can't leave him on the bloody lawn."

"Why not put him in the car and drive him down to the bus stop on Brahmapore Street? Somebody will find him there in the morning. Only we'd better hurry."

"We?"

"Well, you can't carry him alone. Come on. I'll take one arm, you take the other."

Morgan shook his head, inflicting further pain on himself, then gave in. Queenie had her mother's forceful way, there was no doubt about it. Together they dragged Higgins over to the car and hauled him onto the front seat. She carefully knotted the broken strap of her nightgown, to Morgan's relief. "I'd better get his glass eye," Morgan said.

"Better you than me. I draw the line at that."

Morgan retrieved the eye from the paving, came back and tucked it into the pocket of Higgins's dinner jacket. Then he untied Higgins's black bow tie, loosened his collar and removed his false teeth. "We don't want him choking to death," he explained.

Queenie sat in the back seat, hunched over with her arms around her knees, until Morgan reached Brahmapore Street. There they carefully dragged Higgins out of the car and propped him in a sitting position on the bench at the bus stop. His chin fell to his chest, like that of a man who has fallen asleep after a hard night's drinking.

"He'll be safe enough here," Morgan said. "No wog would have the guts to rob a white man in evening dress."

On the way home, Queenie sat in front beside Morgan, apparently unconscious of the fact that she was wearing only a thin nightgown. The breeze caught her hair, and she sighed with pleasure, grateful for the moment of comfort.

"What were you doing awake?" Morgan asked.

"I couldn't sleep."

"It's the heat."

"Yes . . . well, it's not just the heat. I keep thinking about things. . . ."

"What things?"

"Oh, I don't know . . . I feel hot and lonely and bored. When I was little, I could sleep however hot it was. Now I feel so restless at night—as if I itched all over, only I don't." She stretched languidly, then shook out her nightgown to let in the cool breeze. "I wish I were grown-up already," she added.

"You will be soon enough, Queenie. And anyway, it isn't any better."

She looked at him impatiently as he stopped the car in front of the gate. Grown-ups never understand, she thought to herself—not even Morgan, who was, apart from Magda, the most understanding grown-up she knew. In the past year or so it was as if her body had taken on a life of its own, as if it no longer belonged to her. Boys and grown men—even Morgan himself—stared at her with obvious admiration, but the body they admired so much seemed to Queenie like someone else's, as unfamiliar as a stranger.

Morgan leaned over and gave her a quick, uncle-like kiss, which only made her feel worse, though she couldn't say so. He too seemed strained, which was one of the problems. When she was a child, Morgan had snuggled with her, played with her, held her on his lap; now he behaved in her proximity like a man walking on eggshells, as if he was afraid of the consequences of touching her.

"You'd better get back to bed," he said. "I think your Ma had better not hear about *your* part in this."

Queenie nodded. "What about your face?" she asked.

"I'll wash up."

"You can't do it by yourself."

He shrugged. It was true. Morgan wasn't even sure he had the courage to *look* at his face in the mirror, let alone wash it. Together they crept into the house and up the stairs.

In his bedroom, Queenie poured the pitcher of water into the flowered enamel washbasin and carried it over to the bed, where Morgan sat, suddenly drained and exhausted as the adrenaline stopped flowing. In the excitement he had been able to ignore his pain and the other consequences of the fight; now, aching in every muscle, he contemplated the ruin of his evening suit and felt like weeping.

"You'll see," Queenie whispered, guessing what he was thinking. "The ayah can sponge it down, sew it up, and press it with the steam iron tomorrow. It will look like new."

"Perhaps. The shirt is ruined."

"Well, you do have other shirts." Queenie giggled. "At least you haven't lost your teeth."

"I know that, Queenie. What's so funny, though?"

"Higgins hasn't got *his*," she said, giggling. "We forgot to put them in his pocket." She reached into Morgan's jacket and removed Higgins's false teeth, placing them beside the washbasin. "A trophy," she said.

"My word, he'll be angry. Perhaps I should give them back to him. . . ."

"Not on your life, Morgan. Let him eat porridge until he gets a new set. You could give them to Peggy D'Souza!"

Morgan laughed, despite the pain in his lips, and began to take off his collar, placing the gold studs next to Higgins's teeth, which seemed to be smiling cheerfully as they never had in Higgins's mouth.

He watched Queenie wring out the washcloth and lean forward to clean off his face. In the light from his nightlamp, he could see how flushed the child was, no doubt from all this excitement, and then he realized with a slight thrill of alarm and guilty pleasure that he could see her nipples and a small triangular dark patch between her legs quite clearly through the thin cotton. He closed his eyes firmly and tried to put his mind on something else, but he could feel himself hardening and prayed that Queenie wouldn't look down and notice the bulge in his trousers. Luckily her attention was fixed on his face.

"I think tonight had better be a secret between us, Queenie," he said, as the washcloth touched his face.

"Oh, yes," she said, "always."

And then, quite suddenly, as the cold water touched his wounds, Morgan passed out.

When he woke, aching and throbbing from head to foot, it was nearly noon, and he realized, to his sudden horror, that his evening suit had been removed, as well as his torn and bloodied shirt. He was lying on the bed in his undershorts, and as he opened one puffy eye, wincing from the pain, he saw that his patent-leather pumps had been placed neatly beside the washstand, from which Higgins's teeth were grinning at him.

Queenie had undressed him! He felt humiliation, then a certain excitement, then overwhelming guilt at his own feelings.

From now on, he told himself, he would have to be careful.

She wasn't a child anymore.

• • •

Morgan's injuries won him new respect at home. Physical violence as such did not dismay Vicky. Her father had enforced discipline in the Indian railway gangs with his fists. "It's the only language they understand," he often said. "Words are wasted on niggers."

It surprised her that Morgan was following in their father's footsteps, and so tardily at that, but so far as Vicky was concerned, Morgan's black eye, his swollen nose and his puffy lips were wounds of honor, and he found himself being treated, for the first time, with the deference due the man of the house.

It was a new experience, and by no means unpleasant. Even the men Morgan had been to school with, fellows who despised him for playing in a jazz band instead of driving a locomotive and envied the fact that he mixed with the English, clapped him on the back and treated him to a beer.

Magda, who often teased Morgan, now treated him with a certain amused respect, for the general had been a great believer in the value of a beating to keep soldiers, servants, Jews and insolent peasants in line.

Yet, for a hero, he was unexpectedly gloomy, as if the whole incident weighed on his mind. Something, it was clear to Magda, troubled him. She was an expert on the moods of men, if nothing else. "Cheer up," she told him.

Morgan smiled as much as his swollen lips would allow. They were sitting on the veranda, overlooking the site of the now famous encounter, trying to get some relief from the heat. Queenie and her mother sat together on a wicker settee, Ma sewing, her glasses pushed down to the tip of her nose, Queenie resentfully studying her lessons while she tried to pick up a pencil with her toes. Morgan sipped a glass of Tiger beer—a concession on Vicky's part to his new status.

"I'm cheerful enough," he said.

"You should be," Magda said. "The Firpos are taking you back as soon as your lips are healed. And Higgins is gone."

"I know. He did a Burton—packed his bags and ran without even asking for his teeth."

"Good riddance to bad rubbish," Vicky said. "Queenie, stop playing with your toes and put your shoes back on. It's not ladylike to go barefoot like a native."

"Oh, Ma, it's so hot. And this book is so *boring*. I hate arithmetic. What's the point?"

"You won't get a good job if you can't do sums, child. And anyway, you have to pass your exams."

Queenie sighed and moved closer to her mother. "Ma," she said, looking up at her, "there's a theatrical group at school."

"Is there, dear?"

"They put on plays." Queenie did her best to look forlorn. Her best was usually pretty good, but this time Ma went on with her sewing.

"I expect so."

"Can I join it?"

"Not 'can,' dear. 'May.' Of course you may not."

"Why?"

"Because your schoolwork isn't good enough, to begin with. Besides, theatricals aren't at all ladylike. I'm surprised the school allows such a thing."

"Well, they do. Beryl O'Brien is in it, and *her* father is a superintendent of freight and has an office of his own."

"That's as may be. The O'Briens are perfectly respectable, I won't deny that, but just because they allow Beryl to do something foolish is no reason why you should."

"But Ma! They put on all sorts of perfectly *nice* plays. Gilbert and Sullivan. Beryl's mother sewed her a lovely kimono for *The Mikado*—though with a fat little face like hers, she's going to look pretty funny as a Japanese. Still, I suppose the kimono will hide her big bottom."

"We don't speak badly of other people, Queenie. Particularly about things they can't help. Beryl is a very nice little girl. She'll be quite pretty enough once she loses her puppy fat."

"I'm not so sure," Morgan said. "Her mother is built like a water buffalo."

Queenie stared at Morgan, her dark eyes welling with tears of laughter. He noticed for the first time that she no longer had the hands of a schoolgirl. Her fingers were long, thin and tapered; the nails weren't chewed or dirty, as most schoolgirls' were—indeed they were so perfect that he suspected Magda had been giving Queenie manicure lessons. Those same fingers had undressed him when he passed out. He wondered what Queenie had seen and touched as she took off his clothes. He knew her to be innocent, but that did not mean she wasn't normally curious.

He felt himself blushing as she looked at him. His eyes were fixed on her thighs, exposed by the short school dress as she sprawled on the settee, still clutching for the pencil with her toes despite Ma's disapproval.

Morgan realized he was staring back at her and glanced quickly at

Ma to see if she had noticed. She was still intent on her sewing. He looked back at Queenie and cleared his throat. "I don't see anything wrong with Queenie's trying it," he said. He had hoped to produce an effect of stern masculine common sense, but he was aware, even as he spoke, that his voice lacked the ring of authority. He was not used to opposing his sister—certainly not in matters that affected Queenie.

There was a moment of silence, then to his surprise, Vicky raised her head from her sewing, sighed and nodded. "I suppose you're right," she said reluctantly, as if Morgan's new role gave him some special knowledge or wisdom. A tyrant Vicky might be, but she was a tyrant by default. She had been obedient to her stern father and her irresponsible husband; now that Morgan had assumed his proper role as a man, she was prepared to accept his leadership on the same terms.

"I believe it can do her no harm," Morgan said more firmly. "If girls like Beryl O'Brien are in it, there's nothing to worry about." He looked at Queenie, who was staring at him with such passionate gratitude that he broke into a sweat. He forced himself to look into his teacup, but even there he could still see in his mind the gentle curve of Queenie's lips.

"I only hope it doesn't put ideas into the girl's head," Vicky said darkly.

There was no need to worry about *that*, Queenie thought. There were already plenty of ideas in her head, few of which would have pleased her mother. She had no desire to go to work as a typist or a secretary in some stuffy Calcutta office—though admittedly that was a more enticing future than growing up to marry somebody like Paddy O'Brien, Beryl's scrofulous older brother, and to spend the rest of her life looking after the children, while he drank beer with his friends and worried about what would happen when the Indians took over the railways.

Queenie had no great interest in the theater, as such, and did not harbor any fantasies about her talents as an actress, but the theatrical group was a social step in the right direction—she could see that all right—and guessed that Ma would, too, the moment she got over her initial inclination to say no to everything new.

What surprised her was the fact that Morgan had taken her side against Ma. She had stared right at him, hoping for his support, but had not really expected to get it. On the surface, the relationship

between them was the same, but Queenie was aware that at a deeper
level it had shifted. When she looked at him, he had a tendency to
blush. The same sort of thing happened at school, too, for the idea of
joining the theatrical group had not occurred to her spontaneously—
Mr. Pugh himself, who seemed to stare at her almost as much as Morgan did, had suggested it.

Most of the teachers ignored her—she was neither good at games
nor an outstanding pupil. Mr. Pugh, who taught English literature and
music, was an exception. Occasionally his eyes, which were protuberant
and a strange, washed-out blue in color, seemed to focus on her with
alarming intensity. When other teachers did this, it was usually followed by a sharp question or even a rap on the knuckles with a ruler,
but Mr. Pugh merely blinked, swallowed hard, his Adam's apple
bobbing rapidly above the starched high collar and the striped Old
Boy's tie of some English school or college, and went on with his lesson.

He had a habit of staring at her when he recited poetry. Often this
was harmless enough, and even rather pleasant, as when Mr. Pugh fixed
his pale eyes on her and softly read, *"The island-valley of Avalon;*

> *Where falls not hail, or rain, or any snow,*
> *Nor ever wind blows loudly; but it lies*
> *Deep-meadowed, happy, fair, with orchard lawns*
> *And bowery hollows crown'd with summer sea . . ."*

Outside the schoolroom an emaciated cow tore at a sparse brown
patch of dry grass, but Tennyson's lines spoke to Queenie of the
England of her dreams.

At other times, perhaps because of his mood or the heat, Mr. Pugh's
attention would be caught by a line, then his voice rose to a fever-pitch,
much to the alarm of his students. These lines mostly had to do with
women, and whenever Pugh recited from Shakespeare, Queenie trembled, since Shakespeare often set Mr. Pugh off. Once, to her horror,
Pugh had risen to his feet as if he were in pain while reciting from
King Lear, and shouted directly at Queenie: "But to the girdle do the
gods inherit, below lies all the fiend's!"

Happily this anatomical allusion passed over the girls' heads, though
some of them giggled at the word "girdle." Queenie went to the trouble
of finding the line and reading it, but it made no more sense in print
than it had when Pugh shouted it at her, and Magda, whose knowledge
of the theater was better than anyone else's in the house, was not helpful. "All Englishmen hate women," she said.

Queenie sat on Magda's bed, her chin on her knees, watching Magda finish her makeup. She ignored Magda's remark—it was never worthwhile to argue with Magda; she had a way of making it clear when she had pronounced her final judgment on a subject. "Can I try your eye shadow?" Queenie asked.

"No, I'm running short. Anyway, your mother would notice."

"I'd wipe it off."

"Last time you forgot, and she saw it on your pillow. I thought I'd never hear the end of it. 'It will be lipstick next,' she told me. And so it will be, I expect."

"I wish I were old enough to wear makeup. Heather Gomes wears it."

"The little girl with the ugly hair? But she *needs* it, poor thing! She wears Pearl White because her skin is so dark. I see a lot of Anglo-Indian girls wearing it at night. In a certain light it's all right, but when they've danced a little, it begins to run; then they look like lepers. Be grateful you don't need that kind of thing, Queenie. You have beautiful skin. It's quite pale enough. If you take care of it, believe me, it will take care of you."

"Do men like beautiful skin?"

"Yes, of course. Even the ugliest man thinks he's entitled to a beautiful woman—and entitled to be fussy, too! Though it's true that men are such fools—a little bit of makeup, the right dress, a certain way of walking, and they're after you like flies. You'll learn, Queenie." She coughed harshly. "God help us, we all learn."

"Is it nice being with a man?"

"It *can* be nice, yes. My God, what a lot of questions you ask! It depends on the man, and the circumstances. When you're in love, it's wonderful. When you're not—well, you'll find that out, too."

"Were you in love with the general?"

"Of course. But a love like that doesn't come along every day, Queenie. When it does, you have to hold on to it, because it doesn't often last. Other things get in the way."

"What things?"

"War. Revolution. Poverty. Age. Death. Even boredom and unfaithfulness."

"That's sad."

"Yes, I suppose, but life *is* sad. You'll see. Not all the time, however. A beautiful girl like you should be happy."

"I don't think you're right about Mr. Pugh."

"Pugh? What about him?"

"I don't think he hates women."

"Englishmen do, I told you. They can't help it."

"He's always looking at me out of the corner of his eye. And do you know what I heard him say about me to one of the other teachers?"

"How would I know, darling?" Magda asked, staring at herself in the mirror. She sighed, dabbed on a little more eye shadow and hoped it would do.

"He said, 'That girl Queenie Kelley has bedroom eyes.'"

Magda turned and laughed, a deep, guttural laugh which was almost that of a man, somehow not at all an *English* way of laughing. She took a sip of gin and lit another cigarette, then turned back to the mirror.

"My dear child," she said, "you've just had your first grown-up compliment."

CHAPTER 3

"CHANGE AND DECAY all around I see." Cyril Frederick John Fitzroy-Pugh, M.A. (Oxon.) stared out the window of his bungalow at the dusty row of similar houses shimmering in the early morning heat, lit his first cigarette of the day and coughed. His collar chafed, his shirt was already soaking wet and the smell of bacon cooking in the kitchen gave him a sudden, involuntary spasm of nausea.

This was not the India he had dreamed about, a world of Oriental splendor and rich sensuality—in fact it exactly resembled his life in England, except for the climate. He sighed, puffed on his cigarette and waited for his wife to call him to breakfast.

Pugh conjured up silken tents, the whisper of a cool tree-shaded spring, precious jewels glittering in the firelight, a dusky, wanton girl, her bared breasts gleaming smoothly like pearls, her face at once childish and knowing, the diaphanous skirt opening lasciviously as she leaned over him, laughing, while the long, slim fingers grasped him . . . In the dark, the music stopped. The only noise now was the sound of her breathing; he could smell her clean, fresh body, proudly naked, feel her skin against his . . .

"Cyril! Breakfast, dear. The girls are already sitting down." Mrs. Pugh's voice pierced the hot air like the whine of a bullet, but managed at the same time to convey, even in so few words, a wealth of suffering, self-sacrifice and resentment.

Pugh returned regretfully to the real world, realized that he was wet in a way that had nothing to do with the heat, and quickly set about the urgent task of tidying himself up.

He felt no guilt—man, he believed, had desires that must be released. On the other hand, he felt no relief. The thought of Mrs. Pugh,

her bony body all too visible, alas, in her white summer frock, op-
pressed him almost as much as the prospect of sitting down to breakfast with his three lumpish daughters.

Pugh squeezed out the washcloth in the tepid water of his shaving
bowl, realized that the girl in his fantasy very much resembled Queenie
Kelley, then remembered he had left his cigarette burning on the
windowsill. He turned back and discovered that it had already blistered
the varnish, leaving a long, discolored track like that of a snail. He
picked the smoldering stub up with his fingers and burned himself.

He tried to repair the damage to the windowsill with his fingernails,
made it worse, then gave it up. When Mrs. Pugh noticed the blistered
varnish, it would fill her conversation for days. Such small failings on
his part were her only source of pleasure. She would not complain or
accuse; she would simply bring the subject up again and again, until
the mere mention of it became a kind of punishment, a monotonous
torture from which there was no escape this side of the grave.

Pugh buttoned himself, straightened his tie, put on an expression
appropriate to a paterfamilias and schoolmaster, and went downstairs
to join his family.

Unlike most teachers, John Pugh loved young people.

He loved them, in fact, a little more than was seemly, which explained why he was teaching English literature and music in India
rather than England, where his "rapport" (as he liked to call it) with
the young had led to several embarrassing and difficult episodes.

These "misunderstandings," to use Pugh's own description of what
had seemed to most other people serious breaches of conduct, had
made his employment at home increasingly difficult. The authorities
took a dim view of Pugh's "rapport" with his students, and it was
suggested that he would be well advised to leave England if he wished
to pursue his career.

It was all nonsense, of course, as Pugh had explained to his wife
and the authorities. Was not a prophet always without honor in his
own country, he asked rhetorically, as she snuffled into her handkerchief over the thought of disgrace and exile? His methods offended his
colleagues and shocked his superiors. So be it. He succeeded where
they had failed. It was mere jealousy. The charge that he had "interfered" with a thirteen-year-old schoolgirl, he assured her, was a base

canard. Children—girls particularly—had to be put in touch with their own emotions if they were to understand and appreciate poetry and music. The accusation that he had asked the child to take off her clothes was equally baseless—and in any case, was it not ridiculous for children to be covered with layers of heavy wool? There was nothing shameful in nudity—sun and air produced healthy bodies, as music and poetry produced healthy minds. *Mens sana in corpore sano*, he had told the headmaster, as well as the two policemen in raincoats and bowler hats who journeyed down from London to investigate the complaint, but even Latin did not convince them.

At the memory of that unfortunate interview, Pugh's nausea returned.

"Good morning, Cyril," Mrs. Pugh said timidly. She always seemed to be on the verge of crying, though Pugh had long since come to the conclusion that it was an optical illusion caused by the combination of her thick, rimless spectacles and a regrettable tendency toward hay fever.

Pugh repressed a shudder as he sat down. He loathed the name Cyril, and preferred to be called John, a plainer, more masculine name.

His daughters, who had been obliged to wait for him, plunged their spoons greedily into their porridge. They ate as if it might be their last meal. Pugh wondered whether the girls' unseemly passion for food was a form of sexual sublimation, and made a mental note to consult Havelock Ellis at the earliest opportunity. All three girls were depressingly moon-faced, which was hardly surprising, since they stuffed themselves with sweets, despite his lectures on vitamins and nutrition. He wondered if the Kelley girl had a healthy diet.

"Did you sleep well, dear?" Mrs. Pugh asked, interrupting his train of thought as usual. Pugh wondered if it was an unconscious act on her part, or sheer malevolence. She seemed to know so exactly when her interruptions would most distract him that he found it hard to believe they were accidental.

"Quite well," he said untruthfully, for he had spent the night, as always, in an uneasy stupor of heat and sexual fantasy. "And you?" he asked mechanically.

"I had a dreadful headache. And hay fever. I hardly slept a wink."

Pugh nodded with what he hoped would pass for sympathy. Mrs. Pugh never admitted to sleeping well, but as far as Pugh was able to observe, she slept like a log. Certainly the slightest indication of sexual arousal on his part put her to sleep instantly. He prepared to repel further conversation by opening his copy of *The Bengalee*. The headlines told of new strike threats from the All-India Congress Party. Pugh had been an admirer of Gandhi until he arrived in India; experience at first hand with the natives of India had destroyed his faith in self-government as a solution to their problems. They were, by and large, he thought, a cunning, lying, lazy, filthy lot. He saw no reason to believe that Gandhi was any better than his followers.

He turned the page. He noted that an emergency meeting of the Anglo-Indian Committee had once again drawn the viceroy's attention to the difficulties of their position, and wondered if Queenie's family was involved in what appeared to be yet another hopeless attempt to secure special privileges and quotas for the Anglo-Indians.

"I may be late this afternoon," Pugh said, putting down *The Bengalee*. "I'm getting started on our little production of *The Mikado*."

Mrs. Pugh sniffed. "You mustn't overtire yourself, Cyril," she said. "The students take such a lot out of you."

Even while he was starting his battered old motorcar, to take the girls to their school and carry him to his, Pugh pondered this remark.

Was Mrs. Pugh sharper than he thought? He dismissed the idea. All the same, it would cost nothing to be a little more careful.

Then he thought of Queenie, and he whistled above the clatter of the motor all the way to school.

That Queenie had no talent—or at any rate none for performing Gilbert and Sullivan—was immediately clear to Pugh. The girl's assets, considerable as they were, did not include a good singing voice; in fact, she appeared to be tone-deaf.

What she did have, however—and that to an extraordinary degree— was *presence*. She was so beautiful that you couldn't take your eyes off her, but there was more to it than that: somehow she seemed to have a natural sense of how to attract attention to herself. The effect was strengthened by a certain modesty. Queenie seemed genuinely unaware of her beauty, or perhaps she was still simply confused and embarrassed by it.

It did not help that the other girls resented her. Certainly she made them seem unattractive and clumsy by comparison. Most of the girls approached amateur theatricals in much the same spirit as they played field hockey. Queenie seemed as out of place among them as she did on the playing grounds, where her lack of enthusiasm for competitive sports was notorious. Pugh guessed their resentment was because she seemed so much older than she was. She already had a grown-up beauty and the graceful movements of a young woman. She was still a child— but she was determined not to *behave* like a child, which gave her, particularly on stage, a gravity that was entirely inappropriate. No matter how carefully Pugh coached her, she seemed unable to enter into the spirit of the thing, and he found it easy to understand why the other girls thought her "stuck-up."

Nor was the task of directing her made any easier by the fact that he broke out into a sweat every time he touched her. At Saint Anthony's School for Girls it was well known among the older pupils that Mr. Pugh's methods were unorthodox. He stood close to his performers, so close that he often rubbed up against them, and he used his hands to show them how to move and gesture.

The girls did not object or complain. Mr. Pugh was a sahib, and could therefore do no wrong in their eyes, or in their parents'; besides, he showed more interest in them than any of the other teachers, even if that interest was expressed in a somewhat unconventional form. Far from resenting Pugh's attentions, the girls were flattered by them. Membership in the Drama Society was in any case much sought after, if only as a badge of worldly experience, and was generally limited to the "better class" of Anglo-Indian girls.

Queenie did not belong there. Ma was "comfortably off," by the standards of "The Community," but hardly respectable, since she took in lodgers, and it was only at Mr. Pugh's insistence that Queenie had been brought in—which naturally made her even more unpopular.

"Stuck-up chee-chee cow," Heather Gomes whispered, as Queenie went through the motions of playing a Japanese maiden, draped in a singularly unbecoming kimono made up for the play by Mrs. O'Brien, whose sense of color and skill with a needle left much to be desired. Her daughter Beryl giggled as Heather Gomes poked her in the ribs. It was a source of satisfaction to both of them that Queenie, whose skin was so much paler than theirs, seemed unable to grasp the rudiments of acting, nor did it escape their attention that her accent—the telltale Anglo-Indian speech pattern, with its singsong inflections, that strange combination of Cockney and Hindu—was more pronounced than theirs. "She sounds just like a bloody chee-chee, too," Beryl said, just loud enough for Queenie to hear.

Pugh heard it, too. Queenie was holding back her tears—or possibly restraining herself from attacking the two girls, since her fists were tightly clenched. He walked over to her across the improvised stage and put one hand on her shoulder. She looked up at him and Pugh felt his knees grow weak, as if he had been running. Her face was so perfect that it was impossible to think of her as a schoolgirl.

"Pay no attention to them, Miss Kelley," he said in a low voice.

"I can't help it, sir. They hate me."

Pugh was about to say that this wasn't so, but then he reflected that there was probably a certain amount of truth in what Queenie said. If the other girls did not hate her, they certainly didn't *like* her. "Why do you think that is?" he asked.

She looked up at him, her dark eyes wide open in surprise. Most adults would have argued with her, tried to persuade her that it wasn't true, but Pugh took her seriously, and she was grateful for that.

"I don't know," she said. "They always have. Perhaps because Uncle Morgan is a musician and doesn't work on the railway the way everyone else does. Perhaps because my Dad was a jockey. *He* didn't work on the railway either, you see. And they make fun of the way I talk."

Pugh raised one eyebrow in surprise. All Anglo-Indians had such a strong and unmistakable accent that they sounded pretty much alike to him. Perhaps it was true that Queenie's accent was more pronounced than most. He would have to listen more carefully.

"I can't act," she said. "They're right about that."

"Well . . . you don't seem to be having a good time. The whole point of Gilbert and Sullivan is that the cast has to look as if it's enjoying itself just as much as the audience."

"You mean I have to be silly?"

"No. Well, as a matter of fact, yes. The three little maids *are* silly, of course. The whole thing is silly. It's meant to be silly. You have to let yourself go and enjoy being silly, you see. There's nothing wrong in being silly, you know. I'm not sure it isn't the best part of life."

"It isn't grown-up."

Pugh raised an eyebrow—a spectacular gesture, since his eyebrows were almost as bushy as those of Queenie's grandfather, and dark ginger in color. "Why are you so keen to be grown-up?" he asked. "It isn't at all what it's cracked up to be."

"People don't tell grown-ups what they have to do—sir."

"Alas, you're wrong about that, Queenie."

Queenie stared at him. It was the first time Pugh had called her by her first name, and it was strictly against the school rules. It had not occurred to her that Mr. Pugh—a master, a sahib and indisputably a

grown-up—could be influenced just like Morgan. She licked her lips and gave him her undivided attention, and was gratified to see him blush.

Pugh felt his face grow warm—and also felt the eyes of the other pupils staring at his back. He was spending too much time with Queenie, he knew. Even the piano accompanist, Miss Rhys-Mogford, old and half-blind though she might be, was bound to notice. She was already coughing impatiently.

"Come to my room this afternoon after school," he whispered. "We'll talk about the play."

She nodded solemnly and walked off the stage, as Miss Rhys-Mogford crashed into "Three Little Maids from School" again, fortissimo and off-key as always.

Pugh winced. He realized that his face was still warm and found himself wondering what he would say to Queenie.

For a moment it occurred to him that he was getting into deeper water than was prudent, but he dismissed the thought.

Queenie stood in front of him, her hands demurely locked just above the hem of her pleated skirt. Her blazer was unbuttoned, but her school blouse was fastened to the neck.

He wasn't entirely comfortable alone with her. A teacher could get away with a good deal, provided he was never found alone with one of his students. As long as Pugh limited himself to touching the girls when they were in class, or at the Drama Society, or on school outings, he was safe. But a teacher alone with a girl could be accused of anything. In the eyes of many people, the mere fact of his being in this dusty classroom with Queenie, *and* with the door closed, would be proof of criminal intent.

The room had the musty, chalk-dusty, sweaty smell of schoolrooms the world over. On one wall was a tattered, fading world map, the English possessions printed in a particularly poisonous shade of pink and the oceans in pale blue, the two colors apparently covering most of the planet's surface. The school desks, worn by the elbows of countless generations, were covered with inkstains.

Pugh perched against his own table-desk, which wobbled precariously, as one leg was shorter than the others. No matter how many times he pointed this out to Mr. Kalit Singh, the head porter, nothing was done. Singh was a Sikh, who wore his black-dyed beard in a small

net so that it would be sharply pointed for whatever religious cere-
monies Sikhs were obliged to attend. Pugh knew little about Sikhs except that they were warlike, rude and wore their unshorn hair in
turbans. He assumed that their religion was even more barbarous than
most, but his well-meaning inquiries on the subject had apparently
given great offense to Singh, who revenged himself by replying "It shall
be done, sahib" to every request of Pugh's, then ignoring them.

"Will I get a part in the play?" Queenie asked. "Ma will be disappointed if I don't, sir."

"I will put you in the chorus, Queenie. Right at the center. That
should make her happy."

"Was I *that* bad, sir?"

Pugh stood up and walked over to her. "There, there," he said
softly, for she seemed about to cry. Without even thinking about it, he
put his arms around her.

"It's the way I talk, isn't it?"

"Well, you do have an accent, but so do the other girls. It's not by
any means unpleasant, you know. It's a little like Welsh."

"But it's not the proper way to talk, is it?"

"Perhaps not."

"Ma and my Uncle Morgan talk the same way."

"Quite so. The Anglo-Indian accent is quite distinctive. It's a most
interesting subject, in fact . . ."

"If I talked proper, would I have a better part?"

"Properly. It isn't just the accent, Queenie. Amateur theatricals are
supposed to be fun, you see. You have to learn to let yourself go, to
enjoy yourself. . . . Have you heard of Sigmund Freud, Queenie?"

She shook her head.

"He's a very wise man. He divides the human mind into the id and
the ego . . . let me put it more simply. One part of us wants to
behave properly, and the other part wants to have fun. If we re-
press . . . if we don't let the part of us that wants to have fun, *have*
fun—then we become sick."

"Sick how?"

"I don't mean that we become physically sick, Queenie, though that's
possible, by the way—it's called a 'psychosomatic illness.' I mean that
we become sick in our *minds*—bitter, unhappy, unable to enjoy life."

"Like Miss Rhys-Mogford?"

"Exactly." Pugh ran his hands down Queenie's back. She did not
resist. In fact, she appeared to be waiting patiently for his next move.

Beneath the cloth of her blue blazer he could feel—just faintly—the strap of her camisole. His hands trembled slightly and he let them slide down her back until they reached her waist. The flannel was so thick it defeated his sense of touch, and indeed the school uniform was designed with that object in mind. Very slowly he slid one hand a little lower, below the edge of her blazer, and let it rest on the swell of her buttocks. He cursed the stout gray flannel of the school-uniform skirt, his imagination racing to the smooth flesh beneath it, doubtless concealed in a modest but provocative pair of schoolgirl knickers.

For a moment, Pugh was almost blinded by the thought of those unseen undergarments, the demure little elastic bands around the legs, the pattern of embroidered flowers on the waistband, the faint odor of Queenie's womanhood in the clean, freshly laundered cotton—for Queenie had none of the grubbiness most schoolgirls suffered from, and always seemed neater and cleaner than her disheveled and sweaty companions.

Pugh groaned at the pressure in his groin; then, to his horror, he heard the steps of someone in the hall—no doubt Kalit Singh making his rounds inopportunely. He stepped away from Queenie, putting his hands behind his back like the schoolmaster he was.

"Still working, sahib-Pugh?" Singh called from the other side of the door.

"Yes, Mr. Singh," Pugh called back loudly. "I won't be much longer."

Singh dithered for a moment, shuffling his feet.

"I'll lock up myself, Mr. Singh," Pugh shouted. "I won't be long."

"As the sahib wishes." Singh's feet could be heard with diminishing volume as he passed on down the corridor. Pugh breathed a sigh of relief, then turned his attention back to Queenie.

"Can you teach me to speak properly?" she asked.

"What do you mean by 'properly'?" he asked.

"Not like a chee-chee. Like *you*."

"It would take some time . . . private lessons . . ." Pugh turned the matter over in his mind and decided it was an opportunity being presented to him on a silver platter. Her dark eyes were fixed on him from under the thick, curved lashes and her lips were slightly parted. She stood with her toes together, in her school sandals and white socks, like a mute supplicant. "I think it could be managed," he said at last.

Queenie nodded. "Thank you, sir," she said. Her voice was trembling slightly, and Pugh wondered if she would have cried had he decided to say no. Or was she simply pleased that she had won? Did she have any idea of the effect she had on a man? He decided it was unlikely. Part of Queenie's attraction was her innocence.

He reached over and patted her on the shoulder, a firm, school-masterly gesture, well within the bounds of what was permissible, but he was unable to take his hand away. He brushed a speck of imaginary lint off the navy-blue flannel, then his fingertips swept over the lapel and ran lightly across her blouse. The sense of touch, he said to him-self—what wonderful gifts it has to offer us.

"I think a few private lessons will do wonders for you, Queenie," he said. "And when it's just the two of us—you don't have to call me 'sir.' "

"Well, but surely it will cost *something?*" Vicky said doubtfully. "Private lessons don't come cheap, I'm sure."

"Oh, Ma, he's doing it for nothing. He thinks my voice needs im-proving, that's all. He's going to help me get rid of my accent."

"*What* accent, I should like to know? You speak the way we all do."

"I want to speak like a pukka English lady."

"Oh, my. I don't know what will come next."

Morgan looked up from his copy of *The Bengalee*—he was reading with some fascination the account of a "Dastardly Outrage" in which Mr. Justice Simpson was trying to sort out the facts of a case involving one Akbar Kallan, who had found his wife in bed with another man and stabbed her twice in the heart, afterwards wounding his father-in-law, the girl's brother and a certain Sayib Zaniab, who may or may not have been the man whom he had found on top of his wife in his own charpoy.

Counsel for the Crown, Mr. Ram Dass Mehta, had some unkind—and in Morgan's opinion, unwise—words to say about the Muslim propensity for primitive violence and blood feuds. Hindus never knew when to shut up. Morgan had seen plenty of Hindu-Muslim riots in his time, most of them sparked off by nothing worse than Mr. Ram Dass bloody Mehta's ill-chosen words.

"What about these private lessons for our Queenie, Morgan? What do you think?"

Morgan had not been paying close attention, but more than any of them he was aware of the advantages of a "proper" accent. His own was less pronounced than Vicky's, but still noticeable. Queenie would have a better chance at passing as English if she spoke without an Anglo-Indian accent, and it was therefore a blessing if this Pugh wanted to teach her.

He was not surprised that Pugh was doing it for nothing. The English were like that, teachers especially. The pukka sahibs were gentlemen. They did what they thought was right, without asking to be paid or waiting to be thanked. This Pugh was clearly such a one, he guessed, a sahib of the old school, who saw that Queenie was special.

"To talk of money to a man like Pugh would offend him," he said. "He sees that Queenie is gifted. He offers to give her special lessons. We should accept this gratefully."

"Oh, my," Vicky said, "I suppose so. Queenie, child, do thank Mr. Pugh nicely."

But when Magda heard about it, she was skeptical. "Nobody ever does something for nothing," she said, looking up for a moment from her tarot cards, "especially not the English."

"English is a language, Queenie," Pugh said. "We *speak* it, therefore. We don't sing it."

Doubtful as Queenie's acting abilities were, the speed with which her speech improved astonished him.

Even shorn of the Anglo-Indian accent, Queenie's voice retained a slightly musical pitch. She spoke with exaggerated precision, and Pugh's efforts to make her think about the way she used her lips and her tongue had the accidental effect of giving her a slight lisp when she spoke, the inscrutable, fascinating ghost of a smile. Close up, he had come to realize that she was ever so slightly cross-eyed, or perhaps a little shortsighted. When she spoke to him, her eyes seemed to focus on his face with extraordinary intensity because of this defect—and when coupled with the smile, it gave the impression that she was in a state of rapture, hanging on every word from his lips.

It was maddeningly provocative, and all the more so because he had taught it to her without meaning to. From the first, she had submitted to his touch, but without giving anything back. He had not dared to kiss her, but he let his hands roam over her body in an absentminded way, as if he himself hardly even noticed they were doing so. He wondered if it was a game. Was she testing him to see how far he would go? And at what point would she react?

It was a question that Queenie would have found difficult to answer.

She knew perfectly well that Mr. Pugh's fumbling embraces were "wrong," but she wasn't at all sure how to stop them, and it was hardly a problem she could put to her mother or Morgan. She was at that age when she was so self-absorbed that the rest of the world hardly seemed real to her most of the time. She could spend hours examining her own face in the mirror, as if she found it hard to believe it was really hers. She practiced speaking in her "new" voice, to the point where even Grandma begged her to be quiet. When Pugh touched her, Queenie felt nothing, but she had a certain clinical interest in observing what his reaction was. She did not find his attentions particularly pleasant, but she was flattered at the interest he showed in her, and rather interested to discover how very easy it was to provoke it. Besides, he was a grown-up and an Englishman; it was hardly her place to object to his behavior.

"Do you have a boyfriend yet?" he asked her one afternoon, after the lesson.

She giggled. Pugh wondered for an instant if he had used the wrong word. He was by no means an old man, only forty, but schoolgirl vocabulary changed rapidly, and he had no idea what the right word now was.

"No young man at all? A pretty girl like you?"

Queenie shook her head. She did not seem concerned about it.

"I would have thought they'd be queuing up at the door to take you to dances and so on."

"Ma wouldn't approve. She says boys only want one thing."

"Well, I suppose that's true. But they mostly don't get it, so that's all right."

"Anyway, they're all spotty, with nasty hair on their faces because they haven't started to shave yet. When I go dancing, I will go with my Uncle Morgan. He's much handsomer."

"Say it slowly, please, Queenie. Not 'I-*will-go-with* my-*Uncle-*Morgan.*" Say instead, 'I will *go* with my Uncle *Morgan.*'"

"I will *go* with my Uncle *Morgan.*" She smiled slightly as she concentrated.

"Boys are beastly creatures. It's one of the reasons I've always preferred to teach girls. But my point was that desire and curiosity about sex are perfectly natural and healthy, Queenie. Surely you've felt the urge?"

"Urge?"

Pugh strained for another word to make his point but failed. His fingers, he was almost sure, were touching the elastic of her knickers.

Queenie's cheeks, he saw in the dying light, were ever so slightly flushed, though whether from desire or embarrassment it was impossible to say. Queenie closed her eyes, still smiling—a good sign, he told himself.

"Has a man ever kissed you, Queenie?" Pugh asked, leaning down so that his lips were close to hers.

"Only Uncle Morgan." She was astonished at the ease with which she was able to make Pugh treat her like a grown-up. She wondered if Morgan would be as easy.

"Ah," Pugh said, "I meant a *real* kiss!" But just as he was about to show her what he meant, there was a bang on the door and Kalit Singh cried out, "It's late, sahib—I'm locking up."

Pugh straightened up with a surge of panic that quite obliterated his desire. How much, he wondered, did Singh know? And how long would he remain silent about it? It was a risky business, this game with Queenie.

Pugh decided to put a stop to it then and there. Then he looked at Queenie, who was still standing there in her school uniform, the mysterious Mona Lisa smile on her face, and said, "Until tomorrow, Queenie."

In fact, Kalit Singh knew, or suspected, everything, for he was no fool. That evening, seated cross-legged in his two-room flat, he mentioned Pugh-sahib's unseemly passion for the Kelley girl to his wife.

"He touches her with his hands," Singh said, lowering his eyes.

Mrs. Singh shook her head. "No good will come of it," she said. She turned to her four daughters, who were staring at her, their eyes wide open in the flickering light from the kerosene lantern, longing to hear more. "This is not a matter fit for your ears," she said.

But happily Singh had already changed the subject to one of more immediate concern. The British, he reported, had sentenced a Muslim to prison for life for killing his wife—although, even allowing for the fact that he was a filthy Muslim dog, the man had merely been protecting his honor, for he had discovered her in his own charpoy with another man.

"It is said that this Ram Dass called the Muslims pigs without honor there in court, for all to hear."

"So they are."

"Truly. But such things should not be spoken in a place of justice. The Muslims are planning a demonstration tomorrow. Already the shopkeepers in the bazaar are boarding up their windows."

"Will there be a riot?"

"Who can say? In the mosques there is much angry talk. Tomorrow thou and the girls should stay at home."

"And thou?"

Singh finished his meal, dipped his fingers in a bowl of water and shook his head. "Am I not head porter of Saint Anthony's?" he asked indignantly. "My place is there."

He wondered whether he should warn the headmaster that there was trouble brewing in the streets, but decided against it. It was beneath his dignity to pass on rumors. If trouble came, he would guard the school. Such was his duty.

One Sikh was a match for any mob.

"I don't like it," Morgan said. It was late in the afternoon, and even here in Chowringhee the signs of trouble were evident. The policemen were swinging *lathis*—long, brass-tipped wooden staves—and walking nervously in pairs. A long line of lorries had come down the road from the cantonment lines, carrying a battalion of the Duke of Cornwall's Light Infantry in battle dress, the men whistling at the girls and singing, in contrast to the general mood of the day.

That was natural, Morgan reflected. They were English; none of this meant anything to them. Besides, they were soldiers. Drawn up in ranks, with their Lee-Enfield rifles and bayonets, they had nothing to fear from the wogs.

From the veranda, he could see smoke rising from the bazaars and hear the distant noise of shouting and chanted slogans. The Muslim mob, it was said, had marched on Ram Dass Mehta's house, and when it was discovered he had—very wisely—fled, they set it on fire. The riot then proceeded as if by some ancient traditional choreography. The police charged the growing crowds with *lathis*, breaking a few heads, the Hindus seized some luckless Muslims and beat them; then a mob of Muslim fanatics attempted to slaughter a cow outside a Hindu temple in revenge, provoking a counterriot that now engulfed the city streets.

If the British acted quickly enough, Morgan guessed, the riot might peter out, with only a few dozen killed. On the other hand, once enough blood had flowed, anything was possible. In the Amritsar riots, thousands had died.

"Shouldn't Queenie be home by now?" he asked.

Vicky nodded. She was kneading her hands with worry. "I blame myself," she said. "I shouldn't have let her go to school today."

"Oh, if one paid attention to every bazaar rumor . . . But why is she so late?"

"She has a private lesson with Mr. Pugh."

"Ah? Surely then he will have the good sense to bring her home. Besides, the mob won't attack a European girl. There's nothing to worry about."

But Morgan not only could see that his sister was worried; he also had to acknowledge that he was worried himself. This Pugh was, after all, a newcomer to India. He might not realize what was happening out there in the streets. Until you had *seen* a Hindu-Muslim riot, Morgan knew, you could have no idea of the savagery it unleashed. Granted, the mob would not normally attack a young woman in European clothes, but when the police and the army moved in, the riot would spread like ink spilled on blotting paper as the crowds ran through the streets, hurling stones and bottles, breaking windows, attacking anyone in their path. There were—who the hell knew?—half a million maddened, bloodthirsty wogs out there. Anything could happen.

"I'll go and fetch her," he said. "It's getting dark."

Vicky nodded gratefully. "Be careful," she said.

"Oh, I'll be careful. There's nothing to fear."

But as Morgan drove through the brooding, deserted streets, he was afraid. Any sensible person was home at a time like this, with the door barred and a shotgun at hand, if he possessed one. He braked suddenly to avoid a beggar on the street corner, then saw that it was in fact a corpse—some luckless Hindu street cleaner, an outcast who had been beaten to death and mutilated.

In the distance he heard the sharp crack of rifle fire. No doubt the cheerful, red-faced West Country English riflemen of the DCLI were getting a chance to use their Lee-Enfields at last, though it was usual to fire a few volleys in the air before actually shooting into the mob at point-blank range. Sometimes rifle fire—or even machine-gun fire in extreme cases—stopped the mob dead in its tracks, but more often it merely enraged the rioters, who knew the geography of the city better than the English, and flowed through the narrow streets away from the infantry, to reappear suddenly elsewhere on the rampage. The noise of shouting and running feet made him suspect that this was now happening. At any moment they might appear to engulf him. In Decca, a few years ago, a man had been cremated in his own car by the mob. It was not a comforting thought.

Morgan crossed the intersection, speeded up, took a right turn toward the school and found his way blocked by a dozen running, frenzied Muslims, the ragged vanguard of a larger mob. A paving stone crashed against the car, followed by another, which smashed one headlamp.

He hesitated for a fraction of a second. The road was too narrow for him to turn around, but he could possibly reverse fast enough to escape to quieter streets. Then it occurred to him that this was the only direct way to Saint Anthony's School, and he resigned himself, reluctantly and with astonishment, to an act of courage. He would not be doing this, he told himself, for anybody but Queenie, but before he could further analyze his motives, he was into the mob. He hoped she would be grateful. He sounded his horn, stepped on the gas and drove straight into a group of running men, his eyes wide open, his hands gripping the wheel so tightly that his knuckles seemed to him about to burst through the skin.

He felt his right-front mudguard catch one man and send him flying; a brick crashed through the windscreen, showering him with shards of broken glass. Above the noise of the horn and the motor he heard screams, shouts and curses. There was a sickening thump, and for one heart-stopping moment he thought the car was about to stall; then he realized he had struck a man head-on. The man was impaled on the front of the car, his fingers clutched around the headlamps, the dark face staring at Morgan, the mouth wide open, the bloodshot eyes glazed with fear or pain or both. The impact had loosened the man's turban, which was unwrapping in the wind and flapping in Morgan's face.

Morgan took the next corner on two wheels, praying the worn tires would hold; the speed of the turn loosened the man's grip. First one finger, then another, loosened from the headlamps, leaving small bloody streaks on the polished brass, then the man slid out of sight beneath the bonnet of the car, without a sound. Morgan felt a sickening bump as the back wheels rode over something soft, then he was home free, doing sixty miles an hour, with the mob screaming impotently behind him.

He stopped at the corner, untangled the turban, and threw it in the gutter.

Then he leaned over and threw up.

• • •

The school seemed quieter than usual this evening, which was all to the good. Pugh had heard that there was to be a procession of some kind in town, and it seemed to have drawn a great many people away, offering him the opportunity of somewhat greater privacy for what he hoped would be a climactic session with Queenie.

During their lessons he had, for the first time, permitted himself to sit beside her. Gradually, softly, he pressed closer to her, his thigh touching hers, his arm around her. He did not want to hurry things.

"Would you not be more comfortable if you took off your blazer?" he asked. "It's very warm in here."

"We're not supposed to take our blazers off."

"I assure you that it's all right. I shall take off my coat."

Queenie obediently took off the blazer, folded it neatly and went on with her lesson.

Pugh's passion mounted at the sight of Queenie in her blouse, the firm little breasts just visible beneath the thin cotton. He put both arms around her, a trifle more abruptly than he had intended and perhaps too forcefully. For the first time she looked puzzled, even alarmed, but he pressed on, confident that this was the moment.

"First the bee's kiss," he cried, misquoting Browning in his ecstasy. "Now the moth's!"

But as he crushed his mouth against Queenie's, trying to force his tongue between her lips, he felt her try to pull away. Apparently he had crossed the line at last.

"Let yourself go!" he pleaded, the words emerging thickly as they struggled. "Look into my eyes!"

Queenie's eyes, wide open as they were, seemed to be looking at something else; it dawned on him with sudden horror that they were focused on the door.

Morgan stopped his car at the closed gates of the school.

"What news, bahadur-sahib?" Kalit Singh asked. He presented an impressive picture, as he clutched his *lathi*. In anticipation of bloodshed, he had removed his beard-net, and now displayed the perfectly shaped blue-black beard of Sikh warriors, carefully greased into a sharp, curved point.

As Singh leaned over to see who was in the car, he felt a moment of shame. He had thought it was a pukka sahib, and therefore addressed him with the honorific "bahadur" as a hero, and was now dismayed to see that it was merely an Anglo-Indian of no consequence, unworthy of the term.

"Thou hast had an accident?" he asked in Hindi, looking at the damage to the car.

"A misadventure," Morgan replied. He could speak Hindi perfectly well, though he mostly chose not to. At this moment, however, he felt the need for an ally, and a Sikh would do better than nothing. "I knocked down a Muslim."

Singh laughed, politely holding his hand in front of his mouth as was the custom. "Didst thou kill the dog?"

"I believe so. I ran over him."

Singh beamed happily. "But that is splendid!" he said, waving his *lathi* in salute. "Truly thou *art* a bahadur-sahib, as I first guessed. Are the rioters close?"

"A few streets away."

"We two shall defend the school together. We will fight like brothers."

Morgan stared at Singh in dismay. He had no intention of holding off a mob in Singh's company, though no doubt there was nothing Singh would have enjoyed more. Singh even reached into the car and shook Morgan's hand, a gesture which would never have occurred to a Sikh under normal circumstances, since it would call for lengthy and expensive ritual purification. "Of what service can I be to thee?" Singh asked.

"I have a niece here at school—Queenie Kelley. Dost thou know her?"

Singh lowered his eyes and bowed slightly. "How would I not know her? Is it not the head porter's job to know each and every one of the pupils?"

"Knowest thou where she is? I have come to fetch her."

"Wisely. A man must look after his own family. Their safety is his first duty."

"Exactly so. Her mother is concerned."

"I would show thee where she is, but I cannot leave here," Singh said, unlocking the gates. "Drive your motorcar to the front of the big brick building. Go through the main door, and you will find Pugh-sahib's classroom on the left, second door down. The light will be on. And, Bahadur-sahib—" Singh went on with some embarrassment, as if there was more he wanted to say.

"Yes?" Morgan asked impatiently, as he let out the clutch.

"Knock before entering."

There could be no harm, Singh thought, in sparing a brave man pain. Anyone who had killed a Muslim—even an Anglo-Indian—was owed at least that much.

But Morgan was in too much of a hurry to knock.

"I can explain everything," Pugh said, standing up straight. He was a good deal taller than Morgan, and more heavily built, but he showed no signs of fight. On the contrary, he seemed terrified—as well a schoolteacher caught in this situation might be.

As for Morgan, he was too astonished to say a word. He looked at Queenie, who was crying now—from guilt or from fear? he wondered— but the sight of her in Pugh's arms had so enraged Morgan that he hardly knew what he was doing.

"You should have knocked," Pugh said feebly.

"Knock? Man, you ought to be in jail!"

"Acting!" Pugh said wildly, the sweat running down his face. "I was giving her a lesson in acting."

"I'll give you acting, you swine!" Morgan said, all too conscious of the fact that he didn't know what to do. He could hardly do *nothing*— he would lose face in front of Queenie—but the thought of a scandal made him dizzy. What would Vicky say? And who would take his word against Pugh's? He wished he had followed his instincts and stayed at home.

"The girl led me on," Pugh said, and Morgan, whose nerves were already on edge and who half suspected that this was true, suddenly lashed out and landed a clumsy blow to Pugh's head. He had heard about people "seeing red," and assumed it was merely a figure of speech, but for one mindless moment he did actually see red, as if all his anger, jealousy, his pent-up, guilty hunger for Queenie and his wretched feelings of inferiority face to face with a real Englishman had seized control of him.

"Oh, my God, I'm sorry!" he wailed.

But it was too late. The schoolmaster's eyes rolled and he fell to the floor, more from surprise than from the force of the blow. His nose was bleeding, and a livid bruise was already starting to color the right side of his face.

Morgan groaned. He had killed a man this very evening. Now he had hit a schoolmaster—and an Englishman, at that. Doubtless Pugh was right. He *should* have knocked. And besides, Morgan realized, he had hit the poor man as much out of jealousy as righteous indignation. Morgan had caught Pugh doing what he himself had long dreamed about, and the sight of Queenie, her face flushed, her blouse partly untucked, in Pugh's arms, had been more than he could bear. He leaned over and helped Pugh to his feet.

"I'm sorry," Morgan repeated.

"How on earth will I explain this?" Pugh moaned.

Morgan handed Queenie her blazer and thought for a moment. There was no point in creating a scandal. It would damage Queenie's reputation as much as Pugh's—very likely more, in view of the fact that she was an Anglo-Indian.

"Say you got caught in the riot," he suggested. "Tell anybody who asks that someone threw a brick at you."

"What riot?"

"Oh, good God, man. The whole bloody town is on fire! With killings in the street. Sneak out the back way so that nosy parker at the gate doesn't see you in this condition. Then make for home. It will be perfectly safe for a sahib by now."

"Morgan," Queenie said through her tears, "I want to go home."

"That's what I came here for," he said. "But, my God, girl, you have a bloody lot of explaining to do."

"I can't explain this to Ma, Morgan."

"No," Morgan said, "I don't suppose you can. But it's not Ma who is wanting an explanation, you see. It's *me*."

SHAME BLINDED QUEENIE to what would ordinarily have frightened her. She took no notice as Kalit Singh unchained the school gates and expressed his fulsome regrets that Morgan was unable to stay with him and bash in a few Muslim heads.

Queenie huddled in her seat, staring at the shattered windscreen of the car, wishing she were dead. Then it occurred to her that if the riot was as bad as Morgan said, her wish might very well be granted.

She looked at Morgan out of the corner of her eye. He was driving recklessly down the dark back roads, both hands on the steering wheel as the old car skidded around corners and shot through intersections. Queenie sensed his fear, but it didn't make her afraid—she was too worried about what Morgan would do to fear anything else.

The car sped past small groups of policemen and soldiers, moving in to contain the riot. Opposite Saint Swithin's Anglican Church, Morgan was obliged to halt for a convoy of khaki-painted Army lorries rumbling out of the city down Ishapore Turnpike. Each open lorry was packed with Indians who had been arrested. Many were covered with blood, and not a few were badly wounded or had been beaten around the head with *lathis* by the police.

A constable waved Morgan on, and he engaged the gears noisily.

"What will happen to them?" Queenie asked, to break the silence between them.

Morgan shrugged. "Nothing much. They will be detained a few days. People talk a lot of rot about independence for bloody India, but I tell you this, my girl—if the British weren't here, this would happen all the time, and who would stop it? Nobody!"

"Morgan, what happened to the car? Did you hit something?"

"Did I hit something? Too bloody right I did! I hit a wog, that's what I hit. Because your mother is worried, I come out to rescue you in the middle of a riot, and what happens? I am nearly killed, then I run over a man, and when I get to the school I find you in the arms of Mr. Cyril-bloody-Fitzroy-Pugh! A fine night I've had of it!"

"I'm sorry, Morgan."

"Sorry? I'd like to give you 'sorry' my girl, with my hand on your bottom! Your grandfather would have beaten you black and blue, for a bloody fact!"

Queenie sat with her arms wrapped around her, her chin on her knees and her eyes closed. No doubt Morgan was right—her grandfather would certainly have beaten her black and blue, and her father, too, but what did that matter? The old man was merely a sepia photograph in the parlor. He had left India when Ma and Morgan were mere children. Even grandmother could hardly remember him. As for her father, he had simply vanished into some other corner of the British Empire, apparently without regrets.

Queenie felt like crying again but willed herself not to. Had it been *her* fault that Mr. Pugh had kissed her? She had flirted with him, it was true, and it gave her a curious sense of power, but she had not meant it to go so far, or realized how strong his feelings were, since she did not share them. At least Mr. Pugh had treated her like an adult— admittedly with unwelcome results—but now Morgan was treating her like a child again and behaving like one himself, which was worse.

She supposed she should be grateful to Morgan for having saved her in the nick of time, but she was not. For a moment, in the schoolroom, it had seemed to her as if Morgan and Mr. Pugh had been fighting over her, the way she had been told men sometimes did at the bar of the Railway Institute on Saturday nights. She wondered if his anger had been entirely a case of wounded family pride and indignation. Was it possible that he had been *jealous?* She looked at him with new interest, but his expression was hard to read. Mostly he looked tired and miserable, she thought.

He put on the brake and stopped the clattering motor. He seemed in no hurry to get out, and in this instance, Queenie didn't find it difficult to guess what was troubling him.

"What will you say to Ma?" she asked.

He sighed. "I don't know what to tell her, frankly. It puts me in a very delicate position."

"I said I was sorry."

"I should bloody hope so! But I ask you, what bloody good does being sorry do?" He paused, not at all sure how to continue. He was not comfortable playing a parental role, which no longer corresponded at all to his feelings about Queenie. "This comes of your Dad's running away the way he did," he continued sadly. "The night he left, he told me, 'Morgan, look after Queenie for me—be like a father to her.' What would he say to me about this?"

"Was he as handsome as his pictures?"

"This isn't the time to talk about how handsome your Dad was, for goodness' sake! Though in fact he *was* handsome. There's a lot of him in your face." Morgan closed his eyes, as if he were remembering happier days. "I liked him, Queenie. He borrowed five hundred rupees from me," he added sadly. "I shan't see that back again."

"I wish he hadn't run away."

"So do I. But it was that or jail. Still—what a shame! A girl needs a father as much as a boy—perhaps more."

Morgan had been deserted by *his* father, too, Queenie remembered. It was another thing the two of them had in common. She tried to think what life would be like if her father hadn't run away, but she couldn't imagine. What would he have said to her about Mr. Pugh? What would he have done to Mr. Pugh, for that matter? She had heard stories about her Dad's violent Irish temper, and knew there were traces of it in her which even Ma had been unable to suppress. She had something of his pride, too, Ma was fond of saying. Queenie wondered if it was true.

"I'll have to leave school," she said. "I can't go back there. Not after what happened."

A look of exasperation crossed Morgan's face. He was always looking for solutions, compromises, the way out of things. Queenie, like her father, usually slammed head-on into things, and damn the bloody consequences—stubborn as a mule!

"You'll do no such thing," he said.

"I will. I must."

"Listen to me. If you leave school, there will be questions. People will ask why you left. That bloody Sikh will gossip. Somebody will put two and two together. There will be a bloody scandal."

"I don't care. If I do go back, Mr. Pugh will throw me out of the theatrical group—and his classes. The other girls will guess something happened."

"You *have* to go back, girl! What's going to happen to you if you don't? You won't get a job, you know. Do you want to hang around the house until you're old enough to marry somebody here—or become a bloody bar girl? What would people say?"

Queenie looked at him closely, trying to read the meaning of his anger. His fine mustache was beaded with sweat, and his eyes were red-rimmed. Morgan's nerves were like a string; you could pull it only so far before it snapped. It was not *her* reputation he was concerned about, Queenie guessed, but his own. He would not want to be known as a man whose niece had been thrown out of Saint Anthony's for immoral behavior. However much he feared her mother, he feared a family disgrace more. It might take him a while to forgive her for what had happened tonight, but in the meantime it would not be difficult to enlist him as an ally, she sensed. She put her hand on his gently. "I don't want to go back with my tail between my legs," she said quietly.

Morgan looked at her glumly. He did not move his hand. "Pride! Just like your Dad."

"There's nothing wrong with pride."

"For those who can afford it, perhaps."

She squeezed his hand. "I'll only go back if I can be in the play," she said with an implacable determination that reminded Morgan of Ma.

Morgan slumped down in his seat, feeling the sweat running down his back. He was not up to a contest of wills with any woman, and never had been, as he sadly recognized Queenie had already discovered.

"I'll talk to Pugh," he said wearily, wondering just what he'd find to say and why he was doing it. But he knew why. He only had to look at Queenie to know she had the upper hand.

"There's still Ma," he said quietly. He lit a cigarette and stared out at the veranda of the house, then looked over at Queenie, who was still folded up in the seat beside him.

She opened her eyes wide and stared back at him. Even in the dim light from the dashboard he could see a few tears clinging to the long lashes. "Do we have to tell her anything?" she asked.

Morgan was so surprised by the simplicity and cleverness of this suggestion that he didn't even pretend to be shocked. Queenie had a way of getting one step ahead of him. "I suppose you're right," he said reluctantly. Then he put his hand on her cheek, wiped away the tears, and said at last, "Queenie, just tell me one thing—*did* you lead him on?"

. . .

Queenie thought about the question as she undressed for bed and was unable to come up with a satisfactory answer.

Luckily Ma had been so glad to see Queenie home safe and sound that she had failed to notice Morgan's embarrassment. As a rule, Morgan was a bad liar; in more normal circumstances, Ma would have realized that something was being hidden from her, but the news that Morgan had struck and possibly killed a rioter gave Ma more than enough to worry her without asking questions about Queenie. She had visions of the police breaking down the door at any minute, and had been obliged to take a glass of Wincarnis tonic before going to bed early with all the symptoms of a migraine headache that promised to defy Christian Science.

Queenie undressed and put her clothes away neatly. She hung up her school blazer and her skirt, smoothing out the creases and brushing off any lint or dust. Below them she placed her sandals—a source of particular annoyance, since they were very ugly indeed.

She paused before putting on her nightgown and looked at herself in the mirror. The sight never failed to puzzle her. She did not think she was particularly beautiful. Oh, granted she was not fat like loathsome Beryl O'Brien, with big handlebars at her waist and a bulging tummy, nor was she knock-kneed like Heather Gomes. There was nothing *wrong* with her body, in fact, she rather liked it, but it was impossible for her to see what it was that men were apparently so excited about.

Queenie examined herself, trying to be objective about it. She had a small waist, long legs, breasts that were still something of an embarrassment to her, spoiling the firm, flat chest of her childhood and causing her all sorts of unexpected problems. Perhaps they excited men, but they didn't excite Queenie, who still sometimes woke up in the mornings surprised to find them there. Objectively she could see they were firmer and more nicely shaped than most of the other girls', but the thought they would one day hang down, pendulous and unwanted, like Grandma's or Ma's, which were enormous, filled her with dismay. The nipples were small, rosy, almost without an aureole, but all they did was to remind Queenie of their purpose, the whole disgusting business of having babies and feeding them like an animal.

She ran her hands over her breasts, as Mr. Pugh had done, but it was impossible to guess what he had felt that excited him so much. She touched her nipples and stroked them gently, which gave her, she had to admit, a pleasant tingling feeling. Ma had warned her several times not to touch herself, though it was an obscure warning, since she had been unwilling to enlarge on the subject and say *where* she shouldn't touch.

She looked at her image in the mirror. The small triangle of pubic hair seemed to her ugly. Like her breasts, it had simply appeared of its own volition, and it did not seem to her at all beautiful or even an improvement on the smooth skin that had been there before. She could hardly imagine that any man would find it beautiful either.

Queenie had been to the museum in Calcutta, and she had looked at the few art books in the school library. The paintings and sculptures of beautiful women did not include pubic hair. If the ladies in the world's most famous works of art were the standards by which women were judged, then pubic hair must be shameful and ugly.

Even the parts that the pubic hair partially concealed seemed to Queenie far less interesting than what a man had there. Not that *it* was any more beautiful—in fact, it was a good deal uglier, if Morgan's was anything to judge by—but at least it was more impressive. She had examined Morgan when she undressed him after the fight and was fascinated to observe that his thing seemed to have a life of its own. It grew and, changing in consistency and firmness as it did so, it trembled like the living thing it undoubtedly was.

Queenie wondered if Morgan's thing was typical. He had a reputation as a "ladies' man," even, it was rumored, with English ladies, but Queenie had no idea whether Morgan's was larger or smaller than most, or whether they all looked pretty much alike. What, for example, was Mr. Pugh's like?

She decided it was not a subject she wanted to pursue—she had come very close to finding out, after all.

Queenie pointed one leg high in the air—she had to admit that her legs were very nice—supported it with one hand and stared into the mirror. She sighed and let her leg fall back.

There was a knock at the door. "Queenie, dear," Ma asked, "are you decent?"

Queenie hastily pulled on her nightgown. "Yes, Ma," she said.

Ma came in, her vast lace-edged wrapper pulled around her. She seemed distracted, and Queenie wondered for a moment if her mother had guessed what she was doing, or perhaps had even peeked through the keyhole.

Ma peered at her shortsightedly. "You look flushed, dear," she said. "Are you sure you don't have a fever?"

"No, Ma, I'm all right. Is anything the matter?"

"I can't sleep at all, dear. It's been such a worrying day, then your poor Uncle Morgan hitting a man with his car . . ."

"I'm sure nobody will know—or care. I'll bet dozens of Indians were killed today. The police won't notice one more or less."

"I suppose you're right, dear, but still . . . How was your lesson with Mr. Pugh?"

"He says I'm making progress."

"That's nice, dear," Ma said vaguely. "You're lucky to have a gentleman like that take an interest in you. Your father always used to say that you could always trust a real gentleman." Then she started to cry softly. "Oh, Queenie," she asked, "what's to become of us all? If only your Dad were here!"

Queenie put her arms around Ma. It was not often that her mother broke down and cried, but sometimes she couldn't help it, especially when she thought about Dad. It was even harder for Queenie to think of Ma as a woman who needed a man than it was to think of Morgan in a man-woman way, but some instinctive feminine understanding told her this was Ma's problem. Queenie's Dad had been gone for twelve years now, long enough for Ma to have become the corseted dowagerlike figure she now was, but not long enough for her to have stopped missing him.

Queenie had seen photographs of Ma and Dad in Ma's big leather photo album, and the woman in the pictures was a very different person from the one she held in her arms—a thin, beautiful young woman with one hand around her husband's waist, looking up at him with an expression that was at once adoring and satisfied. Tiger Kelley had given Ma something wonderful—some special pleasure or happiness— then taken it away, along with himself, when things turned out badly for him.

No man will ever do that to *me*, Queenie told herself, and lying down on the bed, she snuggled up with her mother to comfort her for the night, happy enough to be a child again, for the time being.

Pugh rose from behind his desk at the knock, and to his horror saw Morgan standing there. He cringed involuntarily. His face was still heavily bruised from the blow Morgan had landed there, and he assumed that Morgan had sought him out in his own home to inflict further damage. "If you lay a hand on me, I'll call the police. For God's sake, shut the door."

Morgan closed the door and gave Pugh what he hoped was a placating smile. He was, in fact, far more terrified than Pugh, and had spent half an hour sitting in the car, sweating in the heat, trying to screw up his courage. Had he not given his promise to Queenie, he would have started up the car and driven home. He feared an argument, the possibility that Pugh would prosecute him, humiliation. And he had been right. Pugh's first thought was to call for the police.

Morgan hurried across the threadbare little carpet to calm Pugh, but it was only when he was within reach of the desk that he realized he had neglected to remove his solar topi—an act of bad manners that caused him to blush beneath his sallow skin.

The effect on Pugh was remarkable, for Pugh took Morgan's embarrassed blush to be a sign of rage, the flush of a man intent on committing mayhem. "Don't hit me," he pleaded.

Morgan, who hadn't the slightest intention of hitting Pugh, took off his hat, held it in his hands for a moment, and put it down on the desk. He realized he had gotten off on the wrong foot. His new reputation as a man of violence was inappropriate here—though it certainly seemed to have made an impression on poor Pugh, who was positively cowering in his chair, his eyes fixed on Morgan's hat as if it were a bomb.

"Be reasonable, man," Morgan said. "I didn't hit you *that* hard."

"Hard enough. I had a bloody difficult time explaining it."

"I told you to say you were hit by a rioter."

"I did. Quite candidly, I don't think my wife believed me. She has a suspicious mind, Mr.—ah . . ."

"Jones. Morgan Jones."

"Mr. Jones. Look, she's going to wonder what we're talking about now, you know. Please go."

"I have to talk to you."

Pugh closed his eyes. He sat quietly, his hands on his desk so as not to provoke Morgan, waiting like a martyr for whatever it was Morgan intended to inflict on him. He had hoped the whole episode would blow over—Queenie would drop out of the Drama Society, there would be no more lessons, perhaps he could even find a way to transfer her with honor to another teacher's class. "I promise not to see the girl again," he said. "You have my word on that."

"But that won't do at all, Mr. Pugh." Morgan's voice rose in alarm. He lowered it to a confidential tone. "That's not what I came here for. Listen, we are both men of the world, damn it, are we not?"

Pugh nodded again, though in fact he was not at all sure what Jones meant by "men of the world," and doubted that either of them was any such thing.

Morgan sat down, crossed his legs, pulled up his trouser creases neatly, revealing a neat pair of spats, and lit a cigarette. "The main thing is to avoid a bloody scandal, don't you agree?" he asked.

"Quite so."

"Our Queenie could make a complaint. That would cause all sorts of problems for you, I think, would it not?"

"Possibly. If she was believed." Now that Morgan was sitting down, Pugh felt more in control of the situation.

"Even if she was not believed, it still wouldn't look good for you, man. Besides, there is a witness to the crime, a member of the family who actually *saw* the whole dastardly outrage with his own eyes."

Pugh closed his eyes for a moment, to think. There was no arguing with Morgan's assessment. Even if he were exonerated, there would certainly be repercussions. He felt himself breaking out in a sweat. "I'm not a rich man," he said, staring at his checkbook on the desk.

Morgan blushed. "Money isn't the thing at all, my dear fellow. We're both gentlemen. No, no, I assure you I don't want your money. But I do have a proposition for you."

Pugh's imagination raced. He had resigned himself to a modest demand for blackmail; now he didn't know what to expect. "What do you have in mind?" he asked. His hands were trembling, and he concealed them in his lap. "And keep your voice down, please."

"Put Queenie back into the bloody play, with a better role."

Pugh leaned forward as if he couldn't believe his ears. "I'd have thought you wanted her out of my sight," he said.

"I do, personally. It's Queenie's idea. She wants to be in your damned play, man. With a better part."

"A *speaking* role?"

"Why not? She speaks much better since your lessons. Is she really that bad?"

Pugh adopted a schoolmasterly pose and placed the tips of his fingers together reflectively. Now that his opinion was being sought about a pupil, he seemed more at ease. "Ours is only a school theater group," he said. "Our standards are not high. Even by those standards, however, Queenie's ability is rather limited. She has many attractions and a lively intelligence, but you may take it from me that an actress is the one thing she won't be."

"I'm not asking you to put her in a West End show, man. The other girls are probably not that good either."

"True. Queenie is so beautiful that her deficiencies stand out, however. But that's not the problem. If I give her a major role, there will be talk of favoritism. It will cause exactly the kind of gossip you and I are trying to avoid."

"Not so much gossip as there will be if she makes a complaint to the headmaster, Mr. Pugh. With me as a witness. Think it over."

Pugh thought it over. "Fair enough," he said, hoping he was home free.

"If I were in your shoes," Morgan added after a pause, "I would have a word with the head porter. He's on to you, make no mistake about that."

"I see. He *has* made a few insinuations . . ."

"Wogs gossip, Mr. Pugh. They can't help it. It's in the blood. Now me, I'm a gentleman, like yourself. I know how to keep my bloody mouth shut. Particularly when it's a question of Queenie's reputation."

"You're very fond of her?"

"Too damn right I am."

"She's a lovely girl."

"She is that," Morgan said with a sigh.

"And apparently strong-minded."

"Too true!" Morgan said sadly, reluctantly acknowledging Queenie's ability to twist him around her little finger, which Pugh had been shrewd enough to guess.

They sat for a moment in the comradely silence of men who were afraid to say no to the women in their lives. Pugh felt a sense of relief flood over him. All things considered, he had scraped out of this one nicely. It would be hard to keep his hands off Queenie, but no doubt there would be other girls. . . .

"Do we have a deal?" Morgan asked.

"Oh, yes," Pugh said, rising from his chair to shake Morgan's hand. He smiled knowingly. "You can tell Queenie we have a deal, Mr. Jones."

"I've never been so happy!" Heather Gomes shouted to Beryl O'Brien, as they wriggled out of their kimonos, revealing gym shorts and blouses beneath.

And probably never will be again, Queenie thought glumly, looking at them. They were a pair of envious, nasty little cows, but she felt no hostility toward them. The fact that she had appeared in the play, and in one of the major roles, should have made her happy—Queenie knew that. But it hadn't. She saw the whole evening so clearly that she might have been looking at it through someone else's eyes. Mr. Pugh drinking himself into a stupor, the bleak Railway Institute Hall, with its dusty wooden floors and British Railway posters of English country scenes, Morgan with his eyes fixed on her, Ma in her best hat, and the rest of the parents and relatives, their faces shiny with sweat, relishing one moment of triumph for their daughters before the girls went on to become typists or marry. They would look back at this moment for years, long after the girls had become fat, tired married women, fanning themselves on their verandas while they waited for their husbands to come home. She was not at all sure what she wanted, but she knew it would have to be better than this.

Queenie's Dad used to call her "Princess" sometimes. She wasn't sure that she remembered his saying it, but everybody had always told her he did, so it had become a kind of memory. Sometimes—tonight particularly—she *felt* like a princess, one in a fairy story who has been mixed up at birth with another baby and given to the wrong parents. A dreadful mistake had been made. She did not belong here, with these people, in this country, where everybody was mean, stifling and mediocre, the world reduced to a narrow strip of land next to the railway lines, the rows of hot, dreary bungalows in which "her" people pretended to be English and hid themselves from India.

The evening had taught one thing, at least—even though she might not be able to sing or act, people *looked* at her. She had received more than her share of applause, and she was surprised at how much she enjoyed it.

She wiped off her makeup, wondering how women could wear such sticky stuff, pulled on her good frock and slipped out of the ladies'. Behind her she could hear the other girls chattering in their singsong voices—probably talking about *her*.

Let them talk, she thought. I'm going to get away from here somehow and leave all of them behind.

One day, she told herself, I'm going Home!

CHAPTER 5

"WOULDN'T IT BE NICE to be rich?" Queenie asked with a sigh.

It had needed a good deal of persuasion to convince Morgan to take her to tea at the Grand Hotel. Almost six months' worth, and even then it was only her fifteenth birthday, for which this was a belated present, which did the trick. She had not been idle during this time. If Pugh had taught her how to speak, it was from Magda that she sought her knowledge of the world—or what Magda called *le monde*, by which she meant clothes, men and manners. Queenie pumped her relentlessly, though much of Magda's information seemed, even to Queenie, somewhat inappropriate. Her experience of *le monde* had been gained in Central Europe before the Great War.

Magda taught Queenie which were the best dressmakers—Worth and Molyneux in Paris, Krivitsky in Vienna, Baum in Budapest—not that Queenie was likely to patronize any of them. Magda showed her how to enter a room—a long, slow glide, back straight, head high and haughty, how to sit down, showing just a flash of leg—"enough to tantalize, but no more"—how to put on just enough lipstick to attract attention, but not so much as to look like what Magda called a "tramp." She taught Queenie how to dress, how to hold her hand out to be kissed, how to wear clothes so that they moved gracefully, in short, how to attract and please a man—except, of course, for the one thing that pleased men most, which Magda, out of fear of Ma, decided Queenie was still too young to know.

Queenie had borrowed one of Magda's dresses to wear for tea at the Grand. It was pale pink, with a short bolero jacket lined in silk, and Queenie was so worried about creasing it that she could hardly bring herself to sit down at all, let alone gracefully. She stepped down the huge, ornate staircase into the Palm Court in such a state of terror that she hardly noticed the fact that every man in the room was looking at her.

In the distance, the bulk of old Fort William, with its crumbling walls and fortifications, loomed above the polo grounds and the race-track, obscured by the smoky haze of the factories and mills on the other side of the Hooghly River. Here, on this unpromising site, Job Charnock had founded the city, briskly replacing the ancient Hindu shrine of the tutelary goddess with a mud-walled fort—and here he had been buried, only to have his body rooted up by the herds of wild hogs which then roamed over what was now a parched, though neatly tended, English park, inappropriately decorated with an obelisk com-memorating the founding of the Calcutta Society for the Prevention of Cruelty to Animals.

Inside the Palm Court it was difficult to imagine the brutality of Calcutta's past, and easy to forget the squalor of its present. Waiters in white jodhpurs, crimson turbans and dark blue knee-length kurtas with gold piping and buttons carried silver tea trays to the bamboo tables, while an Indian string ensemble played selections from Victor Herbert.

Morgan peered into his teacup as if he were reading the leaves. He was ill at ease, not only because he feared being snubbed. There were plenty of people in the room who frequented Firpo's, and would no doubt feel it was cheeky of a jumped-up chee-chee band player to even think of entering the Grand Hotel Palm Court. "Rich?" he asked. "Of course we'd all like to be rich. But we're not so badly off."

"Well, we're not starving, Morgan, I know that, but look at that woman over there. I'll bet that frock wasn't made up on the Singer at home. It looks like a Worth, or a Molyneux." Queenie wondered if she was pronouncing the names correctly. They seemed to have no effect on Morgan, but then he had not spent hours poring over Magda's old fashion magazines. "And that diamond bracelet must have cost a for-tune—if it's real."

Morgan turned his head slightly, trying not to make it obvious he was staring. The woman Queenie was looking at was sitting at the next table. She was tall, thin—and indeed elegantly dressed—with blond hair concealed under a pearl-gray velvet cloche, set off with a large diamond brooch. She might have been thirty-five or a well-preserved forty, or anything in between. Time and the East had not been kind to her skin; her hands were freckled, her neck and the corners of her eyes showed the first signs of deep wrinkles, but the total effect conveyed a certain ruthless sexuality that was obvious to everyone except her companion, a large, overweight, florid Englishman in a white suit, who was eating sandwiches with a passion that suggested he had missed lunch or was not expecting dinner, neither of which was probably the case.

He had pop-eyes, fat, flushed cheeks and a bristly ginger mustache, and his concentration was fixed so firmly on his plate and on the trolley of food next to the table that he seemed oblivious to the woman's presence, let alone her smoldering boredom. She lit a cigarette with a gold lighter, flicked a speck of tobacco off her lips impatiently with the tip of her tongue, placed the cigarette in a gold-and-coral holder, and stared out the window toward the bronze statue of Lord Mayo, whose round, pop-eyed face remarkably resembled that of her companion.

Morgan turned around, blushing. "Oh, they're real diamonds, all right," he said. "You can be sure of that."

"How do you know?"

"That's Mrs. Penelope Daventry. Daventry Street was named after her husband's great-grandfather. He came out in the early eighteen hundreds and started the first big textile mill. He built the old Sans Souci Theater on Park Street, as a matter of fact, then ran off with one of the actresses."

"Did he marry the actress?"

"No, no, in those days nobody *married* actresses, Queenie. It wasn't the thing at all. They lived together for a few years, then her dress caught fire when she brushed up against a candle. She was carried next door to the Archbishop's palace and died in the Archbishop's bed. People said it was the only bed in Calcutta she hadn't been in before!"

"Why do you know so much about the Daventrys?"

Morgan blushed again, deeper this time. "Mrs. Daventry is a friend of mine. Well—let's say an acquaintance."

"And Mr. Daventry?"

"Mr. Daventry I don't know. I've seen him at Firpo's, of course, from time to time."

"I see." Queenie stared at Mrs. Penelope Daventry with renewed interest, ignoring Morgan, who was twisting in his seat and slumping over, presumably in the hope that Mrs. Daventry wouldn't notice him. Mrs. Daventry's nails were long, pointed and bright red, each one a small work of art. Queenie thought of her own neatly trimmed, unvarnished nails, and sighed. Mrs. Daventry's shoes were tiny, pointed gray lizard pumps, the heels as thin as matchsticks, and the straps so narrow that it was impossible to imagine how she managed to fasten the tiny gold buckles, or to walk in those shoes. She wore a plain gold wedding band and a magnificent emerald in a diamond setting that matched—no doubt not by accident—the color of her eyes. Around her left wrist the bracelet of square-cut diamonds and emeralds glittered as she moved. She had the look of an athlete—one of those rich mem-sahibs who rode, played tennis, swam and golfed. Her bare arms were thin, but muscular and sinewy; her long legs, which she was displaying rather obviously, one knee crossed over the other, were slim, firm and elegant. There was not an ounce of superfluous fat on her.

"Are the Daventrys *very* rich?"

"Rich and social. The Calcutta Club, the Turf Club—Daventry's a steward of it—the whole works. Very posh people."

"Do they go to Firpo's often?"

"Sometimes," Morgan said vaguely. "It depends."

"I wish I could go there myself, just once."

Morgan sighed. "It's out of the question," he said. "Your Ma would never allow it."

"She wouldn't have to know."

"It's not a place for a young girl."

"I'm *not* a young girl. Not *that* young, anyhow. Oh, Morgan, I would so love to see you there, just once. I'll bet you look smashing up there on the bandstand."

"Queenie, please . . . don't even think of it!"

"I can't *stop* thinking about it. I'd just come and sit quietly, only to see what it's like. Please, dear, *dear* Morgan."

Queenie leaned across the tea table and gave Morgan a kiss, causing him to blush again. He looked at her sternly, trying to make clear by his expression to anyone who might have seen the kiss that he was merely an uncle, or possibly her father—that this was a family two-some, not some kind of low hanky-panky between a man his age and a young girl. Queenie opened her eyes wide and cupped her chin in her hands, with her elbows on the table, looking straight at Morgan. She slipped one foot out of a shoe, wishing her shoes were as elegant as Mrs. Daventry's, and pinched Morgan's calf with her toes.

"Stop that!" he said.

"I shall pinch you until you say yes."

"I'll think about it," Morgan said, resigning himself to the fact that he had as good as surrendered, and Queenie laughed, knowing she had won, or almost, anyway. Her bell-like laugh echoed above the genteel tinkle of teacups and the string ensemble playing "A Nightingale Sang in Berkeley Square." Then she leaned forward to kiss Morgan again, while she continued to tickle Morgan's leg under the table with her toes. He giggled involuntarily, then he began to laugh with her.

"Oh, Morgan," Queenie said, "I *do* love you."

And Morgan, his laughter stopping, took Queenie's hand in his for a moment, pressing it hard, and said, "I love you, too." He wondered if they meant the same thing by "love," but doubted it. He did not question her innocence any more than he questioned her power over him.

They sat for a moment, looking at each other, hand in hand, as the Daventrys—Mr. Daventry having apparently sated himself at last—passed by the table on their way out.

Daventry stumped along in front of his wife. Mrs. Daventry followed him, slowly and gracefully, her slim body as erect as a guardsman's. She was putting her cigarette holder and lighter into her small beaded bag, when her eyes, as cold and restless as a snake's, focused on Morgan.

"You don't belong here, Morgan," she said quietly, without breaking stride.

And before Morgan could rise out of his chair, she was off, nodding at men all over the room, who dropped their napkins and started to get up at the sight of her.

"What will your poor mother say?" Magda cried.

"She won't know."

"Bite your tongue. Why am I even discussing this with you? I must be mad myself. A girl your age going to a nightclub. *Unglaublich*— unbelievable! It's not that I mind lending you a dress, but the whole idea is crazy."

"Oh, Magda, I only want to see what it's like."

Magda shuffled her tarot deck and picked up a card. "The Queen of Wands reversed," she muttered, holding it up for Queenie to see. "A vengeful, domineering woman, unfaithful and treacherous. Not a good card."

"Who can it be?"

"Not your mother, anyway. That's for sure." Magda carefully stacked the cards, wrapped them in a piece of yellow silk and slipped them into the pocket of her kimono. The Queen of Wands seemed to have depressed her. "I'm not so sure it's a good idea after all," she said.

"Oh, Magda, you promised!"

"I did *not* promise."

"As good as."

Magda sighed. She stabbed out her cigarette in a Benares brass ashtray and lit another. Whenever she looked at Queenie, she saw herself at the same age. Magda's own childhood—not to speak of her whole life—had been so full of disappointments that she was unwilling to inflict one on Queenie, who was biting her lip in apprehension, the tears beginning to form at the corners of those dark, luminous eyes. How many hearts the child will break, Magda thought—and what a dangerous gift that is. "It's against my better judgment," she said, "but take the pink dress. And Queenie, stay out of trouble. . . ."

But before she could finish with her warning, Queenie had thrown her arms around Magda's neck, laughing in triumph, and Magda joined in, feeling as she often did with Queenie, that she too was young again and about to commit her first innocent folly.

After all, Magda told herself, Firpo's isn't an opium den. And with Morgan as chaperon, Queenie couldn't come to any harm. . . .

"Your Ma would bloody well kill you!" Peggy D'Souza shouted, above the noise of the band.

"You're the third person who's told me that."

"Well then. At least you know three people who have some sense, girl. Unless you're including your bloody Uncle Morgan, in which case it's only two. Pink suits you, dear." She stared at the dance floor moodily. "Not much happening tonight. Thank God I'm getting out of here."

"Are you?" Queenie asked, happy to change the subject.

"Too bloody right, Queenie! I'm going Home."

Queenie looked at Peggy with astonishment and not a little envy. "Home? How?"

"I'm engaged. To an Englishman. A pukka businessman. We're going to live in London."

"Can I meet him? Is he here?"

Peggy looked nervous. She stuck one finger in her drink, then licked it. "He's in Bombay—on business," she said. "Just because a girl's engaged doesn't mean she can't have a good time."

"Is he rich?"

"He *will* be when he gets to London. He explained it all to me, did Sid. I can't remember it all, but we'll have pots of money when we get there."

"What's his name, Peggy?"

"Butts, dear. Sid Butts." Peggy looked toward the dance floor, eased her breasts in her brassiere a little with her hands and stood up, smoothing the wrinkles in her satin dress. "I see somebody I know," she said. "You stay here and be good." She plunged off into the darkness, leaving Queenie alone at the table.

Firpo's did not seem tawdry to Queenie: the colored chandeliers, the mottled mirrors, the tented ceiling all seemed to her like a fantasy world, the ultimate grown-up dream. Even the presence of Peggy D'Souza as an off-and-on chaperone did nothing to diminish her enthusiasm.

By midnight the dance floor was jam-packed, the air dense with smoke, the sound of raucous laughter almost drowning out the band. Through the haze of cigarette smoke she could see Morgan, showing off for her benefit on the bandstand by greeting people he knew with a wave and a smile. Peggy had not returned from the dance floor, and Queenie was feeling, for the first time, a slight, gnawing sense of disappointment, the feeling of being left out, like a wallflower at a dance. It was fun to be here and look at the spectacle, but not quite as much fun as it would be to be *part* of it, she thought to herself.

No sooner had this thought crossed her mind than a well-bred English voice said, "I say, haven't we met before?"

Queenie was so startled that she blushed. She hadn't noticed anyone approaching her hideout. She strained her eyes and saw a tall young man in a white mess jacket looking down at her. He had a pleasant English face, a military mustache and the figure of a soldier.

"I don't think so," she said. "I've never been here before."

He emerged from behind a palm tree. "How odd," he said. "I could have sworn I'd seen you before, at any rate . . . at the Calcutta Turf Club perhaps? Or the Polo Grounds?"

"I'm afraid not."

"Dear me, I *know* I've seen you somewhere . . . wait! I have it! You were having tea last week at the Grand, weren't you? Sitting near Pempy Daventry? In the Palm Court?"

Queenie nodded.

The young man smiled with relief. "I say," he said, "how jolly to see you here! I couldn't help noticing you, you know. You were quite the belle of the Palm Court, what? But why are you sitting here by yourself? If you don't mind my asking?"

"I was just watching."

"Oh, quite." He laughed, as if Queenie had made a particularly funny remark. "Oh, I say, that's a good one! I say, I am most *damnably* rude, what? I haven't introduced myself. Nigel Goodboys. Lieutenant, Murray's Jats."

"Murray's Jats?"

"Twentieth Lancers. Indian cavalry. Splendid chaps! Regiment was founded by a chap called Murray, you see, so it's always been called Murray's Jats. Like Skinner's Horse, and so on. New to India?"

"No, not at all."

"Jolly good! I say, though, fair's fair, what? You haven't told me *your* name."

"Queenie."

"Queenie!" he laughed. "Oh that's frightfully jolly. Queenie, indeed! Well, I suppose you'll eventually tell me your real name, but 'Queenie' it is for the moment, eh? No names, no pack drill, as we say in the army. Would you care to dance—*Queenie?*" He laughed again, though Queenie couldn't see what was so funny about her name.

"Well, I don't know . . ." Queenie wanted to dance more than anything in the world, but she had promised Morgan she would sit quietly and stay out of trouble. Still, Goodboys, with his pink face and trim figure, represented just the kind of Englishman she had always dreamed of, young, handsome—and definitely a sahib.

He raised an eyebrow at her hesitation and launched into a new round of more-or-less inarticulate apologies punctuated with hearty laughter. Most of his conversation was interrupted by short laughs, or the word "What?" and the combination of his upper-class English accent, the military habit of breaking everything up into short sentences and a slight public school stutter made it difficult for Queenie to follow him.

"I say," he said, "have I put my foot in it? You're probably waiting for someone, aren't you? I wouldn't want to poach a chap's girl while he's in the loo, or whatever. But the thing is, you've been sitting alone here for some time, so I thought . . . Besides, quite frankly, any chap who'd leave a smashing girl like you alone for more than a minute deserves to have you poached."

Queenie laughed and stood up, noticing the admiration in Goodboys' eyes as she did so. "I *say!*" he said as he looked at her, though whatever he was going to say he left unsaid.

"You came alone yourself?" Queenie asked politely, as she took the arm Lieutenant Goodboys offered her, and allowed him to guide her to the dance floor.

"Not at all," he said, placing one hand against the small of her back and pulling her a little closer to him. "I came with the Daventrys. As a matter of fact."

And as the band started to play, Queenie saw out of the corner of her eye a familiar face—two familiar faces. At a table beside the dance floor, Mr. Daventry sat, looking like an English version of the Buddha, in a white dinner jacket opened to reveal a massive paunch that strained his starched shirt-front, his concentration riveted on the bottle of champagne a waiter was opening to replace the empty one that floated in the ice-bucket on the table.

Beside him, slim, elegant, her bare arms and shoulders revealed by a daring silver gown that seemed almost to have been painted on her body, Mrs. Daventry glared at Queenie in young Goodboys' arms.

"In shallow shoals
English soles
Do it . . ."

Queenie sang to herself as she made her way to the ladies' room. She had danced three consecutive dances with Nigel Goodboys, despite Morgan's disapproving frown from the bandstand. Goodboys had behaved like a perfect gentleman, unlike Mr. Pugh. His left hand had remained firmly against her back, without straying lower for a moment, and though his shirt-front had brushed against her bosom and he had put his cheek next to hers, he was as reassuring as he was charming. He was also a perfect dancer—good enough to make Queenie feel obliged to apologize for her own clumsiness. "No, no," he said, "you're simply tense, that's all." And putting his face close to hers, he whispered the tune until she felt herself relaxing in his arms.

"You see," he said, as they paused between sets, "it's just a question of relaxing, what? Think of it like taking a fence, eh? If you tense up, the horse refuses and off you go. If you relax, you're over it and away. Do much huntin'?"

"I can't ride."

Goodboys roared with laughter. "Oh, my!" he said, "you *are* pulling my leg!"

His expression suddenly became somber, and a guilty look clouded his eyes. "I say," he said, "you'll think me frightfully rude, but I *did* promise I'd dance with Pempy. We've had such a smashing time that I'd quite forgotten. I expect she'll be livid."

Goodboys steered Queenie back to her hidden table, promised to return when he could, and vanished behind the tree to make his apologies to Mrs. Daventry. He did not really seem worried. He was the kind of young man who took it for granted that everything would work out for the best, the typical sahib who believed that God was an Englishman rather like himself, but older. Fortune, women and senior officers had always smiled on Goodboys, and probably always would.

To Queenie, he seemed perfectly splendid. She had never met anyone quite like him before and was unaware that there existed thousands of Englishmen just like him, and that, like young Anglo-Indian girls, they faded early. The pink faces became red, the slim figures vanished in the fat of middle age, the good humor was eroded by drink, promotion and marriage. In ten years' time, Goodboys would probably be a choleric, balding major. He would have his own favorite armchair in the mess, from which he would scowl at the young subalterns over his burra peg; his inspections would sow terror in the hearts of the regiment's sowars and havildars, he would play polo to the point of heatstroke and possibly beyond. To Queenie, however, he was Prince Charming in person—and all the more so since he had accepted her as one of his own!

She watched him vanish into the darkness, then went to the ladies' room to look at herself in the mirror. She found it hard to believe she was still the same person.

Inside, it was more luxurious than she had expected. There was a powder room decorated with gold satin wallpaper, and a gold-painted makeup table with a large, well-lit mirror.

She went into the lavatory, and when she came out found that someone was sitting at the makeup table, her back to Queenie. It was, Queenie saw, a particularly *elegant* back—completely bare, except for two almost invisibly thin silver-beaded shoulder straps. In the mirror Queenie saw the face of Mrs. Penelope Daventry, her eyes fixed on Queenie's reflection. Her compact, a gleaming circle of gold, was open on the table beside her, and she was touching up her lips with bright scarlet lipstick. She had the fierce concentration of someone engaged in a task demanding precision workmanship. She held her breath as she touched the point of lipstick to her lips, tracing the line exactly, then filling in the space below with the careless flourish of someone who has succeeded with the difficult part.

Mrs. Daventry snapped the lipstick case shut and, like a lazy cat, ran the point of her sharp little tongue over her lips to smooth them out. Then she smiled to test her workmanship, lit a cigarette and placed it in her holder. At her elbow was a large whiskey tumbler, half-empty.

Mrs. Daventry turned, took a sip, leaving a rim of scarlet around the edge of the glass, and closed her eyes for a moment as if she was in pain. The heavy diamond bracelet clinked against the glass as she put it down, giving off a musical chime. She looked older than she had in the Palm Court, and her green eyes seemed to have faded slightly. It occurred to Queenie, who felt a sinking sensation in the pit of her stomach, that Mrs. Daventry was drunk.

Queenie edged toward the door, but it was no use. Mrs. Daventry's eyes followed her with much the same effect that a cobra is reputed to have on its prey. In the harsh light of the makeup lamps around the mirror, Mrs. Daventry's face had indeed a certain reptilian quality—a jeweled, watchful, glossy reptile. Queenie almost expected her to hiss at any moment, but instead Mrs. Daventry merely took a deep puff on her cigarette holder, exhaled without blinking and said in her cold, precise voice, "Well, well. The belle of the ball."

"I was just going," Queenie said.

"Were you now? I expect you'll find Nigel Goodboys waiting for you, my girl. He was *very* taken with you."

Mrs. Daventry's voice was like a deadly weapon. It was brittle and polite as only an upper-class English voice can be, but there was no mistaking the hostility it conveyed. She could cut to the bone without ever having to raise her voice.

"I only danced with him twice," Queenie said, as soothingly as she could, trying hard to strike a note of apology without making it sound like a whine. She had no desire to antagonize the older woman, whose world was exactly the one she wanted to enter.

It had no effect. Mrs. Daventry merely smiled unpleasantly, arching her neatly penciled little eyebrows. "Let me tell you something, dear child," she said, in a voice that was at once cordial and menacing. "Keep your little paws off him or I'll scratch your bloody eyes out. I don't take kindly to poaching."

"But he *asked* me to dance with him."

"I'm sure he did, dear. But not without a little encouragement from you, I imagine." She gave a sigh. *"Men!"* she said, with venomous emphasis. "They all make fools of themselves when they see a pretty young girl. However common she is."

"I'm *not* common," Queenie said, startled at her own courage.

Mrs. Daventry stared at Queenie for a moment in silence, examining her from head to toe. "Oh, but you are," she said. "That dreadful pink dress, for one thing—nothing could be more common. I've seen you before, haven't I?"

"I don't think so."

"Oh, yes, dear, I wouldn't forget a face like yours . . . of course! You're the girl who was with Morgan Jones at the Palm Court. Even my dolt of a husband noticed you. Do you know, I could learn to dislike you very much, miss? That's two of my men I've seen you with now. Can't you find one of your own?"

Queenie wondered what men Mrs. Daventry had in mind. It had not occurred to her that Mrs. Daventry might think of Morgan as one of "her men," nor had she ever been exposed to such intense hostility from an adult—Mrs. Daventry was the same age as her mother, after all, however glamorous. She was at once petrified and determined to be polite. "I didn't mean any harm," she said in a small voice, conscious of the fact that she sounded like a child. But the apology had no effect on Mrs. Daventry.

"Harm? Don't give me any of that little-girl crap! I don't know who the hell you are, but if you don't keep off my turf, you'll be bloody sorry. You're playing out of your league, miss. And what's your name, by the way?"

"Queenie."

Mrs. Daventry glared at her balefully. "Queenie. *Queenie?* What the *hell* kind of a name is that?"

"Mine."

"Don't be smart with me, my girl. How did you meet Morgan, may I ask?"

"He's my uncle, Mrs. Daventry."

Mrs. Daventry smiled grimly. She leaned forward and took Queenie's hand, then pulled her closer, examining her as if she were an object for sale. She laughed unpleasantly. "Do you know, I believe you're telling the truth," she said at last. "Morgan's niece! I should have guessed. The dark hair, the cheekbones, the eyes—oh, yes, I see the resemblance now all right. How *dreadfully* funny! Then you're just a bloody little chee-chee, aren't you, passing yourself off for white? I can't wait to tell

Nigel. He can't stand chee-chees, the dear boy. Neither one thing nor the other, he says—the worst of both races, and the best of neither."

Queenie tried to pull away from Mrs. Daventry's grasp, but the woman held her firmly. Laughter and anger had turned her face into a grotesque mask, and suddenly she seemed to Queenie old and ugly, but her grip was as strong as a vise, and the cold, hard fingernails dug into Queenie's wrist.

Queenie felt herself tremble, not so much from fear as from humiliation. In Goodboys' arms she had allowed herself to believe, for a few minutes, that she was as English as he was—but of course she was not, and as long as she stayed in India, she never would be.

"My father was English!" she shouted, conscious as she said it that even that wasn't true—he had been Irish, which in Mrs. Daventry's eyes would be almost as bad as being a chee-chee, if not worse.

"Oh, I can see that," Mrs. Daventry said. "Railway scum, I suppose. Listen to me, you little chee-chee bitch, from now on stick with your own kind!" Her voice had risen now. Before, it had been a low, menacing whisper; now it was an angry shriek, like the sound of the wind in a storm. For the first time, Queenie was frightened.

Mrs. Daventry tightened her grasp. Her mascara was streaked now, either with sweat or tears, and one corner of her scarlet mouth twitched. "You think you've got it all, don't you, you bloody little tart, with your bedroom eyes and your nice juicy tits, and every stupid man in the room staring at you? Never mind. Your kind doesn't last, dear. By the time you're twenty-five you'll be a fat nigger cow, suckling half a dozen half-breed brats! Just like your mother, I daresay."

Queenie hardly even realized she was crying as she struggled to pull free from Mrs. Daventry's hand. She heard someone shout, "Don't you ever speak that way about my Ma!" but the voice didn't sound like hers, for she had never screamed at anyone before—certainly not at a grown-up. Then, without any thought on her part, as if the instincts of her Welsh grandfather and her Irish father had finally emerged in her, she reached back with her left arm and slapped Mrs. Daventry as hard as she could.

There was a moment of silence while Queenie waited for punishment—in what form, she wasn't sure. Would Mrs. Daventry call for the police? Would a thunderbolt from heaven crash down through the quilted-satin ceiling and strike her dead? She was confused, terrified and astonished by what she had done. But nothing happened.

Mrs. Daventry merely sat rooted to the spot, as if the slap had paralyzed her. Her self-possession returned almost instantly, as if it had never abandoned her. Her eyes amidst the ruined mascara were cold and distant. They focused on Queenie as if she were a total stranger, or some inanimate object of no particular interest or value. As if, Queenie realized, a chee-chee girl was beneath her contempt.

"I shall have to do my face over," Mrs. Daventry said calmly.

Queenie went to the door. She was trembling. Despite the heat, she felt numb with cold. She wanted only to be home, away from here, to forget the whole evening—though already she knew that would be impossible. At last she had discovered for herself what it meant to be a chee-chee.

She wondered if she was going to be sick. Above all, she was determined not to show her tears to Mrs. Daventry. She opened the door, the noise of the band suddenly filling the little room, and heard Mrs. Daventry say, in a low, clear voice, speaking into the mirror without turning back to look at her, "I'll make sure every door in Calcutta is closed to you, my girl, you can count on *that*. By the time I've finished with you, there won't be an Englishman or an English firm or an English establishment that will have you. You'd better hurry off and marry a chee-chee engine driver, Queenie—because that's all you're ever going to get. Now close the bloody door behind you."

Queenie ran. She was sobbing now, her face covered with tears. She ran past Alberto Firpo so fast that he hardly even had time to raise one elegant eyebrow, she ran past the bandstand, from which Morgan stared after her in amazement, past the huge Sikh commissionaire, not even hearing him ask, "Taxi, missy-sahib?" and out into the street.

The noises and the smells of Calcutta engulfed her. She was suddenly pressed on all sides, crushed, suffocated by the sheer number of people—most of them, she realized, staring at her, some with curiosity, some with blank indifference. In the dark streets, figures rose up all around her from where they sat huddled like dim shadows, crying, pleading, cursing her.

She ran on past them blindly, trying to escape from these living bundles of rags, turned a corner and found herself in a small square so full of people that it seemed like an anthill of misery. There were beggars everywhere, many displaying hideous deformities, women cradling in their sticklike arms emaciated babies too weak to cry, painted prostitutes with tattooed faces, who grinned and jeered at her, their lips stained purple from chewing betel.

She plunged into a dark alley and bumped headlong into a thickly veiled woman, who hissed at her like a goose, scandalized by the sight of Queenie's exposed face and shoulders.

The heat was unbearable, for this was the week before the monsoon. The entire city, all India, was imprisoned in a cocoon of heat, waiting breathlessly for the rains. To the east, far out over the Bay of Bengal, vast black clouds rose above the sullen, oily sea, flashing with lightning as the monsoon gathered strength. If it was delayed by so much as a few days, the land died, for without the rains, crops failed, wells ran dry, famine raged. A late monsoon meant death to millions. Yet the monsoon itself brought no relief, for the rain came too swiftly and harshly. Floods devastated the countryside, entire islands were washed away, vanishing into the seas with their inhabitants as if they had never existed.

Queenie paused breathlessly. Her head ached, her chest hurt from the exertion of running, she felt the whole weight of India pressing down on her, crushing out her life with its traditions, its monstrous indifference to life and death, its unbreakable social customs that made a mockery of change, hope and youth. There was nothing here for her except humiliation and waste. Tonight, if nothing else, had brought that home to her.

She wiped her eyes and looked around her in despair. She was standing in a fetid alleyway—one of hundreds, perhaps thousands, which ran through the city like a meaningless maze, leading nowhere, unidentifiable except to those who lived there.

Out of the darkness she saw a small group of a dozen or so men rising from the pavement abruptly. They appeared to her to have been sorting out rags, but at the sight of her they broke off whatever they were doing. They shouted at her, but she couldn't understand what they were saying, and as she turned to run, they surrounded her, their long, thin arms reaching out toward her in supplication or anger.

She tripped on the broken, slimy cobblestones and lost a shoe. In the dark cubbyholes on both sides of the alley she could see huddled figures watching her silently. She turned and found herself staring into the hideous face of a beggar, only inches away from her. She recoiled at the stained, rotting stumps of broken teeth, the milky-white cast of blindness in the eyes, the missing earlobes. She could not even tell what sex it was.

A thin hand touched her wrist. Queenie pulled her arm free and ran, but with only one shoe, she stumbled, falling into the darkness. She landed on some unidentifiable, reeking, filthy bundle of rags. Her hand touched something soft, warm and slimy, and she willed herself not to think about what it was, or might be.

Queenie closed her eyes. She heard herself panting hoarsely for breath. At any second she expected to be raped or murdered, but even that prospect was less terrifying than the sheer horror of touching these people—or being touched by them. She felt a hand brush against her arms, tried to scream and heard herself whimper for mercy instead. The hand grasped her upper arm firmly, then a rich, kindly voice said, "Please don't be frightened, missy-sahib. Come with me."

Queenie allowed herself to be helped to her feet, and limped after her rescuer, if he was that. He shuffled along, slightly ahead of her, one hand still guiding her in the darkness, muttering to himself and swinging what appeared to be a stick to ward off the people of the streets, who parted silently to let them pass.

"Where are we going?" Queenie asked, still struggling for breath.

"Patience, patience, missy," the man whispered, fumbling under his clothes for a huge iron key, which he produced like a conjurer, holding it up for her inspection. "Have utmost confidence in your humble servant, Mr. Bos Brammachatrarya."

Mr. Brammachatrarya opened a low, iron-studded door and, with a courtly gesture, ushered Queenie into the light. He followed, closing and carefully bolting the door behind him.

At the sound of the massive bolts closing, Queenie felt herself panicking again, though now that Mr. Brammachatrarya had turned around, he was revealed as something less than a frightening figure. For one thing, he was enormously—grotesquely—fat, so fat that he bore a startling resemblance to the Michelin tire man. For another, like many Indians, he had adopted European clothing without committing himself wholeheartedly to the idea.

It was as if he had felt obliged to make a gesture of respect to the British conquerors by displaying bits and pieces of their alien costume, so that he wore a black suit waistcoat, unbuttoned, over a white dhoti. His legs were encased to the calf in tight white jodhpurs that made them look like huge sausages, but below the calf he sported black silk socks, handsome purple sock suspenders and well-polished English shoes. On his head he wore a white Congress cap, but he carried an unfurled black umbrella in his left hand like a badge of office.

He smiled shyly at Queenie and carefully hung the umbrella on a hook by the door. His face was so round and fat that his eyes were reduced to small, dark slits, in which, however, it was impossible to

ignore, even in Queenie's state, a certain shrewd, steely gleam. He
wore a tiny gold-rimmed pince-nez on his broad nose, the pads sunk
so deeply in the flesh that they simply vanished.

He drew aside a beaded curtain, revealing a small square room that
looked out over a dark courtyard. The floors were covered with carpets
and big, threadbare cushions. There was no European furniture except
for a huge, very old-fashioned safe. On top of the safe was a pair of
enormous rubber galoshes—apparently Mr. Brammachatrarya was prepared for the monsoon. There was a curtained doorway on one side
of the room, behind which it was possible to hear someone breathing
heavily.

Mr. Brammachatrarya gave a low, jerky bow, no doubt the best he
could manage, given his corpulence, seated himself on one of the
cushions, crossing his legs with considerable difficulty and gestured for
Queenie to sit.

"Some refreshment would not be amiss?" Mr. Brammachatrarya
asked, and, without pausing for a reply, he shouted, then clapped his
hands, then shouted even louder, producing from the darkness of the
courtyard outside a torrent of angry protests at the lateness of the hour.

"Tea in a mo'," the fat man said cheerfully, and in Queenie's opinion
optimistically, since there was no sign that his command was being
obeyed.

"Where am I?" she asked.

"Missy, the question is not where but why? The Street of Thieves
is no place for a young lady—not remotely at all."

"I was lost."

Mr. Brammachatrarya smiled benevolently at her, as if the sight of
a young woman in a pink evening dress—sadly stained and bedraggled now—with one shoe missing was perfectly normal. He folded his
hands across his vast belly. "Lost from whence?" he asked.

"I was at Firpo's and stepped out for a breath of fresh air."

Mr. Brammachatrarya laughed. "Ah, Firpo's," he said. "I know the
place! Dancing, eh? Oh, jolly good!"

For a moment Queenie thought he was making fun of her, but he
radiated such enthusiasm and goodwill that she dismissed the notion.

"You know Firpo's?" she asked.

"I know it, to be sure. Who does not know it? I have not been *in*
it, of course. Mere Indians are not welcome there. The pleasures of
such a place are unknown to we poor Hindus, missy. We are ignorant
savages, you see. Our men and women do not dance with each other.

We do not 'trip the light fantastic,' as the poet says. . . . What did you say your name was?"

"I didn't. It's Queenie. Queenie Kelley."

Mr. Brammachatrarya nodded as if the fact had been known to him from the beginning. "Very good," he said, though whether he was signifying his approval of her name or the arrival of tea, it was hard to say—for at that moment, a sulky young man in a dhoti appeared from the courtyard carrying a tray, which he put down on the floor with a crash.

"Thank you," Mr. Brammachatrarya called out serenely at the young man's back. He handed Queenie a soiled china mug without a saucer. "There! Nothing like a nice cup of tea."

"Thank you for saving me."

"You were in no real danger, missy," Mr. Brammachatrarya said, heaping sugar into his own mug.

"It seemed dangerous to me."

"Yes? These are of course very poor people. The poor often seem dangerous to those who are better off, but mostly they are not. They are merely ragpickers, beggars, perhaps petty thieves. Nothing serious . . . but this is *their* street, you see. I fancy your presence there is as unwelcome to them as they would be outside your house. Tell me, won't somebody be looking for you by now?"

It occurred to Queenie for the second time that Mr. Brammachatrarya might not be as benevolent as he looked. She had heard of "white slavers," and while he was anything but white—his skin was the color of dark toffee—he might well trade in white women. She sniffed her tea suspiciously, wondering if it was drugged. Her host looked genuinely alarmed at the gesture.

"Is it not all right?" he asked, his voice rising with concern.

Somewhat ashamed of herself, Queenie nodded. "I expect people *are* looking for me, yes." Even as she said it, Queenie realized that Morgan would probably be too angry to go searching for her and, in any case, would hardly be likely to follow her this deep into the old part of the city. He would surely assume she had made her way home somehow.

Mr. Brammachatrarya recognized a subterfuge when he heard one, but he did not seem offended. "Yes, yes, to be sure," he said cheerfully. "You will be missed by your friends, no doubt. There will be a hue and a cry. Never mind, missy. You drink your tea, then wash up. I will send my boy back with you to guide you safe and sound."

Mr. Brammachatrarya smiled reassuringly, revealing a pair of gold teeth in the center of his mouth. He offered Queenie a plate of sweets. They looked unpleasantly sticky, and a number of flies had become stuck to them, their wings buzzing ineffectually as they tried to pull loose. She shook her head, but Mr. Brammachatrarya took no offense. He put the plate on his knees, and ate the sweets one by one, popping them into his mouth with surprising delicacy. He did not seem to notice the flies.

"I have a sweet tooth," he explained unnecessarily, pausing to lick the powdered sugar off his fingers. "I am only sorry you cannot meet my better half. Mrs. B. is in purdah, and in any case only speaks Hindi."

"I speak Hindi," Queenie said, immediately sorry she had mentioned it.

"Do you now?" he asked. "Jolly good! You were not born in England?"

"No."

"And where do you live, missy?" The broad face of Mr. Brammachatrarya seemed to express a genuine curiosity, as if he were anxious to increase his knowledge of European customs and social life. It occurred to Queenie that he probably had few opportunities to talk to Europeans, and for a moment she was tempted to lie to him—for once she told him where she lived, he would know she was an Anglo-Indian and might well treat her with the contempt of a caste Hindu for a half-caste. But it was impossible for her to lie to the fat man. There was something about him that was too genuinely good-natured for that.

"Chowringhee," Queenie said.

"Ah!" Mr. Brammachatrarya nodded happily, no doubt because his suspicions had been confirmed. "That's nothing to be ashamed of," he said firmly.

Queenie found herself relaxing in his presence. She knew very few educated Indians, and shared many of Morgan's prejudices about them. Mr. Brammachatrarya, however, was obviously a man of considerable charm and intelligence, who seemed happy enough to treat her as an adult. He was neither haughty, like the English, nor touchy and apologetic, like her own people. He seemed quite content to be what he was. She sipped her tea—which was, in fact, delicious.

"If you are Indian born, then nothing here should frighten you," he said. "This is your home."

Queenie shook her head. "England is Home."

"Oh, dear me, no! Forgive me, but it's not so. Part of you is Indian, Miss Queenie. You see I wear the Congress cap?"

"Yes."

"I don't hold with Gandhi completely, you understand. How could I? I am a moneylender. I thrive on other people's misery. That's how *he* would look at it, at any rate. But about some things he is right, I believe. The English will not stay here forever and when they go, we will all have to live here together without them. Your people, too."

"We're not Indian."

Mr. Brammachatrarya shrugged. "Who is?" he asked. His expression was more serious now. "We are Hindu or Muslim or Sikh, or goodness knows what-all. Some of us are—what do you call yourselves?—Domiciled Europeans, or Anglo-Indians, or Eurasians . . . 'A rose by any other name,' as the bard wrote. We won't be Indians, any of us, until the British have gone."

"They'll never go."

"Oh, but they *will*, Miss Queenie. They will. Many of your people know that. Certainly the community leaders—the estimable Mr. Frank Anthony, the distinguished Colonel Gidney—*they* know. They don't like it, mind you, but they know it's coming. When that time comes, you will be Indian, missy, just like the rest of us."

"We were brought up to be English."

"True. And in my opinion, very unwisely. But *are* you English? Do the English clasp you to their bosoms? Are you welcome in their houses and clubs?"

Queenie was about to argue the point; then she remembered Mrs. Daventry and shook her head.

"Accept the fact that you're Indian, and we will accept you. With open arms." Mr. Brammachatrarya opened his arms wide, to make his point.

"Perhaps . . ."

"Not perhaps, missy. Your future is *here*. The sooner you accept it, the better. And when you have, then nothing in the streets will frighten you. Why should it? You will be Indian, too."

Mr. Brammachatrarya leaned forward and patted Queenie's knee. She shook her head. It was a future she could not accept.

"I'm going Home to England," she said stubbornly. And to her surprise she knew she meant it. Nothing would stop her—not after tonight.

"Well, well," he said, "if you *want* to be English, that's the place to go. Some of your people go, it's true. How welcome they are there, I don't know. For a pretty young lady like you, no doubt all things are possible. You may not have a rosy path. . . ."

He clapped his hands and the sulky boy appeared with a bowl of water and a towel. Mr. Brammachatrarya tactfully closed his eyes while Queenie washed her face and straightened her dress. He opened them when she was finished and beamed. "*Much* better," he said. "The boy will fetch you a pair of Mrs. B.'s shoes and show you the way. You will be back—quick as a bird!"

Mr. Brammachatrarya did not get up to see her out—it was not the Hindu custom to do so. He placed both his palms together instead and inclined his head as much as his chins would allow.

"I have had such a jolly time chatting with you," he said, as the boy opened the door for Queenie. "If I can ever be of any service, please let me know. Just come to the old bazaar and ask for me. Any-one will show you to my door."

He rose with surprising speed, vanished behind the curtain and was gone.

Morgan was so relieved to see Queenie reappear safe and sound that he hardly showed any anger at all, though she could tell that it seethed just beneath the surface. He had spent the last hour trying to think of some way to explain to Vicky how he had lost her, and by the time she returned, he was drenched in sweat.

She found him sitting out his break at a small table with Peggy D'Souza, toward whom he had doubtless gravitated for comfort.

"You gave us a right old turn, dearie," Peggy said. "Morgan sent a couple of sweepers out looking for you. Wogs! Fat lot of use *they* were!"

Among the many things that Queenie had learned from Pugh was the ability to hear accents, and differentiate between ways of speaking. It was a two-edged sword. Before her lessons with Pugh, even if she noticed a difference, she didn't attach any particular notions of class or quality to it. Now she was oversensitized. Peggy's way of speaking, she recognized, was hopelessly vulgar, her chee-chee accent so strong that she could never "pass" in England.

Queenie liked Peggy D'Souza, and the thought that Peggy was vul-gar made her feel disloyal and snobbish, and at the same time pleased that *she* spoke better, which made her feel even guiltier. She blushed, angry at herself for blushing. She seemed to blush a lot these days.

"You do well to blush, girl," Morgan said. "Where on earth did you run to?"

Queenie had given the matter some thought on the way back, and decided it would be a mistake to mention that she had slapped Mrs. Daventry. Morgan would very likely assume that *she* had been at fault, not Mrs. Daventry, of whom he was obviously in awe. "I didn't feel well," she said, and blushed again, this time because she had lied.

"No bloody wonder. It's beastly hot." Peggy fanned her bosom—which was lavishly exposed—with a small napkin. She looked out of sorts, Queenie thought; then she realized that Peggy's night was probably a total loss if she was reduced to sitting with Morgan and sharing his worries. "Oh, Peggy, I'm sorry," she said, and meant it.

"What about *me?*" Morgan's petulance was rising to the surface, a storm warning for his anger. Queenie could read the signs: the narrowed eyes, the slight trembling of the lips, the rising singsong pitch of his voice. He was always at his worst when he was afraid he had been made to look like a fool—and certainly her running out of Firpo's must have embarrassed him. "I'm sorry I worried you," she said, reaching over to give his fingers a quick squeeze.

"Where the devil did you *go* out there?"

"I went outside for some fresh air and got lost," Queenie explained, trying to sound as plaintive as possible. She had no wish to add a quarrel with Morgan to the other misfortunes of the night. "Luckily a nice old Hindu gentleman rescued me."

Morgan frowned. "A wog?"

"Well, yes . . . he gave me a nice cup of tea."

"You went to his bloody *house?*"

"Morgan, he was a harmless, fat old man. I'd still be wandering around the bazaar if it wasn't for Mr. Brammachatrarya."

Morgan stared at her in astonishment, then rubbed his eyes with his hands, like a man who has just heard one piece of bad news too many. "My God, girl, you do pick your friends, don't you? The fellow's a notorious thief—a kind of Hindu Fagin."

"Who's Fagin?"

Morgan shook his head. "You ought to read some books, girl," he said, "instead of worrying all the time about how you look and how you sound. Haven't they given you *Oliver Twist* yet at school?"

Queenie blushed. She read well enough, but reading bored her. She had, in fact, been asked to read *Oliver Twist*, and had so far managed to put it off.

"I haven't finished it yet," she lied.

"You haven't bloody *started* it, or you'd know who Fagin was. Honestly, Queenie, if you don't mind your schoolwork, you'll end up like—"

Queenie stared at him, while Morgan fell silent. It was his turn to blush now, since he was about to use Peggy D'Souza as an example of what happened to girls who didn't pass their school-leaving examinations and learn typing. "You still haven't told me who Fagin was," she said, more to help him out than from any curiosity.

"A Jew."

"Mr. Brammachatrarya is a caste Hindu."

"Yes, yes, that's not the point. Fagin in the book is a fence," Morgan said impatiently, and seeing that Queenie was about to ask for an explanation of that, too, he added, "A man who receives stolen goods, you know—who buys what others steal."

"He said he was a moneylender."

"That, too, no doubt. If your Ma knew . . ."

A plump, middle-aged Englishman came over and put his hand on Peggy's shoulder. He paid no attention to Morgan, who might have been invisible as far as the man was concerned. "Care for a dance?" he asked Peggy. He wore gold-rimmed pince-nez with a broad black ribbon that attached them to his lapel. He took them off for a moment, awestruck by the sight of Peggy's bosom from above. He bobbed his head in Queenie's direction. "Hope I'm not interrupting, what?" he said, squeezing the pince-nez back on his fleshy nose again to examine *her*. For a moment, he seemed to be wondering if he had made the wrong choice, then noticed Morgan glaring at him and hastily pulled Peggy's chair back for her.

Morgan lit a cigarette, made a valiant stab at blowing a smoke ring and failed. He didn't have the knack for it, for some reason, and Queenie had come to suspect that it was one of the many small mannerisms he affected to disguise the fact that he was staring at her. Sometimes at home, when she came out of the bath shed in her dressing gown, she would find Morgan sitting on the veranda, practicing his smoke rings and pretending to stare at the trees, but if she turned her head quickly enough, she could see that his eyes were focused on her. At teatime she would look up to see his eyes fixed on her over the top of his newspaper. Now they were aimed at her through the cloud of smoke he had caused.

Their expression was not at all friendly. Morgan often seemed to Queenie to be blaming *her* because he couldn't take his eyes off her, as if it was all her fault, which struck her as unfair, because she couldn't help the way she looked, or the effect it seemed to have on him. And yet she couldn't help flirting a little for his benefit from time to time, if only because she had no one else to try it out on—certainly nobody as "safe" as Morgan.

The glass in front of him was empty. He clicked his fingers at a waiter, and called for another. It occurred to Queenie that he was a little drunk. "Bottoms up," he said, when the waiter rudely slammed his fresh drink down on the table. "Cheeky sod!"

He leaned forward, lowering his voice confidentially. "For God's sake, tell me the truth, now Peggy has gone. Did that chap Goodboys do anything that frightened you? Was he going too far?"

"He was a perfect gentleman."

"They're always the worst kind."

She looked past him at the crowded dance floor, where Peggy D'Souza, also in pink, was smooching with the fat Englishman, while the English ladies sniggered and glared at her. She felt suddenly depressed and exhausted. "Morgan," she said, "I want to go Home."

"You'll have to wait. I'm not off for at least another hour."

"I meant *Home*, Morgan. England."

He sat back and sighed. "We all want to do that, Queenie."

"We all talk about it. Nobody *does* it."

He closed his eyes for a moment. "It isn't so easy, Queenie."

"Peggy is going Home."

"She's lucky. She's marrying an Englishman—this chap Butts."

"I'd marry an Englishman if I had to. Anyone, so long as he took me Home. Besides, what's wrong with marrying an Englishman?"

"Nothing, I suppose. It all depends on the Englishman."

"I wouldn't care. I'd marry anyone to go Home. And I'd do anything."

"Don't talk like that," he said. He wasn't staring at her now—his eyes were sad and affectionate, like the old Morgan, the companion-uncle of her childhood. "Don't ever sell yourself cheap, girl."

"I meant it. I'd do anything for the man who takes me Home. I hate it here."

He put his hand on her forehead, as if he were trying to see whether she had a temperature. "What happened tonight, Queenie?" he asked softly. "I've a right to know."

She bit her lip. He did have a right to know *something*, there was no denying it. Besides, Morgan was better off hearing her side of the story before he got Mrs. Daventry's version from somebody. "Mrs. Daventry told me off in the ladies' for dancing with Nigel Goodboys."

He laughed. "Is that all? She's got a sharp tongue. She *did* look bloody angry, I must say, when she came out of the loo. She had one dance more with Goodboys, then packed it in. Made poor Daventry call for the bill before he'd even had his supper, the fat sod!"

"Morgan—it wasn't funny. She called me a 'bloody little chee-chee.' I've never seen anybody so angry. She threatened me, too."

"*Threatened* you?"

"She said she'd close every door in Calcutta to me."

He fingered his stiff white collar nervously. "I'm sure she didn't mean that," he said miserably. Then he gave a deep sigh and looked down into his drink hopelessly. "My God, what a thing to happen . . ."

"You think she means it?"

He shrugged. "I'm sure her bark is worse than her bite," he said mournfully, unable to disguise from her his opinion that Mrs. Daventry would probably bite as hard as she barked, or harder. "People don't always mean what they say."

"They do when it's something bad," Queenie said, glad that she hadn't told him the whole truth. "Oh, dear, what an evening . . ."

"I'm sorry."

"It's not your fault," Queenie said, rather more sharply than she had intended. Morgan had a habit of saying he was sorry for things that weren't his responsibility. *She* had persuaded him to bring her here; she had danced with Goodboys, fought with Mrs. Daventry and run away. On the other hand, when Morgan *was* in the wrong, he denied it stubbornly and made excuses for himself.

He looked so sorry for himself that Queenie apologized for snapping at him. "Mr. Brammachatrarya said something to me over tea," she explained. "In a way, it was as upsetting as what Mrs. Daventry said. He said when independence comes, we'll all have to learn to be Indian. Do you think that's true, Morgan?"

"Of course not. It's just the kind of thing a cheeky wog would say." Morgan took a last sip at his drink. He looked at Queenie over the rim of the glass, then shook his head sadly. He was never able to lie to her for long. "I suppose it's possible," he admitted. "Of course independence is a long way off. If ever . . ."

"You've always told me it's coming."

"Yes. Well, I suppose it is. It will be a bloodbath, mark my words."

"I wish I could just *go*."

"You're too young . . ."

"I don't want to wait forever. Didn't you want to go, too, at my age?"

"Yes, of course. I still do, damn it all!"

"And you're still here."

There was an uncomfortable silence. Queenie couldn't remember a time when Morgan hadn't talked about going Home, but he also talked about "waiting for the right moment," and she guessed that, left to himself, the right moment would never come. "Going Home" was not something he was prepared to plan or work for—in Morgan's mind it was like winning the lottery. Every day he believed it was just around the corner, and yet, year after year, he had stayed here. He blushed, avoiding her eyes. "It's not that simple," he said softly. "Apart from everything else, there's the question of money."

"We could save up for it, Morgan."

He stared at her in surprise. Over his shoulder, she could see Alberto tapping his watch to show it was time for Morgan to get back to work. "We?" Morgan asked, in a whisper.

"We'll go together," she said firmly. "Alberto's signaling."

"Damn." He stood up, a little unsteadily. "My word, I think you *mean* it, girl."

"Of course I do!"

He nodded. "Well, then," he said, "it's a deal, Queenie. As the Yanks say."

"You promise?"

He seemed taken aback by the serious tone of her voice, but Queenie looked right at him until he blinked. She was not about to let him off the hook. Morgan, she knew, was a man of his word. He thought of himself as a gentleman—besides, he would never be able to break a promise to her.

"I promise," he said unhappily, with the mournful expression of a man who has allowed himself to be caught in a trap.

CHAPTER 6

SHE LOVED BRIGHT COLORS and the sun. Her heart sank when she entered the office with its dark paneling, the sunblinds pulled low against the outside glare, the vast, tufted-leather and mahogany furniture crouching like huge forest animals in the shadows, sofas and armchairs so big that they seemed made for some improbable race of giants. She had learned that the English—the *pukka* English—hated bright colors. Their homes, offices, clubs and railway stations were faithful reproductions of the Victorian buildings they were comfortable in at home.

The faces in the oil portraits on the walls stared down at Queenie with the lofty contempt of the pukka sahib from their heavy, dull-gilt frames. Some of them were clean-shaven and wore powdered wigs, others had the improbably luxuriant beards of the Victorian sahib, but all of them were pink-skinned, pale, blue- or green-eyed, and for a moment it seemed to Queenie that at the sight of her dark hair and eyes, they might shout in chorus, "She's a chee-chee!"

It was not until she sat down that she recognized the fat Englishman behind the desk as the man who had tapped Peggy on the shoulder for a dance at Firpo's. The plump pink face seemed more stern here, where he was in a position of authority, the pukka sahib personified, with his ginger hair, tailored white suit steaming in the heat, red-veined nose and an irritable expression which was intended to show that his time was more valuable than hers.

He did not seem to recognize her, to her relief. Nor was there any reason why he should, Queenie realized—he had only seen her for a few seconds, and over a year ago at that. Besides, now that she had left school, she wore her hair swept up to make herself look older, and a string of artificial pearls, borrowed from Magda for the interview.

Mr. Chubb—as the polished brass nameplate screwed into his door proclaimed his name to be—put his pince-nez on. They steamed up immediately, obliging him to peer over their tops. It occurred to Queenie that her legs were the focus of his attention, not her face, so he would have been hard put to recognize her anyway. To get a better look at them he was obliged to squirm down in his chair, his chin pressed against his chest, his fat red neck bent like that of a contortionist. Maliciously she crossed her legs slowly, pointing one foot toward the carpet. Magda had shown her how that gave the calf a more rounded shape while emphasizing the slimness of the ankle.

That Magda was right was confirmed by Chubb's face. He picked up her job application and turned his attention to it, clearing his throat ostentatiously. He peered over it and scrutinized her face. "Haven't I seen you somewhere before?"

No good could come of admitting that they had met at Firpo's, Queenie decided. "I don't think so, sir."

"I could have sworn . . . I don't usually forget a face . . . particularly not one like yours. . . . Well, never mind. Miss Kelley, is it, eh? Your father is Irish?"

"Yes."

"Well, I'm broad-minded about things like that. You're a Domiciled European." It was not a question but a statement.

She nodded.

"Of course, these days we prefer to hire Indians, to be perfectly frank. Don't like it any more than you do, I daresay, but it's a question of politics. Government keeps talking about independence, you see. A lot of rot, but if it happens, which God forbid, we'll want to have plenty of Indians working here. Protective coloration, so to speak, eh?"

He snorted with laughter, then removed a silk handkerchief from his sleeve and blew his nose loudly. He squinted at the piece of paper in his hands. Queenie wondered if he was having trouble reading her handwriting. Penmanship was not one of her skills. In fact, the more she sought a job, the less confidence she had in *any* of her skills. A short typing course had merely confirmed that she would never master the machine. She was always getting the keys stuck together, and when she made carbon copies, the paper seemed to slip sideways by itself so that the lines ran off at odd angles. Her spelling left much to be desired, too.

Ma accused her of "not putting her heart into it," and Ma was right. Queenie hated the typewriter, the carbon paper that smudged her fingers and, above all, the whole idea of being a typist. She could imagine, just possibly, being a receptionist in a posh office, but most English firms didn't want a Domiciled European as a receptionist, out front where everybody could see her.

"You were at Saint Anthony's?" Chubb asked.

She nodded.

"But you didn't take your school-leaving examination?"

"I *took* it, sir. I just didn't pass it, that's all."

"Usually, we expect a candidate to pass . . . well, never mind . . . typing test . . . I say, not too good, eh?"

"The machine was very stiff, sir. I wasn't used to it."

"I daresay. Don't know much about that kind of thing myself. All the same, Miss Kelley, your qualifications for the job are a little—" he paused for the right word—"slim. Wouldn't you say?"

She nodded sadly. "I'd work hard, sir."

"I'm sure, I'm sure." Chubb put the application down and looked her over from head to toe. Then he stood up, walked around to the other side of the desk and put a damp hand on her shoulder. "Of course that kind of skill isn't everything," he said. "There are more important skills than typing, what?"

"I suppose so."

"Business is no laughing matter, Miss—may I call you Queenie?"

She nodded. His hand was sweaty now. She hoped it wouldn't stain her frock.

"No laughing matter at all, by jove! It's hard work and heavy responsibility. A man in my position doesn't have an easy time of it, I assure you. I'm often here until quite late at night. Then there's the hot season—when the mem-sahib and the children go away to the hills for months on end . . . one gets lonely, but one soldiers on. What one needs is someone to share the burden, someone who's loyal, willing—and *discreet*."

Queenie knew she was getting into deeper water than she cared to with Mr. Chubb, but this was the tenth—or was it the twelfth?—interview she'd had, with no sign of a job yet. She had no difficulty in guessing what Chubb was driving at in his ponderous way, and no intention of filling in the evenings when his wife was away or when he stayed late at the office, but once she was hired, perhaps she could sort all that out. Magda would have an idea—she always knew what to do about such things. "I'm loyal," she said. "And discreet." She left out the matter of whether she was "willing" or not, and Chubb didn't seem to notice.

"Splendid," he said. "Topping." He allowed his hand to run down her back. "Of course you'll be working closely with me, you understand. Personal secretary, and all that. When I work late, *you* work late. You'll have to work on your typing a bit. I'll start you off at five pounds a week, but if things work out, as I hope they will—" he gave her a wink—"you'll find me more than generous. All right?"

Five pounds a week! It seemed to Queenie an enormous sum. There were plenty of grown men in the community who didn't make more than that. Ma would be delighted, even Morgan would be impressed— and besides, Chubb's firm was one of the most famous trading houses in Calcutta. All the girls in her class would be green with envy when they heard she was working there, and for a partner at that, a pukka Englishman.

"All right, sir," she said.

Chubb rubbed his hands together.

He went back to the desk, humming to himself, and picked up her application. "I'll just pop next door and let my senior partner know," he said. "Then I'll have the boy take you down to accounts, so the babus can fill out all the bumf. You just wait there half a mo'."

He leered at her briefly, then went out, leaving Queenie to look at the photographs on his desk. There was a portrait of a severe-looking woman with pearl earrings, glaring disapprovingly at the camera—presumably Mrs. Chubb—and another of two fat, unattractive children on ponies.

The door opened and Chubb came in, clearing his throat. He seemed less jolly now, even a little embarrassed. He sat down behind his desk heavily and gave her a look of frank disapproval.

"I'm afraid there's a snag," Chubb said.

She wondered what the problem was. "Is it my typing?"

"No, no . . . but I'm afraid we can't hire you, Miss Kelley."

"But why ever not? You said you would."

Chubb sighed uncomfortably. He was as disappointed as she was, for different reasons, and a little ashamed as well. "I can't tell you why," he said. "I suspect you already know."

She did *not* know. But now she guessed why it was so hard for her to find a job. "Is it Mrs. Daventry?" she whispered.

Chubb stared out at the window. "We do a lot of business with Daventry's firm," he said reluctantly. "That's all I can say. A word to the wise."

She stood up, trying hard not to cry at the unfairness of it. Chubb rang the bell on his desk to have her shown out. He did not get up. "If I were you, Queenie," he said, "I'd get out of Calcutta while you're still young. You've got the looks, eh? They'll take you a long way. But not here."

She stood in front of his desk, her face hot with anger. "Doesn't anybody have the guts to stand up to Mrs. Daventry?" she asked.

"I gather *you* did. Look where it got you." Chubb's voice was full of contempt now. He had made a fool of himself, offering her the job, then withdrawing it, and he blamed her for his own embarrassment. "Besides," he added, "she's one of us, and you are not—or only partly so, eh?"

Then he turned his eyes to the papers on his desk as the messenger boy came in. "Show Miss Kelley out," he said coldly. He did not say goodbye or even look up at her as she left.

Queenie had never dreamed that she would look back on her school days with fondness, but the year that followed was so full of humiliation, boredom and disappointment that it made school seem idyllic. She had no money beyond what little she received from Ma or cadged from Morgan, and apparently no future.

Worse still, Morgan appeared to be making no progress in fulfilling his promise. Daily he found excuses to put off doing anything about it. He was not even saving money—though, to be fair, there was no way he could have saved enough money to finance the journey.

Her only pleasure was the cinema, for since her fifteenth birthday Ma had been persuaded that a weekly film was in order, provided that it was not too "sensational" and that Morgan or Magda chaperoned her. From the first, the cinema had seemed more real to Queenie than life—at any rate more appealing.

Morgan liked to take Queenie—he enjoyed sitting beside her in the dark and always bought her a box of sweets—but he was usually an irritating companion. He fussed about details and always wanted to know why something had happened, or what it meant, whereas Queenie was content to be swept up by the film itself. Her pleasure was only slightly marred by the knowledge that she was just as beautiful as many of the film stars. Admittedly, she didn't know how to act, not really—but how much did that matter? she wondered. One thing she knew: as long as she stayed in Calcutta, there was not much chance of her being "discovered," as film stars apparently so often were.

She had been so upset at Chubb's rejection that Morgan had taken her to the cinema in midweek—a special treat—to see Marla Negresco in *Royal Wedding*, which proved to be a disappointment. Marla Negresco was undeniably beautiful, though rather plumper than most stars, but she had apparently found the transition from the silents to talkies difficult. Her accent was heavily European, much thicker even than Magda's, and most of what she said was incomprehensible. "She's had it," Morgan said as they tramped out into the rainy night.

On the other side of Corporation Street a poster in the window of Thomas Cook & Son advertised the P & O steamers for the voyage to England. There was a picture of a ship steaming past the white cliffs of Dover. Above it, red letters proclaimed, "Bookings always available."

"Have you seen Mrs. Daventry lately, Morgan?" Queenie asked as they settled into the car.

Morgan stared out through the cracked, rain-washed windshield. On either side of the street were masses of people, their white dhotis contrasting sharply with their black umbrellas so that they almost seemed to be part of the architecture.

He shrugged. "From time to time."

"Does she speak to you?"

"I'm in her bad books, frankly."

"Because of me?"

He nodded. The subject seemed to make him even more gloomy, but she pressed on. "The two of you were—" she sought the right word—"lovers, weren't you?"

"*Really,* Queenie!"

"Well, whatever you want to call it."

Morgan stared out into the rainy street. "We had—a kind of affair, yes. You might say."

"Was she in love with you?"

"I refuse to answer." She glared at him. "Oh, all right. No, she wasn't in love with me, for God's sake."

"And were you in love with *her?*"

"Certainly not," Morgan said primly.

"Well, then . . ."

"People sometimes have an affair that doesn't involve—love. Mrs. Daventry has a lot of affairs that don't involve love."

"I see. Why did it break up, Morgan?"

"It didn't 'break up,' as you put it," Morgan said impatiently. "I used to visit her from time to time. When she *sent* for me, I must admit. In the last few years, less often. Now, not at all."

"Do you miss her?"

"Not at all," Morgan said gamely, but Queenie guessed he did. However difficult Mrs. Daventry might be, she was part of exactly the world he coveted.

"Has she talked to you about me?"

Morgan sighed. "No. She makes a point of ignoring me, I'm afraid. I saw her last week, sitting there with all her diamonds on. I waved to her, and she just turned her head away with a smile."

"I remember her bracelet. It must be worth a fortune."

"I suppose so. Who knows how much such things are worth?"

"Guess."

"I have no idea, for goodness's sake, Queenie . . . thousands of pounds. More than you and I will ever see."

"Enough to get us to England, and then some," Queenie said sadly. "It's so unfair."

Inside the car it was hot, damp and stuffy. Queenie could feel herself beginning to sweat, and hated it. She found it hard to imagine Morgan in bed with Mrs. Daventry. She looked at him out of the corner of her eye, seeing him in a new and more interesting light.

There was no denying that he was handsome, a little like the actor John Gilbert, but thinner, and with the dark, slightly almond-shaped eyes that were, like her own, one of the telltale signs of his ancestry. He had the broad shoulders and narrow waist of her grandfather, judging by photographs of the old man, and though he seldom exercised, his figure was as trim as a soldier's. There was a "sensitive" quality to his face, a certain sadness that she supposed some women must find attractive, if only because it was so unlike the hard, aggressive, self-satisfied faces of their husbands.

Queenie disliked what she secretly thought of as Morgan's defeated "hangdog" look, but she could imagine that a woman who was married to a man like Mr. Daventry might find it a welcome change.

Morgan's hands were those of a musician, with long fingers—even longer than hers. Queenie was proud of her hands, which was yet another reason she hated typing. She closed her eyes and tried to remember Mrs. Daventry's hands. They were long and sinewy, with bright-red nails that would have precluded not only typing but almost anything else that was menial, but what Queenie remembered most clearly was the glittering bracelet, its square-cut diamonds reflecting the light, while the emeralds glowed a cool green. She wondered if Mrs. Daventry took off her bracelet when she was in bed with Morgan. . . .

She opened her eyes. Morgan had halted at the signal of a policeman, who held a black umbrella over his turbaned head with one hand while he signaled to the traffic with the other, his silver whistle clenched between his teeth. On the other side of the street a line of beggars lay stretched on the pavement, sheltering under their umbrellas and feebly shaking their bowls for alms.

"Wouldn't it at least be nice to get out of this city, just once?"

Morgan put the car in gear at the policeman's signal, and glanced at the beggars. One of them in the middle seemed to be dead. His umbrella had slipped and his white, sightless eyes were staring up into the rain. His mouth was open, as if he was trying to drink the raindrops; the rigid hand clutching the umbrella handle was hardly more than a black withered claw. None of the other beggars seemed to have noticed—or more likely they simply didn't care.

"Out of the city? What do you mean?"

"We could go on a picnic. Just the two of us." She lowered her eyelids modestly and allowed her leg to brush ever so gently against Morgan's. She wondered if it was enough. She hoped so. She had no intention of going any further.

"A picnic? Whatever next?"

"Well, why not?" She leaned over and gave him a quick kiss. "Please, Morgan," she whispered.

"Perhaps," he said. He looked at the awful city before them. "If it ever stops raining."

"I can hardly wait."

"I haven't said yes yet."

"As good as," Queenie said triumphantly. She saw in his eyes that he had already conceded. And somewhere in the back of her mind she realized that once Morgan got into the habit of giving in to her about the small things, the large ones would follow.

It was just a question of time.

Like most Calcutta Anglo-Indians, Morgan was essentially a man of the city. India beyond the streets of Calcutta was largely terra incognita to him. A picnic, like a tiger hunt, was a profoundly alien notion, though it was just the kind of thing the British loved—going off to some remote and godforsaken spot to endure discomfort, heat and the presence of natives to eat a meal which any sensible person would prefer to have comfortably at home.

Still, he was anxious to indulge Queenie for reasons which he was unwilling to admit even to himself—and also because he was ashamed that he had made no progress in making any plans at all to go to England. Whenever he thought about it the difficulties seemed overwhelming, and much as he wanted to go himself, it was easier to let the days go by without doing anything.

Morgan contemplated a picnic in the Botanical Gardens, but he knew perfectly well that wouldn't satisfy Queenie, so he consulted Mr. Bisram Chauduri, who managed the Indian help at Firpo's. "There are some nice gardens in Chitpore," Chauduri suggested plaintively.

"Don't be silly, man. Chitpore is still Calcutta. You can see the bloody Oriental Gas Works from the gardens."

Mr. Chauduri wrung his hands. His advice on such matters was seldom requested. He feared being responsible for a disaster.

"I'm taking a young lady," Morgan said, by way of explaining the eccentricity of his request.

Mr. Chauduri smiled broadly as if everything were now clear to him. "Shivapur!" he exclaimed. "It's just the place to take her."

It took almost half an hour to cross the Howrah Bridge, so jammed was it with pedestrians, buses, cars, ox carts and beggars. With its monumental pseudo-Georgian buildings, the eastern side of the Hooghly River was like a shoddy imitation of London, except in the monsoon season when the drains overflowed, turning it into a caricature of Venice as the streets filled with water. The western side was worse. Beyond the Hooghly stretched the docks, the jute mills and the factories, their smoke blending with that of the funeral pyres smoldering on the Burning Ghat, then a vast maze of nameless alleys sprawled for miles, the filthy tenements gradually giving way to small clusters of hovels set in fields of mud or dust, according to the season.

Farther on, the huts and shacks petered out. Now the highway cut across a flat, dusty plain spotted with tiny villages hardly less squalid and impoverished than Calcutta itself.

It was not until they were miles beyond the city limits that Queenie's mood lightened, despite her earlier anticipation of the day. Morgan, who had also cheered up once he was out of the city, drove with one hand on the wheel, his solar topi pushed on the back of his head, whistling through his teeth. He looked like a sahib, and felt like one.

In the back of the car, staring ahead silently, sat the khitmatgar, thoughtfully provided by Mr. Chauduri, holding a picnic hamper on his knees, since it was unthinkable that a sahib—or indeed anyone with even the slightest claim to European descent—should serve his own food. Morgan had succumbed to his presence reluctantly, sacrificing the advantages of privacy to the White Man's Burden.

Initially Queenie had been dismayed by Ahmed's presence, but like most Europeans in India she had the gift of ignoring servants as if they didn't exist—and in any case she was soon grateful enough to have him there, for without his help, Morgan would have been hopelessly lost.

Ahmed seldom spoke, but at the approach of a crossroads, he would gravely clear his throat and mutter, "Left, sahib," or "Right." His manner was deferential, but at the same time conveyed a certain distant authority.

By mid-morning Queenie began to feel at last the presence of something at once familiar and mysterious—the India of legend, untouched by the city and the British. There was nothing romantic about the India Queenie lived in, though even in Chowringhee there were surprises, as if the harsher realities of the brooding, unruly subcontinent were gathered beyond the neat streets and bungalow gardens of the cantonments, ready to intrude at any moment: a vulture dropping a human bone on the lawn, a mad dog roaming the streets, a jackal appearing in the garden or a cobra sighted near the house.

She gasped with pleasure at the sight of a small boy leading two elephants down to a stream for a bath, the great beasts plodding silently through the trees, their trunks waving lazily from side to side, their feet stirring up the dust so that they seemed to be vanishing into a golden haze of their own making. The lead elephant's forehead was painted in bright colors, like a child's drawing, and its eyes were circled in red, giving it the appearance of a huge clown in baggy gray pants.

"Is it painted for a ceremony of some kind?" Queenie asked, but Morgan didn't know—in fact, to her dismay, he clearly regarded the elephant as yet another example of the Indian's distorted sense of priorities. Here was a people who would go to the trouble of painting a bloody elephant while their houses fell down for lack of the most elementary care!

A few miles east of Shivapur, the road narrowed to a track, winding gently through low, rolling hills covered with scrub. At intervals fields had been hacked out—or cemeteries; it was hard to tell which, for here the cemeteries with their low, dried mounds and small markers were often part of a field, as though life and death were simply alternate manifestations of the same spirit.

In the distance Queenie could see a clump of trees—a miracle in this climate, like an oasis in the desert. The car turned down a dirt track, with bamboo on either side making it into a kind of green tunnel, then emerged into a clearing.

"Shivapur," Ahmed announced.

At first Queenie could see little to justify the long, dusty journey. She stepped out of the car and looked around her, then realized that they were at the top of a low hill covered with bamboo and silvery trees. Just below them was the village itself, the reed-and-wattle roofs of the huts blending in so well with the foliage that they were almost invisible. Ahead of her, beyond the edge of the clearing, the temple itself rose from the trees—three strange weathered stone lumps, or so they seemed from a distance—each of them of a different height. They were bullet-shaped, and as one looked more closely at them, they displayed elaborately carved tiers, rather like wedding cakes. Queenie shaded her eyes and saw something move.

"Monkeys!" she shouted, and, as if to confirm the fact, the monkeys broke into a strident burst of chattering and howling, the noise setting off screams of outrage and alarm from the birds in the bamboo thicket.

As usual in India, there was too much of everything. A dozen monkeys would have been ample to provide an interesting spectacle, but there appeared to be hundreds, and judging from the noise of the birds, there were thousands of those hidden in the trees.

"It's beautiful," she said.

"Do you think so? I can't see it, I'm afraid. It's only a native temple covered with bloody monkeys. My God, what a row they make!"

"It's the *place* that's beautiful. Can we go in?"

"Oh, certainly. Why not? But we'll take a stroll and eat something first, I think."

Queenie looked around and saw that Ahmed, with the professional skill of an experienced bearer, was already busy laying out the picnic. He had chosen a large flat rock with a view of the temple and a small stream, and placed on it two cushions, a tablecloth and a bowl of flowers. He had already recruited an old man—who had appeared as if by magic out of the bamboo growth—to hold back any inquisitive villagers, as well as a small boy, perhaps the old man's great-grandson, to perform such tasks as were beneath Ahmed's dignity.

Morgan helped Queenie up onto the rock, and they sat down.

She did not have to guess at the food. It would be chicken and eggs, of course. Ahmed, as a Mohammedan, could not be expected to touch ham, and it was considered bad taste to eat beef for fear of offending the sensibilities of the local Hindus.

"What have we to drink, Ahmed?" Morgan asked.

Ahmed opened the hamper and peered in. "Gin," he said. "Whiskey. A bottle of wine."

"A pink gin, then."

"This is the life," Morgan said, reclining on his pillow. There were moments when he was happy enough to be in India.

"Yes." She moved her pillow next to his and leaned against him. "But I'll bet a picnic in England is even nicer . . . green fields. And swans instead of monkeys."

"And rain, Queenie. It rains there all the time."

"I don't believe that. Anyway, it doesn't matter about rain, Morgan. What kind of a future is there here for us? That's the point."

"I know, I know. But these things take time, Queenie."

"Time? What will time change? I'll be old soon."

"Nonsense." He held his glass out for a refill.

"Morgan," she said, taking the plunge, "I do have an idea about how we can get the money."

"Let's chat about it later, shall we? It's too nice now." He loosened his tie and smiled at her. Queenie was not about to give up so quickly, but then she realized that Ahmed was lurking nearby and decided it might be better to wait until they were alone.

"Can we go and see the temple now?" she asked.

Morgan nodded. Ahmed's preparations were not yet complete, and while Morgan had no curiosity about Hindu religious architecture, he felt the need to move a bit, and to be alone with Queenie.

"We'll go to the temple now," he said to Ahmed. "We'll eat when we come back. Is there any difficulty about getting in?"

Ahmed shook his head. "No, sahib," he said. "There is no difficulty. Most people, however, prefer to eat first and visit the temple later, when it's cooler."

"It seems cool enough to me. We'll go now." Queenie noticed that Morgan seemed slightly unsteady as he climbed down off the rock— the two pink gins on an empty stomach were affecting him more than he realized, and she put her arm in his to steady him as they entered the dark, cool tunnel of bamboos overhanging the dirt path. He held on to her, his face close to hers, and it seemed to her that his grip was harder than necessary.

The bamboo thicket was full of monkeys. "It's like a bloody zoo," Morgan complained, pushing his topi back to mop his brow, but Queenie saw a flash of color ahead, and ran on to look at it. The flash of color resolved itself into a large parrot, which gave a high-pitched scream as she approached it, then suddenly burst into flight, setting off an explosion of noise as birds of every size and color flapped their wings and flew to safety in the higher branches.

The noise was so loud that it startled her. She stood still for a moment, then looked up, shading her eyes. All around her she could see the birds looking down at her, their unblinking round eyes—yellow, orange, red—gleaming like bright dots of color in the leaves and branches. The path forked in front of her.

She took the left fork and found herself on a track that seemed much narrower and even darker. The branches were so low that she had to bend over, and the smell of flowers was almost suffocating.

At the end of the pathway she stopped short in a dazzling circle of sunshine and saw before her the entrance to the temple. The open doorway was dark and oddly shaped, almost like a cave, hidden in a vast, irregular wall of carved stone so thickly covered in vines, moss and leaves that it seemed more like a work of nature than something made or planned by man.

Morgan looked flushed and feverish when he caught up with her. From outside the temple it was possible to imagine that the thick walls and the darkness would make it cooler, but instead the shrine seemed to contain and magnify the heat, like a giant oven.

At first glance there was nothing remarkable about the interior, which was cavelike and unfurnished, lit by hundreds of small, flickering lamps that gave off an overpowering odor of stale butter and burned grease. Overhead there was a dry flutter, as if a colony of bats was stirring, and Queenie was for once grateful for her topi. Morgan, who sensed her fear, put his arm around her, and she was conscious of his body pressing against hers through the thin cotton of her summer dress.

Despite the heat—or perhaps because of it—she felt a certain excitement. There was something peculiarly sensual about being here with Morgan in the dark, surrounded by the glow from the lamps. Morgan seemed to feel this, too, for he held her tightly, one hand reaching down, his fingers gently touching her breast, as if by accident. The sensation was by no means unpleasant, and though she knew she should push him away or tell him to stop, the heat made the effort of resisting seem impossibly difficult.

Queenie felt weak, as if it were *she* who had drunk the gin instead of Morgan. He kissed her, not abruptly, as Mr. Pugh had done, but gently, lingeringly, his lips grazing her cheek. He put both arms around her. Then, as her eyes adjusted to the gloom, she looked over his shoulders and saw that the walls of the shrine were covered in carvings. Against the far wall, its color dim in the feeble light, a huge silk hanging portrayed Shiva. His naked body was a deep blue-black and his face was that of a demon. He seemed to be dancing with majestic grace, while before him men and women, rich and poor, and a dazzling multitude of birds and beasts knelt to adore him.

Striking as it was, the portrait of Shiva was overwhelmed by the figures, thousands of them, intricately carved, totally lifelike, entwined and joined until they vanished in the darkness of the room.

It took a moment for the reality to sink in—for the entire temple was like some imaginative catalog of sexual acts carved in stone, the participants all smiling serenely, even modestly, as if demonstrating some interesting athletic feat for the onlooker—row upon row of carvings, penises, breasts, rounded thighs and buttocks stretching on until they became infinite and meaningless, a vast, silent stone forest of sexuality, reaching to the invisible ceiling, then descending on the other side. As the flames flickered, the figures appeared to move languorously, the trembling shadows giving the momentary illusion of life and passion, so that the whole shrine appeared to be in motion. The illusion lasted only a second—not more—but it was enough to make Queenie dizzy.

The moment passed, and she found herself in Morgan's arms, drenched in sweat. His lips were glued wetly to hers, his breath coming in short, noisy gasps, either from the heat or from guilty passion. "Queenie," he muttered thickly, "Queenie, I love you!"

She was conscious only of the cotton dress clinging damply to her body, the underwear chafing her in the heat, the sheer discomfort of Morgan's embrace. He was so busy pawing her that he had not even noticed the carvings.

She pushed him away, rather harder than she had intended to, and for a moment she expected him to react with anger.

But Morgan had come to his senses. "My God," he said, "I'm sorry." He mopped his face with a pocket handkerchief. "I've got a splitting headache," he said from behind it, his words muffled. "The heat . . ."

"And the gin," she suggested.

"Yes, yes, perhaps . . . That bloody Ahmed should have warned me how hot it was."

"He did, Morgan."

"Did he? I didn't hear him." Morgan took Queenie's hand and squeezed it gently. "I couldn't help myself," he whispered, as if there were people lurking in the shadows who might overhear.

Then his eyes focused on the wall above her head. "Oh, my God!" he wailed. "But all this is filth! What must you have thought of me?"

"It doesn't matter."

"Doesn't *matter?* That bloody man Chauduri should have warned me . . ."

"Morgan, they're only carvings. India is full of things like this."

He wiped the sweat from his face with his sleeve. "It's not what I intended at all."

For a moment Queenie thought he was going to cry from the shock and guilt, and perhaps also because he had at last allowed his feelings for her to escape, only to have them mocked by the place he had chosen.

She took his arm and led him to the doorway. Beyond it the sunlight was dazzling after the gloom of the shrine, and they stood for a moment on the steps, breathing the hot, dry air that now seemed almost refreshing by contrast.

The silence was complete, the bamboos rising like a green wall in front of them, motionless in the windless heat. High overhead, a vulture soared. The blank immensity of the landscape was more threatening than the darkness of the shrine and seemed to make every human desire meaningless—or so it affected Queenie, who felt drained by it.

Now that they were back in the sunlight again, Queenie was able to think. What had happened in the shrine was more than the result of a couple of gins and the heat. She had never doubted that Morgan loved her; she was old enough to realize that he loved her more than an uncle should, and in a different way—but until now she hadn't realized how strong that passion was. "Morgan," she asked, "will you do *anything* for me? Anything I ask?"

Night after night, Queenie puzzled over the next step, and night after night she finally went to sleep without finding it. Sometimes she found work as a "temporary," doing odd jobs of typing, but these jobs seldom lasted long. Even Ma felt that she was "marking time." Peggy D'Souza had gone to England, to everyone's surprise but Ma's, with her Butts, and once a week Ma read aloud a postcard from her describing in a hasty scrawl the many wonders of her new life at Home.

At least once a month Queenie sneaked out of the house after Ma had gone to bed, to join Morgan in Firpo's, where at least she could dance, listen to the music and be seen. Much as Morgan hated it, she seldom lacked for men who wanted to dance with her, and she became increasingly adept at fending off suggestions that she go home with them or for a drive in their cars.

She had persuaded Morgan to put down a deposit on two tickets to England, but she knew it was no more than a token, a small first step that would lead nowhere by itself—though it did have the advantage of committing Morgan, at least in his mind, to what she planned to do.

The rest would take time, and luck, and courage, and she would need to supply the courage for Morgan. She didn't doubt that she had enough to spare for both of them. It was the question of luck that bothered her, that and keeping Morgan's hopes up. Sometimes, on the way home, he would put his arms around her in a frenzy of passion and guilt, but she had so far always been able to bring him back to his senses. Once they were in England, she let it be understood, things might be different—she couldn't promise, but it was possible. . . . And always he backed off, apologetic, wild-eyed, sweaty and willing to promise anything.

She had seen a film about a man who was obsessed by his love for a woman he could never have, and it had seemed to her incomprehensible, even silly, but she understood now what it was about. Morgan was obsessed—perhaps he always had been, and it had only just come to the surface. It was not, she knew, that he couldn't have other women. In his own small way he was a dashing, popular figure, who, if rumor was to be believed, had never experienced any difficulty in getting all the women he wanted—but the only one he wanted was *her*.

He even came into her room at night and stood in the doorway, staring silently at her. But still she hesitated to take the final step, until one night, terrified that Ma would hear them, but determined to have it out with him, Queenie put her arms around him, placed her lips to his ear and told him what she wanted him to do.

He turned pale—as white as the sheets in the moonlight. "You're mad!" he said, so loudly that she put her hand over his mouth.

He lowered his voice. "I couldn't do it," he whispered. "Not in a million years."

"Then I'll marry the first Englishman who asks me. Even if I have to sleep with him first."

She could see the pain in his eyes, but he shook his head. "I won't even discuss it," he said.

But night after night, in her hot stuffy box of a bedroom or at a table behind the potted palms in Firpo's, they discussed it anyway, until gradually, inch by inch, Morgan began to accept the fact that she was right, and that the only questions were "How?" and "When?"

"I can't just ring her out of the blue," Morgan complained.

"Why not?"

Morgan was aghast. "It simply isn't *done*, Queenie."

"Well, you'll have to do it anyway. Write her a note and send it over to her table the next time she comes in." Queenie stared at him for a moment with exasperation; but it was no use shouting at Morgan, she knew that. It would only rattle him further, which was the one thing they didn't need. It had taken her a long time to make Morgan realize that the thing could be done, and that it was his only way out. If he really, truly wanted to go to England with her, this was the only way.

The one thing that gave him courage was his desire for her, but Queenie wasn't at all sure that would carry him the whole way. She took his hand in hers. "Say you want to apologize and explain things to her," she suggested.

"Explain what?"

"Explain about me."

"There's nothing to explain, Queenie. She knows you're my niece."

"She may not believe it. And even if she does, she'll be sure to think there's something more to it than that."

"I still don't think she'd want to see me."

Queenie was unable to prevent an edge of irritation from creeping into her voice. "Morgan," she said, "*believe* me. Mrs. Daventry will see you because she won't be able to resist."

"Resist what?"

"The opportunity to humiliate you, of course. She'll want to gloat over the fact you're crawling back."

It was true. He tried to disguise his annoyance. "And then what?" he asked.

"Then you wait for the right moment."

"But she'll know it was me!"

They had been through this dozens of times before, and yet, Morgan was still resisting. He wanted the plan to be worked out in advance right down to the last detail, step by step, and she knew it couldn't be.

There had to be room for improvisation; some things had to be left to luck.

"She won't know it was you if she's drunk," Queenie said. "Besides, you won't be the only man who's been there, will you, if what you tell me about her is true? Then there are the servants . . . and besides, she's not likely to admit that you were there, is she now? So who can she tell?"

"She'll know." Morgan shuddered slightly. "I don't think I can go through with it."

Queenie put her arms around him and squeezed, but Morgan didn't respond at all. "I *know* you can," she whispered. "Even if she thinks it was you, we'll be on our way to England before she can do anything."

Feeling Queenie's body pressed against his, Morgan felt a sudden spurt of courage. "Oh, damn it," he said, "I'll do it."

Once they were in England, he told himself, they could start a new life together. Just for a moment he allowed himself to imagine it. He would have a job at one of the best clubs, he would be well paid, well dressed, *respected*. In the morning when he came home in a taxi through the clean, rain-washed streets, Queenie would be waiting for him in their flat asleep, or perhaps only pretending to be asleep, in their big bed, her eyes opening as he slipped under the covers to lie beside her, while outside the church bells of London chimed under the cool gray sky. . . .

"What's the bloody worst that can happen?" he asked with a reckless laugh. But even as he said it, he knew the answer.

He could go to jail.

The receipt for the deposit on the tickets to England was in Morgan's jacket pocket. It felt like a lead weight.

When he had removed the envelope addressed to Mrs. Daventry and handed it to a waiter to carry to her table at an appropriate moment, he almost gave the boy the receipt by mistake. He would have to be more careful than that, he knew. His hands were so sweaty, he left damp prints on the paper. He felt like a waiter with his thumb in a plate of soup.

"Don't carry the bloody thing over on a silver platter, for God's sake!" he shouted to the waiter, who smiled and bobbed his turbaned head, his eyes rolling white in the gloom. Morgan handed him a rupee, then hesitated and slipped him another. "Wait until she's alone. Do it discreetly. Can you manage that?"

"Most certainly, sahib."

For an hour or more, as the evening wore on, Morgan could hardly bring himself to look in the direction of Pempy Daventry's table. He cursed himself for trusting a bloody Hindu, who would surely make a balls of the whole thing so that everybody at the table would know she had received a note, and might even ask who it was from. His playing was so erratic that the other members of the band glanced at him in surprise, and even Alberto Firpo, who cared nothing about music as long as it was loud and fast enough to keep the clients dancing, gave a frown of displeasure.

The worst of it was that Mrs. Daventry was quite capable of reading the letter aloud and laughing at it. He could almost hear that cold, precise voice saying, "Oh, my dear, it's from my chee-chee admirer on the bandstand." He could imagine her ridiculing him to her friends. . . . Oh, Morgan knew her all right, and because he did, he was clammy with sweat.

" 'Valencia,' " the bass-fiddle player hissed as he peered myopically at a scrap of paper passed to him by a waiter, carefully holding up a fifty-rupee note so that the other members of the band could see it— for it was the custom to split the tips from requests at the end of the night.

Morgan sighed. It was always the same old songs, night after night. In England, he was sure, nobody would ask for "Valencia"—they would ask for the latest red-hot stuff, and he would give it to them. He wet his lips, raised his saxophone, groaned inwardly as the bandleader sang "In my dreams, it seems I hear you softly call to me."

As Morgan heard the word "Val—encia!" he blew, picking up the rhythm and giving it his best, for it was a tricky moment in the otherwise simple score. He closed his eyes to concentrate, hardly even hearing the words, then swung around to face the dance floor and opened them again.

The dance floor was packed—"Valencia" always brought them to their bloody feet—but on the far side, facing him, Mrs. Daventry sat alone at her table. Methodically she tore up the note the waiter had just handed her. Then she lit a cigarette, placed it in her long holder, looked across the room at Morgan and winked.

• • •

Mrs. Daventry filled her glass from the decanter on the tray-table, examined the level in it carefully and added another finger of Scotch. "Cheers!" she said. "Here's to old times. How's your little spitfire in the pink dress, Morgan? Isn't she a little young for you?"

Her tone was mocking, as it always was when she deliberately used lower-class expressions. It was a way of humiliating Morgan, who wasn't sure just what was wrong with saying "Cheers!" in the first place. Mrs. Daventry took another deep drink, went over to her dressing table, sat down and examined her face, as if Morgan weren't there.

"I don't know what you mean," he said.

"Bollocks! The girl with the bedroom eyes, Morgan! You've been cradle-snatching, my boy."

"Queenie? She's my niece!"

"Queenie." Mrs. Daventry lingered over the name, relishing each syllable. "How divinely vulgar. I don't believe you're her uncle at all, Morgan," she teased.

"Well, you're wrong," he said stiffly. "I am."

"Not that it matters. I could tell you stories about my Uncle Ned and myself, when I was a little girl . . . I used to sit on his lap, you know—he always had a pocketful of sweets for me. Do you know, I was so innocent that I didn't even know what he'd been *doing* until I was sixteen?"

Mrs. Daventry laughed, her voice echoing in the huge bedroom, then she looked at Morgan in the mirror and took another sip of her drink. "Why did you send me a note like this?"

Morgan stared at his hands. This was the hardest part, since it required improvisation. Mrs. Daventry terrified him so much that he could hardly bring himself to look at her. Only the fact that he couldn't face returning to Queenie empty-handed kept him from running. "I've missed you," he said.

She laughed. "Bollocks, Morgan," she said. "Are things going badly for you? Hard up, are you? Hoping to cadge a little money off me, just like the old days? Well, sod off!"

Morgan gritted his teeth. "It's not that at all," he protested. "I'm doing very nicely, as it happens. . . ."

"Oh, yes? Still playing for chicken feed at Firpo's, and as far from England as ever. You'll never get there, Morgan. You haven't got the guts, dear. As for your little slut, I've closed every door to her."

"I know."

"Has she bared her heart to you?"

"Yes. Yes, of course . . . a headstrong girl. I have told her a thousand times to apologize."

"Apologize? I don't want her apologies. I don't need them. I don't need *you*, either."

"Then why did you answer my note?"

Mrs. Daventry stared at her image in the mirror as if she was looking for the answer to that question herself. Her expression was totally self-absorbed as she studied her reflection, the diamond bracelet on her wrist glittering as she played with her hair.

Her room was silver, like her dress—silver-brocaded walls, silver silk cushions, a silver-embroidered silk cover on the enormous bed. Despite the deliberately dim lighting, the entire room seemed lit with a silvery glow, like a cave filled with treasure. Every available surface was covered with expensive objects of crystal, gold, silver or tortoiseshell. Mrs. Daventry's back was bared by her evening gown, and as she leaned forward, Morgan could see the elegant articulation of her spine and shoulders and the long, fine muscles of a natural athlete.

"I wanted to see if you'd crawl back, dear," she said at last. "And you *have*, of course. Now you can get out!"

Morgan was seized by a moment of panic. He could hardly go through with the rest of the plan if he left now, and he couldn't face Queenie if he failed. As for Mrs. Daventry's willingness to see him, Queenie had guessed better than she knew. Of *course* Mrs. Daventry wanted to humiliate him! And as usual, she had succeeded. For a week after receiving his note, she had turned up at Firpo's every night, ignoring him completely. The fifth night, she had sent him a note scrawled on a cocktail napkin with an eyebrow pencil. When he unfolded it, there was only one word: "Wait."

The next night Mrs. Daventry managed to see him for a moment, in the corridor that led to the ladies' room, having sent a waiter over to the bandstand to tell him to wait for her there. The walls were covered with red-flocked velvet, and in the gloom her eyes seemed to shine with a deep red light that Morgan found particularly frightening. "Tomorrow," she said coldly. "Daventry is going to Bombay."

"How shall I get in?"

Mrs. Daventry glared impatiently. She was an expert at planning liaisons, and expected men to be as quick-witted as she was. "Leave your car a few streets away," she whispered. "My maid will let you in the side door. Surely you can't have forgotten, Morgan?"

"I only thought things might have changed."

Mrs. Daventry touched his lips with one long, cool fingernail, then flicked it up sharply, giving him a small, painful scratch.

"Oh dear," she said. "Have I drawn blood? Things *have* changed, Morgan, dear. Things always change. But my arrangements are perfect and unalterable. I don't like to have my little routines upset, you know—not once I'm used to something."

Morgan knew what she meant. He always knew what she meant. Mrs. Daventry's life was complex, like a maze to which she alone had the map. Morgan's role in it had been minor—he was one of many at her beck and call—but he had taken her for granted once too often in the past and had been made to suffer for it. Now he guessed he would have to suffer a little more.

If he wanted to stay here in her bedroom, Morgan realized, he would in fact have to crawl, and while he rebelled inwardly at the thought, he knew there was no choice.

"Please," he said, walking over to her. "Let me stay."

"You're a jumped-up half-caste, Morgan. Worse than that, you're a bore. And you don't know your place, do you? I haven't forgotten that you brought your little slut into the Grand for tea. That's my turf, Morgan, not yours. A dance at the Railway Institute was quite good enough for her then, and now."

"You are right," Morgan said, kneeling beside her, while she continued to study her eyebrows with the close attention of a jeweler looking at a diamond through his loupe, elaborately ignoring him. "Forgive me, I beg you. Let me make it up to you."

"Make it up to me? How?"

Morgan bent forward, on his knees and put his head on her thigh. She ran one hand through his hair, then dug her fingernails hard into his neck. "Poor little Morgan," she cooed huskily. "He's been such a bad boy."

"I have, I have," Morgan whispered, swallowing hard. For a moment he was truly disgusted with himself, almost sick—but it passed, as it always had.

"He'll have to be punished," Mrs. Daventry said, still facing the mirror, as if she were talking to herself. She drained her drink, put the glass down and turned around to face Morgan. She was holding a silver-backed hairbrush tightly in her right hand now, her eyes were wide open and her lips were gently curved in a curious little smile.

"Unhook my dress, Morgan," she said in a commanding voice, tapping the hairbrush hard against his cheek as he kneeled before her.

"Unhook it *carefully*, then get your bloody clothes off. I'm going to teach you a lesson you'll never forget."

Morgan lay awake in the darkened room, listening to the sound of Mrs. Daventry's breathing. He could still feel the sting of her finger-nails on his back. He wondered if he was bleeding on her sheets. No doubt the servants were accustomed to it, he told himself.

He glanced at Mrs. Daventry in the light from the night lamp. He had kept her glass filled from the decanter by the bed and calculated that she had drunk at least four double whiskeys without water, and taken a few puffs of opium—for Mrs. Daventry took a pragmatic view of the Orient and embraced whatever pleasures it offered.

She slept on her side, graceful even when comatose, one arm stretched out languidly, the other tucked under her head, smiling in her sleep. Her clothes were neatly folded on a chair. Disorderly as her sexual life might be, Mrs. Daventry was a stickler for neatness in every other respect. Even before going to bed with a man she would pause to fold her undergarments, smooth out the creases and lay them down in a neat, tidy pile, as if for inspection, on top of a scented silver silk cushion reserved for that purpose. She always removed her jewelry last. Before coming to bed, she liked to stand in front of the mirror for a moment, naked except for her bracelet and ring.

Morgan sighed, contemplated the possibility of skipping the next step, thought of Queenie, then carefully got out of bed. Mrs. Daventry stirred, and he gently covered her, pulling the sheet over her body and tucking it in. She moaned, then lay still again.

He had been through this many times before; it was part of the routine for him to leave in the middle of the night, once she was sound asleep. Mrs. Daventry was not afraid of what the servants would do or say—the maid's silence had long since been bought—but he knew there was no connection in her mind between what she did at night and who she was during the day.

He dressed quietly, delaying the moment he feared, glanced back at the bed to make sure she was still asleep, then screwing up his courage, his knees trembling, his armpits wet with the sweat and smell of fear, he padded softly over to the night table, his shoes in one hand, and picked up the diamond bracelet.

For one moment he stopped and stared at the emerald ring, but the cold green glow of the stone reminded him so sharply of Mrs. Daven-

try's eyes that he couldn't bring himself to touch it. Besides, the brace-let was enough—and dangerous enough as well. He slipped it in his pocket, next to the ticket receipt, slid his feet into his evening pumps and walked to the door.

Morgan heard a murmur from the bed and stopped in terror, his hand on the doorknob, praying that she wouldn't wake up. His hand was so wet with sweat that he could hardly turn the knob, and he longed to put the bracelet back, or drop it on the floor and run.

There was a long, low, deep sigh from the bed, and the soft sound of Mrs. Daventry's slim body rustling against the sheets. Then she fell silent, her regular breathing the only sound in the darkened room, as Morgan finally managed to twist the doorknob open and make his way to the stairs.

He sat in Queenie's bedroom glumly staring at the diamond bracelet glittering at the foot of her bed. The sight depressed him so much that he was unable to move, or even think about his own fear.

"She'll miss it when she wakes up," he said, shutting his eyes as if he hoped it wouldn't be there when he opened them again.

"We talked about that, Morgan. She can't very well go to the police and say you were there. And it could have been one of the ser-vants. . . . We just have to move fast, that's all."

"We'll be caught the moment we try to sell it. I know it."

"Not necessarily," Queenie said. "I know just the man we need. . . ." She picked up the bracelet, fastened it on her wrist and admired it for a moment. It was like a bright circlet of brilliant fire against her skin. She could see her own reflection sharply in every facet of the stones, as if they were hundreds of tiny mirrors. Queenie sighed and took it off. "One day," she said, "I shall have one just like this. Why didn't you take the ring, too?"

"I couldn't."

"Perhaps it's just as well. If she finds the ring, she may think she simply dropped the bracelet somewhere. If they were both missing, she'd know they were stolen right away."

"She'll know anyway."

"Oh, do cheer up, Morgan," Queenie said, tossing the bracelet back toward him. As she threw it, her nightgown slipped, and Morgan saw the tip of one breast. Despite his sexual exhaustion and fear, he man-aged to produce the ghost of a smile. "We're going Home at last,"

Queenie said, laughing, and suddenly Morgan was laughing with her.

After all, he told himself, it's not as if he were really a criminal! In the time he had known Mrs. Daventry, had he not earned the price of the bracelet a hundred times over? "What now?" he asked. And as Queenie began to explain her plan, he realized, with a sinking heart, how much more he would have to risk before he was home free.

"Well," she said abruptly, sensing his hesitation, "I never said it would be easy." She turned off the light, rolled over and closed her eyes. Morgan wanted to talk, but she wasn't in the mood. She was one of those rare people who could always sleep when they wanted to. Like Mrs. Daventry, he realized with an unpleasant start. It never failed to amaze him that women could always go to sleep whatever they had just done. They did not seem to suffer from shame or guilt, as men did. He was briefly envious.

He tiptoed to the door and opened it quietly, knowing that he himself would spend a sleepless night worrying about the next step.

"Morgan," Queenie whispered, "better take the bracelet, don't you think? We don't want Ma to see it."

He came back, slipped it into his pocket and stood there for a moment, hoping she would say something else. But all he heard was Queenie's quiet breathing. She was already asleep.

Mr. Brammachatrarya sat on his moth-eaten cushion as if he had been waiting for Queenie patiently since her last visit. His plump, round face showed no surprise at seeing her again. He was as jolly as ever. Toward Morgan he was so deferential that, had Morgan been less anxious, he would have realized immediately he was being treated with contempt.

Luckily, Queenie thought, Morgan was unaware of Mr. Brammachatrarya's feelings toward him, though the fat moneylender made a point of addressing himself to Queenie.

"To what do I owe this pleasure after such a long time, please?" Brammachatrarya asked in his silky voice. "You are not lost again?"

"No. This time I'm here on business. We, I should say."
Brammachatrarya smiled cheerfully and wriggled his bare toes. "The civilizing art of commerce," he remarked, nodding his head approvingly. "It binds all men—and women—together."

From behind the purdah curtain Queenie heard someone whisper in Hindi, "Get on with it!" Brammachatrarya paid no attention. Like a fisherman on the bank of a stream, he waited peacefully for the fish to swim his way.

"It's a confidential matter," Queenie said, glancing toward the purdah curtain.

"An extremely delicate transaction," Morgan added, trying to capture Brammachatrarya's attention.

Brammachatrarya ignored him. He flashed Queenie a brilliant smile. "What business is not confidential?" he asked. "Or delicate? My mouth is sealed."

She nodded at Morgan, who pulled a folded handkerchief out of his pocket and handed it to her. Queenie placed the handkerchief on the carpet and opened it. A gleam appeared in Brammachatrarya's eyes, but it was merely a reflection from the diamonds. His expression did not change. They sat in silence for a few minutes, since Brammachatrarya was clearly unwilling to be the first to speak.

It was Morgan whose patience broke first. "Well, what do you think, man?" he asked.

Brammachatrarya's eyes remained fixed on Queenie, ignoring both Morgan and the bracelet.

"This is what we came to you about," she said quietly, with a small nod of respect.

Brammachatrarya acknowledged it gravely. "You did well to do so," he said. "I am a jolly good judge of stones, if I do say so by myself. This is a family heirloom, no doubt?"

"What does it matter, man?" Morgan asked. "What's it bloody worth?"

Brammachatrarya leaned over with difficulty, picked up the bracelet gingerly, then held it up to the light and examined each stone. "Some people would ask where it came from," he said, handing it back to Queenie. "But curiosity killed the cat . . . or words to that effect. How much did you want to borrow against it, my dear miss?"

"We were hoping to *sell* it, actually."

"Ah, that's a different color horse! I am merely a poor Hindu moneylender. An object of such great value is beyond my means, I think."

"We had heard otherwise, Mr. Brammachatrarya," Queenie said respectfully.

"Bazaar gossip! Slander put about by spiteful and envious business rivals, that you may be damned sure about. There is too much tongue-wagging and all of it up to no good." Brammachatrarya closed his eyes and sat in silent contemplation of the world's evil for a few moments, his hands clasped across his ample stomach.

He opened his eyes at last and focused them on Queenie. "Of course, you realize that only the stones are of interest? Regrettably the bracelet will have to be broken up . . . I only mention this in case you have a sentimental attachment to the piece."

"None," Morgan said.

"Oh, capital! It's so difficult to put a price on sentiment. As stones, however, I would be willing to give you—oh, five lakhs, let us say."

Morgan turned pale with rage. "That is less than fifteen hundred pounds sterling, man! The bloody thing is worth ten times that."

"Yes? Then you should by all means take it, dear sir, to a jeweler on Corporation Street—with a bill of sale or proof of ownership." Brammachatrarya seemed to lose interest in the whole discussion. He lowered his eyelids as if he were about to take a nap.

"That is robbery, man!" Morgan shouted.

Brammachatrarya opened one eye and shrugged. "Robbery is not a nice word," he said. "In the circumstances."

Queenie leaned over, getting closer to the moneylender, and put one small hand on his. "They say in the bazaar also that Mr. Brammachatrarya is a fair and generous man." Queenie spoke in Hindi.

"They speak the truth."

"They say, too, that he is not a man to take advantage of a young woman in distress."

"This, too, is so," he muttered uncomfortably.

"Can a price be put on gratitude? Perhaps one day even I may be in a position to offer help in some small matter. The young grow older, do they not? Sometimes young women marry great men."

"Truly."

"Even at fifteen lakhs the bracelet would be a bargain—for a man who knew where to sell the stones. A man of knowledge, of patience, of subtlety . . ."

Mr. Brammachatrarya took the bracelet, rose, waddled over to the purdah curtain and slipped it inside. A low voice from behind the flowered curtain whispered something; a plump hand passed the bracelet back. "For you—ten lakhs," Mr. Brammachatrarya said, turning to face Queenie.

Queenie nodded. All things considered, it was not an unreasonable offer.

Brammachatrarya shuffled to the safe, opened it with a big brass key and took out a bundle of notes. He counted out ten thousand rupees, recounted, pausing to lick his fingers, and put the money down in front of Queenie in a neat pile. Then he held the bracelet in front of the purdah curtain. The plump, graceful hand, as dark as his own, reached out, took the bracelet and vanished. It occurred to Queenie that a purdah curtain was better protection than any safe. Nobody would dare to search behind it, not even a policeman.

"A pleasure to do business with you," Mr. Brammachatrarya said briskly. "Good luck in England."

"How did you know we were going Home?" Morgan asked.

"I have a good memory. The young lady confided in me at our first meeting, ages ago."

"We haven't fixed the exact date yet."

Mr. Brammachatrarya shook his head. "I would go soon," he said. "Very soon. Tonight, if possible. Rumors reach even this humble house, my dear sir—and miss. I have heard that a valuable piece of jewelry was stolen from the wife of the great Mr. Daventry. Apparently some low fellow broke into the house and threatened the poor lady. A dastardly outrage! She resisted, but the rotter overpowered her rudely and made off with a bracelet. . . ." Mr. Brammachatrarya coughed gently. "No doubt," he added politely, "it's quite different from this one."

Morgan looked as if he was about to faint. "Do they know who did it?" he asked.

"A musician. Apparently intoxicated. His name escapes me, but happily he was a European of sorts, and not one of our people."

Mr. Brammachatrarya smiled cheerfully, as if he was the bearer of good tidings, while Morgan, the sweat pouring down his face, put his head in his hands and moaned.

Queenie ignored him. It had never occurred to her that Mrs. Daventry would be quick enough to come up with an explanation for Morgan's presence in her room. She had underrated the woman.

She stood up and held the fat man's wrist, her face close to his. "If such a man wanted to leave the country quickly," she said, "could it be done?"

He nodded. "Assuredly so, missy."

"And if a woman went with him? Would there be a way?"

Mr. Brammachatrarya stared at the purdah curtain, then at Queenie, and laughed. "How not?" he asked. "With money, all things are possible.

"How will I find a job without my bloody saxophone?"

"For God's sake, Morgan, when we get to London you can buy a new one. Nobody is going to believe a Hindu traveling with a saxophone."

Morgan shuffled uneasily on the crowded platform. He wore a white dhoti, a European jacket and a Congress cap and carried two bulky Gladstone bags with an umbrella and two blankets strapped to them. It was odd, Queenie thought, that he was quite convincingly Indian in Indian clothing. She knew better than to remark on it. It was not an achievement that would please Morgan.

Queenie was pleased enough with her own disguise. Her body was wrapped in a pink silk sari, while her head was completely covered by a purdah veil. For all practical purposes she was as good as invisible. Every Hindu would ignore her respectfully—as would the Muslims, for to them also the veil was sacred—while to Europeans, she was simply another native and therefore unworthy of notice. She reached out to touch Morgan, but he backed away. "For goodness' sake, Queenie," he whispered, "you know damned well a native woman in purdah would never touch her husband in public."

"I was only trying to warn you." She turned her head toward the big iron gates, where a railway official was examining tickets. Standing beside him were two policemen, and behind the policemen stood Mr. Daventry, his hat pulled low over his eyes as he scrutinized the passengers filing past for the Calcutta-Bombay Mail. He seemed to be in a bad temper, and it was easy to guess that Mrs. Daventry had drafted him for this unwelcome duty.

"He'll recognize me," Morgan wailed, in English.

"Speak Hindi, for God's sake!" Queenie hissed. So far things had gone smoothly, thanks to Mr. Brammachatrarya—and to Magda, whom Queenie had sought out to bring what they needed from home, and to deliver to Ma a brief letter in which Queenie promised to explain matters from England. "You'll break her heart," Magda said, for once unforgivingly, and Queenie knew it was true. But how could she explain what she and Morgan had done—or go back only to find the police waiting?

The notion of a journey across India in flight from the police had never seriously occurred to Queenie in making her plans, but now that it had come to this, she was determined to succeed. Somehow, once they were safe, she would straighten matters out with her mother—she promised herself that.

Impatient as Queenie was with Morgan, she suspected, with a sinking heart, that for once his pessimism was justified. Daventry would surely recognize him, even wearing a Congress cap, if only because Morgan's fear would be obvious to anyone who was looking hard. His eyes were glittering and surrounded with dark, deep circles, like those of someone with a high fever, and his face was deathly pale—which was unfortunate for a man trying to pass himself off as a Hindu. Queenie looked for an alternative, but there was none. To get on the Calcutta-Bombay Mail, they would have to pass the barrier.

"I can't do it," Morgan said. He was paralyzed by fear, and Queenie recognized that at any moment he would give himself up, relieved to have it over with. She could think of nothing to say.

"Do we not know each other, friend?" a voice asked softly. Morgan turned in terror and found himself staring at a vaguely familiar face, much of it concealed by a beard carefully rolled in a beard-net, a heavily waxed mustache and a bulky dark-blue turban.

"Why it's Mr. Singh!" Queenie said, realizing a moment too late, as she saw Mr. Singh's astonishment, that it was hardly a likely remark for a woman in purdah to make.

Singh nodded, took Morgan's hand and stared at his face. "Truly," he said, "it is the brave killer of Muslims! And behind the purdah veil, I think, is Miss Kelley! But why do you travel disguised as Bengali Hindus?"

Morgan's fear seemed to have rendered him speechless, but Queenie, straining to look at Mr. Singh through the narrow slit in her veil, realized that he was wearing a blue kurta with gold buttons, emblazoned with the seal of the Indian Railways, and she felt a small, sudden thrill of hope.

"Do you work for the railway now?" she asked.

"Yes, miss. Mr. Pugh complained that I was spying on him. He also told the headmaster I was rude and insolent, so I was sacked." Mr. Singh spat on the platform, then shrugged. "Worse will come to him, I have no doubt. He is a man of no morals, as I told the guru . . ."

"Yes, surely," Queenie said, interrupting Singh before he lapsed into a side of Sikh eloquence. "Can you get us on the train?"

Singh looked puzzled. "You must buy a ticket," he explained.

"We *have* tickets. There is someone at the barrier we don't want to see."

Mr. Singh glanced toward the barrier, saw Daventry and the policemen. "For my brother, the slayer of Muslims— anything!" Overcome by emotion, Mr. Singh embraced Morgan, then gave Queenie a wink.

"Follow me," he said. "But Miss Kelley-sahib, a word of advice. Walk slowly, please, and behind us a few paces. A woman in purdah follows her husband respectfully, you understand, with humble steps."

Queenie followed, watching Singh guide Morgan by the hand through a maze of piled-up luggage into the station, trying to walk as humbly as possible, until after going through several doors she saw they had emerged onto the platform and the barrier was behind them. In the distance she could see Daventry diligently looking at everyone who passed through the gate, then she was surrounded by the mass of humanity on the platform, pushing, shoving and shouting as they fought their way onto the train, and realized that they were home free at last. They had done it! *She* had done it!

She had always thought that leaving Calcutta would be the happiest moment of her life—but the city was far behind her before she even knew it had gone.

Part Two

RANI

FOR A MOMENT she saw the blazing blue sky, felt the heat, heard the sound of the birds quarreling on the veranda as they swooped in and out of the flowered vines—then she opened her eyes and saw the damp-stained ceiling, smelled the odor of mildew and stale cooking, felt the cold, scratchy boardinghouse sheets, and shivered. No matter how many layers of clothing she put on, Queenie felt cold when she got up. The mornings were the worst—she hated the moment when her feet touched the icy linoleum, which curved and bubbled like the waves at sea—but the afternoons were the dreariest time of the day, eating away at her optimism and mocking the dreams which had brought her here.

Queenie felt like crying, but she knew that would only make her feel worse, besides making her look ugly—for all that mattered, since in this huge, gray, foggy city, her beauty, which she had always counted on to attract attention, seemed hardly even to be noticed, except by the occasional street-corner lout.

She hated London—had hated it at the very first sight of the foggy streets filled with drab crowds hurrying home, the shop windows glowing feebly in the misty twilight, the huge buses reduced to dim red rumbling shapes that seemed to appear from nowhere out of the smoke and fog. She particularly hated this dingy, dark, ugly room, with its broken-down furniture and the hissing gas heater in the fireplace that went out if you forgot to keep enough shillings to feed into the coin slot. She thought about struggling into a heavy skirt and cardigan and pulling on a pair of thick stockings; she hated the feel of wool against her skin. Her wool gloves, which she disliked even more, were suspended from a wire in front of the pale-blue flames of the gas heater, drying from another hopeless morning of job hunting and giving off an odor which Queenie found loathsome. Everything in England seemed to smell of damp wool, as if the entire population consisted of wet sheep.

She pulled her robe around her, put the kettle on the single grease-stained gas ring and sighed. If only she could find a job, she thought to herself. If only *Morgan* could find a job.

At the thought of him she could feel her anger returning, warming up like the gas ring in front of her. If Morgan hadn't behaved so stupidly on the boat, they would be living comfortably now while they looked for work. Queenie knew it was always easier to find a job when you didn't look as if you needed one. She had counted on the fact that Mrs. Daventry's bracelet would give them at least six months to get on their feet—not living like kings, to be sure, but living comfortably and respectably. If only Morgan hadn't ruined everything!

She poured herself a mug of tea and sat down at the small table by the bay window. Outside in the street, she could hear the rumble and the splash of traffic in the rain. Morgan would be soaked when he came back—unless he had stopped in a pub to waste a few precious shillings more of his money—*their* money!—on drink. She looked at the piece of lined paper in front of her, on which she had been trying, day after day, to write to Ma.

There was a click behind her as the gas turned off. She reached into the jar on the table for sixpence and discovered it was empty. She hoped Morgan would at least remember to bring some coins home.

Home, she thought, as a chill began to settle into the room, she was Home at last—and already homesick for India.

The voyage from Bombay to Port Said had been hellish. For safety's sake, they traveled cabin class on an Egyptian passenger-freighter of the Pyramid Lines, where a Hindu couple would attract no special attention. The heat of their tiny cabin was so great that Queenie spent the nights on deck, despite the soot and ash from the funnel that rained down on her, dozing fitfully while Morgan suffered the agonies of seasickness.

In the Indian Ocean several of the steerage passengers collapsed from heatstroke, and one died. A two-day stop for loading freight in Basra made the deck so hot that unwary passengers burned their feet on the deck plates, while the smell of coal dust, greasy mutton curry and fuel oil hung around the ship like a miasma as it wallowed through the soupy water.

The filth and noise of Egypt, when they finally reached it, was beyond anything she had ever experienced, even in Calcutta, and the

French steamer from Alexandria to Marseilles was hardly better, for the ship was infested with bugs of every species and reeked of garlic. At least she was able to drop her disguise after Port Said, while at the same time Morgan recovered some of his spirits now that he was closer to Europe and no longer obliged to dress as a Hindu. Perhaps it was from the sheer relief of having escaped arrest, or because he was ashamed of having lost his courage in front of Queenie, but once he was back among Europeans he became reckless and arrogant, leaving her alone in the cabin while he spent his time drinking in the second-class bar.

The men who gathered there were the muscle of French colonialism, tough, hard-bitten men who had spent a lifetime in the tropics, keeping the "natives" in line. They stared at her with undisguised admiration, and although she could not understand French, she could tell they were talking about her. After five minutes of being stared at and whispered about, she left Morgan to his own devices. A few drinks would do him no harm, she thought.

But she was wrong. The first night out, he did not stumble back into their cabin until one in the morning, and he slept through most of the next day, snoring and groaning in his bunk. She spent the day huddled in a deck chair along with the women and children, while they drank bouillon and tea and prepared their digestive systems for the next meal. The women stared at her with frank hatred, as much because she was English as because she was young and beautiful, but at least she was safe among them from the attentions of the men.

The second night out, Morgan did not return until three in the morning. He sat down on his bed with a sigh and remained motionless for a while, staring at his shoes as if he didn't know how to take them off. He seemed to Queenie less drunk than he had been the night before, but there was something about him that worried her, an aura of shame, fear and guilt which was more frightening than drunkenness.

"Morgan?" she whispered.

He rolled over into his bunk, still wearing his shoes, and buried his face against the wall.

"Morgan! What *is* the matter?"

He groaned, and for a moment Queenie was afraid that he was in serious physical pain. She had read about appendicitis. Had Morgan had his appendix out? Would he have to be operated on before they reached Marseilles, on this filthy boat? "Where does it hurt?" she asked, sitting up in her bunk.

"I'm sorry," he said, his voice muffled by the pillow. "I'm a fool."

"Sorry for *what?*"

"I drank too much . . . I should have known better. . . ."

"Morgan, what happened?"

"They cheated, Queenie. It was bloody robbery, I tell you!"

She stared at his back and felt a sudden spasm of nausea. "You weren't playing cards, were you?" she asked, in a small voice, but she already knew the answer.

"A friendly game . . . nothing wrong with that, Queenie."

"How much did you lose?"

There was a long silence. "I was doing bloody well," Morgan said. "I doubled our money, Queenie. We'll stay at the bloody Savoy when we reach Home, I told myself, and drink champagne."

Queenie hugged her arms around herself, as if she were chilled. I should have guessed, she told herself, I should have stopped it. "How much?" she asked coldly, trying to hide her fear.

When he spoke it was in such a low whisper that she had to strain to hear him. "A thousand pounds," he said.

It was more than half their money. She did not say anything. There was nothing to say. She rose and dressed quickly, forcing herself not to listen to Morgan's pleas for forgiveness and apologies. She walked out, slamming the cabin door behind her, hesitated for a moment, then made her way down the silent, airless corridors to the bar. A sleepy steward with a heavy growth of beard and an unbuttoned white mess jacket raised an eyebrow at her, but she ignored him and walked over to the bar, where three tough-looking men sat, staring at her in the mirror, their backs to her. She could smell the pungent smoke of French cigarettes and the licorice-sweet odor of Pernod.

"I want my money back," she said.

There was a long silence. The barman put down the glass he was polishing and disappeared into the storeroom, shutting the door behind him. The largest of the three men in front of her turned slowly to face her, a cigarette pasted to his lower lip. His black hair was slicked back with so much grease that it shined like oilskin, and his face was hard, muscular and lumpy, as if it were made of badly sorted pieces of rock. His eyes undressed her, and only her anger prevented her from blushing.

"*S'il vous plaît?*" he asked. "*Mes excuses. Je ne comprends pas l'Anglais.*" He shrugged, while his two companions smirked at her in the mirror.

"You spoke enough English to play cards with my uncle."

The big man laughed. "A little, maybe," he admitted. "He is your *oncle?*"

She nodded. Her lips were pressed together in anger.

"And he shares a cabin with his little niece? *Merde alors!* I want to be in your family!"

"You cheated him at cards."

The big man narrowed his eyes. "What it means, 'cheat'?"

"You tricked him."

"*Elle dit que tu l'as triché,*" one of the man's companions explained.

The big man's expression did not change. He walked over to Queenie and took her chin in his big hand, holding her so tightly that she could hardly move. He lowered his head so that he was looking straight into her eyes. "You should be careful not to say things like that to a man, *ma petite.* It would be sad to get your pretty face broken by some *mec* who is not as nice as me."

"I'll go to the captain."

He roared with laughter. "Go, go, see where it gets you, mademoiselle. We had a game of cards. He lost. *Tant pis, c'est la vie.* I'll tell you what," he whispered hoarsely. "I'll make you a *pari.*" He searched for the word in English. "A bet? I throw a coin, yes? Heads, you get back a thousand pounds. Tails, you go to my cabin."

She shook her head so hard that the Frenchman let go. "A proud one," he said. "I like that." He took a wad of money out of his pocket and waved it under her nose. "Do we have a bet?"

"I'm going to the captain," she repeated.

He put the money back in his jacket pocket with a knowing smile. "And what will you tell him, *petite?* That your 'uncle' is a lousy gambler—and a bad loser?" He narrowed his eyes appraisingly and lit a fresh cigarette. "Of course I don't imagine he will take the word of a *métèque*—even such a pretty one—over a fellow Frenchman's."

Queenie knew no French, but she had no difficulty in guessing the meaning of the word. She could read the contempt in his voice. He winked at her. "It's in the blood, *ma fille,* you can't hide it from an old colonial like me. Go back to your uncle—if that's what he is. And tell him not to play cards with strangers in the future." Then he turned his back on her.

She saw her own reflection in the mirror, standing helplessly among the empty tables, on which the stewards had already stacked the chairs. She wondered what it was that had given her away. Her dark hair? The shape of her eyes, or face, or lips? Or was it the way she walked? She could find no answer. It was something she would have to learn in England.

She held back her tears, turned away and retired with what she hoped was dignity. She spent the rest of the night on deck, wrapped in a blanket, until Morgan found her at last, alone and shivering, and, without saying a word, took her by the hand and led her back to her bed, which she didn't leave until the ship docked in Marseilles.

She did not tell Morgan what had happened. She did not speak to him at all on the long train journey from Marseilles to Calais, not even when the train ferry passed the white cliffs of Dover and landed them, at last, in England.

It was not until they reached Victoria Station that she relented, suddenly aware amidst the bustling, busy crowds of London that she would need Morgan's help to survive here. The city seemed so huge, so cold, so dark and busy that she felt dizzy. The buses whizzed past her, looming out of the mist, marked with the names of places that were unknown to her, and might be around the corner or miles away, for all she knew. "Elephant and Castle," "Hammersmith," "Camberley"—she read the signs as the buses passed by the obedient queues of people, wondering if she would ever know how to find her way here; then she saw a bus pass by with a sign that read "West End–Piccadilly" and without even thinking about it, she took Morgan's arm and said, "We're Home!"

He nodded, relieved that she had spoken to him at last.

"We'd best go find Peggy D'Souza," Morgan said, clapping his hands together to warm them up. He didn't own gloves, nor did Queenie, who was shivering in her cotton dress and thin coat, while Morgan fumbled in his pocket for Peggy's address. The fog seemed to eat into her bones, producing a chill that numbed her to everything else. At least, she thought, Peggy would give them a cup of tea and some good advice on where to live. At the thought of the tea she felt less miserable and was even able to take some pleasure in the interminable taxi ride to the Bayswater Road—for the taxi seat was of real leather, and the driver spoke with a Cockney accent which she found incomprehensible. She wondered if he recognized them as foreigners, but he said nothing as he pocketed his tip, touched his cap and chugged off into the fog, leaving them standing outside the low, rusty, cast-iron garden gate of a small, shabby house which seemed identical to its neighbors in the long row.

At the sound of the bell, the door was opened by an elderly woman, her hennaed hair wrapped up in an old cleaning cloth. She clutched a wheezing Pekingese in her arms, and stared through her glasses at Queenie, Morgan and their suitcases with frank hostility.

"What do *you* want?" she asked. "We've got no room." The dog opened one rheumy eye and yapped at Queenie.

"What's its name?" Queenie asked, trying to be pleasant.

"None of your business, miss."

"We were looking for Mrs. Butts."

The old lady squinted at them. She wore a flowered wrapper, stockings that sagged around her ankles and a pair of threadbare carpet slippers. "Who?" the old lady asked.

"Mrs. Butts. Peggy Butts?"

"*Mrs.* Butts, is it? Oh, that's a good one!" The old lady cackled ferociously, showing her false teeth.

"Isn't this her house?" Morgan asked politely. Queenie was acutely conscious of the fact that his accent, unlike hers, remained distinctly noticeable.

"I should say not! It's *my* 'ouse. And if you think I'm 'aving any more of *you* people in it, you've got another think coming."

"We just wanted to see her," Morgan said. "Is she in?"

"I daresay. You a relative of hers?"

"Just a friend from home."

"Home? And where would *that* be, I wonder? Bombay or Calcutta? Third floor on the left. And leave your bags here, *if* you please. You'll not be staying."

As they walked up the steep stairs, feeling their way in the dim light of a single bulb, the old lady slammed the door shut and bolted it. The dog yapped again, and she calmed it until it was merely snuffling and wheezing.

"There, there," Queenie heard her mumble in the dark hall below them. "He's just a bloody wog, dearie, never you mind. And with a girl who should know better! I don't know *what* the world is coming to." Queenie felt a certain relief that she had passed the old woman's scrutiny, then shame at her selfishness.

She knocked at the stained door on the third landing. There was no answer, so she knocked louder. The door opened a crack. "Who the hell is it?" Peggy D'Souza asked.

Queenie stared at her in amazement. Peggy seemed to have aged by years. Her olive skin was concealed beneath a heavy layer of white makeup, her eyes were ringed with dark circles, her mouth was painted with bright red lipstick that failed to disguise the bitterness of her expression. Her false eyelashes were thickly coated with flaking mascara. She seemed to have been crying.

At the sight of Morgan, she smiled mechanically, but then she recognized Queenie and gasped. She pulled the dirty flowered kimono a little tighter around her to hide her breasts. "Why, it's not Ma Kelley's little Queenie, is it?"

Queenie nodded. "Whatever next?" Peggy said. "And Morgan, too, of all people!"

"May we come in?"

Peggy sighed, then shrugged and opened the door wider. Behind her Queenie caught sight of a small, dark, squalid room. A two-bar electric heater glowed in the fireplace. Beside it was a gas ring, attached to a meter, on which a blackened kettle stood. The single washbasin was filled with dirty pots, dishes and glasses. On the rumpled bed, it was just possible to distinguish a man asleep in his trousers and undershirt, a dirty handkerchief spread over his face. The smell of stale cigarette smoke, cheap perfume and cooking was overpowering. The man on the bed groaned and rolled over. "Who the hell's that?" he asked, in a muffled voice.

"Friends," Peggy said.

"Friends, my ass. Tell 'em to stuff a sock in it."

"Wait a mo'," Peggy said. "You got your bloody money's worth." She turned to Queenie, her expression at once shameful and defiant. "What the hell are you two doing here?" she asked.

"We've come Home," Morgan said. "We thought you might be able to give us a little help. We'll be looking for jobs, a place to stay . . ."

Peggy laughed without mirth. "Home? Home is Calcutta, man!"

"What happened to Mr. Butts?" Queenie asked. "Ma said you were living like a princess. She had letters from you."

"Well, I had to write something, didn't I? I couldn't tell the truth. Butts left me cold, ran off with my money—not that I had much, but it was more than *he* had, the lousy, lying sod. Look, I'm keeping my head above water the best I can. But I can't help you. You'll have to go."

"Go where?" Morgan asked. "Where can we stay?"

"Try the Fulham Road, man. There are plenty of places there that take people like us in. You'll do all right. At any rate, Queenie will, with a face like hers."

"Stop nattering, Peggy. I haven't got all day," the man grumbled.

"We thought you might know some people . . ." Queenie started to say, but before she could finish, Peggy D'Souza burst into tears. "If I knew some people, girl, would I be living like this?" she shouted. And as the tears began to run down her cheeks, streaking her makeup, she slammed the door in their faces.

So they had settled down to this miserable existence in a bed-sitter off the Fulham Road. Morgan trudged off daily to look for work, his feet soaking wet in cracked shoes, a tattered map of Central London folded up in his coat pocket to help him find his way. In the mornings, Queenie made her own way from employment agency to employment agency, with decreasing enthusiasm. She had no training to speak of, and less experience. Everywhere she went she was told how grim things were. Jobs were scarce, money was tight, people queued patiently for hours on end for work that hardly paid a living wage.

In India, of course, there had been talk of the economic crisis "at home," but the very poverty of India insulated it from the effects of the world depression. Nothing had prepared Queenie—or Morgan—for the long, drab lines of the unemployed, the sad, polite men with war medals pinned to their threadbare jackets selling pencils or shoelaces in the streets, the signs in shop windows that announced, "Sorry—no jobs here, and no credit." These were the English—a race of sahibs who commanded respect by the color of their skin—and yet here at home, they lived in squalid, hopeless, cold poverty.

In the afternoons Queenie shopped for their supper, all too conscious of the fact that she had few domestic skills. In India there was always somebody poorer than yourself to shop, cook or clean, and among Morgan's many complaints about the way they lived now was the fact that they were obliged to exist on a diet of canned corned beef, chocolate biscuits and tea.

The worst thing about their supper, Queenie thought, was how quickly it was over—for once they had finished eating, there was nothing to do but wait for the embarrassing moment when it was time for bed. She stepped behind a curtain to undress and put on her nightgown, and Morgan reluctantly did the same to put on his pajamas. There was no sofa for him to sleep on, and she could hardly ask him to spend every night on the floor, so they slept uneasily in the same bed, which was not so bad for her, but presented many difficulties for Morgan. Occasionally he would roll over so that his body was pressed close to hers, pretending that it was an accident, but she always pushed him away. Sometimes, when it was more than he could bear to be lying beside her, he would touch her with his hand and ask, "Queenie, do you love me?" and when that happened she would sit up in bed and tell him to behave, which always led to an argument.

If Morgan had been drinking on the way home, he sometimes lost his temper. One night he put his arms around her, his face close to hers in the dark, and tried to kiss her as she struggled to turn her face away from his lips. His breath reeked of whiskey, and for a moment she thought she was going to be sick. "You made me a promise," he hissed.

"I didn't promise anything."

"You bloody did! I nearly went to jail for you, and now you won't even let me *touch* you!"

"Morgan, it's wrong . . ."

"Wrong? It was wrong to steal the bloody bracelet, but I did it."

"*We* did it. And if you hadn't lost our money, we wouldn't be living like this."

"Oh, bugger!" Morgan let her go, sat up in bed, lit a cigarette and coughed harshly. "You always have the last word," he said. "Just like your Ma."

"Well, it's true."

They sat side by side silently for a few minutes, carefully keeping their distance from each other. "Still nothing?" Queenie asked, trying to make peace, since they shared the same bed.

Morgan shrugged. "Not a sausage. I might just as well not have spent forty pounds at the pawnshop on a sax—nobody even wants to hear me play it. You'll have a job before I do, at this rate."

"Not a prayer. I can't even find a job as a shop assistant," she sighed. "These nightclubs you go to," she said, "don't they need girls?"

"Well, yes, I suppose so . . . but you wouldn't want to do that kind of thing, Queenie."

"Why not? It's got to be better than being a shop assistant."

"Some of them are pretty rough places. Not exactly the Café de Paris, you know."

"They have dance hostesses, don't they? I can dance."

Morgan cleared his throat. "That's not usually all they do," he said. "I see."

"Of course the *performers* are another thing entirely. Some of them are pretty respectable, I believe. But it's not at all something for you. . . ."

"Why not?"

"Well, you don't want to be up there on stage with most of your clothes off, do you? It's not Gilbert and bloody Sullivan, you know. Besides, you have to be a singer or a dancer."

"I can dance. I could learn to sing."

"It's daft. Anyway, we're not talking about ballroom dancing, Queenie. Exotic dancing is something quite different."

"Is it difficult?"

"I don't suppose so . . . how would I know? Mostly they just strike attitudes and take their clothes off, except for the chorus line, which is for real dancers. But it's out of the question. What would your Ma say?"

"She isn't here. I don't suppose she'd think it was worse than stealing, anyway."

"You must write to her. She'll forgive you. It's *me* she won't forgive."

Queenie nodded. That was undeniably true, she thought. "I keep trying, but it's hard to know what to say."

"Cheer her up."

"That's the problem. Oh, Morgan, take me with you to the clubs. If I could only get a job as a dancer or something . . . at least it would be a step in the right direction."

"It would be a step in the *wrong* direction," Morgan said firmly, and stubbed out his cigarette, ending the conversation.

Now Queenie stared at the grimy, tear-stained letter to her mother with a growing sense of helplessness. Days had passed by while it sat there, but still she could think of nothing to say. That she was sorry? It was true enough, but would that make up for what she had done? Had the police come tramping through the house, asking questions? She had forced herself not to think about it. And how could she explain that the future here was even grimmer than it had been in India? She decided to wait for better news, hoping there would be some. She tore the paper up.

Would Ma forgive her? What would she say if she could see her now, living in a squalor that grew worse every day, while Morgan drank away what little money they still had?

Queenie's experience with alcohol was limited to what she had heard about her father, but it seemed to her that Morgan was not a good drinker. His hands trembled in the morning, he shaved himself unevenly, leaving small bloody nicks and patches of beard on his cheeks, his eyes were bloodshot and dark-rimmed, which made it all the more difficult to land a job. He chain-smoked, since cigarettes were cheaper than food, and Queenie grew to loathe the smell of tobacco, which clung to her hair no matter how often she washed it and seemed to pervade not only the room, with its sad furniture, but even the few articles of clothing she owned.

Queenie had never known poverty before, and the specter of it terrified her. In India, especially in the narrow world of the Anglo-Indians, there was always somebody to help you when times were bad. Even the poorest had friends, relatives, a community to fall back on, if worse came to worst, for it was not in anybody's interests that an Anglo-Indian should fall to the level of a native. However poor Anglo-Indians might be, they were better off than the Indians, which was a consolation of sorts—and in any case poverty in a warm climate was not so terrifying as it was here, where shelter, clothing and ready money were critical. She felt the stirrings of panic at the thought of what might happen to them when they ran out of money.

She got up and opened a box of chocolate biscuits. On the cover there was a picture of a fat man in Indian clothing being weighed on a huge scale. Above it a banner proclaimed: "Cadman's Chocolate Biscuits—Rich and Dark, like the Aga Khan."

She nibbled at a biscuit, pulling back the curtains to look out at the rainy street and the glow of lights. She heard a key turn in the door, and turned around. To her surprise, Morgan was smiling cheerfully—not his usual sheepish, apologetic grin, but a real smile. In one hand, he carried his saxophone case, with the other he cradled a bottle wrapped in damp brown paper. "A surprise!" he said. He slipped off his wet overcoat and threw it on a chair, missing by a couple of feet, then peeled the brown paper off the bottle. "Champagne!"

"What on earth for, Morgan?"

"Ah," he said, grinning. "That's the surprise. I have—a *job!*"

Queenie felt a sense of relief flood through her. She ran across the room, put both arms around Morgan and hugged him. "What job?" she asked. "Where? How much money are they paying you?"

"In a moment, in a moment." Morgan unfastened the wire around the champagne cork, put his thumbs under it and laughed happily as the foam spurted out, splashing them both. He poured champagne into two chipped toothbrush mugs, handed one to Queenie and clinked his mug against hers. He emptied his own with one gulp, and refilled it. "Five pounds a week," he said proudly. "In a nightclub jazz band, Queenie!"

"What's it called?"

"Club Paradise. It's in Soho, just off Greek Street."

"Is it nicer than Firpo's?"

Morgan drank from his mug and thought for a moment. A shadow of disappointment crossed his face. "No," he said. "Drink up."

It was the first time Queenie had ever drunk champagne—or any other kind of alcohol, for that matter—and the taste seemed to her singularly unpleasant. The bubbles were nice enough, and it was pleasant to feel the foam touch one's nose, but the champagne itself was sickeningly sweet, with a chemical aftertaste that lingered on the tongue. Her expression must have indicated her dismay, for Morgan instantly apologized. "I'm afraid it's not French," he said.

"It's very nice all the same." She was determined to be polite and unwilling to say anything that might change his mood. Reluctantly Queenie emptied her mug, which Morgan instantly refilled.

Queenie sat down on the bed, holding her mug. Her legs felt suddenly weak. She had once heard that drinking on an empty stomach was a mistake. Apparently it was true. She forced herself to think straight, but she felt very tired. "Do you think there's a job for me?" she asked. Her voice sounded strangely muffled and thick, and she wondered if Morgan had noticed.

But he showed no signs of noticing anything—whatever *he* had been drinking before he came home, it had filled him with energy and a kind of high-pitched nervous excitement. "I won't hear of it, Queenie. Are you all right?"

"Yes, of course I'm all right," Queenie said, but she wasn't. In fact, she felt quite sick, but was too proud to admit it.

"It's just that you seem a little tired. Here, let me help you . . ." Morgan sat down beside her on the bed. "Put your feet up," he said. He took her ankles in his hands and lifted her legs up onto the bed. Queenie gave a small groan of relief, which Morgan apparently—or deliberately—misinterpreted, for he unfastened her robe and opened it. "You'll be more comfortable this way," he said.

He took another drink, then put his mug down on the floor. Queenie could see his eyes—they were dark and almost opaque, not at all the gentle, timid eyes she was used to seeing whenever she looked at Morgan. She tried to fasten her robe, but her fingers couldn't manage a knot.

She felt the weight of his body pressing against her, but she couldn't push him off, and suddenly his face was so close to hers that it was out of focus, like a cloud passing in front of the sun, and she felt his lips on hers, his tongue probing into her mouth, his mustache rubbing against her cheek. "Queenie," he groaned. "Queenie, I love you!"

She tried to push him off, fighting for breath, for his mouth was on hers and his weight was pressed against her chest, but Morgan was past noticing. He grabbed the back of her neck with one hand, while with the other he pulled up her nightgown. Without releasing his hold, he squirmed down and kissed her breasts wetly, his breath coming in short gasps.

Queenie could see the top of his head and smell the brilliantine he used on his hair. His mouth tasted of tobacco, liquor and sweet champagne, and for a moment she thought she was going to be sick, but then she felt Morgan's hand plunge between her legs, the fingers digging deep into her flesh, then penetrating her roughly. The pain was so sudden that her nausea vanished instantly.

"You've been wanting this as much as I have," he whispered thickly.

She shook her head, but it did no good. Morgan's weight and his strength were too much for her. She gave a moan of pain and bit him as hard as she could, astonished at her own anger.

"Bitch!" Morgan shouted, and slapped her face. Then, as if he had had enough of the preliminaries, he clamped his hand on her mouth, forcing her head back against the pillow, unbuttoned his trousers, raised himself over her on his elbows and, opening her with his fingers, roughly inserted himself, driving in as deeply as he could with the thrust of his full weight. Queenie gave a howl of pain.

She pounded against his back with her clenched fists and tried to kick him away with her legs, but Morgan's attention was not diverted. He pushed on, groaning slightly himself with pain, for her muscles were instinctively clenched against him, then she felt a sudden, tearing pain as he ruptured her maidenhead, followed almost instantly by a sticky, wet feeling inside her as Morgan reached his climax with a moan.

"My God, but I love you," he said, his voice slurred. Then he rolled off her, took a deep, noisy breath as if he were about to swim underwater, closed his eyes and began to snore. His trousers were still unbuttoned. Queenie, when she opened her eyes and wiped away the tears, could see his limp penis exposed. There were flecks of blood on it and, she supposed, more on her. Now that it was over, she felt a growing panic, as if she were drowning. She couldn't bear the sight of Morgan, or the wretched room he had landed them in—not for a moment longer. She stood up, dressed quickly without looking in the mirror—for she was afraid of what she might see there—and rushed downstairs into the street.

She hardly felt the cold. She walked quickly without even caring what direction she was going in, as long as it took her away from Morgan. She could feel the rain soaking her hair, washing down her face. She didn't mind—she welcomed it, even as she shivered. She had heard about rape—it was the kind of thing the girls whispered about at school. Had Morgan raped her? From the little she knew about it, she supposed so. But if that was the case, why did she feel so ashamed and guilty? Surely it was *his* fault, not hers. There was nobody to ask.

She walked on until her panic gradually subsided. People were staring at her, but she didn't notice them any more than she noticed the brightly lit shop windows of Knightsbridge. She tried to think calmly about her situation, but she already knew the only thing that mattered now was to get away from Morgan. But how? If she left, where would she go? She knew nobody, she had no job, she would be alone in this huge, indifferent city. A taxi splashed her as it passed, but she ignored her wet shoes and stockings. She stopped for a moment in a doorway to shake the water out of her hair. From the next doorway, a fat woman with a garishly painted face glared at her angrily. "Hey, you!" she shouted. "Get off me beat!"

Queenie did not argue. She knew about prostitution in India—there were whole districts devoted to the trade, where the women wore distinct marks—but it had not occurred to her that it existed in England, too, or that it was something a white woman would do. She pondered what the woman would say if she told her that she had just lost her virginity, then decided she was becoming hysterical.

She crossed the street. The sentries were sheltering in their boxes outside the Knightsbridge barracks. She could smell the warm, pungent odor of horses in the stables beyond the gate. One of the sentries winked at her. She wondered if she looked different, if people could somehow tell. . . . She glanced at her reflection in a shop window, but except for the fact that she was drenched, she looked much the same.

She turned from the window and looked across the street. Through the tall windows of the Hyde Park Hotel she could see people dancing, the men in tails, the women in long, formal gowns, swirling in the light from dozens of chandeliers. She could hear the music above the noise of the traffic, and it was as if everything she wanted in life was there, so close she could almost touch it, but beyond her reach.

A low, racy sports car pulled to a sudden stop as the light turned red, sending a spray of water onto the pavement and splashing her legs. The driver unfastened the window on his side and leaned out. "I say," he said, "I *am* sorry. Are you all right?"

She stared at him. He was in evening dress—she could see the black tie and white silk scarf under the drawn-up collar of a trench coat. His blond hair was worn long and carelessly brushed back into small wings above his ears. His face was handsome—not conventionally handsome, like a movie actor's, but *interesting*. What struck Queenie, however, was not his good looks, but his evident concern.

"I'm all right, thank you," she said.

"You ought to go home and dry off," the man said gently; then the light changed to green, and Queenie heard a woman's voice, with the precise, high-pitched tones of the English upper classes, say from the passenger's side of the car, "Oh, *do* come on, Lucien, we'll be late!" The man gave Queenie a disarming smile, as if to apologize for leaving her there in the rain, let out the clutch and shot across the street to the entrance of the hotel. The doorman rushed out with an umbrella to open the door, and a young woman stepped out into the light.

Queenie felt a strange combination of sadness and relief, as if the fact that he had noticed her was a sign of better times to come. She would not run crying back to Ma—she knew that once and for all. She would walk back to their room, have a cup of tea and clean herself up. The thought of confronting Morgan no longer dismayed her. She would have to stay with him until she could get away on her own terms—it would be difficult, perhaps painful, but necessary. Given his capacity for guilt, he was unlikely to do it again, that much she was sure of, but she would know better than to drink—and from now on, he could sleep on the floor.

At least, she told herself, turning toward home, the worst had happened. Now she owed Morgan nothing.

Then it occurred to her there was one thing worse than being raped. She could be pregnant.

"So *nu*? You've only worked here a week and already you've got troubles?"

Solly Goldner sighed wearily and sat down beside Morgan at a small table near the dance floor. He lit a cigar, the plump fingers performing the operation with surprising delicacy. He slipped the matches and a gold penknife back into his waistcoat pocket, examined the tip of the cigar critically and puffed until it was glowing to his satisfaction.

Goldner was fat. Goldner was short. Goldner was ugly. Goldner was balding, though not by any means old. But none of these things was what most people noticed when they first met him, for it was the eyes—wary, unblinking and intense—that caught the attention.

In his native Hungary Goldner had survived the Red Terror of Bela Kun, the White Terror of Admiral Horthy, starvation, anti-Semitic riots and financial chaos, all before he was twenty-one. Since then he had gone bankrupt in Vienna, Berlin and Paris, always managing to get out one step ahead of his creditors—though sometimes it had been a close call. In Paris he ran an international photography agency that eventually attracted the attention of the Brigade de Moeurs, though by the time the fascinated vice squad officers had finished sorting through the boxes of pornographic photographs—which even *they* found impressive—Goldner was already on the cross-Channel steamer, happily puffing his third cigar of the day.

In England, Goldner reverted to his earlier profession of nightclub owner, having no wish to make the acquaintanceship of Scotland Yard's vice squad—not at any rate until he had accumulated enough capital to buy them off.

Like most truly unscrupulous men, Goldner was a sentimentalist, which was why he had agreed to sit down and listen to Morgan's problems. Goldner doubted there was any advantage to be gained from a conversation with Morgan, but he never considered it a waste of time to listen. Most people liked to talk. Goldner preferred to listen.

"Mr. Goldner," Morgan said, lighting a cigarette to calm his nerves—a gesture which Goldner's eyes instantly picked up and assessed—"I wouldn't want you to get the wrong idea. I don't have any complaints about the job."

Goldner nodded slightly, raising one eyebrow just enough to indicate that this wasn't news to him. A *shlep* like this Anglo-Indian was lucky to have a job at all, Goldner told himself, and would hardly be likely to complain about anything—not with the unemployed lining the streets looking for work. He allowed himself to glance quickly around the room. It was still early and most of the tables were empty, but instinct told Goldner it was going to be a slow night. Even the girls at the bar, whose job was to sit down with men and persuade them to order a bottle of champagne, looked depressed—and, Goldner acknowledged to himself, depressing. He made a mental note to have the lights turned down a bit more, then returned his attention to Morgan.

"I have a family problem, Mr. Goldner," Morgan explained.

Goldner's eyes returned to the bar to make sure the girls were drinking only ginger ale. He had no time for family problems. He had hired

Morgan because Morgan came cheap. It occurred to him that this miserable half-*shvartzer* saxophonist might be trying to borrow money with a hard-luck story about his family. Goldner moved swiftly to dispel that hope, if Morgan nurtured it. "A family is a millstone around the neck," Goldner said, moving his outstretched hands palms up in a circle to suggest its heaviness. "The other day Bruno, the headwaiter, came to me in tears. His little girl has to go to hospital. A big expense. I told him, 'Bruno, what has your little girl done for *me*?' "

In the dim pink light Goldner's face had a sallow, sepulchral glow and the heavy beard on his thick jowls took on a sickly green cast. He took a puff on his cigar, then waved it in Morgan's direction, the tip glowing red, to further emphasize his point. "Everybody has to look out for themselves," he added. "The sooner children learn that, the better."

Morgan dabbed at the sweat on his forehead. "Yes, yes," he agreed, his voice rising, "that's my point exactly. I have a young niece who wants to look out for herself. She needs a job."

"A niece? What does she do, this niece?"

"She is a very beautiful young woman."

"That is not necessarily a profession."

"She can sing and dance a little . . . but the main thing is that she's very beautiful. Much more beautiful than any of the girls here."

Goldner sighed. "That wouldn't be difficult, my dear fellow," he said. "And it doesn't really matter anyway. By the time the customers arrive here, all the girls look beautiful to them."

"If you saw her, Mr. Goldner, you'd know she was special. You put her on that stage, and by Jove, they'll break down the doors to get in. There's money in this girl."

"Money?" Goldner asked, savoring the word. He narrowed his eyes and stared at the small stage, where a heavy woman with peroxide-blond hair and a face painted as white as a Kabuki mask had just appeared. A spotlight somewhere at the back of the room was turned on, with a loud hiss, and its beam illuminated her desperate smile, the lines around her eyes caked with makeup, the false eyelashes like thick black caterpillars.

Goldner economized on talent—the money was in the champagne, not the floor show, and most people in England came to nightclubs only because it was impossible to get a drink anywhere else after eleven o'clock. They didn't expect to be entertained, and most of them wouldn't have noticed if they had been.

Still, he had to admit that business was off, and the floor show was unlikely to improve that. Gloomily he watched the woman onstage strip down to a spangled G-string and bra.

"Well," he said sadly, "bring her along, my dear fellow. She can't be worse than Mavis. Mind you, I don't promise anything. Will she take her clothes off?"

Morgan looked shocked. "*All* of them?"

"Don't be silly. This isn't Berlin or Paris. She just has to take off enough to keep the customers awake and drinking."

"She'll do what she's told if she wants to eat," Morgan said bravely, though he was by no means certain that was the case.

Goldner nodded. The strip act was drawing to a lugubrious ending, and it was time for Morgan to get back to the band. "That's the trouble with having relatives, my dear fellow," Goldner said. "They always want to eat. Three times a day!"

Queenie sat silently in the taxi on the way to what he grandly called "her audition." She had no very clear idea of what was expected of her, but whatever it was, she was determined to succeed. She felt like a sailor drowning at sea, reaching out for the lifebuoy that represented the last, slim chance for survival.

"Chin up!" he told her, patting her arm, but she merely drew farther away from him into her corner of the taxi and stared out the rain-washed window at the lights.

She closed her eyes. The last couple of weeks had been such a nightmare that she was hardly able to think about them without feeling sick—and this was not the right time to feel sick, with so much at stake. She did not cry. She did not sulk. She simply refused to talk to Morgan, or even acknowledge his existence. He slept on the floor and daily begged her to forgive him. "I'll forgive you when you've found me a job," she finally told him.

The taxi chugged down Greek Street, took a sharp turn and stopped. The driver flicked up his flag with a ring. "Five bob, guv," he said.

Morgan stepped out and handed him two half crowns and a sixpence. The driver examined the sixpence, leaned over and spat out the window. "Thanks, mate," he sneered.

Morgan stuck his head in. "It's all you bloody deserve, man," he shouted. "You took the long way here. You think I'm a foreigner who doesn't know better? Well, you're bloody wrong, man. Take sixpence and be damned!"

The driver was unimpressed by Morgan's fury. His lumpy red face showed his contempt. He cocked his head to one side as if he were trying to place Morgan's accent. He took the cigarette out of the corner of his mouth, holding the butt between thumb and forefinger. "I don't think you're a bloody foreigner," he said triumphantly. "I think you're a bloody wog." He gave Queenie an appraising stare, and winked. "Why don't you go back where you bloody came from, mate," he growled at Morgan. "We don't need your sodding kind 'ere." He revved his motor and let out the clutch, forcing Morgan to straighten up. "And leave our women alone!" the driver shouted. "It makes me fucking sick to see a nigger with a white girl." He tossed the six-penny bit at Morgan's feet and accelerated noisily down the street, his laughter rising above the squeal of the tires.

Morgan stood on the pavement for a moment, trying to recapture his bedraggled dignity. He looked toward Queenie for support—or perhaps sympathy, she couldn't tell—but she stared ahead as if he didn't exist. She followed him down the steps with a sigh.

"Good evening, miss," the doorman said, doffing his greasy hat, as she passed by him.

She smiled back. In a hundred ways she had come to realize that the English accepted her as one of them, while Morgan was instantly recognized as a half-caste—or at any rate as a "native" of some kind. It was his manner and his accent, more than his appearance, that gave him away, in a country where manners and accent were almost as important as money and appearance. Left to herself, she might easily be accepted as English, provided nobody asked too many questions—and as long as Morgan wasn't around to muddy the waters.

They passed through a narrow hallway decorated with framed eight-by-tens of pouting blondes with too much makeup. A sign above the pictures read, "London's Most Beautiful Girls—Members Only." A tired, washed-out blonde, who was clearly not one of them, leaned on the counter of the cloakroom.

She gave them a theatrical smile, revealing stained, crooked teeth, then seeing that it was only Morgan, she allowed her mouth to settle back to its natural dissatisfied pout, and slumped forward again, resting her big breasts on the counter. "You're early, then?" she said to Morgan. It was amazing, Queenie thought, just how badly most Londoners spoke. She had vaguely assumed that everybody would sound like Mr. Pugh, but what with the Cockneys, the Scots, the impossible grunts and gasps of Geordies and Yorkshiremen, and the singsong lilt of the Welsh, nobody seemed to speak proper England at all. The woman's voice was pure Cockney. Queenie couldn't help thinking that she sounded a lot better, even if she *did* come from India.

"Where's Solly?" Morgan asked.

"*Mister* Goldner is inside. He left word he wasn't to be disturbed."

"He's expecting me."

"Is he now? He didn't say anything to me."

"Mr. Goldner is expecting *me*, I think," Queenie said quietly.

The woman scrutinized her carefully. "I daresay. I should think he'd be happy to see *you*, dear."

Queenie's confidence, such as it was, ebbed as she climbed the worn, steep stairs onto the small stage. She caught her heels, and for a moment she thought she was going to fall on her face, but she recovered, all too conscious of having made an ungraceful and almost disastrous entrance—not that anybody was paying much attention except Morgan, she thought, looking around the room.

It was not an inspiring sight. Goldner, his stout body tightly squeezed into a fashionable dark-breasted suit—or rather one that *would* have been fashionable on anyone else—sat at a small table in the back, going over his account books. He did not look happy.

Morgan sat beside him, trying to attract Goldner's attention to her. For a moment, Queenie felt like a slave being auctioned to an indifferent buyer—a feeling which bore just enough resemblance to her present situation to make her angry.

The lights were turned up, since it was only seven in the evening, and in the glare from the bare bulbs, the Club Paradise seemed to her almost grotesquely tawdry. Goldner relied chiefly on darkness to provide a decor—in working hours the place was plunged into Stygian gloom. The ceiling consisted of several layers of fishing nets, from which were suspended colored glass balls and dusty stuffed fish. When the lights dimmed and blue spots were turned on the ceiling, the effect was like being inside an aquarium. With the lights turned up, it reminded Queenie of a fish market—an impression which was dismayingly reinforced by Goldner's appearance, for the dark, watery, protuberant eyes and the damp, unhealthy pallor of his complexion gave his face a remarkably fishy look. As he puffed on his cigar, even his mouth moved very much like a fish's, the lips parting in soft little gasps. He did not look up from his papers.

Morgan sat next to Goldner, at once apprehensive and ridiculously pleased with himself, Queenie thought—and also somewhat embarrassed by the fact that Goldner was too preoccupied to pay any attention to her. Only the barman and two Levantine waiters had noticed her. They were huddled together behind the bar exchanging comments about her, their hands flashing back and forth as they expressed their admiration. The fact that they had stopped working at last attracted Goldner's attention. He raised his face from his papers, gave them a threatening glance that set them back to polishing glasses, and turned to face Queenie.

"What did I tell you, Mr. Goldner?" Morgan asked.

Goldner pursed his lips and blinked. He was not about to express satisfaction. Satisfaction cost money. It was the first rule of commerce to let the other chap praise his own goods. The buyer's job was to find fault. Goldner looked at Queenie, but could find no obvious faults—if anything, Morgan had undersold her. He examined her more closely. She did not look like Morgan's niece—her skin was as pale as ivory. "Can you sing, dear?" he asked.

Queenie nodded.

"So sing."

Queenie had no illusions about her voice, but she stood up straight, closed her eyes, and sang:

"Every little moment I'm with you, I'm happy,
Every little moment without you, I'm blue . . ."

Without an orchestra to provide rhythm, the pert little song from *Mr. Cinders* sounded flat even to Queenie. Her voice seemed to vanish among the stuffed fish.

"Of course, she'd sound better with an orchestra behind her," Morgan said gamely.

Goldner's face was impassive. He gave Morgan an impatient sidelong look, then rubbed one fat hand over his jowls, as if he were in deep thought. "Do you dance, dear?" he asked. "Try a few steps." His guttural voice was kindly, even gentle, but the weary tone made it all too clear what he thought of Queenie as a singer.

Queenie steeled herself, did a kick and a turn, and felt one heel catch in the uneven boards of the stage. She stumbled, recovered her balance, kicked again and saw, to her horror, her right shoe fly across the room and land at Goldner's feet.

Goldner picked up the shoe, ignoring Morgan, who was trying to explain that Queenie was merely nervous. He stood up, crossed the dance floor, and handed Queenie her shoe. Absurdly she thought of Prince Charming bringing Cinderella her lost slipper. She giggled, a nervous

reaction to sheer despair, then realized that Goldner was staring at her in surprise, and she felt even worse about her failure.

"It's no good, is it?" Queenie asked in a small voice.

Goldner shrugged. "Reita Nugent you're not," he said. "Still, who needs Reita Nugent around here? Take off your clothes, dear."

"Take my clothes off?"

"If you please," Goldner said politely.

"I thought I'd have a costume."

"And so you shall. If you're hired. But first I have to see how you look."

The thought of undressing in front of a stranger—several strangers, if one included the barman and the waiters—paralyzed Queenie. She had never undressed in front of a man before. She looked up at the ceiling, into the glass eyes of the stuffed fish.

"Do I have to?"

"If you want a job."

She wanted a job. She glanced at Morgan, still sitting at the table, nodding his head to encourage her. If she was ever going to get rid of him she would have to take the first step, and if the first step meant undressing, she would have to undress. She thought about her underwear. It was clean, but decidedly unglamorous. "All right," she said. "Do I have to do it in front of Morgan and the waiters?"

Goldner sighed. It never failed to surprise him that women made difficulties about the most trivial details. He was about to point out that if she got the job she'd be taking off her clothes in front of a roomful of strangers, but then he looked at her more carefully. She was a good deal younger than he had thought—at most, seventeen, he guessed—and from the tone of her voice, there was some problem between the girl and Morgan. Goldner had not given much thought to their relationship.

Morgan was recognizably of mixed blood, but the girl could easily pass as English—though there was something about her beauty that was at once intriguing and mysterious, a certain exotic quality that Goldner told himself was money in the bank. Her face was exquisite, so perfect that Goldner was suddenly almost dizzy at the thought of how valuable a property she could be—in the right hands, of course. And without Morgan, who would only be in the way, as well as an inconvenient reminder of her origins.

The soft touch was needed, he decided. He climbed the steps to the stage, wheezing slightly from the effort, and stood facing her so that his bulky body shielded her from Morgan. His expression was kind, re-assuring, almost fatherly. He put one fat, damp hand on her shoulder. "I understand," he said, his voice lowered to a soulful whisper, and without turning back, he shouted, "All of you get out!"

He waited for a moment, then looked around. "You too, Morgan."

Morgan stood up, at once angry and unsure of his ground. "What for? I'm her uncle, damn it. I have a responsibility . . ."

Goldner shrugged. "The young lady doesn't need a chaperon. And she's made her wishes perfectly clear."

Morgan hesitated, visibly lost his nerve and took a few steps toward the door. "I'll be waiting outside," he said, trying to maintain his dignity.

"You do that, my dear fellow," Goldner replied affably, gratified to see the look of gratitude and respect on Queenie's face. He smiled as he heard the door slam. It was amazing how women responded to even the smallest gesture of kindness—and even more amazing that so few men understood this, or could be bothered to try.

"Now let's get on with it," he said gently, and made his way back to the table. "There's just the two of us now. Try to think of me—oh, perhaps as your family doctor."

"I've never taken my clothes off for a doctor," Queenie said, and it was true. In India, doctors still clung to the Victorian tradition and examined their female patients through a gown so as not to offend their modesty. Only Ma, Grandma and of course the ayah had seen Queenie naked.

"What should I do with my clothes?" she asked. Goldner crossed his legs, revealing a handsome pair of mauve ribbed silk socks. "Why, hand them to me, dear. I'll look after them." He was sitting precariously on a small, flimsy chair, his thighs overflowing so far over the edges of the seat he appeared to be levitating. His attitude was that of a man pre-paring himself to watch the unveiling of a memorial stone or a piece of heroic municipal sculpture. His expression was patient, polite and faintly bored, as if he were longing to give a perfunctory round of ap-plause and get home before it rained.

"Do you want me to take my clothes off in any special way?"

"Just take them off the way you normally do," Goldner said, puffing on his cigar. "Nothing fancy. We must learn to walk before we can run."

Queenie nodded. She had always believed that one day she would get her chance, the magic moment that would change her life, and the belief in it was what had brought her all the way to England in the first place. She had never been quite sure how it would take place, or where it would lead, and had certainly never imagined it would involve undressing on a bare stage in a Soho nightclub, but it might be the only chance she would have. On the one hand, there was Goldner, his pudgy hands folded over his belly, waiting for her to take her clothes off; on the other hand was the small room she shared with Morgan and the shame of what had happened there. It was no contest.

She unzipped the back of her dress, leaned forward and pulled it over her head. Goldner's expression did not change. She handed him the dress, holding it out over the lip of the stage. Goldner folded it neatly and placed it on his lap. "Now the slip, please."

Queenie hesitated. She felt no great shame standing in front of Goldner in her slip, but the next step was a big one. She drew the slip over her head by its shoulder straps and closed her eyes. She handed it across to Goldner and stood still, her arms crossed in front of her, conscious of the fact that he would surely notice that her brassiere and her panties were cheap cotton ones. The panties were white, with a design of small pink roses. Her stockings were rolled above the knee, and held in place by elastic garters. Queenie felt herself blushing, and she looked for a reaction on Goldner's face. There was none. He seemed neither interested nor impressed.

Queenie knew very little about strip acts. She had seen a few in films, of course, though they always remained well within the bounds of decency. She gave Goldner what she hoped was a sexy smile, then raised one leg to pull the stocking off slowly.

"That's not necessary," he said. "If you get the job, I'll teach you what to do."

A little disappointed, she continued undressing. She had some difficulty with the bra. She turned her back to Goldner and struggled with the fasteners, but once she had it off, she found she couldn't face him. She could hear him puffing on his cigar, but the thought of standing there in front of him, naked to the waist, was more than she could bear. She made up her mind to do it, closed her eyes, folded her arms in front of her chest and turned around very slowly.

"Continue," Goldner said quietly.

It was cold onstage, but she felt burning hot, as if she had a fever. She wondered if it was possible for one's whole body to blush. Then, somewhere in the back of her mind, she remembered the dancers swirling in the light from the chandeliers in the hotel ballroom, the gleaming Rolls-Royces drawn up in the street outside, the furs and jewels shining on the women as they gathered their long skirts to walk from their cars to the door of the hotel.

She dropped her hands and began to pull down her panties.

"Very, very nice," Goldner said with satisfaction. "You can stop now."

Hastily she pulled the panties back up again. Goldner had seen enough—he'd decided against her before she'd even finished undressing for him. She was outraged at the unfairness of it. She opened her eyes. He was holding her clothes in his lap, neatly folded. "That's it?" she asked.

"That's it."

She put her hands on her hips, forgetting for a moment that her breasts were bare. She was furious with herself—and not a little angry at Goldner, sitting there with her clothes like a frog on a lily pad—that she had missed her chance. At least she wanted to know why. "What did I do wrong?" she asked, surprised at the firmness in her voice.

Goldner looked surprised. "Wrong? There's nothing wrong. I've simply seen enough."

"Do I have a job?"

"Of course you do. I'll tell you a secret—there was never any doubt in my mind."

"Then why did you make me undress?"

"It was a test, dear. That's all. Some young women find it difficult to do this sort of thing. Others enjoy it."

"I didn't enjoy it."

"I know. That's good. The ones who enjoy it are always trouble, you see. They end up sleeping with the customers." He stood up, walked over to the stage and handed her back her clothes. "You can get dressed now, Queenie," he said. "You're a good girl."

She pressed her clothes against her chest, hardly able to believe that her chance had paid off. "I *really* have a job?" she asked.

"Absolutely. You have a very good body, you know . . . and the face is—remarkable! There are all sorts of things you have to learn, of course. . . . Never mind, I'll teach you."

"Will I have to take all my clothes off?"

"Not at all. You'll have a costume that will preserve the legal degree of decency to the letter. The English are prudes at heart. They prefer the illusion of nakedness to the real thing."

"When do I start?"

"Come and see me tomorrow in the afternoon." He paused. "You don't need to bring Morgan with you."

Queenie nodded. The future already seemed much brighter to her. She turned her back to Goldner and started to dress. It was odd, she thought, but she felt more embarrassed dressing in front of a man than taking off her clothes. There was a screen to one side of the stage and she slipped behind it to pull her dress over her head. Then she looked out over the top of it. Goldner was standing up, rubbing his hands together like a man who has just found a shilling on the street. She nerved herself up to ask Goldner the one question that mattered to her most. "How much do I get paid?" she called out boldly.

"Seven pounds a week," he said with a nervous blink.

She said nothing. She was unable to speak. It was an awesome amount—more than even the best-trained typist could hope to make. She could hardly even believe her good luck.

Goldner hesitated, waiting for a reply. "All right," he said, "ten pounds. But that's my best offer. And you'll have to work for it."

She stared at him, embarrassed that he had misinterpreted her silence. Then she smiled. "Thank you," she said.

Goldner sighed with relief. She was a bargain at ten. And he liked the way she had held out to see if he would go higher than seven. It was one thing to be beautiful—but to get to the top a girl needed brains as well. The dumb ones got pregnant or ran off with unsuitable men.

He helped her on with her coat. "Morgan will be waiting outside," he said. "He'll be pleased, I suppose."

"Yes," she said rather glumly.

"You'll tell him about your good fortune?"

Queenie thought for a moment. "If you don't mind, I thought I might say it was seven pounds."

Goldner patted her on the shoulder. "That's the ticket," he said cheerfully.

The girl had a good head on her, he told himself.

She would go a long way.

"Seven pounds a week!" Morgan said. "You should have asked for fifteen. Why didn't you talk to me first?"

Queenie didn't answer. Indeed, she could hardly hear him. The

Painted Lady, on Greek Street, was jam-packed with people having a quick drink at intermission time, and the noise was deafening.

Queenie had seldom been in a pub, but it was not, she decided, one of the English institutions that appealed to her. Morgan could sit in pubs for hours, but Queenie felt more lonely and out of place than ever among all these people who seemed so loudly sure of themselves. She knew nobody in this country and had no real sense of what it was like beyond what she picked up from reading the *Daily Express* and listening to Morgan's account of his day.

"Why didn't you talk to me before accepting the job?" he repeated.

She wondered why Morgan was so upset, then realized what the real problem was—her own salary was more than his. She made as much for taking off her clothes as Morgan made for playing the saxophone—and with the promise of better things to come. Goldner had even given her an advance of one week's salary—a fact which Queenie had prudently withheld from Morgan.

"He offered me the job. I took it. What was there to talk about?"

"You wouldn't have *had* the bloody job without me. You should have let me talk to Goldner."

Queenie sipped her ginger beer. Morgan looked flushed and angry, and she had no desire to provoke a scene in a crowded pub. He knew he had lost face with Goldner. He already suspected he had lost face with Queenie. "I know that," she said quietly, hoping for a truce. "I'm grateful, Morgan."

"I don't need your bloody gratitude," he said thickly, the drink beginning to slow him down, as it always did.

He lit a match with some difficulty, then found he couldn't get the flame anywhere near the tip of the cigarette. He kept trying until he burned his fingers, gave a startled cry of pain and dropped the match. "I burned myself," he said, in the small, surprised voice of a child, but there was no sympathy in Queenie's eyes—a fact which was clear to Morgan, even drunk as he was.

"I thought we'd be happy together," he said. "That's why we came here, you know. We've both got jobs now. We can find a nice place to live, make a life of it . . . I still love you, Queenie. You know that. I'm sorry about what happened."

Queenie knew that all right. Morgan told her he loved her a hundred times a day, and that he was sorry even more often. In India, he had seemed to be older, wiser, more sophisticated, even attractive, but now that she knew she could survive on her own here, he had somehow shrunk to a pathetic figure, a small, mean, frightened man who drank too much and was willing to settle for the most modest and boring of goals, and unlikely to attain even those.

Queenie looked at him with cold objectivity. His tie was askew, revealing the collar stud, his eyes were glazed, his mustache ragged and badly trimmed. He was holding his handkerchief around his burned fingers. The door behind them opened as people began to make their way noisily back to the theaters, and the cool night air sobered Morgan briefly. "I sometimes wish we were back in India," he said softly. "Don't you?"

There was a moment of silence—one of those sudden accidental pauses when everybody in a crowded bar stops talking at the same time. Queenie heard a woman whisper piercingly to her companion, "Do take your eyes off that divine dark-haired girl, Basil! It's madly rude of you!"

The noise level rose again, so Queenie missed Basil's reply, but she heard the woman laugh and caught a few words rising above the din. "I'd give a lot for a face like that," Queenie heard the woman say.

Queenie turned to look at them in the mirror as they left the pub. All she could see of "Basil" was a broad back in a well-tailored overcoat with a velvet collar. His companion was as bright and colorful as one of the gold-and-enamel brooches Queenie had admired in the windows of Asprey's in Bond Street. Her long Nile-green dress was partly covered by a short coat of some fluffy white fur, and she wore an emerald necklace and a tightly fitting hat made of iridescent green feathers.

The woman paused at the door and looked back at Queenie. There was no jealousy or hostility in her eyes—the tiny heart-shaped face, with its scarlet-painted lips, absurdly thin plucked eyebrows and black-rimmed eyes reflected admiration rather than envy. She swept out into the night, leaving behind her, in the stale air of the pub, a trace of expensive scent.

Queenie sniffed it enviously. It was sweet, but almost animal-like, not at all the faded-flower odor of cheap scent. She tried to imprint the smell in her memory for the day when she could afford to buy expensive perfume.

Morgan was still staring at her, waiting for her to say something, his eyes full of guilt, or love—perhaps the two were the same for him. "You could go back," she said quietly.

He laughed harshly. "To jail?"

"You could persuade Mrs. Daventry to drop the charges. Pay her back for the bracelet bit by bit. It's possible."

"Would you go back with me?" he asked.

Queenie shook her head. "I'll never go back."

Morgan picked up his glass and swallowed the rest of his drink. His eyes closed briefly as the whiskey hit his stomach with a jolt that was almost electric, then he waited a second or two for the glow to spread through his body. "Well, that's it, then."

It was as if he'd said, *You'll never get rid of me*, Queenie thought. She had come to England for a chance to escape from drowning in the tight little world of Anglo-Indians, but Morgan had come here for her. However many times he said he was sorry, he could always argue somewhere deep in his mind, she was sure, that he had been justified because she had cheated him of his reward.

"I want to go home now," she said.

"Plenty of time. I'll just have another drink." Morgan stood up, steadied himself and looked toward the bar as if getting there was an athletic feat that required all his concentration. "I say," he said casually, "can you give me a pound?"

Queenie shook her head.

"Didn't Goldner give you a few quid in advance?"

"Of course not."

He swayed back and forth a moment, and it seemed to Queenie that he was about to lose his temper. She struggled not to flinch. She was not afraid of being hit, but she hated the embarrassment of a public scene. Then, surprisingly, Morgan sat down with as much dignity as he could manage.

"Oh, Queenie," he said sadly, "you're a bloody bad liar."

"Trust me, dear."

Queenie wondered if she had a choice. They sat in his basement office at the club. The one small barred window looked out over the areaway and a steep flight of steps. A vividly painted sign read "Club Paradise—Exotic Floor Show—Members Only!"

During working hours a doorman stood outside to explain that a year's membership could be purchased for two guineas. The arcane mysteries of England's licensing laws required this small but profitable subterfuge. A "members only" club could serve liquor at any hour of the day or night, the only inconvenience of the law being that the establishment was also obliged to serve food, which few of the customers wanted, and which put Goldner to the expense of keeping a kitchen staff. He had solved this problem by adding a charge for supper to the bill. Every customer was served a plate of canned corned-beef sandwiches, whether they asked for them or not, and charged one guinea for the privilege. Often a single plate of sandwiches made its way from table to table through the night, since only the most ignorant and foolhardy of customers would touch them. If they were properly dusted off, they could sometimes be used again the next night.

"What's wrong with the name I've got?" she asked.

"My dear, there's nothing *wrong* with it. Onstage, however, it will lack class."

"I've always been called Queenie."

"Yes, and your loved ones will surely wish to continue calling you by that name, which has a certain charm. But you need a stage name. Besides, there's nothing wrong with changing one's name, dear. Look at Lord Montague—he was once Samuel Isaacs. Look at me—I was once Zoltan Goldschmeidner, and a good many other things as well, I might add. What's needed is something that emphasizes your—shall I say *exotic?*—quality. Queenie is too ordinary, believe me. I was thinking that something Oriental might be appropriate."

Queenie felt a sense of outrage. "Oriental?" she asked. "I'm English!"

Goldner peered at her, his face only a few inches from hers. He stuck out his lower lip. "So am I," he said. "I am proud to hold a British passport—so much better than any of my previous ones. But I am merely suggesting your act might have—an Oriental flavor."

"Please, Mr. Goldner . . . my Ma would hate that."

Goldner sat back and examined the ceiling, as if searching for inspiration. "Ah, mothers," he said with a deep sigh, a mournful expression on his face. "What would your mother want most for you, dear? *She would want you to succeed!* Isn't that what every mother wants for her children?"

"Yes. But she wouldn't want people to think I'm Oriental."

"Does she live in this country? No? Then she doesn't have to know, does she? Do you write to her?"

"Well, no . . ."

"You must. You must!" Goldner scolded. "Mothers worry, if they don't hear from their daughters, they worry." Goldner's cheeks glistened. "Sometimes they even make inquiries, write letters to the authorities—that sort of thing." He placed his free hand on his heart. "Do you love your mother, Queenie?"

"Of course I do."

"Then you must promise me to write to her."

"I've been trying, but it's difficult, you see . . ."

"Of course it is. I didn't mean a long letter, my dear. Not at all. I'm sure your mother doesn't want to know everything you're doing. Mothers only want the good news. Send her a postcard, Queenie. To-day. *Lots* of postcards from now on. 'I'm well, I'm happy, I hope you are, I love you,' and so on. That sort of thing . . . Your mother lives in India?"

"Yes," she admitted. She wondered why she had never thought of postcards and decided to buy some on her way home.

Goldner's expression of sentimentality gave way to his usual bland shrewdness. He let go of her hand. "And Morgan is really your uncle?"

"Yes."

"On your mother's side, or your father's?"

"He's my mother's brother."

"I see. And your father? He too lives in India?"

"No. He was Irish." She paused. "I don't know where he is."

Goldner lit a cigar. The problems and prejudices of India were foreign to him, but he had no difficulty in understanding the situation or in appreciating Queenie's reluctance to appear in "exotic" roles. He wondered how dark Queenie's mother was, but as long as she stayed in India, he reflected, it hardly mattered. He puffed on his cigar thought-fully. "You must understand," he said, "that the reason I hired you—and agreed to such a generous salary for a beginner—is that you're spe-cial. You don't look like everybody else. If I wanted a blond English girl, there are dozens to pick from. And for much less than ten pounds a week. The fact that you are a little exotic is what we call in business an asset. Besides, to tell you the truth, I already *have* the costume, you see. Veils and so on. It was the right girl I was looking for. The cos-tume cost me a good deal more than ten pounds. It's easier to find a new girl than to change the costume. You understand me?"

Queenie understood. She nodded.

"Good. I'll tell you something about Englishmen, Queenie. They don't have romantic illusions about their own women. Myself, I find Englishwomen singularly attractive—but the point is that your average Englishman doesn't. He likes a bit of mystery. So we are going to make you mysterious. Not *too* mysterious, of course—he doesn't like out-and-out foreigners, either. We shall say that you're an English girl who learned to dance in India. There you have it. The best of both worlds."

Queenie thought about it, only too aware that it made no sense. English girls in India hardly ever mixed with the natives—it was unthinkable—and the kind of dancing Goldner had in mind, she guessed, was done by nautch girls, strictly for the entertainment of the wealthier Muslims. Still, it was beginning to dawn on her that Goldner was offering her an opportunity to invent a new past for herself—one that did not include Morgan. And apart from Morgan himself, who would question it? There were very few advantages to being Anglo-Indian in India, and fewer still in England.

She tried to imagine some way in which an English girl would have learned how to dance like a Muslim, but drew a blank. "I don't see how it could happen," she said glumly.

"Oh, come now! Everything can happen. In a country like India? I've read my Kipling, you know."

Queenie had read her Kipling, too, since it was a staple at school, but her India was very different from Kipling's. "Calcutta isn't at all like *The Jungle Book*," she explained. "Or *Kim*."

"Forget Calcutta! When people think of India, they think of the maharajahs, tiger hunts, jewels, painted elephants—not Calcutta."

"I did once see a painted elephant. Two, in fact."

"There you are. Be reasonable. Nobody is going to know the truth or ask any questions. You could have been brought up in a maharajah's palace, after all. Who's to say you weren't?"

"I don't see how."

"An adopted child?"

"Why would a maharajah adopt an English girl? It isn't possible, Mr. Goldner. And there are plenty of people in England who know about India, too."

Goldner sighed. "I'm only trying to help," he complained. "Don't the maharajahs have English people in their palaces?"

"I don't know. I've never even *seen* a maharajah. I suppose they have Englishmen to run their armies. . . ." And then it occurred to Queenie that of course that was nearly *always* the case—it was, in fact, such a source of aggravation to the native princes that they were constantly complaining about it as an invasion of their rights. She had seen such stories often in the newspapers, usually on the front page, which faced her at teatime when Morgan opened the paper to look at the race results.

"Your father could be a colonel, a—what do they call them?"

"A sahib?"

"Exactly."

"If he's a colonel, why would I be dancing here?"

Goldner was startled by the girl's common sense, but not by any means deterred. "You ran away from home," he suggested. "It's best to leave the details—fluid. You grew up in the glittering palace of a maharajah—"

"Which one?"

"That's one of the things that we'll leave fluid," Goldner snapped impatiently. "Surrounded by wealth, glamour, brought up in two worlds, known to one and all as . . . What were you known as?"

"I don't know."

"Lakshmi?"

Queenie giggled.

"Hard to pronounce," Goldner muttered, dismissing the thought. "How about Rani? Isn't that what Indian royalty is called?"

Queenie thought about it. "A maharani is the wife of a maharajah, I think," she explained. "A princess would be maharanji. I suppose an English princess would be a maharanji-sahib, or something like that. . . ."

Goldner waved his cigar to show his lack of interest in the finer points of Indian court usage or Hindustani. "Rani will do very nicely. We won't tell them your family name. You don't want to disgrace your father, and so . . . A nice touch."

Queenie struggled for a moment to come to grips with this sudden elevation. She wondered if she could carry it off. The more she thought about it, the less likely it seemed to her that anybody would challenge it. It sounded implausible to her, but apart from that, there were certain obvious attractions. It would be difficult to go through life pretending that she hadn't been born in India or inventing for herself a childhood in some other country. Too much of what she knew—and was—had come from India for her to deny it completely, and she was wise enough to know she could hardly sustain a total fabrication over the long haul. Some Anglo-Indian girls, she had been told, claimed to be Spanish or Italian when they got to England, to explain their dark exotic look, but she didn't know enough about Spain or Italy to run that risk.

She felt a wary sense of relief. All she had to do was to place herself in Goldner's hands and she was no longer an Anglo-Indian—the whole thing was so simple that it almost seemed like a miracle. This was a perfectly acceptable way out of the dilemma, provided nobody probed too deeply into it—and provided Morgan kept his mouth shut, she suddenly realized, with a sinking heart. For it was instantly clear to her that there was no way in which he could fit into the story.

"What about Morgan?" she asked. "He won't like it."

"I'll take care of Morgan. If he wants to work, he'll do as he's told." Goldner's voice held a faint but distinct promise of menace, and it occurred to Queenie that there was a side to his character she hadn't seen yet. She noted the fact for future reference—Goldner was not nearly as soft as he looked. "Of course, he's family, and one has to respect that, but the less he hangs around you, the fewer explanations there will be to make. You understand?"

She understood. She could pretend to be anything she wanted with a fair chance of getting away with it. Morgan couldn't. She nodded.

"It's not uncommon. I have relatives for whom I have the greatest respect, even affection, that I wouldn't let within a mile of me . . . my Aunt Sara, for example—but never mind that." He shuddered. "The point is, let *me* handle Morgan. I'll put it to him that all this is as much in his interest as yours, or mine. Besides—family is family. He ought to be pleased for you."

That seemed unlikely to Queenie, but she indicated that she was happy to let Goldner break the news.

"Splendid." Goldner had a ring of sweat around his forehead. "He *is* your nearest living relative in England, is he not?"

Queenie turned the question over in her mind. It was hard to think of Morgan in that context, but it was undoubtedly true. She wondered what Goldner had in mind, then almost decided she was being suspicious for no reason, except that he had put the question with such elaborate casualness that it was impossible *not* to be suspicious. She wished there were somebody she could trust completely. Morgan she knew she couldn't trust—not anymore. Goldner she *wanted* to trust, but he was a stranger, and hoped to make money out of her.

Quite suddenly she was gripped by a sense of loneliness, but then she told herself she had traveled thousands of miles for this kind of chance—for *any* kind of chance—and it was too late to get cold feet now. She was on her own.

"I like to know as much as I can about the people who work for me, dear—*particularly* when I'm going to invest a good deal of money in their career, as I am in yours. . . . You are how old, by the way?"

"Nineteen."

Goldner smiled sadly. "One should never lie to one's partner, dear, and I want you to think of us, always, as—partners."

"Well, I'm really almost eighteen . . ."

"That's more like it," Goldner said. "Trust—it's the most important thing in business, dear." He turned to his desk and fiddled with the papers on it, then passed Queenie a short, typed document. "Paperwork," he sighed. "So much nonsense about taxes, pension stamps, work permits . . . All governments exist only to make the businessman's life harder. If you'd just sign at the bottom of the page . . ."

Queenie paused for a moment as Goldner handed her his gold fountain pen, the top already unscrewed.

"What am I signing?" she asked.

"A receipt for the ten pounds I have given you in advance. Also, you give me the right to use photographs of you to advertise the show, for publicity, and so on . . . a mere formality. Read it, read it, dear."

"Shouldn't I talk to Morgan?"

"If you like." Goldner seemed indifferent to the suggestion. His voice became a few degrees cooler. "Frankly, I think you'd do better to follow *my* advice than his."

He looked disappointed rather than annoyed, but there was no doubt about his displeasure. "I can do so much for you, Queenie, and I will. But I can't do it if you have to go running back to Morgan over every little detail. After all, even if he *is* your uncle, he doesn't own you, does he?"

"No, he doesn't own me," Queenie said, and to prove it, both to Goldner and herself, she signed her name boldly.

Goldner's good humor returned instantly. "If you would just initial the stamps at the top, please. There, and *there* . . . splendid. I'll have a word with Morgan later on. Leave it all to me. Wait until you see your costume!"

He retrieved his fountain pen from her hand, carefully screwed the cap on and returned it to his pocket. The signed document he placed on the desk, next to another, bulkier one in a pale-blue binder threaded with red silk tape.

It occurred to Queenie that so far there had been no mention of what she was expected to do onstage. Goldner did not seem worried, but she asked him anyway. She had no desire to make a fool of herself in front of an audience, even for ten pounds a week.

He looked surprised. "Do? My dear, you'll walk slowly onto the stage, take your clothes off very slowly and gracefully, then put them back on again, even more slowly. That's all."

"I don't have to do a dance?"

"No dance. You do what I tell you. Just remember to pick out one man in the audience and look right at him all the time."

"It doesn't sound like much of an act."

"It isn't, dear. It's *you* they'll be coming to see, not the act. They'll be coming to see the most beautiful girl in London, Queenie. And though it will probably cost me money sooner or later to tell you this—they won't be disappointed."

CHAPTER 8

THE FOURSOME SAT at a table near the stage. At the sight of them through the peephole in the door to his office, Goldner emerged to greet them personally. He knew ladies when he saw them, which admittedly wasn't often. Both women wore evening gowns and fur wraps. He suspected they were slumming; from the sound of their laughter, he was right.

He did not take offense—the rich had atrocious manners everywhere, indeed, the richer the worse—but he was not in business for his ego. Once a few rich people came, if only to laugh, others would follow.

Goldner moved quickly toward them, the smile incandescent on his fat face, his arms outstretched as if he were about to give them communion. Like many fat men he had tiny feet, and in his working clothes—a dinner jacket and a starched white shirt and waistcoat—he looked like a penguin hurrying to greet a party of explorers at the edge of his ice floe.

By the time he arrived at the table, he was sweating so heavily that he had to pause and mop his face. He gave a deep bow in the general direction of the ladies. He pulled back their chairs and helped to seat them, clucking softly in what passed for admiration of their elegance and beauty.

Surreptitiously he ran his palm over their furs. Certain things could not be faked, he knew, and good mink was one of them. His fingertips told him that these two young women were rich, or had rich lovers or fathers, since neither of them wore a wedding ring. They had the look of debutantes, though he judged them to be in their mid-twenties. A certain theatrical quality suggested they might be actresses, but probably the kind with rich fathers.

He kissed the hand of each, busied himself with lighting their cigarettes, and only then turned and shook the hand of the taller of the two men. "What brings *you* here, Lucien?" he asked.

The young man laughed. He was tall—he towered above Goldner—and so handsome that the only flaw in his face was a certain self-satisfaction. There was a hint of self-indulgence in the lips, but the dark-blue eyes were intelligent and self-mocking, with an intensity that suggested he was something more than just a spoiled, pretty young man—a young man on the make perhaps. He wore his well-cut clothes with a carelessness that suggested an artist rather than a socialite.

"*La nostalgie de la boue, mon cher,*" he said. "What else?" His French was flawless—clearly not a second language—but the restraint of his gestures was entirely English. "These ladies wanted to see the lower depths of Soho. They're bored with Mayfair, Goldner. They yearn for the lowlife. So naturally I brought them here. I suspect they will be disappointed—in fact, I see they already are. Is there any chance you will be raided by the police tonight?"

"Not much, my dear Lucien—considering what I pay them."

"A pity. Under the circumstances. It would have spiced up the evening for them. May I introduce you, *cher* Goldner? Lady Cynthia Daintry, Miss Margot Feral—and Mr. Basil Goulandris. Goulandris, I'm sure, is a familiar name to you."

"Indeed!" Goldner said with something approaching reverence. He stared at the bottle of champagne the headwaiter was revolving in an ice bucket, his hand artfully spread to conceal the label. Goldner frowned. "Bring a bottle of *French* champagne," he said. "With my compliments."

Lucien raised an eyebrow and gave Goldner an ironic smile. Basil Goulandris took no notice, however. He was accustomed to being offered a bottle of champagne wherever he went. There wasn't a restaurant or a nightclub in London that would have dared to present him with a check, nor did he pay for cigarettes, flowers, liquor, food, theater tickets, cars or clothes. He was always accompanied by a beautiful woman, although his companion this evening, Miss Feral, was somewhat overshadowed by Lady Cynthia, who glittered like a bird of paradise.

Goulandris was big, red-faced, overweight, with the complexion and the irritable temper of a heavy drinker. He stared for a moment at the cigar case protruding from Goldner's pocket, until Goldner pulled it out and handed it over.

Goulandris removed a cigar, sniffed it, clipped the end and waited while Goldner lit it for him. He gave a couple of puffs, took the other cigar, slipped it into his pocket and gave the empty case back to Goldner. He did not thank him. "I don't know what the hell we're doing in this hole," he said. "There's no story here."

"The ladies wanted to see Soho."

"It's a waste of bloody time."

"Not tonight, it's not," Goldner said. "I have a new artiste." He joined his thumb and forefinger in a circle and brought his fingers to his lips with an audible kiss, like a chef expressing satisfaction with his own work. "You will be astonished," he continued. "You have never in your life seen a girl like this one!"

Goulandris yawned. "What is the name of this wonder?"

"Rani."

Goulandris laughed harshly, a grating, croaking, booming sound that was louder than the pop of the champagne cork as the headwaiter levered it out of the bottle. "She'll have to be quite something to overcome that!"

Lucien removed Lady Cynthia's hand from his shoulder, kissed it, then clasped it firmly in his fingers. It was not so much a gesture of affection as a way of getting her to stop touching him.

"We shall see," he said.

Queenie faced the dusty curtains and held her breath. She did not share Goldner's enthusiasm for her costume, which consisted mostly of unwieldy layers of transparent, flesh-colored gauze bordered in embroidered gold thread. On her head she wore a piece of costume jewelry of vaguely Oriental design, from which more gauze veils were suspended, covering her face.

The whole thing, she thought, was like wearing a tent. Even after a week, she was still not used to the way it scratched against her skin. Underneath it she wore a flesh colored G-string and two round pieces of costume jewelry pasted to her breasts, barely covering her nipples. Goldner's warning rang in her ears—she was to move slowly, do nothing fancy and keep her eyes on the audience. "Ten minutes," he had said, right from the beginning. "That's all you get, and all you need." And he had been right.

It had taken Queenie some time to understand what Goldner was after. He *wanted* her costume to be concealing, so that she would appear to the audience at first as a tentlike figure shrouded in flowing gauze that rippled in the air, clinging to her just long enough to suggest the body beneath. Goldner knew what he had, and he calculated that a degree of suspense would lend drama to Queenie's appearance. "Make them wait for it," he told her. "Don't be in a hurry."

He firmly discouraged any attempts on her part to behave like a stripper. "Strippers we've got," he had said, "and who cares?" She was to be, as he put it, the Asprey's, the Cartier, of his place. "When you go to a cheap jewelry shop," he explained, "they show you glass cases full of flashy jewelry, as if they want to blind you so you don't look too closely at the goods. But when you go to a shop like Cartier"—his voice dropped as if he were describing Lourdes—"they show you *one* piece at a time on a black velvet tray. That's all. Class, you see."

Queenie listened. She saw. She had not chosen this particular way out of obscurity, but since it was the only one she had been offered, she was determined to make the best of it. Hidden away at the back of the room, she watched the other acts, and she soon understood exactly what Goldner meant. It was not just that the girls couldn't hold a candle to her—they threw themselves heart and soul into the grim struggle to capture the attention of the audience, shaking their breasts, sticking their bottoms out, tossing their undergarments out to the far corners of the room, but the harder they worked, the more they tried to please, the less the audience was interested. If she tried to do the same, she would be nothing more than another strip act. She made up her mind: she would not try to please the customers; she would *conquer* them. Her act would have to be herself—it was all she had.

She practiced it at home, watching herself in the cracked and mottled pier glass, trying to make every movement as restrained and graceful as possible. It was not a nautch dancer that she was trying to imitate—the gyrating, plump "belly dancer" of the East—but rather the stylized grace of Balinese temple dancers, photographs of whom Goldner had dug up for her.

He had given her the key to her own act, but it was she who provided the details, taking the bus in the mornings to the Museum of Natural History, where Goldner had suggested she might find more and better photographs. For the first time in her life, she was interested in something, to her own surprise—and for the first time, too, sadly aware of her own lack of education. All over the world, it seemed, there were cultures in which beauty was worshipped for its own sake. She marveled at the costumes, the fantasies of makeup, the elaborate ritual

movements, haunted by the idea that if someone could only show her
how to draw all these elements together, she could be twice as good. As
she stood in the musty halls of the museum, or alone in her room in
front of the mirror, she also came to believe it was *possible*.

Now that she had a goal, life with Morgan was easier—besides, so
far, their hours were different. She worked during the day, rehearsing
with Goldner, while Morgan slept. By the time he arrived home she
had been asleep for hours, and sometimes she did not even hear him
settle down on the floor with a groan. Whatever Goldner had told him
seemed to have worked—he was resentful, but otherwise on his best
behavior. At times she caught a note of triumph in his voice, or a quick,
sly glance in her direction, as if Morgan had done something particularly clever that he was keeping secret from her, something at her expense—but she was too busy to pay much attention. Some nights he
did not come home at all, and she did not ask him where he had
been—she was merely relieved to have the room to herself.

The first night she did the show, she was almost paralyzed with stage
fright, but there were so few people in the room that it was not, she
discovered, all that different from practicing at home. She moved with
exaggerated slowness, afraid of tripping or making a fool of herself in
some way, and the more slowly she moved, the quieter the customers
became. It was not until the curtain came down after her first show
that Queenie realized she had succeeded. She had stepped out there
into the stage light, without smiling or wiggling her hips, and made
them look at *her*—made them feel, in fact, that they were privileged
to do so.

Still, she was cautious. Every night she waited for the spell to break,
for someone to laugh or shout a rude remark or give her a catcall. So
far it had never happened, but tonight, as she did every night, Queenie
trembled for fear the moment would come.

The curtains parted. The orchestra—she could hear Morgan's saxophone—slipped into a vaguely Oriental theme. Queenie moved forward into the glare of the spotlight, which momentarily blinded her.
She stood for a moment in the middle of the stage, breathing deeply
and waiting for her eyes to adjust to the light.

Queenie could sense that everyone in the room was staring at her—
this happened every night, and it still surprised her. She breathed out
slowly, feeling the usual tremors of stage fright in her knees, then
slowly, carefully, unfastened the veil over her face and dropped it to
the floor. She did it in extreme slow motion, making a complete turn

so that when she faced the audience again, her face was visible to them for the first time.

She stood motionless, the huge dark eyes looking out toward the audience. Queenie was following Goldner's advice, trying to find one person to look at, as she always did. In the dark beyond the spotlights, however, the faces in the audience were scarcely more than pale blurs.

The light shifted slightly. Suddenly she saw a young man sitting not more than a few feet away from her, beside the stage. He had long blond hair brushed back sleekly, dark-blue eyes that were wide open in astonishment, and a fine straight nose. His lips were sensual for a man's—not thick, but perfectly shaped, with a deep V-shaped notch in the upper one. His skin was pale in the bright light, but had the undertones of a healthy outdoor man. It was, she suddenly realized, a face she had seen before, in the rain, the night Morgan had attacked her.

Queenie stared back at him, reached up to her shoulder, and removed the first layer of her flowing veils.

She would undress for him.

"I've seen her before somewhere," Lady Cynthia said. "Basil, darling, *haven't* we seen her before?"

Goulandris stared at the figure on the stage and shrugged. "It's possible," he admitted. "She *does* seem familiar. She's got a good face. I wonder who she is."

"She looks quite common to me," Miss Feral said. "A little Oriental blood there. Bedroom eyes, as my father would say."

Goulandris ignored her. He looked around the room to see if there was anybody important here. He found nobody. He was not surprised. "Let's go on to the Four Hundred or the C de P," he said.

"Oh *let's*," Lady Cynthia agreed, her voice rising in a clear, high-pitched bell-like tone. "Apart from the girl, this is all *too* depressing. And why on earth has the waiter brought us this ghastly plate of sandwiches?"

But Lucien paid no attention. His eyes were fixed on the stage, locked to Queenie's as she removed her first veil, folded it with slow, schoolgirl neatness and leaned over gracefully to place it on the floor. Her eyes never left his face for an instant.

"My dear," Lady Cynthia shrilled. "She's staring at you quite shamelessly! Do you know her? Is she someone you've photographed?"

Lucien shook his head. He was still holding Lady Cynthia's fingers.

"I still can't help thinking I've seen her somewhere before. I say, *do* stop squeezing my fingers. You're hurting me."

Lucien let go of her fingers. He hadn't even noticed he was holding them.

"It went well," Goldner said. He was sitting in his shirt-sleeves counting the receipts, a bottle of brandy in front of him. He wore purple sleeve garters.

Queenie had sensed this herself, though she didn't know why yet. The audience had been quiet, almost hushed, even when it was so late that the only customers were people willing to go anywhere as long as they could continue drinking. "I just did what you told me to," she said.

Goldner looked up from his accounts. "You're a good girl, Queenie."

"I looked at just one person in the audience each time. Who was the young man in the front at the first show?"

Goldner hesitated. "Which young man?" he asked.

"The good-looking one, sitting next to the lady with the beautiful clothes."

Goldner sighed. "Lucien Chambrun. Were you looking at *him*, my dear? The one you should have been looking at was Basil Goulandris. Still, you could hardly have known. . . . It was my fault entirely. I must remember to point out the right person for you to look at for each show."

Queenie was about to ask why Lucien Chambrun wasn't the right man to have looked at, but she saw Morgan standing in the door, looking at his watch and signaling for her to leave.

Goldner glanced toward him and frowned. "You'd better go now," he said.

There was no point in making Morgan angry, Goldner told himself—not so long as he was still needed, anyway. . . .

"What's the bloody meaning of this?" Morgan asked the next morning. He pushed the newspaper into Queenie's face so she couldn't even see what it was that had caught his eye.

She took the paper out of his hands and held it at a reasonable distance from her nose.

The headlines of the column read "Basil's Corner." Above it was a grainy, though somewhat flattering, photograph of the bulky red-faced man she had seen with Lucien Chambrun. She read the column quickly. Toward the end was a single paragraph, badly smudged by Morgan's damp fingers.

"The fashionables are going—of all places—to Soho these days, or rather nights. Seen at the Club Paradise (no, you've never heard of it before) were the lovely Lady Cynthia Daintry, daughter of the Marquess of Arlington by his second wife, and Miss Margot Feral, a 'close friend' of Dominick Vale, escorted by photographer Lucien Chambrun. . . . And what draws 'the fast set' to darkest Greek Street? The lovely Rani, whose exotic dance and striking beauty lit up the evening. And who is Rani, the girl with the bedroom eyes and the million-pound future? Only yours truly knows the story, as usual. But I can report that her father is a burra sahib of the Raj, and that Rani was brought up as a princess in the palace of a maharajah. Rumor has it that the maharajah wanted to keep this sultry English rose in his harem, so she was sent to London to avoid a diplomatic incident. If her father ever discovers what she's doing here, there'll be H—— to pay! Which is why her real name's a secret."

At first Queenie couldn't believe it. Then she read it again, blushing. It was a sign—the first sign—that she was going to make it, that the risk and the long journey were going to pay off, that the future would be the kind of life she had always dreamed about. She wished she could send the piece to Ma, but since it was based on a total lie about who she was, it seemed unwise, and even unkind.

She was not foolish enough to suppose that one mention in a column would do it, or that it would happen overnight, but at least she was on the way. For a moment Queenie was tempted to hug Morgan, to share her triumph with him, but he stared at her glumly. "How could you tell such lies?" he asked. "And without even mentioning it to me?"

"It's just a story, Morgan. There's nothing wrong with publicity. Anyway, it was Mr. Goldner who gave this man Goulandris the story, not me."

"Mr. Goldner this, Mr. Goldner that," Morgan said angrily. "You've got him twisted around your little finger, just like that fellow Pugh."

"It's nothing like that!" Queenie cried, furious with Morgan for spoiling her moment of happiness, but Morgan seemed to realize he had gone too far and muttered an apology. Queenie sighed. Morgan knew he was being left behind. And no doubt he had been told that his job depended on keeping his mouth shut. He could hardly be expected to be happy about her success in the circumstances, she told herself.

She knew she would have to find a place to live without Morgan very soon, and that it would be a painful and difficult moment.

She was interested to learn that Lucien Chambrun was a photographer. She wondered what it would be like to have her picture in the newspapers.

She decided it would be very nice indeed.

The next night he was there again. Once again he was dressed in white tie and tails, but this time he was alone. He sat motionless through Queenie's performance. He did not touch his champagne.

Goldner had not provided much in the way of dressing rooms for his performers. Part of the basement was partitioned off with sheets of unfinished plywood and curtains, forming a series of cubicles, each of which contained a chair, a dressing table and a mirror. Between performances, Queenie was in the habit of sitting in her cubicle wearing an old terry-cloth robe, since her costume, with its elaborate layers of veils, was hardly suitable for lounging. Goldner had warned her never to mix with the customers. She read movie magazines and experimented with her makeup, but it was a lonely place to be, since the other girls, who envied her solo role, ignored her.

What they resented most was her beauty. Most of them had long since lost their figures to drink, hard living and a diet of cheap, starchy food. In six-inch heels and black mesh stockings, their legs were presentable, from a distance even sexy, but when they took the stockings off between shows, they puffed out like fat sausages, crisscrossed with the deeply indented pattern of the mesh. Their lives had been reduced to a losing struggle against gravity. One look at Queenie undermined all their hard work. They loathed her on sight.

Queenie longed for companionship but knew there was no way she could expect to find it among her brassy-haired fellow workers. She did not think of herself as a standoffish kind of person, and their hostility had caught her by surprise, doubly hurtful and puzzling because she so desperately needed a friend. There was nobody she could talk to about what Morgan had done to her.

The curtain of her small cell was drawn back. A scrofulous-looking youth in a blue uniform handed her a huge bouquet of roses with an envelope pinned to the wrapping. She gave him sixpence, which he pocketed without saying thank you. Tipping was something she would have to learn about.

The writing paper was so thick that it must have cost a shilling a sheet. When she unfolded it, she found a copy of the story from "Basil's Corner," roughly torn out of the newspaper. The note itself, scrawled in a large, firm hand, merely read, "For Rani—the beginning!" It was unsigned.

Queenie held the flowers next to her face and smelled them. Nobody had ever sent her flowers before, and the smooth, glossy buds seemed like the promise of a new and different life. She tried to imagine how much they had cost, but she had no idea.

She had nothing to put the flowers in, so she propped them up on the makeup table next to her jar of cold cream, while she struggled into her veils for the next performance.

She looked at herself in the cracked, pitted mirror before putting the veil over her face. She would always be beautiful, she decided.

It was just a question of willpower.

When she appeared for her last performance of the night, Queenie was disappointed to see that Lucien Chambrun had gone. The table he had been sitting at was empty, and she found herself looking at it as she took off her veils, as if Chambrun were still sitting there. Soon it was taken by a well-dressed couple, fat and middle-aged, who stared at her without demonstrating any degree of pleasure—as if she were a church or a museum that had to be seen because it was on their tour. Queenie looked around and realized that the room was full of equally well-dressed people, most of them just as politely bored with themselves and the world as was this couple. The place was packed. In the dark, beyond the footlights, she could see Goldner moving from table to table, bowing and rubbing his hands together, like a man on whom fortune has at last smiled.

At the end of her performance, the audience applauded her quite warmly—these were the kind of people who had manners, unlike Goldner's usual "members," who either whistled, shouted or snored, depending on how drunk they were.

She peeked through the curtains. She could see Morgan and the rest of the band. He looked sullen and angry. He had wanted success for himself almost as much as he wanted her. He picked up his saxophone and began to play, too loudly and off-key, either as an act of defiance or because he was drunk.

She made her way down the grimy, rusted iron circular stairway to the basement, pulled back the curtain and realized that something was missing. For a moment, she couldn't imagine what it was, then it dawned on her—the flowers were gone, together with the note.

She tore back the curtain of the next dressing room. It was larger than hers—she was privileged to have her own room, small as it was. Three of the girls were sitting at a long plywood dressing table. One of them wore a stained kimono. The other two were naked except for their G-strings. The large blond woman named Mavis was bent over, a cigarette glued to the corner of her lips, carefully trimming her toenails. Mavis did not look up. "What the 'ell do you want?" she asked.

"Who took my flowers?"

"'Ear that? She wants to know what happened to her bloody flowers." The other two women shrugged. "Are you accusing *us* of stealing your flowers, Miss-bloody-Rani?" Mavis put down her nail scissors and stood up. She pulled the G-string down with one hand and gave herself a leisurely scratch. The coarse intimacy of the gesture revolted Queenie—she had no experience of seeing other women naked. In the harsh light from the bare overhead bulbs, Mavis' peroxided hair had a lifeless yellow glow that bore no resemblance to any normal coloring and stood out in startling contrast to the darker hair between her thighs. "Bugger off, you stuck-up cunt!" Mavis said. The others laughed harshly.

"I'm not going until I know who took my flowers."

"I don't have to take that from *you,* nor from any other *nigger.*" The word paralyzed Queenie. She wanted to run, but knew she had to stand her ground.

Mavis removed the cigarette from her lips with the thumb and forefinger of her left hand and spat a fleck of tobacco on the floor in front of Queenie's silver slippers. "Daughter of an English officer, indeed! Brought up as a bloody princess, my ass! I know all about you, my girl. Your pal Morgan told me the whole bloody story." Mavis pulled the G-string up with a sharp snap of the elastic strings.

Queenie stared at her. Her throat was so dry that for a moment she was unable to speak. "I don't know what you mean."

"The 'ell you don't!" Mavis put both hands beneath her heavy breasts and pushed them up, so that the nipples were pointing in Queenie's direction. "Morgan knows a real woman when he sees one." Mavis laughed harshly. "I'll tell you what happened to your flowers: your precious Morgan dumped them in the bloody rubbish bin. Now get out—Miss Rani!"

Mavis turned her back on Queenie and sat down in front of the dressing table. Queenie could see the three women's eyes staring at her in the reflection from the mirror. They were cold, hostile and triumphant. She felt like crying but couldn't bear the thought of these women seeing her tears.

Queenie plunged through the curtain blindly. Behind her the three women were laughing. She stood in the corridor for a moment, feeling more alone than ever. She wasn't shocked that Morgan had been sleeping with Mavis—after all, Queenie had made it clear *she* wasn't going to sleep with him—but to have told Mavis the truth about her was an act of betrayal as bad as raping her, the one thing she had never dreamed he would do, and for which, she knew, she would never forgive him.

Shaking, she opened the curtain of her dressing cubicle. A low, quiet voice in the half-darkness said, "I see my flowers aren't here. Is that a bad sign?"

Queenie was too startled to find a stranger in her dressing room to say anything, but the voice seemed to her strangely familiar. Then, as she blinked away her tears, she saw it was Lucien Chambrun, sitting on her chair, his feet on her dressing table beside his top hat and an ice bucket with a bottle of champagne and two glasses.

Quite suddenly she forgot about Morgan.

Close up, she found Chambrun even better-looking than he had seemed from the stage—or the pavement. His smile was warm, relaxed, faintly ironic, as if he was aware that his presence here in this shabby dressing room, his feet in black patent-leather dancing pumps resting on Queenie's makeshift dressing table, was pleasantly ridiculous, just the kind of romantic, spur-of-the-moment thing his friends would doubtless laugh about.

His feet were beautifully shaped—indeed, Queenie had never seen such narrow feet on a man. He seemed to notice them himself—at any rate, he looked at them with a certain amount of satisfaction long enough to realize they were in the wrong place. Hastily he put them on the ground and stood up, with a low bow that brought his head briefly to the same level as Queenie's, for he was considerably taller.

"Ah," he said, "you're so beautiful that I quite forgot my manners." He laughed as if he and Queenie were sharing a joke together, then took her hand, brought it to his lips and kissed it. His lips were pleasantly warm and dry. "Try not to hold your hand out so stiffly," he said.

"When a man picks up your hand, relax the muscles. The hand shouldn't be limp, you understand, nor rigid. . . . Most English-women haven't a clue. It's like picking up a piece of dried fish."

"You seem to know a lot about it." Queenie was startled that Chambrun was so free with his advice, but intrigued despite herself—these were exactly the kinds of things she wanted to learn.

"I'm half French. It's in the blood. The English know nothing about hand-kissing. Or food. Or women."

Chambrun opened the champagne swiftly and efficiently, without noise or drama, holding a handkerchief around the bottle as he un-corked it.

He filled two glasses expertly, handed one to Queenie and clicked his against hers. "Why were you crying?" he asked.

She almost denied it but changed her mind. "It's nothing," she said.

"An unhappy love affair?"

There seemed no point in telling him the truth. "No, no. Nothing like that. Were you responsible for that story?"

"I cannot tell a lie. At any rate to *you.* Yes, I was."

"Is Basil Goulandris a friend of yours? Mr. Goldner was very impressed."

"The word 'friend' cannot be used in the same breath with Basil. *Nobody* is a friend of Basil's—but of course everybody who matters knows him. I have done a few favors for Basil—now he has done a favor for me. I imagine he got fifty pounds or so from Goldner as well."

Queenie was slightly disappointed to learn the mechanics of getting a story in a gossip column. She had hoped that Goulandris had really been impressed by her—instead, it was a question of bribes and favors.

Chambrun noticed. He had the quick sensitivity of a man who genu-inely likes women. "Don't worry," he said. "You made an impression on Goulandris. He's corrupt, but he's not totally without integrity."

"Why did you do it for me?"

Chambrun indicated by lifting his glass that she should drink up, and drained his in one gulp. "That's a more difficult question," he said. "I had a certain instinct about you. Besides, I'll be quite honest: I like beautiful young women."

Queenie laughed. Chambrun was disarmingly frank. She found it hard to judge his age—certainly he was well under thirty—but she recognized a certain adolescent, playful quality in him, though whether it was real or simply something he was deliberately putting on for her benefit, because of her own youth, was impossible to tell.

"Did you like my act?" she asked.

Chambrun laughed. "How could I not enjoy watching you undress?" Then his expression became more serious. Queenie noticed a change in his eyes, as if they were focusing on her with a different kind of interest—a detached, professional concentration. Nobody had ever looked at her that way before, and the intensity of it took her by surprise.

Chambrun rubbed his chin thoughtfully, cocked his head, moved to one side to take a closer look at her profile, then pushed the shade back to expose the bare bulb of the light so he could see her better. He said nothing—his concentration was total. For a full minute he looked at her, as if she were simply an object on display, then he sighed. "The *act?* It's an act. Forget the act. You have great possibilities, you know. A face like yours is worth—God knows how much. Smile."

She smiled.

"Not like that. Smile as if you had something to smile about."

She tried again.

"Better," he said, but he was clearly not satisfied. "The makeup is all wrong, of course."

He might have been talking to himself, Queenie thought a little resentfully. She glanced in the mirror. She could see nothing wrong with her makeup.

His deep violet-blue eyes warmed as he smiled again. "Forgive me," he said, taking her hand. "I was thinking about how to photograph you. But that's not why I came here."

"Why *did* you come here, then?" she asked.

"Because I had to. Something about your face haunted me. As if I'd seen it before . . . When I saw you on the stage for the first time, in all these ridiculous veils, I thought you were the most beautiful woman I'd ever seen. Since then I've been thinking about you all the time. It's bad for my health and my work. So here I am, you see. Will you come and have supper with me?"

"It's very late . . ."

"What does that have to do with it? Are you hungry?"

"Yes. No. I don't know." Most of the time she was ravenous, so much so that she was sometimes even tempted to eat Goldner's sandwiches. It was nearly two in the morning, and it seemed to her unlikely that there were any restaurants open—which was a pity, since now that Chambrun had mentioned food, she was starving. "I could eat a horse," she said.

"That won't be necessary. And in England you'd be stoned to death. Drink up your champagne."

"I don't like champagne much."

"Nonsense! Everybody likes champagne. This isn't Goldner's Romanian swill. It's Dom Perignon. Try it."

Queenie sipped it. After a moment, she decided it was unlike the champagne Morgan had brought to the flat. She drained the glass.

"You see?" It occurred to Queenie that a part of Chambrun's charm came from the fact that he was so obviously used to getting his own way. He seemed to take it for granted that people would agree with him and fit into his plans—and very likely most did, she thought, especially women.

"I can't dress unless you go outside," she said.

He showed no inclination to leave. "I've already seen you take your clothes off. Twice, in fact," he said.

"That's different."

"I'll turn my back and close my eyes," he said. "I promise. But hurry. I'm hungry, too, Rani."

"That isn't really my name."

"Ah? I didn't suppose it was, actually. What *is* your name?"

She hesitated. "Queenie Kelley."

To her relief, he didn't laugh. "Mine is Lucien Chambrun," he said, with a slight bow. "Now that we've introduced ourselves—kindly get out of that costume. I will turn my back and think about supper."

He turned to the wall. Queenie hesitated, then began to remove her veils, hanging them up carefully. She stood almost naked for a moment, then carefully pulled off the small rhinestone circles that covered her nipples, an operation which was always slightly painful unless it was done just right, as they were held on by adhesive. She paused for a moment, wondering if Chambrun could see her in the mirror—then she decided that she didn't care if he could.

A pipe clanked loudly overhead, and somewhere in the depths of the basement a toilet flushed with a roar. She felt a sudden spasm of irritation at the grubbiness of the place and longed to get out of it. She struggled into her underwear, pulled on her stockings, did a quick pirouette in front of the mirror to check that her seams were straight, and began to slip her dress over her head.

On the other side of the curtain, someone coughed. "What's bloody keeping you?" she heard Morgan ask impatiently. "It's time to go home."

She heard him pull back the curtain, then give a small gasp of surprise and anger. The dress was still around her head, and she had no difficulty imagining the scene from Morgan's point of view, or his reaction to it. She pulled it down quickly, tearing a seam.

"Who the hell is this?" Morgan asked. Now that she could see him, Queenie could tell he had been drinking. His face was flushed, and his eyes had a guilty look despite his anger.

Chambrun turned around, uncovered his eyes and smiled, as if his good nature extended even to Morgan. "I haven't had the pleasure," he said warily, extending his hand toward Morgan, who ignored it.

"What's *he* doing here?" Morgan asked. His voice was blurred and thick.

"I invited him in."

"Well, invite him bloody out!"

Queenie stared at him in sudden fury. "The hell I will," she shouted. "Get out yourself, man!"

The words were stronger than she had ever used, but the tone was Ma's, and the accent Anglo-Indian. It was enough to startle Morgan. Like a man whose bluff has been called, he backed down instantly.

Chambrun put on his silk top hat, tilted it at a rakish angle and twisted his scarf around his neck. "It's been a pleasure to meet you," he said to Morgan, as if they had become the greatest of friends.

He took Queenie's coat off the hook, draped it over her shoulders—a gesture which was at once gallant and proprietorial—and picked up the champagne bucket.

"We must be going now," he said, and without pausing for an argument or further explanations, he took Queenie by the arm and pushed her past Morgan and through the curtain.

"Just a moment," Morgan called out, following them down the hall with drunken clumsiness, but Chambrun hurried Queenie up the stairs as if he hadn't heard him, his hand firmly holding her elbow. Without breaking stride, he pushed open the kitchen door, walked past the cook, who was mopping up the floor, and handed him the bottle of champagne and a pound note. "If anyone asks, you never saw us, my friend," he said.

The cook examined the bottle of champagne and nodded. "The back door is unlocked," he whispered, winking.

Outside in the street, a long, low sports car was parked. Chambrun opened the passenger door, emptied the ice bucket into the gutter, climbed in beside Queenie and accelerated with a roar as soon as the engine had started. "Who on earth was that?" he asked.

Queenie knew it was a question that would have to be answered sooner or later, but now that the moment arrived, she took a wild plunge. Later, she reasoned, she could always explain things to Chambrun if explanations seemed necessary. "He's a family friend," she said.

"Your guardian? That sort of thing?"

"That sort of thing, yes."

"He seemed very angry, this family friend."

"He drinks. It's a long story."

Chambrun nodded. Experience had taught him that when a woman was obviously lying it was wiser not to pursue the matter. "At least he's not your husband," he said.

"Did you think he was?"

"No, but one never knows. Listen, there's no place decent open at this time of night. We'll go to my flat and have supper there, all right?"

Queenie hesitated. She *wanted* to go to Chambrun's flat—in any case there was no place else to go, unless she went home to face Morgan. All the same, a cautious instinct told her to protest. "I'm not sure . . ." she said.

Chambrun drove with the same kind of impetuosity that he showed in his dealings with Queenie. She had never been in a fast sports car before. The speed would have made her uneasy, yet the excitement of sitting next to Chambrun in a car that must have cost several thousand pounds blunted her fear. The seats were made of rich leather, the dashboard was some kind of polished wood studded with instruments that gleamed in the darkness. Inside the car, speeding down the deserted streets, it was possible to imagine that she was rich.

"Oh, come now!" Chambrun said. "There's nothing wrong in having supper with a man in his flat. Not nowadays. You must have done it before."

"Of course I have!" she said indignantly. She hoped he wouldn't guess she was lying.

Queenie was fascinated by Chambrun's flat. One corner of the living room was obviously his working space; a camera stood on a tripod, facing a white backdrop and a three-sided mirror. The rest of the room was expensively overfurnished: there were Persian carpets on the floor, one on top of the other, two and three deep; a life-size marble nude served as a hatstand; the sofas were submerged in cushions, rugs, fur blankets, newspapers, books, magazines and clothing. Everywhere there was evidence of a comfortable bachelor life and of idiosyncratic taste.

Chambrun's preoccupation with women was on lavish display: against the walls were stacks of mounted enlargements, all of them photographs of women, some portraits, others nudes. One of them was of a thin, elegant blond woman, lying on her back in an ecstatic pose. Queenie recognized the face: it was the young woman who had been with Chambrun at the club the first night he came. It was signed "Cynthia." The name was followed by a long row of x's.

While Chambrun busied himself in the kitchen, Queenie examined the living room with curiosity, looking for clues to his character. That he led an intense social life was clear. His mantelpiece was stacked with heavy gilt-edged invitations of every size and shape, some formal ("The Marquess and Marchioness of Arlington take pleasure in inviting *Mr. Lucien Chambrun* . . ."), others bearing breathless personal messages in sprawling, feminine hands ("Do *please* come, darling . . .").

One invitation to a dinner party had a woman's garter pinned to it. A purple-inked handwritten note zigzagging carelessly across the invitations read, "You're a beast, but you're forgiven if you come, so don't be late, kisses."

It was signed "Cynthia," so boldly that the pen had left a big blot next to the name. Queenie noted that the invitation had been for this evening.

There were invitations to dinners, invitations to dances, so many invitations to cocktail parties that she couldn't begin to count them, invitations to art exhibits, film premieres, to vernissages. What on earth was a vernissage, she wondered? She felt a familiar impatience with her own ignorance. There was so much to learn!

Above the mantelpiece, singularly incongruous in these surroundings, was a large formal oil painting of a magnificently dressed young woman, with the swan neck, the classical profile and the tiny waist of an Edwardian beauty. The face and eyes were identical to Chambrun's; even the easy sensual smile—no more than the ghost of a smile on the woman in the painting—was similar.

Immediately below it was a small, ornately framed sepia photograph of a plump, bearded old gentleman holding a pug dog in his lap and smoking a cigar. The face was familiar, and she looked at it more closely. The inscription on the photograph read, "To my dearest Elsie, Affectionately, Bertie."

With a start Queenie realized that the face was familiar because she had seen it all her life on coins and statues in India—for it was undoubtedly that of the late King Edward VII.

The desk—an elegant antique which even Queenie, who knew nothing about furniture, could tell must be valuable—was littered with papers: bills, letters, tearsheets from *Vogue* and *Bazaar*. A camera had been placed on top of a pile of correspondence as a paperweight. The typed letter on top bore the instantly recognizable roaring lion trademark of MGM, embossed in gold at the top, and the words "Metro-Goldwyn-Mayer Studios."

Of the letter itself, only the bottom portion was visible. Feeling slightly ashamed of her curiosity, she read:

> . . . but what more can one say about Los Angeles? How to describe the heat, the *sauve qui peut* greed, the absence of intellectual stimulation? Your dear father would have *hated* it here. As for me, I feel like Joseph in Egypt—except that here Pharaoh is Jewish, too. . . .

Queenie couldn't summon up the courage to turn the page over—it was one thing to read a letter that had been accidentally exposed, and quite another to do so deliberately. In any case, she was spared further temptation by the return of Chambrun, who kicked open the kitchen door and came in carrying a silver tray.

"Find anything interesting?" he asked cheerfully. "There's not much here, but it's the best I could do on short notice."

Queenie blushed. "No, no," she said. "I wasn't looking . . ."

"Of course you were. And quite right, too. I always read other people's mail. It's so much more interesting than one's own."

Chambrun opened a bottle of champagne. Beside it on the tray was a plate of thinly sliced chicken, bread, cheese and fruit. "I try to keep things simple, since I mostly eat out. Every day Miss Hamlyn, my housekeeper, cooks a chicken for me, slices it and puts it in the refrigerator. Sometimes I eat it, sometimes I don't—but the important thing is that it's always there."

"What about her day off?"

Lucien looked at her with some surprise. The girl showed signs of a practical mind. *"Touché!"* he said, laughing. "Before her day off she cooks *two* chickens."

Queenie pointed toward the oil painting over the mantelpiece. "Is that your mother?"

"Yes. She was a great beauty."

"And isn't that a picture of the king?"

Chambrun nodded. "It's him all right. My mother was one of the king's last mistresses. She was young, beautiful, married to a perfectly respectable gentleman—an M.P., actually. She attracted the king's attention at a dinner party, and they fell in love. Of course, her husband accepted the whole thing with good grace, you understand. It was something of an honor—in fact, he became a baronet and later a peer on the strength of it."

"He was rewarded for letting his wife sleep with the king?"

"Not at all. He was merely rewarded for not making a public scandal about it. The scandal came later. After the king died, my mother was heartbroken. She went to live in France for a while and fell in love with a French painter, Leon Chambrun—quite a good painter, as a matter of fact."

Chambrun waved toward the far wall, where there hung a large, bright painting of a picnic in an olive grove. A woman with her golden hair let down around her face was holding a small boy in a sailor suit. In the foreground was a checkered cloth, with baskets of fruit and cheeses, a vase of flowers; in the background the bright-blue horizon of the sea stretched across the canvas.

"That's me," Chambrun said. "My father always preferred domestic subjects. He was a gentle, talented man. He was a friend of Picasso, but he didn't have Picasso's anger—or genius, I suppose. He was very good at stage design. He even did some film work for David Konig. Konig loved him. Everybody did."

"David Konig?" Queenie asked. "Isn't he the film director?"

"Of course. You know his work?"

"I saw *Royal Wedding*. Marla Negresco was awful."

Chambrun shrugged. "Do you really think so? She was very beautiful, you know. It wasn't the kind of beauty that lasts, unfortunately. *Royal Wedding* might have been all right without her—but poor Konig didn't have a choice. He was married to the lady, so he had to put her in the picture. It's a pity. His early stuff was wonderful. *Love in the Morning* was a masterpiece. *The Last Goodbye*—even better."

"I didn't see those. Are you in films?"

He waved his hand. "A little bit. I would like to do more. Perhaps I will. . . . Do you know, you have beautiful hands?"

He took her right hand in his and examined it carefully, bringing it closer to his face. Then he gently kissed it, sitting down beside her on the sofa. He kissed her wrist, then her forearm, then her elbow.

They were the first enjoyable kisses Queenie had ever received, and she did not struggle when Chambrun finally leaned forward and kissed her lightly on the lips. When he raised his head, she didn't move. It was not that she was afraid—to her embarrassment, she did not know what to do. She arched her neck back and closed her eyes, wondering if he would guess how inexperienced she was.

"Open your eyes when you kiss me," Chambrun whispered. "When a woman closes her eyes, she's always holding something back—or thinking about someone else."

"I'm not thinking of anyone else."

"Good."

For years, Queenie had wondered what it would be like to go to bed with a man. She could not believe that her one experience with Morgan was the way it was supposed to be. She felt Lucien's arms around her and his lips on hers, and decided it was very nice indeed, so nice in fact, that she almost hoped he would stop there. She supposed she ought to offer some kind of resistance or struggle—surely that was what was expected of her?—but she felt no inclination to do so.

"You'll spend the night?" he asked in a low whisper. And as she kissed him, she heard herself say, "Yes, yes, I will," happy that the whole night stretched before her, willing to let him do whatever he wanted.

"I think we'd be more comfortable in bed with our clothes off, don't you?" he asked gently. Lucien straightened up and took off his tie. He looked at her shrewdly. "You haven't done this kind of thing often, have you?" he asked. He seemed amused.

Queenie blushed. She was afraid he might refuse to go on—perhaps even refuse to let her stay. She did not want to admit that she had never done it, but she thought it might be even worse to say that she had. "I'm not a virgin, if that's what you mean," she said boldly.

"It wasn't what I meant at all, as a matter of fact." Lucien kicked off his patent-leather pumps and curled his toes. He gave a small sigh of relief. "But now that you mention it, the thought does occur to me . . ."

"Well, I'm not. And would it matter?"

"Not in the least." He leaned over and kissed her gently on the forehead. "The bedroom door is over there, on the right. Go in and make yourself comfortable, and I'll join you in a moment."

Queenie stared at him, astonished that he had guessed so easily that she didn't want to go into the bedroom and undress in front of him.

He handed her handbag to her. "The bathroom is in there," he said. "You can't miss it."

She took the handbag and walked to the bedroom, wondering why he thought she needed it. Before she slipped into his bed, she folded up her clothes neatly, then turned off the light.

• • •

Queenie watched Lucien sleeping, in the gray light of dawn that fil-tered in through the half-drawn curtains. She herself was not sleepy, could not even *think* about sleeping, in fact.

She felt no shame or guilt. Whatever she had expected from sex, it had not been this deep feeling of contentment and pleasure with her *own* body.

Lucien had helped her make that discovery. He had not forced him-self on her—on the contrary, he had stroked and touched her, whisper-ing encouragement all the time, until she had drawn him into her with her hands. Then he guided her movements, his hands clasped hard on her buttocks, until she was caught up in the rhythm of her own pleasure and knew that she was, in fact, holding nothing back, could not if she tried.

Her eyes had been open.

Now she looked at him, lying beside her, and for the first time it oc-curred to Queenie that men were beautiful in their own way. Most were not, of course—but then neither were most women. Lucien's body fasci-nated her, but more fascinating than that was the way their bodies seemed to fit together, comfortably, naturally, without awkwardness, as if they had been designed with that in mind.

Already his face was covered by a pale, golden stubble of beard, a familiar process which suddenly seemed to Queenie magical, as if he had grown it as a surprise for her, and she reached out to stroke it.

He opened his eyes. "You should be sleeping," he said.

"I'm not tired."

Lucien stretched lazily, kissed her and put one arm around her, draw-ing her closer to him.

Queenie ached from head to foot, but it was a warm, pleasant kind of ache. Now that she knew what making love was like, she could hardly imagine how it had been possible to live without doing it. There were parts of her body he had touched that she hadn't even known *existed*, and she had done things that she wouldn't have believed were possible only a few hours ago.

Lucien felt his beard and sighed. "I shall have to get you home," he said. A look of concern crossed his face. "Will there be explanations? Problems?"

Queenie thought about the question reluctantly, unwilling to return to the demands of ordinary life. "I don't want to go home," she said.

He raised an eyebrow. "You're living with your—ah, *guardian?* The dark gentleman with the mustache?"

"Yes. It's a long story. . . ."

"I have all the time in the world for it."

Queenie was suddenly awake, as if someone had dashed ice-cold water on her. How much could she tell him? How much would he understand? Lucien had given her a taste of the life she wanted, not just in bed, but in the obvious ease with which he moved from one world to another. She did not know much about him, but from the way he lived it was obvious that he was at home in society and on familiar terms even with people like David Konig. She felt as if she had one foot on the bottom rung of a ladder. She wanted to climb higher. Above all, she didn't want the ladder pulled away.

"He was supposed to look after me when I came here."

"From India?"

She nodded. She tried to think of some way in which Morgan could be fitted into the story that had appeared in Basil Goulandris's column and decided the less said, the better. "At first, he behaved very well," she whispered, snuggling as close to Lucien as she could get. "But then he began to change . . ."

"Change?"

She put her arms around him. "He began to look at me all the time. Sometimes, when he was drinking, he hit me . . ." She wished she could tell him the truth but was afraid it would disgust him.

Lucien stroked her gently. "I think I see," he said quietly. "Did he, ah . . ."

She settled for a half-truth. "He tried."

"There, there," Lucien said. To her relief, his curiosity about her past was limited. "There's nothing to be afraid of now." The telephone beside the bed rang shrilly. "Damn!" he said, and picked it up. He listened for a moment, and Queenie saw his expression change—he seemed guilty and embarrassed. She guessed he wanted to be alone to take the call, but decided to press herself against him more closely than ever.

He closed his eyes in concentration. "I thought it was *tonight*. . . . No. no, of course you couldn't reach me, I was working in the dark-room. . . . Of *course* I'm sorry, darling. . . . Of course I realize being sorry doesn't help. . . . No, no, I wish to God I could, but lunch is out of the question, I'm afraid . . . I have a deadline . . . I don't know about dinner. . . . Oh, now look here, there's no point in getting hysterical. . . . Hello?"

He put the receiver back and opened his eyes. "She hung up."

"Oh, dear. It's my fault."

"Not at all. It's mine."

"Who was it?" Queenie asked, aware even as she asked the question that she was perhaps going too far. But to her relief Lucien wasn't annoyed.

"Cynthia Daintry. In a rage. I was supposed to be at her dinner party last night."

"Is she the blond lady you were with at the club? The one with all the jewels?"

"Exactly."

"She's very pretty. Will she forgive you?"

"Possibly. Very likely. I think that would depend on my future behavior, though."

Queenie wondered whether it would help to cry. Then, at the thought of going home to Morgan—and being pushed out of Lucien's world— she found it impossible not to. "I'll get dressed," she whispered, hoping he would say no.

"And go back to this man Morgan? I won't hear of it. You'll stay."

"And Cynthia?"

Lucien got out of bed and slipped on his dressing gown. "I've had enough of Cynthia's jealous rages, to tell you the truth."

He looked out the window, happy to turn his attention elsewhere. "The light is good," he said. "It would be a shame to waste it. We'll take a few pictures."

"But I'm not dressed. Or made up."

"That's the point." He was impatient now, a professional who didn't like to be interrupted or questioned. "All that will come later," he explained grudgingly. "Slip on a shirt, a dressing gown, anything . . . you'll find a spare toothbrush in the bathroom closet. And a hairbrush. But hurry. I never like to waste good light."

She did as she was told. There was not just one toothbrush in the cabinet but a whole box of them, brand-new in their cellophane wrappers. As she brushed her teeth, she wondered if Cynthia hadn't good reason to be jealous even before last night.

When she came out, Lucien was loading a camera. He looked at her and gave a small nod of satisfaction. "This afternoon we'll go out and do some shopping," he said. "Then I want you to meet a friend of mine."

"Who?"

"A man called Dominick Vale. I think he could do a lot for you. In front of the white dropcloth, please . . . just there. . . . Do you have a lot of things at home?"

"I wouldn't call it 'home,'" Queenie said, suddenly conscious of the fact that it would be a mistake to let Lucien know that she and Morgan shared one small room, or to let him see it. "It's just a small flat," she explained. "I have a couple of suitcases there, that's all. Why?"

"Because if you're *not* going home, we'll have to pick your things up. Or start out from scratch."

"I'd rather start out from scratch."

"It's always the best way," he said gravely. Then he began to click the shutter of his camera, moving back and forth as he changed focus and angle. "You're smiling now!" he shouted at her. "Just the way I asked you to in your dressing room."

It was because she had something to smile *about*, Queenie told herself. He was going to let her stay!

"Is Mr. Vale expecting you?"

"Tell him it's me. And that it's important."

"Very good, sir.'

The man in footman's livery gave a perfunctory bow. Despite the powdered wig and silk knee breeches, he had the appearance of a prizefighter. As he whispered into the ivory telephone which sat incongruously on an inlaid eighteenth-century gaming table in the hall, the receiver almost vanished in his huge hand, as if it were a toy.

"'E says to go up, Mr. Chambrun. You know the way."

Queenie stared around her in awe. For years, Morgan had spun his fantasies about the Café de Paris. She knew its history from countless hot evenings listening to Morgan on the veranda.

In this beautiful Georgian mansion everybody in London who was rich, famous or celebrated gathered at night to dance beneath chandeliers that had once belonged to His Royal Highness the Duke of York, to eat in the famous Mirror Room, with its glittering candelabras, and to watch a "floor show" (the very phrase had been invented here) that rivaled those in Paris.

The Prince of Wales appeared nightly whenever he was in London, accompanied by his equerry, Major "Fruity" Metcalfe, to dance with Mrs. Dudley Ward, whose unfortunate husband was obliged to doze wearily at his table until the Prince had made a night of it. The Maharajah of Baroda had a regular table, as did the Maharajahs of Kashmir and Jaipur and the Aga Khan—who once enlivened the evening by tossing gold coins at the girls in the chorus, and was said to have thrown away the equivalent of ten thousand pounds before he grew bored with the game.

Most of what was written about Vale was speculative, since he was obsessively secretive about his origins. He was variously alleged to be the natural son of a "royal person" and the child of an immigrant Armenian rug peddler. He denied none of these rumors and was suspected by many to have inspired them.

Even the rich feared him—he was known to have a violent temper, people whispered that he carried a gun, and it was said that he would go to any lengths to destroy a man—or woman—who crossed him. Like a shark, he swam in the dark waters of society, occasionally snapping up a victim.

"An unexpected pleasure," Vale said quietly, rising from behind his desk to shake Lucien's hand and kiss Queenie's. He was immensely tall, with the chest and shoulders of a weight lifter, yet he dressed with an elegance that made his powerful body seem oddly sinister. More sinister still were his thick, black eyebrows, which met in the middle of his brow, giving him a permanent scowl. The pale eyes beneath the famous eyebrows had all the warmth of a couple of oysters on the half-shell, and the lugubrious tone of Vale's voice, combined with his elegant formal suit, suggested to Queenie an undertaker rather than a nightclub proprietor.

"We're not disturbing you, Dominick?" Lucien asked.

"Not at all," Vale replied courteously. "I was alone." He suffered from nasal catarrh; he breathed noisily and gave an occasional loud snuffle to clear his nose. He seemed unaware of the habit, or perhaps simply didn't care whether other people found it offensive or not. He helped himself to a peppermint lozenge from a silver-gilt box. The smell was medicinal and by no means pleasant.

Queenie could hardly help noticing that there were two glasses on the desk, both of them still quite fresh, with unmelted ice cubes. Behind Vale, a door was slightly ajar, as if someone had made a hasty exit and neglected to close it. Vale glanced at a gold lighter, studded with diamonds, on the desk. He picked it up, as if he was wondering what to do with it. He clicked it several times. He cleared his throat loudly. The door shut gently, closed by some unseen hand.

Everything about him was shiny and expensive—even his fingernails were polished to a high gloss. He put the lighter back on the desk and stared at it for a moment as if he had never seen it before, or was in some way surprised to find it in his hand. Queenie stared at it too—it was the kind of object that was difficult *not* to stare at—and saw that the diamonds spelled out the initials "R.B." She guessed that whoever had been with Vale had left the lighter behind.

"I wanted you to meet a friend of mine," Lucien said. "Queenie Kelley."

Vale inclined his head gravely toward Queenie and gave a loud sniff. "Delighted," he said. Queenie didn't think he looked delighted at all—he had, on the contrary, the look of a man who has been interrupted in the middle of something more important. He gave a furtive glance at the door behind him, as if he wanted to make sure it was shut. "Is Miss Kelley seeking employment?" he asked.

"I have a job," she said. It took a certain amount of courage to speak up—something about Vale made her skin crawl.

"Queenie is working at Goldner's place," Lucien said.

Vale lifted a heavy eyebrow. "The famous Rani? Who so impressed Basil Goulandris?" He stared at her with slightly more interest than before. "I must say, he didn't do you justice."

He leaned back and turned his attention to Lucien, as if he'd seen as much of her as he needed to. "She has possibilities," he admitted grudgingly.

"Possibilities? She's perfect!"

"You're a romantic," Vale said with distaste, as if it were a disease. "There is such a thing as a perfect diamond. There is no such thing as a perfect person. Unfortunately. However, she approaches perfection rather more closely than the previous young lady you brought me."

Queenie gave Lucien a startled look. It had not occurred to her that Lucien made a practice of bringing girls to Vale.

Vale gave a faint smile, she supposed because he had intended to embarrass Lucien, and had succeeded. Having done so, he moved to repair the damage. "Perhaps I should explain," he went on, "that Lucien does a little talent scouting for me. Nothing formal, you understand, Miss Kelley. We're old friends, Lucien and I. One hand washes the other. My clientele is rich, famous, *bored*. The best is hardly even good enough for them—they're used to the best, you see. They demand novelty, something different, something new. To work here is to be seen by everybody that matters."

"It can lead to great things," Lucien said.

"Who can tell?" Vale said, standing up to indicate that it was time for them to leave. He did not, Queenie noted, ask *her* to think about anything—the idea that she might not want to work here obviously did not occur to him.

He did not open the door for them. He simply pushed a button on his desk and it swung open. As it clicked shut behind them, Queenie heard Vale sniffle noisily; then a rich, deep, unfamiliar theatrical voice asked, "Have they gone yet?"

She wondered whose presence it was that Vale had been at such pains to hide.

Queenie sat in the car surrounded by boxes bearing the names of some of Bond Street's most expensive shops—names which were well known even in India. She was still irritated with Lucien and suspected that his generosity was merely a form of apology.

"You might have told me it was a kind of audition," she said.

"I explained. It was merely an introduction to a friend. I had no idea he would bring up the subject right away. You should be pleased— it shows how impressed Vale was."

"I didn't like him."

"Nobody does. Well, I do, a little . . . but it doesn't matter. From time to time I tip Dominick off to someone who might be right for the club. Is that so terrible? It's a favor to a friend."

"What does he do for you?"

Lucien slammed on the brakes, pulled over to the curb and turned to face her. "He pays me a finder's fee. Since you ask. A man has to make a living."

"I see."

"You think that's why I came backstage? You're wrong. I could have gone to Dominick without even *meeting* you. And by the way—the finder's fee hardly pays for my bill at the club. I'm not intending to get rich on you, you know. Is that what you thought?"

"It crossed my mind."

"For someone so young you have a suspicious mind. You will have to learn to trust people. At any rate, you will have to learn to trust me."

He started the car again.

"If Mr. Vale wants me . . ." she began.

"He will want you."

". . . what do I do about Mr. Goldner?"

"You give him two weeks' notice, in the nicest possible way."

Queenie wished she had been more careful when she signed the receipt for her first week's pay. In retrospect, it seemed a rather bulky document for such a simple purpose. She wondered if it was worth asking Lucien about it, but just then he pulled the car over as another shop caught his attention.

He shopped much the same way that he drove—which impressed Queenie so much that she would probably have forgiven him by the end of the day even without his explanation. He entered a shop like a whirlwind, demanding and receiving instant attention. He was not interested in things that had to be made to order, or even altered. The moment something attracted his attention, he would grab it, send Queenie off to try it on, then examine her carefully when she returned. If he was pleased, he bought it. If he was not, he explained to her exactly why it didn't suit her. He had strong opinions about everything. He loathed prints, fussiness of any kind, and costume jewelry. "It's better to have nothing than fakes," he said. "The real thing will come soon enough."

It did not occur to Queenie to ask if he could afford this lavish spending spree. Lucien seemed totally indifferent to the cost of things. His extravagance set off a small, irritating note of alarm in her head, for while Queenie was eager to learn everything she could about life, she recognized in herself a certain instinctive caution about money, even before she had any.

In the meantime she was learning about clothes. At Molyneux, Lucien bought her an evening gown of black silk chiffon, which made a startling contrast to her pale skin, though it took half an hour to talk her out of pink. At Asprey's he bought her a handbag of gleaming crocodile for day wear and an evening bag of gilt and silver beads. At Rayne's, he painstakingly chose shoes for her. At Marie de France, he chose lingerie for her and reluctantly indulged her taste for pink.

At Massey & Cunningham he bought cosmetics. He knew more about rouge, powder, mascara and lipstick than Queenie did, and enjoyed teaching her the finer points of makeup. "A woman's face is a work of art," he said, gently touching her face with his fingertips to show her how to trace just the slightest shadow of rouge with a sable brush to emphasize her cheekbones. Queenie tried a dozen perfumes, dabbing a drop of each one on her wrist to warm it, as the saleslady taught her, until she recognized the scent she had smelled that evening in the Painted Lady, which had then seemed to represent everything that was sophisticated and expensive.

"Schiaparelli?" Lucien said, raising one eyebrow in surprise. "You are sure you don't prefer the Chanel?"

She shook her head. She knew exactly what she wanted and was determined to have it.

Lucien nodded at the saleslady, who wrapped up the elegant little
frosted bottle with its elaborately flowered cap. "It's strange," he said.
"Cynthia always uses exactly the same scent. . . ."

She held her wrist to her nose. The smell made her realize for the
first time what it must be like to be happily drunk. She felt dizzy with
pleasure and put her arms around Lucien and kissed him, right there
in the cluttered, old-fashioned, elegant shop, to the shock of the saleslady, and to Lucien's discomfort.

"Do I take it that I'm forgiven?" he asked.

She kissed him again. "You're forgiven."

"And am I trusted?"

"You're trusted."

"Then you can trust me to take you home," he said. "We have just
time enough to unpack these things, make love and get you to Goldner's for your first show, with perhaps a few minutes to spare for a bite
to eat and a look at the photographs."

It was the first time he had suggested that his flat was her home.

That was almost enough to make her forget that in a few hours she
would have to face Morgan again.

"He's gone," Goldner said.

"You sacked him?"

"I threatened to—and worse, I don't mind admitting. We had an
agreement that he wasn't to blab about you, so I took the liberty of reminding him about it rather firmly."

It crossed Queenie's mind that Goldner might mean he had given
Morgan a beating, but Goldner hardly seemed the type. He caught her
look and shrugged. "Not myself," he said, looking hurt. "And nothing
ambitious. Merely a warning. He should be able to play the saxophone
in a week or two, I imagine. Perhaps sooner."

Much as Queenie had come to dislike Morgan, the thought of him
being beaten by a professional thug dismayed her. "Where is he?" she
asked.

"That's the question. It seems I made an error of judgment. He ran
off with Mavis, who is no great loss—but he took a hundred pounds
from the till before he went. And that's on top of what I already gave
him. He'll be far away by now, I daresay. . . ."

"To India?"

"Hardly with Mavis, I think."

For a moment, Queenie felt a cold shiver of loneliness. Compared to Morgan, Goldner and even Lucien were strangers. However badly he had behaved, he was family. She had no wish to see him in jail.

"Did you tell the police?"

"Not yet."

"Please don't."

"It's my duty."

"As a favor to me . . ."

Goldner sighed. "Family sentiment! I respect it. I understand it. I *share* it. But it's always a mistake. You're much better off without him, believe me. Still—for you, I'll do it. You'll pay me the hundred pounds back out of your earnings—shall we say two pounds a week?—and I will forget my civic duty."

"That seems a little steep," Queenie said cautiously.

"Steep? I don't think so. If I don't tell the police, I can't collect the insurance. A hundred pounds is a lot of money."

Queenie almost cried at the thought of losing a hundred pounds, but she knew she owed Morgan at least that. Then she thought about what Goldner had said and realized he had let slip a surprising fact. "Speaking of money," she said quietly, "did you just mention you *gave* him some? Apart from what he stole?"

Goldner smiled. He dabbed his forehead with a handkerchief. "Oh, dear," he said. "That was a slip of the tongue on my part. But I suppose you had to know sooner or later, my dear. I bought out his share of your contract."

She gave him a stony look "What contract?"

"Why, dear—the contract I signed with Morgan on your behalf. You're under age, you see. As your nearest relative, your uncle was entitled to sign for you. With your best interests at heart, you may be sure."

"That's ridiculous," Queenie said angrily.

"Not at all. You even signed a consent to it, with a down payment of ten pounds, which you accepted. It's all perfectly legal. It will survive the scrutiny of any court in the land."

It was another betrayal, Queenie thought. She tried to think of someone to whom she could turn for help. There was nobody. Lucien, she already guessed, would hardly be a match for Goldner when it came to something like this. Morgan had signed her away without even telling her, then fled, leaving her to pick up the pieces.

"You must learn to look on the bright side of things," Goldner said. "I have a stake in your career. You can count on me to push it."

"How much of a stake?" Queenie asked, deciding she might as well know the worst.

"Fifty percent," Goldner said modestly. "I had twenty-five and so did Morgan. The poor chap needed ready cash, so I bought his twenty-five. Not that it will do him much good, I should think. Mavis is a frightful little gold digger."

"So you take half of whatever I make?"

"Just so. Not from your salary here, of course. That's *yours*, my dear. But we must think big. Who knows? There may be all sorts of good things in store. Motion pictures, the stage, advertisements . . . the opportunities are excellent, in my opinion. For both of us," he said, opening his arms wide to demonstrate their scope.

She was not impressed. Everybody talked about her brilliant future and wanted a part of it, but she was still making ten pounds a week, from which Goldner proposed to take two. She knew when she was beaten—she guessed that Goldner's document had been drawn up carefully and that she couldn't fight it by herself—but she was determined to score at least a small victory. "For how long am I supposed to be—your slave?" she asked, surprised by the harsh tone of her voice.

It surprised Goldner, too. He had expected hysterics and tears. Her resolution and cold anger gave him the feeling there was trouble to come. "Don't think of it that way, dear," he said. "It's a partnership, not slavery. When you are twenty-one, you're free and clear. That gives us three or four years to get to know each other. By then, who knows? You may be so grateful to old Solly for what he's done for you that you'll want to renew . . ."

She knew it all now, and it was a bitter pill. She swallowed it. There was no choice. One thing was for sure, she decided—she was not going to call him "Solly," or think of him as "old Solly." He would remain Mr. Goldner.

"Since we're partners, Mr. Goldner," she said, "there are a few things I'd like to discuss."

"Anything." Goldner gave her an uneasy smile.

"I want a decent dressing room."

"You have it. What else?"

She did not smile. She wanted to see how far she could push him. "And surely if we're *partners*, we ought to split responsibility for the money Morgan stole? That's only fair."

Goldner raised an eyebrow. He wished he hadn't used the word "partner." "I don't see the fairness of that at all, dear," he said.

Queenie walked to the door and looked through the peephole at the audience beginning to gather—not a bad house, she thought, for the first show. She knew there was no point in being upset or shouting, and even less point in crying. That would be what Goldner expected her to do. Besides, she had an ace up her sleeve, as poor Morgan would have said. Goldner had his piece of paper, but what he *didn't* know was that she had a place to go now, someone who would look after her. She wouldn't starve. "All this has given me a headache," she said.

"You shall have an aspirin, dear," Goldner said generously, fumbling in his desk drawer. "When you get out there, you'll be fine."

"I don't think I can do it, Mr. Goldner. Not the way my head feels."

Goldner sat there for a moment, holding the white pill in the palm of his hand like a religious offering. "You can't disappoint your audience, dear."

"Yes I can."

"If you don't go on, you don't get paid."

"I don't care."

He looked at her carefully and noticed for the first time that she was wearing new shoes—*expensive* new shoes, to judge from the sheen of them. He poured a glass of water and took the aspirin himself. He wondered who had bought the shoes for her. He hoped it was not a lawyer. He should have guessed that Queenie would soon have a man in her life. It was inevitable, but he had not thought it would happen so quickly. . . .

He belched slightly from the aspirin. "Perhaps you have a point," he conceded. "As a gesture of friendship, I am willing to split the hundred pounds Morgan stole from me."

Queenie said nothing. She closed her eyes as if she were in pain.

"Or even overlook the whole matter," Goldner continued. "After all, what's a hundred pounds between partners?"

"I'd better get changed," she said.

She was delighted to hear Goldner sigh with relief as she closed the door behind her. On the way down to the basement, she paused beside the telephone. There was a limit to the amount of pressure she could put on Goldner as long as she wanted to work—but there was at least one person who could raise the pressure very considerably if he cared to.

She put two pennies in the slot, dialed the number of the Café de Paris and asked for Dominick Vale.

It did not take Goldner more than twenty-four hours to discover that Queenie was living with Lucien Chambrun. He was not displeased.

Lucien's interest would not conflict with his own, or threaten it. On the contrary, with any luck, his photographs would make Queenie an even more valuable property. He made a note to have a man-to-man chat with Lucien at the earliest opportunity. Lucien, Goldner told himself, was a reasonable man—his services could always be useful for keeping Queenie in line.

He mused over his good fortune as he counted the night's receipts, snapping a rubber band around each packet of notes. The sound of the rubber bands was music to his ears. On the strength of it he poured himself a brandy and lit a new cigar. There was a knock at the door. He hastily stuffed the money into his pockets and waddled over to unlock it.

The eye that greeted him when he stared through the peephole was pale gray and totally expressionless. He stood on tiptoe for a better look and saw a white tie and the flash of a diamond shirt stud. Armed robbers, Goldner knew, did not wear full evening dress or diamond studs. He opened the door, and for a moment he almost wished it had been a robber. Dominick Vale stood there towering over him, an evening cape draped over his broad shoulders, his gloves and a top hat held elegantly in his left hand. In his right hand he carried a gold-knobbed dress cane that was suspiciously thick. It looked heavy enough to be a weapon, and Goldner presumed it was. Vale gave a loud sniff by way of a greeting.

"Why, it's Mr. Vale," Goldner said, feigning a delight he was far from feeling. "To what do I owe this honor?"

"You're a lucky man, Goldner."

"If you say so, Mr. Vale."

"I say so. Think of it. You have two legs to walk on. You own a nice little place that hasn't burned down—it's shocking how easily a fire gets started in these old buildings. You don't have any trouble with the police. I call all that lucky. Wouldn't you?"

"I have nothing to fear."

"Oh, come off it, Goldner. Everybody has something to fear. *You* certainly do."

"And what might that be?"

"Me."

Goldner acknowledged the truth of this with a shrug. He wondered what Vale wanted. He decided he would know soon enough. "I'm a reasonable man," he said.

"Of course you are. So am I. I want Miss Kelley."

"Ah. She's under contract to me, you know."

"I know. You got some fellow named Morgan Jones to sign for her and bought him out for peanuts. A slimy piece of work, Goldner. But farsighted. I'll give you that."

"You seem very well informed."

"Yes. The young lady told me the whole sorry story."

Goldner sat down. He had underestimated Queenie again. He reached into his drawer and pulled out the bulky contract. "It's all perfectly legal," he said, placing it on the desk.

Vale pushed it off the desk with the tip of his cane. "Paper!" he said with a sniff. "Paper doesn't bruise or bleed."

Goldner knew when he was beaten, but he was a resourceful man, and not easily frightened. He had been intimidated and threatened by stronger people than Vale in his time, and had long since discovered that there was usually a bargain to be made. He picked the contract up. "True," he said. "But ink is more valuable than blood. Let us say that I tear this document up—with its signatures. You then have to draw up a new one. The girl is not stupid. She *might* go to a lawyer. And she has Chambrun to advise her—not that he's much of a businessman, and admittedly he's a friend of yours. But still, would you get such good terms as these? I doubt it, frankly. And she's under age. With Morgan gone, who would sign for her? You'd have to find her mother, Mr. Vale, and who knows what that would uncover? Why throw away a perfectly good document when it's binding?"

Vale sniffled. He took a small gold box from the pocket of his white waistcoat and put a peppermint in his mouth. "Go on," he said. "I'm listening."

"After all, she'll attract more attention at your place than at mine. I have no objection to showcasing my investment. Or to a partnership."

Vale inspected his fingernails. They seemed to satisfy him. He nodded. "Sixty-forty," he said. "Of your half."

"Fifty-fifty."

"I've been looking for a man to help me with my other interests, Goldner. I have investments in other clubs, you know—places that aren't at all like the C de P. Some of them—" he corrected himself— "*many* of them, I wouldn't want my name connected with directly. The right man could do very well for himself."

"I assume the right man would be someone who is already in the business, with a place of his own? Somebody with no visible connection to you? Somebody discreet?"

"Something like that."

"Sixty-forty it is," Goldner said happily. Thanks to Queenie, he had a foothold in the big time at last.

CHAPTER 9

WITHIN A MONTH, Queenie had accustomed herself to the first taste of real fame. It did not compensate her for the discovery that Vale, instead of tearing up her contract with Goldner, had merely made himself a part of it. She was well paid now—a hundred pounds a week was more than she had ever dreamed of—even if Goldner *did* take half of it. Still, there was no point in being angry over something she couldn't change, as Lucien repeatedly pointed out to her. She must be patient. Her time would come.

Patience was not one of Queenie's virtues, but having no choice, she forced herself to make it one, telling herself that things were not, after all, so bad—she had a lover, she had money, and she was rapidly becoming the talk of London. Her elegant new dressing room, on the same floor as Vale's office, was filled with flowers. Hourly, they poured in, with cards bearing the names of celebrities, maharajahs, millionaires, peers and the aristocracy of half a dozen defunct European monarchies.

At the end of the first week, the Prince of Wales sent roses, delivered by the long-suffering Major Metcalfe himself. The next week the Aga Khan sent a bouquet so large that it was impossible to get it through the door. From Prince Michael of Romania came a floral wreath in the shape of the royal coat of arms, to which was pinned an envelope that contained the torn half of a hundred-pound note, with a letter in which the Prince tactfully offered to deliver the other half when Queenie visited his suite at the Connaught. One admirer even sent her a pet cockatoo, which had to be removed to the zoo after a diamond brooch had been unfastened from its claw. She returned the diamond brooch with many regrets.

Flattering as such offers were, they did not turn Queenie's head. She was not naive—or, at any rate, she told herself, she was *less* naive. The men who sent flowers, cards and champagne wanted to sleep with her, but she had no desire to sleep with *them*. Once she did, she would be just another pretty girl around London. Besides, she was happy with Lucien.

For the first time in her life, she was living in a constant state of sexual arousal. She could think of nothing else, and the moments (which were few) when she and Lucien were not making love, or at least touching, feeling, kissing each other, seemed to her totally wasted.

Her inexhaustible capacity for pleasure astonished her. Sometimes she would fall asleep instantly after making love, like someone diving into a warm, silent sea, but even when she only slept for a few hours, as was often the case, she was never tired. The act of love seemed to fill her with energy, so much so that she frequently wandered naked and restless around the flat at night, sometimes pausing in the kitchen to finish whatever scraps of food she could find, sometimes wrapping herself in one of the terry-cloth bathrobes that hung on the towel rack in the bathroom to stare out the window until dawn brought the milkman and his horse clattering down the rain-washed street.

She loved the time she spent caring for the body that now gave her so much pleasure—and gave so much to Lucien, as well. She had always had a passion for cleanliness, but it was now becoming, as Queenie herself recognized, something of a mania. Once a day she washed her hair—something of a task, given its length and heaviness. Her toenails were shaped and lacquered to gleaming perfection, and the soles of her feet were carefully pumiced to keep them soft and smooth. After every bath she rubbed Vaseline into her skin, slowly, patiently, with small, gentle circular motions of her fingers, and to keep her face from drying out, she never washed it with soap, but massaged Nivea cream into it instead, until her cheeks and forehead glowed like white jade.

She was learning, in front of the mirror, to analyze her own beauty. It was, after all, a valuable and irreplaceable asset, and not to be treated carelessly. She searched endlessly for flaws and found few, completely self-absorbed in a task that was almost as fascinating to her as sex, and not always easily distinguishable from it. The fact that she was slightly cross-eyed, which Lucien pointed out one day when he was photographing her, concerned her deeply. Luckily this was not easily noticed from a distance, but when she looked at herself close up in his magnifying shaving mirror, the defect seemed to her so obvious and ugly that she took to wearing dark glasses during the day.

It was easy to grow used to the good things of life—but Queenie soon discovered this only sharpened her desire for more. Lucien was generous, and at last she had some money of her own, but she still felt a stab of envy when she saw a woman in a beautiful fur coat or wearing expensive jewelry. Every night she performed for the rich. She longed to be among them. Her beauty was her passport—all she had, and, she hoped, all she needed, and through Lucien's eyes and photographs she began to study it seriously, as a banker might learn about money.

She also came to understand the serious side of Lucien's character—for he too was a perfectionist in his own profession. He liked to pretend that he lived an idle playboy's life, and to the casual eye he did, but once he settled down to work, he was totally absorbed in it, and could go on for hours at a stretch, seeking the image he wanted. He was the darling of the magazine editors, and his fees were the highest in London, for it was said that he could bring out the beauty in even the plainest of women. The techniques of his work mystified Queenie, but the results did not, and when he talked about line, form, detail and lighting, she struggled to understand and learn.

Patiently, from behind the camera, he explained to her how he worked, until, bit by bit, day by day, she began to understand that he was an artist who had invented his own style. He had been, he told her, one of the first glamour photographers to give up the bulky view camera, mounted on a tripod, that kept the photographer at a distance from his subject, hidden under a black viewing cloth. Lucien believed in mobility, agility, contact between subject and artist. Liberated from the clumsy fixed camera, he moved around his subject constantly, kneeling, lying down, jumping on and off ladders, clicking away all the time in a whirl of movement.

At first, the magazines, particularly Vogue, had insisted on the traditional eight-by-ten negatives, without which it was believed impossible to obtain high-quality reproduction, but Lucien cared nothing about sharpness or grain—he loved movement, he explained to her, the swirl of clothes, the sudden dramatic effect. Gradually he had won the editors over, for his photographs were electric, sexy, alive, new, in a business where novelty was all.

Yet by now he was already bored with them—perhaps precisely because he had succeeded so quickly. It was the motion pictures that fascinated him, with their awesome possibilities for movement, speed, life—but movie producers were, if anything, even more wedded to conventional photography than magazine editors. Lucien told her about the film he had shot in Paris with Cocteau, in which the entire story was shown through the hero's eyes, the audience seeing only what *he* saw. But this only made him all the more unemployable in the major studios, he complained, where experimentation of this kind was frowned upon or ignored.

Now he photographed Queenie night and day. Her face became his obsession, a challenge that absorbed and at the same time stimulated all his energy. He was determined to capture the elusive quality of her beauty, to discover its secrets, to produce the one image that would *be* Queenie, now and forever—but he was never satisfied.

Others were more easily impressed. Queenie's photograph taken as she swung her head toward the camera as if something in that direction had startled her caused a sensation among the *Vogue* editors. The high, domed forehead, the immense eyes, wide open in surprise, the full, dark lips slightly parted as if in anticipation of a lover's kiss—Lucien had captured them all in a photograph that was blurred with her movement, except for the eyes, which seemed to stare out of the photograph with a sharpness and an intimacy that was startlingly sexual. For *Bazaar* he photographed Queenie in a pond, her body hidden in the water, her head sticking out, face up, lips parted, eyes glowing, among the water lilies, as if she were one of them herself. She was cold, wet and terrified of the brackish water, but none of that showed in the photographs. She was becoming a professional.

Every few days Lucien made a selection of his photographs, those that came closest to the ideal he had in mind, slipped them in an envelope and took it to the post office on the King's Road. In a bold, careless hand that covered the entire envelope, he wrote:

Mr. David Konig,
MGM Studios
Culver City
Los Angeles, California, U.S.A. Airmail
PERSONAL

So far there had been no reply.

Goldner handed her the letter. The faded blue envelope, smudged and wrinkled from the long journey, bore Indian stamps. It had been addressed to her in care of Goldner, for that had seemed to Queenie the safest thing to do when she started sending Ma postcards. She had kept them simple: "I love you, I'm working, I'm sorry"—but as the weeks passed by she came to believe there would never be a reply, that Ma had decided not to forgive her.

The letter was proof at last that she was wrong. She tore it open, scanning the close, finely written lines (Ma's penmanship was as precise and careful as everything else she did, but so densely packed as to be almost illegible). She read it to the end before she realized that Ma had simply refused to come to terms with what had happened, as if she had applied to Queenie's actions the same principles that Mary Baker Eddy had taught her to apply to sickness.

There was no mention of the theft, or of its consequences, no complaint, no hint of hurt or anger. Ma wrote as if Queenie and Morgan had gone Home in a perfectly respectable fashion, asked after the health of Peggy D'Souza and sent her love. It was as if she had succeeded in putting the reality out of her mind—or was it, Queenie wondered, because she simply could not bear to live with it?

There was no point, she realized, in trying to write to Ma about the truth, if Ma was determined to reject it. One day perhaps she could explain everything to her, make it up to her somehow. In the meantime there seemed no reason not to let Ma at least share in her success, whatever she might think of it. She decided to send her the newspaper clippings. Ma may as well have the pleasure, at least, of knowing that her Queenie was becoming famous.

And yet the letter disturbed her. She read it over and over again, after Goldner had taken his leave, searching for some hint of what Ma *really* thought; but she could find none.

She slipped the letter into the pocket of her dressing gown—a present from Lucien. It was not the only thing that troubled her. After their second night together, Lucien had asked her, with an unconvincing attempt at making the question casual, whether she had taken any "precautions." She knew that "precautions" were necessary, but she had no clear idea what they were and assumed it was up to the man. Ma had been as closed on the subject then as she was in the letter now.

Her confusion must have shown on her face, for Lucien blushed for the first time since she had met him. "When you went to the bathroom, with your handbag . . ." he muttered in some embarrassment, "you didn't . . ."

She shook her head.

"You don't have a . . . that is to say, you haven't been to a doctor . . ."

"Of course I haven't. Why should I?"

"I see. Then I had better take some precautions, I think. You'd better go to someone, though. There's quite a simple method that most women use . . . a doctor can explain it better than I can. Max Drymond is the man to see. Give him a call and say you're a friend of mine."

Queenie had nodded. In the middle of all her happiness she found it easy to put off seeing Drymond, and, in any case, Lucien seemed to have taken care of the problem. Occasionally, he grumbled about using what he called a "condom," and Queenie herself at first found the whole business mildly distasteful, but like so many other things, she quickly became used to it. She was afraid that any change might spoil her happiness.

Every day she told herself to make an appointment with Dr. Drymond, and every day she put it off. She knew that missing a period was the first sign of being pregnant. She hoped there were other reasons for missing one as well.

The nights when Lucien was working were lonely, and Queenie often wished there was somebody to talk to. Vale did not encourage "the help" to mix, either with each other or with "the guests," as he referred to his customers. Queenie had only to push a button to call her dresser or a maid, but like all Vale's staff, they were uncommunicative.

Vale himself was an invisible presence. Occasionally she heard a sniffle in the hall that signified he was on his way to or from his office, or a faint odor of peppermint that signified his recent passage. If he had a private life, it was carefully concealed. He appeared to live on the premises, but where his private quarters were—and what he did there—was one of the many mysteries of the place.

"Excuse me," she heard someone say. The voice was deep, richly modulated, sonorous. It seemed to her that she had heard it before, but she couldn't place it. It was not a voice you could forget, and yet she could not, for the life of her, put a face to it.

She turned to see who had entered her dressing room without knocking, and found herself staring at a well-dressed young man in the doorway with the fly of his trousers unbuttoned and his penis in hand.

She was too startled to say anything. She had no experience with perverts as such, though she had heard about them. The young man did not, however, seem to her particularly threatening, or even really perverted. His eyes had the slightly unfocused look common to men who are more drunk than they think they are, but this did not detract from his good looks. The face was solid, square and strongly masculine except for the nose, which was small and curiously feminine.

"Must have opened the wrong door," the man explained, dwelling lovingly on each syllable. "Thought this was the gents'."

"Well, as you see, it's not."

"Quite. Too many flowers, for one thing. Oh, I say, do forgive me . . ." He pushed his penis back into his trousers and fumbled clumsily with his buttons, succeeding after two tries in getting them fastened in the right holes. "Owe you an apology," he said. "Didn't mean to shock you."

"You didn't shock me. It's nothing I haven't seen before."

He laughed. Even his laughter seemed theatrical, as if it were something he had learned for a part. He paused, an actor giving the audience time to applaud. "Do you mind if I sit down?" he asked, and did so before she could reply, dropping heavily into the chair beside her dressing table with a sigh of relief. "I shall have to find the gents' soon, but it feels damned good to take the weight off my feet."

He affected an old-fashioned Victorian accent so perfectly that for a moment Queenie was almost convinced he was some gouty old character from Dickens; then he winked to dispel the illusion and, switching effortlessly to perfect Cockney, said, "Cor, you *are* a smasher, ain't you?" He dropped this pose and returned to his normal voice. "I believe you are the famous Rani?"

"That's not my real name." Whoever he was, she decided, he was charming.

"Well, of course it's not, love. My real name isn't Richard Beaumont, either."

"*The* Richard Beaumont?" Beaumont she had heard of—he was the talk of London, an actor who was at once a matinee idol and a tragedian in the grand tradition. Even Lucien, who knew him well, talked about him in tones of awe. Every newspaper was full of speculation about his forthcoming production of *Romeo and Juliet*—as well as gossip that he was being seen in the company of Cynthia Daintry. She looked at him with sharpened interest. Lucien was reticent on the subject of Cynthia, but Queenie had a natural desire to know more about the woman she had replaced. She decided it could do no harm to flirt a little with Beaumont.

"*The* Richard Beaumont, yes," he said gravely. "None other. Except *my* real name is Sidney Lumley—so you see we have something in common. Not many people are born with names that look good on the marquee. I hardly supposed you were born 'Rani'—or 'The Girl with the Bedroom Eyes' either!"

She blushed. The phrase seemed destined to stick to her forever. Vale's club was too elegant to have a sign outside, but he promoted her as "The Girl with the Bedroom Eyes" in the newspapers.

"Oh, I wouldn't worry, darling," Beaumont said, his eyes on her face. "Sex sells tickets, even for *Hamlet*. Put a pretty girl in as your Ophelia and you double the take—it's a well-known fact. What *is* your real name, by the way?"

"Queenie."

"Much better than Sidney. Still, not a name to put in lights, I agree. I must confess that I've been dying to meet you."

"You have?"

"Absolutely. Cynthia Daintry very nearly drove me *mad* talking about you, dear girl. She couldn't believe anybody could turn Lucien's head quite so fast, you know. Looking at you, I can quite see how it would be possible."

"Was she very upset?"

"No woman likes to lose a man, darling. Even one she's tired of. There was a time when Cynthia would have married Lucien. If he'd asked. And everyone expected him to ask, not just poor Cynthia. Her father is the Marquess of Arlington, you know . . . pots of money, stately home, chairman of this and that, Tory kingmaker, the lot. And she's damned attractive. A little high-strung, of course, but that's breeding for you. How *is* Lucien, by the way? He seems to have dropped out of sight."

"He couldn't be better."

"Splendid. One can see why. Do you often sit here in the evenings all alone?"

"When Lucien isn't here, yes. . . ."

"I am the same. I sometimes think my dressing room is my home. You wouldn't have a drink by any chance, would you?"

"I'm afraid not. I can ring for one."

A faint look of apprehension clouded Beaumont's face. "No, no," he said. "Don't do that." She was fascinated to see that his expressions, like his voice, were larger than life. When he smiled, he made a small performance of it, as if he were determined that his face should register exactly the emotion he wanted to convey. She wondered if he practiced in front of a mirror. "I caught your act, by the way," he said. "As the Americans put it."

"And what did you think?" she asked boldly.

"It's damned clever, speaking as one professional to another. You can't dance—neither can I, by the way—so you pose. I reached much the same conclusion about myself, years ago. Either one *is* a dancer, or one isn't. Ralph Richardson once told me, 'I'm frightfully clumsy, Dickie, so I stand pat, like a bloody statue, and make the audience look at me.' You've learned how to make them look at you, dear girl. That's half the battle. Or perhaps you always knew how to do that," he added shrewdly. "Have you ever thought about acting?"

"Well, yes—but not the stage kind."

"Films? Films are easy. Very boring, unlike the stage, but the money is good. You'd probably do well in Hollywood. All those *gentlemen* out there understand the value of beauty." Beaumont drawled out the word "gentlemen" with obvious irony and a certain contempt.

"Braverman, Mayer, Cohn, Konig—they're all men who appreciate 'pee–ootee,' if nothing else." He winked at her as he gave the word a foreign pronunciation. "I was over there myself to make a couple of films, you know. Braverman thought I was too pretty, and Mayer thought I was too ugly. Nobody cared whether or not I could act, of course, except Konig, but he was taking a nosedive, as they say there—three flops in a row and a bad marriage . . . I can't *tell* you how glad I was to get back to the stage."

"I'd love to see you act."

"My dear, you've just *seen* me act."

She laughed. He was right, of course. Richard Beaumont was simply one of his roles. She wondered what the real man was like behind the carefully crafted presence, and if he ever revealed it. Whatever the truth was, she liked him—he was the first person who had talked to her as one professional to another.

"Will you come and see me again?" she asked.

"If you get yourself a bottle of gin, with pleasure. And tell Lucien to take you out a bit and show you off. He can't keep you all to himself forever. Besides, the best way of getting ahead, darling, is to be seen in the right places."

"I thought this *was* the right place."

"It's one of them, granted. Is Lucien still trying to get into film work?"

"He talks about it, yes."

Beaumont smiled. "He may get there sooner than he thinks, now that he's found you. Your face is going to carry you a long, *long* way, Queenie. Farther than you think, I daresay. Farther than *he* thinks, for that matter. . . . I don't say you can be a Duse or a Bernhardt, that's a question of genius and training—but you can act well enough for the pictures. Make the jump, my dear, make it soon—before the public gets bored with what you're doing."

"Do you often give good advice to strangers?" she asked.

"No, I'm saving that for my old age. When I'm immensely distinguished and besieged by young actors and actresses seeking my words of wisdom." He hunched himself over and transformed himself, without apparent effort, into a vain and pompous old man, puffing out his cheeks and affecting an expression that was at once crafty and senile. "I shall give the same horsepiss my elders gave me, I imagine."

He dropped the pose as quickly as he had assumed it. "The truth is, I expected to find your performance the usual dreary piece of titillation, a slice of after-dinner glamour for the rich, and instead I was rather moved. Hello, I say to myself, this girl has *presence*; she's altogether too good for this bunch of stuffed shirts and their ghastly wives and girlfriends. I misjudged you. So did Cynthia, I daresay."

"What does *she* think?"

"That you're a man-stealing bitch, of course. But I rather suspect that isn't true, either. Lucien's been looking for his Galatea for a long time."

Before Queenie could decide whether or not to ask who or what Galatea was, Beaumont reached into his pocket and produced a cigarette lighter. He fondled it for a moment, as if it was something more than an expensive trinket—a talisman, perhaps, or the memento of a personal relationship. Queenie realized she had seen it before, in Vale's hands, when she first met him, and suddenly she recognized the voice. It was Beaumont who had been hidden away in the back room.

"Do you come here often?" she asked, her curiosity aroused.

Beaumont flicked open the diamond-studded lighter and lit his cigarette. He glanced at his wristwatch, which Queenie guessed was probably even more expensive than his lighter. The intricate band was a goldsmith's work of art, like nothing she had ever seen. Beaumont seemed to feel he had stayed too long. He pulled down his cuff, hiding the watch, and rose to his feet. "Very seldom," he said. "This is the first time in ages."

She watched his eyes. However good he was as an actor, he was not much of a liar, she decided.

• • •

Though Vale was seldom in view, he had a way of appearing occasionally from nowhere, silently, without warning. If he saw something that displeased him, he never said anything. The dark eyes unblinkingly registered the fault, whatever it was. Retribution, Queenie suspected from the terror of the staff, would come at some later time, probably long after the culprit had forgotten about it.

He materialized the night after Beaumont's visit, announcing his presence with a small sniff. One moment she was standing alone in the wings in costume, ready to go on in a few minutes, the next he was standing beside her in the shadows. He was wearing his usual working clothes—evening dress, a black tie and patent-leather pumps. "A good house," he said.

She nodded.

"Of course that isn't what makes the money," Vale went on.

"What does then?" She was curious to know.

"The gambling, upstairs. The point is to get them in the right mood. A few bottles of champagne, a little caviar, a good show—and before you know it, they're ready for a little chemmy or a turn at roulette."

"You mean my job is to get them in the mood?"

"Exactly so. You pull them in and establish a certain mood . . . forbidden pleasures. . . . On the whole, the English don't find anything much fun unless it's illegal." He looked at his watch, a thin disk of gold with a band made of tiny overlapping gold scales like those of a snake. Queenie stared at it. It was exactly like Beaumont's, she noticed. "What a beautiful wristwatch," she said.

Vale glanced at it as if he'd never seen it before. He gave a tight, thin smile—as near as he had ever come in her presence to registering pleasure. "Unusual, isn't it?" he asked. "I had it made for me at Cartier, in Paris. The old man who did it is dead now. This is the only one of its kind—he never made another."

It was on the tip of her tongue to say that she had seen its twin the night before, but she instantly thought the better of it. Whatever the relationship was between the two men, Vale was obviously determined to keep it secret, and it took very little imagination to guess he would be unhappy to learn that she knew about it.

"We'll need to restage the act and get a new costume," Vale said, "before people get bored with it."

He was echoing what Beaumont had said, Queenie thought—and suddenly realized that Beaumont must have been on his way to see Vale when he stopped in to see her. She wondered if he had really been looking for the gents', or whether that, too, was a lie.

"I'll talk to Lucien about it," Vale continued. "He may have some ideas. Is he here tonight?"

"He's working. He'll be here later on."

"You've quite reformed him, you know. He used to be at every party in town. Now he's actually *working*, for a change."

"Cynthia wouldn't let him work?"

"She liked to show him off. Mostly to annoy her father, I suppose."

"I wouldn't mind being shown off myself."

Vale nodded. "Ah, well, there's nothing more tiresome than a love nest after the first week. He's an artist in his own way, you know. You have to make allowances for that. When he gets involved in something, he can't tear himself away. And of course he's in love with his subject." Vale's expression suggested that he regarded being in love as something faintly vulgar. He sniffed. "He probably wants to keep you all to himself," he said. "Don't let him. Tell him to take you out a bit. Princess Tanya Ouspenskaya is giving a party Sunday. I'm sure Lucien is invited, and if he's not, it won't matter."

"He didn't mention it. I expect he'll want to stay home anyway."

Vale laughed. "What a lot you have to learn. Lean on him a bit, my dear. Men never know what they want to do until a woman tells them!"

"Who is Princess Tanya Ouspenskaya?" Queenie had a certain amount of difficulty with the name. She hoped she had it right.

"The grande dame of the arty set. Just right for your social debut, I would think. A great friend of Cynthia's father, by the way. Oddly enough, he loves the theater. I suppose that's why Cynthia's determined to be an actress. . . ."

"Is she good?" She was slightly dizzy at the way everybody seemed connected in Vale's world—and Lucien's, too, for that matter. It dawned on her that London society was a small world, and that she would eventually have to navigate in it unless she intended to spend the rest of her life in Lucien's flat.

Vale chewed on a peppermint thoughtfully. "Cynthia? She's not bad," he allowed. "Basically a talented amateur, like so many English actresses. The Royal Academy of Dramatic Arts has become a kind of superior finishing school, you know, full of rich girls who don't know what else to do with themselves. It still produces a real actor every now and again, like Dickie Beaumont, but I'm afraid poor Cynthia is a more typical product. Of course her looks help. Not that she's beautiful, like you, but she's pretty, like a piece of good china. She has a half sister who was quite stunning, but then she went off and married some rich oaf in India. What *was* her name?" He closed his eyes for a moment. "Penelope," he said. "Penelope Daventry. Did you ever meet her in India?"

Queenie could feel herself breaking out in a cold sweat. She wondered if Vale was taunting her, but nothing showed on his face. "You don't look well," he said. "You should be careful not to get chilled. You're no good to me sick."

He pulled the curtain to one side and peered out.

"Time for you to thrill the idle rich."

For the first time since she had arrived at the Café de Paris, she went through her act without looking at the audience, as if she was afraid that Mrs. Daventry might appear at any moment to accuse her of being an imposter—or a thief.

It was not until the end of her act that she began to regain control of herself. She swept to the front of the stage and looked down at the nearest tables. In the center of the room, Richard Beaumont and Dominick Vale were seated on either side of Cynthia Daintry. Cynthia's hand was on Beaumont's—even from the stage, Queenie could see the glitter of diamonds on her fingers and wrist. Cynthia was looking at the stage, but Beaumont and Vale were facing each other, and for one quick moment Queenie thought they were sharing a joke. She realized it was a look of complicity that flashed between them, so quickly that Cynthia was oblivious to it—then it passed, and Beaumont leaned over to whisper something to Cynthia.

The world was a more complicated place than she had thought, Queenie told herself.

"Out?" Lucien asked, wiping his hands on a darkroom towel. "Of course we can go out. The only thing is that I had in mind doing some pictures of you for French *Vogue* on Sunday. . . ."

"I'd rather go out." She smiled at Lucien, but her tone was firm. She lifted the hem of her dressing gown a little and crossed her legs. It had never occurred to her in a precise way to use sex to get what she wanted out of Lucien—it was too spontaneous for that, and besides, she enjoyed it as much as he did—but without being too obvious about it, she wanted to make it clear to him that her wishes counted for something. Rather to her surprise, Lucien caved in instantly. She took note of the fact for future reference.

"Did you have something in mind?" he asked.

Queenie had taken the trouble to go through the pile of invitations on his mantelpiece. "Tanya Ouspenskaya is giving a party Sunday, I hear," she said, doing her best to make the statement as timid as possible.

Lucien made a face. "My God! It will be a madhouse. Hundreds of people. And the same old people, too."

"They won't be the same old people to me."

"No," he said. "I suppose not." Now that he had given in, he looked a little sulky. Queenie gave him a quick kiss. Physical contact seemed to cheer him up. "It's a perfect opportunity to wear your Molyneux . . ."

"The invitation says 'informal.' "

"You've been looking at my mail . . . well, why not? God knows I can't be bothered to. Let me put your mind at rest—Tanya's idea of informality is not wearing a tiara."

Queenie laughed. "Who is she?"

"She used to be a great beauty . . . She's an old woman now, but immensely rich and chic. She knows everybody. She was born a princess but her husband was a fur trader in Russia before the Revolution, though he also dabbled in oil, banking, God knows what else. . . . He was cut to pieces by a speedboat propeller in Cannes, while he was swimming. Afterward she became the mistress of Lord Fleet, the newspaper tycoon. Fleet would have married her except that he went mad. He ended his life locked up in one room of his own mansion in a straitjacket under the delusion that he was Marie Antoinette waiting to be guillotined, poor man. Still, he left Tanya a fortune while he was still allowed to sign things."

"What a lot you know about people, darling," Queenie said. She knew she was flattering him, but it was true. Lucien was a mine of gossip. As a photographer of beautiful women—or women who wanted to look beautiful—he had entry to every social set.

"I know a lot of people, it's true," he said, as if it was a cross he had to bear. "That's the trouble with London. It's a big city, but a small world. In many ways, I was better off living in Paris."

Queenie nodded. It was a wish that Lucien expressed frequently, and she had come to understand that Paris represented for him an *idea*, not a place. He talked often of taking a small studio on the Left Bank and devoting himself to "serious" photography—by which he meant photographing something other than beautiful women—but at the same time, he liked being part of the London social scene and was unwilling to give up the glamour and the easy money. She wanted that kind of glamour and success so much for herself that it was hard for her to understand how Lucien could even talk about throwing it away to live in a cold-water garret. She had no romantic illusions about poverty. "Will Richard Beaumont be at the party?"

"Beaumont? Perhaps. She collects talented people like a big-game hunter. You've met him?"

"He's sometimes at the club."

"Is he? I wouldn't have thought it was his kind of thing at all. That must be Cynthia's influence."

"Isn't he a friend of Vale's?"

"Oh, hardly. Vale is altogether too flashy for Beaumont. He's a genius onstage, but a bit of a prig and a social climber off it. He wants his knighthood too badly to make a friend of a man like Dominick. That's why Cynthia is perfect for him: she's a peer's daughter."

"She certainly seems to have moved fast," Queenie said. She was surprised that for once she knew something Lucien didn't.

"She knows a rising star when she sees one." Lucien spoke with just a trace of bitterness. Queenie guessed that Lucien was a little disappointed to have been replaced so quickly in Cynthia's affections. She wondered if he was having second thoughts about turning down a peer's daughter. She stretched out her legs, confident that they were a good deal better than Cynthia's.

She was the most beautiful woman there. True, she felt hopelessly out of place among all these glittering people who knew each other and everybody else; true, she was suffering from a slight feeling of nausea, which seemed to be happening more and more often lately; true, her Molyneux gown, which had seemed so elegant in the shop, was upstaged by the clothes of at least half a dozen women who were wearing the latest couturier fashions from Paris; true also, she had no jewelry, in a roomful of women whose necks and wrists flashed like signal lamps—but none of that mattered, for at the sight of her the room fell silent for a moment. Then the noise resumed, at a higher, more deafening pitch, as the other guests tried to pretend that they hadn't been staring at her.

Lucien pushed her into the crowd so quickly that she scarcely even noticed the faces before her. She had never seen such a lot of kissing in her life—though nobody, of course, was kissing *her*—or heard the word "darling" used so frequently. Shy and ill at ease, she stood beside Lucien silently, while he introduced her to so many people that their names were blurred in her mind.

Her silence, as it happened, unintentionally created a sensation. With her long black hair, her huge dark eyes and perfect beauty, she seemed at once mysterious and haughty to everyone except Tanya Ouspenskaya, who recognized Queenie's state for what it was: social stage fright.

Immensely fat, white-haired, her face still showing traces of its former beauty, clad in a billowing black silk gown large enough to make a fair-sized tent, she took Queenie's wrist in one pudgy jeweled hand and pulled her over to a small sofa, away from the crowd. She dropped into it with a sigh of relief, flattening the cushions with her weight, and patted the small space beside her to indicate that Queenie should sit. She lit a cigarette, then put on her gold-rimmed pince-nez and peered at Queenie closely. The eyes, magnified by the thick lenses, were startlingly shrewd.

"You're even more beautiful than they said. Are you in love with Lucien?"

"Well . . ."

"No, no, don't deny it. And don't tell me to mind my own business. At my age, other people's business is more interesting than my own. Lucien is a dear boy, and really quite talented, so it's perfectly natural for you to be in love with him. But with a face like yours, you'll have your pick of men, so for God's sake don't marry him. Take my advice: marry for money. Not, of course, that Lucien is the marrying kind, now that I think of it. His father once painted me. He was not the marrying kind, either, I remember . . . though that never prevents men from marrying, alas. . . . Ah, *there's* someone you should meet."

She waved imperiously, layers of black silk fluttering like banners from her heavy arm, and a short, dark-haired young man appeared out of the crowd at her bidding.

"Have you met Miss—ah—Rani?" the princess asked.

Queenie had not faced up to the difficulty of being introduced in public by her stage name. She hated the fact that it made her sound foreign and decided that from now on she would make sure she was introduced as Queenie Kelley.

Cantor peered through his tinted gold-rimmed spectacles at her, squinting slightly. "I can't say I have," he said. His accent was peculiar, and he spoke in a low, rasping voice that Queenie found hard to understand. She guessed that he was American—the first one she had ever met. She had expected Americans to be taller, and was slightly disappointed. His skin was tanned to the color of old mahogany, and his hair was black and slicked back until it gleamed like polished glass. On each hand he wore a large gold ring; on the right wrist he had a gold chain, on the left a gold watch. He glittered like a jeweler's window. Short as he was, he gave off an impression of enormous strength and power—not just physical power, but the power of a man accustomed to getting his own way.

"This is Myron Cantor," Princess Ouspenskaya said. "He's an agent. From America. Rani dances at the Café de Paris."

"No kidding? I haven't seen you, Rani, but I'll make a point of it. I just got here a day ago, on the *Mauretania*, and my goddam stomach still feels like I was at sea. What a crossing! I came over with Barney Balaban. He was still throwing up when we checked into Claridge's."

He paused, possibly for breath, since he spoke in a rapid staccato, running his words together as if he wanted to say as much as he could before he was interrupted. "You know, you're a great-looking girl, Rani. If your act is any good I could book you anywhere in New York." He examined her more closely, then smiled, exposing the most perfect set of teeth Queenie had ever seen in a man. "Tell you the goddam truth, I could probably book you even if the act stinks. How much are they paying you?"

Queenie hesitated. She had been brought up not to talk about money; she was reluctant to discuss it with a stranger, and in front of the Princess as well.

"Come on," Cantor said, "don't be bashful about money! That's the trouble with everybody here—they think money's a dirty word. Money is the cleanest word I know. How does fifty thousand goddam dollars a year sound to you?"

Queenie stared at him. "Ten thousand pounds a year," the Princess explained helpfully, closing her eyes as if in ecstasy.

"It sounds like a lot of money to me, Mr. Cantor," Queenie said with interest.

"I can get you fifty easy, honey. I'll come around to the Café de Paris, catch your act. I'll bring Barney along if he's stopped tossing his cookies."

"Who's Barney?"

"Who's Barney? He's a goddam movie producer, that's who he is. The son of a bitch is over here looking for talent—not that he'd recognize it if he saw it, you understand—but from looks like yours he knows." He lit a cigarette and stared at her through the smoke. "I can tell you're a smart cookie, so I'll level with you. You ever heard of David Konig?"

She nodded.

"He's looking for a girl. I've got a hunch I could sell him on you. Meet me tomorrow afternoon at Claridge's, four o'clock. We'll talk some more. Just the two of us, sweetheart."

Before she could answer, Lucien appeared. It was easy enough to see that the sight of Queenie deep in conversation with Myron Cantor did not please him.

"Hello, Myron," he said without warmth.

The two men shook hands. Cantor was a good six inches shorter than Lucien, but he adopted a Napoleonic pose to make up for the difference in height and Lucien winced at the American's bone-crushing handshake.

"You two have met?" Lucien asked.

Cantor nodded. He put both hands into his pockets and jingled his change. His eyes were wary. "We were talking. She a friend of yours?"

"Yes. You could say that."

Myron Cantor grinned. He gave Lucien a man-to-man wink as if to show he wasn't the kind of guy to steal somebody else's girl. "Give me a call at Claridge's, Lucien," he said, tactfully acknowledging Lucien's proprietorship of Queenie. "Maybe we could talk a little business. I saw your friend Konig in L.A., by the way."

"Did you?" Lucien asked, his voice tight.

"He's looking for talent. Though after the last couple of movies he made, I think he's washed up." Cantor gave Queenie a wink, then turned back to Lucien. "You got yourself a great little girl here," he said. "Hold on to her. And Rani—don't forget what we talked about. I'll be seeing you." Cantor bowed slightly to the Princess and vanished back into the crowd.

"You don't seem to like him," Queenie said. "Have you known him long?"

Lucien shrugged. "We met in Paris briefly a few years ago. He was handling some Negro jazz musicians then. He's the worst kind of flesh peddler."

"I thought he was quite interesting. He said I could be making fifty thousand dollars in America. Do you think that's true?"

"If you did, Cantor would steal every penny of it. Did he ask you to meet him at Claridge's?"

"Yes."

"If you went, he'd chase you around his suite. He's well known for it."

"Personally," the Princess said, "I rather *like* him. Such an energetic young man! He rather reminds me of my late husband . . ."

The Princess rose to her feet, a procedure which required Lucien's help. "I must circulate," she groaned. She leaned on Queenie's arm. "So must you, *chérie*. It's the first law of society. Beautiful young women can't sit and gossip with an old woman like me. It's not fair to the men." She leaned closer. "If you ever need to talk to a friend, come. *Sans cérémonie*," the Princess added, not bothering to inquire if Queenie spoke French.

"I will," Queenie said, kissing the old woman.

"Especially if you're in trouble," the Princess said, her face severe for a moment.

"What trouble?" Lucien asked. "She has me."

The Princess tapped him on the wrist with her pince-nez, then held her hand out to be kissed with the imperious grace of a woman who had once been one of the great beauties of the Imperial Court. "All men are the same," she said. "If they love a woman, they think that's all she needs."

Lucien laughed and kissed her hand.

She pointed her pince-nez at Queenie. "When you have trouble with this fellow, you come to me. As for love—when you're my age, you realize it's nothing but trouble. The sleepless nights, the dramas, the lies . . . what a lot of trouble!" She winked at Queenie. "But how one misses it."

She moved forward toward her other guests, then paused and turned back to glare at Lucien. "Lucien," she said, "you be careful. Don't keep this one in a cage. Caged birds fly away as soon as someone opens the door."

Early the next morning, while Queenie was still asleep, Lucien drove to the post office on the Haymarket, which was open twenty-four hours a day, and wrote a cable for the sleepy clerk. It read: "DAVID KONIG METRO CULVER CITY, CALIFORNIA USA STOP HAVE YOU SEEN PHOTOS I SENT STOP BALABAN IN TOWN WITH CANTOR STOP THEY MAY SNAP HER UP STOP COME AT ONCE STOP CHAMBRUN."

Lucien stood there for a moment. He wondered if the cable was too peremptory—Konig was not a man who liked to be pressured or hur-

ried into things. But then he decided the tone was probably just right.

Konig would come. Lucien could feel it in his bones. When he did, he would make Queenie a star. Lucien would direct her, they would both become rich and famous—he had no doubts about any of it at all.

Of course, she was very young—*that* sometimes concerned him. She was impressionable, easy prey for men like Cantor. A close call, he told himself. He would have to make sure people like that were kept away from her in future. . . .

Queenie didn't like being told what to do—not even by Lucien—but she was sensible enough to know when it was necessary to give in. That Cantor might chase her around his suite seemed to her altogether likely, but nothing she couldn't deal with if it happened. Besides, she was curious to hear more about that glittering world he was a part of, or *seemed* to be a part of, if he was to be believed. She felt badly about the possibility that he had spent the afternoon alone in the hotel, waiting for her, but there was no point in provoking Lucien, she decided, and in any event, she had another, more pressing, problem on her mind.

It was nothing she could discuss with Lucien—she didn't even know how to begin. She needed a friend, so with some misgivings she summoned up her courage to pay a call on the Princess Ouspenskaya, feeling slightly guilty that she hadn't told Lucien where she was going.

The big house on Eaton Place was more like an embassy than a private residence, and once she had been admitted by the elderly, fussy butler, Queenie realized that she had no memory of what the interior was like. The small sitting room into which the butler showed her was furnished with such a profusion of chairs, sofas, coffee tables, writing desks and footstools that it was almost impossible to move in a straight line. The walls, however, were what caught her attention—indeed they would catch anyone's attention, for they were covered with the most striking and bizarre modern paintings, most of them unframed. The contrast between the furniture and the art on the walls was so startling that Queenie stopped to look around her in amazement, causing the butler, who had apparently mastered the art of sleepwalking, to bump into her.

"You're admiring my paintings, child," the Princess said. She was lying on a sofa in one corner of the room, hidden from sight and draped in a wool afghan which she was apparently still knitting, for she was holding the needles in her heavily ringed fingers, and she wore two pairs of spectacles, one on top of the other.

"They took me by surprise."

"Excellent! That's what they're supposed to do."

"Tea, mum?" the butler asked, shifting from one foot to the other.

"Of *course*, tea. What do you think? Sit down next to me, dear. Which one do you like best?"

"I'm not sure I like any of them."

"Good! Most people feel obliged to say something polite, which is silly. Paintings like this are not supposed to be liked. They are supposed to *shock*. People expect paintings to be pretty, particularly here in England. But art is not pretty."

"They don't seem to go very well with the furniture."

"That doesn't matter. You take that Kandinsky over there," the Princess said, pointing a knitting needle at what seemed to Queenie a ferocious and possibly obscene blob of color. "It wouldn't go well with anything. The truth is that my late husband collected antique furniture, and I collect modern paintings. He liked to spend his days in the showrooms. I liked to spend mine visiting artists. The secret of a happy marriage is to have different interests—and a lot of money, of course. . . . What kind of trouble are you in?"

Before Queenie could answer, the butler arrived with a silver tea tray, coughed and left. The Princess poured Queenie's tea, then poured her own from a separate teapot. It did not escape Queenie's attention that the Princess's "tea" was colorless and smelled very much like gin.

"What makes you think I'm in trouble?" she asked.

"You're young. You're beautiful. A handsome young man is in love with you. Why else would you visit an old woman like me in the middle of the afternoon? Surely Lucien hasn't lost interest in you already?"

Queenie paused for a moment, sitting on her chair like a schoolgirl, with her knees pressed together and her hands in her lap. "I think I'm pregnant," she said.

The old woman stared at her through the double spectacles. "That *is* a problem," she said. "I don't suppose Lucien will be pleased. One doesn't detect in him the paternal instinct."

"It may not be his."

The Princess took this calmly. "That's an even greater problem. Of course, you know men can't always tell. . . . The wife says, 'Look, he has your mouth,' or whatever, and they believe it. Or choose to believe it, anyway. . . . None of the Glazunov children resemble each other at all—*or* their poor father. . . ."

Queenie didn't doubt this was true, in general and in the Glazunov family, whoever they were, but her own case was more difficult. If it was Morgan's child—and the dates made it certain that it was—there was always the chance it would be dark. It was the curse of Anglo-Indian life. Two fair-skinned Anglo-Indians could still produce a child that was black, and it often happened in large families that while some of the children were so fair-skinned they could pass for English, others were as black as the natives, or blacker. If she was bearing Morgan's child, it might be all too evident to Lucien that it wasn't his, and she was therefore determined not to have it.

"I don't want a baby."

"You'd be surprised how few women do. What makes you think I can help you?"

"I don't know anybody else. Not really. One of the girls at the Café de Paris told me to drink a bottle of gin and lie in a hot bath, but I threw up before anything happened. Lucien told me to go and see a Dr. Drymond, but I was afraid I was pregnant, and I didn't want to *know*. I don't suppose he would be . . ."

"No. Forget Drymond. I know him. A good doctor, but not at all the man for what you have in mind. How many periods have you missed, may I ask?"

"Two."

"*Two?* You have left it a little late, you know!"

Queenie blushed. "Well, I thought the first one I missed might just be nerves. When I missed the second, I couldn't fool myself anymore."

"Pretty soon you won't fool anyone, my dear. I shall see what I can do."

"I feel so *stupid*."

"A waste of time. Go. I'll find the name of a reliable person. You may kiss me on the cheek."

"You've been very kind."

"Not at all. I enjoy meddling in other people's lives, child. It's much more interesting than knitting. You'll hear from me tomorrow, or the day after."

"Telephone, Miss Rani." The page, a wizened dwarf in livery (Vale had a taste for the grotesque), pointed to an upholstered sedan chair which served as a telephone booth. He leered at Queenie as she squeezed into it in her wrapper. She waved him away and slammed the flimsy door in his face. She didn't want to share whatever it was

Princess Ouspenskaya had to tell her with one of Vale's people, particularly the dwarf, whom she loathed, suspecting that he spied on her
through the keyhole of her dressing-room door, which she had finally
plugged with cotton wool.

"Princess?" she said. But the voice was so familiar—and unexpected—that Queenie almost dropped the receiver. "Hello?" Morgan
said. "Hello? Queenie? I need your help."

Queenie nearly panicked in the warren of streets around Shepherd's
Market. Morgan's instructions had been hasty and partly incoherent.
He sounded drunk, but even had he been more precise, Queenie was
too flustered to pay strict attention.

She peered at the numbers of the run-down houses that seemed to
have been decaying since the eighteenth century and were probably
decayed even then. The intervening centuries had blackened the brick
and given the plaster a leprous glow, while the houses themselves were
as twisted as hunchbacks, leaning against each other for support. The
few streetlights, converted gas lamps, gave off hardly more than a feeble
orange flicker. The doorways were so dark that it was possible to read
the numbers only by striking a match.

Beside each door was a row of tarnished bells, most of them bearing
a stained and tattered card or a scrap of paper scrawled with inscrip-
tions like "Doreen gives French lessons, three rings" or "Maureen
teaches discipline, third floor left." The malodorous alleyways were like
caves, and the few shadowy figures in them walked close to the walls,
their faces shielded from view, peering at the cards and bells intently.

Queenie found the number she was looking for. One of the bells
was marked "Mavis—fourth floor," without any indication of Mavis's
specialty, if any. She pushed open the door and made her way up the
narrow stairs. A man emerged from the dark, paused as she squeezed
past him, covering his face with his hat, and said, "I wish I'd seen *you*
before I spent my money, love." On the fourth-floor landing Queenie
found a door unlocked. She turned the knob and opened it.

The room was so small that it was almost completely filled by the
bed. A curtain made of old sheets was stretched across one side of it
suspended from a string. The fireplace was incongruously large—some
landlord in the dim past must have partitioned off a fair-sized bedroom
to make two rooms and left the original fireplace untouched. Now it
contained only a rusty gas ring glowing with a faint blue light, its pipe

attached to a coin meter, although the polished steel poker and fire tongs were still propped against the wall, reminders of some more gracious age. There was nothing on the walls but a calendar featuring an improbably long-legged blond girl putting on her stockings. "Morgan?" Queenie whispered.

The curtain moved, and Morgan appeared, lurching slightly. "Hello, Queenie," he said. "I've been a bloody fool."

Then he started to cry.

Queenie wanted to cry, too, but forced herself not to. Morgan, who had always been so dapper even when things were at their worst, looked like a derelict. His mustache was ragged and unkempt, his eyes red-rimmed, he needed a shave, and he seemed to have slept in his clothes, which were stained, creased and in need of repair. He had lost several buttons, and the threads that had attached them were hanging loose. His shirt collar was missing, as were his cuff links and his collar studs, and one of his shoelaces had been broken and clumsily reknotted. He stood there in the sordid little room beside the filthy, unmade bed, his hands trembling and tears running down his sallow cheeks. "Have you got a shilling for the gas meter?" he asked. "I'm cold."

She fished a shilling from her handbag and fed it into the meter. The gas ring gave off a nauseating puff, then warmed to a slightly more steady glow, though it did little to raise the temperature of the room.

"What happened?" she asked.

Morgan searched his pockets, produced a cigarette and lit it. He breathed the smoke in hungrily, his eyes closed, as if he hoped to warm himself from the inside out. "Mavis took off," he said. "With all my money. She didn't even leave me a shilling for the bloody gas!"

"When did you last eat?"

"I had a tin of sardines today. Or yesterday, perhaps. I don't remember."

Morgan shuffled over to the bedside table and picked up a bottle of gin. He examined it carefully. There was about an inch left in the bottle. He poured it into a dirty mug, then came back to Queenie. He moved like an old man, but the gin seemed to revive him slightly. He lifted the mug toward Queenie in an ironic toast. "So you're working at the Café de Paris," he said. "Congratulations. It's funny. I dreamed all my life of playing at the Café de Paris, and now *you're* there, and I'm *here*. . . ." He swung the mug around to encompass the room, spilling gin on his hand. "Down at the bottom, Queenie." He was slipping into a mood of sloppy sentimentality.

"I'll lend you the money, Morgan."

At the mention of money, his mood changed instantly to anger, catching her by surprise. She had forgotten what it was like to deal with a man who was drunk. "Lend? You ought to *give* me money, girl! Without me, you'd still be sitting on your ass in Calcutta. Stuff your bloody loan!"

"Then I'll give it to you. It would get you back to India."

"Come off it. I wouldn't get on the bloody boat. They'd be waiting for me with handcuffs."

"Goldner isn't going to press charges, Morgan."

"Isn't he though? Is that what he told you? He went to the police all right."

"He promised he wouldn't. I asked him."

"Well, if he didn't, somebody did. The word's out all over London that the rozzers are looking for me. That's the reason Mavis scarpered. Or one of the reasons, the bloody bitch. I'll tell you one thing, straight: I'm not bloody well going to prison."

"I'll straighten it out."

"Very much obliged, I'm sure. I don't need you to straighten things out for me. You get a couple of hundred quid together, come with me, and we'll make a run for France. They never pay attention to the Channel boats, and they won't be looking for a married couple."

"That's ridiculous. I'm not going. Why should I? You signed away my future without even telling me."

Morgan closed his eyes. His anger had ebbed, as if he had suddenly lost the energy to keep it going. "I did it for your sake," he said quietly. "I was afraid of losing you."

To her horror, Queenie realized he was probably telling the truth. It was not that he had wanted to cheat or exploit her. He had simply wanted to bind her, to keep some kind of control over her life. "You never *had* me, Morgan," she said.

He banged the mug down and turned to face her, his anger returning, stronger this time. "You're mine, Queenie," he said. "You always were."

She turned toward the door and felt his hand grab her coat.

"You owe it to me," he said. "Get the money. Quickly! We'll go tomorrow."

Queenie pulled away from him, but drunk as he was, Morgan was too fast for her. He grabbed her by the waist, and twisting against her body with all his weight, he shoved her away from the door. Queenie was caught off guard. She flailed at his head with her handbag and missed, scattering the contents across the floor. Morgan wrenched it away from her, and pushed her against the bed. He slid one leg behind hers, and forced her down.

"Is he that much better in bed than me?" he asked, his breath coming in sharp gasps.

"Let go of me, Morgan!"

"You never gave me a bloody chance."

He tore at her dress, while she tried to knee him in the groin, but he was too quick for that. His face was unrecognizable—fury, disappointment, failure had given him a kind of terrible false strength, and for the first time it occurred to Queenie that she might be in danger.

She froze at the thought of being beaten or raped, or perhaps even murdered on this filthy bed, with the unwashed smell of Mavis in her nostrils. It was not only fear that petrified her, but the horror of being dragged back into the rancid, drab, squalid world of failure from which she had so recently escaped. There was only one thing she could think of to stop him. "Morgan," she shouted, "I'm pregnant!"

He stopped for a moment in surprise, though he didn't let her go. "You're *what*?"

"I'm going to have a baby. I think it's yours."

"*Ours*, you mean. All the more reason to make a run for France. You can get a job in Paris. I'll find something there to do . . ."

Queenie took advantage of the pause. She slipped out from under him and ran for the door. To her horror, she felt herself losing her balance as Morgan grabbed her. "Queenie," he shouted, "I *love* you!"

She saw his face, full of passion and hatred, as if he could no longer tell the one from the other, looking down on her as he reached for his belt buckle. Lunging desperately to one side, she grabbed the polished iron poker, felt its weight pull against her muscles and swung it upward at him with all her strength.

There was a noise like a ripe piece of fruit falling to the ground, a sound at once solid and liquid. Morgan's eyes rolled in his head so that she could see only the whites. A thin streak of pink froth appeared at one corner of his mouth. He seemed to be trying to swallow it, then his Adam's apple stopped moving and he gave a sigh like a man who has been woken up before dawn out of a deep sleep—but instead of waking, he dropped heavily to his knees, then rolled over on his side. His fingertips tapped against the floor noiselessly for a moment, then his feet in the down-at-the-heels shoes gave a few spasmodic jerks.

He made a sound like nothing she had ever heard—a low, deep, heavy cough, slow and infinitely sad, as if his last breath was leaving his body reluctantly. Then he was still.

Vale stared at the body with ill-concealed distaste, as if Morgan had been guilty of some breach of good manners by dying. His hands were jammed deep in the pockets of his black Chesterfield and he wore a homburg pulled low over his face, so that its brim joined his heavy eyebrows. "You did quite right to telephone me," he said.

She felt too sick to say anything. She had spent an hour lying on the floor in agony and fear, knowing she needed help, and fearing most of all that Lucien would see her like this. Deep inside her body, she had been wracked with a sharp, tearing pain that made her cry out for help, then bite her lips until they bled. She guessed what was happening to her, and the shame of it was so terrible that it almost overwhelmed the horror of Morgan's death. There was nothing Lucien could do for her—she knew that. Vale was the only person who could deal with what she had done.

He looked around the room, as if the sight of Morgan no longer interested him. "Where did all the blood come from? Did you stab him as well as hit him with a poker?"

"I think I've miscarried." Queenie huddled in a corner, wrapped in Morgan's raincoat. The sheer effort of crawling downstairs to the coin box in the dark hall had drained her last reserves of courage.

Vale popped a peppermint into his mouth and chewed it thoughtfully. "How revolting," he said, with some satisfaction. "What an interesting life you seem to have led for one so young."

"I didn't mean to kill him."

"It doesn't matter whether you meant to or not. You did."

"What am I going to do?"

"Stop blubbering, for a start. It gets on my nerves. Did anybody know you were coming here?"

"No."

"Very good. Then the sensible thing to do is to tidy things up and dispose of your uncle."

"What about the police?"

"The *police?* Do you want to stand trial for murder, Queenie?"

She shook her head.

He put his hands into his pockets and jingled his change. In his own way, Vale seemed to be having a good time. "My chauffeur and I can take care of Morgan," he said, touching the body with the toe of his patent-leather evening pumps. "In the meantime, our friend Goldner can cope with *you.* He's on his way."

"He's coming here?"

"Goldner's a practical man, dear. Something like this won't shock him. He'll take you back to Lucien's flat with some sort of story. You felt unwell at the club, he rushed you to the doctor. . . . The fewer people who know about this, the better. Especially Lucien." Vale whistled tunelessly for a moment. "I have an investment in you to protect. Don't you forget it, my girl. You're going to be worth a good deal of money one of these days. Besides, I don't want headlines saying that my lead dancer killed her own uncle in a scrubber's flat. That kind of thing frightens off customers—and gets the police all hot and bothered. What's done is done. Your friend will simply have to vanish, that's all there is to it."

"How?"

Vale's curiously opaque eyes flickered slightly. He gave her a thin smile. "The less you know, the better off you are."

Queenie guessed there was some truth to that. She wondered how much of what Vale said was true. Certainly he would want to avoid a scandal, and he would jump at any opportunity to make his hold over her more secure, but she could guess that his motives were at the same time more obscure. Violence and danger apparently did not frighten him—she had never seen him in a better mood. She had no doubt that he would use all this against her somehow, but it was too late to worry about that now. She needed help. If he was not the Good Samaritan, he would have to do.

He raised a gloved finger to his lips and frowned. "I hear Goldner coming," he whispered. "Or someone else—I wonder."

Vale reached into his pocket. His right hand, in a tightly fitting gray suede glove, reappeared holding a gleaming, nickel-plated automatic pistol. "Get behind the bloody curtain," he hissed. He slid over to the wall, so he would be hidden when the door opened. He cocked the pistol with a loud click and pointed it toward the door.

She heard the noise of footsteps outside and froze. She imagined it was the police—or worse yet, Lucien. She could feel the blood on her legs. It had soaked through her dress, and she was reluctant to let Vale, whose fastidiousness was so evident, see her in this state.

"Get behind the bloody curtain," he whispered, "or I'll shoot you."

She looked at him, standing there in his elegant clothes, holding the bright little gun pointed at her, and rose to her feet. She wondered if she would ever get rid of him now.

Goldner was dripping with sweat despite the cold. "You should have called *me*," he told Queenie.

Vale grinned—a singularly disagreeable baring of the teeth, like that of a shark rising to the surface. "Well, she called *me*," he said. "And quite right, too. Listen, old man, you don't want a scandal any more than I do. Get the little lady back to Lucien."

"She needs a doctor." Goldner's dislike of Vale was evident, even to Queenie in her present state, but like Vale, he did not seem particularly shocked at the sight of a corpse. No doubt Goldner had seen plenty of violence in his time.

Vale slipped the pistol back into his pocket. "Take her to Drymond," he said. "He owes me a favor, the good doctor. Tell him you're collecting on my behalf."

"I don't like it."

"Don't be an old woman. We're partners now. There's no better way to preserve a partnership than sharing a guilty secret. Why don't you make yourself useful? Gather up her things, then get her off to Drymond. And invent a story for Lucien, there's a good chap. Leave Braddock and me to do the rough stuff."

Vale was cheerful enough when he was in charge of things. He summoned the chauffeur and pointed to the body on the floor.

Queenie noticed it was the same man who normally guarded the entrance to the club, but instead of his usual livery, he was now wearing a black uniform with flared breeches, gleaming patent-leather leggings, black gloves and a chauffeur's peaked cap decorated with a black rosette.

He was so large that he seemed to fill the doorway. He, too, showed no surprise at the sight of Morgan's body. He leaned over and flipped Morgan onto his back with a loud thump. He looked at Morgan's face and whistled. "Nice work," he said, with admiration.

"We can do without your professional opinion, Braddock. The lady acted in self-defense."

Braddock grunted. "Very good, sir," he said. "May I ask what she 'it 'im with?'"

"The poker," Queenie said.

Braddock stared at it. "That'll do the job every time." He looked around the flat. "We'd best wipe everything off before we go. Fingerprints."

"Just so," Vale said. "I had the same thought in mind. Goldner, off you go. Braddock, go downstairs and have a quick look in the basement."

"Surely the police will ask questions when they find his body?" Goldner asked.

Vale laughed. Queenie had never seen him in such high spirits. "Don't worry about that, Goldner," he said.

Queenie turned her head to look at the body. She wanted to close her eyes, but she felt an irresistible urge to see Morgan's face one more time. His eyes were wide open, but it was the face of a stranger, fixed in a twisted smile. He looked as if he knew some secret and was trying to hide it for as long as possible.

"What he wanted most, all his life, was to live in England," she whispered.

"Well, he'll be *buried* here, anyway!" Vale said cheerfully.

Queenie heard a bell ringing. It seemed to be coming from somewhere deep inside her head.

She hovered reluctantly on the edge of waking. Somewhere in the back of her mind nightmare images swirled dimly. She tried to put them together, like pieces of a jigsaw puzzle, but they drifted apart with each ring of the bell.

She remembered the bland, smooth face of Dr. Drymond staring down at her, then the sharp prick of a hypodermic needle. She had a fleeting impression of a glaring white room, full of chrome and glass, and the sharp click of medical instruments being dropped in a sterilizing tray. The click of the instruments merged in her mind with the insistent high-pitched chirp of the telephone bell going on and on until it seemed to be drilling into her head, like the brain-fever birds in the hot season at home. She remembered Morgan and suddenly felt a grief so strong that she could hardly breathe. With each ring she felt pain like a jagged piece of broken glass stabbing her brain, until she could no longer stand it.

Queenie tried to roll over, but felt a new pain, this time in her groin. She groaned and tried to lift her arm. It seemed to be tied down. She opened her eyes and saw that a needle had been inserted into her wrist, from which a thin rubber hose coiled up to a bottle suspended over her head. She felt an urgent need to stop the noise. She managed to slide sideways far enough to knock the receiver off its hook and wedge it against her ear on the pillow. An unfamiliar voice said "Hello?" twice.

Queenie tried to frame a reply, but her throat was so dry she could hardly raise her voice above a whisper, and there was a curious, chemical taste in her mouth that made her want to throw up. She gagged for a moment, and tried to say "Sorry." Even to her own ears, it hardly sounded like a human voice.

"Is this Flaxman 5165?" the man asked.

"Yes. Going. To. Be. Sick," Queenie mumbled. It took an age to get the words out. Her tongue felt as if it were made of lead.

"What did you say?" The voice on the other end of the line had the low, calm pitch of a man who seldom needed to raise it, though somewhere behind the precisely articulated English was the trace of some other more exotic, glottal language. "Hello, what did you say?" he repeated.

"Leave. Me. Alone."

"Is this Mr. Chambrun's number?"

Queenie struggled to reply. Her mind worked as sluggishly as her tongue. Queenie heard the door open. A nurse stuck her head in, and said, "Oh dear, we're not supposed to be talking on the telephone. Doctor wants us to rest."

"It. Was. Ringing."

"I thought it had been removed." The nurse walked over to the bed and took the receiver out of Queenie's hand. Queenie stared at the woman's bosom in the starched uniform. Nurse's posture was awesomely commanding. It was impossible not to trust her. Queenie felt herself drifting off again. "Ma," she said, holding nurse's wrist, "I didn't mean to." Then she closed her eyes and returned to her nightmares.

"This is Mr. Lucien Chambrun's residence," nurse said crisply.

"What happened to the other lady—the one who wants to be left alone?"

"The young lady is resting."

"Listen, give please a message to Mr. Chambrun. Can you do that?"

"Certainly."

"Tell him to telephone me at Claridge's. Say Mr. David Konig called."

"Cohen?"

The voice was patient, as if the man was used to being misheard, though by no means prepared to let the mistake pass. "Konig," he said. He spelled it out slowly, letter by letter.

"K as in 'king'?" nurse asked.

"Exactly," David Konig said with a chuckle of satisfaction. "As in— *king*."

Part Three

DAWN

CHAPTER 10

"MY DEAR BOY. Everybody has domestic problems. There's no need to apologize."

"A minor operation—nothing serious. She was taken ill at work. She'll be on her feet in a few days. You'll see for yourself: she's everything I promised."

"I hope so. My God, what an awful climate! I had forgotten what England is like. Who is now the best tailor?"

"Huntsman, I suppose. Perhaps Poole."

"I shall have some suits made. And shoes, of course. What's playing in the theater?"

"Not much worthwhile. The only real sensation is Dickie Beaumont as Romeo. Everybody's talking about him."

"He's that good?"

"Basil Goulandris managed to sneak into a rehearsal. He was overwhelmed."

"Goulandris is a gossip columnist, not a critic, Lucien."

"True, but Basil is no fool. Beaumont plays Romeo with tremendous sexual passion—not at all the lovesick adolescent. Margot Feral's Juliet, I'm not so sure about. It's hard to imagine *her* as a virgin in love."

"So few actresses can play innocence convincingly. . . . I should like to see Beaumont again."

"That's not difficult. He's an old friend of mine. As a matter of fact, he and Cynthia Daintry are now having—an affair. She sits in the audience every night, just to make sure Margot keeps the kisses at a professional level."

"Cynthia Daintry is the one with the wealthy father?"

"The Marquess of Arlington, yes."

"How interesting. Shakespeare is intriguing. Why pay good money to develop a new story when you can use an old one for nothing? Sex and culture—an irresistible combination. Who is the best bootmaker, do you think? Lobb or Peal?"

"Both are good. Barney Balaban goes to Peal. Somebody saw him there the other day, trying to persuade them to make him a pair of black suede evening shoes."

"If Peal makes shoes for Barney—I'll go to Lobb. I don't want my lasts on the same shelf with his."

Lucien glanced at the mass of Vuitton luggage that filled one corner of the living room. It included two large steamer trunks. There seemed to be shoes all over the place, each with a monogrammed wooden tree and protected by matching knitted traveling bags.

The telephone buzzed discreetly. "Excuse me," his host said, then turned his attention to the telephone call, closing his eyes from fatigue or perhaps simply to concentrate.

Lucien scrutinized the luggage as his companion picked up the receiver. One piece of luggage was open—a small attaché case with gold-plated locks and its own traveling cover of dove-gray suede. It was lined in cedar, with a humidifier built into the lid, and it contained a dozen boxes of Dunhill Montecristo #1s. A leather duffel bag was partly unzipped, revealing that its owner traveled with his own monogrammed sheets, pillows and pillowcases.

"David Konig here," he said. His voice was low, musical, effortlessly charming and persuasive. "My dear fellow! How very kind of you . . . What an unexpected pleasure . . ." The accent was decidedly foreign, despite his fluency. It conveyed a depth of sincerity by no means mirrored in Konig's expression as he spoke and listened.

"Naturally you're the one person in London whom I want to see," he continued. "I was in fact just about to call you when you rang."

Konig listened for a moment. Lucien had forgotten how much Konig resembled a Renaissance prince or cardinal—his face was at once voluptuous, cunning and powerful. "I wouldn't have dreamed of coming to *you* with a venture like this," he went on affably. "It's much too risky. Yes. Yes? Well of course the potential is fantastic, I can't deny it, but substantial sums will be required. And films are a risky business. . . . Frankly, I didn't think you would be interested, or had that kind of capital at your disposal . . ."

Konig winked at Lucien, the receiver held tightly against his right ear. "Of *course*," he continued, his voice full of remorse. "I didn't mean to hurt your feelings. The problem is that I *did* discuss it already—with Victor Rothschild. I happened to meet him on the boat. . . . Can I stall him? I could try. My dear fellow, what are friends for? Dinner? With the greatest pleasure. And my regards to your lovely wife. . . ."

"*Did* you talk to Rothschild about your plans?" Lucien asked.

Konig replaced the receiver with a sigh. "He was on the boat," he replied enigmatically. "I couldn't remember the name of that fellow's wife. I must find out before dinner."

"I still don't see why it wouldn't be just as easy to begin with one film."

"Nobody wants to invest in only one film, Lucien. They want an ambitious program: six major films, a studio, a chance to get in on the ground floor of something big. They need a star, too. Britain's answer to Garbo, or Dietrich, or Crawford . . . The newspapers will love it. The British film industry hardly exists. Why? Because nobody wants to see British films. And why is that? Because the only British stars worth a damn are in Hollywood. With the right kind of face, there'll be no problem raising money. Men are more interested in pretty girls than in balance sheets—even bankers."

"I'm telling you, David—this one has a face that's worth millions. It's unbelievable the way she photographs."

"Can she act?"

"Does it matter?"

Konig thought about it seriously. "No. In fact sometimes it's better if a woman *can't* act. She has less to unlearn."

"There's nobody in this country who knows how to build a star," Lucien said tactfully. "You have the field to yourself."

"Building a star—it's an art, not a business. Very few people know how. One has to start off with nothing, like a sculptor with a block of clay. That was my mistake with Marla—she was already famous, at least in Central Europe."

"Is the divorce final?"

"Nothing in marriage is final except death," Konig said with a wry smile. He was silent for a moment. "The moment you let a star become more important than you are," he added, "it's all over. Look at Mauritz Stiller and Garbo. *She* became a big star in Hollywood—nobody even wanted to talk to *him*. When he had lunch at the MGM commissary, the waitresses wouldn't even take his order. Or Josi von Sternberg and Dietrich. He *invented* her—and now they send a Rolls-

Royce for Dietrich, while poor Sternberg doesn't even have his own parking place at the studio. Of course Stiller and Sternberg both made the same mistake."

"What was that?"

He smiled. "They fell in love with their star. A director should never fall in love with his leading lady. It's always fatal."

"He's an older man."

"Older than what?"

"Older than me, for example. But very distinguished."

"But I feel so ugly!"

It was not so much that Queenie felt ugly as that she looked subtly different—even to herself. For the first few days after what she referred to as "her operation," she had been too weak to look in the mirror, and frightened of what she'd find there, as if the death of Morgan would somehow be recognizable in her face or eyes. It seemed to her that her face was haunted. Her eyes were larger and darker than ever, the skin more translucent, the bones somehow finer and more sharply defined. She had lost weight, and while she had never been fat, the loss of just a few pounds was enough to alter the angles of her face dramatically.

It was as if it had acquired depth in the faint imprint of tragic experience. Her face was no longer merely beautiful; it was that of a *woman*—a woman capable of great passion, a woman with secrets to conceal, a woman who knew something about life. It puzzled Lucien, who attributed the change to the miscarriage.

"Don't be foolish, Queenie," Lucien said. "You're more beautiful now than ever."

She gave him a quick kiss—which he deserved. He had been unfailingly sympathetic throughout her illness. She guessed—for it was not the kind of thing that Lucien liked discussing—that he was not altogether unhappy she had lost the child, whose paternity he had never questioned—but all the same she had thought it best to keep to herself Dr. Drymond's verdict that she could never have another.

She had not asked about its color, but the expression on Drymond's face and the puzzled faces of the nurses made her suspect that it had been noticeably dark. Under the circumstances Drymond's verdict was a relief. Pregnancy was not an experience she wanted to repeat, and not only because it had been uncomfortable and humiliating. Whatever she could achieve for herself—and she felt, somehow, a tingling sensation that she was on the threshold of things she hardly even dared to dream of—a black baby would destroy it all, and the risk was always there, part of the heritage that she was so rapidly leaving behind her.

She adjusted the neckline of the pink silk evening dress Lucien had bought her as a get-well present—despite his dislike of the color—and followed him into a private elevator. Lucien, resplendent in a dinner jacket, pressed a button and the lift rose with a subdued hum. Lucien pulled back the gate and knocked on the door. A peephole opened and the door swung open, revealing Braddock, in livery and a powdered wig, bowing them in. Queenie felt a moment of fear at the sight of him, but his face was expressionless. Behind him, in a large room paneled in light wood and lit by chandeliers, were half a dozen gaming tables. There was very little noise—a low hum of conversation, the click of the ball at the roulette table, the sound of cards being shuffled and chips counted. The air was cool and scented slightly with the odors of cut flowers, expensive cigars and brandy. The Oriental rugs were so thick that Queenie's feet sank into them.

"*Rien ne va plus,*" one of the croupiers called softly, smiling at an elderly American woman with blue hair whose wrists, fingers and neck were so thickly covered with diamonds that she resembled a reptile with fabulous scales. Queenie stared for a moment at the seamed neck and the age-spotted hands. The woman blew a jet of cigarette smoke out of her nostrils and tapped one clawlike scarlet fingernail against the green baize as the ball clicked around the wheel. She sat as motionless as a gaudy bird of prey, staring at the wheel until it slowed to a stop. "*Vingt-et-un,*" the croupier said.

He raked in a large pile of chips, giving the woman a brief, professionally sympathetic smile, then pushed an even larger pile toward the man sitting opposite her. The woman looked up from the table. Her cold gray eyes focused on Queenie. She turned to the man who had won, and in a rasping chainsmoker's voice she growled, "Pink must be your lucky color."

"I hope so," the man said quietly, puffing on his cigar.

"*Faites vos jeux,*" the croupier called.

"Give me ten thousand dollars' worth of chips," the woman said.

"Who's that?" Queenie whispered.

"Mrs. Sigsbee Wolff. From Los Angeles. Her husband owns half the city. Konig is the man who just won. Ah, he's seen us."

Konig rose, dropping a couple of chips into the croupier's slot as a tip, and moved toward them. He was not an old man by any means, Queenie thought, but he seemed to walk with a certain slow dignity, like a figure in a procession. She could imagine him wearing robes and carrying a bishop's crook. He walked with a slight stoop, so Queenie did not realize how tall he was until he was only a few feet away. His face seemed to her like that of an aging and benevolent lion: a mane of sandy hair, beginning to turn gray, a powerful nose, high cheekbones that were almost Oriental. All his features were on a massive scale, in keeping with the nose.

Even in the subdued light of Vale's gaming room, Konig's pallor was remarkable. Yet he did not look ill—on the contrary, he projected an aura of energy so powerful that by comparison everybody else in the room seemed to her half-asleep, even Mrs. Sigsbee Wolff, who had put on her glasses to study Queenie more closely, displaying a curiosity so fierce that her eyes seemed to be gleaming with the same hard light as her diamonds.

"Enchanting," Konig said, kissing Queenie's hand. "Let's sit down and chat."

He led them past the roulette table into the adjoining card room, pausing on the way to give Mrs. Wolff a good-luck kiss on the cheek, which she acknowledged by waving at him, her bracelets clinking against each other like dry bones. He stood in front of the fireplace for a moment, warming himself; without his having given any visible command, two footmen appeared to arrange the chairs in a comfortable half-circle, while a waiter set up a low table and placed on it a silver tray bearing a bottle of champagne on ice, a tin of caviar in a silver ice bowl, hot toast wrapped in a starched napkin and a vase with one red rose.

Konig picked up the bottle of champagne and examined it carefully, holding it so close to his face that Queenie thought he was about to kiss it. He was clearly nearsighted—his glasses were so thick that his eyes seemed to be sealed behind them, like olives in a jar. He stuck his lower lip out. "The 1929 is a better year, but we shall have to rough it—I must speak to this Vale." She caught him glancing at her out of the corner of his eye from behind the bottle. She wondered if the whole performance was just a ruse to get a closer look at her.

He nodded to the waiter, who opened the bottle and poured. Konig gave a small sign of satisfaction, tasted his wine, stuck his lower lip out even further and drained the glass. "Are you interested in wine, my dear young lady?" he asked, as Queenie sipped hers.

Something about Konig's manner warned her not to pretend to a knowledge she didn't possess. "I don't know much about it," she said. "I've only drunk champagne so far."

"An excellent start. You can't develop expensive habits too young. If you wait until you can afford them, it's too late to enjoy them. It's nice to know something about wine, but not too much, of course. There's no bore like a wine bore. . . ."

Behind the thick lenses the hazel eyes were watchful, even a little malicious. She wondered if he had been giving her an opportunity to make a fool of herself. There was no doubt in her mind that he was testing her.

"You weren't born in England," he said. It was not a question. He had an ear for language, as well as an eye for women.

She thought quickly and decided to tell the truth. "No. In India."

"How wonderful! As a child I adored reading Kipling. *Kim*. My God, what a book! I read it in Hungarian, of course. When I read it again in English a few years ago, it didn't seem the same to me. Then I realized it wasn't because the book had changed, or even because of the difference in the languages—it was *me* that had changed. That's sad, isn't it? I always believed that when I grew old I'd be very wise. People would come to me for advice, and I'd know everything. But here I am, fifty years old—nobody comes to me for anything and I don't know a bloody thing."

Konig helped himself to caviar. Queenie was fascinated—she had never seen anyone eat caviar before as if it were ordinary food. He put several spoonfuls on a piece of toast until it was thickly covered, carefully squeezed a few drops of lemon juice on it and ate it as if it were bread and butter, washing it down with another glass of champagne. "Gambling makes me hungry," he said.

"I am the same. It's the fear of losing," Lucien said.

Konig considered the remark, then shook his head. "I don't think it can be that," he said. "I always expect to win. Do you know that in California they take perfectly good caviar and cover it with sour cream, chopped onions and chopped hardboiled eggs?" He shuddered.

"America must be fascinating," Queenie said, with a display of enthusiasm that seemed appropriate.

Konig was not impressed. He shrugged. "Well, of course, it's where the money is. I find it a singularly uninteresting country, myself. If you want to meet *interesting* Americans, you have to go to Paris. You know, Freud visited America. When he was asked what he thought of it, he said, 'America is a colossal mistake.' He was right. Of course, the truth is the entire twentieth century is a mistake so far, in no small part because of Freud. When I was in Vienna, I went to him."

"As a patient?" Queenie asked. She dimly remembered Freud's name—it was part of Pugh's credo. She wondered if she was being tactless. Surely Freud was a sex doctor of some kind?

To her relief, Konig did not take offense. "No, no, I wanted Freud to write a script for a movie about psychoanalysis—a man living out the Oedipus story, in modern Vienna or Berlin. Freud had some good ideas. Unfortunately we couldn't agree on terms. A pity . . ." Konig stared at Queenie over his glass. His eyes narrowed. "The forehead could be wonderful," he said to Lucien. "A real Renaissance forehead. An Andrea del Sarto madonna."

"The forehead is very good. The whole face . . ." For a moment Queenie felt a brief flash of resentment at being again discussed like an object on display, or a prize animal. Konig noticed and gave her a smile of apology.

"We'll have to see," he said. "Tests. We can't tell anything without tests. Still photographs mean nothing. Film is a different medium." He turned to her as if he wanted to make sure she wasn't left out of the conversation. "I have seen quite beautiful women photograph very badly in films. And sometimes the reverse. In Berlin I had Dietrich under contract, you know, as a bit player. Sternberg saw her and said, 'My dear David, I want her for my film.' I thought he was crazy, so I let him have her. And all of a sudden—*The Blue Angel!*"

Konig looked somber. "Of course, I got ten percent of the gross for the lend-out," he said, "but I missed a star." He reached out his hand and gently touched Queenie's cheek. "You have wonderful bones."

"Wait until you see how they photograph," Lucien said, but Konig ignored him. His attention was fixed on Queenie, and for a moment she thought he was in a trance of some kind. His fingers were remarkably delicate for a man's. He traced her cheek line, then nodded, his lower lip stuck out. "So you'd like to be a star, would you?" he asked softly.

"Yes," she replied firmly.

"It's not what it's cracked up to be. Nothing is. Still, there are worse fates." He took his fingers off her cheek and picked up his champagne glass. His mood seemed to have become suddenly somber, and she wondered if she had said the wrong thing. "Of course, it takes more than beauty."

"Who will photograph the test?" Lucien asked, a trace of anxiety in his voice.

Konig gave him a feline smile. "Vilmos Szabothy is in Paris. If I asked him, he would come over. For nobody else. But for me—he would do it. Szabothy is the best still. Did you know, he's the one who discovered that the right side of Garbo's face photographs better than the left? Nobody else had noticed. Of course, he's impossible to work with. He's been thrown off every lot in Hollywood."

Lucien leaned forward. His face was red. "I want to do Queenie's test myself," he said loudly.

Konig smiled. "Szabothy is good."

"I'm better."

"Szabothy is cheap. He can't work in Hollywood anymore. He could be had—for almost nothing."

"I'll do it for nothing," Lucien said. He lit a cigarette, then stubbed it out immediately. "Besides, Queenie won't test without me."

She stared at him in amazement and anger, though Lucien was so intent on Konig that he didn't notice. Konig, cool as a cucumber, noticed at once. His face expressed nothing, but his eyes focused on her.

She was so furious that she was speechless. Like Morgan, Lucien was selfishly spoiling her chance—and making her look like a child or an idiot as well, for she could hardly quarrel with him in front of Konig. There was a moment of silence; then Konig winked at her, and she realized that this, too, was a kind of test. "All right," he agreed, pointing his cigar at Lucien, "maybe it's not such a bad idea. The stills were good—even great. I'll tell you what we'll do: Szabothy will test her, so will you. Then we can see which is best." He turned to Queenie. "Is that all right with you, dear?"

"I'll do whatever *you* want," she said firmly, giving Lucien a black look.

"Splendid. That's settled, then."

"Do I have to rehearse? Or learn a part?"

Konig stood up, brushing a few stray eggs of caviar from his dinner jacket with a napkin. He suddenly seemed to have lost interest, as if details bored him. Queenie was sorry she had asked any questions. "Leave all that to me," he said impatiently. "I don't like to plan far ahead. In life, the important things must be left to chance. Now, if you'll forgive me, I must get back to the tables. I promised Mrs. Wolff a little baccarat before the night is out."

Konig put his arm out for Queenie—a gesture of courtesy which she had seen in films but never in real life. Hoping that she was doing the right thing, she slipped her arm under his and walked to the door with him, Lucien trailing behind. Konig moved at a serene, stately pace, while the liveried servants lined up on either side of him, bowing.

Konig paused and leaned over toward Queenie as they entered the larger room, so that they were framed in the doorway between two candelabras. "When you go into a room—always make an entrance. Pause briefly. Keep your head up, like so." He raised his chin, smiling slightly, to show what he meant. "You see, there's an art to everything, even entering a room. Do you love Lucien?"

She nodded without much enthusiasm, caught a little off balance by the abrupt change of subject. She was not about to forgive Lucien quickly or easily for treating her like a child.

"He's a good boy," Konig said equivocally. "Of course he too has a lot to learn. You shouldn't be angry with him about what he said just now, by the way."

"What makes you think I am?"

"I know women. In the final analysis, they're the only thing worth knowing. Lucien is a young man. He has his career to make. He has helped you, so far—perhaps one day you will have to help him. That is how it should be."

Konig moved briskly to the roulette table, still arm-in-arm with Queenie, and stared at the wheel. "How old are you?" he asked.

"Eighteen."

He raised an eyebrow.

"Seventeen."

"All women lie about their age. When they're young they increase it; after twenty-five they diminish it. I don't know what they do after forty, since I've never met a woman who admits to *being* forty. . . . Are you lucky?"

"I've never been rich enough to gamble. And I would hate losing."

"Nonsense. You may not have played cards or roulette, but everybody gambles. You gambled when you came here to see me. Lucien gambled when he said you wouldn't test without him. Gambling is another word for life. Here at a roulette table, however, one can test one's luck in its purest form. No intelligence is required. *Dix-sept!*"

Konig dropped a pile of chips onto the table without counting them. The croupier reached across with his stick, and pushed them onto seventeen, counting them as he stacked them on the number 17. "A thousand pounds, Mr. Konig?"

Konig shrugged. "If you say so."

"Seventeen came up twice in the past fifteen minutes," Mrs. Wolff said. "It won't come up a third time."

"I like long odds, my dear."

"You can kiss your thousand pounds goodbye, David."

"*Rien ne va plus!*" the croupier called, and spun the wheel. Queenie felt an involuntary spasm of excitement and fear. It was not her money, and it was not her bet, but she sensed that in some way a great deal more was riding on it than money.

The wheel spun. Konig's expression did not change. His mind seemed to be elsewhere. Of course, Queenie told herself, a thousand pounds was not that much money to a man like Konig, but even so, one might have supposed he would show *some* interest. She squeezed his arm. The ball bounced and clattered around the spinning wheel with a dry rattle that seemed to be the only noise in the room.

Queenie closed her eyes. She heard a clink. "*Dix-sept,*" the croupier said.

"*Mazel tov*, David," Mrs. Wolff said. "You stick with that girl."

"I believe you may be right," Konig said to her, kissing Queenie's hand.

"Don't worry about a thing," Konig told her. "Half of what they say about Szabothy is untrue."

"Which half?"

"The good half, frankly. But he knows what he's doing. That's the important thing. All directors are crazy anyway, except me, and I don't want to direct anymore."

"Is it true he hates women?"

"No, no. He hates everybody! He's of the old school—he demands obedience. In Hollywood they nicknamed him 'The Swine.' His bark is worse than his bite, you'll see."

They were sitting on canvas chairs in a gloomy corner of the cavernous sound stage at Elstree Studios, outside London, which Konig had borrowed for his tests. Konig's chair had a canvas pocket hung from one arm for his scripts. On the back of it his name was painted. Nothing was painted on the back of Queenie's chair. Konig peered at the catalog of a rare-book sale at Sotheby's, holding it close to his eyes and marking off the items that interested him with a gold pencil.

"A first edition of Céline's *Voyage au Bout de la Nuit* . . . It had a great influence on me when I was a young man in Paris. Should I bid a hundred pounds for it, do you think?"

"It seems like a lot of money for an old book."

He stared at her over the top of his thick glasses. "You're quite right.

It does seem like a lot of money for a book." He drew a line through Céline. "I must ask your advice more often. . . . Ah, here he comes."

Queenie looked up. For a moment she didn't know whether to laugh or be afraid. Szabothy stood in the stage light, glaring at Konig as if he were determined to live up to his legend. He was over six feet tall in his gleaming cavalry boots. He wore riding breeches and a black leather trench coat, belted so tightly around his wasp waist that the slightest movement caused him to creak like a tree in the wind. Around his neck a long white aviator's scarf was loosely knotted.

She had been told that in the winter he covered his head with a leather pilot's helmet, while in the summer, or when he was working under the heat of the lights, he knotted a red silk bandanna around it. He was wearing the helmet now and carrying a riding crop in his black-gloved hands. He tucked the crop under one arm, unbuckled the helmet and took it off, revealing a shiny, shaven scalp.

His face seemed designed to inspire terror. It was square, jowly, the color and texture of unfinished concrete, the cheeks slashed with dueling scars. He had a roll of fat at the back of his neck, like a Prussian general, and he wore a monocle in one eye. A gold slave bracelet sparkled in the light. He wore it over his glove.

"Excuse me," Konig whispered. "The mountain must go to Mahomet." He rose, smiling, his arms extended as if he were giving a papal blessing. He walked over to Szabothy, who hadn't moved. He embraced him. "*Servus*, my friend," he said.

Szabothy did not return the greeting. He surveyed the sound stage, the lights reflecting from his monocle. "I cannot work here," he said. To Queenie's surprise, his voice was high-pitched and squeaky, like that of a cartoon character.

Konig made a gesture of sympathy. "It isn't MGM. I admit it."

"Forget MGM! Even the Pathé Studio in Paris is better."

"It's only a test, Vilmos."

"What do you mean, 'only'? A test is a test. It's film. The studio is primitive. The English know nothing about film."

"You're right, of course, Vilmos. But from you, they'll *learn*."

Szabothy bared his teeth. "They think I know fuck nothing," he said. "I teach them I know fuck all!"

There was a dead silence, broken only by a nervous giggle from Queenie. Szabothy turned his monocle toward her. "What is this?" he asked with distaste.

"Miss Kelley. She is doing a test for you."

Szabothy grimaced. "The eyes are okay, but the profile stinks." He reached out with his riding crop and pulled the bodice of Queenie's costume down a bit, exposing her cleavage. "The breasts are so-so. I've seen better. We could get Sigrid Berg, you know. Why bother with a test?"

"Because I want one, Vilmos. I think she might be right for us."

"Not in one million years."

"With all respect and admiration—I disagree."

Szabothy shrugged. He rocked back and forth on his heels for a moment, creaking like a ship in full sail. "It's your money, Konig," he said at last.

She knew instinctively that he would do everything he could to make her fail.

The heat and glare of the lights was more than Queenie had bargained for. High above her on the catwalks, she could just make out the dark outlines of the grips, adjusting the kliegs, focusing the spots, tending the enormous white-hot blaze that was concentrated on her.

Szabothy was unsatisfied. "Kill two, up five, somewhere there's a light fading, goddammit," he chanted through his megaphone, while the grips doused the lights, readjusted them and turned them back on, cursing monotonously as they worked.

Queenie shivered in the moments of darkness, feeling the goose bumps rise on her bare arms, only to break into a sweat when the lights were on.

The workmen and the technicians smoked, chatted with each other and went about their business without paying the slightest attention to her, except for the occasional warning to watch out for the electric cables or to mind her back as they carried some piece of equipment past her. Konig seemed absorbed in his book. A production assistant sat next to him, holding a stopwatch. A secretary sat behind him, filing her nails, a steno pad in her lap. A young man stood behind him with a telephone. Next to Konig was a folding table with a Thermos of hot coffee, the day's newspapers and several folders of mail. He read on undisturbed.

Szabothy hardly looked at her. He stood beside the camera cursing unintelligibly in several languages, ignoring her completely.

She had been dressed in a low-cut white evening gown chosen by Konig from the wardrobe department. Her hair had been swept up in an elaborate coiffure. When Konig saw it, he sent her back to have it done more simply. When she reappeared on the set an hour later, Szabothy and Konig interrupted their conversation only long enough to send her back to have it redone the way it was before. She had expected to be coached, be told what to do, encouraged—instead she was treated like a piece of furniture that had been delivered to the wrong address.

The makeup man, who had done her face over a dozen times, shrugged sympathetically as he dusted more powder on her shoulders to hide the sheen of perspiration. "It's always this way," he whispered. "They never know what they bloody want. . . . Konig tested Margot Feral yesterday, and we were here until midnight! Well, it's overtime, but I'd just as soon not have the money and get home for supper, thank you very much, all the same."

"Konig tested Margot Feral?" Queenie asked, trying not to sound surprised.

"And Cynthia Daintry," the makeup man said. "Such lovely English skin . . ."

She was furious, though she kept it to herself. It had not occurred to her that Konig, who seemed so sympathetic, was hedging his bets quite so widely. She had no difficulty in guessing that he had been just as sympathetic to his other candidates.

For the first time she wondered if she really had a chance. Margot Feral was an experienced actress, after all, and so was Cynthia Daintry—in addition to having a rich father. Was Konig merely testing her as a favor to Lucien?

For a moment she had allowed herself to trust Konig. Now she was angry with herself for being so stupid—so angry that she didn't even notice that Szabothy was towering over here, flexing his crop.

"We are ready when you are," he said.

She was not about to let Szabothy walk all over her, she decided. After all, what did she have to lose? "I've been ready for hours."

"You had something better to do, perhaps? An actress's job is to wait. But you are not even an actress yet." Szabothy scrutinized her carefully. "Beauty!" he said, spitting out the word as if it were an insult. "You think that's all there is to it? Beauty is nothing. Let's get on with it. I will ask you to do something simple. You will go over to that chair behind you. You will stand by it. When I say 'Action,' you will walk to the marker, turn toward me, smile and hold your arms out as if I were the man you love. Is this understood?"

Queenie looked down at the cross on the floor, two strips of white electrician's tape, and nodded.

Szabothy glared at her. "You think you understand? You don't understand a thing yet." He turned on his heels and went back to the camera. "To the chair!" he bellowed.

One of the assistants slipped a frame-finder around Szabothy's neck, like a chain of office. Even from a distance, Queenie could see that his manner had changed now that he was ready to shoot. His concentration was absolute. He studied her through his finder, framing her from several different angles, each time bending down to check what he saw against the view from the camera. Szabothy took a deep breath. "Lights!" he called.

From all over the studio lights blazed, instantly raising the temperature. "Camera!" The clapper boy hit his two pieces of wood together sharply, then sprinted out of the way, though apparently not fast enough to satisfy Szabothy, who gave him a fierce glare. "Action!" he shrieked, pointing his riding crop at Queenie.

The task had not seemed to her difficult when Szabothy had described it—in fact, it seemed almost laughably easy. Now, with the lights glaring at her from every direction and the camera focused on her, its round glass lens as black and menacing as the barrel of a gun, she suddenly felt awkward and foolish. She knew that behind the blazing lights there were at least two dozen people—experienced professionals—looking at her, among them Konig, who had at last put his book down.

Every step seemed to take forever. Her feet seemed to weigh a hundred pounds each. The mark seemed to be miles away, and she was beginning to wonder if she would ever get there when she heard Szabothy call out: "Cut! You missed your mark, goddamn it!"

Queenie looked behind her and saw to her astonishment that she was a good three feet beyond the taped cross. She felt a sinking sensation in the pit of her stomach—this wasn't going to be as easy as it looked.

"We are waiting," Szabothy called. She walked back to the chair, where the makeup man waited for her, beginning to realize that each "take," however short, could go on for ages—the lights had to be cut, her costume checked, her makeup freshened to remove any trace of perspiration, her hair redone if there was even a single strand out of place. Szabothy stared into space, putting on a display of long-suffering patience that convinced no one.

This time, she swore to herself, she would get it right. She advanced toward the marker determined to hit like a professional. As she advanced toward the camera, she could see it gleaming on the floor, the white tape reflecting the kliegs. She was almost there when Szabothy called out, "Cut!"

She stared at him. He gave her a wolfish smile. "You are looking at the floor," he said. "Are you by any chance afraid of stepping in dog shit?"

"I was looking for the marker," she said, gritting her teeth.

"Ah? You think the public wants to see you staring at your feet? Your lover has just come into the room. You look where? At the floor? You are not a virgin, are you?"

Queenie felt herself blush. From the shadows she heard laughter.

"You will blush when I tell you to blush. Not before. A woman who is waiting for her lover is not a virgin. She feels excitement, pleasure, anticipation. When she looks up and sees it is him, her face lights up. You understand this?"

She nodded.

"You understand *nothing*. Go *do* it! Look at me! Imagine I am anyone you please. Go on, we haven't got all day."

She went back to the chair, walked toward Szabothy and smiled, opening her arms. "Take little steps, goddammit, you're not playing hockey. You're a lady. You know what a lady is? Again, again, *again!* Watch!"

To her astonishment, Szabothy shoved her out of the way, marched to the chair and did it himself, an expression of beatific pleasure on his face. He hit the mark dead-on, holding his arms out as if he were about to embrace her. "Makeup!" he shouted. "We try again."

He cut the next three takes before she even reached the mark, then paused to shout at David Konig in some foreign language. Konig's face, even from a distance, reflected a combination of long-suffering patience and almost saintly sympathy. He shrugged, he held his hands up like a man volunteering to be crucified, he clasped Szabothy's hands in his, then he rose, put his arms around the taller man and guided him back to the camera.

The takes began to pass like a blur for Queenie. She had no idea what time it was. Again and again she did the same small, meaningless scene. She knew she was doing it better and better, fueled by a growing hatred for Szabothy, whose icy contempt she found even more unbearable than the moments when he lost his temper. "If you want to cry, *cry!*" he shouted.

She glared at him. "I'm not going to cry," she said more firmly than she felt.

Szabothy tapped his thigh with his crop. "You ought to cry! You have no place here. It's all a mistake. Go home. Get married. Have babies. Why waste your time? Or more important, *mine*. Again, please."

She was, in fact, very close to crying. She could feel the tears building up in her eyes, but held them back. She was so anxious to get the take right this time that she moved too soon. She heard Szabothy's scream of rage. He slashed at the camera with his riding crop. Two takes later, he broke the riding crop in half with his gloved hands. Even from backstage, Queenie could hear him grinding his teeth. She gave a sigh of relief when he broke the crop—but the relief was short-lived, for an assistant appeared in a few moments with a new one.

Still, Queenie stubbornly refused to cry. She felt helpless and persecuted, particularly since Konig seemed to be taking no notice at all of Szabothy's behavior. Then she stopped thinking about Szabothy and blindly repeated the scene once more, knowing it was hopeless—so hopeless, in fact, that she burst into tears when it was over, in anticipation of another outburst from him.

"That wasn't bad," she heard Konig whisper as the lights dimmed. And from behind the camera, she heard Szabothy, his voice hoarse from exhaustion, mutter, "It was shit—but if it's the best we can do, print the fucking thing!"

In the small, dark projection room, Konig, Lucien and Szabothy watched the rushes. Konig sat in a leather easy chair, smoking a cigar, still wearing his hat and his overcoat. At times he seemed to be asleep, but his relaxed attitude was deceptive—here he was in his element, the eyes behind the thick glasses fixed unblinkingly on the screen as he puffed on the cigar with small, soft noises.

"Play the last one again," Konig called out to the projectionist.

They watched in silence, Szabothy staring at the screen like a man facing a firing squad—or possibly commanding one.

"Again."

Three times more they watched the last take. Konig pushed a button beside him and the lights went on. "You're a genius," he said to Szabothy.

"Yes. But it's still shit."

"No, no, not altogether. You've somehow brought out of her a performance. The first takes were awful, I grant you—but in the last one, you begin to believe she's a young girl in love. . . ."

"Maybe. But she's ugly."

"Surely not?"

"She squints."

Konig thought for a moment. He dimmed the lights and had the last take played once more. He sighed regretfully. "You're right. She does squint a bit. A pity."

Lucien cleared his throat. "It isn't a squint," he objected. "Queenie is slightly—very slightly—cross-eyed. Or nearsighted. I'm not sure which. You have to know how to photograph her in close-ups. If you do it the right way, the effect is very sexy."

"A squint is a squint," Szabothy said. "Stars don't squint."

"You're prejudiced, my dear Lucien," Konig said sympathetically. "It's hard to be objective when you're in love."

"Let me photograph her tomorrow. I know her better than anyone. I know just what her eyes can do."

Szabothy yawned. "It's a waste of time. We could get Sigrid Berg over here tomorrow with one call from me."

Konig sat motionless for a few seconds, apparently deep in thought. He avoided Lucien's eyes.

"You promised me I could test her," Lucien said.

Konig shrugged. "Did I?"

"Yes."

"In front of witnesses?"

"In front of Queenie."

There was a pause while Konig thought. He nodded to Lucien. "Very well, Lucien, test her then."

"You're a sentimentalist, David," Szabothy said with contempt.

"Never!" Konig said amiably. But he wondered if it was true. For some reason he *wanted* the girl to succeed.

Queenie was in makeup at the studio by six in the morning.

When she had thought of the movie business, she had assumed that actresses led lives of unimaginable luxury, but sleeping late was apparently not one of the luxuries.

Since this was to be Lucien's test, he was determined to supervise every detail. If Szabothy was interested in the way she moved, Lucien was concerned with the way she *looked*. When he saw her made up, he shook his head. The dark line of pancake makeup under her cheek-bones did not satisfy him. He erased it with a piece of tissue, to the annoyance of the makeup man. He tried a line of silver-white instead, like a bold, feathered stripe, on each side of her face. The makeup man nodded. He was a professional and could see what was on Lucien's mind, which was more than Queenie could. To her, the effect was garish, like a clown's face, and she said so. "We're trying to please the camera, not you," he said patiently.

He put his finger in a pot of mascara and created two smudges on either side of her nose. To Queenie it looked as if her nose was dirty, but she decided not to object a second time.

Lucien wiped his fingers, then examined her closely, holding her chin so that he could turn her face from side to side in the bright makeup lights. "What we are creating here is an illusion—an image that will appear real, better than real—on the screen. Your nose photographs a little too flat in the close-ups, for example. I noticed this yesterday. I'm not criticizing. It's a beautiful nose, but the camera doesn't catch it. So I create the illusion of shadows to emphasize it. In the mirror, it looks exaggerated, but on film you will have—the perfect nose!"

When it came to her eyes, he and the makeup man bent over, heads touching, like a pair of diamond merchants examining a precious stone. Her eyelids were painted a translucent white, to give added contrast to her dark eyes, but Lucien was not content. "Fish scales," he whispered. The makeup man produced a small jar and unscrewed it, releasing a powerful odor of stale fish. He rubbed the powdered fish scales together between his fingertips, worked them into a dab of Max Factor silver-white eyelid cream and smoothed the mixture onto Queenie's eyelids with a sable brush. "Lovely," he said with a grudging approval of Lucien's expertise.

Lucien was equally fussy about Queenie's costume. Never mind how uncomfortable it was—he made the wardrobe mistress pull apart the seams and restitch them so there would be no wrinkles, so that Juliet's silk gown fitted Queenie like a second skin. "She won't be able to move, sir," the wardrobe mistress protested. "The seams will tear the first time she walks."

"So you'll sew them back up again after each take," Lucien said with a shrug. "Listen," he whispered to Queenie, bending over so that his mouth was next to her ear, their faces reflected in the makeup mirror, his earnest and preoccupied, hers painted like a doll's so that she barely recognized herself. "When I move in for a close-up, don't stare at the camera lens. Look *beyond* it, into the distance."

"Why? Szabothy told me to look at the camera."

"Why? *Why?* Trust me, Queenie! When you look at an object close to you, your eyes converge a bit. You've noticed? Of course you have—all those hours in front of the mirror! The camera picks that up as a squint. It exaggerates. Normally it wouldn't matter. But this is film. *Everything* matters. Even perfection isn't good enough."

"It certainly wasn't good enough for Szabothy."

"Forget Szabothy. He's a bastard, but Konig is twice the perfectionist Szabothy is. He just doesn't show it. Besides, I told you—the last take wasn't bad. Konig was impressed. If he hadn't been, we wouldn't be here today, believe me."

"I wish I'd seen it. At least I'd know what I did wrong."

"You'll see mine. Listen, whatever happened to your guardian, what's his name?"

Queenie stared at him in sudden alarm. She felt her throat go dry. Had Vale talked to Lucien? she wondered. She looked hard at Lucien, but she could find nothing in his expression except mild curiosity and realized her sudden reaction of fear could only arouse his suspicion. "Morgan?" she said, trying to sound natural, even indifferent. "He went abroad, I expect, after what happened at Goldner's. Why?"

"No reason," Lucien said, though he clearly *had* a reason for asking. There was a knock on the door, and a voice said, "Mr. Konig is waiting."

Lucien and the makeup man guided her out in front of the lights. "Do what I say, and don't worry," Lucien said, as he walked over to the camera.

Again and again she ran toward him, stopping on the mark and looking over his shoulder, but he was never satisfied.

She had long since learned that she couldn't *try* to achieve the kind of expression he was looking for—it had to come naturally, from inside her, and the knowledge that her career, and perhaps his, depended on this test made her all too conscious of where she was and what she was doing. The previous day's shooting had left her exhausted, and today's was proving to be even more of a strain. She could hear Szabothy, an unwelcome bystander, cracking his knuckles and muttering to Konig in German.

She heard Szabothy laugh, then the slap of the clapper board again. Her mind went blank, as if none of them were there, and she moved to play the scene for what must now be the twentieth time, though she had long since lost count.

Then quite suddenly, in a quiet whisper, invisible behind the glare of the lights, Lucien said, "Look, Queenie, there's Morgan!" and she turned helplessly toward the camera, her mouth slightly parted, her eyes wide open in surprise and horror. "Cut!" he shouted. "Print it!"

She stared at him in fury. He did not know about Morgan, she was sure of that, but he had known the mention of his name would be enough to produce a reaction of surprise and fear, though he had underestimated the effect. "You tricked me," she said, her voice trembling. "If you ever do that again, I'll kill you."

Lucien put his arms around her. She could feel the cold metal of the viewfinder around his neck against her breasts. "I'll never *need* to do it again, Queenie."

Queenie sat in the back of the projection room staring at the screen in astonishment.

It was impossible to believe that the face on it was her own. The face that now filled the screen, with the dark, luminous eyes wide open in astonishment and the lips parted just slightly, was more than beautiful—it seemed almost unreal, perfect beyond any human face. The flaws she found in herself when she looked in the mirror were either removed by makeup and Lucien's lighting or turned into assets. Her eyes seemed focused on some invisible point of desire or fear.

In front of her the three men sat silently. They played the test several times. Konig puffed on his cigar. Lucien whistled through his teeth. Szabothy cracked his knuckles. They played it again. Nobody said anything.

Konig turned the lights on. He stood up, adjusted his overcoat and made his way up the aisle slowly, leaning on his cane as if he were exhausted. Szabothy and Lucien did not follow him. There was something in Konig's face that made it clear he did not wish for company.

When he reached Queenie, he paused. "I have something for you," he said, as if he had just remembered. He reached into his overcoat pocket and took out a small package wrapped in brown paper. He handed it to her. He looked up at the ceiling. "We'll have to change your name, of course. We'll discuss all that at lunch tomorrow."

Queenie hardly knew what to say, but it didn't matter, since Konig proceeded up the aisle and out the door without pause, to his waiting limousine. She tore open the package.

It was a first-edition copy of Céline's *Voyage au Bout de la Nuit*. Fastened to it was a card on which Konig had scrawled his initials.

CHAPTER 11

THE TABLE WAS SET for two in the sunny, glassed-in terrace of Konig's suite at Claridge's when Queenie arrived at one o'clock. Lucien had preceded her by some hours and was already deep in conversation with Szabothy and a trio of voluble, sad-eyed Central Europeans, who rose abruptly to their feet as she entered the room, bowing, smiling and making small sounds of approval, or, possibly, greeting, since they seemed to know little English. Konig rose, too, kissed her hand and introduced Queenie to the Central Europeans, whose names were un-pronounceable to her, though by their accents and the way they talked to Konig, she guessed they were Hungarians. With a wave of his hand he conjured up a waiter bearing a silver tray with flutes of champagne. "A toast," he said, "to Queenie."

"To-Kveeny!" the Hungarians murmured, a look of ecstatic pleasure on their faces. A pause ensued, during which each of them approached her with a flashing smile to click his glass against hers, then against Konig's.

"They work on a story," Konig explained.

"Do they speak English?"

"Why should they speak English? We'll get someone who knows English to work with them. A story is a story. Come, let's eat lunch."

"What about Lucien?"

"He is working. He can eat with them. Anyway, he and Szabothy have to learn to get along with each other. The director and the camera-man always hate each other, that's normal—but they mustn't sabotage each other."

"Lucien is going to shoot the film?" She noticed that Konig didn't discuss his decisions—he simply assumed that everyone would fall in with them.

Konig shrugged. "Since the two of you come as a package, why not? Anyway, he's better with the camera than Szabothy, for you. A cameraman can be in love with the star. The director, no. Lucien knows how to make you look beautiful. Szabothy will make you act. I will make you a star." He did not mention what *she* was supposed to do.

As they sat down, Konig smiled with pleasure at the table. There were cold cuts, sausages of every description, smoked goose, pâtés, more breads than she had ever seen before, radishes, green peppers, ham of several different kinds and a cold roast chicken.

"I'm afraid I eat rather simply," Konig apologized. "For you, I've ordered consommé, a grilled Dover sole and *fraises de bois*—I had them brought over from Paris this morning. Altogether a more suitable meal for a star."

It was the first time she had been called a "star." She knew it was premature, but she still savored the moment. "Do you eat like this every day?"

"Yes. It's not that I eat all that much, you understand, though I have a healthy appetite, thank God—but when you have been as poor as I was, the sight of all this food is comforting. Money they can take away from you. Diamonds and gold can be stolen. Women often leave you. But a full stomach is *yours*."

"Were you very poor?"

"Very. Sometimes there wasn't enough food—often, in fact—and my mother would hide some of her share and give it to me later. Poor woman! She loved me as only a mother can—selflessly, completely and without wanting anything in return. She died before I was successful enough to give her a comfortable life."

Konig sipped his champagne glumly, having apparently talked himself into a brief depression. "I think about her for ten minutes every day," he said simply.

She wondered if this was scheduled for the same time every day, but decided not to ask. "My own mother was very similar."

"Was? She's dead?" Konig asked in alarm.

"No, no. I simply haven't seen her for a long time."

"You were poor, too?"

"Not as poor as you, but quite poor, I suppose."

"Then we have something in common. I'm glad. I have never trusted people who were born with money. I prefer the *nouveaux riches*—they haven't become bored with money. In any case, better *nouveau* than never."

"I haven't any money to speak of."

"You will. This much I can promise you."

She looked at her plate while this sank in. She supposed she should talk to him about money, but it wasn't easy to know how. "Shouldn't I have an agent?" she asked, taking a bite of sole. Having been brought up in India, she had no taste for fish, and had only tried it to be polite. To her surprise, however, it was delicious, and she said so.

Konig beamed his approval. "What is expensive is generally good. I can think of very few exceptions. People think it's vulgar to choose the most expensive wine or the most expensive dish on the menu— but most of the time the one that's the most expensive is the best. . . . You don't need an agent. I don't say this to cheat you, but as a matter of plain fact. You are under contract to Dominick Vale and a certain Solomon Goldner. If I could, I would buy them out, but they're not willing to be bought. So I'll have to negotiate with them, and you can be sure they'll ask the highest possible price."

"They take half."

"I know. It's not unusual. I had Caresse Rosay under contract at one hundred thousand dollars a year, and lent her to Zukor at Paramount for two years at two hundred thousand a year. I made a profit of two hundred thousand. She was furious, but you have to keep in mind that I made her a star. I had a right to something for that. Not that it did Zukor any good. She made two flops . . ."

"Vale and Goldner aren't going to make me a star," she said, trying not to show how impressed she was by the numbers Konig threw about so freely.

Konig stared at her through his thick glasses. "You're shrewder than I thought. True, they're getting—what do you call it in English? A free run?"

"A free *ride*."

"Thank you. Let me handle Vale and Goldner."

Queenie didn't doubt Konig's ability to handle them. On the other hand, she was in no position to tell him that she was afraid of Vale, or why. "Vale won't be easy to do business with," she warned.

"Leave it to me. In the meantime, I will pay you ten thousand pounds a year for the first year. We'll have a three-year contract. If we make a picture, the second year will be fifteen, the third year will be twenty. . . . You don't look overjoyed."

In fact, Queenie had been calculating in her head that Vale and Goldner would take half of it. "It's a lot less than Caresse Rosay was getting," she said.

Konig looked at her sharply. "She was already a star—all right, a fading one, I admit, but not an unknown. Listen to me: you're going to make a lot of money, I promise you that. I'm going to build a whole production schedule around you. Be patient. After all, why take a lot of money now, when you have to split it fifty-fifty with Vale and Goldner? Wait a bit. Get rid of them first."

Queenie nodded, impressed. The idea had not occurred to her. Konig seemed to have an answer for everything. She wondered if he was taking advantage of her, but he had the gift of charm to such a degree that she found herself trusting him—or wanting to trust him. Besides, he was offering her a lot more than money. "Whatever you say," she murmured, lowering her eyes modestly.

Konig lifted his champagne flute. "To our mutual success." He drank, then looked at her with the expression of a wise owl, which he slightly resembled from the front with his round glasses and his slightly jowly face. "You are saying to yourself, he's charming, but can I trust him? No? Yes. Listen to me: I don't cheat actresses or actors until they have become very successful. At that point, they have lawyers, agents, they can look after themselves. I am like Robin Hood. I only steal from the rich."

"Do you give to the poor?"

"Ah, no. That far I don't go."

Konig sniffed his coffee and ordered a cognac. "Now about your name . . ."

"Which one?"

"Both. Rani won't do, for a start."

"It was Goldner's idea because I was born in India."

Konig showed no interest at all in the circumstances of Queenie's birth. Experience had taught him that most actresses and all stars lied about this, usually for good reasons. "Forget it," he said. "The Americans hate the British colonies."

"My real name is Queenie Kelley. Why not just use that?"

"It sounds Irish. The English hate the Irish."

"My mother's name was Jones, if that's a help."

Konig grimaced. "They hate the Welsh, too."

They sat in silence. He rose and went over to the window, staring out at the rooftops of Mayfair. "These things are always difficult," he murmured, his back to her. "But they matter. A star's name has to have *magic*. When I first met Marla, her name was Esther Weisz. I took 'Negresco' from the name of my favorite hotel in Cannes," he added, with a note of pride.

"And Marla?"

"Ah. That was a mistake—or rather, an accident. I had the idea of calling her 'Maria,' but my handwriting is so bad that the secretary read it as 'Marla,' so it was announced that way to the press. Esther was furious. She cut up a dozen of my best silk shirts from Knize with a razor, but it was too late. Eventually she fell in love with it."

"And with you?"

"Yes. There are certain kinds of love, however, that are like—a crown of thorns."

"But you miss her?"

Konig nodded. "Like a hair shirt. For twenty years one scratches—then one takes it off and instead of relief, there's a sense of loss. . . ."

The telephone buzzed. Konig gave Queenie an apologetic smile and picked up the receiver. "From California? Mr. Fairbanks? I'll take it." He listened intently, putting one hand over his other ear. "Douglas, my boy! How's the weather? You're having breakfast by the pool? No, here it's raining, of course. What else?"

He listened for a few minutes while Queenie played with her coffee spoon. The notion of telephoning from California to London astounded her. She knew it was possible, of course, but the idea of doing it—or of wasting money discussing the weather—was hard to grasp. Konig, on the other hand, seemed to be in no hurry. She had always believed that one day she would reach this world. Thanks to Konig, she was almost there—yet she knew almost nothing about him. She wondered what his private life was like, if, indeed, he had one.

"I miss the avocados," he said into the phone. "And you, of course, dear friend . . . Distribution? I haven't thought that far yet . . . Well, to be quite frank, I did discuss it briefly with L. B. before I left, but nothing was written in stone . . . My dear boy, i'd much rather be with United Artists, that goes without saying—but would Charlie agree?"

Konig closed his eyes. With a telephone in his hand, he seemed to be concentrating so fiercely that Queenie wasn't sure he realized she was still there. "So talk to Chaplin. And to Sam. A star? I *have* a star. Give my love to Mary. Tell her I miss her parties . . . No, no, I'll come back, you'll see . . . I'll beat the bastards at their own game!" he added, with a ferocity that startled Queenie.

For the first time, Queenie realized just how vast and complicated Konig's business affairs were. Dominick Vale was more powerful than Goldner, but Konig lived in a world beyond the reach of either of them. She knew very little about the motion picture business, but she knew who Douglas Fairbanks, Mary Pickford and Charlie Chaplin were, and Konig was apparently on friendly and equal terms with them.

Konig hung up. He poured himself a fresh cup of coffee. "It's a funny business. Do you know, they say that Fairbanks is a Hungarian Jew? Who knows? In the movies, whatever seems real is fake—and naturally what seems most fake is sometimes real. Fairbanks and I were going to make a film together a few years ago. What was it called? *Darkest Before Dawn*, I think . . ."

Konig stared at Queenie, then put down his cup and clapped his hands together as if he were applauding himself. "Dawn!" he announced triumphantly. "Not a bad name."

"Dawn?"

"Yes, yes—you know. When the sun comes up . . ."

"Dawn Kelley sounds silly."

"Of course it does. Dawn Kelley is out of the question. It has to be Dawn something else . . ." He stared around the room, but nothing seemed to inspire him. He looked down at his cuffs, pursed his lips as he noticed his cuff links and said, "Sapphire?"

"I beg your pardon?"

"The stone. Like my cuff links. 'Dawn Sapphire.' It's not bad at all. Really rather classy." Konig looked at Queenie for a moment as if he were trying to see whether the name fit her, then he sighed with regret and stubbed out his cigar. "It won't do," he said sadly. "It sounds Jewish. People will think it's 'S–A–F–I–R–E.' A pity."

"I was rather taken with it."

"Believe me. Both the English *and* the Americans hate Jews, so it's out of the question."

"What about 'Emerald'? I've always wanted to own emeralds."

"Diamonds are a much better investment, darling. Never buy stones of color. They don't keep their value. No, Dawn Emerald doesn't seem right to me, either."

She could not help noticing he had called her "darling"—a theatrical convention, of course.

"Sometimes it helps to read poetry," Konig said—and Queenie had a sudden, bright vision of herself in the stifling schoolroom, the dust blowing through the open windows, and Mr. Pugh staring at her from the blackboard, the sweat pouring down his face, for in Konig's eyes she had caught for one instant the same expression of desire, like a flash

of light reflecting off a mirror as the sun catches it. If nothing else, it
jogged her memory:

"The island valley of Avalon," she recited, "Where falls not rain,
or hail, or any snow . . ."

"Avalon?" Konig asked, puzzled. "I went there once on Jesse Lasky's
yacht. It's on Catalina. A most unpleasant day. One of the girls on
board tried to commit suicide by eating a champagne glass."

"It's from Tennyson." Queenie felt rather proud of herself.

"A mediocre poet."

Konig closed his eyes in thought, opened them, got up, walked over
to the window, and came back to the table. He reached down and
took Queenie's hand. He kissed it. "You have beautiful hands," he
said, holding hers as if he was unwilling to let them go. "We'll have to
make sure Lucien gets your hands into the close-ups as often as possible. Bathe them in fresh cream. So 'Dawn Avalon' it is! Let's hope
the rest goes this easily!"

He led her to the door and opened it. The telephone was buzzing
incessantly. A liveried hotel servant waited patiently, holding a silver
tray piled high with letters, cables and telephone messages. Two men
in dark suits with briefcases waited on the sofa, looking nervous and
out of place. "Bankers," Konig whispered. "There's so much to do. . . .
Do you have enough clothes?"

"Well, I don't know . . ."

"No woman ever has enough clothes. A film star needs even more.
Go shopping." He reached into his pocket and produced an enormous
wad of five-pound notes. He handed it to her without even looking at
it. Then, before she could say anything, he was on his way, arms outstretched to greet the bankers.

Konig was like a magician, she thought, waving his wand to produce
a new and more glamorous future for her—one so different that it
would blot out the past. . . .

She could hardly wait.

Queenie had never ridden in a Rolls-Royce before and was doing her
best not to show it. Konig—who no doubt never rode in anything else—
was sitting in front, beside the chauffeur. The invitation to accompany
him to the theater had been delivered at the last minute so that
Queenie had been obliged to dress in a hurry. She wore a long pink
evening dress, white gloves, pink shoes and a white coat, cut like a cape,

with gold trim, that Lucien had chosen. She hoped the effect was glamorous enough to suit Konig. She wished she owned a fur coat and some decent jewelry. She could not help noticing that Konig's overcoat was mink-lined, with an astrakhan collar.

She sat next to Lucien in the back of the big car. There were small cut-crystal bud vases on either side of the doors, each with a perfect red rose in it. The interior smelled of rich leather, cigars and perfume.

Konig looked back at her in the rearview mirror. "Pink suits you," he said. "You should always wear it."

Lucien rolled his eyes. He had fought a losing battle with her over this question, and he was now irrevocably defeated. Queenie smiled triumphantly.

"What *Romeo and Juliet* proves is that nothing beats a good story. A boy and a girl meet and fall in love. Their families object. What more do you need? Of course, with Beaumont in it, the play is about Romeo. Margot Feral isn't in the same class with him. In a movie, it should be the other way around."

"Are you thinking of making it?" Queenie asked boldly.

"It crossed my mind. Why bake a new cake when there's a perfectly good one sitting on the shelf? For a picture one would have to change the emphasis. A girl falls in love, grows up too quickly, dies because of it . . . Well, why not? I might get Cecil Beaton to do costumes. He's good. Or Bakst, if I can tear him away from the Ballet Russe."

"Beaton would be easier to work with," Lucien chimed in.

"I don't care about that. Talented people are always difficult to work with. Bakst designed some wonderful costumes for me when I did *Scheherazade* in Berlin in the twenties. Unfortunately they were so heavy that the actors fainted when we turned the lights on. Eventually we had to put blocks of ice on the set, and blow air over them with big electric fans. Perhaps Beaton's a better choice. . . ."

Konig fell silent. He was smoking his cigar, seemingly indifferent to the crowds hurrying through the rain or huddled in doorways, for it was pouring and traffic was at a standstill. The lights of Piccadilly were reflected in the wet streets and pavements, filling the big car with garish flashes of light. Queenie huddled in the back, embarrassed that people stared in through the windows, their faces expressing a mixture of curiosity and envy—even hatred, it seemed to her at times. She decided not to allow it to spoil her pleasure.

The car pulled up slowly to the theater, attracting the attention of a few dozen people who were sheltering from the rain. The commissionaire rushed forward, opening an umbrella, at the sight of the Rolls-Royce. He held it up over Queenie's head as she stepped out onto the pavement, her little silk shoes gleaming in the marquee lights, her pink dress flashing like a bird's bright plumage against the rain-spotted, somber black of the Rolls.

The crowd gave an involuntary gasp of admiration. It increased in volume as Queenie was joined by Lucien and Konig, who followed her across the pavement in a small procession, gallantly leaving the commissionaire's umbrella to her. "Who *is* she?" a woman's voice called in the crowd.

And just as she was making her entrance into the lobby, Queenie heard a loud Cockney voice, tinged with contempt and disappointment, reply, "Pay no attention, dearie—she's nobody!"

But not for long, Queenie told herself.

Beaumont onstage was something of a revelation to Queenie. It was not just the voice that impressed—his energy, the precision of his movements, the control of his expression made him seem larger than life. She recognized his skill, aware now of her own deficiencies. His body and his face were like an orchestra which he commanded at will, making the whole performance seem effortless and natural.

Beaumont had given himself a sharply ridged straight nose for the role and had padded out his shoulders. With his waist pulled in he looked like an athlete, and he played Romeo with such physical vitality that when they joined him in his dressing room he was soaked in sweat and trembling with exhaustion, like an Olympic miler. He greeted her amiably enough, but without enthusiasm. Toward Konig he displayed a certain wary caution that bordered on outright hostility.

Konig paid no attention. The flow of his enthusiasm was positively lyrical. He digressed learnedly on other Romeos he had seen, on the stage and on the screen, comparing them unfavorably to Beaumont's. Beaumont listened, but his expression was mulish. He poured himself a drink but did not offer one to Konig. He drained it and poured another. "You're too kind," he said, dismissing Konig's flattery.

Konig shrugged, undaunted. "Not *nearly* kind enough. You were magnificent. I thought to myself, If only one could put this on film. In Hollywood, you know, they would say it's impossible. Too theatrical. They'd tell you the audience doesn't want to see the classics anymore. . . ."

"I expect they're right."

"They're wrong. They believe the audience is stupid. I don't think so, myself."

Beaumont dabbed at his face with a piece of cotton wool, removing his makeup with a precise circular motion. "You know, I've been there," he said quietly. "I hated every minute of it. Barney Balaban was here a couple of weeks ago with some dreadful little man called Cantor. I couldn't get him out of my dressing room. He must have sat there for an hour telling me how much he liked my performance—though what he can have seen of it, I don't know. I saw him in the third row, snoring away, dead to the world."

Beaumont massaged his face with cold cream, then wiped it off. Queenie recognized that Beaumont was in the process of transforming himself again. He poured himself another drink and slipped effortlessly into one of his favorite roles: the baffled English gentleman, a figure straight out of P. G. Wodehouse, none too bright, a little awed by foreigners but polite to the point of paralysis.

He did it quite well, she thought, except that his eyes glittered with wicked amusement. It was a game. She wondered if Konig knew that Beaumont was pulling his leg. If so, he gave no sign of it.

"Did Balaban make you an offer?" he asked.

"Now that you mention it, he did. Quite a generous offer, too." Beaumont smiled fatuously. "Well, they're a generous people, aren't they?"

He left the question hanging in the air, and anyone less sensitive to racial innuendo than Queenie might not have picked up on it. She had no strong feelings about Jews herself. The topic was hardly a burning issue in India, where there were so many other racial and religious differences to worry about, and almost no Jews. If Morgan had not pointed out that Goldner was Jewish, she would hardly have noticed, and Konig's somewhat exotic character seemed to her more European than anything else. She wondered if he would take offense, but he merely smiled and said, "Americans? Yes, I've always found them so." Having neatly deflected Beaumont's remark, he removed a cigar from his crocodile-skin case and examined it. "Whatever Balaban offered, I'll double it."

Beaumont's pose as a comic Englishman evaporated. *"Double?"*

"Whatever it was. If it's money that matters."

Beaumont hunted through the debris on his dressing table, found another glass and poured a Scotch for Konig. "Of course it matters.

You of all people know that! But I'm an actor, not a trained seal. I went to Hollywood once, and they didn't know what to do with me. I don't want to go back again. Certainly not now."

Konig held one finger up like a schoolmaster. "First of all, forget Hollywood. I'm going to make films *here*." He held up a second finger to make a V. "Second—I'm not an idiot like Balaban. You're an artist. You'll have the last word on what you do."

"There's a film industry here already, Konig. Romantic comedies. *Maytime in Mayfair*. Murder mysteries with comic butlers. Small potatoes."

"You don't need palm trees to make films. Only money—and talent, of course. The money is the easy part."

"Not in the theater it isn't." Beaumont looked glumly at Konig's fingers, then shook his head. "I won't say it isn't a tempting idea, Konig—but the truth is I have other plans."

"My dear boy, I'm sure I can accommodate them. Just tell me what they are."

Beaumont cleared his throat. "I promised to do a play with Cynthia Daintry, you see."

Konig heaved a sigh. His expression was sympathetic, as if he understood everything there was to know about making promises to women—which was probably the case, Queenie thought. "So make a film with her instead," he said casually.

Queenie felt a sudden stab of betrayal, so sharp that she almost bit her tongue. She had trusted Konig, and now he was selling her out, just to get Beaumont. She gave him a look of sheer rage—she couldn't help it—but Konig didn't seem to notice. He puffed contently on his cigar, like a man who has just picked up the winning card and is savoring the moment before calling "Gin."

Beaumont gathered his dressing gown around him and stood up. "I hate to say no, but I must. I'm afraid someone has already agreed to back me in the play."

"Who is it? One can always get out of an obligation like that."

Beaumont shook his head. "Not this one," he said firmly. "I'm not at liberty to talk about it." Despite her anger, Queenie detected a trace of fear in Beaumont's voice, as if he had already said more than he wanted to. He took his watch out of the pocket of his dressing gown and glanced at it. The sight of it seemed to increase his anxiety. "I must be getting dressed," he said abruptly.

After they had taken their leave of Beaumont, Konig stood for a moment in the dingy backstage corridor. "I must be getting old," he said. "I thought I had him. I was sure of it." He glanced at Queenie. "Didn't you think he wanted to accept?"

"I've no idea." She made no effort to hide the bitterness she felt—Konig had been quite willing to discard her without a thought when it suited his purpose.

He raised an eyebrow. "You're angry."

"No, I'm not." She knew there was no point in denying it—in fact, she *wanted* Konig to know she was angry—but at the same time she hated the idea of letting him know how weak and helpless she felt. Her career was in his hands; she had no more power over him than a child over its parents.

He looked at her sternly. "Don't lie to me," he said. He pushed open the stage door and walked out into the alley without pausing to let her go first—a small discourtesy, which she recognized instantly as an expression of his irritation.

"Lucien," he said, "go find the bloody car." He peered at her impatiently over the top of his spectacles as Lucien went off obediently to find the chauffeur. "You must understand—I need Beaumont. There are others, of course, but he's the best. I can't put two unknowns in a film. It's too risky. Even *one* unknown is a problem."

"Cynthia's not *completely* unknown," she spat out.

"Cynthia?" Konig sighed. "Let me just say right now, before Lucien comes back: If there's one thing I can't stand in a woman, it's stupidity. It's stupid not to trust me. It's also stupid not to listen carefully. I told Beaumont I'd make a film with him and with Cynthia, yes? I did *not* say it would be the first one, or even the second."

He stepped toward the Rolls as it stopped in front of him. "On the other hand," he went on, settling into the front seat without opening the door for her, "I don't know why I should bother to explain myself to you. Claridge's first," he told the driver.

Queenie felt relieved and unutterably stupid—once again, though she had no experience in the matter, it was as if she had offended her father. "I'm sorry," she said.

"Sorry for what?" Lucien asked, as the big car glided out into the Piccadilly traffic.

"It doesn't matter," Konig said, from the front seat. He did not look back. "Who *is* Beaumont's mysterious backer?"

"It could be any number of people," Lucien said. "There are a dozen producers who'd be happy to be."

"There would be no reason to make a secret of it, however. The first thing a producer would do is announce it. So it's somebody out of the ordinary."

Queenie stared at the back of Konig's head—or rather, his hat, for he had jammed his black homburg on. "I think I can guess," she said, anxious to make a peace offering.

Konig did not respond except for a puff of cigar smoke.

"I think it's Dominick Vale."

Lucien frowned. "That's foolish," he said. "Vale isn't at all interested in the theater. And he hardly knows Beaumont. They're acquaintances. That's all."

"That's not so, Lucien. They're—friends."

"Nonsense. They have nothing in common."

She was about to say that he was wrong about that, too, when Konig finally turned around. "What makes you think it's Vale?" he asked.

"An instinct." She was reluctant to tell Konig just how close the two men were—particularly in front of Lucien.

"Life has taught me many things," Konig said. "One of them is that there's no such thing as a woman's instinct. It's just a woman's way of not telling how she found something out. You say Vale is close to Beaumont? How close?"

"Very close. And you could see Beaumont was afraid to talk about it. That makes sense. Most people are afraid of Vale."

"Are they? How interesting. He didn't strike me as someone who's particularly fearsome—but then I've worked with people like Marty Braverman and Louis B. Mayer, so perhaps I wouldn't notice. Are *you* afraid of him?"

Queenie swallowed the truth. "No, but I've nothing to be afraid of him *about*." She wished it were so and felt sorry she'd brought the subject up with someone as acute as Konig.

"But perhaps Beaumont has something to be afraid about, eh?" He chuckled, delighted by his own conclusion, then turned back to face the windshield as the car pulled up in front of the hotel. He got out onto the pavement and took off his hat. "Take care of Dawn, Lucien. She's going to be a valuable property."

Lucien took her hand and smiled. "Dawn! I can't get used to it. For me she's still Queenie."

Konig smiled. "No, no, Lucien. She's outgrown Queenie. You'll see. You'll get used to the change. More quickly than you think."

Then, with remarkable speed for such a sedentary man, he turned and vanished into the hotel, so fast that Queenie almost imagined his grin had remained behind, like that of the Cheshire Cat in *Alice in Wonderland*. She had told him very little about Beaumont and Vale, but for a man like Konig it was probably enough. He would work out the rest, and would know what to do with it, she was sure of that. She traced the words "Dawn Avalon" in the condensation on the window with her fingertip.

She decided she liked it a lot better than "Queenie."

Konig was right, she thought. Lucien would have to get used to it.

Queenie stared at the front page of the *Evening Standard*.

THE GIRL WITH THE
MILLION POUND FACE.
KONIG REVEALS "STABLE"
OF BRITISH PLAYERS

She read the piece aloud to Lucien as they sat in his car.

In my exclusive interview with film mogul David Konig, [Basil Goulandris had written] he let me in on the Big Secret. His film version of Shakespeare's *Romeo and Juliet* will star Richard Beaumont and a beautiful newcomer—Dawn Avalon.

Interviewed in his penthouse suite at Claridge's, Konig told your *Standard* reporter: "She has a face worth millions. Every Hollywood studio wants her at any price, but I am saying no. I want to make British films with British stars."

As for *Romeo and Juliet*, Konig is currently negotiating with George Bernard Shaw to write the adaptation. Picasso has been approached to do the scenery, and the costumes will be created by Léon Bakst, of the Ballet Russe. "Stravinsky wants to do the music," Konig revealed, "but I am talking to Benjamin Britten and William Walton, since I prefer a British composer. . . .

Lucien snorted in disgust. "That's typical of Konig! He'll announce anything to make the headlines. He hasn't even *talked* to Picasso, I know that for a fact!"

Queenie ignored him and looked at her photograph. It was one taken by Lucien. At this very moment, she told herself, millions of people—5,234,897, according to the claim above the *Standard*'s banner—were looking at her, presumably with envy. She could hardly wait to send it to Ma.

"Good *evening*, Miss Avalon!" The commissionaire standing outside the entrance to Claridge's doffed his brown top hat with a flourish. He signaled to the doorman to open the door so that Dawn wouldn't have to pause, even for a second, as she swept from the car into the lobby. "Good evening, Miss Avalon," the doorman said, bowing.

"*Good* evening, Miss Avalon," the liveried footman in his silk stockings and powdered wig whispered, as he took them up in the lift.

"*Bon soir, Mademoiselle Avalon*," the maître d'hôtel said, opening the door to Konig's suite. He took her fur coat—for Konig had borrowed a mink coat from the studio wardrobe department for her use on the grounds that no star should be without one.

"Good evening, darling!" Konig held his arms wide to greet her. He embraced her, kissed her on both cheeks and put out his arm for her. Then, as if he had just remembered something he had forgotten to do, he nodded at Lucien.

Queenie knew that Lucien hated Konig's dinner parties—he complained that they were boring, stuffy and interminable, and she had to admit he was right to some degree. Lucien's real complaint, however, lay in the knowledge that he was invited only because of her. Konig always placed her at his right, next to his most important guest, while Lucien was relegated to the bottom of the table along with the less important bankers and their stodgy wives.

As Konig led her around the room, Queenie saw that the guests were his usual mix of money and power: Sir Hugh Pomfrett, of Hambro's Bank; Sir Conop Guthrie, Chairman of the Board of the Prudential; Victor de Rothschild; a couple of City financiers—hard-faced men who looked uneasy in this glittering company; a rising Conservative politician; Basil Goulandris, accompanying a press lord to whom Konig deferred as if he were the Pope. To keep these people amused, Konig had also invited Princess Ouspenskaya, Cecil Beaton, a distinguished novelist, the conductor of the London Philharmonic and, Queenie supposed, her and Lucien.

As Konig moved her from guest to guest, he whispered instructions to her. "Tell Mrs. Pomfrett how much you like her brooch. . . . Be particularly nice to Lord Woodlake—he owns three newspapers. . . . If that pompous Fascist Gorse talks to you about politics, try to look interested. . . ."

"I see from the papers you managed to persuade Dickie Beaumont."

"To persuade him? Not exactly. Thanks to you, I found the person who *could* persuade him, however. . . ."

"Vale? Was he helpful?"

"Helpful? I suppose so. Like most people, he had his price."

"What was that?"

Konig chuckled. "He wants to get in on the ground floor. Well, why not? I'd as soon sell Vale a few shares as anyone else."

"I'm not sure I understand . . ."

"Financial matters? Luckily, you don't need to. But it's really very simple. If you tried to borrow a hundred thousand pounds or so from a man like Vale, he'd throw you out of his office. But if you let him have one hundred thousand nicely printed shares of your company and a seat on the board of directors—it's a whole different story. Beaumont and Cynthia are coming tonight, by the way."

If there was anybody Queenie didn't want to meet, it was Cynthia—she feared a scene or a quarrel, which would make her look ridiculous, but it was not until after dinner, when the ladies withdrew to leave the gentlemen to their brandy, cigars and politics—an English tradition which bored Lucien and, indeed, Konig, though he disguised his boredom better—that she had to face the necessity of talking to Cynthia.

"Sit down next to me," the Princess said in her usual commanding voice. Queenie did as she was told and found herself squeezed in on the sofa between the Princess and Cynthia Daintry. "There," the Princess said. "God protect me from the wives of bankers and politicians. You know Cynthia, darling?"

Cynthia's sophistication and glamour had always terrified Queenie, from a distance. She was blond, blue-eyed, indisputably English, dressed with an extravagance and a natural chic that made her the darling of *Tatler* and *Vogue*. As the daughter of a wealthy marquess, her place in the English class system was secure, and she did not hesitate to show it—or perhaps it was simply something she couldn't hide even had she wanted to. Queenie's experience of aristocrats was limited, but even at first sight, before she knew who Cynthia *was*, she had envied Cynthia's apparently unaffected sense of superiority—the brittle, upper-class laugh, the knife-edged precision of her speech, the ice-cold blue eyes that seemed to treat the rest of the world as if it had been made for her amusement.

There was no denying, Queenie thought, that she was more beautiful than Cynthia—and still Cynthia frightened her. It was not simply that she was Penelope Daventry's half sister, though that was hard to overlook—it was the fear that Cynthia, like Mrs. Daventry, might put her in "her place," with a word, a look of contempt, a cutting laugh. Queenie knew she could defend herself against most things, but not against ridicule. She suspected Cynthia of a quick wit.

Cynthia was not in the mood to display it at Queenie's expense, however. "I'm so pleased to meet you at last, darling. You're *much* more beautiful than I thought you were," she said. "Pink suits you, too. Lucien was thunderstruck when he saw you at that dreadful little nightclub. I was madly annoyed with him. He couldn't take his eyes off you. Ah, well, it was all for the best. . . ."

"I wish the men would hurry up," the Princess said, fidgeting with her cordial glass. She hated being separated from the men as much as Konig hated being separated from the women.

"Not I. It's such a relief to be rid of them." Cynthia lit a cigarette despite the fact that the previous one was still smoldering in the ashtray. "Has Konig made a pass at you, Queenie?" she asked. "You don't mind if I call you Queenie, do you?"

"I would prefer Dawn, frankly."

Cynthia raised an eyebrow. "Yes, I can understand that. My nickname was Muffin, and my father still calls me that to this day. I hated it as a child, and I still do. Which, I suppose, is why he does it. Dawn it is."

"Thank you. Konig hasn't made a pass at me, no."

"Thank God. I've been waiting for him to make a pass at me, you see—and he's behaved like such a perfect gentleman that I'd begun to think he didn't like me. I mean, most movie producers begin that way, before even saying 'How d'you do?' Perhaps he really *is* a perfect gentleman. How boring."

Queenie sensed with relief that Cynthia was willing to accept her on an equal footing. Close up, there was something about her that was too bright and fragile for comfort, like an expensive piece of crystal that looked as if it might break at a touch. Her skin was so pale that it was almost transparent, and there was something about her china-blue eyes that suggested she always walked at the thin edge of hysteria.

"God, I hate parties like this," she said, signaling for the waiter to refill her brandy glass. It occurred to Queenie that she might be a little drunk. "Don't you?"

Queenie gave it a moment's thought and decided that she didn't hate them at all. "Actually, I quite like them," she said.

"How *lucky* you are! How on earth do you get Lucien to come? That's what I'd like to know. I used to have to move heaven and earth to get him to a dinner party."

"I think that's Konig's doing, not mine. Lucien doesn't feel he can say no to him."

"Neither does anybody else, apparently. It seems we're all going to be working for him. One big happy family. I say, where's that bloody waiter?" She gulped the rest of her drink down, then held up the glass, which the waiter hurried over to refill. Queenie, who felt dizzy on one glass of champagne, was both impressed and horrified. "Does Lucien still have that photograph of me?" Cynthia asked.

"He *did*. I made him put it away, frankly."

"Thank God! I must have been mad to pose for it. Are all those stories about your growing up in a maharajah's court true?"

Queenie was tempted to admit they weren't, but knew better. She nodded.

"You're so lucky," Cynthia said. "My childhood was unutterably boring—nothing but nannies, ponies and boarding schools. I always wanted to run away with the Gypsies, but I didn't have the courage, so I went on the stage instead. Unfortunately, instead of Daddy's being infuriated, he was delighted. I'd quite overlooked the fact he's stage-struck himself, so as an act of rebellion it fizzled. I expect that's why I took up with Lucien—that *did* annoy him no end."

"Were you very much in love with him?" Queenie was astonished at the way Cynthia discussed her own life so openly with a total stranger. It was as if she had no small talk but herself.

"Yes. Head over heels, literally. Well, he's divine in bed, of course . . . as you know. But I don't think he was in love with *me*— and of course, when things are one-sided, they always go bad very fast, don't they, darling? When you popped up, I was so angry I could have *killed* you—but of course I was just hanging on to something that wasn't there."

"All this talk about love makes me feel even older than I am," the Princess said. "When you're my age, food is more important! Isn't Konig a wonderful host? It's so seldom that one gets really *good* caviar. . . . Of course, he's Jewish. I've never understood anti-Semitism, myself. It was one of the poor Czar's most foolish ideas. The Jews were exactly what Russia needed most . . . ah, here come the men, at last."

Cynthia put down her glass. "We must chat again soon, darling," she said to Queenie breathlessly, then rose, a trifle unsteadily at first, and rushed across the room to put her arms around Richard Beaumont in a burst of affection that seemed to embarrass him more than it pleased him.

"I hope she's not going to make the same mistake again," the Princess said, examining the scene through her lorgnette. "Though I suppose it's inevitable. People *always* make the same mistakes over and over again."

Queenie wondered how much the Princess knew about Beaumont. "Why is it a mistake?" she asked, aware that she was fishing for an answer that would confirm her own suspicions.

"Because he's English. He's talented, attractive, charming—and knows nothing about women. She's beautiful, she has a rich father who loves the theater, and she's passionately in love with him—it must seem like a very attractive proposition to Beaumont, but the poor man doesn't have a clue what's in store for him. To be the object of someone else's grand passion—it's not an enviable fate."

For a moment, Queenie thought of Morgan. "Grand passion" seemed a rather highfalutin phrase to describe his feelings for her, but she supposed that they were just that, whatever words were used. Was she Lucien's "grand passion"? To the extent that he was capable of one, it seemed possible. Had she herself ever felt a "grand passion"? She would have to admit that she had not, if it meant sacrificing everything for the sake of one person.

From the far side of the room she could see Konig signaling her. "Go, go," the Princess said. "Konig wants to show you off. You won't raise any money for him sitting here with an old woman like me."

"It's more interesting sitting with you."

"Of course it is, darling, but it's not what you're here for." She tilted her head, as a sign that Queenie should kiss her on the cheek.

The room was beginning to fill up with more guests, who had been invited for after dinner. Konig, she had already discovered, disliked going to bed, and would do almost anything to postpone the moment when he was left alone in his suite. Instead of letting his dinner parties break up at eleven o'clock, he usually invited a second group of guests, people who had been dining elsewhere, or had been at the theater—actors, politicians arriving from a late-night sitting at the House of Commons, artists and writers. When *they* left, Konig settled down to play poker or chemin de fer until dawn with whatever rich insomniacs he could persuade to stay.

A man turned toward her as she crossed the room and she found herself face to face with Dominick Vale. He did not look happy.

"You've been meddling in my affairs," he said quietly.

"I don't know what you mean."

"I think you do. Were you sneaking around backstage, spying on me?"

"Of course not."

"Then how do you account for Konig's turning up in my office with the idea that Dickie Beaumont won't make a move without consulting me?"

"It seems to be true. He's doing the film. David says you're putting money into his company."

"Oh, it's *David* now, is it? As it happens, I advise Beaumont from time to time. On business matters. It's not something that's generally known. It's not something I *want* generally known. Is that understood?"

"Of course it's understood."

"I'm so pleased. We all have our little secrets." Vale gave her a ghostly, acid smile. "Yours, I would say, is more delicate than most."

Konig was gesturing at her impatiently, but she stood frozen for a moment, numb with fear, staring at Vale's broad back. The only way to safety was ahead—she knew that.

She would have to be so successful, so famous, so secure, that Vale wouldn't *dare* threaten her. Summoning up all her courage, she gave Konig a dazzling smile and moved toward him, slipping her arm into his.

CHAPTER 12

BECAUSE KONIG WAS SHORT of capital, it had been decided to begin with the last scenes of his *Romeo and Juliet*, leaving the more expensive crowd shots until later, a procedure which was by no means unusual in the movie business, but which made it difficult for Queenie to develop any understanding of what she was doing, or why. She supposed a more sympathetic director might have explained things to her, but sympathy was not a part of Szabothy's method. He required absolute obedience.

She hated being shouted at and hated being treated like an idiot even more. Worse yet, she felt betrayed. Konig, once he had set things in motion, vanished. His days were spent with financiers and bankers; his mind had already jumped to the next film, or beyond that to his ambitious plans for what the press was calling "Hollywood-on-the-Thames."

Without Konig to supervise him, Szabothy turned his undivided attention on her. One memorable day, she did thirty-seven takes of a one-minute scene without satisfying him, until her nerve finally broke, and she ran off the stage. When she came back, led by the makeup man and the wardrobe mistress like a virgin about to be sacrificed to the gods, Szabothy merely lifted an eyebrow and asked, "Now you've had a good cry, are you ready to work some more?"

Dawn glared at him. "I didn't run because I wanted to cry." She paused. "I ran because I wanted to kill you." "Bravo!" Szabothy said, his voice flat with distaste. "There's hope yet that you'll be an actress."

The infuriating thing was that she knew she was getting better—despite Szabothy, not *because* of him.

Szabothy's demands seemed designed to make her uncomfortable.

Small feet in women were an obsession with him and he insisted on her wearing shoes that were a size too small, with strange, curved high heels that he alleged were authentic for the period—though she suspected he was merely providing her with another difficulty to overcome as she swayed and rocked on them like a ship in a high sea.

Daily she suffered, unable to decide what to do to save herself. She did not dare complain to Konig about Szabothy, for at the back of her mind was the suspicion that Konig might be testing her in some way, trying to see if she could "take it," and that complaining would seem to him unprofessional. Neither Lucien nor Beaumont was in a position to help her much with Szabothy, since he despised cameramen and boasted that he never "took any shit from actors," however distinguished.

She sat gloomily, massaging her aching feet, on the first day of the third week of shooting, knowing that her career was going down the drain because of Szabothy—but it was not until she heard his voice tearing at her like a buzz saw from the depths of the cavernous sound stage that she realized how close she was to giving up.

"All of us are waiting for you to get this right, Miss Queenie," he shouted. "It's not so difficult. A child could do it. You hear a noise. You think it's your nurse, with news about your lover. You look up. You turn your face to the right, because that's where the door is. Is this too much to ask? Do you think people will come to see this film because you are blinking like a stupid cow? You are waiting for news."

Queenie bit her lip. It was only a minor annoyance that Szabothy called her "Queenie" or "Miss Queenie," instead of Dawn, except for the fact that because *he* did, so did most of the crew.

"I'm looking as sad as I can."

"Sad? You are *nothing*. You are a pretty face, that's all. You do what I tell you. And—Miss Queenie—don't look toward Chambrun when I'm talking to you. He is not directing this picture. I am."

She silently cursed the absent Konig. Wearily she went through the scene again, knowing that whatever she did, it wouldn't satisfy him, and it was with a certain bitter sense of triumph that she heard him cry "Cut!" before she was halfway through.

He walked over to her, his leather coat creaking ominously, and stood silently. For a moment she felt fear, but she knew instinctively that the only way to beat Szabothy was to provoke him.

Szabothy pointed his riding crop at her until its tip almost touched her face.

"You stupid cow," he hissed. She wondered if he dared use it, then decided there was only one way to find out. She seized the tip of the crop, pulled it out of his hand, and threw it as far as she could.

There was a sudden silence onstage, broken only by the clatter of the crop as it landed in the scenery. She watched Szabothy's face. It turned from its usual putty color to crimson, then went white. His cheek muscles worked as if he were chewing his own tongue. Then he drew himself up to his full height, drew off his left glove and with a snap that echoed from one end of the stage to the other, he slapped her across the cheek. *"Miststück!"* he cried. *"Was fällt dir ein!"*

She could feel her cheeks burning, but win or lose, she knew she had beaten Szabothy. He had crossed the line, taken that one step too far that would put him hopelessly in the wrong. She gave him such a look of hatred that he took a step backward.

"You're through!" he hissed, but there was fear in his eyes. A director could shout at an actress, insult her, ridicule her. There was no precedent for *hitting* an actress, however, not even in Hollywood.

Szabothy put his glove back on, and for a second she thought he might be about to hit her again. She could see Lucien, apparently recovering his wits, about to lunge at Szabothy; then a deep voice emerged from the dark at the far end of the stage.

Konig stepped into the light. "Stop! No fighting, please," he said quietly. His gray homburg was tilted back rakishly on his forehead. He was leaning on his cane, his overcoat thrown over his shoulders like a magician's cape. He reached down and picked up the crop. He handed it back to Szabothy. He looked at him wearily, shaking his head; then he sighed. "I hear you're not happy with the rushes," he said calmly.

"They're the best I can do with what I've got. You need a new star."

"Yes? I can understand you wouldn't be happy with them. No perfectionist is ever happy with his own work. But there's a bigger problem, I'm afraid."

"What's that?"

"I'm not happy with them. I hate to say this, but I think what we need—is not a new star, but a new director."

"There's nobody as good as me, Konig. That's a fact."

"It's a fact, Vilmos. I acknowledge it. But you aren't getting the best out of Dawn. That too is a fact. I apologize. It was my mistake. To put it bluntly: You're fired."

Szabothy stared at Konig for a moment, then shrugged. He recognized the voice of authority when he heard it.

"Very well," he said quietly. "I'll finish the day's shooting. Then you can replace me. But you're making a mistake."

"Maybe. Probably. But you don't need to stay, Vilmos. To tell you the truth, your replacement is already here, ready to go to work."

Szabothy flushed. "You already *hired* somebody?" He was indignant, his eyes glittered with rage. "Who is it? What second-rate *Dreck* director have you hidden away, Konig? Tell me so I can spit on him!"

"It's me," Konig said simply.

There was a long silence. Szabothy sighed, like a blowfish deflating. "You've been away from it too long." His voice was suddenly gentle, even kind, as if he were genuinely concerned. "Anyway, you can't finance, produce *and* direct, David. Nobody can. You've been behind a desk, in board meetings, sitting with bankers, for too many years now. You've forgotten what this is like, my friend."

Szabothy waved toward the lights, crackling now as they cooled off, at the camera on its dolly, at the floor, so crisscrossed with electrical cables that only an experienced hand could walk across the stage without falling. In the single rehearsal light, center stage, Queenie stood, her hands clenched, while all around her in the twilight at least a hundred people—grips, propmen, hairdressers, gaffers, laborers, sound men, technicians, men and women whose skills ranged from the mundane to the esoteric—waited for the orders that would send them back to work, a small army temporarily deprived of its commander.

"It will kill you," Szabothy said. "Don't do it to yourself, David."

"I'm not afraid of directing my own film, Vilmos. I'm not that old."

"I wasn't thinking of that." Szabothy looked at Queenie, then shook his head sadly. "You're too old for *that*, my friend."

Konig turned pale. "*Servus*, Vilmos," he said abruptly, a trace of anger in his voice for the first time.

Szabothy shrugged. He took off the red bandanna tied around his head. "I'll just get my hat."

"Never mind. I've already had it put in your car."

Konig walked over and stood beside Szabothy's chair. An assistant removed the canvas back and replaced it with a strip of canvas on which DAVID KONIG had been lettered.

Another assistant handed Konig a copy of the shooting script and a frame viewer on a black string, which he hung around Konig's neck respectfully.

Konig snapped his fingers and the camera boom descended. He swung into the seat and fastened the safety strap over his suit jacket, then nodded his head.

Queenie watched him soar high above her. It was as if Konig needed to study the scene from a distance—or perhaps he simply wanted to be alone for a moment, high above the floor of the sound stage.

He sighed, lit a cigar, then picked up the megaphone and in a soft voice, magnified by the instrument, called out, "Lights! Makeup for *Miss Avalon!* Let's get back to work."

"Bring me in close," he said, and swung silently down until he was suspended just above the floor, his head level with hers. "This too will pass," he said. "Why are you standing on your toes like that?"

"My feet hurt."

Konig raised an eyebrow.

"My shoes are too small," she explained.

"Take them off. Your feet don't show in this shot." He puffed on his cigar. "I owe you an apology." He did not wait for her to accept it. "Szabothy was the wrong choice. These things happen in this bloody business." He closed his eyes. "All right, it's late at night," he said. "You are cold, alone, frightened. You are waiting for news from the man you love—who loves *you!* You hear a noise at the door. Your whole body responds."

"But what do I *do?*"

Konig was patient. "It doesn't matter what you do. It's what you *feel.* If you feel what I am talking about, you will do the right thing automatically. Be *yourself!* Have you ever been frightened and lonely—Dawn?"

"Yes," she said in a small voice.

"So. Be frightened and lonely now." He stepped down and relinquished his seat on the camera boom to Lucien. "Give me a tight frame," he said, sitting down in his canvas chair with his hands folded over his cane. "Action," he called.

She heard the clapper board and looked toward Konig. Her face was full of gratitude—had he not fired the odious Szabothy?—and as she turned her head she opened her eyes wide, for he was smiling at her with approval. Or was it something more? she wondered.

And suddenly it was as if she understood what he wanted, she *felt* it, and she threw her arms toward the door as if beyond it was everything she wanted out of life—fame, wealth, success, security—and she ran toward it, while Lucien tracked the camera boom alongside her, so close that he could have touched her.

"Cut," she heard Konig say, a note of satisfaction in his voice. "It's a take. Print it."

And from all over the sound stage she heard the sound of applause, quietly at first, then loudly. She knew it was in part for Konig—that after years of producing he had returned to the point from which he had begun, before she was even born. The crew had just witnessed a comeback that would pass into legend, a scene directed by a man who had made his first film before the Great War, one of the pioneers. But she also knew some part of the applause was for her.

Konig rose stiffly to his feet and joined in the applause. He stepped into the floodlight, took her hand and kissed it. He looked at her and smiled.

"Thank you, Dawn," he said simply. "You have proved me right."

Queenie had her own chair now. On the back it bore her name: DAWN AVALON. Above it was a star.

She sat huddled in it, cold and numb with fatigue, a coat thrown over her shoulders. Beside her, on Konig's chair, was a copy of the *Daily Express*. She picked it up to find herself looking at a photograph of David Konig. "DAVID KONIG LAUNCHES KING FILMS," the caption read.

She turned the page. "Impresario David Konig," the story went on, "announced today the launching of an all-British film company with a capital of over a million pounds. Mr. Konig is personally directing the company's first film, *Romeo and Juliet*, starring Richard Beaumont and the glamorous newcomer Dawn Avalon. Future features will star Lady Cynthia Daintry and Margot Feral, and will include an epic film version of *War and Peace*. The directors of King Films Ltd. include the Marquess of Arlington (Honorary Chairman), Mr. Dominick Vale and Mr. Solomon Goldner. See financial pages for further details."

Queenie turned to the financial page, where the same story was repeated in greater detail, much of it incomprehensible to her. She gathered that Konig had gracefully accepted the post of managing director, and in that capacity had announced King Films' purchase of the old Pathé-Gaumont movie studios at Teddington from Sigsbee Wolff, the California film and real estate magnate, who had briefly flirted with film production in England. Konig promised to make them "the most up-to-date in the world." Corbusier, he revealed, was already working on the drawings.

The object and central figure of all this publicity stood in one corner of the dark sound stage, deep in conversation with the head studio carpenter, who was complaining that his men were exhausted. Given Konig's accent and the head carpenter's Cockney, communication between the two seemed unlikely, but Queenie saw from the distance that they had reached an understanding, which didn't surprise her at all. Konig implored, pleaded, cajoled, charmed, and by the time he was finished, the head carpenter was smoking one of Konig's huge cigars and his men had resumed hammering.

Konig's taste for the grandiose was remarkable. When he saw the set for the ball scene, he simply shook his head and said, "Make it bigger."

The next day they showed him a set that was twice as big. He glanced at it with displeasure. "Bigger still," he said, then turned back to his catalog of rare books.

The carpenters labored all night, but in the morning Konig merely turned to the exhausted art director and said, "Thank you, dear boy. But when I say big, I mean *big!*" And one more time, it was rebuilt, to become the largest set in the history of English film production.

Konig did not count the cost. When he saw her costumes, he was dissatisfied. "Something isn't right," he complained. "She doesn't look happy enough. . . ." He examined the one she was wearing, peered at her coiffure, sat staring at her makeup despondently. Then his eyes lit up behind the thick glasses. "The necklace!" he said. "The bloody thing's costume jewelry."

"Of course it is, Mr. Konig," the designer protested. "But it photographs like the real thing."

"Perhaps. But it doesn't *feel* like the real thing. No woman can feel truly happy in fake jewelry, my friend."

Within an hour a man arrived from Cartier, in a black morning coat and striped trousers, carrying a small black briefcase, which he opened with a key, to reveal a priceless diamond necklace cradled in a black velvet cushion. "It's insured for one hundred thousand pounds," he said nervously.

"Don't bother me with details." Konig placed the necklace around Dawn's neck, expertly fastening the clasp. "That's better," he said.

To her surprise, he was right. The scene, as she had learned to say, "played itself," and she had never looked more beautiful.

Konig was *always* right, Queenie thought, as he came over and sat down heavily beside her. He looked exhausted, but then he always looked that way. "I've been reading all about you," she said.

"Yes? It makes a nice story, doesn't it? Some of it is even true."

"It sounds very impressive. What does it all mean?"

Konig shrugged. "The truth is less impressive. I don't have nearly enough money for what I plan to do. But the rest will come. The important thing is to finish this bloody film. Once you've got people to put up money, it's no great trick to get more—but you have to show them that something is *happening*, or they get nervous."

"Why on earth do you need Goldner?"

"I persuaded him to put up a little capital. He's a useful man to have on the Board, I think. He has a lot of common sense—and anyway, we need a Jew. Nobody in England would trust a board of directors that didn't have at least one Jewish name on it. The English have a touching faith in the business sense of the Jewish people. Soon it will be time to show you off a bit. I'll have a word with Basil. I've hired him, you know. A fox to guard the chickens. But we'll see. It's time we did some column planting. . . ."

"Show me off? How?" She wondered what column planting was, but didn't want to ask too many questions at once.

"You should be seen at parties, at the theater, at movie premieres. What you do here in front of the camera, that's important—but it's only half the job. What do you do in the evenings?"

"Lucien and I go home. We're both tired after ten or twelve hours here. And happy to go to bed," she added, conscious even as the words left her mouth that it was the wrong thing to say.

"*Mazel tov*," Konig said, a certain amount of envy showing on his face. "But unfortunately, that won't do at all! To begin with—stars are never tired. Not in public, anyway. They're not supposed to get sick or be depressed, either. The public expects you to be beautiful and happy one hundred percent of the time. And they have the right to expect that, Dawn. They are the ones who buy the tickets, you see. You can do anything you want, provided you don't shatter their illusions. I'll tell Basil to draw up a social schedule for you."

"I'd better warn Lucien."

Konig shrugged. "Oh, there's no need to bother him," he said lightly, putting his hand on hers.

"He doesn't give a damn how much things cost," Basil Goulandris said admiringly. "When he hired me, we had a brief chat about my expenses. Do you know what he told me? 'I shall only worry if they're too low'! Of course, it's not his money he's spending, but still . . ."

"Whose money *is* he spending?" Queenie asked, looking around Goulandris's new office, which resembled an art gallery. Goulandris himself, for that matter, positively glowed with prosperity. He wore a flower in the buttonhole of his lapel, and seemed to have put on about ten pounds.

He winked. "Vale's. Your chum Goldner's. Arlington's. He'd spend mine, if he could get me to buy a few shares, or yours. The bulk of it is from the banks and Prudential Insurance. Konig could charm money out of an empty safe, once he put his mind to it."

"*You* seem to be living well."

Goulandris surveyed his new domain with unconcealed satisfaction. "Not so bad, thank you. I'll tell you something I've learned. People like Konig always do themselves proud—nothing but the best. As a result, they have no respect at all for people who don't. There's no point in trying to economize when you're working for a man who despises economies. . . . You're doing nicely yourself, if I may say so."

"I suppose . . . I haven't had the time to think about it much. I always thought that I'd go on a shopping spree when I had the money to do it, but I've either been too busy or too tired."

"The price of fame, dear. Well I've been hard at work making you famous, so you can blame me. I think Konig is getting his money's worth, if I do say so myself. Have you seen this?" He opened the *Daily Express* to William Hickey's column and passed it to her. There was a photograph of Konig and Queenie at the opening night of Noel Coward's new play. Queenie looked at it carefully. She decided she had worn the pink Molyneux once too often. She would need more clothes—far more. She made a note to talk to Konig about it.

"How's Lucien?" Goulandris asked.

"Fine." It was not entirely true. Lucien was, in fact, more than a little irritable. Konig kept her out until late at night, "showing her off," as he said, while Lucien worked at the studio, stuck away with the cutter.

"That's good. I only asked because some of the publicity might annoy him."

"Why would he be annoyed?"

Goulandris handed her a folder of clippings. Peter Pindar, in the *Daily Mail*, had also run a photograph of Dawn, over an item that read, "Heads were whirling at the sight of lovely Dawn Avalon, when she arrived at Emerald Cunard's smart-set party to say goodbye to Mrs. Sigsbee Wolff, who returns to California tomorrow. Miss Avalon, a vision in pink, arrived on the arm of Mr. Konig. There are rumors that his head is whirling, too, and no wonder. . . ."

The *Evening Standard* had a photograph of Konig, Beaumont and Dawn on the set of *Romeo and Juliet*. Beaumont and Dawn were in costume. Konig stood between them, his arm around Dawn's bare shoulder. She was looking up at him, laughing, the dark eyes glistening with admiration, even in the smudged newspaper photograph. Konig's cigar was tilted at a jaunty angle. Behind them, out of focus and unidentified, Lucien was visible, his face partly blocked by the camera. The caption read: "THREE'S A CROWD?"

"I see what you mean," she said, handing it back. "Do I have you to thank for that?"

"Not at all. My colleagues—*former* colleagues—draw their own conclusions. No romance, no story. That's the rule of the game. Of course a scandal is better, but we don't want *that*, do we? Ah, here's the Great Man himself, late as usual."

The door opened and Konig came in. He kissed her hand, nodded to Goulandris and sat down in a leather armchair with obvious relief.

"Before I forget," he said to her, "you need some new clothes. You've been photographed in that Molyneux at least twice. That won't do. A star should never wear the same dress twice in a row."

As usual, she thought, he was one step ahead of her. She wondered if it was Konig who had planted the stories or given the reporters their "angle"? On the whole, she doubted it—not that she would put it past him. She could see, looking at the photographs, that the strength of her own feelings for Konig, however ambiguous, were simply too obvious to miss.

What those feelings were, she found it hard to define for sure, and was reluctant to consider too deeply. Konig fascinated her, with his wizard's power to get things done and his charm. How could she not be grateful to the man who was determined to make her a star, and willing to spend a fortune to prove himself right?

"All this is very well, so far as it goes, David," Goulandris said, patting his clipping folders, "but the papers will want to know more about Queenie. Her childhood, and so on."

"In the first place, from now on, it's *Dawn*. How many times do I have to say it? This 'Queenie' business has got to stop." He frowned at her. "You, too. So long as you think of yourself as Queenie, everybody else will. As for the childhood—we have whatever we need. The English parents in India, the maharajah's court, it's all fine."

"Which maharajah? People are bound to ask."

Konig looked at her.

She thought about lying, but decided it was too risky. If she mentioned a maharajah and he denied the story, there would be endless and embarrassing repercussions. "I'd rather not say."

Konig lit a cigar. He did not press her on the point. "I think it's obvious that Dawn doesn't want to cause embarrassment to her parents . . . and so on. A little mystery doesn't hurt, Basil."

"Not so long as there are no unpleasant surprises."

Konig acknowledged the wisdom of that. "Are there any unpleasant surprises, darling?" he asked.

"No," she lied. It was easy enough to see that Konig didn't believe her, but he had his own secrets in this area, as she had learned from listening to him. His childhood and past were subjects on which he was adamantly unforthcoming, and on the rare occasions when he talked about them, he made his origins more obscure by contradicting himself recklessly. When a reporter once asked whether he had anything to hide, Konig replied, perhaps truthfully, "Not anything, my dear fellow—everything!"

She thought Konig probably recognized in her a kindred spirit. He had invented himself, and was now busy reinventing her. He had no interest at all in what she had been or what she had done before. He preferred to start with a clean slate, or as clean as he could wipe it.

"Too much detail is always dangerous," he said. "The public cares about the present—and maybe a little bit about the future. About the past, hardly at all. Nobody will care that you worked at Goldner's. Stars are discovered in places you wouldn't believe. What matters is to put on a good show."

That she had already learned from him. Konig did not believe that a star should ever be mistaken for an ordinary person. Stars, in his view, did not ride on buses (or even in taxis), have children, wear casual old clothes or allow themselves to be seen in public, much less photographed, without their makeup. Konig insisted on her being driven in a studio car, and also came up with the notion that it should be a white limousine instead of the usual black one, in much the same casual way that he decided her favorite flower should be white gardenias, which seemed to him to have a certain exotic appeal, and which Queenie now found floating in bowls wherever she went.

"They're asking what your plans are now," Goulandris said.

"Tell them I just bought *Grounds for Divorce*."

"For how much?"

"Fifty thousand pounds."

"That's a lot of money for a play."

"It would be, if it were true. Still, who will deny it? Not the author, poor fellow. It will raise his price for the next one."

Goulandris puffed out his cheeks. "It's not bad. Cynthia Daintry wanted that part, you know."

"I know, but it's better for Dawn . . . A sexy drawing-room comedy—the English love that kind of thing. Get us tickets for tomorrow night, Basil. Dawn had better see it."

He did not ask her if she was free. She could hardly help noticing his proprietorial manner, but she didn't mind it. There was something to be said for letting Konig run her life for her, since he did such a good job of it.

"Will you direct it?" she asked, giving Konig a smile that was at once intimate and appealing.

He usually hated direct questions, but he accepted them from her—most of the time. Sometimes when he was not in the mood for them, he stuck his lower lip out and frowned. This time, apparently, the question pleased him. "I might," he said. "Would you like me to?"

She nodded. It was true, too. Konig knew how to direct her. The last thing she wanted was another Szabothy.

"We'll see," he said. "God knows I've never felt younger. It's better than going to a spa. We could put in some marvelous bedroom scenes—sexy, but in very good taste. They'll love them in Hollywood, darling. We'll have somebody make you the most wonderful lingerie. Basil, find out who's the best in Paris. . . ." He closed his eyes for a moment. "Why are there no good stories around?" he asked, as if Goulandris were responsible.

"I read a nice little story the other day," Goulandris said. "It's about a woman who kills her husband while they're on safari."

"By Hemingway? I read it. I had the same thought myself. One could change the story to make it more English."

"It would be good for Beaumont. He's champing at the bit."

"Let him champ. We'll find something for him."

Goulandris was not about to be put off. "That's not the problem, David. He wants to make a film with Cynthia. He promised her that, you know. *You* promised him that."

"Please stop reminding me of my promises. Nothing is more tiresome." Konig got up and paced around the room. "An African picture should be like a Guys sketch, you know . . . spare, harsh, the small, precise detail that conveys terror. 'Fear in a handful of dust,' as Browning wrote. . ."

"Yeats," she said automatically.

He stared at her. "First Tennyson, now Yeats! You're full of surprises. Do you read a lot of poetry?"

"No, but I had a schoolmaster in India who read it aloud to me."

"At the maharajah's court?" Konig asked, with a feline smile. He walked over and put a hand on her shoulder. "I like the idea of doing a film in the colonies. It's cheap to go on location there. It's patriotic. There's nothing like a little flag-waving for raising money. Cynthia might be quite good as the woman, too. She's blond, blue-eyed, the perfect spoiled rich English bitch. . . ."

"I don't think she's that at all," Queenie said.

"Granted, but she *looks* that way. Beaumont could play the husband if we build up the part. Or the white hunter?"

"The white hunter," Queenie said. "Is it the romantic role?"

"Bravo! You're beginning to understand the picture business. We can get a big American star to play the husband. That's the way to get American distribution. Here we will say it's a Richard Beaumont film. In America we'll say it's a Gary Cooper picture, or whoever. Will Beaumont want to go to Africa, though? I don't see him happy about spending two or three months in the bush, frankly . . ."

"Nairobi is hardly 'the bush,' David," Goulandris said.

"I could have a chat with Cynthia," Queenie suggested. "She might be able to persuade him."

"Excellent. Do it! I should make you my assistant. But it would be a waste. Is it lunchtime? I'm starved."

Goulandris looked at his watch. "Twelve-thirty."

"Book a table, Basil, at the Ritz Grill. We can show Dawn off. Be sure to write the name of the headwaiter down for me, so I remember it. There's only one problem."

"With the Ritz?"

"No, no, with Africa. Who's going to direct? Whatever you say about Nairobi, I'm not going out there myself. It's a job for a young man with stamina. I'd like to find somebody new."

Queenie felt his hand move down her back, gently. He did not seem to be aware of what he was doing. He appeared lost in thought, as if he were reviewing all the directors he knew, but she knew that Konig was not the kind of man to do anything by chance or accident. The sensation was by no means disagreeable. It was a gesture of intimacy and trust. She knew that she had only to move or lean forward and Konig would withdraw his hand. She didn't move.

"Of course, there's one possibility . . ." Konig increased the pressure slightly, like a man calming a horse. "I've been thinking of giving Lucien a chance to direct."

Goulandris looked startled. "Isn't that a little risky?"

"I don't mind risks. The boy wants to direct. He's young, healthy— the climate and the problems won't matter to him. Besides, we can take it by stages. He could go to Africa to shoot locations and background. That should give us some idea of whether he could do it. If we don't go ahead, I can always sell the footage in Hollywood for stock. At worst, one would break even. He'd need an experienced production manager to look after things, but that's no problem. I know just the right man."

He looked down at Queenie with a kindly smile. Behind the glasses, however, his eyes were hard. He was putting her to the test. If she objected, Lucien would lose his chance to direct, and Konig would very likely turn his attentions to some other woman—he was not a man to play a losing hand beyond reason. If she agreed, he would have her to himself for several months. It was nicely thought out. "What would you think, Dawn?" he asked, his long, sensitive fingers following the line of her spine. They were surprisingly strong.

"He'd jump at the chance, I think. It's what he's always wanted."

"And how about *you?* The two of you would be separated for some time. I can't spare you. We have publicity to do. And a new picture to begin. It's a lot to ask, I know . . . a big sacrifice. Would you mind very much?"

She looked up at Konig. "I would never stand in his way, David," she said. She had never called him "David" to his face before. "It won't be forever, after all."

Konig looked at her, then nodded. He had heard what he wanted to hear. "You'll miss him, that goes without saying, but you'll be busy, and so will he. That's the nature of the profession. In any case, I'll look after you . . ."

He took his hand off her back. "We'll go to lunch now." He took her hand, giving her fingers a slight squeeze. "I feel I've made the right decision," he said cheerfully, putting his arm around her as they walked to the door.

But she knew it was as much *she* who had made the decision as Konig.

"You'll spoil my makeup." She was standing in front of the bathroom mirror, her eyes narrowed with concentration.

Lucien wrapped a towel around his waist, partly concealing the beginning of an erection. He tried to cover his embarrassment by pretending that he hadn't been serious about it in the first place. "Where are you off to?" he asked sharply.

"Lunch with some American journalists. David's car is picking me up at one."

"Queenie—why not cancel? We'll go to bed. Or you can simply turn up late. People always expect a star to be late—or at any rate, American journalists do."

She was never late. Certain fragments of Ma's teachings remained sacred to her, chief among them politeness, neatness, cleanliness and punctuality. These had been drummed into her by Ma so hard that they were now part of the bedrock of her character. She could no more be late than stop breathing. "I can't do that," she said firmly, finishing off her lips with a flourish that was like a dismissal.

He did not move. "A few months ago you wouldn't have said no."

She examined her eyebrows carefully. "A few months ago I wasn't a film star. Listen, Lucien, I'm not saying I don't want to go to bed with you. I'm not saying I don't enjoy going to bed with you. I'm only saying that I can't go to bed with you *now*."

"I no longer understand what you want, Queenie."

She paused, sighed and looked at him in the mirror. "Among other things, I want not to be taken for granted."

She leaned over as if she were reaching down to touch her toes, and slipped her bra on. It was something she did naturally, but she was not unaware that it was, from Lucien's point of view, a gesture that seemed full of erotic implications, perhaps because when she leaned over like that her breasts, which were quite small, hung down and seemed larger than they were, firm, delicately balanced, perfectly shaped.

He stood there for a moment, looking at her. She was naked, except for the bra. "Ah, Queenie," he said, "what's to become of us?"

But Queenie was angry with him. Like Morgan, Lucien was unable to conceal the fact that he resented her success—he wanted her all to himself, on his terms. She slipped on her panties, with a snap of elastic. "Dawn," she said, firmly correcting him.

A week later they sat side by side in the white limousine.

For once there was no rain. The big car crawled slowly through a traffic jam, turned into Leicester Square, inched forward toward the Odeon Theater. Ahead she could see the beams of two giant searchlights playing on the low clouds—a touch Konig had imported from Hollywood. The entire square was full of cars, people in evening dress, crowds of onlookers behind barricades, policemen on foot and mounted policemen, the row of chauffeur-driven limousines lining up slowly to discharge their occupants at the glittering marquee, which was banked with flowers.

A huge billboard above the marquee showed her face, fifty feet high, the eyes giant in the glare of the lights, but still recognizably *hers*, the lips, a yard wide, parted slightly as if she were about to be kissed.

A brilliantly uniformed commissionaire opened the door. "Good luck, darling," Lucien whispered, but she hardly heard him, for as she stepped out onto the pavement, where David Konig waited for her in white tie and tails, a row of trumpeters in medieval costume raised their instruments and blew a fanfare. The light was so bright that she could see nothing. Everywhere there were flashbulbs popping, some of them only inches from her face.

She smiled into the dazzling glare, saw the gleam of Konig's silver hair, and aimed for that, conscious only of the need not to trip on her long pink evening dress, which seemed to be trailing feathers and panels in every direction.

She heard a voice from the crowd cry out to ask some unseen person, "Who's *that?*"

And a second voice, as loud and clear as a bell in the silence that followed the fanfare, called back, "Don't be bloody silly—that's *Dawn Avalon*, of course!"

As Konig took her by the arm to lead her into the foyer, she heard a wave of applause.

Queenie Kelley was behind her at last.

CHAPTER 13

"I HAVE NEVER READ such reviews," Konig said, polishing his reading glasses with a silk handkerchief. "The *Daily Express* says: 'The British film industry comes of age at last!' About me, they say: 'Hats off to David Konig!' That's nice. About you, Dawn, they say: 'Dawn Avalon's luminous performance takes her in one leap to the highest reaches of stardom!' Not bad. By noon the bloody phones will be ringing from all over the world. You'd better warn the secretaries, Basil."

"I took the liberty of hiring two extra operators to handle the switchboard and take messages."

"Good boy! First-rate thinking. And it shows a certain amount of optimism, too. I like that. Dawn, darling, come sit by me and read about your triumph. It's not every day that all the newspapers in the country will have something so nice to say about you—so come and enjoy it. My God, I feel twenty years younger!"

"You *look* younger," Dawn said. "Though how that's possible at this hour of the morning, I don't know."

"You are too kind." Konig kissed her hand as she sat down beside him on the sofa. He did not release it. "Did you have a good time?"

"I've never had a better time in my life!" It was true. The audience made the difference—all the difference in the world. She had seen herself in Konig's rushes and in the countless jigsaw puzzles that constituted a film in the making, but Konig's belief that you never knew what you had until you had an audience turned out to be true. For the first time she was able to see her performance as a whole, and she was impressed. She knew that much of it was Konig's direction and cutting—unlike Szabothy, he had been shrewd enough to let her be herself as much as possible. The expressions, mannerisms, gestures were hers. It was *her* the audience was applauding, not Juliet. Looking at the film, feeling the reaction of the audience, it was as if she had been seeing herself for the first time.

Dawn glanced at the *Daily Mail.* "KONIG'S TRIUMPH!" the headline read. "A BRITISH ROMEO AND JULIET THAT CHALLENGES HOLLYWOOD!" There was a photograph of her embracing Richard Beaumont. The caption proclaimed, "Dawn Avalon—Britain's answer to Garbo?"

"It looks as if you've won your gamble."

Konig looked at her and chuckled. He leaned close to her, his lips against her ear. "I'll tell you a secret," he whispered. "The papers are wrong. You can't beat Hollywood from here. They can only be frightened a bit. Eventually one has to go back and beat the bastards at their own game. But this is a start. We'd better start planning some new films for you, fast. But first there's something else we have to do. Not here."

"What's that?"

"We're going to New York, Dawn. For an even bigger premiere than this. You've never been to America?"

"America? Never. I've hardly gotten used to being in England yet."

"You'll probably hate it. Most intelligent people do. But in our business, darling, it's where we all have to go, sooner or later. Five days at sea will give us a chance to talk. You'll see—it's very pleasant."

"The only time I was on a boat I hated it."

"You were seasick?"

"No," she lied. "I was angry and frightened. Are we all going?"

Konig raised an eyebrow. "All? You and me—and Basil, of course."

"Lucien won't like that, you know."

"Do *you* mind?"

She thought a moment before answering. She did mind—perhaps not as much as she should, but still, some. "I don't want him to be angry with me."

"He won't be. As a matter of fact, I've already told him. I broke the news about Africa to him tonight. He is delighted. He didn't want to leave you here—he was worried you'd be lonely, but I said I'd take you with me to America on a publicity trip, to take your mind off his absence. I told him that Basil and I would look after you. . . . So you see? Everything is in order. Did you have your little chat with Cynthia?"

"Yes."

"And?"

"She'll talk to Beaumont. She thinks he'll make a fuss, but he'll go."

"What did you tell her?"

"That she'll never get him to pop the question until she gets him out of London."

Konig laughed. "Very true," he said. "It's surprising how a bit of travel changes things."

She could tell it wasn't Cynthia and Beaumont he was thinking about.

"Africa!" Lucien exclaimed, his voice unsteady with excitement. "My God, what an opportunity! Think of the backgrounds—wild, savage, barbaric. I feel like Gauguin. And do you know what else Konig told me? 'Lucien,' he said, 'take your time, don't economize on film. . . .'

"I'm to make preparations immediately. Konig's already assigned an assistant to travel with me and look after the details. A chap named Kraus. I've already been thinking about it. Kenya, in my opinion, may be too tame, too spoiled by civilization. . . . If I don't find what I'm looking for there, I might go down into the Congo, or perhaps to Uganda."

She pulled her dress over her head. She wished that Lucien was a little more excited about her triumph than about his trip to Africa. She was tired, but at the same time so happy that her whole body seemed to tingle with excitement. She threw the dress down, stretched out her arms and kissed him.

But though he put his arms around her and kissed her back, Lucien did not seem to be paying any attention. His mind was on Africa and on the chance he had finally been given to direct a picture. He hardly even noticed that she was aroused. "It's been a long day," he said. "You must be tired, too." And with that Lucien lay down on the bed and closed his eyes.

Dawn lay awake for an hour. She was not angry at Lucien, nor indeed angry at all, but she felt one part of her life—the part that she had until recently thought was the most important—slipping away from her. Konig had offered them both the chance to be a success, and both of them had seized it, even though it might mean losing each other.

She decided to make love to Lucien in the morning—but when morning came she was awakened by a telephone call from Konig, who wanted her to get ready "immediately" for a press conference; then

Basil Goulandris called to discuss a whole string of luncheons and dinners. By the time she had finished with her calls, Lucien was already up
and shaving, for he had appointments at the Royal Geographical Society to seek the advice of old Africa hands; then he was due at the Tech-
nicolor labs in Islington, where his film was being prepared in specially
sealed boxes to protect it from the heat and the humidity. His day was
as busy as Dawn's.

One morning two large envelopes arrived at the flat, delivered by special messenger. Lucien's contained five thousand pounds' worth of travelers checks, a bundle of tickets and several thick folders of documents.
Queenie's contained a first-class round-trip ticket to New York on the
Mauretania and a British passport made out to "Dawn Avalon."

She wondered how Konig had managed to fix *that*. Dawn's birth-
place was listed as Calcutta. Her parents were described as "British subjects." If only Ma knew, Queenie thought, that she had at last escaped
from the stigma of being Anglo-Indian, at least on paper. It was ironic
that David Konig could fix for Dawn, with one stroke of the pen, what
generations of Anglo-Indians had longed for.

But even as she looked at her picture—a glamorous studio shot, the
sultriness of which seemed distinctly inappropriate to a passport photograph—she saw Lucien, beside her on the bed, going through his
papers. He was surrounded by guidebooks, obscure works of ethnology
in several languages, technical papers from film and camera manufac-
turers, huge maps on which he had circled with a grease pencil places
that were meaningless to her, totally absorbed in his new adventure.

She was a little disappointed that Lucien seemed to be leaving with
so little regret and emotion. He loved her—she knew that—but like
most men he had no difficulty in putting his career ahead of a woman,
or forgetting about her when he was busy. But was she so different
herself?

Impulsively she put her arms around him and kissed him, pulling
him away from his papers onto the bed with her.

It was as if she was saying goodbye, not just to him, but to a part of
her life. For a moment, she wished she could have both—the bright
future Konig was offering *and* Lucien—but already she knew that was
impossible.

"We'll eat at the captain's table the first night out. After that, a bit
more informally, I hope." Konig scanned the printed list of first-class

passengers myopically, then sneezed. "Too many bloody flowers," he complained.

For an hour or more her stewardess had been busy placing them in vases, and was now unpacking her trunk. In the adjoining suite, Konig's steward was laying out his evening clothes. The purser of the *Mauretania* had sent champagne and caviar. The captain had sent an invitation to dine at his table and another bottle of champagne.

"Tina von Arx is on board," Konig said. "I hear she's having a love affair with someone in New York. Gunther Dobrolyubov. Somebody told me his boyfriend left him . . . and Jaime Tristán Cuehna y Platino is on board too. . . . We shall have some interesting card games, I think." Konig not only seemed to know everybody on board; he tactfully paid Dawn the compliment of pretending she knew as much about them as he did.

"Hmm," he murmured, "here's an old friend of yours. Mr. Solomon Goldner."

Dawn fought down a brief moment of panic. "What on earth can he be going to New York for?"

"He's bought into a few movie theaters. He has ambitions to become a big exhibitor—even, eventually, a distributor. I'm encouraging him. An association with a British distributor who has an interest in King Films, however small, would be useful for the future. If you don't mind, we'll dine with him—perhaps tomorrow. I don't think we'll find *him* at the captain's table."

Konig glanced at a basket of fruit. He got up and removed the card, scrawled his name and a couple of lines on a piece of notepaper, and rang for the steward. "Take this to Mr. Goldner's cabin," he ordered.

"Apart from you, Basil and Goldner, I don't know a soul on board."

"Ah. But they know *you*. That's the advantage of being a star." Konig glanced out the porthole. "It's getting dark. We're well clear of Le Havre by now. I'm going to have my bath and change. Shall I lock the door between our suites?"

"That doesn't seem necessary."

"No. If you need me, knock."

Konig rose, adjusted his steps to the movement of the ship and paused. He picked up a wooden box. "A mistake," he said. "These are from the American distributors. You got the box of cigars, so I expect I'll find a bottle of perfume for you in my bathroom."

"I'll pick it up later."

He nodded and closed the door behind him softly, carrying the cigars. Dawn rang for the stewardess to draw her bath—she had already learned that it was not something you were supposed to do for yourself when you traveled first class.

Dawn was used to attention, but she was not yet accustomed to receiving it from the rich. As she descended the gala staircase, she heard the name "Dawn Avalon" being repeated all over the saloon, like a chant. She was a curiosity, like something on a tourist's guide map. She felt a real, warm pleasure at being recognized. She wondered if it would wear off in time. She doubted it.

She walked toward the captain's table, pretending to ignore the buzz of interest around her. Konig himself had selected her pale-pink evening gown, which floated around her as she moved, in a swirl of silk chiffon, and Goulandris had borrowed a diamond necklace for her use during the voyage that was big enough to cause comment even here, where most women had plenty of diamonds themselves.

The captain rose to greet her as a waiter pulled back her chair. She placed her silver-beaded bag on the table, exchanged a few words with the captain, who promised her a smooth crossing as if he had arranged it personally with God, and glanced around at her fellow guests. A thin, elegant, silver-haired man with doe eyes and a narrow mustache dyed black introduced himself as Jaime Cuehna y Platino. To Dawn's surprise, Gunther Dobrolyubov, despite the loss of his boyfriend, turned out to be a cheerful, plump gentleman in his mid-sixties, who showed no hint of homosexuality except for a solid-gold slave bracelet around his right wrist and a tendency to stare soulfully at the waiters when he thought nobody was looking. It was easy to forget, when she was alone with Konig, that most of the people he knew were his own age—he talked about their love affairs and problems as if they were in their twenties. She had expected these people to be glamorous from the way Konig talked about them, and was disappointed to find they were merely rich and elderly.

Konig had deliberately staged her entrance so that they arrived a few minutes late, but there was still one empty seat at the table, immediately across from her. Dawn turned to thank the waiter as he helped her to caviar and noticed that the men at the table were all making a perfunctory gesture of rising, flexing their knees and raising themselves up, with varying degrees of difficulty, a few inches off their chairs. Only the captain felt obliged to actually rise to his feet.

Dawn turned to smile at the newcomer, caught a flash of silver and green, and found herself looking directly into the eyes of Penelope Daventry.

For a brief moment, Dawn panicked. The pupils of Mrs. Daventry's remarkable green eyes, like those of a cat, seemed to narrow as she looked at Dawn, until they were merely black, threatening pinpoints.

Dawn gave a small gasp and overturned her glass of champagne. She felt herself flushing, and at the same time her bare shoulders shivered as if she had been touched by an icy breeze. Even in her confusion, Dawn couldn't help noticing that she and Mrs. Daventry were the only women in the room whose shoulders were completely bare. Mrs. Daventry's dress exposed her small, firm breasts almost to the nipples, then swept down to leave her back bare, kept in place by some miracle of dressmaking. Her emerald earrings were enormous.

Dawn, still shivering slightly as the waiters put fresh napkins down over the champagne she had spilled, looked down involuntarily at Mrs. Daventry's wrist and, to her horror, saw the familiar bracelet, the emeralds matching exactly the color of Mrs. Daventry's eyes, the diamonds glittering just as brilliantly as they had when Morgan had placed it on her bed a lifetime ago. She stared at it, wide-eyed.

Mrs. Daventry's eyes flickered. "It's a nice piece, isn't it?" she asked, in her low, husky voice. She lit a cigarette, ignoring the captain's frown, and examined the men around the table quickly. She paused for a moment to look at Konig, but then dismissed him, along with the rest, and smiled without parting her lips at Jaime Cuehna y Platino, who was seated next to her. Once she had his attention, she relaxed and turned back to Dawn.

"I couldn't help admiring it." Dawn felt a certain numb despair at the thought that Mrs. Daventry was playing with her like a cat with a mouse, but she could see no way to escape.

"It's been in the family for years. Actually, it was once stolen and we had to buy it back. I felt quite *naked* without it." Mrs. Daventry laughed. Dawn was unable to manage much more than a strained smile in return—her head ached and her mouth was dry with fear. "You must know my half sister, Cynthia Daintry?"

"I know her quite well."

"I hear she's off to Africa with Richard Beaumont. Lucky girl. My father told me you were born in India, Miss Avalon?"

"Yes." Dawn stared at her plate waiting for Mrs. Daventry to drop her bombshell and beginning to wish she would hurry up and get it over with. The waiter had taken away her caviar untouched. There was a plate of soup in front of her, but she had no appetite for it, or anything else.

"Oh, I'm so glad. I live there myself. Since we know so many of the same people, I'm sure we have a lot in common. I hope we'll have a chance to chat during the crossing."

Dawn kept her eyes on her plate, though the sight of the soup made her want to throw up. "That would be nice . . . though I don't remember much about India. It's been a long, *long* time since I was there."

"Ah," Mrs. Daventry said, "but childhood memories are the best, aren't they? Speaking of diamonds, that's a very handsome necklace."

"Thank you," Dawn said, resisting the urge to confess they weren't her own.

Mrs. Daventry reached across and patted her hand. The big ring flashed in the candlelight. The older woman's hand was cool and dry, but Dawn felt as if she had been burned by its touch. She waited for the inevitable explosion of Mrs. Daventry's anger, but the older woman merely smiled. "You have a great career ahead of you, I can tell that. I envy you. To be beautiful *and* have a great talent is a rare combination. I can't tell you what a pleasure it was to learn you were on the ship. When I saw the picture, I told myself—there's something special about this girl, it's almost as if I *know* her. And now I do. But I mustn't monopolize you, dear."

She gave Dawn another smile and turned to address herself to Jaime Cuehna y Platino, who had been admiring her bosom and shoulders for the past five minutes with such concentration that Dawn was surprised he had been able to find his mouth with his spoon. Mrs. Daventry extended an unlit cigarette in his direction and stared into his eyes as he lit it.

Coolly, slowly, the impassive green eyes examined him, and as Dawn turned to make polite conversation with Gunther Dobrolyubov, she heard Mrs. Daventry, apparently satisfied with her inventory of Platino's assets, say to him, "You must tell me all about South America— I'm *dying* to hear about it . . ."

Dawn, who seldom drank more than a few sips, drained her glass of champagne and asked for another.

It took three glasses to make her stop trembling.

·   ·   ·

She lay on her bed, unable to sleep. Every time she closed her eyes, she was terrified by nightmare visions.

When she opened them, she felt worse. She repeated the entire conversation with Mrs. Daventry over and over again in her mind, searching for hidden meanings. Mrs. Daventry was malicious enough to play with her, Dawn knew that—and knew she had five days to do it. Sooner or later, she was bound to recognize Queenie in Dawn, if she hadn't immediately.

For a moment, she thought of Morgan. He had been the only person she could talk to about that part of her life. The thought of Morgan made her feel even worse. She pushed it away.

Nausea from the champagne, combined with the movement of the ship, clawed at her stomach. The captain's promise had apparently been optimistic, for the *Mauretania* wallowed in a heavy sea, the silence broken with each slow roll by the sound of china and glassware breaking and the regular, mournful bellow of the foghorn.

Dawn rose unsteadily to her feet, felt her way around the stateroom toward the bathroom door, slipped and grazed her knee against a table, overturning a bowl of flowers. The water splashed over her bare feet. She tried to get up but her feet slipped on the wet floor as the ship shuddered, hesitated in the waves, then righted itself slowly, sending another bowl of flowers crashing to the floor.

She had fled from the saloon after dinner, pleading a headache. The sooner she was out of Mrs. Daventry's sight, the better, she had thought, but now it seemed a mistake. At least there was company in the saloon, and enough going on to take her mind off her fears. Konig would probably be there all night, slumped in a chair with his brandy, coffee and cigar, deep in a game of cards with Jaime Tristán Cuehna y Platino.

Dawn hesitated to ring for the stewardess at this time of the night; then she reflected that she was now a star, and anyway it was the stewardess' job. Blindly she groped for the bell, but before she found it, she heard a knock on the door. Thinking it was probably the stewardess, coming to see if she needed anything, Dawn called out, "Come in."

But it was the communicating door between the two suites that opened, not the door to the passageway, and in the rectangle of soft light she saw David Konig's silhouette and heard him say, "My God, are you all right?"

She groaned. "I fell."

"Let me help you up." He edged his way into the room, leaned over with one hand on the rail and helped Dawn to her feet with the other.

"I heard a noise and thought you were still up," he explained. "I thought I'd see if you were all right—and give you your perfume."

He made his way through the door with admirable balance and returned a moment later with a huge bottle of Schiaparelli and two capsules. He poured Dawn a glass of Evian water. "Take these," he ordered.

She swallowed them obediently.

"I thought you were never seasick?"

"I drank too much champagne."

"The sleeping pills will help. Sometimes sleep is the best thing."

"I've never taken sleeping pills before."

"You're lucky. I take them often—particularly since the divorce."

"You can't sleep?"

"I sleep—badly, let's say. When you're lonely, it's hard to sleep. What frightened you at dinner?"

"What made you think I was frightened?"

"I know these things. I don't believe it can have been any of the men. Dobrolyubov is a queer. Platino is merely a rich South American, a kind of Don Juan in reverse—he is pursued and seduced by women, and always runs away. . . . Mrs. Daventry, the woman with the sharp teeth and the body of a sexual athlete? Is *she* the person who frightened you?"

"Perhaps. I think she probably reminded me of someone else. I've never met her before."

Konig nodded. He didn't believe her, but on the other hand he was too polite to express disbelief. "You're cold," he said, letting the matter drop. "And the floor is wet in here."

"I tipped over some of the flowers."

"Come into my stateroom and dry your feet. I'll get someone to clear all this up." He led her through the doorway and into his bedroom. She sat down on the bed while Konig went to fetch a towel. His pale-yellow silk pajamas with the initials D K embroidered in blue on the breast pocket were laid out on the bed, neatly pressed. Konig returned with the towel and handed it to Dawn. "Are you all right?" he asked.

"No."

"Still sick? Shall I get a doctor?"

"I'm not sick. I'm frightened."

"It's not easy to be a star at your age. And being beautiful isn't always an easy thing, either. It's all happened very fast, hasn't it? And there are things—I'm not prying, mind—that you wish you hadn't done?"

She nodded. She was crying now.

"This happens to everybody. It's not so terrible. You close one part of your life and go on to the next part. It's the only way. Looking back, feeling guilt—all that is a waste of time."

More than anything else, she wanted to be comforted. She put her arms around Konig and leaned against him. "There, there." He put his arms around her. "Cry a little. It can't hurt."

"I hate crying."

"At times it's the only sensible thing to do."

The ship gave a sudden heave as if it were going to plunge to the bottom of the sea, and Konig, his glasses askew, fell onto the bed so hard that he gave a grunt of surprise, followed by another as Dawn landed on top of him.

He was lying on his cigars and messages, which were now strewn across the bed. His face was red. Konig opened his eyes and said, "You knocked my breath out. I think you broke the cigars in my pocket, too."

"I'm sorry."

"Never mind."

He pulled himself up to a sitting position, took off his coat and unfastened his tie. He had some difficulty reaching his shoes. Dawn stretched out one arm and slipped them off. With his jacket removed, Konig's waist was noticeably thicker, and even the mild physical exertion of undressing seemed to make him breathe harder. Dawn pressed herself against him, savoring the warmth of human contact, and felt something cold and hard against her stomach.

"My watch," Konig said. "This is foolish." He stood up, swaying with the increasingly violent movements of the ship, picked up his pajamas and modestly retired to the bathroom, clutching the handrail to support himself. He returned a few moments later wearing the yellow pajamas, his hair neatly brushed, and lay down beside her again. He peered nearsightedly at the night table, selected two pills from an assortment of bottles that were rolling back and forth on its surface and swallowed them with a sip of Evian water.

Dawn snuggled close to him and put her arms around him again. They lay together for a time, Konig on his back, Dawn pressed against his side, as the ship wallowed and pitched. Konig's eyes were open, but he seemed to be dozing, despite the noise of objects sliding and banging against each other, the groans of the ship's structure and the occasional sharp crash of breaking glass.

More out of gratitude than desire, but with a certain curiosity, she ran her hand over Konig's chest. She was surprised at how hairy it was. She was not sure she liked the sensation. The flesh beneath the hair was soft. Without his well-tailored suit, Konig's body seemed to sag and spread in several directions.

He was not exactly *fat*—but there was undoubtedly more of him than was good for his health. She ran her hand lower down, unbuttoning his pajama top. She was playing with him, teasing him to see what his reaction would be.

He sighed heavily. "You're very sweet. But it's no good."

"What's no good?"

Another sigh. "To be frank, dear child, since the divorce . . . I don't know how to tell you this . . . it's shameful . . ."

"I won't be shocked. I'm not a child."

"You are. A very lovely child, however. . . . The truth is, ever since Marla and I broke up—I've been quite impotent." Konig stared ahead toward the small blue night-light. His face expressed a resigned stoicism that was at once appealing and, in the circumstances, slightly ridiculous.

Dawn leaned her chin on his chest. *"Completely?"* She realized, a moment too late, that her tone of curiosity might seem to him impolite, or possibly unfeeling. "I'm so sorry," she added quickly.

"Nothing helps," he said. "You lie there quietly. I'll stroke your back. You'll sleep."

"Is there nothing I can do?"

"Others have tried. It's hopeless. Vandergraf, in New York, gave me vitamin shots. B-One, B-God-knows what . . . nothing. It's psychological, I'm afraid. Pressure, overwork, age, the divorce . . ."

"My poor David." She pressed against him.

"It's kind of you, but it's no good. Don't embarrass me further, please."

"I only want to help. Let me try."

"If you insist. But it won't do any good."

She twisted around. From Lucien she had learned what men liked, and while she still felt a few qualms about doing it, she no longer felt any real repugnance.

"My God!" he whispered, as if in prayer. "I think I feel something!"

She was glad for him, and happier still when she could stop. She rolled over next to him, still dizzy from the champagne and the pills, and fell asleep gratefully.

. . .

In the morning the ship ran smoothly again. Dawn woke to the gentle vibration of the turbines—and to Konig's snores, for he was asleep on his back, his mouth wide open and his head propped against the pillows. Except for his snoring, Konig might easily have been mistaken for a corpse laid out for a funeral. Was this, too, she wondered, a sign of age? She rose, made her way to the bathroom, washed the makeup off her face and slipped on one of Konig's silk robes. Her head was absolutely clear. Despite the champagne, she felt no hangover—whatever Konig's pills were, they worked.

Dawn opened the door to her suite as quietly as possible, but the noise woke Konig, who stirred majestically and opened one eye.

"What time is it?" he asked.

"Eight."

"So early?"

"I'm an early riser, usually."

"Me, not. Come over here and sit down. We'll order breakfast."

Obediently she sat down on the bed beside him. Her underpants, she noticed, were crumpled up next to the pillows. She decided not to think about how they got there.

"I don't apologize for last night," Konig said, holding her hand. "It was wonderful. And I will tell you something: I was attracted to you from the very first."

"I know."

"Yes, I suppose so. Women always know these things." Konig sighed. He rummaged through his collection of bottles, selected two large red capsules and washed them down with a sip of water. "Wake-up pills," he explained. "In half an hour, I'll be ready for anything. *Almost* anything, anyway . . . You don't seem happy."

She shrugged. Konig had an uncomfortable ability to guess what she was thinking or feeling.

"You are thinking about Lucien, I suppose?"

"Well . . . yes," she admitted reluctantly.

He put his hand on hers. "Let's put it this way. Last night you were tired, frightened, a little drunk. What happened between us—it was not such a big thing. Even Lucien would understand that it could happen once, especially on a ship. . . . So if we say, well, it only happened once, and from now on it won't happen again, there is no harm done. You understand?"

"I understand."

"The problem is that I would like it to continue. That wouldn't be so easy to explain to Lucien."

"No. It wouldn't."

"I want you to myself, Dawn. I'm not a young man, I know, but I can offer you certain—compensations."

"You're not that old, David," Dawn said, though with his gray skin and silver stubble Konig looked very old indeed. She knew what she was being offered. Konig would make her a star—he might do that anyway because it was in his interest—but if she left Lucien for him, he would do much more. He would take her into his world, among rich, powerful people, and give her a place there. She would not have to be afraid of anybody—not even Mrs. Daventry.

She leaned over and kissed him. "I'll think about it."

But both of them knew she had already made up her mind.

"To your health!" Solly Goldner lifted his glass and sipped his wine. "Not bad."

"Not *bad*? It's excellent. There's no point in ordering the most expensive wines on a ship. The movement is bad for the wine. A robust, simple wine, on the other hand, survives . . ."

"As *we* have, Mr. Konig," Goldner said with a flattering smile.

Konig nodded. "Exactly, Goldner. We understand the art of survival, you and I."

She understood it as well as either of them, Dawn thought. The three of them—Konig, Goldner and Dawn—were seated at a table in the center of the saloon. It had cost Konig twenty pounds to square things with the purser, as well as a long conversation with the captain, to whom he had explained that Dawn craved privacy—that while she was grateful to be at the captain's table, she preferred to eat without having to make conversation with strangers.

He got rid of Mrs. Daventry, at least for the moment, by sending Jaime Tristán Cuehna y Platino a magnum of Dom Perignon and a kilo of caviar—rightly calculating that the combination of champagne, caviar and sex would keep Mrs. Daventry and Platino locked up in either his stateroom or hers for at least a day or two.

Goldner was unchanged since the days when Dawn had danced for him at the Club Paradise, but in some indefinable way he showed the traces of prosperity. There was a gloss to his plump cheeks, and his dinner jacket was new. He wore a lavender orchid in his buttonhole, carefully chosen, she was sure, to match his socks and handkerchief.

Konig treated him with his usual politeness, but not as an equal.

"Dawn and I were delighted to find you on board," Konig said, examining his smoked trout like a surgeon—he had a horror of choking on fishbones.

Dawn picked at her own food. She did not share Konig's delight. "You look as if you're doing well, Mr. Goldner," she said.

"We have prospered together, Queenie." He gave her a knowing look. "I should say 'Dawn,' of course."

It was true, she thought. She had given Goldner an opportunity to get into the big time, with Vale, and now he was on his way to even bigger and better things. Without her—and the contract he had so skillfully extracted from Morgan—Goldner would still be peddling sandwiches in his club. Once again she felt the old resentment at having been used, but there was still nothing she could do about it. "I'm sure we'll continue to," she said, flashing Goldner a dazzling smile.

"So am I." He smiled back.

Konig followed this exchange with wary interest. "I have to admit, frankly," he said, "that Dawn's loyalty never fails to amaze me. Most stars can't wait to drop the people who helped them in the beginning—particularly when there's a questionable contract hanging over them that costs them money."

"There's nothing questionable about it," Goldner said firmly.

Konig shrugged. "Please don't insult my intelligence." He examined the foie gras that was held in front of him on a silver platter for his inspection. "The color is nice and pink. In America it's always gray, like the muck that comes out of cans . . ." He took a piece of toast, then frowned at the waiter. "The toast isn't hot enough. Bring some more, please. . . . You took advantage of her, Goldner. You and this fellow Jones. What's become of him, by the way? One would have expected him to appear out of the woodwork at the first sign of Dawn's success."

"He went abroad," Goldner said. "I wouldn't know where to find him. Not that I want to."

Dawn gave him a warning glance. Happily, Konig's curiosity was limited—or perhaps he limited it deliberately.

"What takes you to New York?" Konig asked, changing the subject, to Dawn's relief.

"Loew's has several theaters in England that are losing money. They could be picked up at a very advantageous price. The managers steal Loew's blind. Someone who was on the spot could make money out of them."

Konig was obviously impressed. "Would you like me to say a word on your behalf to Schenck? He owes me a few favors."

"That would be most kind—David. But there's something else I want to talk to you about. Confidentially."

Konig watched carefully as the waiters served roast beef from a huge silver trolley. "And what is that?"

Goldner looked at Dawn.

"It's all right. Dawn is not only beautiful, she also knows how to keep her mouth shut."

"That I know." Goldner tasted his Yorkshire pudding, then moved it to the side of the plate with his fork. "Between the three of us, then," he said, "Vale is talking to people in the City about taking over King Films."

Konig showed no surprise. "Did he talk to you, too?"

"Yes."

"And what did you say?"

"I listened."

Konig nodded.

"With the right kind of backing," Goldner went on, "Vale could do it. You don't have enough shares to beat him on your own."

"True. That's always the danger of using other people's money. Why didn't you go along with him, Goldner?"

"I haven't said I wouldn't. But I don't like him. He's a dangerous man. Eventually he'd push me out." Goldner looked at Dawn. "Are you sure we should be discussing all this in front of Dawn?"

"It's time she learned how things work. I have no secrets from her. Well, not many, anyway." He sighed. "It's always such a bloody business, having partners. I needed Dawn, so I made a deal with you, Goldner, and your damned friend Vale. I needed a studio and some real capital, so I had to make deals with the banks, and a few of Vale's friends in the City, and the Prudential Insurance Company . . ." He poked through a basket of fresh fruit, selected an apple and handed it to the waiter to be peeled for him. "Until I start to show a substantial profit," he added with unexpected savagery, "they own my *balls!* It's not the best time for me to fight off Vale."

"He knows that. He's a thug," Goldner said. "A thug who knows a lot of important people."

"All of whom are afraid of him. Well, I know thugs, too, but they're on the other side of the Atlantic. And it's not the moment. When big money is pouring in, you can call for help and get it—but not before. If you call for help before, you end up losing everything." He ate his apple slowly, then wiped his mouth. "I'm grateful to you for telling me all this, but you may have picked the losing side."

Goldner leaned forward, dropped his voice to a whisper. "Vale has his weaknesses. He owns a lot of questionable businesses . . . night-clubs that are fronts for gambling, prostitution, and so on. Unfortunately that kind of thing is hard to prove. He's too smart to have any of it traceable to him. Of course, if one looks hard enough, everyone has something to hide, don't they? A financial scandal, little girls . . ." He coughed. "With Vale it's not little girls, but you know what I mean."

"I know exactly what you mean. You're surely not suggesting that I blackmail him?"

Goldner chose a cognac from the tray held before him by the wine steward. "That's not a nice word to use," he said reproachfully. "I'm only trying to be helpful."

Konig selected a *grand fin*, sniffed it and sighed. "Would it work? That's the question." He turned to Dawn. "What do you think, darling?" he asked.

Was this the way everybody did business? she wondered, trying to decide what to say. She had acquired a good deal of respect for Konig's survival instinct, but she hadn't realized quite how far he was prepared to go. The idea of blackmailing Vale apparently did not shock him, but she knew better than Konig did just how dangerous it would be to try. Vale would fight back—and she could guess whom he would attack first! Would Konig have any use for her if he learned about Morgan's death? She could guess the answer to that, too.

She glared at Goldner, who should have known better than to bring the subject up. "No," she said firmly. "It wouldn't work, David. You can't frighten Vale. You'd either have to buy him off or do something that destroys him."

"From the mouth of babes," Konig said, beaming. "I'll think about it, Goldner. We'll wait and see. I don't like taking that kind of risk. With a man like Vale, there's always someone around who has enough to fear from him to take the risk."

He gave Goldner a knowing smile. "It's just a question of finding the right person." He lifted a brandy glass in benediction. "Someone who has a *lot* to lose."

Dawn and Goldner glanced at each other. They both knew, she thought, who had the most to lose if Vale turned nasty under pressure.

She wondered if Konig knew too.

Konig sat in Dawn's sitting room, his feet on a stool. He had taken his shoes and his black tie off and was smoking a cigar. "Sit down next to me. Have you given any thought to what we discussed this morning?" He had apparently put Vale out of his mind.

"A little. But I'm bad about making long-term decisions."

"So forget about the long term. Let's take it step by step." He put his arm around her shoulder and held her chin up close to him. He kissed her gently. "Will you spend the night with me again?"

She nodded. That decision she had already made.

She followed him into his stateroom. All around her was the evidence of Konig's sleeplessness, as well as the settled habits of a man who was used to having things exactly as he wanted them. Even here, she noticed, despite the luxuries of first-class travel, the bed had been made with his own pale-blue sheets and pillows embroidered with his initials. Dawn wondered if everybody rich lived this way. She stretched, enjoying the cool, smooth feel of Konig's sheets, and decided it wasn't such a bad way to live.

She looked at Konig's watch, which he had put down next to the fruit. It was gold, wafer-thin, with twelve large diamonds instead of numbers, and a ring of diamonds around the edge. She reached across and ran her fingers over it. The diamonds were cold and hard.

DAWN'S STAR RISES!
KONIG MAKES COMEBACK!
Romeo & Juliet Box Office Knock-out at Roxy!

"Variety loves us," Konig said. He had settled into the St. Regis Hotel as if it were home—indeed, any first-class hotel was home to him.

Goulandris, sleeker and plumper than ever, passed another paper to Konig, pointing to a review with a neatly varnished fingernail. "It's not just the trades. Look at The Times."

Konig peered at it through his reading glasses. He frowned. "What's so wonderful about it?" Konig asked. " 'Veteran moviemaker David Konig's return to directing is a deft popularization of Shakespeare's play, but throughout one can see the traces of Vilmos Szabothy's genius, and only wish one could have seen his work without the addition of Konig's *Schlag* . . .'"

"What's *Schlag*?" Dawn asked.

"Whipped cream."

"Otherwise, it's a money review," Goulandris said.

Konig held *The Times* to his nose. "'The most exciting face of the decade—a Juliet to dream about.'"

"You can't complain about that," Dawn said.

Konig smiled gracefully. "Darling, I'm delighted for you. I have been a producer for too long, complaining about director's egos—now I've got one myself again. I'd forgotten what it was like to be a director. But as a producer . . ." Konig stood up and put his arms around her. "My congratulations. You've taken New York by storm." He paused. "And not only New York. Tonight we're having dinner with Sigsbee Wolff."

"Golly!" Goulandris said. Dawn had never seen him so impressed. She wondered why.

Then she realized that he was not so much impressed as *scared*.

Even at "21" Dawn attracted attention.

"The man with the telephone at his table is Walter Winchell," Konig whispered to her.

"He looks like a thug."

"He *is* a thug. Smile at him."

She smiled. Winchell was talking on his telephone; the glaucous eyes, curiously devoid of life, restlessly moved back and forth as if he was afraid of missing anything. He caught her smile, waved to her and went on with his conversation.

Konig seated Dawn, threw up his hands as if he were overjoyed to see Winchell, made a motion to indicate that he would talk to him later, then sat down and ordered a dry martini.

"In America," he said, "I do as the Americans do. The food being what it is, it's best to stun the taste buds with a cocktail before dinner. The only things to eat here are the hamburgers. . . . Here comes Wolff."

Konig stood again. In the doorway, a tall black chauffeur appeared, pushing a wheelchair in front of him. The figure in the chair seemed so old that Dawn found it impossible to estimate his age. He might be a man of seventy in bad health, or perhaps even ninety or a hundred—there was no way to guess. From the waist up he was neatly dressed in a dark-blue suit, a white shirt and a polka-dot bow tie. From the waist down, his legs were covered in a navy-blue cashmere blanket, except for his feet, on which he wore old-fashioned ankle-length lace-up black boots. Even the soles were highly polished—presumably because he was unable to walk on them. Wolff's face was colorless, his lips were blue, his gnarled, age-freckled hands trembled. He had a hearing aid in each ear. His eyes, however, were bright enough to dispel the notion that Wolff was the feeble geriatric case he appeared to be at first glance.

He was pushed to the table. He dismissed the chauffeur. His entrance had caused almost as much of a stir as Dawn's—indeed, Winchell had put down his telephone, as if the mere sight of Wolff was news in itself.

"You're even more beautiful than you are on the screen," Wolff said to Dawn, reaching across to kiss her hand. His fingers, she noticed, were unpleasantly cold. His voice was a low, rasping growl, and he spoke with a curious accent that was peculiar to New York, so that the word "beautiful" came out sounding like "bee–oot–i–fool."

"You make me wish I was young again," he croaked. "Of course, every goddam thing makes me wish I was young again . . ."

Wolff's voice rose and fell, so that parts of his sentence seemed to vanish into some deep well. Since he was deaf, it made no difference to him. *He* knew what he was saying. Dawn assumed correctly that he was flattering her, and smiled.

He smiled back—or at least he bared a set of startling white dentures. His facial muscles showed the effects of a bad stroke.

A martini was produced for him. He tasted it and sent it back. Another was brought. He nodded with satisfaction. "Dey tasted beddah when dey used bat-tub gin."

"Sigsbee made a fortune during Prohibition," Konig explained.

"Bet your ass."

"That must have been a tough business."

Wolff patted her hand gallantly. "Lidd-el goil—it was only tough on the guys who tried to compete with me."

"Mr. Joseph Kennedy was one of Sigsbee's partners. Sigsbee and Kennedy once bought RKO together."

"Joe was a competitor at foist. But he's a smart guy. We made a deal. Smart guys always know when to make a deal." Wolff leaned over in his wheelchair and pinched Dawn's cheek. He gave a cackle that approximated a laugh. "Your friend David, Miss Avalon—he's a smart guy, too. I only deal with smart guys."

"Sigsbee and I tried to take over Empire Pictures together a few years ago." Konig smiled at Wolff, who nodded back and seemed unable to stop nodding for an embarrassingly long time.

"And what happened?"

"We lost. They brought in the big guns. The Bank of America. The Morgan Bank. One of the opposition persuaded the FBI to leak some documents about Sigsbee to the SEC . . ."

"It was all bullshit! I didn't do nothing worse than a lot of other guys."

"Of *course* you didn't, Sigsbee. I know that. Everybody knows that. Now we have an opportunity to try again. If you're still interested . . ."

"I'm interested," Wolff muttered irritably. "I wouldn't be here otherwise."

"Have you always been interested in the movie business, Mr. Wolff?" Dawn asked politely.

Wolff made a noise that was barely distinguishable as human speech. She shook her head to indicate that she hadn't understood, and leaned closer. Wolff grabbed the front of her dress with his clawlike fingers and pulled her even closer to him. "I don't give a shit anymore about the movies, doll-ing," he said, speaking slowly, his lips carefully framing every syllable. "I just want to kill the bastards who fucked me last time out."

"I'll drink to that," Konig said, clicking his fingers to summon the captain to the table with menus.

Much of what Konig and Wolff had to say to each other passed over Dawn's head, though she was beginning to understand more about business than either of the men knew. She kept her ears open. She had a good memory, and when something puzzled her, she asked Konig to explain it later, which he was happy to do.

She understood enough to guess that Wolff regarded Konig as his protégé. From Goulandris she had learned that Wolff was enormously rich. He had arrived in Los Angeles along with the pioneer moviemakers, but he had seen the potential of the orange groves, the truck farms in the San Fernando Valley, the barren hills inhabited by snakes, coyotes, Gila monsters and a few drunken Indians. The land he had bought for a song (though Goulandris hinted that Wolff's methods of persuading the original owners to sell bordered on the brutal and unscrupulous) now bore offices, houses, oil wells and supermarkets instead of fruit, but Wolff still retained, as his one surviving passion, an interest in the movie business. He wanted to own a studio.

All this she knew. From the conversation, she gathered that Konig's English venture was a springboard from which he hoped to launch his return to a larger stage. Konig had been defeated in his attempt to take over Empire and reduced to working as a producer at MGM, where he had chafed under Mayer's abrasive, despotic rule. Like Napoleon on Elba, he was building up a small empire while he brooded over his plans to seize the larger one he craved. King Films might be a gamble, and even a desperate one, but its success would launch him on a larger gamble still, with Wolff as his none too silent partner.

Wolff ate sparingly. She guessed that it was less his appetite that was at fault than his ability to handle a knife and fork. He disguised the fact that his hands trembled by ordering soft food and picking at it delicately.

"How's Empire doing?" Konig asked.

"Lousy. Marty Braverman's a shmuck. *You* know that."

"He's a shmuck who managed to hold on to his studio, Sigsbee."

"I didn't say he wasn't tough. He's tough. But when it comes to running the fucking studio, he's a shmuck. Two million dollars in *Messalina,* for chrissake! With Ina Blaze in the lead, and a script you wouldn't piss on. And you know why."

"I know why."

"He's *shtupping* Ina Blaze. A two million dollar *shtup!* And he's got his nephew—a goddam cloak-and-suiter from New York—running the accounting department, stealing the company blind. His wife's cousin is the comptroller. They throw the money up in the air and what sticks to the ceiling is the stockholders' dividend. Marty's ripe for the plucking, Konig. Believe me."

"I believe you."

"You'd better. Isn't that Winchell over there, waving at you? You better go talk to him. The son of a bitch is a troublemaker. Go give the fucker something he can print about Dawn and tell him to keep my name out of his column."

"Will he do that?"

Wolff chuckled. It was a sound like a drain emptying, devoid of any suggestion of mirth. It turned into a cough, and for a moment Dawn thought he was going to choke to death. She patted him on the back until he wheezed a little and began to breathe normally again. "Thanks," he said. "He'll do it, Konig! I got more on Winchell than he has on me, and he knows it. You tell him to phone me at the Plaza. I'll give him some dirt on Marty Braverman."

Konig rose, smiled at Dawn and made his way through the crowd to Winchell's table.

"You *shtupping* Konig?" Wolff asked. He had ordered a piece of cheesecake and was spooning it into his mouth with obvious pleasure.

The question caught her by surprise. "I don't know why you should think that."

"Because I've still got eyes, that's why. The rest of me may be shot, but I can *see, bubby.*"

"I don't think it's any of your business."

"You're wrong about that, too. Everything to do with Konig is my business. Don't get me wrong. I got nothing against Konig *shtupping* you. He's a lucky man. I wish I could still do it, but this is it for me— a piece of goddamn cheesecake. Age stinks. Take it from me."

She nodded warily, wishing Konig would hurry back. She was not willing to take anything from Sigsbee Wolff.

"Konig thinks you could be a big star, you know that?"

"I know."

"*You* think you could be a big star? He needs a big star."

"I hope so."

Wolff laughed again. He wheezed. He panted. His eyes ran. He seemed to be enjoying himself. "You *hope* so, kiddo? You got to believe it! You want to be a star, you got to be a killer. Are you a killer?"

She looked at him steadily, not even bothering to hide her dislike. "I can be," she said flatly.

He stared at her for a moment, then nodded. "I believe you, *bubby.*" He patted his mouth with his napkin, scattering crumbs onto his lap. "Konig thinks you're going to be a big star. I don't say the potential ain't there. It's there all right—I could see that right away, and I'm half blind. But you need Konig, little lady, and don't you forget it. And remember one more thing: I need him, too. So you be nice to him, you understand?"

"I'll take good care not to make David unhappy."

"That's my goil!" Wolff exclaimed.

As Konig returned to the table, the chauffeur appeared to wheel Wolff to his limousine. It had been a long evening for a man his age, he told her, giving her a dry, cold kiss. His hand, the fingers vibrating with a life of their own, touched her cheek, then dropped down and ran lightly over her breasts.

"I've enjoyed every minute of it, though," Wolff growled. Then he signaled the chauffeur to move him. The crowd opened before him, backing away in awe, and a moment later he was gone.

For a moment, Dawn expected to smell brimstone in the wake of his departure, but there was nothing to signal Wolff's passage except the faint tracks of his tires on the carpet.

Dawn looked out at the lights of New York from the window of Konig's sitting room in the St. Regis. Konig stood by the fireplace, reading his cables and messages. "What did you think of Wolff?"

"I thought he was the most horrible man I've ever met."

'Mmm." Konig did not seem surprised or upset. "He often gives that impression at the first meeting."

"Then he grows on you?"

"Not—necessarily. Myself, I like the old devil. But it's like Hungarian cooking—not everybody's taste."

"Do you trust him?"

"No, of course not. If one had to do business with people one trusted, there'd be no business. He has sound instincts. *That* I trust."

"Do you really need him?"

"To remain in England, no. For what I want to do here, yes. In California, I'm an outsider. So is Wolff, so we're natural allies. 'The enemy of my enemy is my friend,' as I believe the Arabs say. . . . Listen, I'm grateful to you. You charmed the old man. That isn't easy to do." He opened an envelope with his cigar clipper and frowned. "A cable from Lucien," he said, holding it up. "He's in the Congo. My God, his cast hasn't even arrived, and he wants more film shipped to him. I sent Kraus along to control him, but they must *both* have gone mad!"

"Is he well?" She tried to make the question as casual as she could.

"He seems to be. 'DESCENDING CONGO STOP MAGNIFICENT FOOTAGE STOP SHIP MORE FILM TO LEOPOLDVILLE STOP ALSO AT LEAST $5,000 STOP BOATS AND PORTERS EXPENSIVE STOP MY HEALTH GOOD STOP REGARDS CHAMBRUN.' "

"Not a word about me. You'd think he'd at least say he missed me."

"Why wouldn't he miss you? The question is, Do you miss *him*?"

She looked him right in the eye. "Frankly, yes," she admitted. "Sometimes."

Konig tore the cable up, poured himself a brandy and took off his reading glasses. "Good," he said. "If you'd said no to please me, I would have known you were lying. Do you love him?"

"I don't know."

"And me?"

"I don't know that either, David. Not yet."

"I'm not talking about grand passion, you know. That's for the movies. Affection, need, respect—given enough time, they become love."

"Affection, need and respect—all that, I have."

Konig seemed satisfied. He reached into his pocket and produced a red leather box. "You've made me very happy. A star should have diamonds, after all. So I went to Cartier and bought this."

He handed the box to Dawn. She opened it. Inside was a diamond necklace. She stared at it.

It was much bigger than Mrs. Daventry's.

They made love that night, but despite the necklace, Dawn felt no sexual passion. She tried, but it was simply not there to feel. She did not think it was Konig's fault. He was a considerate and experienced lover, but it made no difference. She was surprised at how disappointed she was.

She woke early in the morning, went into the living room and stood naked before the ornate mirror. She put the necklace on. It gleamed coldly against her skin. She looked out the window at the streets far below.

There were certain sacrifices—adjustments, Konig would call them—that had to be made, she understood that. She missed Lucien sexually the way she thought an addict must feel when deprived of a drug.

She took off the necklace and picked up the morning newspapers, which had been left in the foyer. Her eye caught Winchell's byline, and she turned to his column. She saw her name.

"Film mogul David Konig was beaming as he entered '21.' Why not? The most beautiful girl in the place was on his arm: Dawn Avalon, the English star. From the way she looked at him—this is one girl whose heart belongs to Daddy. Ain't love wonderful?"

Lower down was another familiar name. "Rumor hath it that Empire Pictures bossman Marty Braverman's private life is raising eyebrows in Tinsel City—and among the major Empire stockholders. Moviegoers turned thumbs down on Marty's toga epic *Messalina*, but he's announced plans to make two more pictures with Ina Blaze. . . . Maybe Marty should read up on what happened to Nero. . . ."

Nowhere was Sigsbee Wolff's name mentioned.

CHAPTER 14

DAWN SWEPT INTO the waiting room of Konig's office on Grafton Street. Both his secretaries rose to their feet. "Oh, Miss Avalon," they chorused, "how *beautiful* you look!"

Dawn smiled at them. Konig had impressed on her the importance of the human touch. She asked after Miss Bigelow's mother and Miss Musgrave's ailing cat.

Miss Bigelow, a plump, motherly woman in her late fifties, was Konig's senior secretary. She guarded Konig like a watchdog, and her first reaction to Dawn had inevitably been one of suspicion and barely concealed hostility. Dawn had set out on a campaign to win her over with small presents and small talk, but it had taken her a while to realize that the key to Miss Bigelow's heart was to share her concern for David Konig's health and well-being.

"How is he feeling?" she asked. There was no other "he" in Miss Bigelow's life.

"He looks much better today. He was so tired yesterday, poor man. Well, they don't leave him alone, you know . . ."

Dawn nodded sympathetically. Just at the moment, she knew, "they" were bankers and accountants, Konig's natural antagonists.

"Has the hotel finished the work on your dressing room yet?" Miss Bigelow inquired. From the moment they returned to England, Konig complained that Dawn was living ("camping out," as he put it) in Lucien's flat. It was unseemly, he argued, and inappropriate to her new condition. There was nobody to take messages; she had no maid; it was dangerous for a beautiful young woman to live alone. He insisted that Dawn move into a suite of her own at Claridge's, where she would be comfortable, protected by layers of servants and porters and have the comforts of room service and a maid.

Almost effortlessly, without any consciousness of having made a major decision about her life, Dawn found herself living in the suite adjoining Konig's.

Within a week it was difficult for Dawn to remember what it was like *not* to have a maid on call twenty-four hours a day, to press, clean, tidy up. As if by magic, her wardrobe seemed to expand to take up the maid's time, filling the capacious closets of the suite. Konig, who was never satisfied with anything no matter how luxurious, had the hotel rebuild her dressing room, which did not seem to him glamorous enough for a star. He wanted the entire job completed in two days, and it was—though when it was finished Dawn was surprised to see that a mirrored door now connected their two suites directly, a perfect example of Konig's roundabout way of getting what he wanted. She indicated to Miss Bigelow that the job was done.

"I'm sure he'll be finished in a moment," Miss Bigelow said. "What a lovely dress!"

Dawn thanked her. She was wearing a new silver-fox wrap over a chic black suit and a black hat with a veil held back by a diamond clip. On the side of the hat a single plume of glossy black feathers was pinned with a spray of diamonds—yet another gift from Konig.

The exact implications of these gifts was something she preferred not to think about. With each expensive present she accepted, the relationship became more binding.

By his silence on the subject, Konig made it clear enough that he was not anxious to discuss it. Why should he? It suited him very well. Occasionally, in the long nights when she lay awake beside Konig, who had knocked himself out with a sleeping pill, she found herself wondering if this was what she really wanted out of life, but having come this far, she was determined to make the best of it. "Is he very busy today, Miss Bigelow?" she asked.

"We're *always* busy. And we've had a *very* difficult morning."

Miss Bigelow liked to refer to herself and Konig as if they constituted a single person. "We had Mr. Wolff on the telephone from California for ages," she continued. "And the accountants were here, asking all sorts of questions about the African picture. . . . Apparently Mr. Chambrun is spending a fortune out there. It's all very worrisome for poor Mr. Konig."

"Has there been much mail from Mr. Chambrun?"

"No, not much at all. Just the usual cables."

"He didn't send any messages for me, by any chance, did he?"

Miss Bigelow shook her head. "None at all, Miss Avalon." Miss Bigelow disapproved of Dawn's curiosity about Lucien. As far as she was concerned, Dawn now belonged to David Konig. "I hear Mr. Beaumont and Lady Cynthia are to be married before they go to Africa?" Miss Bigelow asked. She had an unquenchable thirst for romantic gossip, and information was the best way of keeping on her right side.

"It's true, Miss Bigelow." It was not only true, but a source of some embarrassment to Dawn, who knew more about the bridegroom than the bride did. She had been astonished to hear that Beaumont had actually proposed. When she discovered that Beaumont had made no plans for a honeymoon, she suggested to Konig that it would be a nice gesture to send them off to Africa at his expense a few weeks before shooting was to begin. Grand gestures appealed to Konig automatically, and he went into action immediately. They would have a royal honeymoon! Cables were sent, telephone calls placed to remote corners of the world, and by the end of the day the Beaumonts were committed to a luxurious cruise up the Nile and a safari for two in Kenya.

"She's a lucky girl," Miss Bigelow said. "Mr. Beaumont is such a handsome man. And such a *gentleman,* for an actor. Did you hear about the present Mr. Vale gave them?"

Dawn had not.

"A lovely little house. Right next door to his own. I know people say he has a bad reputation, but I must say it's a *princely* gift, isn't it?"

It was. Dawn thought of the door Konig had artfully contrived to have built to connect their suites. She wondered if Vale had the same thing in mind.

Miss Bigelow looked up. "Here he is," she whispered, as if she were announcing the Second Coming.

The door opened. From the depths of the room there was the sound of English voices raised a fraction in protest. Dawn heard someone say, "Oh, but Mr. Konig, I really must object . . ." Someone else interrupted: "Sooner or later the shareholders are bound to ask where their money went, Mr. Konig . . ." Konig appeared in the doorway, his cigar at a jaunty angle. "Thank you, gentlemen," he said. "Ah, here's Miss Avalon," he said, as if he was surprised to see her waiting. "Come in, come in."

There were half a dozen people in the room, all of them with the tight faces of men whose patience has been sorely tried. Their expressions were as dark and funereal as their suits, but at the sight of Dawn they rose to their feet with embarrassed smiles. She knew what was going on in their minds—a financial meeting was no place for a woman, and she had no business interrupting it.

David, she thought, looked exhausted. His face was white, and his fingers trembled as he lit a fresh cigar. She wondered how many he had smoked already. "I was just telling Sir Conop Guthrie and his associates about our plans," he said, giving her a warning look.

Sir Conop wore a monocle, a high, stiff white collar, a flower in his buttonhole and a gold watch-chain with a Masonic fob. His face might have been carved out of cheap soap.

Konig smiled genially. "I take it you've all seen *Grounds for Divorce?*" he asked. "No? But you *must!* I will send you all tickets—and for your wives, as well, naturally. Miss Avalon is preparing herself for the film version—a beautiful woman whose husband believes she's unfaithful when she isn't . . . We'll open with Dawn's face, filling the screen, then cut to her husband, who's sitting in his office . . . what do you call a lawyer's office in this country?"

"Chambers," Sir Conop snapped.

"Thank you, *thank* you, dear Sir Conop. You should come and write scripts for me. He is in his—chambers, exactly—opening a letter. It is marked 'personal.' He reads it quickly. There is a look of horror on his face. He tears it up. Then he gets down on his hands and knees, this well-dressed, handsome man, picks the pieces of paper up off the carpet, puts them together again like a—what do you call those damned things with pictures on them?"

"Jigsaw puzzles."

"Thank you, my friend. He puts them together like a jigsaw puzzle and reads the letter again, then he sits down at his desk and cries, and the screen fills up with Dawn's face again . . ."

"Then what happens?" Sir Conop asked, fascinated in spite of himself.

"I won't spoil the play for you. But you only have to look at Miss Avalon to know we'll earn our money back, in this country alone. The rest of the world will be pure profit. Sugar on the cake."

"Icing," Sir Conop corrected. "Will it cost a lot to make the film?"

Konig shrugged. "Cost? It costs the same to make a bad picture as it does to make a good one. The main thing is that we have Miss Avalon. The moment I saw the play, I knew it was for her. Didn't I, darling?"

She caught her cue, and gave him an affectionate smile. "It's the role of a lifetime," she said. She reached out and touched Sir Conop on the shoulder. "You must come and see me while we're shooting it."

"A good idea," Konig said sagely. "You gentlemen should come to the studio and see where the money goes. You'll be my guests for lunch, of course."

A thin man in the corner cleared his throat nervously. "Most kind," he said, "but there's still a real question in my mind about continuing. We've already poured in a fortune, with nothing to show for it. And now you're asking for more. And at the rate this man Vale is buying up shares, you'll soon have no control of your own company."

Dawn stared at him. She blinked her eyes rapidly, as if on the verge of tears. She took a lace handkerchief out of her pocket and dabbed them away. She gave him a look of such passionate, helpless appeal that it would have done credit to a Calcutta beggar child. He blushed. "Of course I understand it's a risky business," he stammered.

"Nothing ventured, nothing gained," Sir Conop said. His associates nodded as if they were awestruck by the originality of his thought.

Konig looked grave. He went over to the window and stared out at the street. "I don't want you to think I'm not grateful," he said mournfully. "I have many burdens, and the one that weighs most heavily on me is your generosity. But it's your *confidence* that matters to me, gentlemen, not your money. Sometimes I ask myself, Am I the right man for the job? Perhaps I'm too old? I'm wasteful—that's true. It's a wasteful business. Listen: The best thing you could do is to put King Films in bankruptcy. You'll get a shilling on the pound, or whatever. It's unfortunate, but these things happen. I'll go and live in the south of France. Perhaps I'll write a book. I might grow something. Olives, perhaps. Or grapes, for my own wine. Why not? I was born on a farm. You'd be doing me a favor."

"My dear fellow," Sir Conop said. "You mustn't think of it."

"I think of it constantly. It wouldn't be such a bad life. Perhaps my friends—my *real* friends, like you, Sir Conop—would visit me from time to time for a simple meal, a glass of my own wine. . . . I would miss Miss Avalon, of course, but I couldn't stand in the way of her career. I could sell her contract to Mayer or Selznick tomorrow for a quarter of a million pounds . . ."

He paused, while the figure sank in. "Of course, that's small potatoes. After *Grounds for Divorce*, I want to put her in a big historical film. *Cyrano*, maybe, with a big American male star . . . maybe Douglas Fairbanks, if he's not too old."

"Lady Guthrie is a great fan of his."

"There you are! Lady Guthrie shall do all my casting for me. Then a light comedy. There's a nice little play called *Champagne for the Ladies*—a beautiful, scheming marriage-breaker gets her . . . what's the bloody word?"

"Comeuppance?" Dawn suggested.

"Exactly. And I just bought *The Temptress*, this new novel everyone's talking about . . . you know it?"

"Lady Guthrie read it. Couldn't tear herself away from the bloody thing. Not much of a novel reader myself. Fond of John Buchan."

Konig clapped his hands together in ecstasy. "So am I! I've always wanted to make one of Buchan's adventure stories. Sir Conop, you and I will have a quiet lunch at your club and talk about Buchan. *The Riddle of the Sands*—what a movie *that* would make, eh? Of course, my dream is to make *Anna Karenina*, with Dawn. What an Anna she'd make—imagine that face, surrounded by furs, the eyes, as she looks out of the window of her carriage—a sensation!"

It was the first Dawn had heard of this ambitious program for her future—which she took with a grain of salt.

"Of course that's all in the past now," Konig said, a trace of bitterness in his voice. "It's a pity. Miss Avalon will go to America, to make money for MGM. I will retire. . . . Ah well, this isn't the first time I've failed."

"You haven't failed." Dawn said.

Konig put his arms around her. "You're wrong, darling," he said. "Ask these gentlemen."

Sir Conop cleared his throat. "Perhaps we're premature," he suggested. "As you say, it's not an ordinary business. We might review the matter in another six months . . . would that be enough time, Mr. Konig?"

Konig shrugged. "Time isn't the problem."

"No, quite . . . would two hundred thousand pounds keep things going? *If* we could see our way to doing it?"

"If you could see your way to putting up five hundred thousand, we'd have a better chance."

"Three-fifty," Sir Conop said firmly. "But we want you in charge. No more trouble from Vale." His associates nodded gravely.

"Agreed, gentlemen," Konig said cheerfully, recognizing a final offer when he heard it. "You've persuaded me."

Konig descended the steps to the courtyard slowly, like an old man.

With Dawn at his side, her arm in his, he looked like an invalid, an impression made all the more striking by his cane.

"Shouldn't you have asked them to lunch?"

He shook his head. "No, no. The moment they offered the money was the time to shake hands and say goodbye. At lunch the whole subject would come up all over again. They might have had second thoughts."

The Rolls appeared. Konig slumped against the seat. "We're going to the Ivy," he said with a touch of weariness. "You can show off your new hat to Noel Coward. You were wonderful in there with Sir Conop," he said. "We should be partners, you and I."

She took his hand. "We almost are."

He was silent. She knew that marriage was one of Konig's few admitted fears. He had failed at it once, and the failure had scarred him deeply. He joked about it, but behind the joking there were doubts— and *self*-doubts, too, she suspected.

She wiped away the condensation from the window and stared out at the street. "What are you going to do about Vale?" she asked.

Konig made a face as if he'd just bitten a lemon. "He's not an easy man to deal with, your friend Vale. He's smart and greedy. He has— what's the phrase?—a chip on his shoulder. He made a terrible fuss about my sending Dickie Beaumont and Cynthia off to Africa for their honeymoon before they start shooting the film. I happened to mention that it was your idea. It made him even more angry."

"How angry?" she asked, trying not to sound as alarmed as she felt.

"Spitting angry. We had a very unpleasant scene, as a matter of fact. . . . Well, I don't mind unpleasant scenes, but I won't stand for his trying to undermine me."

Dawn shivered, despite the heated car and the fur coat. "He's always been a self-dramatizer and a bully."

"A bully, yes. A self-dramatizer, I'm not so sure. I know the type. Hollywood is full of them—Aaron Diamond, Lou Bioff, even Sigsbee Wolff, I suppose . . . gangsters. Or ex-gangsters. Of course, only in England would you find a homosexual gangster—but a gangster is a gangster, whatever he does in bed. . . . You're shivering," he said. He rapped on the window that separated them from the chauffeur. "Turn the heat up," he shouted. "And get a move on, damn it! It's after one." He looked at his folder again. "Another cable from Lucien . . . that boy has shot enough footage to circle the globe. In my day, one counted it by the inch. Have you heard from him?"

"Not a thing."

Konig sighed. "He's young, he's busy, he's making his career . . . and of course communications are poor. I hear from Kraus, of course. The tests from Kenya and the Congo were wonderful. I'll screen them for you. Though now Lucien wants to go to the Sudan—apparently the natives are still quite unspoiled there, though why a lack of civilization should be thought *unspoiled* I don't know."

"The Sudan—it seems a long way away."

"It is," Konig said, with some satisfaction. "It definitely is."

Goldner was sweating heavily despite the cold. She could hardly see him, but at frequent intervals he dabbed his forehead with a silk handkerchief. Inside the Fusilier it was almost impenetrably dark, which was why he had suggested it as a meeting place.

"I have as much at stake as you do," Goldner began.

She nodded. "You bet you do. You were *there*. You took me to the doctor in your car. If Vale makes trouble for me, there'll be trouble for you."

Goldner's eyes took on the pleading quality of a spaniel's. "It was merely an act of charity on my part. I helped you in your moment of need. Besides, I doubt that anybody saw me come or go."

"You never know. All I'm saying is that if I have a problem—*you'll* have one. You've made a great deal of money out of me so far. You're going to make a lot more. You have to put a stop to Vale."

"I hear the same thing from your friend Konig. I notice he doesn't want to get *his* hands dirty."

"Surely you can see that the less he knows about this, the better? For all of us. Any kind of scandal, and he'll go back to America, or to France, and make films there. There must be *something* you can do."

"I fail to see what. I'm not a gangster like Vale. Or Sigsbee Wolff. I can't have him rubbed out, or whatever the Americans call it. . . ."

"You could threaten him. His private life ought to make him vulnerable, surely?"

"Vale's discreet. And quite apart from that, you have to bear in mind that in England nobody takes homosexuality seriously. There are homosexuals in the *Cabinet*, for God's sake! So long as they don't get caught, nobody pays much attention."

Dawn put one black-gloved hand on Goldner's. "And what if Vale *was* caught?" she asked quietly. "A public scandal like that would mean the end of him, wouldn't it? Nobody would do business with him."

Goldner downed his Scotch and soda in one gulp. "It's risky," he said. "And difficult."

"Not as risky as doing nothing."

"It wouldn't be easy to find the right—bait."

"In your clubs? Surely you can think of someone?"

"It would cost a good deal of money."

"Think of it as an investment. What if you had a distribution deal with King Films?"

"You *have* picked up the jargon. It's tempting, but I don't think Konig would offer me one, do you?"

"He might if *I* asked."

"Yes," Goldner said thoughtfully, peering at her face through the gloom. "I suppose he might. Well, I'll do my best."

"I hope so," Dawn said. "For both our sakes." She stood up, slipped a pair of dark glasses on, pulled her veil down a little lower and walked out into the biting wind. She hardly even noticed it.

By the time she reached Claridge's she was frozen. When she had first met Lucien, he used to warm her up by putting his arms around her and taking her to bed. Konig, she knew, would be in a meeting, surrounded by scriptwriters or accountants or set designers. For a brief moment, she longed for a different kind of warmth; then she plunged into the lobby of Claridge's and stood for a moment in front of the fire.

It didn't help.

In Léopoldville the temperature was almost sixty degrees hotter than in London. The heat burned clouds of steam off the oily, torpid surface of the Congo River until the whole city was blanketed in a hot, thick, malodorous fog, like a giant laundry room. Slowly the sun drew the mist into the air, creating an unimaginable humidity. For a few hours the bright, blinding glare turned the whole city white, the rooftops, the cracked pavements and the great river itself shimmering like molten metal and making even the most ordinary objects—knives, spoons, café chairs—so hot that they burned the flesh. Then the amount of moisture became too much for the air to carry. It solidified itself into huge black roiling thunderclouds, flashing sullen bursts of lightning across the darkening sky. Thunder echoed in the distance, silencing the screeches of the birds and monkeys in the trees, and suddenly the moisture descended as violent rain, so heavy that it was almost possible to believe the river itself was rising into the sky in a solid mass of water, until the rain stopped, the sun came out and the whole process began again.

Lucien sat on the terrace of the Hotel Albert, his lunch moldering on the plate before him under a cloud of flies. He sipped his beer. It was lukewarm. He clicked his fingers at one of the boys lounging insolently on the terrace.

"*Encore une bière,*" he said. "*Bien glacée cette fois.*"

The boy shrugged. Beads of sweat glittered on his black face. He had tribal scars on his cheeks. "*Pas de glace,*" he said. "*L'éléctricité est en panne.*"

Lucien nodded, without surprise. In Léopoldville everything was always *en panne.* Things broke down. It was the heat, the humidity, the lethargic, resentful natives, or perhaps simply the sullen immensity of the Congo itself.

Almost everybody who visited the Congo hated it. He loved it. Here in Africa, like so many Europeans before him, he had rediscovered himself. He was hot, weary, often uncomfortable, yet the continent had reawakened the artist in him. He felt ten years younger. He did not need praise from Konig in London. He knew his work was good—better than good, in fact. It was as if the heat had purged him of a decade of easy, shallow success. He was transformed.

Occasionally, in the long nights, as he lay listening to the noise of the jungle, he wished he could share this transformation with Queenie. He had written to her about it, but she had not replied—not that Lucien was by any means sure she would or could understand, for her star was rising in exactly the world he was turning away from.

Lucien heard a taxi door slam. A moment later Kraus appeared on the steps to the terrace, dressed as usual in a suit of some heavy, stiff gray material and a collar and tie. Kraus carried a panama hat in one hand. Under his arm was a worn, bulging leather briefcase, like the kind of bag European children took to school. And indeed there was something childlike about Kraus. He had a baby's big domed head, sparsely covered with straight thinning blond hair, and below it a pale, sharp, narrow, small-featured face. On meeting him your first thought was that he needed a good meal—unless you happened to notice that the pale eyes behind the thick, round, wire-rimmed spectacles were very definitely those of an adult, however frail. Everything about Kraus was small—the schoolboy wrists, the bony fingers, with the nails bitten to the quick, the colorless eyebrows. Anywhere in the world he would have been recognized as a refugee.

Kraus was energetic, efficient, tireless and unfailingly calm. Lucien had hated him on sight.

Time and the companionship of travel had softened Lucien's initial dislike of the little man. Kraus had no romantic illusions about Africa or anything else. His job was to arrange things, however improbable, difficult or senseless. He was the perfect production assistant.

Kraus spoke five or six languages—even when he didn't know the language, he could still haggle over a bill, negotiate for extras, produce five hundred tribesmen in full regalia, a herd of elephants or anything else that was required.

Konig had brought Kraus out of Europe some years before, for reasons which were unclear, had discovered his abilities and found him work. Kraus now worshipped his benefactor even from afar.

He put his hat down carefully on the table. He clicked his fingers at the boy.

"Clear this up," he said, pointing to the food on the table with distaste. "Immediately!"

As if Kraus had galvanized him to life, the boy quickly removed the dishes and wiped the tablecloth clean, smiling broadly. It never failed to astonish Lucien that Kraus had such natural authority, despite his appearance.

"You have to keep after these people," Kraus said. "They have no sense of discipline."

Lucien shrugged. That, as it happened, was exactly what he liked about the natives. "Any news?" he asked.

"Mr. Konig cabled. We're to go on to the Sudan."

"The Sudan? But it's a thousand miles away. Whatever for?"

Kraus shrugged. "He was quite specific. He says the natives are unspoiled there."

"What's the quickest way to get there?"

"There isn't a quick way. Nobody was even sure it could be done. However, I had a word with the manager at Cook's. A typical Belgian colonial type, but I set him straight. We leave tomorrow. There's a train service from here to Uganda."

"What's it like?"

"There are first-class accommodations for Europeans. Not that *that* means much. We'll spend the night in Kikiwisha, where there's a government lodge—pretty primitive, I imagine. Then the next day we'll go through Kasai Province to Bukavu. There's some kind of a hotel in Bukavu, apparently. Then to Kibombo, lay over in Ruanda for a couple of days, and try to get transport to Kampala. After that it gets rough."

"How rough?"

"Nobody can say. We may have to spend some time in Juba—nobody seems to know much about the train schedule here."

"What's in Juba?"

"Nothing."

"There must be *something*."

"I don't think so. It's six hundred miles to Khartoum, and there's nothing from one end of the line to the other but sand. I can't help feeling it would have been easier to make this picture in California."

"You wouldn't have the natives, Kraus. Were there any other messages?"

Kraus pulled a piece of paper out of his pocket. "Just Mr. Konig's cable. He liked the tests."

"Nothing from Miss Kelley?"

"Pardon?"

"Miss *Avalon*."

"I'm afraid not."

"You sent my cable?"

"Of course," Kraus said. He crumpled up the piece of paper and signaled the boy to remove it. Kraus had a passion for neatness. Rather than sit at a table with a dirty ashtray, Kraus would clean it himself. The boy brought his tea.

Kraus wondered what would happen when Lucien found out, as he surely would, that his cables and letters to Queenie had never been sent. No doubt there would be hell to pay, but Kraus took his orders from Konig, and was merely doing what he'd been told. Konig's instructions had been explicit.

Kraus's conscience was clear.

Refinanced, Konig plunged into his next film. Dawn thought his pace would have killed a younger man—it was very nearly killing *her*. He had two directors working on *Grounds for Divorce*, and he himself appeared, usually late at night, to direct the more important scenes in which she appeared. He had four pictures going simultaneously, including the African film, two of them being shot in the new studio he was building, on half-completed sound stages. He did not interrupt his round of dinner parties—nothing could be allowed to stand in the way of his social life, since it was the keystone of his financing—but when the last guest had left, he settled down to work with his screenwriters, dictating pages of script changes, revising scenarios, pacing back and forth in the living room, puffing on his cigar until the air was blue and heavy with smoke.

Though her own life was caught up in his plans, she seldom saw him. A studio car picked her up at Claridge's in the morning while it was still dark, and she seldom returned until late at night, just in time to put in an appearance at the tail end of Konig's dinner parties, "like a girl jumping out of a cake," as Goulandris put it.

Most nights she was asleep long before he came to bed with a groan of fatigue. It amused her to imagine how different their life together really was from what Konig's dinner guests no doubt imagined it to be. Sometimes, however, she fell asleep dreaming of Lucien's hard, muscular body lying beside her.

She knew it was irrational to feel anger at Lucien—after all, she had chosen Konig herself—but she could not help being amazed and hurt by the fact that he had apparently dropped her without a thought the moment he was out of England. That disturbed her more than anything. If she could make a mistake like that, then how could she ever trust her instincts?

One night, she woke as Konig slipped into bed. He gave a sigh, propped himself against the pillows, poured a glass of ice water from the carafe next to his side of the bed and took a pill. "You're very late tonight," she said, yawning.

"I didn't mean to wake you."

"Did you take a sleeping pill?"

"Yes. Not that they do much bloody good. I told my fool of a doctor that I need something stronger, but he says what I have will put a horse to sleep. Unfortunately, I'm not a horse. He should have been a vet. . . . You know, I'm tired of living like this, in a hotel. It's very comfortable, of course, but I wouldn't mind a place of my own—*our* own. Perhaps I'd sleep better in my own bed. . . ."

Dawn was no longer sleepy. She sat up and pulled the covers around her.

"I thought of a flat," he went on. "But I don't like apartments much. One has neighbors. It's all right in New York or Berlin, where everybody lives that way, but in London a house is much nicer. How would you like that?"

She knew the answer to that. "I'm not sure I'd feel right about it, David," she said.

He raised an eyebrow. He selected another grape. "You don't like houses?"

"I like houses, yes. That's not the point."

"What exactly *is* the point?"

"I have the suite next to yours here at Claridge's. People may guess we have a—relationship, but they don't really know. If we move into a house together, there won't be any doubt in anybody's mind, will there?"

"None at all," he said. He paused. "You think it would look better if we were married?"

"I don't think I'd do it if we weren't married."

"And if I asked you to marry me, what would you say?"

"I don't know. You haven't asked me." She wanted to hear a direct offer, knowing how circuitous Konig's approach to things was.

"I'm asking now."

"I don't think I can marry you just so we can move to a house, David. Surely there's more to marriage than that?"

"Oh, yes," he said with a sigh, "I know all that. What if I were to tell you that I love you? I'm not good at these things, you know, but it's true. What if I were to say that I need you? Lately, I've grown used to not being lonely. I don't ever want to be lonely again." He frowned. "I also don't like being hurt. I'm not going to ask you if you love me, but if you have any doubts, now is the time, please. Not later. Are you still in love with Lucien?"

"I'm not sure I ever was. And he's certainly not in love with *me*."

"Good. Then in that case, will you marry me?"

She said yes—as she had always known she would.

"It will have to be a quiet marriage, I'm afraid. No press, no publicity. If Marla gets wind of it, she'll be on the next boat to make a scene. . . . You don't mind that?"

"I don't mind," Dawn said. She knew perfectly well that the disparity of age between them was bound to cause comment. It could hardly be the kind of romantic ceremony girls were said to dream of, with the bridegroom in his fifties and the ink hardly dry on his California divorce papers. She wondered what Ma would say when she saw the clippings. But what could Ma understand of her life now? It was as impossible to explain as Morgan's disappearance, about which Ma had first asked questions, then apparently decided to put out of her mind, as she did everything she didn't want to know.

Konig leaned over and kissed her. "Now I'll tell you the truth," he said. "I already bought the house and put it in your name. It's a bargain. The Spanish Ambassador owned it, so it's going cheap."

She laughed. "You knew I'd say yes?"

"Shall we say—I was willing to take the gamble?" He removed a small red leather box from the pocket of his Charvet dressing gown. "I even bought the ring." He opened the box and slipped the ring on her finger. It fit perfectly. That was the kind of detail David would hardly overlook, she thought.

He closed his eyes for a moment, then shook his head. "Damn," he said, "I took my wake-up pill instead of my sleeping pill—no wonder I'm wide-awake!"

She felt his hands on her breasts, his breath on her cheeks. She put her arms around him. Despite the fact that he brushed his teeth meticulously, she could still feel the faint taste of cigars on his lips. She tried to put it out of her mind, and thought about the future instead. As Mrs. David Konig, she would be secure, rich, protected always by Konig's power and money.

Outside Caxton Hall, the reporters and photographers were standing three deep on the pavement, a living barrier between the Konigs and their waiting car. Even Konig had not been able to keep the wedding a complete secret, though he had managed to do so just long enough to keep Marla away. Dawn clutched his arm as the flashbulbs went off.

"Where are you going for your honeymoon?" a reporter shouted.

"That's a secret," Konig said. "We'd like a little peace and quiet."

"What did you give Dawn for a wedding present?"

"I followed the tradition," Konig said. "Something old, something borrowed, something blue, something new, isn't that it?"

"What was it?"

"I gave Mrs. Konig a Van Gogh still life—'Blue gloves, with flowers.' And a diamond bracelet. And a sable coat."

"That's something old all right, and something new," the reporter said. "What's borrowed?"

"The money to pay for it, of course!" Konig shouted, and stepped into the Rolls.

The honeymoon was staged by Konig at his usual breakneck pace. No sooner had they arrived in Paris on their first day than he was on the telephone arranging dinner parties, fittings for her with the major couturiers, interviews with the French film journalists. She had hoped for a day or two of peace, to share her first visit to Paris with him quietly. Perhaps it would have done no good, but given time, closeness and the novelty of being married, she thought she might have come to love him that first night in Paris, or even the second. Certainly, she *wanted* to, for she could not easily bring herself to accept the fact that she had married him for his money, or for her career, or because she was angry at Lucien.

But the moment they were installed in their suite at the Ritz, with the flowers, the champagne and the caviar, compliments of the manager, he was on the telephone. Lubitsch was in town? He must come to dinner, too! And Jean Renoir, of course, if he was free, and Tanya Ouspenskaya, how not? And by the time the car picked them up, Konig had ordered a table for twelve at Maxim's.

Even when they arrived at the Hotel du Cap in Antibes, Konig seemed unable to relax. He needed company—and the company of his wife, however young and beautiful, was not enough. . . .

Dawn had forgotten what it was like to be warm. Every day she rose early, walked down through the rows of orange trees and *oliviers* to the rocks and lay down in their private cabana to sunbathe. She was a poor swimmer—there had been no opportunity to learn in India—so daily she took a swimming lesson from the teacher in the heated salt-water pool before anybody else in the hotel was even awake.

Konig himself seldom rose before noon or made an appearance at the cabana before lunchtime. It was not until the evening that Konig came to life. The waiting limousine took them to dine in Cannes, Nice or Monte Carlo, then on to the casino, where Konig invariably played baccarat until one or two in the morning. There were seldom fewer than six for dinner, which only a short time ago would have scared Queenie—but she was now Dawn. Konig had taught her the art of conversation; above all, he had taught her that a beautiful woman can never say anything wrong. "However rich, famous and successful people are," he said, "they never lose their awe of beauty. It's the only democratic instinct left in the upper classes."

And it was true. Cocteau joined them for dinner and made a drawing of her on a napkin. Winston Churchill, who dined with them at the Hotel de Paris in Monte Carlo with a party of people from Lord Camrose's yacht, gave her his set piece on his charge at the battle of Omdurman and told Konig she knew more about India than the Viceroy. Marcel Pagnol offered to write a play for her. Even Noel Coward, who had fled for the evening from the Villa Mauresque, where he was staying with Willy Maugham, was so impressed by Dawn that he wrote a song for her on the spot and insisted on taking over the restaurant's piano to sing it.

It should have been an idyllic time, and to all appearances it was, but Dawn recognized, lying on her mat in the sun, that marrying David had changed their relationship. It was not just that she felt no passion for him—she had faced that at the very beginning, or rather, decided *not* to face it in the hope that she could live with the fact. It had been easy enough to live with on a temporary basis, but the permanency of marriage made it much harder than she had imagined. More difficult to cope with was the effect of marriage on Konig. Before she had enjoyed an anomalous—certainly an ambiguous—role in his life; now she was his wife. She had become, with a stroke of the pen, part of Konig's image, along with the Rolls-Royce, the dinner parties and the carefully tailored suits. He fussed endlessly about what she should say or wear or do.

To give Konig credit—and she was determined to give him credit— he was unaware of the change himself. He seemed unconscious of the distance he had put between them, or perhaps it was something he simply couldn't help.

He settled himself down beside her in a deck chair. A servant tilted the parasol so that he was in the shade. A waiter put a tray with coffee and ice water beside him. The beach boy brought him a telephone, a pack of cards and a list of the day's arrivals in the hotel. Konig lit a cigar and replaced his ordinary glasses with tinted ones. He did not seem to Dawn to look well—true, he never looked well, but there was something bothering him, a tightness around the mouth, a slight flush on his cheeks, that prompted her to ask how he was feeling.

He waved is cigar to indicate that his health was not an issue. "We'll be staying on here a few days more than I expected," he said.

"I thought you wanted to finish *Grounds for Divorce?*"

"I do. But a few days more in the sun won't do either of us any harm."

"Did you speak to London this morning?"

"What makes you think I did?"

"I heard the concierge putting through the call on my way down."

"A man should have no secrets from his wife. Do you know why? Because it isn't possible to *keep* any secrets from a wife. . . . In London, it's raining, it's about forty degrees, and the work on the house is going to take twice as long as I thought—and probably cost three times the estimate. If we're lucky."

"It's not like you to worry about money, David."

"Who's worried?"

"*You* are, I think. It shows in your face."

Konig leaned forward in his chair. He glanced around him to see that nobody was within listening distance. "It's not a good time to be in London," he said. "It seems your friend Vale ran into a bit of trouble."

Even in the heat of the sun, Dawn felt a chill. She looked up to see if a cloud had passed over her, but the sky was a perfect, clear blue. "What kind of trouble, David?"

"The usual sordid English sex scandal. A boy complained to the police that he was homosexually assaulted by Vale. Unfortunately for Vale, when the police found him for questioning, he was in one of those nightclubs for men with—special tastes. . . ."

"He owns several of them."

"Yes? I had no idea," Konig said, with an expression in which shock and indignation were artfully combined. Clearly he was determined to play the role of an innocent, even with her.

"What will happen to him?" There was, Dawn recognized, a slight edge of hysteria in her voice.

Konig looked at her shrewdly. "I'm surprised you care. I had the impression that you and Vale were hardly the best of friends."

She struggled to sound calm. Goldner had given her no warning. "I was just interested. Will he go to prison?"

"He'd have to be tried first. England isn't Germany, after all. But in fact Vale behaved sensibly. He took the night train for Paris and vanished from sight. I imagine his friends helped him to leave. I suspect they *urged* him to leave—and even made it worth his while to go, quickly and quietly. A lot of people with well-known names must have been desperate to get him out of the country before he talked to the police. . . . Of course, he'll have to resign his directorship, and so on. Including King Films."

"How convenient."

"Isn't it? One is sorry for the poor man—but on the other hand it will be a great relief not to have him around trying to push me out of my own company."

"Where will he go?"

Konig shrugged. "If he's smart—and he *is* smart—he'll sell off everything and start all over again somewhere else. There's a market everywhere for what Vale sells. If I were him, I'd go to America. He'd do very well there. . . ."

The farther away, the better, Dawn thought. She thanked God that Vale had no way of connecting his downfall to her. At worst, he might suspect Goldner, but he would have no reason to think that she had anything to do with it. She felt warmer, and even a little hungry. She rolled over and took a piece of fruit from the basket beside Konig. "It's funny," she said. "When we were going to America—remember?—we talked about Vale's weaknesses at dinner with Goldner. I remember your saying later that if a man has something he really has to hide, he can do it for years—but it will still bring him down in the end."

"I don't remember talking about Vale at all," Konig said firmly. His expression was absolutely sincere. He frowned as if he were trying to jog his memory. "No," he said, "I can't remember a thing. Of course it's true about hiding something. In the end, it's what we've hidden best—the thing we've buried deepest—that comes back to haunt us every time."

He paused, puffing his cigar. "It's true of all men." Another pause. "And women, too."

He blew a smoke ring in the still, hot air. He seemed to be waiting for a reply, but she had nothing to say.

The lights from the crystal chandelier reflected from the polished surface of a dining table that stretched the length of the room. There were twenty guests for dinner, many of them unknown to Dawn. She was the hostess—and the main attraction—but she had nothing to do with the guest list, the food or the wines, all of which were chosen by Konig, who, in deep conversation with his new political friends, sat at the far end of the immense table, which had cost ten thousand pounds at Christie's and had once graced the Duke of Albany's house. Nineteen thirty-eight was the year of Munich, and everywhere there was talk of war. All London was split between the appeasers, who supported Neville Chamberlain, and the anti-appeasers, who believed in resistance and Winston Churchill.

Konig, for once, had chosen the unpopular side. He was enough of a Jew to sense that no deal was possible with Hitler—none that would include people like him, at any rate. His dinner parties included those who favored war—heavyset hard-faced men with money behind them, who saw the chance for a sudden rise to power in the gathering storm.

Dawn had no interest in politics and rather liked Neville Chamberlain—at any rate, she liked him better than the loud-voiced, self-confident politicians who gathered nightly at Konig's table to ridicule the Prime Minister and gloat over the approach of a war which other, younger men would have to fight. She kept her opinions to herself, which was by no means difficult to do, since Konig's friends treated her as if she were some particularly valuable and fragile ornament.

"They don't have the ships!"

"They don't have the tanks!"

"They don't have the guts!" she heard them grumble as she made her way upstairs to bed, her departure unnoticed. Churchill smoked cigars, Konig smoked cigars, Beaverbrook, Bracken, Duff Cooper, Arlington, they all smoked cigars. No matter how many times a day she bathed and shampooed, the smell of cigars seemed to cling to her. Konig usually retired late to his own bedroom, long after she was asleep, and rose hours after she was already awake and dressed. He was always tired, but that was hardly surprising: his new studio was almost completed and he had half a dozen films in production. The new studio, together with his ambitious production schedule, was draining capital at a dizzying rate, and he was borrowing against his debts, counting on the fact that he already owed so much nobody could afford to let him go under.

He did not let these concerns stand in the way of his other ambitions. Konig and Sigsbee Wolff were busy buying up shares in Empire Pictures, carefully assigning the transactions to middlemen so as not to arouse Marty Braverman's suspicions. Dawn knew from the dinner-table conversation that Goldner was one of these anonymous investors, and strongly suspected that Kraus, Konig's weasel-faced hatchet man, was another—certainly Kraus was around the house a lot and often closeted with Konig. Once or twice he was even asked to dinner, turning up in a dinner jacket several sizes too large that had obviously been rented.

"He gives me the creeps," Cynthia Beaumont said at dinner one evening.

Now that the Beaumonts were back, with *Safari* (as Lucien's film had been retitled) finally completed, they too became habitués of Konig's dinner table. The film did little for Cynthia's reputation—most of the critics had dismissed her as "an attractive blond lightweight," but Beaumont's performance dazzled everyone, and he was assured of a career as a major film star. His scenes, the *Daily Express* critic reported, "fairly crackled with white-hot masculine energy." Lucien's direction was also much admired, and even though some critics complained that much of the film looked like a beautiful travelogue, he was praised as "a director of promise."

Cynthia seemed as arrogant and beautiful as ever, at first glance, but there were shadows under her eyes, a curious tightening of the mouth— and she drank. She neither hid her drinking nor made a point of it, but by the end of the evening she usually required help to walk to the car. Her laughter had a hysterical quality to it, like breaking glass, and she chainsmoked restlessly, sometimes lighting a fresh cigarette only a minute after she had lit the previous one, so that the tablecloth around her was quickly disfigured with ashes and small burns.

Tonight she was in control of herself so far—much to Dawn's relief. "Kraus gives me the creeps, too," she said.

Cynthia giggled. "He was a perfect swine in Africa. Always sneaking around like a divorce detective. Lucien hated him."

"That's not hard to understand. How *was* Lucien? He seems to have vanished."

"He grew a beard. It rather suited him, I think. No longer the dashing pretty boy. Africa does that to men, somehow. Most men, anyway. He was pretty gloomy at first."

"That doesn't sound like Lucien."

"Well he was pining, darling. For you. Not a word, not a letter, he used to tell me every morning at breakfast. He took it quite hard, you know. . . ."

"I didn't hear from *him*."

Cynthia looked puzzled. She hesitated, then emptied her glass. "That wasn't the story *he* told me. How odd. . . . Who is that dreadful man staring at me from the middle of the table?"

"Sir Conop Guthrie. Why hasn't Lucien come back, Cynthia? He didn't even show up for the opening of his own picture." She tried to make the question sound casual. She was not sure she had succeeded, but Cynthia didn't seem to notice.

"Well, darling, in the first place, he's gone off to scout for locations. He's smitten with the idea of doing *Heart of Darkness* in the Congo. A bloody depressing book, if you ask me, and no part in it for a woman. He's gone bonkers over Africa. I can't think why. I hated every square inch of it myself. Everybody out there is frightfully middle-class, except for the blacks, of course. . . ."

Cynthia snapped her fingers at the butler, who raised an eyebrow and half filled her glass. "Word must be getting around," she said. "I can see Dickie's been talking to Konig about my drinking."

"Fill Lady Cynthia's glass up," Dawn ordered.

"Thank you, darling. The shameful thing about drinking is that the servants are the first to know. And they're always such dreadful prudes about it . . . What were you asking me?"

"Why Lucien hasn't come home."

"Oh, yes, of course. Well, one reason, darling, is that I think your marriage took him a little bit by surprise. The torch still burns. For you, I mean. Which should be madly flattering."

"It shouldn't have surprised him. I wrote to him."

Cynthia drained her glass, shut her eyes for a moment, then lit another cigarette. She had a certain amount of trouble finding the end of it, but finally she succeeded, took a deep drag, then stubbed it out in her plate. "Did you, darling?" Cynthia looked more distracted than ever.

"I wrote to him. He never answered."

"The mails are dreadful out there."

"Surely not *that* dreadful?" Clearly Cynthia was hiding something. She was a bad liar, too, or an unwilling one, more likely.

"Awful!" Cynthia said. "Things get lost all the time. You must have had *some* letters from him, darling. At the beginning he was scribbling away all the time."

"How did you post your letters?" Dawn asked, trying to sound casual. "I suppose they don't have red pillar boxes out there, do they?"

"No, no. One gave them to Kraus, and he put them in the pouch. He took care of everything."

"I see," Dawn said—and she did. It was only a suspicion, but it was a suspicion that made sense, and when something made sense, it was usually true. She was surprised that she hadn't guessed it before— perhaps she simply hadn't wanted to guess it. "Where is Lucien now? Still in Africa?"

"He *was* going to Paris, I think. There are some French producers who were very interested in his work. You'll never guess who we saw in Paris on our way back, by the way—Dominick Vale, of all people. Looking absolutely splendid, right there at Fouquet's. Not a bit guilty, in fact."

"Did you talk to him?" Dawn asked, with an effort to appear casual.

"We had dinner with him. You know what chums he and Dickie

are. He had some very unpleasant things to say about *you*, darling. He seems to blame you for what happened."

"That's nonsense!"

"I expect so. Oh, why don't those dreadful men shut up?"

"There'll be war by thirty-nine," they heard Brendan Bracken say, his loud voice booming above the rest of the conversation. "Heard it from a chap who was in Berlin last week. They'll wait until the autumn, when they have the harvest in."

Cynthia's china-blue eyes were slightly clouded but still able to focus. "Do you think there'll be a war, Dawn?" she asked.

"I hope not."

"Really? I'm looking forward to it myself. It can't possibly be as boring as peace, can it? What does David think?"

"He thinks there will be war."

"So does Dickie. Do you know what he did? He went off and took a reserve commission in the RAF Auxiliary. I think he fancied the uniform, frankly."

"I don't think that's fair, Cynthia."

"Don't you? But you're not *married* to him, darling, are you? There he is, the most handsome man in England. He has only to step on stage in his tights, darling, and ladies of all ages positively wet their seats, but when we're in bed together, I don't—feel—a—thing!"

Cynthia laughed—a brittle, high-pitched sound which seemed to contain not the slightest suggestion of humor and which rose to a shattering crescendo that brought conversation to a sudden, embarrassing stop, followed by its immediate resumption, as if everybody else at the table wanted to pretend nothing had happened.

"Don't make a scene," Dawn whispered.

Cynthia snuffled slightly into her napkin, then seemed to regain control of herself. "Of course not," she said, her pretty face suddenly bitter. "No scenes. This is England. It's all right to talk about making war, but we don't make *scenes*."

"Cynthia, darling, perhaps you just haven't given him a chance. Why don't you go away, just the two of you?"

Cynthia lit another cigarette and stared thoughtfully at Dawn. "You haven't understood me," she said, her voice low this time. "I don't mind so much that Dickie can't satisfy *me*—though I wouldn't have thought that was so bloody much to ask. I can't satisfy *him!* When he's in bed with me, he just isn't there. It's as if he were going through the motions. You can't have any idea what it's like."

"Perhaps I can," Dawn said so quietly that Cynthia didn't hear her.

"It was a mistake," Konig said. "I admit it."

"You cheated me. And it wasn't even necessary."

"I didn't know that. It was insurance." He stood in the darkened living room, his black tie undone.

"I don't think that's a decent excuse." It was the first time she had ever challenged him.

He blushed slightly. "It isn't the first thing I've done that I'm ashamed of," he said. Did he feel guilty because he had stopped her letters and Lucien's, Dawn wondered—or only because she had found out? She wondered what Lucien had said in his letters. Would it have made a difference?

Konig poured himself a drink. He was drinking more lately. It never seemed to have much effect on him except to slow him down, so that he did everything in slow motion. "I'll make it up to you," he said.

She was silent. David was not stupid enough to believe he could buy his way out of a quarrel with her, but when he was tired—as he was these days—he had neither the time nor the patience for anything else.

"I think I'll sleep in my bedroom, for the time being," she said. "I'd rather be alone."

Konig did not argue the point. He gave a weary shrug, turned his back to her and helped himself to the one ice cube—never more, never less—that he always put in his Scotch and soda. She heard the hiss of the soda siphon, and turned to go upstairs.

She wondered if he was relieved at her decision to sleep alone. It had not occurred to her until then that David might have been making love to her out of the same sense of obligation that she felt toward him.

Nineteen thirty-nine was the year of grim preparations for a war which everybody knew was coming and nobody wanted to think about. Gas masks were issued to everybody, together with leaflets describing the various gruesome symptoms that could be expected following a gas attack; sandbags, fire extinguishers, shovels and pails appeared in the hallways and entrances of office buildings; house owners were urged to construct shelters in their gardens. In the parks, centuries-old lawns were dug up to site antiaircraft guns, and Konig's new studio, just completed, was in the process of being camouflaged. All over London busybodies and snoops began to join strange organizations identified only by letters—ARP or CAD—and flushed with the authority of their new armbands and steel helmets took to pestering their neighbors about fire precautions, blackout curtains or the presence of spies.

It was sufficient to ask for directions in a foreign accent to be arrested, and Konig's three scriptwriters were picked up almost every day by zealous spy-watchers, until Konig solved the problem by drafting them into the studio's volunteer fire-fighting force, which entitled them to armbands and helmets of their own.

In some ways Konig had nothing to complain about. The closer war came, the more people wanted to forget about it. The cinemas had never done better business, and Dawn—beautiful, glamorous and sophisticated—was exactly what they wanted to take their minds off the dangers of nerve gas, massed aerial bombing and Nazi storm troopers parachuting into England disguised as nuns. Her reputation was growing in America, but here in England Dawn was already a major star, and a secretary was employed full time at Grafton Street to answer her fan mail, which far exceeded that of the Prime Minister after Munich.

Yet the approach of war was not Konig's chief concern. No matter how successful his films were, they could never earn enough to pay off the vast organization he had built; even his legendary skill at juggling figures could not conceal from his investors that King Films was foundering under the weight of the studio—and its managing director's extravagant habits. Konig's strategy in dealing with this problem was instinctive. He doubled his bet.

He would produce a major epic—a picture that would capture once and for all the world market for British films. He would use Dawn Avalon and Richard Beaumont to ensure its box-office success and would pour all his remaining resources into one huge movie. At the same time he would make his bid for Empire Pictures, using King Films as a means of acquiring a foothold in Hollywood for his British investors.

He reasoned, with some justification, that the banks, the Treasury, Bracken, perhaps even Goldner and his new Jewish friends in the City, would be happy enough to overlook the financial problems of King Films if they were offered a chance to acquire a major Hollywood studio—nor would it be difficult for him to persuade them that with Sigsbee Wolff "in his pocket," the thing could be done. With a little

luck—and a new infusion of capital—they would own Empire Pictures—not only the studio, but, more important, Empire's distribution
company—thus opening up the entire American market to British
films, while at the same time retaining the English studio.

Since Goldner himself was already acquiring English theaters and
preparing to become an independent distributor, the English-speaking
world would be theirs to control. At one stroke, a British group would
end the hegemony of the American majors over world film distribution
and seize a commanding position in America itself. It did not escape
Dawn's attention that Goldner's good fortune—and to some degree even
Konig's—was her doing. Now that she was twenty-one, and free of her
old contract, she was earning money for Konig, after all.

Under the circumstances it was scarcely surprising, even to Dawn,
that her husband had little time for her, and she herself was in any
case busy enough as his leading star. What was more worrying was
that he didn't have enough time to devote to the epic picture she was
to star in.

After rejecting *Cyrano* as too subtle for an English-speaking audience, and *War and Peace* as too ambitious, he chose *King Solomon's
Mines*, the rights to which he had picked up cheaply years before.
Konig had come close to making it several times, and the more he
thought about it, the better it seemed. It was escapism, adventure,
romance—exactly what people wanted to see on the eve of war. That
it would also be expensive and difficult to make he refused to acknowledge or even discuss. He was like a man who has set himself a gigantic
task and hopes, by delaying it, to escape from it—but by now he had
announced it. The newspapers, even the government, had applauded
his courage. He was trapped.

The one thing he feared was attempting to direct the picture himself—that, he knew, was beyond his resources. He had made epics
before—a long time ago. He knew the human cost all too well. Besides, he complained, it was not his métier: he was not Cecil B.
De Mille, after all. But finding a director was by no means easy. No
major American director wanted to come to England at a time when
war was about to break out, and no English director had the experience
for this kind of thing—or rather, they had the wrong kind of experience, Konig said, correcting himself. They were used to thinking
small, whereas what was needed was a man who could think big. He
went over the problem again and again, even with Dawn, but he found
no solution.

One night she found him slumped in front of the fire in his study, his eyes closed. He heard her and stirred wearily. She came over and stood behind him. "You're up late," he said.

"I couldn't sleep. I came down for a cup of tea."

"We have servants, you know."

"I know."

"You mustn't hesitate to wake them up. God knows they get paid enough."

"I know that, too. I simply prefer making my own tea. It's a habit."

She put her hand on the back of his neck. He groaned. "I shall have to do it myself," he said.

"Was John Mammon no good?" she asked. Konig had screened several of Mammon's pictures and had even journeyed out, tonight, for a quiet dinner à deux at Mammon's country house—a sign of his desperation, for Konig almost never ate at other people's houses or visited the country. "Everybody says he has a lot of experience."

"Experience? He has a *lot* of experience—in making flops. Experienced directors take the easy way out. They imitate other people—or worse yet, they imitate themselves. We need somebody who has a flair for the savage, somebody who can make an improbable adventure story seem *real*. . . ."

There was a long silence, broken only by Konig's labored breathing.

"There's Lucien," she suggested quietly.

He said nothing.

"If his new picture is as good as *Safari* . . ."

"It is, to be honest. I had it screened for me."

"He might be able to do it."

"As it happens, he's exactly the right man." Konig straightened his neck and moved his head back and forth. "But," he said, holding up his hands as if he were fending off an attacker. "But . . ."

"But what?"

"*But!* Do I really want him directing you? Do *you* really want that? Jealousy is a ridiculous emotion, but painful at my age. I don't want to add it to my troubles."

"He's the right man, David. The right man for the job."

He did not ask her if he could trust her with Lucien. She was glad, since she didn't know the answer herself. Konig, who had sent Lucien away and kept them apart, would now have to bring him back and take the risk of losing her. It was a kind of justice, she thought.

"Would he come back, though?" Konig asked. "He's got commitments. And I hear he's still bitter about our marriage."

She knew the answer to that. "He would if I asked him."

Konig nodded. "True," he said. His expression was mournful. He knew she was right, he knew he had no choice, and he knew he was taking a risk. "Write to him. Better yet, cable him. I don't want to know what you say, or how you do it—but get him here. I'll do the rest."

He stood up, put his arm around her and walked over to the huge ornate staircase. He was so tired that he paused for breath on the way upstairs. He pressed her hand. "It's been a long time since we slept together," he said. "A very long time."

In the dim light of the stairs he seemed so exhausted that it was difficult to remember how energetic and charming he could be when he was with other people. She had no desire to sleep with him, but she understood—or thought she understood—the reason he had brought the subject up. He would always be jealous of Lucien. He needed now to reaffirm his possession of her. She did not argue the point. There were times in marriage when it was better to give in, and this was one of them.

He followed her into her bedroom, still breathing hard. He sat down on the bed and pulled off his shoes. "I have a secret to tell you," he said. "Nobody must know this, but I've been offered a knighthood."

She stared at him in astonishment. Konig had a reputation for being able to fix anything, but a title seemed beyond even his capacity for pulling strings. "But that's wonderful, David!"

He smiled as if he had done it just to please her. "It's basically a way of affirming the government's faith in the British film industry. A little flag-waving. Besides, politically, it doesn't look bad to give a knighthood to a Hungarian and a Jew. The Americans will love it—American Jews, particularly. It's one in the eye for Hitler. . . ."

"You deserve it on your own merits."

"You're very sweet. I wish that were true. Chamberlain owes Churchill a favor—never mind why. I did a few favors for Churchill, so he owes *me* one. In England a knighthood is the traditional way for politicians to pay their debts. I can't deny that I'm pleased. You'll be known as Lady Konig, of course," he added.

"I shall find it difficult to get used to that."

"Nonsense. You'll get used to it in no time. You got used to being Dawn quickly enough. Naturally we shall both have to be careful. The Palace is very stuffy about these things. A bad story in the papers, even the wrong kind of gossip, could kill the whole thing."

He might as well have said, "No affairs, please, or you'll ruin my chances." She resented the warning. Dawn sat down and began to wipe off her makeup. "You don't have to worry about me," she said.

"It was merely an observation," he said wearily. "I'm not worried."

She turned around and looked at him. Whatever the difficulties between them, he had once again performed a miracle, at least in part for her. He had made her Dawn Avalon, the star. Now he was about to transform her into Lady Konig, which was a long way from Queenie Kelley! She got up, slipped out of her clothes, put on her dressing gown and lay down beside him. Not to sleep with him tonight, when he had given her the news of his knighthood, would be to widen the breach between them until it could no longer be bridged.

That night they slept in the same bed for the first time since they had quarreled over Lucien's letters. David had never made love to her with more feeling, gentleness or affection—not since the first time, on the *Mauretania.*

And when he was done, and asleep, Dawn got out of bed, went into the bathroom, looked at herself in the mirror and cried.

The postman, a grizzled veteran with an impenetrable meridional accent, had bicycled all the way from Antibes to deliver the cable, on the instructions of the concierge at the Hotel du Cap, pushing his bicycle up the steeper hills. In the heat it was a slow trip. The postman did not complain, but he presented the flimsy piece of folded pale-blue paper to Lucien with such elaborate ceremony, unbuckling his patent-leather shoulder pouch and fussing over Lucien's signature on the receipt, that Lucien felt obliged to offer the old man a drink.

"I wouldn't say no, Monsieur Chambrun." He pronounced it "Chambrung," in the manner of the region. He took off his kepi, stroked the ends of his mustache, sat down gratefully and sipped his pastis while Lucien read the cable.

"Not bad news, I hope?" the postman asked, brushing a few drops of moisture off his mustache. "That's the worst part of this job, bringing people bad news."

"It's not bad news, no. It's wonderful news! I knew it would come, sooner or later. I have to go back to England, that's all."

"You'd better book a seat quickly. The Americans are going back to America, the English are going home—soon there'll be no business here at all. Poor France!"

"War hasn't been declared yet, has it?"

"Not yet, but it will be today. Just between us, the telegrams are all ready to go for calling up the reserves. By tomorrow we'll be mobilized. What a mess that will be! Well, thank God I'm too old for this war. I was in the last one."

"I hope this one doesn't last four years."

"Not a chance, *monsieur*. Last time, the Boches invaded France. This time they're only invading Poland. If they want Poland, let them have it. Who gives a shit about Poland?"

Lucien nodded. He did not disagree. He went upstairs to pack.

At the Nice railway station, the postman's comment about foreigners proved to be correct. The train to Paris was packed with a glittering, polyglot assortment of people bound for home. The corridors were jammed with piles of Vuitton luggage, the atmosphere was heady with the aroma of good cigars and expensive perfume.

The walls were covered with mobilization posters, which had been hastily pasted up overnight. There were few patriotic slogans in sight. At Lyon someone had hung a banner that read: *"Nous gagnerons parce que nous sommes les plus forts."* It did not, Lucien thought, have the Napoleonic ring—in fact, it contradicted the general opinion. It was possible to hope that France would win because she was in the right, or simply because she was France, but not because the French were strongest. One only had to look at the sad, cynical faces of the troops to know they believed nothing of the sort.

In Paris, Lucien waited for an hour to change trains. Already the confusion of war had set in. Thousands of men in uniforms that dated from the last war milled about, looking for someone in authority to direct them to their units. The noise, heat and chaos were unbearable. If the first hours of mobilization were this disorganized, the French army might have other shortcomings as well, Lucien decided.

Shouldering his own luggage—for there were no porters—Lucien pushed his way onto the Calais train, squeezed himself into a corner and fell asleep. By tomorrow he would be in London. He would go directly to see Queenie.

When Lucien reached Calais, it was dark—a peculiar threatening darkness, for a blackout had been hastily imposed in case of air raids before any thought had been given to how travelers would find their way. The *gare maritime* was in almost total darkness, and it was impossible to move without stumbling over people, luggage, freight and sleeping soldiers. All over the station people cursed, cried out in pain or begged for directions in several languages. The casualties of war already included innumerable sprained ankles, cuts and bruises.

Lucien moved forward slowly, surrounded on all sides by English tourists with their children. He saw, in the dim light, a little girl with a sand pail and shovel who had the same coloring as Queenie. He felt, quite suddenly, such a longing to be with her that he was almost dizzy.

It took all of an hour before he reached the front of his line and handed his dark blue-and-gold passport to a *gendarme*. The *gendarme* peered at the passport, shined a flashlight in Lucien's face to compare it with the photograph in the passport, put the passport back on the table and picked up his rubber stamp. "How long have you been in France, *monsieur?*"

"Several months."

"Where?"

"Paris and Antibes."

"A vacation?"

"*Les vacances, oui.*"

"Ah, *monsieur* speaks French."

"My father was French, *monsieur le gendarme.*"

"That explains it. Chambrun is a French name."

"He was a painter."

The *gendarme's* dark eyes studied Lucien carefully. He seemed delighted. "Not *the* Chambrun? Who painted '*La femme nue avec des fleurs*'?"

"*Exactement.*"

The *gendarme* touched his forefinger and his thumb in a circle and kissed them in a gesture of admiration, then shook Lucien's hand warmly. "A truly gifted painter. What an eye for the female form! One stands in awe. You were born in . . ."

"Paris. If you'll look, it says so in my passport."

The *gendarme* examined the passport, wetting his fingers with his tongue to flip the pages. "*Très, très bien.* That's exactly what it says. And yet *monsieur* is British?"

"My mother was British. I was registered as a British subject at birth at the consulate in Paris when I was born. It was my mother's wish."

The *gendarme* shrugged. He put the passport down on the table and closed it. "Nevertheless—while respecting the delicacy of your mother's sentiments, I have to observe that *monsieur* is a French citizen."

"But you can see for yourself. My passport lists me as British by birth!"

"That is what your passport says. But *monsieur* is on French soil. In the eyes of the Republic *monsieur* is as French as I am. Your father was French—a great French artist. You were born in France. Therefore, you are French. To please your mother, your father permitted you to acquire a second nationality—hers. That is perfectly in order. But the father's nationality naturally comes first in the eyes of the law."

"Look, even if this is so, I'm sure it can be worked out. I'll stop by at the French consulate in London and get all this cleared up. In the meantime, I have to get home. I have a cable here from Dawn Avalon, the film star."

The *gendarme* raised an eyebrow. "My congratulations," he said. "You're a lucky man. However, strictly speaking, you are also a deserter. As a French citizen, you should have registered for military service. *Has monsieur* registered?"

"Look here, of course I haven't . . ."

"Ah!" The *gendarme* sighed. He waved to a couple of men in belted raincoats and bowler hats who were standing in the shadows behind him. He picked up the passport and handed it to them. He whispered to the taller of them, indicating the relevant information on the passport with his forefinger.

"This is outrageous!" Lucien said. "I demand to see the British consul immediately. I have urgent business at home."

The two men took up stations on either side of him. They were less friendly than the *gendarme*, who gave Lucien a shrug of regret, holding up his hands, palms facing outward, to express his inability to help.

"Your business, whatever it is, will have to wait until the war is over," the larger of the two detectives said.

"I insist on talking to the consul!" Then Lucien felt a hand grasp his wrist in a viselike lock and heard the second detective growl, "Shut the fuck up, *espèce de con*, or I'll knee you in the balls."

In the dim light of the far corner of the shed, Lucien could see where he was being led. Parked by the doorway was a gray van with barred windows, and beside it stood two enormous men in the uniform of the French military police. As they saw him approach, they stamped out their cigarettes on the concrete floor. One of them unshouldered his rifle. The other reached down and unfastened something shiny from his belt.

To his horror, Lucien realized that it was a chain.

. . .

"Nobody seems to know *where* he bloody is," Basil Goulandris told Konig.

They were sitting in the office on Grafton Street. The blackout curtains had been drawn, the windows and mirrors were crisscrossed with sticky tape to prevent flying glass shards in the event of bomb concussion. In the corner of the room was a bucket of sand and a fire extinguisher. Konig was looking glumly at his gas mask in its brown canvas carrying bag. "Do you think it will work?" he asked.

Goulandris stared at his own. "I don't suppose so," he said. "Bracken doesn't think they'll use gas, actually."

"What the hell does he know?" Konig snapped.

"True. Somebody told me Cecil Beaton heard the Nazis were sending homosexuals to concentration camps. He tried to get his doctor to give him suicide pills—one for him, one for his boyfriend. When the boyfriend found out, he was livid. He said Cecil could do as he pleased, but *he* wasn't going to hold hands with Cecil and die. He walked out with all Cecil's Charvet ties and some rather nice pieces of jewelry . . ."

"Madness! I still can't understand why Lucien would simply vanish just when we need him."

"It's wartime. Anything can happen."

"War—don't talk to me about war. I remember the last one, for God's sake! If we don't get this bloody picture made, we'll be in bankruptcy! And if we're in bankruptcy, I don't think there's much chance of acquiring Empire Pictures, do you?"

"None."

"There you are. In that case, a lot of people will be angry. If all else fails, I suppose I could ask my doctor for a suicide pill, like poor Beaton. *My* doctor is a German Jew, so he's probably got a supply on hand for himself. . . ."

Konig took a cigar from the box on his desk, lit it and blew out a cloud of smoke. He seemed momentarily revived by it. "I've failed before," he said briskly. "This time I'm not so sure I could recover from it. I'm the wrong age. And the war complicates things. I hate to even think about it, but we may have to go to California."

"People will say you're running away."

"I am, dear boy. But not from the war. Here I can do nothing. There I can make the picture—and perhaps take over Empire Pictures. It's the only way to get the wolves off my back. People can say what they bloody please. My job is to make movies—and money. Besides, Dawn is our biggest asset at the moment. What good is she to us here? Do you see her making training films for the army or wrapping bandages? Now is the time to take her to California and make her a real star, war or no war."

"It won't do her reputation here much good, you know."

"Nonsense, Basil. Don't make me teach you your own business. People will forgive anything in a star."

Dawn was tired of Konig's telling her what to do, as if she would always, automatically, accept his judgment. She had no fears herself about going to Hollywood—it was the only place where you could become a star, in the full sense of the word. Konig was right about that. Nor was she reluctant to leave England—others were going, after all. Vivien Leigh and Laurence Olivier were in California and so was Leslie Howard. Dickie Beaumont had already agreed to go. No doubt there would be criticism, but it could be handled. . . .

What she *did* feel badly about was Lucien. There were rumors that he had been arrested as a spy, or jailed because his papers were not in order. The French, having in all likelihood made a mistake, were covering their tracks by pretending that nothing had happened. She could not help feeling responsible.

She stared at Konig angrily. His weariness and exasperation had become so constant that she was no longer impressed, and while she was willing to make allowances for the strain of Konig's present situation, she was beginning to feel that her life was singularly free of just those pleasures that youth, beauty and fame entitled her to.

"Send Kraus to find out what happened," she said stubbornly.

"I can't *spare* Kraus! Besides, Kraus can't risk it. If the Germans invade France—and nothing is more likely, despite what the papers say—he'd be arrested by the Gestapo and put in a camp."

"Then send Goulandris."

Konig rolled his eyes. "May I ask why you have this sudden concern for Lucien? I thought it was over between you."

"It is. But I owe him this, at least."

Dawn knew it went deeper than that. She had been responsible for Morgan's death, and while she had learned to live with that, she had no desire to be responsible for whatever had happened—or was going to happen—to Lucien. She did not want to feel she was in some way jinxed, a kind of bad-luck token to the men in her life. It was not so much a question of guilt as of a vague, superstitious fear that her own happiness would be compromised.

She pulled on her long black gloves and looked at herself in the mirror. The car was waiting to take them back to the house. She wore a black hat with a veil. Her sable coat was draped on a chair. Konig had succeeded in transforming her into what he wanted—a lady, in fact, as well as a star—but the next step she would have to take for herself.

She stood as he draped the fur coat over her shoulders. She could see his face in the mirror, gray, lined and visibly resentful. He did not like being pushed into bargaining with her. He would have to put up with it.

"Send Goulandris to look for Lucien, and I'll go to California," she said.

For a moment, Konig's face betrayed his sudden anger. Then he paused, calculated, as she knew he would, and surrendered with a weary nod.

She took his arm and went downstairs with him. Outside, a flock of reporters waited. "There's Dawn Avalon," she heard them shout as the flashbulbs began to go off. She smiled triumphantly, posing for a moment before Konig helped her into the Rolls.

Once they would have photographed Konig, and asked who *she* was—if they even bothered to do that. Now it was Konig they ignored, as if he were merely her companion.

CHAPTER 15

"Isn't it *divine?*" Mr. Snayde exclaimed excitedly, as the car pulled up in front of the house.

Dawn took off her sunglasses. It was exactly the way she had always dreamed of living. Set in a forest of palm and eucalyptus trees and surrounded by high walls and a formal garden, the house seemed to have been designed by someone who wanted to combine every form of European architecture in one building. It had mullioned windows and Tudor beams, Norman towers and Gothic arches, Spanish tiles and Moorish courtyards with fountains. The garage, big enough to hold a dozen cars, was a thatched cottage covered with ivy and roses; the pool house was built in the shape of a Greek temple, and the pool itself was a vast Roman folly, with marble statues rising above the blue, chlorinated water. She was impressed.

Snayde positively leaped from the car, like Peter Pan levitating in a pantomime. He was a diminutive hummingbird of a man, dressed in a suit that appeared to be made from shimmering emerald-green silk, with contrasting stitching. He wore a pink shirt and a gold bracelet; his enthusiasm was so intense that it gave Dawn a headache. "Louis B. Mayer's house is just down the road," Snayde announced reverently. "Mr. Zukor's house is the next one down, though you can't see it from here. Marty Braverman lives over there. What can I tell you? The cream of the cream."

Konig nodded gloomily. Dawn wished he were more enthusiastic.

"Francis X. Bushman used to live here," Snayde said. He seemed about to cross himself. "There's a projection room, of course. And a gymnasium. And a bowling alley in the basement."

"I love it," Dawn said.

"I just knew you would," Snayde said ecstatically. "It had *you* written all over it!"

Konig looked at the house, sighed and got back into the limousine. He sat down heavily.

"My God, I hope not," he said in a low voice; then he looked at Dawn's face. "We'll take it," he growled.

Dawn's days were scheduled like those of a royal personage. She was to meet Hedda Hopper for lunch at the Polo Lounge of the Beverly Hills Hotel, then go off to have photographs taken—after which, tea with Louella Parsons, home to change into formal clothes for a premiere at Grauman's Chinese Theater, and from there to a black-tie dinner party at Chasen's—a typical day. What little time she had to herself, she devoted to driving lessons, without telling Konig. Within a few days of her arrival in Los Angeles, she realized that there was no freedom here for anyone who couldn't drive a car.

Konig moved into his new house without ceremony. He left the Beverly Hills Hotel one morning in his limousine, and in the evening the limousine took him home. He scarcely seemed to notice the difference, which was a tribute to the efficiency of Miss Bigelow, who had arrived from England by sea to take charge of Konig's life again. As if by magic, his suits and shirts were moved from the hotel into the closets of his new bedroom. Servants appeared, hired by Miss Bigelow, to staff the house and kitchen. The pool was cleaned, Konig's toothbrush was placed on the sink. When he reached the front door, it was opened by an English butler he had never seen before, who bowed low and said, "Good evening, Sir David."

In the drawing room, the drinks tray was ready. Miss Bigelow was standing beside it. "Is everything satisfactory, Sir David?" she asked.

"Yes, yes, Bigelow," Konig said impatiently. He looked around the drawing room. "The Van Gogh should be hung a little lower, I think. Perhaps an inch or two."

"I'll see to it, Sir David."

"Who are all those damned Orientals in the garden? I thought I was in Japan when I came up the drive."

"The gardeners, Sir David. They're all Japanese."

"Well, for God's sake ask them not to bow when I come home, Bigelow! I'm not the Mikado."

"I'll make a point of it, Sir David."

"Where is Lady Konig?"

"Upstairs, Sir David."

Konig walked to the door and stopped. "How the bloody hell do I get upstairs?" he asked. "I don't even know where my own bedroom is."

Miss Bigelow led the way up a staircase that would have served very well for a procession of medieval monks. She pointed to a door. Konig opened it. "Have them bring me up a whiskey," he said. "One of us is going to need it."

Dawn was lying in the bathtub, her long hair wrapped in a towel.

"May I come in?" he asked.

She nodded. He sat down on the toilet seat. There was another knock on the door. He opened it a crack, reached out his hand, took the whiskey off the butler's tray and slammed the door shut.

"You've had a good day?" he asked.

"Terrible. One boring thing after another."

"It's part of the profession. It's easier if you learn to like it."

"Tea with a reporter from a woman's magazine? She wanted to know what it was like being married to an older man."

"I hope you didn't tell her. . . ." He laughed uneasily. It was a sensitive subject—so sensitive, indeed, that both of them recognized it would be fatal to discuss it. He sipped his whiskey. "Miss Bigelow said she couldn't reach you this afternoon. I can't think what you find to do here."

Dawn made a note to deal with Miss Bigelow. She had nothing to hide, but she resented being spied on by Konig's staff. "I've been learning to drive," she said.

Konig looked astonished. He had never learned to drive himself, and considered it a vastly dangerous mystery, like flying an airplane. "You should have talked to me about it," he said. "It's very dangerous. If you had an accident . . . my God!"

"David, *everybody* here drives."

"Marlene Dietrich doesn't. Her chauffeur drives her. Or her husband, if it's the chauffeur's day off . . . What do you want to drive for, anyway? You have a studio car and a driver."

"I want to come and go as I please."

"Come and go? Where? Why? People have accidents. Breakdowns. I won't hear of it."

"David, I'm not going to be driven everywhere like an old person. It's a perfectly normal thing to do. I'm going to get my driver's license. And I want a car of my own. If you won't buy me one, I'll buy one myself."

"You don't have a bank account."

"I want a bank account, too."

"For God's sake! What for? You can charge everything to me."

"Because I'd like to have something of my *own*."

She heard him sigh through the steam. "Perhaps it was a mistake, coming here to America . . . all right, I give in. I haven't the energy to argue. In any case, I have news . . ."

"Good news?"

"Not good, no. But not bad. Goulandris is back. He arrived in New York yesterday on his way here. I spoke to him."

Dawn sat up, emerging from the surface of the bubble bath, her breasts exposed. "Did he find Lucien? Is he all right?"

"He didn't *speak* to him—but he's all right. It seems the French arrested Lucien. They claimed he was a French citizen."

"He's in prison?"

"No, no, not as bad as that. They put him in the army and sent him off to Algeria for training. They wouldn't let Goulandris go to Algeria to see him—it's a military zone. But the authorities say he's in good health."

"Is there any way to get him out?"

"Yes, I think so. Goulandris talked to Duff Cooper at the British Embassy and had dinner with René Poisson, who supposedly has the ear of Reynaud's mistress . . . In France something can always be done if one knows the right person's mistress. Anyway, not to make a long story of it—the French will let Lucien go back to England. He'll have to stay in the army for a while—a question of saving face for the French, you understand—but he'll be released on the grounds of ill health."

"How long will it take?"

"Not too long. At most another five or six months, maybe less. Hopefully, they'll ship him back to France soon, so at least he'll be comfortable."

Dawn covered her breasts with soap bubbles, conscious of the fact that Konig was looking at them. "David, I'm grateful to you."

"I'm going to change now. We dine at David Selznick's. The usual people. The usual awful meal. The usual collection of second-rate Impressionists. The usual movie after dinner . . ."

He closed the door and went off to his own bath. Dawn soaped herself vigorously. As usual, he had not discussed his plans with her, but she was able to guess much of what he was doing. It was, like most of Konig's schemes, the work of a clever, instinctive juggler. The audience saw only the dazzling speed of the act, but Dawn understood the patience, the skill and the cold daring that lay behind it. He deceived everyone but himself.

The only thing he made no allowance for was her own growing realization that she was the keystone of his plans.

He needed her now—she knew that. She could see it in his face when he talked to her. Konig usually managed to conceal his fears, but for the first time she could tell that he was afraid.

He came downstairs dressed in a white dinner jacket, looking every inch the Hollywood tycoon. He loathed white dinner jackets, but it was the custom of the place.

He saw Miss Bigelow waiting in the hall. "The towel rack in my bathroom isn't hot enough," he complained. "It needs more steam, or whatever the hell."

"I'll have it seen to, Sir David."

"Tomorrow morning we'll talk to the cook. We should plan a few dinner parties right away. We'll need champagne—cases of it. . . . Oh, before I forget. Buy Lady Konig a car tomorrow."

"What kind, Sir David?"

"How should I know? It shouldn't be too big . . . one of those— what are they called? The kind with the top that folds down?"

"A convertible, I believe, Sir David."

"Exactly. Buy her a convertible. A Cadillac. And Bigelow—no bright colors, please. White, perhaps. After all, we don't want people looking at the car—we want them looking at Dawn."

At the Selznicks' there was no doubt that everybody was looking at Dawn.

In a town where physical beauty was commonplace, a commodity bought and sold every day, Dawn attracted admiration—even awe. She easily upstaged Selznick's "blue period" Picasso, which rose noiselessly at the push of a button to reveal the square glass window of the projection booth. Dawn was not enough of an art connoisseur to appreciate the look of amusement that crossed Konig's face when he saw it.

It was the one thing he liked about Hollywood—vulgarity was, in his opinion, the only redeeming feature of the place.

The food seemed as odd to Dawn as the Picasso on rails. The soup was made of fruit and had a flower floating in it. The salad was covered with shaved nuts and the lamb was served with a slice of pineapple. The dessert consisted of huge tasteless strawberries covered with sour cream and brown sugar.

"I want a loan-out of her," she heard Selznick whisper to Konig over dinner.

"Not yet, my boy. When I'm ready, you'll pay through the nose."

She strained to hear more, above the noise of conversation, ignoring the man on her right, a short, balding bespectacled man, half pixie, half gnome.

Dawn listened to David and Selznick with fascination—and some anger, since it was she who was being bought and sold. A star's success, she knew, was rated by the number and size of his or her "loan-outs." Konig had, in fact, no serious intention at present of loaning her out to anyone—let alone a rival like Selznick—but he was constantly testing the market. She turned to give her full attention to her dinner partner— and realized he was so short that Selznick—always the thoughtful host—had provided two petit-point cushions for him to sit on.

"Is Konig going to loan you out to Selznick?" he asked in a gravelly voice. "Take away my soup and bring it back without the goddamned flower," he growled to the waiter. "I want to eat flowers, I'll grow wings and become a goddamned bee. My name's Aaron Diamond. I guess you've heard of me."

"No. As a matter of fact, I haven't, Mr. Diamond."

Diamond looked incredulous—a feat he accomplished with ease, through the largest pair of spectacles Dawn had ever seen. The frames were solid gold, and looked so heavy that it was hard to imagine how his nose could bear the weight. The thick glass magnified his eyes, which combined charm and cunning to an extraordinary degree. "No kidding!" he said. "I must be slipping. Well, of course, you're new in town. I'm a lawyer. You *have* to be a lawyer to do business with some of the creeps in this town. I handle Gable. I handle Crawford. Nothing but the best. I don't handle bums and losers. There's no percentage in that. . . . Hey, aren't those the Beaumonts, just coming in?"

Selznick waved to Cynthia and Richard Beaumont, who waved back, made their apologies and sat down.

"They look like they've been fighting," Diamond said. "Trouble in Paradise!" He had a birdlike intensity, though Dawn was hard put to

decide what kind of bird she had in mind. The eyes behind the thick
glasses were certainly as sharp as a falcon's, and there was indeed something predatory in the shape of his mouth, with its thin, colorless lips.
He had the obligatory Beverly Hills tan, as if his face had been baked
in an oven and basted, and teeth of a whiteness so improbable she
suspected they were real. Beneath the gruff and prickly exterior, she
intuitively detected a streak of hidden kindness.

It had been a month or more since she had seen Cynthia. There
were dark circles under the china-blue eyes and her cheeks were flushed.
She waved at Dawn, tipped over a glass, dabbed at the pool of water
with a napkin and upset the saltcellar. She sent a pinch of salt flying
over the wrong shoulder and into the face of the Selznicks' butler.
Beaumont glared at her grimly as he described the failure of their car
to start—a story which Cynthia seemed about to contradict until he
gave her a warning look to shut up.

"She likes the sauce?" Diamond asked.

"Sauce?" Dawn still had trouble understanding Americans—and
Diamond's vocabulary was more bizarre than most, as well as spoken
in a low growl at high speed. His lips did not seem to move at all
when he spoke, as if the mere fact that he was talking to her at all was
something he wanted to keep secret.

"What's the matter with you? Sauce! She drinks, right?"

Diamond's diagnosis, she decided, was all too correct, but before she
could deny it, Diamond growled again. The hard little eyes missed nothing, least of all a chance to take over the conversation. Diamond was
apparently so quick that he could tell when the person he was talking
to was about to pause for breath, and he instantly took the initiative—
like an athlete, he was off and running with what he had to say, often
with a complete change in direction. She decided it would take a good
deal of practice to hold her own with him in conversation. "Don't bullshit me, honey," he said, "I know a drinker when I see one. Half this
town is tanked most of the goddam time. Don't get me wrong. I got
nothing against booze, but boozers are a pain in the ass. You drink?"

She took a deep breath. "Well, no . . ."

"That's what I mean. You're too smart. I like smart people. You
got smarts, you got the world by the balls, know what I mean?" As he
talked, he examined the silver carefully, picking it up to study the
hallmarks. When he was through, he breathed on each piece and
polished it with his napkin. "You're going to *need* smarts, married to
Konig."

Dawn examined her companion with interest. Small as he was, he had the hands of a much larger man, so well manicured that they might have been fabricated by Fabergé. It was difficult to guess Diamond's age, if only because she could not imagine him as a young man with a full head of hair. He had apparently succeeded in transforming himself into a timeless object, like a piece of antique furniture, lovingly polished, carefully preserved, but still in daily use.

"Why don't you trust my husband, Mr. Diamond?"

"Call me Aaron. I don't trust *any* producer. They're all *gonievim* at heart. It's in the blood. Konig is smarter than most of them, and a lot more classy—but that only makes him harder to trust. I mean, he's playing games with Sigsbee Wolff."

"You don't like Sigsbee—Aaron?"

"What's to like? He wants to buy Empire. That's okay by me— Marty Braverman is a shmuck. But if Sigsbee went after the company by himself, everybody would shout murder. I mean, the guy's a gangster. So he brings in Konig and the British as a front."

"Frankly, I don't care much one way or the other. But David does."

"Good luck to him! If Sigsbee manages to stay alive, they might even bring it off."

"Well, he's certainly *old*, but he doesn't seem any worse than he was the first time I met him."

"That's not the kind of staying alive I mean, kiddo. Sigsbee's got partners. He wants to put money in movies, but there are other guys who think it's a better idea to put the money into gambling—Vegas, Reno, Tahoe. . . . You been out to Reno?"

"No. I haven't seen much of the country yet."

"You gotta go. I was there last week. There's a guy out there building a big hotel. Terrific place! I met him, but I can't remember his name. He's British, I know that."

"Really?"

"Sure. Listen, you ever want an agent, you come see me, okay? So long as you're working for your husband, you don't need me, but if there's ever any—ah . . ."

"Trouble in Paradise?"

"If that happens—and it's not exactly unknown out here—telephone me. Right away. And don't let him loan you out without talking to me. It'll be free of charge, kiddo. On the house."

Diamond turned to speak to the woman on his right, while Dawn turned to make polite conversation with the man on the other side of her, a heavyset producer with bulging pop-eyes like those of an exotic Japanese goldfish, who had been eying her breasts unashamedly throughout the first course.

But before they had exchanged more than a few words, Diamond clicked his fingers and tapped her on the shoulder.

"I remembered," he said. "The Brit's name in Reno. It's Vale. Dominick Vale."

Dawn was not yet used to the Hollywood custom of showing a movie immediately after dinner.

No sooner was coffee served at the Selznicks' than the Picasso rose, the screen appeared and the lights dimmed. Conversation stopped, to most people's relief.

Those who were tired could look forward to a good sleep before the drive home. It was possible, she knew, even usual, to arrive for dinner at seven, sit down to dinner at eight, watch a picture and be home before eleven. This was a company town—most people who were working had to be up at dawn, and social life was adjusted accordingly.

Konig withdrew to the card room after the movie had started, where those who were too powerful to have to be at the studio early gathered to drink, gamble and talk shop. Dawn sat down next to Cynthia as the lights began to dim. She noted with alarm that Cynthia was holding a tumblerful of brandy. She lay on her side on a sofa, her long silk dress clinging to her body so that it was molded to her flat stomach and her thighs. She had taken her shoes off.

"You look comfortable," Dawn said.

"And provocatively sexy."

"And provocatively sexy, too."

"Thank you. A fat lot of good it does me. I'd heard that all sorts of sexy things go on during these screenings—very discreetly, of course— but so far it's been rather a disappointment. Everybody seems madly tired."

Dawn curled up close to Cynthia so they could whisper together.

"Half the men here are secretly queer," Cynthia complained. "The other half get so much sex from girls who want to break into the movies that they're spoiled."

"Are things as bad as that with you and Dickie?"

"Oh, my dear, they couldn't be more awful. He's out all hours of the night, and hasn't the slightest use for me. Of course he claims it's work—production meetings, script meetings . . . oh, he covers his tracks well, but I can tell—he's got another woman. One always can tell when one's husband has another woman, which is a pity, because of course it's the one thing one doesn't want to *know*."

"How can you be so sure, Cynthia?"

"Well, he certainly isn't sleeping with me, darling. And besides—he was away for a couple of days last week, supposedly meeting with some people in San Francisco who want to finance a Shakespearean festival out here, and when he came back, do you know what I found in his pocket?"

"No. What?"

"A book of matches from some hotel in Reno. Now why the hell would he lie about a thing like that?"

And Dawn turned away to watch the screen, a sinking feeling in her heart. She knew just why Dickie Beaumont had gone to Reno. Dominick Vale had reemerged in his life.

She wondered how long it would be before he reemerged in *hers*.

The movie was innocuous, but Dawn felt grateful for it, since it gave her an excuse to break off her conversation with Cynthia, who got up several times to refill her glass. Much as she liked Cynthia, it was more interesting to talk to men.

Men controlled the world, whether it was movies, banking or journalism—even here in Hollywood, where the whole industry revolved around the sex and glamour of a few female stars. A beautiful woman earned a fantastic salary—ten thousand dollars a week was not uncommon—but no matter how much money she earned, she was never the one who made the decisions or shared in the profits.

She had learned a lot about money from Konig. All the same, she was nervous. She had no money of her own to speak of. Now that she was over twenty-one, Konig controlled her, handled her finances and negotiated her contracts. In every sense of the word she belonged to him. As long as she was married to him she could spend money like a millionairess, without any complaint from him, but if she left Konig—or if something happened to him—she might easily find herself in the clutches of somebody like Marty Braverman or David Selznick. She made a mental note to talk to Aaron Diamond again as soon as possible, only too well aware that Konig would regard it as an act of betrayal.

A voice interrupted her train of thought, and she realized that Cynthia was still whispering to her. "Jesus, you can't *believe* how hard I've tried," she was saying, the low voice slurred slightly with drink. "It's humiliating to have to seduce your own husband—and fail." Her voice dropped until Dawn had to strain to hear it. Cynthia gulped her drink down and rose unsteadily for more. "It's enough to give a girl the pips."

Dawn watched her stumble across the room, tripping over people's feet. There was a muffled crack as Cynthia dropped her glass on the carpet. "Oh *shit!*" she hissed loudly. In the dark somebody got up to help her. "Fuck off!" Cynthia said, and walked out of the room, slamming the door.

Dawn sighed in the dark. Was there anybody here, she wondered, who had a happy sex life? Cynthia's problems were worse than most, but not at all uncommon. The men were busy working, and they took their pleasures quickly with starlets; the wives drank, spent money and had affairs, either with men in "the industry" who were just as busy as their husbands or with the kind of handsome young men who came to service the pool. Was she that much better off herself? She set off in search of Cynthia.

"She was asleep in the Selznicks' bed?"

"Fast asleep."

"One day there'll be trouble."

"There already is."

"Not the kind that matters." Konig stared out the window of the limousine. "How I hate palm trees," he said glumly.

"Cynthia is desperately unhappy."

Konig nodded. "I don't understand why Dickie doesn't try to stop her from drinking. Quite the contrary—he asked the butler to bring her a double Scotch when they arrived."

"I didn't notice."

"I did. It's just the opposite of what makes sense—unless he's *encouraging* her to drink."

"Why on earth would he do that?"

"Oh, I can think of so many reasons. It makes him look like a martyr. It gets her off his back, no doubt. You and I know what's wrong with that marriage, but to the rest of the world it will look as if it's her fault, not his . . . Still, I wouldn't have credited Dickie with that kind of diabolical imagination, would you?"

The limousine pulled up to the marble steps of their house—she could not bring herself as yet to think of it as their home. Konig seemed more tired than usual. His face was the color of parchment. He climbed the steps slowly and stiffly. She put her arm in his to help him, but he brushed it away. "There's no need for that," he said. "I'm not an invalid."

In the front hall, Dawn stood for a moment as Konig caught up with her. Then she noticed a couple of suitcases—one a cheap fiber valise, the other a Vuitton bag plastered with stickers from famous hotels.

Konig quickened his pace. Whoever the visitors were, he was obviously expecting them—though, once again, he had said nothing about it to her.

He opened the door to the living room. Basil Goulandris lifted his glass in greeting. From the armchair where he had been sitting, hidden from view, Kraus rose to his feet and clicked his heels.

"What's the news from New York?" Konig asked Kraus impatiently.

Kraus waved his hand in the air gently, like a pilot describing a maneuver. He glanced at Dawn as if he were unwilling to say too much in front of her. "Not too bad," he said, his expression as mournful as ever. "I think we can count on just enough shares."

"So it's good news?"

"It's not bad, Sir David, but it will be touch and go."

Konig looked better already. Some of the color had returned to his face.

Dawn looked at Goulandris, who gave her a wink. "You heard I found Lucien for you?" he asked.

It seemed like news from a lifetime ago, but still she wanted to know all the details. There were days when she never thought about him at all. There were other times, particularly at night, when she thought about nothing else.

"He's well, he's well. I can't tell you what a time I had tracking him down to North Africa! They're going to put him somewhere quiet in France. The Ardennes, I think. A rest camp. It's a battalion of artists, writers, sculptors, Nobel Prize-winning refugees and so on. . . . Of course the whole thing is a farce. Both sides are looking for a way out without fighting."

"When will they let him go?" Dawn asked.

"April. Or May. Not long."

Konig stood up. "I'm going to bed," he said. "We'll talk tomorrow.

By the way, John Mammon is on his way over from England. I've decided to start filming again."

"I thought you said he was a mediocrity," Dawn said, surprised that Konig had made a decision like that without telling her—and that he was going ahead with the picture at all.

"He is a mediocrity. But he's fast. Anyway, now is not the time to stop. I've got financing for the picture, I've got you, I've got Dickie, so we have to make it—quickly." He turned to Kraus. "Braverman is on the ropes. One more push and I'll have a seat on his board—with enough stock behind me to take over Empire. It's not the time to take a rest. Or fail. Or get a bad press. Just now there's too much at stake. Above all, what I don't want are surprises. You'll see to that, Kraus?"

"Absolutely, Sir David."

"Then goodnight." Konig slowly climbed the stairs, pausing halfway for breath.

"He doesn't look well," Goulandris said to Dawn.

"He's tired."

Kraus walked to the window and stared out into the darkness. "It's an amazing place," he said. "Imagine— you can buy fresh oranges, right off the trees, a dozen for a quarter!"

"Kraus has been brooding all the way from New York," Goulandris explained. "It was a bloody depressing trip."

Kraus did not take offense. He turned around, the thin, pinched face serious, as if he alone understood the gravity of the situation. "I merely meant that here everything seems possible. It's the sunshine, I expect. Sir David finishes his film, gets a seat on the board of Empire—boy meets girl, happy ending. . . . In New York, however, they take a less rosy view. They think maybe he's too old and spread too thin to make a big picture. And if it *is* finished, they think maybe it will be a flop. And they talk a lot about Sigsbee Wolff. They don't know if they can trust Sir David, but they *know* they can't trust Wolff."

"People always talk a lot about Sigsbee Wolff," Goulandris said, trying as usual to ignore bad news.

"Yes, but this time they're already talking about him in the past tense. There are rumors his associates don't share Wolff's enthusiasm for the motion picture industry. They are more interested in gambling."

"Businessmen disagree sometimes. They compromise. So what?"

"Wolff's associates aren't ordinary businessmen, Basil. They want to build casinos. He wants to make movies. It won't be settled by a compromise. A couple of people at the Morgan Bank told me there was a big fight about some hotel that's going up in Reno. Sigsbee was against it. His friends were for it. He lost, and it's been built." He paused and rubbed his frail hands together. "What's more worrying, frankly, is that the front man turns out to be—Dominick Vale."

Goulandris poured himself a stiff drink. The news did not seem to surprise him.

"I hope Sir David knows what he's doing," Kraus said.

"So do we all. In the meantime, you'd better tell him about Vale tomorrow. Another worry for the old man . . ."

"Is it a serious worry, Basil? Compared with all the others, I mean?" Dawn asked.

"Vale knows how to run a gambling operation. That's a valuable skill. Gambling is still a grubby business here—bookies, numbers, small-time hoods . . . Vale runs the kind of place where the very rich can drop a hundred thousand dollars in a single night—and have a good time doing it. To answer your question, my dear Dawn, Vale's one of those chaps who knows a lot about people—and wouldn't hesitate to use what he knows."

Dawn looked at him in silence for a moment, remembering that she had more to hide than anyone else in the room.

"I think I'll have a drink," she said—she who never drank as a rule— and realized that Kraus and Goulandris were staring at her in surprise.

They were sitting on the terrace overlooking the gardens, with the pool gleaming in the sun. The flowers, the birds and the sun reminded her of India, as so much of California did—but an India without poverty or discomfort. She crumbled up a piece of toast and threw it out for the birds, which fluttered their wings restlessly but stayed in the bushes. "I don't think they're as hungry in Bel Air as they are in India," she said.

"I suppose not," Goulandris said. "Who is? I say, look at this!" Goulandris, who had been reading the trades with his breakfast, handed her *Variety*. "BRAVERMAN NIXES RUMOR," the headline read. Below it Marty Braverman was quoted in an exclusive story, which described him as "Empire's embattled Czar."

" 'Konig gets a seat on the board over my dead body,' " Dawn read aloud. " 'The guy's not qualified, and his financial support comes from a bunch of hoods and foreigners. There have been vicious rumors spread about me which are one hundred percent not true. Konig is beneath my contempt.' "

In the *Los Angeles Times* there was a photograph of Marty Braverman and Ina Blaze. Braverman was lunging at the photographer, his eyes popping and his mouth wide open. Ina Blaze was clutching a miniature poodle and a handbag in front of her face. The caption read: "JUST GOOD FRIENDS?"

The story, however, while steering just short of libel, suggested that Braverman had used Empire's money to buy Ina Blaze a million-dollar house in Malibu. In the *Herald-Examiner*, a more enterprising photographer had caught Mrs. Braverman, a plump, hard-looking blond matron in her late forties, wearing slacks and a full-length mink coat, getting into a limousine outside Chasen's in the company of a dour, heavyset man who was described as the "divorce lawyer to the stars."

"There's a nice story about a stockholders' revolt brewing at Empire on the financial page," Goulandris said with satisfaction. "And a story in *The New York Times* about a few stockholders suing Braverman for malfeasance. Nice work, if I do say so myself."

"You've certainly been busy, Basil," she said.

"As a bee."

"What happens next?"

"That's not my department. Konig and Wolff do the heavyweight stuff. I merely plant stories."

"I suppose I'd better go. I have a costume fitting."

"Ah, yes. The picture. Are you happy to be going back to work?"

"I think so. It will take my mind off—things. . . ."

Goulandris gathered up his papers. "Never brood. Basil's first law. But if you want my advice, old darling—be happy with what you've got."

"Why shouldn't I be happy here?"

"I don't know. But nobody *is*. You don't seem to be. And people like Konig aren't concerned with happiness, you see." Goulandris stood up, brushing the crumbs off his trousers. "They think it's something they'll take up later in life, after they retire. Like golf. Don't make the same mistake, Dawn."

"I won't," she said. But she wondered if she hadn't already made it.

"He's like a guy who can't get out of the house because he hasn't decided if he should take his umbrella with him or not," Aaron Diamond said. "Will it rain, won't it rain? He's a *putz*."

"He's got a good eye," Dawn said loyally, though in fact she had come to the conclusion that Mammon was a dithering bore.

Mammon, as it turned out, was a perfectly competent director, but seemed to have very little grasp of the story or control over the material.

It was a mystery how Diamond managed to get onto sets during filming, even "closed" sets. He seemed to enjoy a kind of informal *laissez-passer* throughout the industry, and his presence was welcomed, whereas other agents would be handed over to the studio police. Now that he was Beaumont's agent, he at least had a reason for being here, but he spent most of his time sitting with Dawn, when he wasn't using a studio telephone to conduct his business.

He acted as if he were already her agent, confidant and closest adviser, which was his usual way of acquiring clients. People simply got used to thinking of him as their agent. He had made several deals for Gable—good ones, too—before Gable finally said, "Hey, but you're not my agent!" "Aren't I?" Diamond asked in his raspy voice. Gable shrugged his shoulders, ordered another drink and said, "I guess you are now."

Dawn found herself in much the same position. Diamond behaved as if she were his client, and gradually she accepted the fact that she *was*.

"I guess you'll be celebrating tonight," he said. He had his own chair next to Dawn's, with two cushions on it. On the canvas back he had gotten somebody to paint "10%."

"Why?"

"Don't you read the trades?"

"No."

"Jesus! At least get somebody to tell you what's *in* them every morning. I got a secretary who reads me the stuff I need to know while I'm having a bath."

"She stands outside the door and reads to you?"

"Nah, she sits on the can. I'm not shy. Here, have a look at this."

Dawn looked at the story in *Variety*. For a moment it made no sense to her. "KONIG AND BRAVERMAN PACT!" the headline read. Then below: "Marty Braverman, the President of Empire Pictures, announced today that Sir David Konig, the Managing Director of England's King Films, would join the board of Empire Pictures immediately. 'I have the greatest admiration for Sir David,' Braverman said in an exclusive interview. 'He is a brilliant filmmaker. His experience and wisdom will be valuable assets to our company. Empire will be immensely strengthened by his participation, which is only dependent on certain financial details that are being worked out now.'

"Sir David, reached at his Bel Air home, said: 'Marty Braverman is a warm human being. I look forward to working with him to make Empire an even better company than it has been.'

"There are rumors that as soon as Sir David and his associates have completed their financial dealings, he will take control of Empire, with a majority of the stock behind him, and that Braverman has already accepted in principle the role of Honorary Chairman of the Board, leaving the presidency to Sir David. Also in line for seats on the new board are Sigsbee Wolff, the Los Angeles real estate tycoon; E. P. Kraus, one of Sir David's long-time production associates; and Mr. Solomon Goldner, the English theater magnate . . ."

Dawn looked at him in amazement. All this was news to her.

"Didn't Konig tell you this was happening?"

She didn't want Diamond to know that Konig had left her in the dark—he hadn't even told her about Goldner—so she covered up quickly. "He left a message for me, but I was doing a scene when he called. I must telephone him."

"Screw that! Go home and give the guy a kiss. I never thought he'd bring it off. Tell you the truth, I still have my doubts, but I guess I'm wrong. Sigsbee must have more clout that I thought. . . ."

"Is it true?"

"It's true."

Konig put his arms around Dawn and kissed her. His fatigue and irritation seemed to have vanished. He looked ten years younger.

"I'm glad for you," she said. But, in fact, she was furious. He had deliberately concealed his negotiations from her, as if she couldn't be trusted.

"I know. And I'm grateful to you. It's been a difficult time. But now the gamble has paid off. In a month's time, this picture will be in the can, for better or worse, and with Empire, I can do anything I want. Twenty, thirty pictures a year, international distribution of our own, and one day, when the war is over, unlimited growth . . . I have plans . . . my God, I can't even begin to tell you what plans! We'll do things nobody has ever *dreamed* of before. I'm sorry I left you in the dark, but there were things it was better you didn't know . . ."

"We should celebrate." She wondered what "things." It didn't seem the moment to ask.

"We will, we will! Tonight. In the meantime, I have to talk to

Sigsbee. . . . There are several large blocks of shares we have to buy up. Let's have some champagne."

Konig rang for the butler, who appeared a few moments later with a bottle of champagne, followed by Goulandris, smiling cheerfully.

"A triumph!" He lifted his glass to toast Konig.

Dawn lifted hers, too. The three of them were about to drink when Kraus appeared, walking across the big living room so quickly that nobody noticed his ashen face.

"Ah, Kraus," Konig called, "a glass! You're just in time to drink with us."

But Kraus's hands were locked together like those of a man in prayer. He did not reach for the glass that was offered to him. He seemed, it suddenly occurred to Dawn, to have been crying. "Is something the matter?" she asked.

There was a long silence as the four of them stood waiting for the answer. The sun was going down. The twilight made the room seem even larger. A slight breeze ruffled the curtains and brought with it the scent of jasmine and oranges. Outside was the gentle sibilant rhythmic sound of lawn sprinklers.

Kraus's prominent Adam's apple bobbed once or twice. "It's Sigsbee Wolff," he said at last.

Konig stared at him. "What about Sigsbee? I spoke to him only an hour ago."

"He's in—his swimming pool."

"Sigsbee? *Swimming?* Why would he be swimming?"

"He wasn't swimming, Sir David. Somebody tied him into his wheelchair and pushed it into the pool. He went straight to the bottom of the deep end. The gardener found him. He thought he saw something at the bottom of the pool, so he looked over the side and— there was Mr. Wolff looking up at him."

There was a splintering crash.

Konig had dropped the bottle.

"How bad is it?"

Konig shook his head. He seemed perfectly in control of himself. Nothing brought out the stoic side of his character better than defeat.

His expression was remote. He was not about to share the catastrophe with her. "Perhaps it's not too bad. It depends if I can keep the pieces together for a few days. That won't be easy. Go to bed. Don't worry about it. You need your sleep if you're going to work in the morning."

Dawn touched his hand, but he didn't respond. Clearly he wanted to be alone for now.

The moment passed. As she went upstairs, leaving him in the library to his thoughts, she knew it would never return. For a brief instant, she had been ready to take him upstairs to bed. But Konig had chosen to maintain his lonely dignity, and she left him to it.

The next few days had the quality of a nightmare, for Konig elected to face the problems of Wolff's death by a public display of confidence. Every night he and Dawn dined out at Romanoff's, Chasen's or the Brown Derby. They went to every dinner party and even went dancing, though Konig hated dancing as a rule.

He looked fit, happy, energetic, the very picture of a successful film entrepreneur married to a successful star. It was a brilliant and convincing performance, though Dawn could see what it cost him—for as soon as he was seated in the limousine for the ride back to the house, he put his head against the back of the seat, closed his eyes and gave a long sigh of relief and fatigue.

In the mornings, he salvaged his energies by working in bed, Miss Bigelow sitting by his side with her steno pad and a basketful of mail. In the afternoons, he met with lawyers, bankers, financial people—long meetings behind closed doors, the substance of which he refused to discuss with Dawn.

"Sigsbee isn't the only one who's in over his head," Aaron Diamond said to her on the set one afternoon.

"David has always managed to produce a last-minute miracle. It's his specialty."

"He brings this one off, it'll make Lourdes look like small potatoes. You want my advice, kiddo, take your jewelry down to a bank and rent a safe-deposit box in your own name. Better yet, in somebody else's name."

"Surely things aren't going to be as bad as that, Aaron?"

"Worse. You can get away with anything in this town, but there are three exceptions. Don't fool around with a girl who belongs to a studio head. Don't cheat at cards. And don't try and take over somebody else's company and fail. Konig had Marty Braverman by the balls. Then somebody gave Sigsbee a swimming lesson, so Konig had to let go. So long as Konig had Sigsbee behind him and was winning, people were happy to lend him money. They're going to want it back in a hurry. And he's only got one quick source of income now, sweetie."

"What's that?"

"You."

Late that night, Konig came to Dawn's bedroom. He was fully dressed. He did not look at her. He wandered around the room as if he were appraising the furniture.

"I'm sorry to disturb you," he said, "but we have to talk."

Dawn sat up. Konig picked up a bottle of lotion and read the label. Whatever he had to say, he was reluctant to begin.

"What about?"

"I've been talking to Selznick," Konig said. "And a few other people. About you."

"Which other people?"

"Marty Braverman, for one. He's interested in a long-term loan-out. Four pictures. Maybe five. He has a great deal of confidence in your box-office potential."

She was outraged. "You can't be serious! You yourself told me that Braverman is a pig!"

"So he is. But now he's our pig. Be sensible. I can get two or three million dollars for a four-picture deal—maybe more. It wouldn't solve all my problems, unfortunately, but it would take some of the heat off me."

"David, I don't want to be sold off to Marty Braverman—of all people—for four pictures. You can't trade me off like a piece of furniture."

"Like a piece of furniture? No. But I *can* trade you off. We have a contract."

"And we're married."

He sighed wearily. "Listen, it's a question of survival. I don't like it any better than you do."

"Whose survival? Yours or mine?"

"Ours."

"David. One movie, maybe. I'm not unreasonable. I'm grateful to you for a lot of things. But make it one movie, and for God's sake, *not* to Braverman. At least let it be someone with a little taste, someone we can *talk* to about the picture, the script, the director . . ."

He did not look her in the eye. She realized, with a sinking feeling, that he couldn't. "I've already agreed with Braverman in principle," he said quietly. "We have a deal. It's just a question of working out the details."

"I won't do it."

Konig shrugged. "We'll see," he said. "I hoped it wouldn't come to this, but since it has—let me remind you again that I own your contract. There is nothing in it to prevent me from making a deal with Braverman."

She felt a cold rage—not since Morgan's betrayal had she felt such anger. Konig—who claimed to love her—was ready to throw her to the wolves now that he was in trouble. "So *I* do four pictures, and *you* get two or three million dollars."

"*We* get it. With that I can perhaps hold things together long enough to find new financing."

She shook her head. "I'll get a lawyer, David, if I have to. I'll break the contract."

"You can try, by all means." His face was white. He turned on his heel and left, slamming the door.

Dawn picked up the telephone and dialed Aaron Diamond. His answering service said he was at the Polo Lounge. She was about to dial the number; then she realized that since sleep was out of the question, she might as well go to see him. She hadn't come this far, made so many compromises, taken so many risks, merely to be trapped again, sold off to Braverman for Konig's convenience. She dressed quickly, went downstairs and started her car.

By the time she was speeding down Sunset Boulevard, Dawn felt better. She was not normally a confident driver, but she loved speed. She hit seventy on Sunset before she realized that she was driving far beyond her skill and experience. It was one of the strange things about living in Southern California—movement solved your problems better than anything else. Driving through Beverly Hills with the top down, the wind in her hair, and the smell of the trees and flowers all around her gave Dawn the illusion of freedom, so much so that she relinquished the car to the doorman at the Beverly Hills Hotel with some reluctance. It was the one sense in which Los Angeles was magic.

In the darkness of the Polo Lounge, she searched for Diamond, and finally found him at a small table with a telephone and an attractive young woman wearing a mink coat despite the heat.

Diamond showed no surprise at the sight of Dawn, nor did he seem upset at having his date interrupted. He recognized a business problem when he saw it and accepted the fact that it took precedence over pleasure, even at this hour of the night. He was a professional.

"Take a walk," he said to the woman, who shrugged without resentment and went off to the bar as if she were used to being dismissed.

"You were right," Dawn said.

"I figured. Look, the guy's your husband, but he's a Hungarian, you know what I mean? He can't help it. You know what they say about Hungarians."

Dawn shook her head, more out of irritation than because she didn't know. Diamond had a way of getting off the track at just the moment when she most wanted him to concentrate.

"'A Hungarian goes into a revolving door behind you—and comes out ahead of you.'" He laughed. "What's the matter, kiddo? Loosen up. Point is, Konig wouldn't think twice about selling you out if it was the only way to survive. He may be a knight, but he's got the soul of a con man—all Hungarians do. Hell, when Konig was here before, story was he used to seduce girls by telling them he was impotent. He'd sit there and say, 'I'm sorry, dear, but you see it's no good . . . I haven't been able to do anything for years . . . nothing helps . . .' They'd feel sorry for the poor guy, right? And for a woman, it's kind of a challenge, right? So before you know it, they'd have their goddam clothes off and Konig would be saying 'My God, it's a miracle—I'm starting to feel something. . . .' What's the matter? You look like you've just seen a ghost."

Dawn bit her lip. It was another humiliation. She had been naive enough to fall for a piece of deception so well known that it had apparently become a Hollywood legend, part of the vast body of Konig folklore. She was not about to admit it to Diamond, however. "Aaron," she said, as firmly as she could, "just tell me what to *do*."

He shrugged. He enjoyed playing the jester, but he knew when it was time to settle down to serious business. And as she leaned forward to hear what he had to say—for when Diamond was discussing business, his voice descended to a gravelly, confidential whisper—she saw, dimly and for one brief moment, reflected in the dark, antiqued mirror on the wall in front of her, three men rise, still deep in conversation, and leave the room. One of them was Kraus, his spectacles gleaming. The other was Basil Goulandris. Between them, his hands in his pockets, was a large, well-dressed, dark-haired man, whose hard, suspicious eyes flashed in the mirror. He looked very much to her like Dominick Vale.

Dawn turned to look at the table they had just left, just in time to
see Marty Braverman, his cigar a dot of glowing red in the dark, sign
the check and make his way out past the bar.

She realized Konig was in worse trouble than even *he* knew. She
wondered if she should warn him, but in her anger she decided to
wait and see.

"It's merely a question of keeping up appearances," Konig said
stiffly. "This is as much in your interest as mine."

Dawn said nothing. Now that her anger had cooled slightly, she
was able to face the facts, if not to act on them. Konig's ship was
sinking. Should she go down on it with him? Should she warn him?
Was there a way off before it went down? And of course there was,
with Konig, always the possibility, however remote, that he would
save himself at the last minute in another of his triumphant *tours de
force*. Diamond's advice to her had been succinct. "Walk out, make
your own deal, sue him for divorce—all those English contracts probably won't stand up over here, and with community property, you get
half of what he's got, if he's got anything."

It was easier said than done, she thought. Konig had pushed her too
far, and she could not forgive him for that, but there was a part of her
which still acknowledged him as Sir David Konig, the miracle worker.
She dreaded the inevitable complications, but she was determined not
to make peace on any terms but her own. "Just so there's no misunderstanding," she said, "I won't agree to a loan-out. I'll fight you, David,
if I have to."

"That's understood," he said grimly. In the dim light of the
limousine's interior he looked awful. His face was gray and lined, as
if he had aged ten years overnight. His lips were blue and his eyes
red-rimmed. When he lit a cigar, his hands trembled. He wore a dark
suit that gave him a funereal air. Dawn had dressed according to the
fashion of the place, in pink silk pajamas with wide trousers, high-
heeled gold sandals and a diamond necklace. She wore sunglasses, as
everyone did here, even at night, and a fur coat over her shoulders.
They made a peculiar couple, she thought—Konig dressed as if he
were in mourning, while she glittered from head to toe.

Outside Chasen's a small crowd of fans and autograph hunters
waited. She knew they were not here for her specifically. They were
like predators—willing to snap up anything that came along. She

emerged from the car, took off her sunglasses and gave them a dazzling smile.

She pushed her way through the crowd to the door, followed by Konig, who was walking as if each step required a superhuman effort. Usually he took her arm when she was surrounded by fans, giving a proprietorial smile and sometimes even joking with the autograph hunters. He was apparently not in the mood tonight.

No sooner were they in the restaurant, however, than he seemed to revive. *His* audience was here, after all, not outside. His color returned, he smiled, he walked the room shaking hands with people he knew. They were twelve for dinner, including the Beaumonts, the Selznicks and a couple of people whom Dawn hardly knew. Konig, by the sheer force of his will and personality, managed to put on a perfect performance as a host. Nobody looking at him could have imagined that he was teetering on the brink of ruin, or that he and Dawn were at odds with each other. His anecdotes had never been funnier or told with more energy. His charm put everyone at his ease—sitting at the head of the table, he seemed like the king for whom his company had been named.

He had ordered a flaming soufflé for dessert, and watched with apparent pleasure as the brandy caught fire and illuminated the whole table in its sudden glow. His face was flushed. He seemed to stiffen, as if he was afraid of the heat. Then, with an apologetic smile, he excused himself. "I must make a call," he said, as the dessert was served, still flickering with blue flames.

He stood up, walked to the other end of the table, leaned over and kissed Dawn's hand. He held it a moment. There was a glint of amusement in his eyes, as if he knew a secret, or was about to play a practical joke. He walked through the crowded room, nodding to people he knew, mounted the steps quickly, his hand on the railing, and vanished from sight.

It was half an hour before the headwaiter appeared, his face white. He stood there for a moment, his hands clutched in front of him, then he leaned over and whispered to Dawn.

"There's been a—problem, Miss Avalon," he said.

"I'm sorry, Miss Avalon." The chauffeur was standing in the parking lot, holding his cap.

"What happened?"

"Sir David came out of the restaurant and got into the car. 'Where to?' I asked him. 'Cedars of Lebanon, you idiot,' he told me. 'I've had a heart attack.' So I drove him to the hospital as fast as I could."

"And . . ."

"He died in the back of the car."

Dawn stared at the limousine. The door was open. One of Konig's patent-leather pumps was on the floor.

It occurred to her that Konig had probably had his heart attack at the table while the dessert was being served. He had willed himself to stand up, to walk over and kiss her hand, to leave the room on his own two feet and die in his car.

Dignity had been important to him to the very end.

Part Four

THE
PRINCESS

CHAPTER 16

"I NEED HELP."

Aaron Diamond inclined his head, his scalp gleaming as if it had just been polished with bowling-ball wax.

For once, to Dawn's relief, he did not tell a joke or rush off at a tangent. Funerals depressed him—even that of Konig, whom he scarcely knew. At the funeral service he had wept uncontrollably—afflicted, as he later confessed to Dawn, by the notion that a man who had money, fame and a beautiful wife could die just like anybody else. Once the service was over, he swept her through a side door in the Chapel of the Stars, deftly avoiding the press, and took her back to his office, where he left her sitting while he changed his clothes, as if he was afraid they had been contaminated.

Outside, the palm trees wilted in the California heat. Inside, there was the smell of polished leather and wood, the heavy tick of antique grandfather clocks, the dull gleam of polished brass and copper. Diamond's office on South Rodeo Drive looked like a movie set. Everywhere she looked there was fumed oak, red leather, brass lamps, hunting prints, heavy Victorian furniture. Everything was designed to convey an impression of solidity, old money, respectability—everything, that is, except Diamond himself.

"What kind of help? You're a rich widow."

She shook her head, dislodging her veil. She removed the hat and put it on Diamond's desk, along with a large black handbag, which looked more suitable for a voyage than a funeral. "Apparently not. I had a session with the accountants, Aaron. There's nothing there except debts."

"There's the house. The paintings. Your jewelry."

"The bank owns the house. *And* there's a second mortgage on it. The paintings haven't been paid for, except for my Van Gogh—and I expect David's creditors will have their hands on that by tomorrow. The jewelry, too, unless I move fast."

"Jesus! I figured Konig was good for a million, at least."

"So did everybody. He lived by appearances, Aaron. I'm going to have to do the same."

"What do you want me to do?"

"Start negotiating with Marty Braverman."

Diamond raised an eyebrow—or the place where an eyebrow would have been if he'd had one. "I thought that was your beef against Konig."

"It was. I didn't want to be sold off to Braverman. But now I need a contract, Aaron. If I can get a four-picture deal, I'll take it. For the right price. And with approval of the pictures."

Diamond whistled. "That's not going to be easy to get you, kiddo."

"All we have to do is negotiate from strength, Aaron."

"*What* strength, chrissake?"

"He *needs* me. You know that. Empire can't go on making pictures with Ina Blaze forever."

"True. Good point. But you need him, too. Konig's picture is down the drain. Marty's not really a shmuck, you know. He hears you're in financial trouble, he's going to offer us *bubkes*."

"Aaron," she whispered, "he's not *going* to find out. I haven't been married to David Konig without learning something from him. That's why I need your help."

He cocked his head at her like a hungry sparrow. "Shoot."

"I'm going to sell the jewelry, Aaron."

He pulled a face. "The moment you do that, everybody in town will know you're broke."

"Not if I go out every night wearing paste replicas. Nobody has to know the real stones are in New York."

Diamond put on his tinted glasses. "I wonder how many years it is for concealing assets from creditors. I probably used to know. Well, what the fuck . . . I know a couple of guys who can do the job— diamond merchants from Amsterdam, refugees. The problem is how you get them out of the vault. Everything's going to be sealed tight."

"I know," Dawn said grimly. "I went to the vault."

"When somebody dies, the goddamned bank seals the box."

"I was there at nine o'clock the morning after David's death. I thought by the time they'd read the news and made a few phone calls it would be noon, or, at best, eleven o'clock—and I was right. I took my key, opened the box, and that was that. I cleaned it out."

"Where are they now?" Diamond asked.

Dawn opened her handbag and emptied it onto Diamond's desk. For a moment or two he simply stared at the jewels, then he picked up a necklace and weighed it in his hand. "Jesus," he whispered. "What are we talking about? In round numbers?"

"The whole lot is insured for three million dollars."

"You get a third of that, you'll be lucky. You know that?"

"I know. It's a pity, but it can't be helped. Your friends can simply take the stones out of their settings and replace them with paste. That way I can have the whole lot back in twenty-four hours with nobody the wiser."

"You've done this kind of thing before?"

"I've had a little previous experience, yes," Dawn said cautiously. "A long time ago. And in another country. Aaron, there's another thing—I want to sell the Van Gogh. That's mine, whatever David's creditors say."

"That's easy. But how are you going to get it out of the house? I'll bet they're watching night and day."

"They are. There's a couple of cars parked opposite the end of the drive. Men from the bank, I suppose."

"Or the IRS. Or Sigsbee Wolff's estate. Or who the hell knows. . . . Cases like these, though, it's the goddam servants are the problem. That's the first thing the creditors do—*schmeer* the servants to tip them off if anything is missing."

Dawn took a color photograph out of her bag and passed it to Diamond. "Here's the picture," she said. "And the dimensions. Can you find somebody at one of the studios who can do a copy overnight?"

He nodded. "For five hundred bucks, there are guys at the Disney Studio who'll do anything. It won't fool an appraiser, though."

"It doesn't have to. It only needs to fool the servants. Have him do it on canvas; you'll bring it over in your briefcase, and while we're having tea we'll switch the paintings in the frame. Thank God it's small. How do we get a valuation on it?"

"Mayer Meyerman can handle the whole thing—he's opened a gallery here. My guess is that you're talking two, two-fifty, tops. Let's say you come out with a million plus, if we're lucky. What are you going to do with it?"

"Live like a rich widow while you negotiate. Keep the house for a while. And the servants. I'll look for a smaller house—because this one is too big for me, *not* because I can't afford it, or because the bank is taking it over. The less I need Braverman, the more he's going to want me."

Diamond grinned. "Konig should have listened to you more often."

"He *couldn't*. He made me a star. He couldn't ever forget that—or let me forget it."

"So he didn't talk to you about business?"

"He did, of course. What else was there to talk about, at the end? But he kept the cards that mattered close to his chest, if that's what you mean."

"I don't *know* what I mean. I'm asking. It's going to take years for the lawyers to straighten things out. Konig probably had companies all over the place. A guy like that, he must have kept all the details in his head."

"He did."

"He ever ask you to sign anything?"

"Of course."

"Corporate stuff? Documents? Things that had to be witnessed or notarized?"

"Sometimes. He didn't like questions about that kind of thing. He incorporated me—he said it would be useful for taxes. And he had me made an American citizen."

"How the hell did he do *that*?"

"He pulled a few strings. You know what David was like—he knew Bob Sherwood and Harry Hopkins in the White House. He thought it would be a good idea for one of us to be American. A nice man from the Justice Department came around and filled out the papers, and I went downtown the next day and appeared before a judge."

"I need the files, I'm going to be any help to you about Konig's business." Diamond opened his desk drawer and shoveled the jewelry into it. He slammed it shut. He watched her carefully. "You want a receipt?"

She shook her head, knowing that Diamond was testing her. He was, she guessed, the kind of man who would do anything for someone who trusted him, and nothing for someone who didn't. She calculated the risk. "I don't need a receipt," she said.

Diamond stood up and showed her to the door. "You're learning. Anybody asks me, I never saw the fucking things."

All the way back in the car, Dawn wondered how she could simply have handed Aaron Diamond three million dollars in jewels. And yet she knew the answer. Sometimes you had to take a risk and gamble everything on instinct.

It was not until she went into Konig's study that she discovered the filing cabinets were empty.

Somebody was thinking as quickly as she was.

Braverman's desk was white. It was built in the shape of a half circle. It was raised on a dais. It was solid, so that from below one saw only his shoulders and his bald head. Behind his desk, with its row of white telephones, he looked as if he could hold off an army single-handed.

It was rumored that he never left it to greet a visitor. For Dawn, he stood up. He even stepped down off his dais and shook her hand. He did not bother shaking Diamond's hand. He only shook hands with men on making a deal.

For the past three weeks he had been talking to Diamond, while Dawn went out every night, her paste diamonds in glittering evidence, putting on a front. Diamond had announced that she was thinking of retiring. He had announced that she was thinking of donating Konig's paintings to the Los Angeles museum. He had announced that she was returning scripts unread, sure proof that she was in no financial need.

To Marty Braverman, he had confided that his client might accept a deal if the terms were right. He knew that behind Braverman's facade was a studio without a star. Years ago Braverman had committed the basic error of making Ina Blaze his mistress, then compounded it by putting her in movie after movie, despite slumping box-office returns and terrible reviews. Ina's career was going down the tubes, and Empire was going down with it, as well as Braverman's reputation and marriage.

The Empire lot was one of the largest in town, but behind the high white, flower-covered pseudo-Spanish walls, topped with Moorish tiles, there was nothing. Half the sound stages were empty, the water tank, big enough for a full-scale naval battle, was drained, the wind whistled through the empty buildings of Empire's Western town with its hitching posts and saloon; even the Empire "Young Talent" program, designed to train starlets, had degenerated into one of the town's better-known call-girl syndicates.

Still, Braverman's ego was undiminished. He was a mogul, a czar, boss of a major studio, a man used to making or breaking careers on a whim. He had, step by step, given in to Diamond's demands, making each concession with the maximum amount of histrionics and threats, while Diamond made sure that Dawn was seen dining at the Selznicks', the Mayers', the Goldwyns' and both Warner brothers'.

Braverman had agreed to a three-picture deal, but it took two weeks to get him to accept a two-million-dollar price tag. On the subject of Dawn's approval of scripts, however, Braverman was adamant. He had never given an actress anything of the kind, and he was not about to start.

Courtliness was not one of the virtues to which Braverman aspired. He had agreed to meet with Dawn reluctantly, and he came straight to the point. "Nobody tells me what to do on my fucking lot," he growled.

"We *know* that, Marty," Diamond said.

"Shut up, Diamond. You want something to do, go over to the Disney lot. They're casting for the seven fucking dwarfs, you could start a new career. I'm talking to your client."

"I know it, too," Dawn said respectfully. She had thought it wise to dress for the occasion in clothes that David Konig would have approved. A dark-blue silk suit from Chanel, a severe little hat that pulled her hair back, emphasizing her cheekbones, very little makeup, a single row of pearls around her neck. She wore long dark-blue suede gloves. She was every inch the lady and the widow.

She put one gloved hand on Braverman's. Close up, Braverman looked as if he had been carved out of rock by an untalented sculptor. In an industry where most of the giants were hardly taller than Aaron Diamond, Braverman was the exception. He was well over six feet tall, with the build—and apparently the coat—of an aging gorilla. The backs of his hands were so hairy that Dawn felt a certain repugnance in touching him.

He was tanned to the color of a mahogany dining table, and his eyes were small, dark and cunning, rimmed in red like those of some wild animal caught in a trap. It was not warm in his office, but he seemed to be sweating as if he were in a steam bath. He was, Dawn concluded to her own surprise, afraid.

Afraid of what, she wondered? Hardly of *her*. Braverman's reputation with women was part of Hollywood legend. In the old days, before Ina Blaze had clipped his wings, he boasted that he slept with every star who worked on the Empire lot, as if he enjoyed *droit de seigneur* as part of his contract.

It was not her he was afraid of, Dawn concluded. It was his own board. Braverman had held on to his control of the studio by the skin of his teeth. If it hadn't been for Sigsbee Wolff's death, David Konig would have been sitting in this office. Braverman needed a hit and he needed a star, and he must need both of them much more than anyone had guessed.

"David always spoke so highly of you," she said. "I want us to work together the same way."

Braverman eyed her suspiciously. "What way was that?"

"We were partners."

"I got partners. I wish to fuck I didn't."

"I don't mean that kind of partner, Marty. You don't mind my calling you 'Marty,' do you?"

"Anything."

"I *relied* on David, Marty. People say he invented me. It's not entirely true, but there's some truth in it. He knew what I could do, and he knew how to use me. And he knew there was no point in putting me in a picture where I couldn't be myself. So we talked about it. We made the decisions together. I just don't want to be handed over to a producer I don't even know, or given a part that's no good for me, that's all. I want the same kind of relationship with you that I had with David."

Braverman thought about it. "You were married to him, chrissake. You ain't married to me."

"Well, I *know* that . . . I just want the feeling that you are going to be looking after me *personally*, Marty. That I can come to you directly if I'm not happy."

"See me anytime," he said. "But don't give me no shit. Not for the kind of money I'm paying."

"I hear rumors you've hired a new head of production, Marty," Diamond interjected. "We just want to make sure Dawn gets the full attention of the man at the top, not some guy who's new to the lot."

Braverman stubbed his cigar into the ashtray so hard that it broke. He picked a new one out of the silver humidor on the glass coffee table, bit the end off and spat into the ashtray. "Listen, Diamond," he said, "a studio this size needs a head of production. I can't do every fucking pain-in-the-ass thing myself, can I?"

"No argument, Marty."

"Anybody thinks the goddamned board pushed this down my throat, they're wrong!"

"Nobody thinks that, Marty," Dawn said, guessing that this was exactly what had happened. She wondered who Braverman had picked for the job, and why anybody would want it.

"I went along with the board because it was the right thing to do. I still call the shots."

"Of course you do," Diamond said soothingly.

"That's why I want it in the contract that you and I, Marty, just the *two* of us, will work out what I'm going to do. I'm not coming here because of Empire. I'm coming here because of Marty Braverman."

"Selznick wanted her, Marty. Mayer wanted her. Harry Cohn wants her. She wants you."

"Did they want her two million bucks' worth?" Braverman asked shrewdly. "Cohn's a fucking cheapskate. Selznick don't have that kind of money. And Mayer wouldn't give a contract like that because all his other stars would want the same."

"The money's not the point," Dawn said. "David left me all the money I need, Marty. The money is just a question of prestige. I want the assurance that we'll be making major pictures together, that you and I will mutually approve my roles—not some producer or studio chief or committee. *Us.*"

She watched Braverman's face as he reduced his cigar to a soggy mess. What she was offering him was the chance to cut the balls off his new studio chief before he had even arrived on the lot, in the one big decision that really mattered. She was giving Braverman a chance to increase his power, at just the moment when it was about to be taken away from him.

"You got a deal." He shook Dawn's hand, then stood up and solemnly shook Diamond's.

Braverman was a man of the old school for whom nothing was sacred until he had touched flesh. He would break every clause in a contract without thinking twice about it, but he would never go back on a handshake.

"So who's the new production head, Marty?" Diamond asked.

"Can you keep a secret?" Braverman asked with a cunning smile.

"I'm a lawyer."

"That don't mean shit. I'll tell you anyway. It's going to be announced this afternoon, so what the fuck? The board wanted me to hire somebody, so I did. They left the choice to me. I hired my son-in-law."

A look of puzzlement crossed Diamond's face. "Marty," he said, "you don't have a son-in-law."

Braverman laughed. "As of yesterday, I have a *future* son-in-law. My daughter is engaged to Myron Cantor."

Dawn stared at him. "You mean *Myron Cantor* is going to be running the studio?"

"*I'm* going to be running the studio. He reports to me."

"But he's an agent."

"Nobody's perfect. He's a bright boy. He'll learn."

"I know him," Dawn said. She wondered if Cantor still remembered how she had stood him up. Then it occurred to her that he would hardly remember her as Rani, the exotic dancer, after all these years. It was unlikely he would make the connection, she thought—and if he did, what would it matter? He would be just as anxious to have people forget that he had been a bright young agent trying to hustle his way up as she was to keep her own past hidden—or at least obscure.

When she thought of putting her future in the hands of Marty Braverman and his new son-in-law, she realized how much she missed David Konig. After the first shock, she had felt grief, not suddenly, but like a growing pain that wouldn't go away. Now she felt fear.

She was in the hands of strangers. The only person she could really trust, once again, was herself.

The headlines showed bold black arrows marking the German sweep into France. All the maps placed one thick arrow in the Ardennes, where the main thrust of the Germans' Panzer forces had broken through what was described as "weak French defenses." She wondered if Lucien was part of them.

Other reports hinted of confusion, retreat and collapse. The radio reporters spoke of long lines of weary French troops clogging the roads, of Stukas appearing unopposed out of the hot, cloudless summer sky to bomb and strafe them, of disaster, humiliation and death. At night, lying awake in the house David had left her along with his debts, she thought about Lucien. She felt guilty about both of them, and sometimes wished either one of them were here. The loneliness was more than she could bear at times, and after a couple of weeks she dismissed Miss Bigelow and accepted Cynthia's invitation to stay with the Beaumonts until she found a house of her own. To her surprise, she needed Cynthia as much as Cynthia needed her.

All over Los Angeles the German exiles and refugees listened to the news and congratulated themselves on having escaped from Europe in time, though many suffered for friends, family, loved ones, while the French suffered for the defeat of their country and from the guilt of being here in safety. The British, who were the most numerous, suffered the most because they could still choose to go home.

At the Los Angeles Cricket Club, C. Aubrey Smith, the doyen of British society in Los Angeles, assured them that they were doing more for their country here, serving as an example of British talent and culture in American films, than they could possibly do at home, but not everybody was reassured by this convenient argument. To the doubters, Smith replied, "Look at Beaumont, man! If *he* can stay here and work, so can you."

But Beaumont refused to advise his fellow countrymen or explain his own position, least of all to Cynthia, who accused him daily of cowardice, against Dawn's advice. Cynthia was drinking more heavily than ever, with a desperation that made every dinner party a high-tension drama and every evening at home—not that Beaumont was home much—an agony. Drunk or sober, she wanted to go back to England with him as if sharing the war would solve the problems of sharing a bed.

Dawn forced herself to smile, as she dined with the Beaumonts and Aaron Diamond one evening at Chasen's, but there was no way she could paper over the hostility between them. Cynthia knocked back her second brandy—on top of three double Scotches and at least half a bottle of wine—and said, "I want to go home."

"In a few moments, dear one," Beaumont replied nervously, hoping to avoid a scene.

"I don't mean back to the bloody house. I mean *home*. England."

"We'll talk about it later, dearest," Beaumont said, trying to resume his conversation with Diamond.

"Fuck that! We'll talk about it *now*. What do you call a man who won't go home even when his country needs him, Aaron?"

Diamond took off his glasses and thought for a moment. "Prudent?" he suggested.

Cynthia laughed, the sound rising in intensity until Dawn thought her glass would shatter. "No," Cynthia said. "A *coward!*"

She drained the last few drops from her glass and called for another drink, her voice echoing in what was now a stony silence. "Don't you think so, Dawn? After all, *you're* British. Don't you want to go home?"

"It's different for me," she told Cynthia with a warning frown. "I'm not a man."

"Oh, that's all right, Dawn, darling," Cynthia said sweetly. "Neither is Dickie, apparently, when it comes to king and country."

Dawn momentarily regretted that she had accepted the Beaumonts' hospitality. She had quickly discovered that both Beaumonts wanted to have a referee under their roof. Beaumont hoped Dawn would calm Cynthia down, while Cynthia wanted somebody to whom she could explain "her side of the story," in the odd hours when she was sober. It was not a happy position for a guest; Dawn longed to find her own house, and was almost tempted to move back into Konig's mansion.

Beaumont turned white at the insult. He stood up. Cynthia gave him an insolent stare, her large pale-blue eyes mocking him. "You don't have the guts to hit me," she said with a giggle.

Dawn guessed she was wrong a moment before Cynthia did—but Beaumont's hand was stopped in midair six inches before it reached Cynthia's face. "Not in public!" Diamond whispered quietly to Beaumont, pushing him back into his chair with surprising strength for such a small man. "You want to take her home and beat the shit out of her, that's okay with me—it might even be the smart thing to do. But you do it *here*, and by tomorrow you'll be on the front page of every paper in the country."

Beaumont nodded wearily. There was a moment of strained silence; then Cynthia took out her compact, refurbished her makeup with trembling fingers and snapped it shut. She rose. "It's been a lovely evening, darlings," she said brightly. "We must do it again soon!"

Then her eyes closed and she slipped to the floor.

Beaumont sighed, and lit a cigarette with his lighter. Dawn caught its gold flash, and guessed why Beaumont didn't want to go home to England.

It was curious, Dawn thought, how easy it was to become lazy in Los Angeles. Her new state of widowhood was a kind of limbo from which she had no doubt she would eventually emerge, but in the meantime there was little for her to do. Diamond was working out the details of her deal with Empire; the lawyers were wrangling about Konig's estate; Kraus and Goulandris had vanished, no doubt trying to put as much distance between themselves and Konig's affairs as possible; Billy Sofkin, the decorator to the stars, had at last found her a house on the beach at the Malibu colony and was busy redecorating it—but most of this activity, however much it concerned her, did not really require her presence. She rose late, sunbathed by the pool, and waited for Cynthia to come down for her first Bloody Mary of the day.

Dawn counted the days until her house was ready. She longed to be in it, by herself, with only the sound of the surf for company.

She longed for it particularly one night when Cynthia decided she would force herself to stay up and wait for Dickie to return. "I'm going to have it out with him," she said. "He's seeing another woman."

Dawn sighed. She wondered if this might be the right moment to tell Cynthia the truth about Beaumont, but the more she thought about it, the less it seemed like a good idea. The truth scarcely seemed likely to improve the situation.

At midnight, Dawn gave up the vigil thankfully, made her excuses and crept up to bed. It was nearly two o'clock when Cynthia woke her. "There are some men outside," she said. "I can hear voices. You don't suppose it's burglars, do you?"

Dawn shook her head. "I expect it's Dickie," she said sleepily.

"No, it isn't. I heard a man's voice quite distinctly, and it wasn't his."

"Then call the police. Or wake up the servants."

But Cynthia did neither. She stumbled out of the room to her own bedroom, followed by Dawn, and turned on the big outdoor floodlights. Instinctively Dawn pushed in front of her, opening the heavy curtains just wide enough so that she could see out.

The lawn, the pool, the long driveway were suddenly illuminated, and there, harshly outlined in the glare, their arms around each other in a passionate embrace, were Richard Beaumont and Dominick Vale.

Beaumont's back was turned toward them. He had one hand behind Vale's head, pressing his face close as they kissed. Just then Vale pulled back and looked over Beaumont's shoulder, straight up at the window, his cold, pale eyes wide open as in a flashbulb photograph. He gave a smile and shrugged, as if to apologize for an unfortunate display of bad manners. Then he made a gesture of tipping an imaginary hat in her direction, turned on his heel, stepped into the shadows and was gone. The lights went out, and although the whole scene had taken only a couple of seconds, and the air outside was moist and warm, Dawn was shivering. When she turned, Cynthia's face was expressionless. Dawn hoped she had seen nothing—she had tried to block the view—but she could read nothing in Cynthia's eyes.

"I'm going to have another drink and go to bed," Cynthia said. Her hands were trembling.

"Don't you think you've had enough?"

"Don't *you* start, darling." Cynthia filled her glass.

"Drinking won't help."

"That's easy for you to say. You don't drink." She drained her glass in one quick gulp, coughed and put it down carefully on a coaster. Even drunk and in despair, Cynthia was not the kind of person to leave a wet glass on polished furniture. "It's the nights I can't stand," she said. "I want to touch him, and he hates it when I do. He tried to hide it, but I can tell."

"Then don't touch him. Sleep in a separate bedroom."

"I can't do that either. You don't have a sleeping pill, do you?"

"There are some in the bathroom. I got them after David's death, but I don't use them."

"Thanks," Cynthia said. She took the bottle and went off, closing the door quietly behind her.

Later that night, Dawn woke to hear the sound of a quarrel. She heard a slap, then silence, and decided not to interfere. In the morning, just as the pool boy was cleaning the pool, Cynthia Beaumont made her first suicide attempt. When she woke up in Cedars of Lebanon Hospital and realized to her disappointment that she was still alive, she took Dawn's hand, and in a voice that was reduced to hardly more than a whisper after the pills and the stomach pump, said, "Never mind, darling. Sorry I used your pills. Sooner or later I'll get it right, if I keep on trying."

Dawn had no doubt she would.

Shirley Braverman's wedding was so expensive that it dwarfed the bride, who was not all that tall to begin with. The ostentation was remarkable, even for a studio head, but it was generally acknowledged that Braverman had more than a demonstration of paternal love in mind. He was celebrating his own victory.

Sigsbee Wolff and David Konig had tried to take Empire over. They had failed, and died—an even greater failure, in fact, the ultimate one. Braverman, though diminished in authority and prestige, survived. That was worth a few hundred thousand dollars, which he would charge to the studio anyway. Besides, he was more anxious to display his son-in-law in the best light than to please his daughter, or even his wife.

It was Cantor whom the guests had come to meet and congratulate, not Shirley, and of the many benefits that would accrue to him as chief of production of Empire Pictures, marriage to Shirley Braverman was not, in most people's minds, the most important of them.

Dawn recognized him immediately. He had put on weight—not much, but enough to give him that smooth look of a successful studio executive. His black hair was slicked back as flat and shiny as ever, as if the top of his head had been hand-lacquered like a Chinese box. The dark feral eyes were still penetrating. "We've met before," he said, staring at her. He snapped his fingers a couple of times to jog his memory. "London. Some big party. You were with a photographer."

She nodded. There was no point in denying it. "You have a good memory," she said. "That was a long time ago."

"Four or five years. You were the most beautiful woman I'd ever seen, so I'm not likely to forget it. You're still the most beautiful woman I've ever seen, as a matter of fact. You stood me up. I sat at Claridge's all goddamned evening waiting for you, you know. . . ."

"I'm sorry I wasted your evening."

"No big deal. It happens." Behind the predatory eyes there was the flash of something that Dawn recognized as a bruised ego. She guessed that Cantor was not the kind of man who forgot, or forgave, any kind of slight from a woman. "I'm glad we're going to be working together," he said. "Hiring you was the second smartest thing Marty has done in years."

"What was the first?"

"Hiring *me*. We're going to make a great team, you and I, you'll see. I'm going to do things Konig never dreamed of. I want to show we can make a star just as well as MGM can."

Dawn frowned. "I'm a star already, Myron."

He backed off a little. "Well, sure you are . . . don't get me wrong. But I mean the real thing: fan clubs, mobs every time you go somewhere, people naming their kids after you . . . Being a star doesn't have anything to do with making movies. Gloria Swanson is a star and she hasn't made a picture in years."

"It's all in the roles, Myron. Find me the right roles first."

He shrugged. "You're wrong. It's the *publicity* that matters. That's why Konig could only take you so far. He knew all about pictures, but he thought publicity was just something you do after the movie's already in the can. I believe in *starting* with publicity—the big, early buildup." He paused for breath. "Why'd you stand me up?"

"I never said I'd come."

He clicked his fingers. "Lucien Chambrun! That was the name of the photographer, right?" Cantor did not pause for a reply. "What happened to him?"

"He's in France . . . in the army. . . ."

"Tough. He was a pretty good cameraman. He was here, I'd use him. You read *Flames of Passion?*"

The swift change in subjects was typical of Cantor—and of Hollywood. It was, as Dawn had discovered, a place in which people's attention spans were measured in seconds or even fractions of a second. She also knew the rules: you never said you hadn't seen or read anything. "What did *you* think of it?" she asked, lobbing the ball, she hoped, into Cantor's court.

To her relief, he did not lob it back. "History!" he exclaimed. "Patriotism! A good love story! People want to be proud of America. That's why it's a number one best-seller. It'll make a great movie, don't you think?"

She smiled enthusiastically. "That's the first thing I thought."

"Of *course* you did. You're smart."

"Have you bought it?"

Cantor's face darkened. "Marty bought it. He lucked into the property. Didn't even read the goddamn thing." He lowered his voice to a whisper. "The truth is, Marty's not on top of things the way he used to be. Just between us."

"He seemed pretty sharp to me." These were dangerous waters, and Dawn had no wish to tread in them. She looked around the party. "Which one is Shirley?" she asked.

"Over there, standing next to her father." Cantor nodded in the direction of the house, where the Bravermans were assembled in an uneasy group under an awning. Shirley was short, dark and plump, with her mother's hard eyes and her father's heavy beak of a nose. She still had the prettiness of youth, but it was not the kind that would last. She wore a diamond choker so big that from a distance it looked like a surgical collar.

"She's very pretty."

Cantor shrugged. Shirley Braverman's prettiness was not the subject of his attention. "I guess it must be lonely for you, now that Sir David is—gone," he said. "We ought to get together—have lunch or dinner, talk about what you're going to do."

"Well, as soon as my contract is signed . . ."

"We don't have to wait for that. You know how long the boilerplate takes. Tell you what. I want to talk to Beaumont. We'll all have dinner together." He stood close to her, one arm around her shoulder. "Hey!" he whispered. "That thing at Claridge's. No hard feelings. Maybe we'll try a replay."

She felt his hand drop lower down her back and moved away from him. She made a mental note to buy *Flames of Passion* on the way home.

Wrapped up in her own affairs, Dawn had failed to follow the publishing story of the year, most of which she was able to get, in a breathless, condensed form, from Aaron Diamond, who claimed to be responsible for having mentioned it to Braverman in the first place.

Flames of Passion had captured more people's attention than the Second World War. It was the work of a seventy-year-old Cleveland schoolteacher, who had written the book in her spare time, writing, rewriting and revising it for ten years, happily unaware that she had inadvertently stolen most of the plot from *War and Peace* and transposed it to Virginia in the Revolutionary War.

The manuscript, when completed, moldered in a cardboard box in her attic for several years more until a chance encounter with Emmett Lincoln Starr, the New York publisher, who was lecturing at the Cleveland Art Institute on "Writing in America" (a subject on which he was as ignorant as his audience), encouraged the old lady to dust off her life's work and leave it at Starr's hotel.

In normal circumstances Starr would never have read Maybelle Faith Darling's manuscript, and had had no intention of doing so when the bellboy brought the heavy box up to his room. Chance, however, felled him with a mild cold and an upset stomach. He was confined to his bed in Cleveland, and since the alternative to reading Mrs. Darling's manuscript was to spend the next twenty-four hours in a state of terminal boredom, he opened the box and took out a few pages.

The next morning he negotiated a five-thousand-dollar advance for all rights with the astonished Mrs. Darling, and returned to New York with a book that convinced his editors he had been drunk in Cleveland or was simply losing his mind, but within six weeks of publication it was the hottest novel in the history of American fiction—in every sense of the word, since it was banned in Boston, Atlanta and Mrs. Darling's native Cleveland.

For over a year it was at the top of the best-seller lists. All over the country, women named their infant daughters Caresse, after the novel's heroine. The "Caresse look" swept the fashion world—women everywhere took to wearing long, full skirts and plunging necklines, while hair stylists offered the "Caresse wave," after the heroine's flowing blond curls. Builders hastened to add a white-pillared portico to their houses to simulate the facade of "Alma," the Carson manor, and a country which had largely forgotten the Revolution suddenly rediscovered it as seen through the eyes of a woman who was simultaneously in love with a British officer and an American hero, and who went to bed with both of them—to the horror of ministers of every faith, who preached against the book from their pulpits, thereby guaranteeing its success.

Starr sold the motion picture rights to Braverman for the unheard of amount of two hundred and fifty thousand dollars, and Braverman had promised the millions of readers of *Flames of Passion* an absolutely "authentic" movie version of the novel—a promise which was swiftly to prove both rash and costly. Braverman, with an old-time showman's instinct, had promised a nationwide talent contest for the perfect Caresse. Unluckily the contest turned into a hot potato when the newspapers discovered that some of Empire's talent scouts were asking the younger and better-looking contestants for the role to take off their clothes as part of the "talent test."

Braverman had invented the talent contest. Now he was stuck with it. Stubbornly he refused to give in and admit he had made a mistake.

"It doesn't make sense," Myron Cantor told him over a predinner drink in the pool house of the Braverman home in Bel Air.

"How's Shirley?"

Cantor sighed. Braverman was an expert at changing the subject when it suited him. "How should she be? She's fine. Listen, Marty, forget the talent contest. It backfired, okay? The girls were balling the talent scouts. Well, shit, what can you expect? Besides, it's no way to pick a star for a big movie. Even if we control who wins the fucking thing, we still end up with an amateur. We're going to spend four–five million dollars, let's at least start with somebody who has a track record."

"I promised the American public a contest," Braverman said, putting one hand over his heart as if he were taking the oath of allegiance to the flag. "They expect us to use the winner."

"We give the winner a four-year contract and find her a part. She won't complain. We'll say we found someone so right for the part we couldn't say no. The public will accept that."

"They'll lynch us."

"They'll forget. You know that."

Braverman knew. More important, he knew he didn't have a choice. Cantor's star was rising. He had taken over the studio in a blaze of publicity, most of it self-created. The other members of the Empire board were as impressed by Cantor's energy as the industry was. Cantor had anointed himself as a genius, and Braverman, whose loathing for his son-in-law grew with each new story and press release about him, was in no position to resist—he had a stake in his son-in-law's success, and though it would have given him a good deal of pleasure to see Cantor fail, it was not in his interest that Cantor should do so. Besides, Cantor was right.

"So, okay. You got a point. But who have we got? There's Ina Blaze . . ."

Cantor stared at his father-in-law, who shrugged sadly. "Okay, forget Ina," he said. "We could get a loan-out. L. B. might let us have Joan Crawford for one picture."

"She's too old."

"Tallulah Bankhead?"

"She comes across as a dyke, chrissake!"

"Rita Hayworth?"

"She's wrong for the part." He took a deep breath. "I want Dawn Avalon."

Braverman puffed out his cheeks. "I got other plans for her."

"What other plans?"

"She's beautiful, she's sophisticated. She should do pictures like Garbo's. She's all wrong for *Flames*."

"She's a star. We need a star. So let's use her."

"She's not a blonde. The public expects a blonde."

"We can rewrite around that. No sweat."

"Anyway, she's not a big star yet. International market—yes. But with this goddamn war on, there's no international market. She should be built slowly so the American public gets to know her better."

"I had her pictures screened for me, Marty. She could do it."

"Her accent is all wrong."

"It's a period picture. We'll coach her. It's the right decision, Marty."

Braverman's face turned red. "It's *my* decision. I decide what she does."

"With her approval."

"That means shit."

Cantor sighed. Arguing with Braverman was like taking on a buffalo head-on. Once Braverman's ego and authority had been challenged, he was immovable. Dawn Avalon was his personal possession—he had signed her, and he was quite capable of letting her sit unused rather than give her up to Cantor.

He took a sniff from his inhaler and decided there was only one person who could change Braverman's mind.

Dawn was not kept waiting—a fact which astonished Cantor's secretaries, who were accustomed to complaints from stars, many of whom cooled their heels for hours in Cantor's luxurious anteroom. Since Cantor's office had another entrance leading directly onto the lot, they often waited without even realizing that he wasn't in his office.

In the two months since he had taken over the studio, Cantor's arrogance and rudeness had become legendary. In fact, he was simply a man who operated on his own strict order of priorities. If there was a problem with a script on an important picture, Cantor might spend two days and nights locked in his office with a team of writers, while outside the door actors, actresses, producers, agents waited in vain to see him.

Cantor's energy was the talk of the town. He worked around the clock, dictating memos that were sometimes twenty or thirty pages long, on everything from costume to history. He was a man who had at last found his true calling—*nudzhing,* as Aaron Diamond put it to Dawn, telling other people how to do their job. "The guy's a full-time, twenty-four-hour-a-day *nudzh,*" he said. "With any luck he'll burn out in a year or two."

On the rare occasions when Cantor's path crossed Dawn's, it seemed to her he was likely to burn out sooner than that. From time to time, his energy level ebbed alarmingly, like a light bulb burning out, leaving him so exhausted that he was unable to speak. When that happened, it was rumored, a couple of pep pills brought him back to life in no time at all. Around the studio brass, Cantor's use of Benzedrine was no secret—he recommended it to everyone, and went through half a dozen inhalers a day, sniffing at one every time he felt depressed or tired. Outside his own inner circle of gofers and yes-men, it was supposed that Cantor suffered from a sinus condition.

He was, all too clearly, in the process of turning himself into a legend in one leap, with one spectacular movie.

Nothing could be done without Cantor's approval. Unlike his father-in-law, who was only interested in what he liked to call "the big picture," Cantor was interested in everything. He personally allotted the studio parking spaces. He went through the contact sheets of the studio photographs to pick out publicity stills, screened the rushes of every movie in production at Empire, approved the menus for the commissary and dictated whole scenes overnight for his scriptwriters.

When Dawn entered his office, he was stretched out in a barber's chair, his face covered with a white towel like that of a corpse. A studio barber was shaving him while a studio manicurist worked on his nails. At his feet, the studio shoeshine boy knelt as if in prayer, breathing on Cantor's handmade glove-leather moccasins to bring them to a final mirrorlike gloss.

Cantor signaled the barber to take the hot towel off his eyes. They were dull and red-rimmed with fatigue. "Sit down," he said flatly, then realizing that Dawn might think he was rude, he added with more enthusiasm, "You're looking great, kid. Want something to drink? Coffee?"

"Tea, please."

"Tea!" Cantor bellowed in the direction of his desk, where the loudspeaker hummed slightly and a muffled voice answered, "Right away, Mr. Cantor."

"I keep forgetting you're a Brit."

"I'm not anymore. I took out American citizenship. David thought it would be a good idea."

"Yeah? I guess it is at that. Listen. I'm going to come right to the point. I want you to play Caresse. You interested?"

Dawn had thought about it for weeks. It was, in many respects, a leap into the unknown. When she signed with Empire, she had in mind three or four movies with major established directors and producers, and the kind of glamorous parts that she played best. She tried to imagine herself as the tomboy daughter of a Virginia squire. It was not easy to imagine. Then, too, Cantor was a problem—this was the first picture he would control, his debut, and he had elected to take on for it one of the biggest, most complex properties ever to be filmed—like a man who decides to learn how to walk a high-wire by crossing Niagara Falls on his first attempt. There was every possibility he would fall, particularly since Braverman, at some level of his mind, *wanted* him to fall.

Those were the negatives. The positive was that Caresse was the most sought-after role in Hollywood. If Cantor succeeded, whoever played Caresse had a chance to be the biggest star in movie history.

She asked herself what David would have advised her to do, but she already knew the answer. He believed in long-shot gambles. Still, she knew better than to leap at the offer. "It's a good part for somebody," she said.

"It's a *great* part, goddamn it!"

"What happened to Marty's talent contest?"

"So far as I'm concerned, you just won it."

"I'm not sure I could handle the accent."

"We'd get you a teacher. We can always write in a few lines to explain you were sent away to school in England . . . some shit like that. No big deal."

Cantor took a sniff from his inhaler to reinforce his optimism. His eyes brightened immediately. He got up and walked quickly around his office, the barber's smock flowing behind him like a druid's robes. "Goddamn sinus," he complained. "I ought to go to the Springs for a couple of days, breathe some clean air . . . Wanna come with me?"

Dawn shook her head. She had no intention of going to Palm Springs with Cantor. Luckily, the Benzedrine produced in Cantor such a blaze of instant energy that he hardly reacted at all to her refusal.

"Listen," he said, "it's the part of the century. You turn it down, you'll be making the mistake of a lifetime."

"And if I do take it?"

"You can write your ticket. Name your own price. If this works, I'll be running the goddamn company, not just the studio. I'll tear up your contract—whatever it is. You can name your own terms. You'll be the most famous woman in the world."

"I thought I *was* famous, Myron. It's not exactly my first movie."

He sat down next to her with a sigh. "I know all that," he said, "but it's not the same thing. Okay, you were a star in England, and your movies did pretty well here, but when I'm through with you, more people will know your name than the goddamn President's. England, you could walk down the street, go shopping, stuff like that, right? Nobody would pay any attention, right? Here, after this picture, you'd be mobbed!"

Cantor clicked his fingers restlessly, then signaled the barber to remove the smock from his shoulders. "Come with me," he said. He led the way to a door and opened it. Dawn followed him and found herself in an immense bathroom. One end was fitted out like a health spa, with a Swedish shower, a sauna and a massage table. Cantor closed the door and sat down on the toilet seat. He indicated that Dawn could perch on the side of the tub. "We can talk privately here," he said.

"Is there something we have to talk privately about?"

"You bet your ass. We're going to put four–five million dollars, maybe more, in this fucking picture. Caresse Carson is America's best-loved heroine since Betsy Ross."

"Who was Betsy Ross?"

"She sewed the first flag. Made it out of her own underwear. I saw a movie about it once, when I was a kid. Listen: there are Caresse Carson fan clubs, Caresse Carson comic books, Caresse Carson look-alike contests—there's even a high school in Richmond named after her. She nearly got voted 'Woman of the Year' by the readers of *Time* magazine. They know everything about Caresse—even the fact that she has a seventeen-inch waist and a size five-and-a-half triple-A foot. So they're going to want to know everything about *you*—from your bra size to your grades in kindergarten. *And* where you were born. The press is going to be looking at your past for dirt. If we're going to work together, I have to know: Are they going to find any?"

"I can't think what you mean," she said firmly.

Cantor looked at her impatiently. He fortified himself with another sniff from his inhaler, then threw it away and opened a new tube. "These goddamn things don't last," he complained. "Okay. So what do we tell them?"

"I was born in India. My parents were British. My father was an officer in the service of a maharajah. He died when I was young. I came to England with a relative, studied drama, became a dancer—against my family's wishes. Then I met David." She spoke with absolute conviction. In many ways the past that had been invented for her was more real to her now, she thought, than her own. She had come to *believe* in it.

Cantor looked thoughtful. "India may be a problem," he said. "Americans aren't crazy about the goddamn British colonies. People figure it's okay for us to whip niggers in the South, but it's not okay for the British to whip niggers in the colonies."

"I grew up with Indians," Dawn said, which was no more than the truth, though not in the way she hoped Cantor would take it.

"Like Kim," Cantor said, brightening as he always did when he found a movie to explain what he or someone else meant. Cantor saw all life in terms of movies. Heroism was *Beau Geste*. Friendship was

The Four Horsemen of the Apocalypse. Motherhood was *Stella Dallas*. Movies explained everything—in the end they *were* everything.

"Or Wee Willie Winkie," he added happily, already imagining Dawn's childhood in terms of Shirley Temple saluting C. Aubrey Smith in the British India of so many Hollywood epics. He could see it all clearly in his mind: The little girl holding her father's hand, she in her white dress, under the hot sun—he magnificent in his glittering uniform, the stern, just sahib, beloved by his native troopers. He thought of *Elephant Boy*, of *Gunga Din*, of *Lives of a Bengal Lancer*. "Did you used to ride on elephants?" he asked.

"Not often," Dawn said, trying to keep a straight face.

"The Taj Mahal, the Raj, snake charmers . . . it's not bad. We can do something with it."

Cantor closed his eyes for a moment and tried to imagine his publicity campaign. His enthusiasm wavered slightly. India was exotic all right, but was it too exotic? Then he opened his eyes, looked at Dawn and decided it was worth a shot.

"Okay," he said. "We'll do some tests."

Dawn looked him in the eye. "I don't test."

"Everybody tests, for God's sake. You know that."

"I don't. I've *been* tested. You've seen my pictures."

To her surprise, Cantor showed no anger. On the contrary, he seemed impressed. "You win," he said. "What the hell. It would probably be a waste of time. Besides," he added, already running with the ball, "we can say you were so right for the part we didn't bother testing. We found Caresse! What's to test?" He paused for a moment, fumbling for his inhaler. "There's only one small problem. You have to talk to Marty."

"Why me? What for?" she asked warily.

"Because it's in your contract. And because if I talk to him, he'll say no."

Little as Dawn relished the prospect, she nodded. "How much is he against it?"

Cantor waved his hand from side to side, as if it were a ship in a stormy sea. "*Mezzo-mezzo. Comme ci, comme ça*. He could be persuaded. But not by me."

Cantor's eyes seemed to have gone glassy. Dawn wondered if he was about to faint for some reason, but he recovered, his mind immediately shooting off at a tangent. "Did I ask you to come to Palm Springs with me?"

"Yes. I said no, Myron."

"Did you? I forgot. I get these blank spells. You're probably right. I couldn't get away to the Springs anyway. Too much to do. And Shirley would want to come along . . ." He sighed. "You should have come to Claridge's. We'd have been great together. I'm never wrong about these things."

Dawn decided it was time to leave. "I'm sure you're right," she said cautiously—there was no point in antagonizing him—"but now you're married, and I'm a widow, so it's just one of those things we'll always have to wonder about. Best that way, perhaps . . ."

"The hell with that. How long has Konig been dead?" he asked.

Dawn looked puzzled. "Three months, more or less . . ."

Cantor took a sniff. He took his glasses off, like a man preparing himself for a fistfight. "Poor kid," he said. He slipped off the toilet seat and fell to his knees in front of Dawn, clasping his arms around her in an attempt to pull her down onto the bathmat. "You want it as much as I do," he whispered hoarsely. "I could tell that in London, chrissake!"

Dawn was not only startled but afraid of losing her balance and toppling over backward into the tub. She had a sudden vision of herself with a broken back. It seemed safer to fall forward, even if it meant wrestling with Cantor on the floor. She felt the zipper of her dress tear, then she was on the floor, while Cantor struggled to get on top of her.

"You and I were made for each other," Cantor said in a fuzzy voice, unconsciously picking up a line of dialogue from the movies, as he always did in moments of passion or importance—but Dawn managed to brace herself against the side of the bathtub just long enough to push Cantor off. To her astonishment, he rolled over onto the mat and lay there on his back, his eyes closed.

She suspected a trap. Then, as she began to get to her feet cautiously, Cantor began to snore gently, his chest rising and falling, and she realized he was fast asleep.

She straightened her dress as best she could, though there was nothing she could do about the runs in her stockings or the torn zipper, and stepped out of the bathroom, leaving Cantor to his dreams.

She and Cantor would have to come to terms with each other, she decided.

She still wanted this picture.

.   .   .

"I think of you like a daughter," Braverman said, coming down from behind his monstrous desk. His expression was mournful, as if paternity were a heavy burden. He placed one hand on his heart. "And if you were my daughter, I would say to you: 'Don't do this, darling!'"

"You let your daughter marry him."

Braverman rolled his eyes. "It's not that I have anything against Myron. He's a splendid young man. He's my own son-in-law. I think of him like a son, in fact. But he's going too fast. He should learn to run the studio first. He wanted to produce *Flames* himself, and I said okay—but he's putting his whole goddamn life on one movie."

"That's why it might work, don't you think? I read the script. It's good."

"It's too long. I told him that. He don't listen to me. He don't listen to *anyone*. Believe me: Forget it! I got two or three scripts that are perfect for you."

"I read them."

"So?"

"They're good, it's true. But I think I could play Caresse, Marty."

"She's American, for chrissake."

"That doesn't matter. Who knows how Americans spoke in the eighteenth century? They probably sounded pretty much like the English. And I can work on the accent. The point is—she's a young woman whose beauty gets her into trouble, and who has to learn how to look out for herself the hard way. She's in love with two strong men, on different sides, and though she doesn't know it, she's stronger than either of them. She's a *survivor*, Marty."

"Is that the way Myron sees the story?"

"No. That's the way I see it."

She waited for Braverman to explode with rage, but he seemed distracted, as if something else was on his mind.

He walked over to the window and stared out at the palm trees. He turned and came back to her, a look of elephantine caution on his face. "How long has David been dead?" he asked.

She wondered what he had in mind, hoping that it wasn't the prelude to another assault.

"About three months. Why?"

"I guess the lawyers are still straightening things out."

"Well, yes. It's all rather complicated. That's why I want to get to work. I'm tired of sitting around talking to them every day."

"He left you everything?"

Dawn approached the question carefully. Had Braverman found out that she had pulled a fast one on him? That Konig's estate was mostly debts and problems? She put on a sad expression, as if the subject were too painful to discuss, and hoped he'd pass on to the next question and reveal what he had in mind.

"He must have had investments all over the place."

"Well, yes. Here and in England, certainly. King Films alone is enough to keep the lawyers busy for months."

"They'll bleed you dry. I hate fucking lawyers. Listen, I know more about business than the lawyers do. You come to me for advice."

"Well, that's very generous of you . . ."

"I told you: you're like a daughter. David's stock, for example. Don't listen to *anybody*. Come to me. I'll tell you what to do. Like your own father."

"Stock?"

"Shares, you call them in England."

"David wasn't very keen about the stock market, Marty. He got badly burned out here in twenty-nine. He lost millions of dollars in the crash."

"I know. I remember. Sigsbee Wolff told him to get out of the market, and he didn't listen. What the hell—a lot of guys didn't listen. I wasn't thinking of that kind of stock. David owned a piece of this, a piece of that . . ." Braverman exuded a false geniality that was positively alarming. He patted her hand and gave her what he probably thought was a winning smile. "Don't listen to the lawyers," he said. "You come straight to me."

In fact, Dawn had been too wrapped up in the problems of what Konig owed to think much about the larger question of what he owned. Braverman's interest set off a small, persistent alarm in her head—she would have to find out what it was that he wanted so badly to see. In the meantime she took advantage of his curiosity. "I'm sure I'll need all the advice I can get," she said diplomatically.

"Count on me."

"It's a promise." She paused. "About the picture, Marty . . ."

He opened his arms, as if he were blessing her. "You want to do it, go ahead. Just come to me before you do anything. I want us to be *partners*, Dawn." He winked alarmingly. "You know what I mean?"

She didn't. But she meant to find out.

. . .

Cantor's decision to use Dawn was a shrewd gamble. It would also, in years to come, be part of motion picture history. Cantor would eventually claim that he had never met Dawn previously—that Aaron Diamond had brought her to visit the set of Alma while they were shooting exteriors, and at the sight of Dawn standing on the steps of the house, Cantor had whispered, "There's Caresse!"

The story became part of Cantor's legend, as well as Diamond's (though in *his* version, he had said to Cantor, "Here's your Caresse, Myron.").

Under Cantor's supervision, she rapidly became the most photographed woman in America. *Life* photographed her new Malibu beach house—she appeared on the cover in a memorable picture, standing in the water looking out to sea, with the ends of her long gauze beach robe fluttering in the breeze as if she were in flight. *Vogue* sent Munkacsi himself out to do a photo essay on Dawn. For *Harper's Bazaar* she was photographed in a gold sari and diamonds, her long black hair drawn back tightly to accentuate her features, standing next to a live Bengal tiger, which had been suitably drugged for the occasion.

To Hedda Hopper she confided, at Cantor's suggestion, that her childhood dream had been to come to America. To Louella Parsons she confided that she had no plans for remarriage as yet. Her childhood as a "fairy-tale princess" in a maharajah's court captured the imagination of the public, as well as the reporters, and since India was exotic, bizarre and far away, no embarrassing details were sought or found.

Daily she went through her paces at the studio, the task of filming made more complicated by the fact that Cantor seemed unable to settle on a director or a script. He had so identified himself with the picture that he insisted on second-guessing the director down to the smallest details. By the hour, memos arrived on the set in which Cantor elaborated at length on the motivations of the characters or suggested last-minute changes in dialogue. Roddy Lackrack resigned after two weeks. Zoltan Daranyi collapsed from exhaustion and rage and had to be removed in a studio ambulance. James Chase de Witt survived almost a month, but the strain was too great, and after fifteen faithful years of AA, he was discovered in a bar on Sepulveda Avenue, hopelessly drunk at ten o'clock in the morning.

Since no director of the first rank would now touch a picture that was widely regarded as a disaster-in-the-making, Cantor eventually settled on Roger Aptgeld.

"But he's a hack!" Braverman protested. Cantor was not impressed or moved. He knew Aptgeld was a hack, but he was also a professional, and being a hack, he would take orders and leave the big decisions to Cantor.

With Aptgeld in charge, the picture proceeded smoothly. Dawn had no difficulty working with him, for he was soft-spoken, patient and in awe of his surroundings and responsibilities. Besides, Cantor knew exactly what he wanted, which made her task easier. Each night he rehearsed her in his office, acting out the parts himself, until she began to feel she *was* Caresse. Even Cantor was satisfied in the end, though he complained from time to time that she didn't seem to photograph as well as she had in her earlier pictures. Still, the difference was negligible—and she photographed a lot better than anybody else in Hollywood, as she pointed out to him sharply.

Cantor played the rushes over and over again in his private screening room. There was something about her beauty that challenged and at the same time frightened him. The big, dark eyes in that perfect oval face seemed to reflect exactly what he was thinking when he looked at her, and gave back nothing more than mild amusement, as if Dawn were telling him he was out of her league. Whenever he moved his knee next to hers she smiled and moved her leg away.

At the end of the working day, Cantor had her driven home in his limousine. The driver dropped him off at his Bel Air house, then made a silent U-turn and drove down Sunset Boulevard to take Dawn to Malibu.

Every night Cantor prayed that Shirley would be asleep, so he could take a sleeping pill, dictate a few memos in his study, then slip quietly into bed when the pill began to take effect and go to sleep. But Shirley had staying power. Most nights she was awake, propped up against the pale-blue satin pillows in their big bed, reading a book. Years ago, her mother had told her that the best way to keep a marriage going was to give a man what he wanted, and they all wanted the same thing.

Cantor, however tired and unwilling he might be, was invariably obliged to put on a show of ardor when he came to bed. He had no illusions that he was giving pleasure to Shirley, but it was expected of him, and to the best of his ability he obliged. Not to do so would require explanations.

He had discovered that thinking of Dawn invariably helped. He closed his eyes and formed a mental image of her face, her slim waist, her long legs, and in no time at all he had an erection. If he thought about her undressing—imagining the smooth, rounded buttocks, the dark strip of hair between her legs, the small, firm white breasts—he could usually manage to come within a minute or two, so he could roll over and get some peace.

He had everything a man needed, he sometimes told himself.

But not what he wanted.

"What do you think of Dick Beaumont?" Cantor asked, as he sat down in the limousine beside Dawn. At night the car was always pulled up next to the secret exit from his office, so he could leave without having to pass through his waiting room. His assistants followed him at a run to the car, while Cantor fired off his last-minute instructions, rolling down the window so that he could shout a few orders at them as the driver started the car and pulled away. Occasionally his secretary ran alongside, throwing messages and envelopes into the car like confetti at a wedding.

"He's a great actor."

"Yeah. I wanted a loan-out on Gable, but L. B. said no, the cocksucker. . . ." Cantor glanced at a few messages and crumpled them up. His restless energy never failed to make Dawn nervous at close quarters. "I hear Beaumont's marriage is on the goddamn rocks."

"That doesn't affect his acting. Besides, he seems to have turned over a new leaf. He's spending more time at home."

That, at any rate, was the truth, Dawn thought. Beaumont was playing the devoted husband since Cynthia's suicide attempt. And being the actor he was, he made a good job of it. He had convinced everybody except Cynthia.

"Would you be comfortable working with him?"

"I'm always comfortable with Dickie. We go back a long way."

"Were you and him . . ." Cantor gave a grotesque, confidential wink.

"No."

"I was just asking," Cantor said mildly. It was as close as he was able to come to apologizing. He had made his apologies for the scene in the bathroom by sending Dawn flowers and champagne. She guessed he was not so much ashamed of having attacked her as of having failed to complete the attack, since he never missed an opportunity of telling her how tired he was now. He had fallen into the habit of confiding in her. His manner had become almost proprietorial, as if they had in fact consummated their relationship. "Jesus, I'm tired," he said, slumping in his seat and putting one listless hand on Dawn's knee, as if he expected her to pat it.

"You ought to get a rest," she said.

"I'd be bored. You know, this whole fucking business is crazy. As if I don't have enough *tsuris* to begin with, Braverman calls a goddamn board meeting every five minutes. Shit, he can't make a movie to save his life, but you'd think he could at least take care of what's happened to the goddamn stock. . . ."

"What's the problem?"

"The problem? The problem is that I haven't got time to sit there. Half the board is old *cockers* who got nothing to do but sit around the Hillcrest Country Club all day—Braverman's steam room buddies. The rest are bankers who get paid for being there. . . . What did your husband do with his stock anyway, chrissake?"

"What stock?" She was listening carefully now.

"He was buying stock like crazy for a while there—with Sigsbee Wolff."

"I don't know much about these things," she said, affecting a carelessness she didn't feel. "He bought a lot of stock, mostly on margin. He spent hours every day on the telephone, buying and selling. I assume it's all gone."

"You're probably right. I can't see a guy like Konig putting up his own money for anything. The executors haven't found anything?"

"They're still trying to work out how many companies David owned. Why?" she was fully alert now, but Cantor was apparently not prepared to pursue the subject.

"No reason," he said. "It's probably just some shitty mistake in paperwork. Marty's put so many of his goddamned relatives into the company that nobody can find anything." Cantor quickly changed the subject. "What I need is an assistant I can *trust*," he said. "Somebody from the outside, who doesn't owe Marty anything."

"There must be someone, Myron."

"Yeah. My problem is I'm looking for someone honest and loyal."

The limousine swept up the driveway of Cantor's house between the rows of palm trees. He glanced up and saw that Shirley's bedroom light was still on. He sighed. He leaned close and put his hand on

Dawn's leg, more firmly this time. A faint aura of cigar smoke clung to him, reminding her of David and his friends—of the endless enormous meals, the talk about money and deals and politics late into the night. For a moment she had a terrible feeling of loneliness, as if she were wasting her life. She wished she were anywhere else but in this limousine with Myron Cantor breathing down her neck.

"Give me another chance, Dawn," he whispered.

Dawn nodded toward the chauffeur. "Not here, Myron, please! Besides, I'm a widow, for heaven's sake. And we're parked right outside your front door."

Even Cantor saw the logic of this. He backed off slightly. "Listen: I can wait. There's no point in rushing things." And before Dawn could say there was no point in his waiting, he kissed her, opened the car door and stepped briskly out before the marble steps of his house.

He stuck his head in through the open car window. "I'm not the kind of guy you think I am," he whispered. "Grief I understand, I respect. I don't think you should mourn too long personally, but mourn, mourn, as long as you have to. I'll be waiting. I'm a very patient guy, when I have to be."

"Myron," she said. "That's sweet of you, but you're wasting your time." She raised the window, giving Cantor the choice of backing off or being guillotined.

Still, she was grateful to him, she thought, as the big car slipped down the gently curved driveway. Was it possible that David had died still in possession of his Empire stock? It seemed unlikely to her, but of course it was possible, given the complexity of his affairs. No doubt the answer had been in the files.

There was one person who would know.

She decided to have Aaron Diamond track him down.

CHAPTER 17

ON THE SUNLIT TERRACE of Dawn's beach house, Kraus cut a ridiculous figure, even for Hollywood. The thin, ferretlike, earnest face was unchanged, the complexion as pasty as ever, but he had made several concessions to the climate and local custom. He wore huaraches on his feet, carried a panama hat which he seemed reluctant to put down, and had discarded his double-breasted European suit for a white linen jacket with mother-of-pearl buttons. He seemed nervous.

"You're sure you won't have something to drink?" Dawn asked.

Kraus nodded. "So kind," he muttered. "A little water, perhaps." He seemed grateful for the interruption.

"What have you been doing?"

"Since Sir David's death?" Kraus arranged his features into an expression of grief. "I've been packaging entertainment for hotels. And casinos."

Dawn gave him a hard stare. "You're working for Dominick Vale, aren't you?"

Kraus wiped his forehead. "One has to eat," he said.

Dawn sipped her tea. "I can't think why you should, Kraus. As soon as David was in trouble, you ran off like a rat leaving . . ."

"The sinking boat." Like most Central Europeans, Kraus's command of English colloquialisms was confident but erratic. "Yes. I admit it. I was terrified. First Sigsbee, then Konig. . . . Well, we all make mistakes, even Sir David. I know why you sent for me. Listen to me, please. Is there worry at Empire about the stock?"

She narrowed her eyes. "Maybe. What *is* it about Empire? Nobody can leave it alone."

"It's a beached whale. A major studio with enormous assets and a weak management—except for Cantor. Its stock is undervalued. And

Braverman's margin of control is paper-thin—he holds onto the company by putting his cronies on the board and letting them loot it. Look at it this way," Kraus continued, with increasing enthusiasm. "Because of the way the stock is distributed, somebody could take control of a major studio for a comparatively *small* investment. Then you spin off some of the assets you don't need—and now you own the whole thing, for free! After that, all you have to do is turn it around, which isn't all that difficult. America won't stay out of the war forever. And what do people do in wartime?"

"Get killed, I suppose," she said impatiently. "I don't see what that has to do with it."

"In Europe they get killed, yes. But not here. Here, they will need entertainment, escapism, something to take their minds off the war. They'll go to the movies. Business will double. At the right price, Empire could be a gold mine."

"That's what David used to say."

"Of course he did. Sir David was no fool."

"He also used to say that once you owned Empire, you could borrow a fortune by listing their inventory of properties and the film library as assets, even though they've been written off years ago."

Kraus blinked. He took another sip of water. "My congratulations! You learned a thing or two from him."

She stood up in her beach robe and stretched. "It all sounds fascinating." She yawned.

"I owe everything to Sir David," Kraus said. "I ask myself, if he were alive, what would he want me to do? He would want me to be honest with you, I think."

"Very likely. And are you *going* to be honest?"

"I have many problems . . ."

"So do we all, Kraus."

"If war comes, there's a possibility I'll be deported. Or interned."

"I don't think it's going to happen, Kraus. Nobody I know thinks that."

He shrugged. "I hope you're right. Myself, I think it *will* happen. Vale offered to help me with the Justice Department. Now he's backing off, giving me excuses . . ."

"What does this have to do with me?"

"I need somebody to help with my American citizenship. And I need a job. Both of these things, I think you could do—or somebody at Empire. What I have in mind is an exchange, Lady Konig."

"An exchange for what?"

"Information, to begin with." Kraus opened his briefcase. He drew out a thick envelope and put it on his lap. He placed the tips of his fingers together like a schoolmaster about to give a lecture. "How much do you know about Konig's shares in Empire?" he asked.

It was the third time she had been asked that question. Her hunch had been right. If Kraus had the answer, there was no point in pretending to further ignorance. "Suppose you tell me," she said. "After all, you emptied out David's files."

Kraus blushed. "It seemed the prudent thing to do."

"I suppose you offered them to Vale?"

"No, not exactly. I hinted that I knew where they were. That was enough to get me a job. I have come to the conclusion, however, that Vale and I are not going to—hit it off. I think your side is safer, in the long run." He paused and took a sip of water. "Did Sir David ever discuss these shares with you?"

"Not really. I don't suppose he thought I'd be interested. Or that I'd understand. Perhaps he thought I was better off not knowing."

Kraus smiled gently. "About that I suspect he was right, poor man. You have a better head for these things than Sir David knew—or *wanted* to know, I suppose. . . . You remember that he set up a corporation for you?"

"Yes, of course. He explained *that* to me. I remember signing the papers. He arranged for me to become an American citizen at the same time . . . but it was chiefly a way of reducing my taxes."

"True. It's quite common here. Avalon Pictures, Inc., owned the exclusive right to your services. If Empire had hired you for a three-picture deal while Sir David was still alive, for example, they would have signed with Avalon Pictures, not with you personally. Of course, you're the major stockholder in Avalon Pictures." Kraus beamed as he held up a thin blue folder. "Sir David didn't believe in making things easy for his creditors."

"I know all that. What's the point? Avalon Pictures' only asset was me. It was just a way of reducing taxes."

"Not quite. Sir David was very anxious to protect himself. I expect that was his reason for wanting you to take out American citizenship. He had many obligations, as you know. Just before he died, he transferred his shares in Empire to Avalon Pictures. No doubt it was a temporary measure, so he could claim he didn't own them, if he had to. In any event, he died before he could take the next step. So, my dear lady, you are now the full owner of Avalon Pictures. And Avalon Pictures is the owner of record of—nearly one million shares of Empire."

Dawn stared at him in astonishment.

"It makes you a significant factor in Empire's affairs," Kraus continued. "You don't have enough shares to get rid of Braverman—but anybody who wanted to take over the company would have to reckon with you."

"I see," Dawn said.

Kraus put the envelope on the table, like a man placing his chips on the baize of a roulette table. "Do we have a deal?"

"I'll need some proof of what you've got."

He opened the envelope, took out a photocopy and handed it to her. He had come prepared.

She glanced at it, and recognized Braverman's spiky signature. "Myron Cantor is looking for an assistant producer," she said evenly.

"I had hoped for better."

"You've got to start somewhere. Working for the head of production of Empire is a good beginning."

Kraus gave a thin smile. "Depending on the salary and so forth, it might do . . . I'd want a contract, of course. And somebody would have to look after my immigration problems. That should be no problem for a major studio."

"I'll be in touch."

"Of course." Kraus bowed courteously. "It's going to be a pleasure working with you again," he said. "Just like the old days."

Dawn stared at the photocopy in her hand. "No," she said without sadness, "it's not going to be like the old days at all."

Aaron Diamond held the photocopy up to his face, then sat silently for a moment, like a tiny Buddha. "Holy shit!" he said.

"Does it make me a rich woman?"

"Well, yes and no. One thing's for sure. It makes you a woman with a lot of enemies."

"Surely the stock is worth a lot of money."

"I don't know what Empire is selling for today. I'll get my secretary to check on the New York price. But it's not much. Three, three-fifty a share, maybe. It went up to ten or eleven when Sigsbee and your husband were playing around with it, but a lot of people got burned then. It moved up a little with all the publicity about *Flames of Passion*—but so long as Braverman is chairman, the price isn't going to change much."

"Still, that's three and a half million dollars."

"Sure. But the moment you start to sell any significant amount of it, the price is going to take a dive." Diamond picked up the photocopy and examined it with an expression of distaste on his face. He put it back on his desk again. "You want to sell," he said, "you either have to sell to Marty Braverman or to one of Marty Braverman's enemies. Tough choice to make. In the right circumstances, like a takeover, you could just about name your own price. But in the open market, you got zip."

"Braverman must know I have them, surely?"

"No. If he did, he'd have been on the phone with an offer. Konig didn't reregister the stock, you see. He simply assigned it to Avalon. So far as Marty knows, it's part of Konig's estate. He's probably waiting for a call from a lawyer or an executor when the estate's affairs are cleared up a little—if that ever happens. There's so much litigation around Konig's estate that Braverman's got to figure it may take years before it's sorted out, and in the meantime this stock can't be voted against him. Out of sight is out of mind."

"When will he find out?"

"When we reregister the stock. *If* we reregister it."

"We don't have to?"

"No. We can sit on it for a while. Why stir up trouble we don't need? Sooner or later somebody is going to put two and two together and come looking for it—then we'll find out what it's worth to them. Or you might play it a different way."

"What way would that be, Aaron?"

"Take the long-term view. You might end up sitting in Marty Braverman's chair one day." He laughed.

It wasn't until she had left Diamond's office that he realized she hadn't smiled.

"The rushes look good," Cantor said, at the wheel of his personal golf cart.

"It's been a long time since I worked."

"You wouldn't know it. The love scenes are terrific." He turned to smile at her, narrowly missing a crowd of extras in battle costume, complete with flags and swords.

It was ironic, Dawn thought, that her big scene in *Flames of Passion* was the moment when Caresse Carson, watching the flames destroy her beloved Alma, turns to face the camera and says, "Love is everything."

The line had caught the imagination of millions of readers, most of them women—and since Cantor felt his whole multimillion-dollar picture would rest on the way women reacted to the line, he and Dawn had rehearsed it a thousand times. Aptgeld shot it as a close-up, shot it as a long shot, shot it back-lit, shot it with a pan, but Cantor continued to agonize over the scene. He knew those millions of women would be crouching tensely in their seats, holding their breath, waiting to hear that one line—and if they didn't like the way Dawn said it, or the way it was shot, he was dead.

He pulled to a stop by the awning of the commissary and sat for a moment. Dawn had no choice but to wait, since her costume, with its layers of silk, made it impossible for her to get out of the golf cart without Cantor's help. She wished she had decided to eat alone in her dressing room.

"I owe you," Cantor said.

"For what?"

"This guy Kraus is a real find."

"I told you so."

"You were right."

"He was trained by David."

"David this, David that . . . that's all I hear from you. . . ." He sighed. "You also got Marty off my back."

"That was easy."

He raised an eyebrow. "I know better. Mind you, he's so busy now trying to hang on to the chairmanship that he doesn't have any time left to get in my way. My mother-in-law thinks he's going to have a nervous breakdown. I wouldn't be surprised. The poor guy's got a nagging wife *and* a nagging mistress: the worst of both worlds!"

"I thought he'd reconciled with Estelle?"

"It's more like a truce. No shooting, but nobody's unloaded their gun. Ina's furious with him because you're the big star at Empire now. And Estelle figures she's owed a certain amount of suffering for taking him back. I get daily bulletins from Shirley. She takes her mother's side, which just goes to show how wrong Freud was about fathers and daughters. It's a case of like mother, like daughter—they're not the kind of women who forgive and forget, I'll tell you that."

"Not many are, Myron."

"I guess . . . Let's go eat." Cantor stepped out and helped Dawn as she struggled to the ground in her long dress. He put one arm around her waist to steady her, and as she swung herself out of the cart to the pavement, he leaned forward to take advantage of their closeness and kissed her. She jabbed him with one gloved hand and he straightened up with an apologetic smile. Over his shoulder she saw a big La Salle limousine pass slowly by.

In the back, staring at her with undisguised hatred, sat Estelle Braverman and her daughter.

Cantor defied convention. Most movies proceed by orderly stages. He was still shooting and reshooting while the movie was being scored. He tested it with different endings. He threw them out and reshot the ending. Then he tinkered with the opening. He had so much at stake that he was unable to let go of it.

He tested each new version as if it were an experimental airplane. The routine was always the same. Kraus would pick a movie theater somewhere in Los Angeles and announce a "sneak preview." A full audience was guaranteed by the advance offer of free dishes. Dishes were one of Cantor's obsessions—dishes and glassware—because they brought in the older people, the married couples, and kept out the kids. "Everybody in Los Angeles is going to be eating off glass dinner plates before this movie is released," Aaron Diamond grumbled to Dawn.

Dawn had tried to avoid the sneaks, if only because Cantor's nervous tension built up to a crescendo for each one. The distributors were screaming for the movie, she knew, as were Braverman, the Empire board of directors and the exhibitors, yet Cantor went on, day after day, cutting whole scenes and even writing fresh dialogue, while Empire's stock, its price now dependent on the success of a single picture, sagged daily on Wall Street, pulled down by rumors that *Flames* was a bomb, so bad that the studio was unwilling to release it.

For Pasadena, with its upper-middle-class family audience, Cantor insisted she be present, and rather than fight about it, she gave in. She managed, at least, to get Aaron Diamond to take her—sitting in the limousine with Cantor, in his present state of anxiety, would be like sitting next to a time bomb.

It had been a long time since Dawn had been in a movie theater except for gala previews. People who made movies seldom if ever went to them, in the usual sense. It was curious, she thought, that all her childhood feelings of magic revived in the gilded lobby with its Egyptian columns and potted palms. "You want any popcorn?" Diamond asked, but popcorn was not part of Dawn's moviegoing experience.

There was a hushed silence as she walked into the theater itself. She heard the audience whispering her name, and she smiled at them, standing for a minute so they could see her. Then she sat down, prepared to enjoy herself, as the big Wurlitzer organ descended into the stage with a last flourish, its colored lights glowing in the semidarkness, while the dusty red-and-gold curtains drew back to reveal the screen.

The credits came on. There was applause at her name. When Cantor's name flashed by ("A Myron B. Cantor Production, produced by MYRON B. CANTOR"—when, she wondered, had he decided to invent a middle initial for himself?) there were a few discreet hisses, no doubt from some of the Empire people who were taking advantage of the darkness to express their feelings about Cantor.

Then the sound track rose, with the score for *Flames of Passion*, and Dawn found herself staring at her own face, magnified a thousand times. The camera rolled back to reveal her full-length, in a bare-shouldered eighteenth-century dress of silk and lace. It rolled back even farther to show her descending the magnificent staircase of the Carson mansion. All eyes were on her as she stopped halfway down and looked into the crowd. Her eye caught Richard Beaumont, splendid in the gold-and-scarlet coat of a British officer, then as she looked past him at a handsome young man in a severe black coat, her expression became more serious, the camera moved in to a close-up, and, with one quick change of expression, she indicated to the audience that there were two men in her life.

She had seen the rushes. She had rehearsed the scene again and again. It had been shot and reshot from different angles at least twenty times. She knew every frame of it by heart. But seeing herself on screen in a movie theater, as part of the audience, was a different experience. She was drawn into the movie as if it were fresh to her, and at the same time she could see that her performance was even better than she had hoped. The camera caught her beauty, but it went deeper. With one brief, sideways look, almost effortlessly, she conveyed a certain shrewdness, a hint of duplicity and cunning in the character; then she erased it with a smile as she reached the bottom of the staircase. There was no doubt about it: she had given Cantor what he wanted. It was up to the rest of the film whether his gamble had succeeded or not.

"Money in the bank," Diamond whispered through a mouthful of popcorn. "They got you cheap, kiddo."

In the gloom she could see Cantor and Kraus, huddled over a notepad. No doubt Cantor was still dictating changes, but as the movie progressed, Dawn doubted that they would be necessary. It held up.

When her face filled the screen and she whispered, above the swelling music (she must talk to Cantor, she decided, about toning that down in the final print), "Love—is everything!" she found herself crying like every other woman in the audience. As the lights went on, and she turned to Aaron Diamond, she saw to her astonishment that he was crying, too, tears running down his glossy cheeks from behind the thick spectacles.

She did not need to stay to watch the audience fill out questionnaires. She knew it was a hit. She put her arms around Cantor and kissed him. "Leave it alone, Myron," she told him. He nodded numbly.

"*If* they like it, maybe . . . there are still a million things to fix . . ."

"They'll like it. There wasn't any noise in the house. David always said you could tell by that. If they don't fidget, and if they applaud at the end—you have a hit."

"There were a couple of scenes I'd like to switch around . . ."

"It isn't necessary. The music is too loud at the end, though. It covers my line."

Cantor nodded toward Kraus. "Make a note," he barked. Then he smiled. "You know something? It's just the kind of thing a star would pick out. So, congratulations. You're a star!"

"I already was, Myron."

"Not like this, honey!"

It was true. She could hardly move through the lobby as people came up to her, asking for autographs or simply staring at her. She could feel their hands touching her dress, stroking her fur coat, plucking at her hair. A man pressed a miniature Bible into her hand. A woman grabbed her arm, an expression of blind ecstasy on her face, like somebody worshipping at the shrine of a saint. People began to push and shove each other, forcing their way forward for a closer look. A woman tripped and fell with a startled cry. Nobody helped her up—she was as trapped by the press of bodies as Dawn was herself.

Diamond was an old hand at this kind of thing. He grabbed Dawn's arm, and pushed his way through to the door, where the security guards cleared a space. Outside on the pavement, the crowd was even bigger, drawn by whatever mysterious rumor brings fans out to the right place at the right time. There was a sea of faces beneath the marquee, a mob of people shouting, "Dawn, Dawn, *Dawn*." Two rows of burly cops forming a narrow path to the car. "Smile, wave, and run like hell," Diamond ordered. She did as she was told.

It wasn't until she was in the car that she realized two or three people had managed to cut away pieces of her dress. She closed her eyes and put her head back on the seat. There was something in her hand.

She opened her eyes and looked at the tiny Bible. On the flyleaf an un-steady hand had written with painstaking care, in miniature letters, "Repent, for the day of judgment is at hand." She passed it to Dia-mond, who looked at it with distaste.

"You know what I'm going to do?" he asked, putting the Bible in his pocket.

"No," she said, "I don't." Most of Diamond's questions were rhetori-cal and demanded no answer.

"I'm going to buy myself some Empire stock, that's what I'm going to do. First thing in the morning." He took the Bible out again, pro-duced a gold pen, made a note on the title page and tore it out.

"What about *my* stock?"

"Sit on it. It's going to go up. The moment this picture is released, there are going to be people out there trying to take over Empire again. When that happens, you can name your own price. It's your goddamn studio, we play our cards right . . . listen, you're not playing around with Cantor, are you?"

The question took Dawn by surprise. Her mind was on her stock. "Good heavens, no, Aaron. What makes you think that? He's been after me to sleep with him since the first day we met, but that's just another one of his fantasies."

Diamond nodded. "You can't knock him for that. I mean, as fan-tasies go, it's pretty normal. The only reason I asked is Shirley Cantor has her ax out for you all over town. And her mother, too."

She laughed. "It's all nonsense. Believe me, Myron is not my type."

"You'd be surprised. I could tell you stories . . . If women stuck to their types, nobody would ever get laid."

"Aaron, Shirley doesn't have any reason to be jealous of me. And anyway, my private life is my business."

"Well, sure. All I'm trying to say is, be careful. You saw those peo-ple back there in the lobby, the street. Fans—they're all crazies. But they can turn nasty, and don't you ever forget it. They'll name their kids after you, wait in the rain for hours just to see you—but one bad scandal, and they'll turn on you. That's why you've got a morals clause in your contract."

"A morals clause? I didn't see it."

"It's buried in the goddamn boilerplate. *Nobody* sees it. But it's there. A studio can cancel a contract if there's any kind of moral prob-lem. Not that I'm suggesting there is. I just don't like hearing that Shirley and Estelle are badmouthing you."

"It will pass, Aaron. Myron's infatuated, but that's because we're working together. I think he's one of those men who always has to be in love with his star. The next picture, it will be someone else."

"Maybe you're right. But remember, it's okay to make enemies in this business—but never make enemies of the goddamn wives, if you can help it. You're getting all kinds of good publicity, and that's great. But you'd be surprised how quickly it can go the other way, kiddo." He stared at the moonlit Pacific as they crested Sunset Boulevard and turned onto the Coast Highway for Malibu. "It can wash you right out to sea," he said, his tone unusually serious for such a flippant man. "I've seen it happen."

"I'll be careful, Aaron," she said firmly. She felt a sudden, strong resentment, not so much against him as against the fact that an amorphous rumor, a piece of idiotic gossip, could damage her career, however untrue it was. She made up her mind she was not going to be another victim.

As soon as the moment was ripe, she would confront Braverman with her stock. In the end, that was what mattered: how much control you had. A star was just a hired hand, no matter how much he or she was paid. A major stockholder was someone to be reckoned with.

Their arrival at Richmond airport caused a riot; the crowds outside the theater had been so large that the governor called in the National Guard to surround the building. For a short time it had been thrilling, but then it became frightening—for she sensed that beneath all that hysteria was a hard core of envy. She had experienced crowds and riots in India as a child just enough to know how quickly the mob's mood could change, how unexpectedly a mood of holiday-making gaiety and good humor could erupt into savagery. She told herself that Americans were different, but at bottom she doubted it.

On Richard Beaumont, the experience had a more traumatic effect. The crowds terrified him. He needed at least two or three stiff drinks to face them. Worse still, Cantor had insisted that Cynthia accompany him. He wanted no scandals to mar his opening, and the Beaumonts were therefore under strict orders to play the loving couple. Just in case there were problems, a male nurse from the "rest home" in which Cynthia had recovered from her suicide attempt accompanied them—though Cynthia made a point of ignoring him.

Dawn glanced behind her toward the back of the chartered airplane and saw that Cynthia was asleep—which was hardly surprising, considering the number of pills she was taking to see her through the tour.

Cynthia's way of dealing with her suicide attempt was to ignore that it had happened. It was an accident, like falling off a horse, and the less attention paid to it, the better. She would not talk about it, even to Dawn, who had grave doubts about the wisdom of Cynthia's accompanying her husband on a tour that was exhausting and terrifying—and said so.

As for Beaumont, his nerves were pulled taut as piano wires by whatever combination of guilt, anger and fear he was concealing. Offstage he was, as Dawn knew well, enigmatic and subject to fits of instability—or lack of focus, to be more exact, as if he were constantly looking for some clue to his role. He required direction, in private life as much as on the stage, and Cynthia was in no position to give it, nor would he accept it from Cantor.

Surprisingly, Cynthia stood up well under the strain—rather better than Beaumont did, in fact. Perhaps it was the pills, Dawn thought, but there were moments when she herself was glad to be alone with Cynthia, who wanted nothing from her. It sometimes astonished Dawn just how much she cared about Cynthia—she had very little experience of friendship, particularly with women. She made sure that Cynthia was in sight whenever it was possible.

Cynthia doubled as a kind of chaperon. By staying close to Dawn, she made it difficult for Cantor to make a pass at her—though that proved unnecessary, for since they had left Los Angeles, his attitude toward her had been withdrawn and cold, as if he was holding back his anger at being turned down. He pushed himself forward at her side whenever there were crowds of reporters around; otherwise he kept to himself.

"I feel rotten," he said, now that he had her next to him, a note of self-pity in his voice. "Not that anyone cares."

Dawn decided to deflect this approach, if possible. She knew very well what was troubling Cantor, and it was the last thing she wanted to discuss. "It's pointless to complain about the reviews, Myron. From what I've seen, they're wonderful."

"That's not what I'm feeling rotten about, and you know it. You've been giving me the cold shoulder ever since we left L.A. *Before* we left L.A., in fact."

"Well, you've been in a lousy mood . . ."

"That's why, goddammit! It's driving me crazy. We're in the same hotel, but when I call your room, what do I get? Cynthia, for chrissake! I mean, have a heart. At least let's talk."

Dawn realized that Cantor, his patience apparently at an end, had her trapped this time. She could hardly squeeze past him, since he had dropped himself down, uninvited, into the aisle seat.

She wondered if it was worth pressing the button to call the stewardess for a cup of coffee, but decided that would only make him angry.

"I wish you'd drop the whole subject, Myron," she said firmly. "For both our sakes."

"Don't threaten me."

She sighed. "I'm not *threatening* you . . . I'm simply trying to make you understand we're not going to have an affair. . . ."

"You wanted me in London. I could tell. What's the problem? Now that you're a star and a goddamn lady, you think you're too good for me?"

"It's not that at all . . ."

"Goddamn right! You didn't feel that way in my office."

"Myron. You attacked me in your *bath*room, for God's sake! I pushed you off. You fell asleep."

"That's not the way I remember it."

"Well, that's the way it was. Have you any idea the things Shirley and your mother-in-law are saying about me? That's *your* doing, Myron! You're going around pretending that we're having an affair, and you know it isn't true. I think that's despicable. And I'll tell you what: If you don't leave me alone, I'm going to see Shirley when I get back to L.A. and tell her the truth."

"The hell with Shirley! I can take care of Shirley, if that's what's worrying you."

"I doubt that, Myron. But it's not what's worrying me. And lower your voice. Unless you want everyone to know what we're talking about."

Cantor turned red—he hated being told what to do. However, he lowered his voice to a rough whisper, and leaned over close to her. "Every time I go to bed with Shirley," he said, "I'm thinking about you. It's killing me."

"I don't want to *know* about it, Myron."

But Cantor, having made what seemed to him a romantic declaration, was unstoppable. "Hell—" he continued—"and not just with Shirley! Every time I *shtup*, it's you I'm dreaming of *shtupping*. Have you any idea what that's like?"

"Well, no . . ."

"It's hell, that's what it's like. I think I'm in love with you." He said it as if he were suffering from some rare and fatal disease.

The stewardess leaned over his shoulder. "We're coming in, Mr.

Cantor, so could you and Miss Avalon fasten your seat belts?" she said. Cantor's face turned red. "We're *talking*, goddammit," he shouted. "How dare you interrupt us!"

"I'm only asking you to fasten your seat belts."

"I rented this fucking airplane, chrissake, crew and all. You work for *me*! I don't have to fasten my seat belt if I don't want to."

"Suit yourself," the stewardess said with a look of disgust. Dawn fastened her seat belt with a loud click, just to show whose side she was on.

"I don't like to be pushed around," Cantor explained to Dawn as the plane bumped down the wet runway toward the waiting crowd. "Not by *anybody!*"

"Nor me," she said firmly.

He stood up, ignoring her remark, as well as the stewardess's warning to stay seated until the aircraft came to a halt. "*Nobody* says 'no' to Myron Cantor," he growled, then looked toward the back of the cabin and frowned. "You better get back there and talk to Cynthia. She looks to me like she's been drinking. Where the hell could she have gotten it? That goddamn nurse is supposed to keep his eyes open."

Dawn knew the answer to that. The cut-glass perfume bottles in Cynthia's makeup case were full of liquor.

"Go help out," Cantor ordered, lighting a cigar despite the stewardess's frown. "If there's one thing I don't want, it's a goddamn scandal."

Cantor had hired the Plaza's main ballroom, then, panicked by the possibility that he would be unable to fill it, had sent out twice as many invitations as he originally intended to, with the result that it was almost impossible to move or breathe in the crush of freeloaders. At one end of the big room, Dawn, Beaumont and Cynthia stood beside Cantor in front of an unruly crowd of photographers and reporters, while Kraus, with the help of the hotel staff and the studio publicity men, tried to keep the guests away from the stars.

It was one in the morning before the press left, and by that time Cynthia's sedation had worn off. In the noisy crowd of guests that swirled in front of Dawn and Cantor, she appeared from time to time, dancing with total strangers, and finally with one of the waiters, her body pressed tightly against his. Dawn felt a sudden stab of guilt at having let Cynthia out of her sight.

"Where the fuck is Beaumont?" Cantor growled. "We've got a problem."

"I don't think it's one Dickie could solve."

"You British! We've got to get her out of here."

"I think she'd make a scene, Myron."

"She's making a scene *now*, for chrissake. She's practically jerking that guy off in front of half New York. Where's her goddamn nurse, for that matter?"

"*You* decided she could handle this without him tonight, Myron."

"I must have been out of my fucking mind. I'm going to ask her to dance with me. I'll move her out toward the door. Wait for me there. Then we'll get her upstairs and put her to bed."

Cantor, when his own interests were at stake, was a man of action. It took him all of two minutes to cut in on the waiter, to whom he palmed a hundred-dollar bill, and without too much trouble he took his place, squeezing his body hard against Cynthia.

He pushed her through the crowd on the dance floor as if she were a hostage, then, when they reached the door, he took one arm and Dawn the other, and together they dragged Cynthia into the corridor.

A man in a dinner jacket followed them into the lobby. "Got a problem?" he asked. He had the plump, pasty face of a hotel banquet manager, with the sad, dark eyes of a man who has seen everything more than once, and hasn't liked any of it.

Cantor handed him another hundred-dollar bill. "We want to get the lady up to her room quietly," he said. "She's not feeling well."

The man nodded. "Follow me," he said. He led them down the corridor, pushed open a fire door and rang for the service elevator. When it came, he handed the elevator operator a ten, nodding to Cantor to indicate that this treat was on him.

"What floor?"

"Twenty," Cantor said.

"Get your fucking hands off me," Cynthia said.

"Things like this happen in hotels all the time," the man said philosophically.

"Sod off!" Cynthia said.

The elevator bounced to a stop, and the grill doors crashed open. "Here we are," the man said. "No one the wiser." He peered at the service operator's denim overalls and said, "Thanks, Harry." He followed Cantor down the hall to the Beaumonts' suite, then patted his pockets. "Damn!" he said, "I don't have a passkey."

"We can go through my suite," Dawn said. She unlocked the door while the two men followed behind her, supporting Cynthia on either side. At the far end of the suite, Dawn unlocked the connecting door to the Beaumonts' suite. She opened it and Cynthia stumbled through it, stood for a moment as if rooted to the spot, then screamed.

On the bed, in the light of the bedside reading lamps, Richard Beaumont lay on his stomach, naked except for a pair of black silk socks and his evening shirt. On top of him, his face contracted with pleasure or pain, was Cynthia's male nurse.

The scream was followed by a ghastly silence. Then Cantor said, "Oh, Jesus!"

"I'm going to be sick," Cynthia said in a quiet voice.

Dawn led her to the bathroom, then went back into her suite, where Cantor and the banquet manager were standing together, already deep in conversation.

"We've got a problem," Cantor said.

"I would say so," the man said quietly.

"How much of a problem?"

"That's hard to say."

Cantor took a roll of bills from his pocket and peeled off five hundred dollars.

The man pretended not to have seen them.

"How much, for chrissake?" Cantor asked.

"How much have you got there?"

"Don't be greedy, goddammit. I can get you canned."

"And I can go to Walter Winchell and tell him what I saw, Mr. Cantor."

"He'd never print it. He couldn't."

"Maybe. Maybe not. He could *hint* at it."

Cantor sighed. He tossed the roll at the man without counting it.

Dawn went back to the bathroom and tried the door. It was locked. She called out to Cynthia, but there was no reply from the other side. She banged on the door.

Cantor and the banquet manager appeared at the sound.

"She's locked herself in," Dawn said.

Cantor banged on the door. "Open the fucking door, honey!" he shouted. When that had no effect, he leaned over, his lips at the keyhole, and whispered in a more winning tone. "Please open up, baby—

we're here to help you." There was no answer. "Cunt!" he said, straightening up.

"I can go get a passkey," the banquet manager said.

Cantor nodded. Then, from outside, there was the noise of police sirens. Cantor's doughy face turned white. He kicked the door, then backed off and gave it a blow with his shoulder that made him grunt with pain. Muttering what might have been a prayer to himself, he took a gold nail file out of his pocket and jimmied the lock with the dexterity of a man who has done it before.

The door opened. He pushed his way in, followed by Dawn. The white marble-tiled bathroom was empty. For a split second Dawn thought there must be another door—prayed there was.

But there was none. The window was wide open, the filmy curtains blowing in the breeze.

One of Cynthia's pale-blue silk evening shoes was on the windowsill.

"He wants to see you right away," Kraus said. His eyes were so pale that the whites seemed darker than the pupils. There were deep circles under them.

Dawn thought she probably didn't look much better. The one thing she hadn't brought with her to New York was a black suit or dress, and she had begun the day at Mainbocher's, hastily outfitting herself for mourning. It was no disadvantage that Mainbocher had insisted on selling her a black hat with a veil—there were reporters everywhere, and she had been obliged to enter the Empire Pictures Building on Fifth Avenue by the freight entrance and go up to Cantor's fifteenth floor New York office on the service elevator.

"There can't be any more bad news."

"One wouldn't think so, no. But there is, judging from the tone of Myron's voice."

"Where's Dickie?"

"*That's* been taken care of, at least—thank God! He left for England early this morning, on the Pan American Clipper. He's going to join the Royal Air Force, so he'll be safely out of sight." Kraus took off his glasses and rubbed his eyes. "You'd better go in."

"Sit down," Cantor said. There was a slight tremor at one corner of his mouth. Several patchy places on his face showed where he had scraped himself shaving. He looked like a man on the verge of collapse.

"Are things that bad, Myron?" she asked, trying to be sympathetic.

"Not as bad as they're going to get."

"Cynthia's dead. I can't think about anything else."

"You'd better start thinking fast. There's a rumor going around that the reason she threw herself out of the window was because she discovered you and Dickie in bed with each other."

Dawn pulled back her veil and stared at him in astonishment. "That's ridiculous."

He shrugged. "People didn't *know* he was a faggot. Hell, *Cynthia* didn't know! As rumors go, it makes a lot more sense than most."

She had to admit, on reflection, that Cantor was right. Cynthia was known to be suicidal—the sight of her best friend in bed with her husband might have been enough to make her kill herself. It would add up—to those who didn't know the truth.

"Who's spreading the rumor, Myron?" she asked quietly. It crossed her mind that Cantor might have done it himself. Anything would be better, from his point of view, than a homosexual scandal that involved his leading man.

He broke the pencil he was holding. "I'm not too sure . . ."

"Come off it, Myron. You *know*. I can see that. Did your people think it up?"

"No . . ."

Oddly enough, she thought, he looked as if he was telling the truth. "What happened to the male nurse, by the way?" she asked, watching him closely.

Cantor sighed. "I gave him a couple of thousand bucks and told him to vanish. I guess he did."

"I see. And let me guess. The banquet manager has vanished, too?"

"I thought it was the smart thing to do."

"And Dickie is off somewhere in England. So it would be my word against—whose, Myron?"

He stood up and walked over to the window. "Jesus," he said, "what a way to go! Do you think she knew what was happening on the way down?"

"I don't want to think about it at all, Myron. I asked a question."

"Okay. Shirley started the rumor. She talked to Louella and it's all over Hollywood by now. Tomorrow it will be all over the country."

"It's just a rumor. I'll deny it."

"Sure. The more you deny it, the more people will believe it's true." He turned away from the window and faced her, his hands in his pockets. "Look," he said, "everything is a two-way street, know what I mean? I'll tell Shirley to shut up. I'll even make her retract the story. I can do that, you know. And if I can't, her father can. I'll do that for you—but only if there's a little understanding between us. . . ." He lit a cigar, eying her shrewdly through the smoke.

She shook her head. She was prepared to do a great many things for her career, but sleeping with Myron Cantor was not one of them. She decided to stall him, however, for the moment. "This is hardly the time to talk about it," she said. "Not with poor Cynthia hardly even cold in her grave yet . . ."

"She isn't *in* her goddamn grave. She's still at Frank E. Campbell's."

Cantor came over and stood next to her, his feet apart like a boxer's. For a moment, Dawn thought he was going to hit her. She stood up quickly, but he merely pointed his cigar at her. "I can help with this," he said. "But with me against you, you're washed up. Think about it. Don't make me do that, kiddo."

"I told you once before, Myron. I don't like threats."

"You picked the wrong guy to play hardball with, baby. I can make sure you never work in Hollywood again."

"Oh, piss off!" Dawn said. "Use that line on starlets. There's no clause in my contract that says I have to sleep with you."

"Give me one good reason why you won't," Cantor shouted.

"Because you're an ugly, conceited, overbearing little man, Myron, that's *one* reason. And because—when it comes to bed, I think you probably talk a bigger game than you play."

He put down his cigar and grabbed Dawn's wrist, his eyes unfocused with rage, like those of a man who has just been hit on the head, or drunk a bottle of liquor against the clock on a bet.

His grasp was harder than she would have expected. She tried to pull away, but couldn't—Cantor was holding her tightly, his face close to hers. She knew he was on the edge of violence, but strangely she felt no fear. A year ago, two years ago, she would have been frightened, but not anymore. She grabbed Cantor's cigar from the ashtray where he had placed it, jabbed its glowing end as hard as she could into his crotch, and held it there.

There was no immediate effect. Cantor was so busy trying to make up his mind whether to hit her or kiss her that it was several seconds before he noticed the smell of burning cloth. Even then, though he was puzzled, he didn't react. Then he felt the warmth and gave a blood-curdling scream as the cigar burned its way through to his flesh. He leaped backward, releasing her from his grasp, and clutched his crotch, burning his hand, so that he screamed again.

Dawn watched the scene calmly. She was confident that Cantor's private parts, for what they were worth—and obviously they were worth a good deal to Cantor, to judge from the high-pitched terror of his voice—had not been seriously damaged.

He was struggling to say something, but between his groans and a steady, inventive stream of curses, it was difficult to make any sense of it. She listened more carefully and caught the word "Help!" Obligingly she took the stopper out of Cantor's gold-plated Thermos pitcher and tossed a full quart of ice water at his crotch. He gave another scream, then retreated behind his desk. From the expression on his face, his terror was giving way to humiliation.

Dawn took her handbag and walked to the door.

"I'll send a check for a new pair of trousers, Myron. Will a hundred dollars do it?"

Cantor sat down, realized he was about to ruin the pale-cream sueded pigskin desk chair and stood up again, one hand held in front of him like a fig leaf. He was trembling.

"You go fuck yourself. You can kiss Hollywood goodbye. You have a morals clause in your contract, baby. This rumor is all I need to suspend you."

"I couldn't care less, Myron. Empire isn't the only studio in town."

"Don't be so goddamn sure. You haven't got Konig around to protect you anymore. Believe me, there won't be a studio in town will touch you, when I'm through."

The sooner she was back in Los Angeles to talk it over with Diamond, the better, she decided. After all, she had cards of her own to play.

She walked out without looking back.

"Look at the bright side," Aaron Diamond said on the telephone. "Even Fatty Arbuckle made it back." He paused and coughed. "Under a different name, of course," he added cautiously.

If there was a bright side, Dawn couldn't find it. Cynthia had been ignored by most people in Hollywood while she was alive; now that she was dead, she was being treated like a martyr. The story of her death took on an instant life of its own—people embellished it with details, claimed to know someone who "was there," swore that they had known Dawn and Dickie Beaumont were having an affair for *months*. . . .

She was determined to fight back. Her stock was in Aaron Diamond's hands. Now was the time to use it. No sooner had she reached Los Angeles than she ordered Diamond to find Cynthia's nurse. If he could be bribed to vanish, he could almost certainly be paid to tell the truth—or a part of it, anyway.

"It's worth a shot," Diamond agreed, but for three days she heard no further news from him on the subject. The house was surrounded by reporters—she could not leave it without flashbulbs popping in her face and a running barrage of questions, but the worst of it was not the press but the fans, who, as Diamond had predicted, turned against her.

All day long a small group of them stood outside her house, staring at its whitewashed walls like the chorus in a Greek drama, waiting for her to show her face. Across the highway, one man stood for hours every day, holding a sign that read, "Repent, for the wages of sin are death." Dawn, who had found in Los Angeles a kind of freedom, now found herself trapped in her own house. Even the few friends she had "in the industry" were anxious to keep their distance.

Inside the house it was dark, the curtains pulled tight. People strolling along the beach stopped to gawk, some of them even bringing binoculars. She glared at them from behind the gauze drapes with anger—these were not fans; these were the people who lived in Malibu, movie people, her own kind, invading her privacy just as surely as the man across the highway with his hand-lettered sign, or the reporters lying in wait for her at the end of the driveway.

On the third night, when the telephone rang, she picked it up with a certain reluctance. Like most stars she had an unlisted number, but it was not impossible for people to reach unlisted numbers—they were in address books and on the desks of too many secretaries at the studio to be fully secure. She picked the receiver up gingerly and to her relief heard Diamond's rasping voice.

"I got him, kiddo," he said. "He's in my office. I'll send a car for you."

"Will he tell the truth?"

"Maybe. He'll say you weren't in bed with Beaumont. He won't say *he* was. You can't blame him for that."

"It's a start."

"It'll cost ten thousand dollars. It's not negotiable."

"Pay it."

"I already did. Half now, half when he's gone public for us."

"I'm on the way."

"Hey! Don't do that. I'll send the car, have it parked a couple of houses down the road. Walk down the beach, the driver will be waiting. Nobody will even know you've left the house . . ."

She felt a sudden, overwhelming need for release, for freedom. She had had enough of being a prisoner in her own house. "Don't bother, Aaron. I'll be there in half an hour."

She tied a scarf around her long hair, put on a pair of sunglasses and walked to the garage. As quietly as she could, she opened the garage door and peered out into the dimly lit alley. At the end of it she could see the glow of a few cigarettes—the press was still waiting, by now, no doubt, reduced to a few patient second-stringers. She did not turn the garage lights on. With a growing feeling of excitement, she stepped into the big white convertible and pressed the starter. All she had to do was to clear her name and use her stock. She could hardly wait to see Cantor's face when she told him he was working for her. She had all the cards in her hand, at last.

The engine turned over quietly—the car was worth every penny David Konig had paid for it with such reluctance. Even in gear, the noise was hardly more than a whisper, drowned out by the monotonous booming of the surf.

She did not turn the car's lights on. If the press got in her way, she would knock them down, just the way Morgan had driven through the rioters so long ago in Calcutta.

She breathed deeply, bit her lip, stabbed down on the accelerator, and felt the big car lurch down the narrow alleyway, barely clearing the walls. She heard shouts, a flashbulb popped, she saw a man throw his cigarette away in panic and take a flying leap up the trellised wall, scrambling to reach the top, his face white with fear; then she was out of the alley. She speeded forward, causing the reporters to run for cover again, backed up, shot forward and found the way clear to the Pacific Coast Highway. She heard someone laughing, then she realized that it was herself. Her hands were trembling, but she held the big car steady at sixty miles an hour, suddenly free again.

For the first time in three days, she felt her optimism returning. She would attack the rumors head-on. She would confront Marty Braverman with her stock. She would *not* be defeated. She could smell the honeysuckle and the oleander in the evening air, drowning out the salt smell as she pulled away from the sea and into the outskirts of Santa Monica. Behind her a car closed in, climbing fast. It shot by her, and a man leaned out with a press camera. The flash momentarily blinded her. She speeded up, for there was another car behind her now—in fact, as she looked in the mirror, there was a long row of cars, at least a dozen. The press was on the move.

Dawn was not a confident driver, but anger made her reckless. She took a sharp right down a dark residential street without slowing down, slewed left, then left again, then sharp right onto Sunset, where she put her foot down hard.

There was nothing behind her. Then she saw the headlights of a car turning onto Sunset, and guessed that at least one reporter had managed to follow her. There was a turn ahead, and she took it at high speed, determined to throw off her last pursuer. She skidded into a side street, looked back in the mirror, then turned to look ahead of her and saw an ancient sedan moving slowly down the center of the road, straddling the white line. Her headlights caught the astonished face of an old lady, with glasses and blue-rinsed hair, her eyes wide—but before she could open her mouth to scream, Dawn had twisted the Cadillac sideways, missing the other car by inches.

She was sober now, her excitement drained away by fear. She would drive the rest of the way at thirty miles an hour, she told herself, and the hell with the press! But when she put her foot on the brake, the car skidded sharply, bouncing up onto the pavement, out of control.

She held on to the wheel for dear life, but it no longer seemed connected to the steering. She saw a carefully manicured lawn, a child's bicycle, a red fire hydrant, illuminated in the white beams of the headlights. The car was spinning now, almost as if it were in slow motion. She saw a palm tree in front of her, appearing suddenly in her path as if it had grown out of the ground like something in a Disney nature film, but before it had even registered on her mind that she was going to hit it (or was it going to hit her?) she heard a noise like a thousand dishes breaking and felt something like a stinging rain on her face.

There was the sound of someone moaning, a sharp metallic noise as a piece of chrome fell off the car and rolled out onto the concrete pavement; then she realized her face was wet and wondered why she hadn't noticed it was raining. Was that the reason the car skidded? The rain was warm—even hot.

It was all very mysterious and thinking about it made her tired. She went to sleep. In her dreams she heard people talking in hushed whispers, felt a needle prick into her arm. Somewhere there was a ringing bell, the wail of sirens, muted, and yet somehow very loud. She dreamed she was in a gleaming white room, with rows of powerful lamps overhead—was it a movie set of some kind? She saw strange shapes in white gowns, moving through a kind of fog, and then heard a voice counting backward from ten.

Why backward, she wondered? Then she noticed the harsh, rhythmic sound of someone breathing deeply and the feel of something cold and clammy over her face. "Jesus, what a mess," she thought she heard someone say—an unfamiliar, ghostly voice, in the far distance, almost as if it were coming from underwater.

Was it the owner of the lawn she had ruined? She tried to apologize, but the words wouldn't come, though she did hear somebody say, "Sorry," again and again, in a voice so thin and frail that she couldn't recognize it.

CHAPTER 18

THERE WERE NO MIRRORS allowed in Dr. Echeverría's clinic. His patients would see themselves only when the doctor ordered it, not before. He took photographs of them before he began the treatment, so they would remember what they had looked like when it came time to pay the bill. When he judged it was time for a patient to look at the new face he had created, Dr. Echeverría always made a small ceremony of it, unveiling the mirror in his own office (which was normally covered with a heavy curtain) as if he were presenting an object of art.

No sooner had Dawn arrived at the *clínica* in Cuernavaca in the doctor's Rolls than she was brought to his office. He greeted her with grave courtesy from behind his massive antique desk. His eyes were dark, sad, soulful, as if he had absorbed all the suffering of his patients; his features were craggy—a nose like a jagged fragment of marble, a powerful chin, heavy sensual lips. His head was massive, the chest and shoulders those of a wrestler or a weight lifter, but his hands, in startling contrast, were long and fine, the hands of a violinist or a concert pianist, with long, graceful fingers and the blunt, sensible nails of a surgeon.

He was vain about his hands, she could tell that at a glance from the way he used them to express himself, occasionally lowering his eyes to admire them, as if they were someone else's. It was not until he stood up that she realized what should have been obvious when she first entered the room: Echeverría was a dwarf. The leonine head and huge torso were supported on the tiny legs of a child, as if his upper body had been created by a sculptor in the heroic mold, who had left the task unfinished.

Her eyes must have registered shock, for Echeverría smiled—he had wonderful teeth, strong, white and even—and gave a small shrug.

"When I first began to do cosmetic surgery," he said, "there was much criticism. Surgery was for saving lives, not for the trivial purpose of making people happier or more beautiful. A colleague told me, 'It's not medicine's task to change what nature has done, for frivolous reasons.'" Echeverría laughed. He had a low, deep voice and his laughter was like the boom of the surf. "Who knows better than me that nature doesn't always do her job properly? Sometimes she needs help. As for man-made problems, those we are surely free to correct. How long is it since—your accident?"

"A month." She had woken from an uneasy sleep to see Aaron Diamond sitting beside her, holding her hand. There was no pain—only the thin, sour taste of nausea from the anesthetic, and the sudden terror of realizing that her face was wrapped in bandages. He had patted her hand and promised her she'd be fine, but his eyes told the story—he could not look at her while he was speaking.

Against everybody's advice, she had insisted on seeing her face two days later, when the bandages were changed. She had stared for a second at the unfamiliar apparition in the nurse's hand mirror, suddenly numb with shock and grief. Her face was crisscrossed with livid scars, her lips were black and puffy, there were deep, purple bruises under her eyes. She closed them against the sight. She had not looked at her face since.

Echeverría turned on a battery of powerful lights, aimed them directly at her, then pulled over a stool, adjusted it for height and sat down in front of her, so close that they might have been lovers. Gently he removed her veil, then cut away the bandages, which he dropped on the floor. For a full minute he simply looked at her, then he ran his fingers over her cheeks with a touch so light that she was hardly aware of it. "The bandages have been changed every day?" he asked.

She nodded. Daily the nurse had pulled them away, washed her face with a saline solution and rebandaged it. Dawn had closed her eyes so she would not have to see the nurse's expression. She did not want to see pity there. She refused to see any visitors except for Diamond. She did not want to hear any news. No announcements were made to the press—only those who were close to her knew that her face had been damaged. She took refuge in Diamond's house in Palm Springs like a wounded animal, lying in a darkened room, wondering if she would ever be able to appear in public again.

Echeverría smiled encouragingly. "Have you been reading the newspapers?" he asked.

She shook her head. She wanted to hear his opinion about her face.

"What a sensation you're making. 'Star's mystery disappearance.' Half the press is looking for you, the other half is making up stories about you. . . . You were very lucky. To go through a windshield, face first . . . it's not exactly a beauty treatment."

"I know. I saw it."

"Ah. You looked. Well, that's inevitable. Curiosity is natural. Even when we don't want to know, we can't help looking. And what did you see?"

She did not reply. She had seen the end of everything that mattered to her.

"You saw something ugly where there had once been great beauty," Echeverría said, answering his own question. "Well, the healing process isn't pretty. What did the doctors in Los Angeles say?"

"That I was lucky to be alive."

"That's true. Of course, doctors always say that. What else?"

"That there would be some permanent scarring." She remembered the surgeon, a big, bluff, hearty man, a golf player or weekend yachtsman, from the look of him, saying to her, "You'll still be a great-looking woman, so don't worry. You may have some problems with close-ups—but hell, that's what makeup is for."

She had asked him about plastic surgery, but he merely shrugged. "You're better off living with the scars," he had advised. "You'll get used to them. Hell, nobody's perfect. Most of those plastic surgeons are quacks anyway."

"Permanent scarring!" Echeverría chuckled. "Well, he was tactless, but in a way it's true. We can't remove scars from the skin. But we *can* reduce them to the point where they become invisible. *You* will know they're there. God will know. But nobody else will know, except me. They did a decent job of patching you up, you know. That's a plus. If you were a man, I would say, 'Go home, leave it alone.' The lines will be faint, not too obvious except in a bright light—no big deal, as Americans are so fond of saying."

"I want to look exactly the way I did."

"You're looking for a miracle? Well, that's what we perform here. I must warn you, however—it will be a long and painful treatment. There are risks. You may wish you'd been willing to settle for something less than perfection."

"No," Dawn said. "That's what I've come here for."

"Very well. It will be expensive—I should add that. And there are no guarantees."

"I don't care what it costs."

"I wouldn't want you to think it's entirely a matter of greed. Who knows what my services are worth? Only the patient can judge. But we provide here an establishment—an environment—in which our patients can feel at home. You will have a suite of rooms overlooking a beautiful garden, a personal maid, who is even now unpacking your bags, your own private terrace, so you don't have to see the other patients if you don't want to. There is a first-rate chef, a hairdresser, a manicurist, even a cosmetician. We have a sauna, a heated swimming pool, tennis courts, a gymnasium, a diet expert—though you don't need *his* services, I think. All this costs money. About the telephone system, there is nothing I can do—it is slow and inefficient. This is Mexico."

"I won't be getting many calls. Only my lawyer knows I'm here."

He nodded, and glanced at her file. "And under the name of—"

"Miss Kelley."

"The staff is discreet, I assure you. They are well paid, precisely to ensure their discretion." Echeverría leaned over and examined her face again, this time at greater length. He took a long, thin needle from his pocket, dipped it into a jar of sterilizer and touched it against the scars, barely pricking the surface. "You feel it?"

"Yes."

"Good! The tissue is still alive." He switched off the lights. "The skin!" he exclaimed with enthusiasm. "It is one of nature's wonders—maybe the *most* wonderful. Thinner than the finest paper, elastic, unbelievably strong, self-lubricating, self-repairing—it even has a memory of its own! The hardest skin to work with is that of Anglo-Saxons, particularly those with light skin color and blond hair. Their skin is fragile, almost brittle. It does not heal easily, particularly if it has been repeatedly tanned. The skin of tropical or Mediterranean peoples is much tougher, more resilient. It responds better to treatment. You are English, I believe?"

"I was. I'm American now."

"I mean you were born English. The skin doesn't care about the name on your passport."

"Yes."

Echeverría shook his finger at her like a schoolteacher. "Listen to me," he said. "Between us, there is no room for the small vanities. I have to know what I'm dealing with. This is not English skin. The color, the thickness, the elasticity, the slight oiliness . . . It's wonderful skin, you're lucky to have it, but your parents weren't English."

"My father was. Well, he was Irish, at any rate."

"And your mother?"

There was a long silence. She found it impossible to lie to Echeverría. His eyes demanded truth. "Half Indian," she whispered. "I was born in Calcutta."

"Ah!" he said triumphantly. "I should have guessed. The coloring is not unlike that of certain of our mestizos, but finer, much finer. Mixed blood is nothing to be ashamed of. In Brazil, for example, people are proud of it. But I see it gives you trouble?"

"It wasn't anything to be proud of in India, Doctor. It isn't in England, either. And in the United States, even less so."

"Anglo-Saxon madness! It takes a certain mixture of the races to produce good skin, you see—just the way the best wine is made from a combination of different grapes. Anglo-Saxon skin evolved because the people lived in a climate where there was very little sun. In Ireland, where it rains all the time, you see young women with the most beautiful skin, like pearl, like *milk*—but when these same people move to the subtropics, to places like California or Mexico, they lie in the sun and bake their skin until it's dry, cracked and brown. White skin is a freak of nature, dear lady—a genetic mutation evolved in a bad climate. If your mother weren't Indian, you would have these scars on your face for life. As it is, we have something here to work with, thank God."

For the first time in weeks, Dawn laughed, despite the lingering pain she felt when her skin moved. "You're very persuasive," she said. "But it's not something that's easy for me to admit."

"I saw that."

"In fact, Doctor, you're the first person I've ever admitted it to."

"I'm honored. Listen, I'm not stupid. You're a movie star. You don't want your fans to know you're of mixed blood. Maybe you don't want the men in your life to know, also. That's possible, though in my opinion, it's silly. Well—in commerce and in love a certain discretion is sometimes necessary, I admit. But you shouldn't think they're *right*, Lady Konig. One must always accept what one is, without shame, even if one has to lie about it."

"It's not easy . . ."

Echeverría stood up. He smiled gently. On his feet, his head was at the same height as hers, though she was sitting down. "Easy?" he asked. His voice was humorous and kind. "Who says it's easy?"

He sat down at his desk. Behind it, with his big shoulders and *beau-laid* face, it would have been impossible to guess that he was in any way abnormal. "You've heard of dermabrasion?" he asked.

She shook her head.

"It's a new technique. It requires time, and great delicacy. There is a certain danger of infection. We go one small step at a time, therefore. It is not a big dramatic procedure. If you had a problem with your nose, or some gross trauma, I could perform one big miraculous operation, and you'd think I was a genius. Instead, day by day, I'm going to reduce your scars. It will be boring, and sometimes painful. You'll become impatient. You'll wonder if I know what I'm doing. Be assured in advance—that's normal. I will start by cutting away the scar tissue where it's raised above the level of the skin—that's the most delicate kind of surgery. I will close the incisions with stitches that are so fine they will be almost invisible. Then all that must heal. We'll change the bandages constantly, many times a day. When the healing process has begun, we'll rub your face with Vitamin E to keep the skin supple, and with a sulfurated saline solution to prevent infection. You will hate the smell—the Vitamin E comes from fish oil, I'm afraid. You will follow a strict diet, no stimulants, and stay out of the sun. When I think you're ready, I will then begin to abrade the damaged surface of the skin, only a small area at a time, again and again, like a carpenter turning a rough plank of wood into a beautiful table. The one thing I have to ask you is that you don't look at your face during the process. It won't be a pretty sight, and any kind of shock or depression on your part hinders the process. The skin is affected by the moods, just like the rest of the body. You will have to trust me. I'll decide when you're ready to look at what I've done."

"I trust you," Dawn said. And for the first time since her accident, she felt hope. She would put everything else out of her mind, out of her life.

She would stay here as long as it was necessary.

The terrace of Dawn's suite looked out over a broad expanse of carefully trimmed lawn. At the far end there was a luxuriant tropical garden. Exotic birds—cranes, parrots, peacocks, Chinese pheasants—strutted across the lawn or perched among the flowering trees. At dawn, the gardeners silently made their way across the lawn, brushing it with whisk brooms, trimming it by hand, tending it with such care that it almost seemed that they were performing a religious rite.

Dawn took her walk then, when the rest of the patients were still asleep and she had the garden to herself. The crystalline pool, set in solid rock, steamed in the early-morning sun. Around it was a sculpture garden—male and female nudes, in bronze and marble, heroically proportioned and flawlessly beautiful, like a temple of youth. Dawn wondered if they had been chosen by Dr. Echeverría, for they seemed to symbolize exactly the grace and perfection his own body lacked. At the end of the garden was a high wall, and beyond it a grove of eucalyptus trees, a glimpse of an even more luxurious garden and the red-tiled roof of what appeared to be a vast Spanish castle.

In the evenings she sat on her terrace, looking across the garden with curiosity. Echeverría often joined her there. He nodded approvingly as a servant wheeled Dawn's supper in on a trolley. He ate simply himself, and preferred his patients to do the same, though they could order anything they wanted. "Fruit, vegetables, a little chicken," he said. "You eat sensibly."

"I always have."

"That's good. The worst part of my work is that my patients go back to their lives and destroy it. I do what I can with the flesh, the skin—then the patient goes home and drinks, smokes, eats too much, and it's all for nothing. Of course, they come back, but each time I can do less."

"Nobody can stay young forever, I suppose. Even with your help."

"Well, that's easy for you to say. You are twenty-four years old. At twenty-four, youth seems to stretch on forever. The aging process has hardly even begun. Yet that's the time to start thinking about it. There's no reason why one can't be youthful forever. But one has to approach it with discipline."

"How?" she asked, fascinated by the idea—and also by the passion in Echeverría's voice. When he talked about beauty, he was mesmerizing: his eyes took on a hypnotic quality, the muscles in his face tightened as if he were a prophet, he touched his hands together gently, at the fingertips, as if there were an electric current between them.

She could not help wondering if he was like other men—if his sexuality was normal, like his shoulders and head, or dwarfed, like his legs.

"I will teach you what I know," he said. "But tell me this: Do you enjoy life? You are twenty-four. I've read about your life. No doubt much of what I read is untrue, but still—you married a man thirty years older. You have worked hard to become a star, and now it's been taken away from you. If there is a man in your life, you've never mentioned him, so I conclude there isn't. What did you tell me when you arrived? The only person who would call you here was your lawyer? I don't call that enjoyment. You have cut yourself off from your past, your childhood, your ancestry, but what have you put in their place? Your career? Money? Fame? Look what happens. When I give you back your beauty, what will you do with it?"

"I thought I'd go back and start again," she said defensively. Aaron Diamond telephoned daily to urge the same thing.

"I can repair your face. Already, there's tremendous progress. I can teach you how to eat, how to exercise, the importance of rest—all child's play. But to be beautiful, the body needs more. It needs love, happiness, sex, *joy*, just as much as it needs restraint and moderation. More, maybe."

"I think I had that once. Or almost had it."

"And then?"

"And then other things got in the way. It didn't seem to be what mattered."

"To desire beauty for its own sake is destructive. The purpose of beauty is happiness. It should make you happy. It should make other people happy. Otherwise it's just a burden, one that gets increasingly hard to bear as the years go by. I wanted to be a psychoanalyst, you know. It's more important to repair the mind than the face. But I couldn't stand hearing an endless stream of people's guilts and fears every day. So much guilt. So much fear. In the end, even in training, it weighed me down. I couldn't breathe. . . . You have no children, I think?"

"I had a miscarriage. The doctor said I would never be able to have children after that."

Echeverría shook his head. "I've seen your medical records, you know. I doubt that he was right. The English are light-years behind in this sort of thing. Today it's just a question of a simple operation. The odds are, you could have all the children you want. . . ."

"I don't want any." It was obvious from her tone that Dawn was displeased by the news. As long as it was physically impossible to have children, the matter was closed, and no fault of hers. She had no desire to learn that it was her choice.

Echeverría noticed, as he noticed everything. "Children can be a great comfort," he said.

"Not to someone of mixed blood—as you tactfully put it."

"Ah." He sighed. "Myself, I'm in favor of life in any form—or color. But then you might say that I have a special interest in the subject. In the old days, I'd have been left out on a mountaintop to die. . . . However, there's nothing worse than doing something that will make you unhappy—I agree with that. Unhappiness is a great sin when it can be avoided—a waste of life. . . . You know that big house over there, the one like a castle?"

She was relieved at the change of subject. "On the other side of the wall?"

"Exactly. La Casa de Oro. It's Prince Charles Corsini's house. You know him?"

She shook her head.

"The banking family. He's immensely rich. A rather ambiguous reputation, but I've always found him charming, personally. His wife died in a boating accident a year or so ago, and Corsini never recovered from it. He wouldn't *let* himself recover from it, you see. He's seldom here—the house sits unused. He's given up his polo ponies, he doesn't go out to parties, he's buried himself in his banks, here, in Argentina, God knows where else. . . . He feels guilty, so he can't stop grieving. But it's a pointless exercise. He *wills* himself to be unhappy, you see. . . . If grief and guilt could bring people back to life, there'd be no need for graves. . . .

"I must leave you to your sleep," he said reluctantly. "Another four weeks, perhaps five, and I'll be done. You can look at your face then. After that, you can go out, walk around, get used to the world again. Small steps at first, you understand."

Dawn smiled at him. "I shall find it hard to leave here."

"No," he said, standing up. He kissed her hand with grave courtesy. "When you see your face, you'll be anxious to leave and get back to life. That's my reward—and my pain."

Dawn rang for the servant to take away her meal. She stared out into the darkness. Mexico was like the India of her childhood—night came instantly, and brought with it total darkness and silence.

In the distance, beyond the trees, she thought she saw a light in the Corsini house—Casa de Oro, was it called?—but when she looked again it was gone.

"It's a miracle!" she said, grasping his hand.

"No. It's discipline on your part, skill on mine. If you were to look very carefully, under bright lights, you would see faint traces of my handiwork. Think of it as my signature, like an artist's on a painting."

"It's not my face anymore," she said. "It's yours."

"Ours," he corrected. "Go out, go shopping, go to the market, a little at a time. Get used to being seen. You can wear a veil to begin with. The skin is still delicate. I don't want it exposed to the sun, or to too much dust. No makeup. The time for that will come, but for the moment, the skin must breathe. We must still keep it bandaged part of the time—but less and less. My work is done. Yours is just beginning."

"I wish I could *say* it's your work. Nobody will know."

He shrugged, then turned off the bright lights. "You'll know," he said. "I'll know. That's enough."

He pressed the bell on his desk for the nurse and turned away from her to look out the window.

For a moment she felt his loneliness, but already there was a part of her mind that was making plans, thinking about the future, impatient to be back in Los Angeles. She wanted to rush over and kiss him, but she knew it was impossible.

She followed the nurse down the hall.

That night he did not come to dine with her.

Each day, like a swimmer going deeper into the water, she went out into the crowded streets of Cuernavaca, accompanied by her maid. At first she was terrified of being recognized, and even more terrified of an accident—of anything touching her face, or striking it.

Gradually, both fears subsided. Cuernavaca was full of rich foreigners. The natives had better things to do than to gawk at them, and were too courteous to do so anyway. To avoid her own kind of people, who might recognize her or even try to talk to her, Dawn went early every morning to the market. She did not need to shop, but it was something to do, a pleasure she had never had the time for in Los Angeles or London. She felt strangely at home among the stalls and the crowds, as if her life had come full circle, for the market reminded her of India: the flowers, the noise, the clamorous beggars, even the smells, were all unmistakably familiar. She wore a long, bright-pink robe, almost like a sari, and wound a white silk scarf around her head. Except for her sunglasses, she might almost have been a Hindu lady in purdah shopping in the bazaar.

She selected a mango, smelling it, squeezing it gently with her fingers.

She pulled back her scarf and pushed her sunglasses back to pick the coins out of her purse, and as she lifted her head, she suddenly realized a man was staring at her. Damn! she thought. She had been recognized.

She wondered if he was a journalist, but no journalist would be as well dressed as this man was. Besides, the expression on his face was not one of curiosity, or even surprise, but of intense shock, even terror, as if he had just seen a ghost.

Was he someone she knew? He was standing under an awning, in the shadows, so it was hard to tell. He seemed in his forties, tall—about six feet, more or less, she guessed—with the slim waist and broad shoulders of an athlete. What she could see of his face under the brim of an expensive panama hat was handsome.

For a moment she was tempted to say something to him—it had been a long time since she had talked to anyone but Dr. Echeverría— but when she moved, he gave an embarrassed, apologetic smile, as if he was ashamed of staring at her so obviously, or perhaps relieved that she *wasn't* a ghost, then stepped back into the shadows and vanished among the market stalls.

She handed the mango to the maid, and more out of curiosity than anything else, made her way through the market in the same direction the man had taken.

Around the corner, in a narrow street behind a church, was a gun-metal-gray Rolls-Royce. A chauffeur in livery was just shutting the door. Behind the pale smoked glass of the passenger compartment, she saw the man who had been looking at her. His head was back against the seat and he was wiping his face with a handkerchief, as if he had only just escaped from some terrible accident by the skin of his teeth. Then the motor started and the big car glided off, honking the crowds away.

He did not look back.

He did not appear again in the marketplace in the days that followed. Dawn was surprised by her own disappointment.

She did not mention the incident to Dr. Echeverría, whose manner was ever so slightly cooler. She knew it was nearly time to go, but every day she hesitated, unwilling to pick up the telephone and start making arrangements with Aaron Diamond. The picture of the stranger haunted her. She felt she could not leave until she knew who he was, yet he remained invisible—though once she saw his Rolls-Royce from a distance, moving down a side street at a stately pace.

She had almost given up hope; then, a week after she had seen the man, he suddenly emerged from a small doorway in the garden wall while she was taking her early-morning walk.

At first she thought it was one of the gardeners, for she only saw a tall figure standing by the wall in a kind of niche. Behind him was a wrought-iron gate. *"Buenos días,"* she said, but then she heard a strange voice, not at all Spanish in tone, say "Good morning," and looked up to see him.

Despite the early hour, he was again faultlessly dressed—a dove-gray suit, a white shirt, a black tie—strange clothes for a resort. He was not wearing a hat this time. His hair was blond, straight and combed back. The face was strong, handsome, but by no means conventionally attractive in the way of Hollywood leading men. The nose was far too large and skewed to one side; the mouth, too, seemed large, with deep lines on either side of it, though the most noticeable feature of his face, apart from the eyes, were the high, prominent cheekbones.

Together with the sharp, predatory nose, they gave the man the look of a bird of prey which has just flapped its way back to its perch with a rabbit in its talons, a look which was at once expectant and wary. His eyes were startling: a smoky, grayish-blue color, which seemed to reflect the sky; his ears had very small lobes and were pressed so flat against his head that his silver-blond hair hid them almost completely under two elegantly shaped winglets ending in points very much like feathers. The comparison was an apt one, Dawn decided. Whoever the man was, he had the look of an eagle.

"Prince Charles Corsini," he said. "I owe you an apology."

She laughed—he seemed unnaturally serious. "You might have given me a lift home from the market!"

He smiled, a little uncertainly. She wondered if his understanding of English was as good as she had assumed. He had perfect teeth. "You must have thought me damnably rude," he said. "Staring at you like that. The fact is, you reminded me of someone I knew. Of course, I suppose you're used to people staring at you. . . ."

"Not quite like that, actually. How did you know I was here?"

"It's a small town, Lady Konig," he said vaguely.

She raised an eyebrow. "Oh, dear," she said. "I was hoping nobody would recognize me. I've been admiring your garden every morning."

"Yes? You must come and see it. But I'm interrupting your walk, I think."

"I don't mind. You can join me if you have nothing better to do."

"I have nothing better to do at all," he said. "Normally I'm not an early riser." He offered her his arm. "Have you been here long, in Cuernavaca?"

"Nearly three months."

"Three months! You must have been terribly bored. It's not the most exciting place in the world."

"I was—recovering from an illness."

"Ah. Echeverría is a remarkable fellow, is he not? I sold him this house, you know, when he decided to open a clinic."

"You're in real estate?"

"No, no. I *own* a lot of real estate, here, there, everywhere, but I'm really an investment banker. People here were against having a clinic— the rich always hate change. I did not agree. Echeverría is a genius. So I sold him this. Often I used to walk over here in the evenings for a chat with him." He lit a cigarette. "Not that I've ever followed his advice," he added, with a laugh.

"He said you hadn't been living here for some time."

"It's true. This isn't really my home. My father came here to escape from the winter in Argentina—not that the winters there are so bad, but he loved the sun. He was Italian, from Naples."

"You sound as if you were educated in England."

"Yes. A most unpleasant experience, by the way. Beatings and cold baths. Luckily, another boy taught me how to feign the symptoms of asthma, for a price. At the drop of a hat I could produce a coughing fit until I was blue in the face. I even scared myself. So my parents sent me to school in Switzerland, where I was much happier. You have no idea how difficult it is to be a foreigner in England when you're young."

"Oh, I think I do. I wouldn't have thought an Italian prince would have been thought all that foreign, though. . . ."

"Being a prince only made it worse, I can assure you. That was bad enough, but coming from Buenos Aires I was treated as a dago as well, you see. A wop, a dago and a prince . . . a heavy cross for a schoolboy to bear."

"Then you're actually Argentinian?"

Corsini shrugged evasively. There was apparently no such thing as a simple answer where questions about his life were concerned. "I was born in Argentina," he explained. "I still have many interests there. In fact, I have the honor to be the Consul General of Monaco to Argentina—a post which does not require my residence in Buenos Aires, happily. My deputy does whatever little work is involved, but I have a Monegasque diplomatic passport. I am welcome everywhere." He paused and corrected himself. "Almost everywhere, that is. . . . Nobody hates Monaco. In this century nothing is more important than picking the right nationality."

"You seem to have thought of everything."

"I try. As a banker, it's second nature."

"You don't look like a banker."

"I take that as a compliment. But mine is not the kind of bank where you go to cash a check or take out a loan to buy a car. It's a small private-investment bank. I know everybody thinks bankers are dull, but it's not at all true, you know. Banking is a very romantic business, really. All good bankers are romantics. Will you have lunch with me tomorrow?"

For the first time in many years she felt a sudden excitement about a man. Corsini had walked her around the garden back to the gate. Behind him, the turrets of his house rose above the trees. White doves nestled on the tiles. "Yes," she said. "Yes, I'd love to."

He bowed and kissed her hand, holding it in his fingers just an instant longer than formality required. Then he was gone.

It was amazing, she thought, how slowly the rest of the day passed.

"Corsini? Forget it!" Aaron Diamond squawked, his voice barely discernible over the telephone. He was irritable. He had telephoned—at some inconvenience to himself, since it took hours to get a call through. He had been cut off three times already. "We got important things to discuss," he said. "You better get back here fast . . . fantastic box office . . ." His voice died out, though she caught the words, "Myron," "Marty," and "stock." Then Diamond came back again, suddenly clear. "I don't want to go into more detail over the goddamn phone."

"Who *is* Corsini, Aaron? I've only just met him today. I'm having lunch with him tomorrow."

"For God's sake, don't get mixed up with Corsini, kiddo. Do yourself a favor."

Dawn was in bed, the telephone receiver pressed hard against her ear. "I'm not 'mixed up' with him, Aaron. I was only curious."

Diamond either didn't hear this or didn't believe it. His voice rose and fell abruptly as he continued his warning in more detail, most of it lost in static. Despite the bad connection, she could hear his anxiety. ". . . Bank of Europe and the Americas . . . Just a front for Corsini . . . The Rio de Plata Bank . . . There was almost a revolution—

or maybe there *was* one, I can't remember . . . Of course his father
was a swindler on a giant scale . . . Vatican money, and worse. . . ."

"Aaron, I only asked who he is. How do you know so much about
his business life?"

"I read *The Wall Street Journal* and the financial pages, for chrissake, which is more than you do. *Everybody* knows about Corsini. He's
bad news. They say Princess Corsini killed herself, you know."

"The mother?"

"What mother? The *wife!*"

At first sight, Corsini's house was gloomy enough to be the cause
of a domestic tragedy. Hidden by trees, it seemed unnaturally large for
a resort town like Cuernavaca. From some angles it resembled a Ba-
varian castle; from others, a Spanish monastery.

Corsini greeted her in a hall that would have been appropriate as the
setting for a joust.

"Unusual, isn't it?" he said, following Dawn's eyes as she stared at it.
"My father bought the whole hall in Belgium, and had it shipped over
here and reassembled. It took two years to do."

"He must have been a remarkable man."

"Remarkable? I would say so. This is nothing. In Buenos Aires he
built a much bigger house than this. He liked things to be *solid*, you
see. . . ."

Corsini led her through a succession of large rooms full of heavy,
bulky antique furniture. They did not pause until they reached a
smaller room, overlooking the garden, which Corsini seemed to have
made his own. It was painted white, furnished with a few impeccable
antique pieces and decorated as if he had set out, in sheer desperation,
to prove that he existed as a separate person in his father's house.

Against one wall was a cabinet full of sporting trophies, a theme du-
plicated in the thicket of silver-framed photographs on every flat surface. There was Corsini playing polo, Corsini golfing, Corsini taking a
horse over a fence, Corsini skeet-shooting, Corsini in a race car, Corsini
leaning against the wing of an airplane, Corsini standing alone, or with
his team-members, wearing the costume of every imaginable expensive
and dangerous sport.

In some of the photographs, the more informal ones, there was a
young woman beside him, fashionably dressed and jeweled. She had

long, dark hair, full lips, a small, oval face with high cheekbones. The expression in the large dark eyes was remote, even when she was smiling, as if she had no connection at all to the event that was being photographed, or perhaps to Corsini.

The young woman was at once beautiful and eerie. Dawn studied her with a certain amount of curiosity while Corsini prepared two Margaritas at the bar, wondering if this was the wife who had committed suicide, and if so, why. There were no clues in the face or the pictures.

It was not until Corsini returned with the drinks that Dawn realized she had missed the most important fact about the late Princess Corsini, if it was she.

She had exactly resembled Dawn!

They ate in the garden, overlooking a swimming pool that seemed large enough to drydock a battleship, except that it was full of small marble islands, each one bearing a massive sculpture in the Roman style: gods, goddesses, cherubs, lifesize horses, dolphins and grotesque monsters writhed, fought, embraced and spouted water. "A folly," Corsini said apologetically. "My father had it built as a birthday present for my mother. Unfortunately, most of it is useless. She couldn't swim, you see, so half the pool is built to a wading depth."

"Your father must have been very rich."

"Grotesquely so. He had a natural talent for making money. Even his mistakes usually turned out to be profitable. Not for other people, you understand, but for *him*. I am the same way myself. It's the Midas touch. I should have thought your late husband had it, too."

"Not really. David's gift was for *spending* money."

"Ah, that's quite a different talent. I am lucky. I have the gift for both. Of course, this war is a damned nuisance. I wouldn't normally be here at all. I have a lovely apartment in Paris, where I've lived for years. Frankly, I don't find South America a stimulating continent. The polo in Argentina is first-class, but you can't play polo all day. Unfortunately."

"You're not fond of Cuernavaca, either?"

Corsini shrugged. "I came here to check on certain properties I have. I had intended to stay a day or two." He leaned forward, his eyes bluer than ever in the reflected light from the pool. "To be honest," he said, "I stayed on only because I saw you."

In a large, ornate cage behind them, cockatoos and macaws sat. Dawn felt Corsini's hand touch hers. It was a warm, strong hand, and the feeling was by no means unpleasant. "Are you staying here long?" he asked, his fingers still on hers, touching them with a gentle pressure.

"I haven't decided."

"Stay awhile," Corsini said quietly. "It would give me great pleasure to show you around. There is much to be seen in Mexico. I don't think you'd be bored."

She hesitated. She knew it was important for her to get back to Los Angeles and her affairs. Then she looked at Corsini and shook her head. "I haven't any immediate plans."

He smiled. "Excellent," he said. He took a cigarette from the silver box beside his plate. A servant ran from the terrace to light it. "I'm wonderful at making plans."

It was true. Nothing was left to chance, yet she never had the feeling of being hurried or overtired. Partly it was the fact that he had innumerable people in his service, or obligated to him, or anxious to please him. In a country where money and influence counted for everything, he appeared to have both. Museums in Mexico City were opened for them at night so they could look at the treasures there in peace and quiet, accompanied by the Minister of Culture himself. Churches and monasteries that were closed to the public were opened for Corsini, with a monsignor or a bishop to act as a guide.

Everywhere they went, a car waited, with a chauffeur in white and a bodyguard in a dark suit. In the back of the car there was always a crystal vase of flowers. In Guanajuato, where a nineteenth-century governor who admired all things French had caused a replica of the Opéra in Paris to be built, they watched a performance of La Bohème, alone in the vast, ornate auditorium, a bottle of champagne between them, while Corsini cried unashamedly—for he was a man of deep and unaffected sentimentality about music.

Dawn had been debating for days whether she should provoke Corsini into making love to her—was that, she asked herself, what he needed or expected? She felt a passion for him which she was sure—or almost sure—he shared, yet something held him back. They returned one evening to their hotel in Mexico City, after an elegant dinner party at the Portages', where Corsini, as always, had been solicitous, polite and charming, in his curiously reserved way. He kissed her goodnight, and she went to her suite. She took off her makeup and slipped into a nightgown, then heard a gentle knock at the door. "Come in," she said, thinking it was the hotel maid.

But when she turned around, it was Corsini, still in evening dress and carrying two flutes of champagne. He put them down, walked over to her and kissed her. It was a very different kind of kiss from the one she had received a few minutes before. She wondered if her scars were visible, but he gave no indication that he had noticed them.

"I've been thinking . . ." he said.

She gave him a searching look.

"I've been thinking—it's time I told you I love you. I knew it right away, you know," he said. "At first sight."

"What took you so long to say it, then? Did you want to be sure?"

"No, no. I was always sure. I wanted *you* to be sure. I felt you needed time. Sometimes, when things move too quickly, they end quickly. . . ."

Charles took off his jacket and put it on the back of a chair. He was not the kind of man to leave his clothes on the floor. Then he lifted her up and carried her to the bed. As she helped him undress, feeling his arms around her, running her own hands down his muscular back, Dawn wondered, for just one moment, whether in his mind it was her he was making love to or someone else, the other woman in the photograph, who had committed suicide—and whom he had never, in the ten days they had known each other, once mentioned. Then as she was overcome by pleasure, she realized that she didn't care.

If there was one subject that gave Dawn trouble, it was love. Corsini said he was in love with her, but what did that mean to him? What she felt for Charles Corsini was far stronger, whatever it was, than anything she had ever felt before—strong enough to frighten her, for she wanted him, despite his secrets, the mystery of the wife he never mentioned, the possibility, if Diamond was right, that he was a swindler on a colossal scale.

She did not even want to know the truth about him—if there was an unpleasant truth. He was rich, attractive, charming, fascinating—and he loved her. More important, she was beginning to accept that *she* loved *him*.

Daily now, the telephone messages from Aaron Diamond were appearing, picked up from the clinic by Charles's servants. She knew she had to go back, and yet she allowed Charles to persuade her to stay. Every day she mentioned that she would have to go home soon, and every day he smiled agreeably and found something new to show her, something new to do.

One day, toward the end of the third week since they had met, she finally forced herself to confront him. They were dining in the garden of his house, surrounded by flowers and the scent of honeysuckle, while she talked about the future, the need to make a decision. She must leave, she told him, by the end of the week at the latest. He nodded, as if he had finally accepted the fact. He whispered to one of the servants, who returned in a few minutes with a package.

Charles rose from his seat, drew her to her feet and kissed her. Then he slit the paper open with a silver-gilt fruit knife and handed it to her. She reached in, pulled out a flat black leather box and opened it. Nestled in the dark velvet was a diamond-and-emerald necklace, with stones so large and perfect that it surpassed any piece of jewelry she had ever seen.

She stared at Charles, who gave a small shrug, almost as if he were apologizing for the gift. Then he gently placed it around her neck and nodded with satisfaction. "It was my mother's," he said. "I don't think it would be possible to assemble such stones today. Even then, it wasn't easy. My father gave Stern, in Amsterdam, the first stone and asked him to find a dozen that matched it perfectly. It took Stern five years to collect the diamonds. He rejected hundreds that were almost right, but had the wrong color, or simply didn't please him. The emeralds my father found in Brazil. Stern rejected dozens of them, too, until he was satisfied he had a perfect match. The gold for the mountings, by the way, came from one of my father's own mines. He knew that would please my mother. He was a very sentimental man."

Dawn felt the weight of the necklace around her neck. The stones were cold when Charles had placed it there, but they seemed to warm to the temperature of her skin. She felt herself beginning to cry. "I can't accept it," she said, although even as she said it she knew that she could, and must.

Charles looked at her, for once very seriously, and in a low voice said, "I beg you to." Then he took her hand, slipped an emerald ring on her finger and whispered, "I want you to marry me."

"Yes," Dawn said, astonished at the sound of the word in her own ears.

He took the ring off. "It will need to be made a size smaller," he said. "It too was my mother's. I'll have it seen to tomorrow."

Dawn was struck by the ease with which he could turn his mind to practical questions, even at a moment of high emotion. Then it occurred to her how little she really knew about the man who was to be her new husband. In three weeks, she had learned next to nothing. . . .

She put the thought out of her mind firmly.

One of the servants brought her the letter. Dawn was lying in the sun by the pool, spending a rare day by herself while Charles went about his business, whatever it was. He sometimes left her little messages, but the handwriting on the stationery of Las Mañanitas hotel was not his. She tore the envelope open and read the note. Within an hour, she was dressed and on her way to the hotel.

At Las Mañanitas lunch was being served. Dawn walked through the crowded garden from table to table, ignoring the admiring glances of the men, but there was no sign of the man she was looking for. Then she saw him, sitting by himself at a small table under an umbrella, far away from the noise and the music. He took off his sunglasses and waved his newspaper at her, then rose as she sat down, clicking his heels.

"You look wonderful!" Kraus exclaimed. "Not better than ever, that's impossible, but as good as ever. I've had a difficult time finding you. You're not staying at the clinic anymore?"

Dawn ordered a glass of orange juice from the waiter. "I've been busy."

"*Here?* Anyway, I telephoned the clinic. They said you'd gone. Finally, somebody told me where you were, but I couldn't find out what the telephone number is. I know Diamond thought it was a good idea for you to keep away from the press, but don't you think you're going too far?"

"I'd forgotten all about the press, actually."

"Diamond's been going *crazy*. Finally, I agreed to come down here and find you."

"Has Cantor changed his mind? You can tell him to go to hell."

"No, no . . . he's still furious, of course, but that's not the point."

"You're still working for him?"

"Not exactly. Myron's temperament is not that of a businessman or a manager—as I don't need to tell you. I am now doing at the studio all the things that bore him. I report to him, naturally. But I also report directly to Braverman and the board—which Cantor doesn't know. That's why I'm here. The studio is in trouble."

"I thought *Flames of Passion* was a hit."

"It is. The unfortunate publicity about you even helped business. But Cantor's no good at providing product. No studio can survive on one big picture a year. It's been, what? A couple of months since it opened. The trades are asking what's next. We need lots of pictures— steady, reliable merchandise. . . . So the stock is slipping, there's a cash-flow problem, Braverman is sending up smoke signals to Wall Street for help. . . ."

"I don't see what that has to do with me."

"Don't you? You've been down here too long. You have a substantial interest in the studio, dear lady. You stand to lose a fortune if things go on as they are. And anyway, the other shoe has finally dropped."

"What shoe?"

"Braverman has guessed you have Konig's stock. He's terrified you'll sell it to one of the sharks that are circling around him. Of which there are plenty—your old friend Dominick Vale among them, which shouldn't surprise you. He's busy buying up stock. People like that can smell blood in the water from miles away."

"Vale? Why Vale?"

"Why not? He has hotels, casinos, partners with access to plenty of cash—most of it illegal, but never mind. They'd love to own a studio."

"And exactly what is it that you think I should do, Kraus?"

"Sell your shares to Braverman, of course. He'll pay almost anything, I assure you. His control is paper-thin, as things stand. With your shares he'd be secure. And he could force Cantor to back down over your contract. That could be made part of the deal."

"And if I don't want to sell?"

"There'll be great pressure on you to sell—some of it possibly un- pleasant. My advice is to sell out to Braverman, fast, for a good price. You'll be rich, you can resume your career, and there's nothing anyone can do about it."

"What does Diamond think?"

"Much the same. That's why he . . ." Kraus fanned himself with his panama hat. A strolling guitarist stopped by their table, smiled and began to play. Kraus handed him a five-dollar bill. "Please go away— V*aya!*"

"I'll think about it."

"For how long, please? This is an urgent matter. Perhaps I've failed to make that clear?"

"You've made it clear enough. I still want to think it over. And perhaps talk to someone about it."

Kraus looked alarmed. "Forgive me, but it's also a *confidential* matter. Speed *and* secrecy are necessary."

"I understand that."

"You have to trust me, Dawn. I've taken a considerable risk to myself in coming down here."

"I appreciate that, Kraus."

Kraus nodded. "There's another piece of news, by the way."

He glanced around the garden. He seemed reluctant to get on to the next piece of news. "I suppose it's restful down here," he said, glaring at the peacocks on the lawn. "You are still under treatment? When can you come home?"

"Any time. I've been traveling. Kraus, I did do something quite out of the ordinary a few days ago. You're the first person I've told, but I think you should know. . . ."

"What's that?" he asked.

She hesitated for a moment. "I got married," she said.

Kraus stared at her. "*Married?* What do you mean, you got married?"

"You know: marriage. 'For better or for worse,' and so on. Except they don't say that in Mexico. The Minister of Justice married us. He wore a red-white-and-green sash. He looked very nervous, poor man, until I explained that I was a widow. He thought I'd been *divorced*, you see, because I'm a movie star. This is still a very Catholic country."

Kraus was flustered. "Fascinating. If I may be permitted to congratulate you . . . Who is the—ah, your husband?" He dabbed at his forehead with a paper napkin.

"I've got a new title. I'm no longer Lady Konig, Kraus—I'm Princess Corsini now. What do you think of that?"

Whatever Kraus thought of it, he seemed unable for the moment to express his feelings, or even breathe. His face turned the color of skimmed milk, and his eyes opened wide, like those of a fish that has just been hooked. "Charles Corsini, oh, my *God!*" he croaked.

"What on earth is the matter, Kraus?"

But Kraus had regained control over himself at last. "I've been rude," he said between gasps. "I'm sure Corsini must be a man of great charm . . . every happiness . . . needless to say . . ."

"I didn't mean to shock you with the news."

"No, no. My fault. No doubt much of what they say about him is untrue."

"What *do* they say about him?"

"He has a reputation for a certain ruthlessness in business, Dawn . . . exaggerated, I'm sure . . . in America, they blow these things up out of all proportion. I imagine he's learned his lesson."

"*What* lesson?"

"He was involved in a famous financial scandal, you know. Then, right in the middle of it, his wife—ah, died. . . ."

"Aaron said she committed suicide."

"That was the verdict, I think . . . although. . . . Listen, I must be getting back to Los Angeles. I have a plane waiting for me in Mexico City. . . ." Kraus stood up, his pale eyes flickering back and forth, as if he didn't want to look straight at Dawn. "I have a piece of news that isn't about business . . . I don't know if this is an appropriate moment—under the circumstances. Lucien is alive."

"Alive? Thank God! Where?" It was the one piece of good news wanting to make her happiness complete.

"He's a prisoner of war."

"Have you heard from him?"

"No. Basil Goulandris told me. It's perhaps not the most opportune time to give you the news."

"Of *course* it is. I'm so pleased to hear he's all right."

"It may be a long war," Kraus said ambiguously, but before he could pursue the subject, a chauffeur in livery appeared on the steps.

"Charles must be looking for me," Dawn said. She gave Kraus a quick kiss. "I'll think about what you told me."

"Do," he said with unusual firmness. "Think *hard!*"

He made his way out through the hotel to the street, where his own car and driver waited. He could imagine what Braverman's reaction to the news would be—all but the most powerful Wall Street financiers trembled at the mention of Corsini's name.

He felt a headache coming on and he opened the window. The dust on the narrow highway was so bad that he rolled the window up again and resigned himself to several hours of suffering. He wondered how much Dawn knew about her new husband.

There was one consolation, he told himself, trying to think clearly despite the throbbing pain in his head. At least Corsini couldn't get back into the United States. The Department of Justice would never give him a visa.

Then he gave a groan so loud that the driver stared at him in the rearview mirror. For despite Corsini's reputation—despite the long record of raids, speculations, asset-stripping, dubious stock issues and even more dubious foreign connections, even despite the bankruptcies and scandals that so often followed in the wake of his financial activities—there was in fact one way Corsini could enter the United States— one way that nobody could stop him.

He could marry an American citizen!

CHAPTER 19

IT DID NOT TAKE DAWN more than a few days of marriage to realize that while Charles Corsini liked to give the appearance of a man who has nothing to do but amuse himself—and others—it was a deceptive pose. She was anxious to get back to Hollywood, her career and her stock, but Charles seemed happy to let the days pass by, busy in his own way, finding ever more elaborate ways of putting her off.

From time to time he retired to his study to make telephone calls or receive visitors, most of them men in dark suits who arrived by limousine. Hidden away in the depths of the big house was a small staff of secretaries and assistants, who appeared from time to time with black leather folders full of papers for Charles to read or sign.

He made no secret of the fact that details bored him, as did everyday routine. The bulk of his banking affairs ran smoothly without him. Charles was not interested in what he called "nuts and bolts." He sometimes bought companies without knowing or caring what they produced. He seemed to have no special skills or knowledge, certainly no interest in visiting factories or examining their products. It was the balance sheet that interested him—the long rows of close-packed numbers, with their footnotes and asterisks had an implacable logic that appealed to him, a poetry to which he responded naturally.

"It's like reading music," he explained. "Some people can look at a score and in their heads they hear the subtleties of the music, the nuances the composer intended, without hearing the piece played—indeed it may never be played so well, so sensitively, as it was in their heads, and perhaps it never can be. . . ."

He gazed out over his garden, as if it too were the balance sheet of something. "They say Beethoven played on a keyboard without strings," he said, to himself as much as to her. "Silent music . . . And yet people say bankers are dull."

Charles was certainly not dull; he was complex, a man of deep passions, who worked overtime to conceal the fact. His easygoing charm concealed a streak of jealousy, as Dawn discovered the night of Kraus's visit.

"You met a friend today?" he asked. He was smiling, but the pale gray-blue eyes were narrowed, as if he were about to judge whether or not her explanation was satisfactory. Obviously news of her visit to Las Mañanitas had reached him via the chauffeur or the hotel staff.

She nodded. "A business acquaintance. Eberhart Kraus. He used to be David's assistant."

"You should have invited him to dinner, darling."

"He couldn't stay. He only flew down here to give me a message."

Charles raised an eyebrow. He threw some nuts at the birds on the lawn. He did not show any particular interest, but his expression was wary. "This man Cantor has relented, perhaps?"

Dawn had often discussed with him her problems with Cantor. Charles was sympathetic and understanding—he had experienced much the same kind of thing himself, he said. One had to be patient. "No," she replied. "Cantor is still making trouble. What's worrying Kraus is my shares in Empire."

"Shares?" Charles seemed to perk up at the word.

"When I arrived in California, David set up a corporation for me, you see. . . ."

Corsini nodded. "Sensible," he said. "It would have saved you quite a bit in taxes. Of course, California is not the best place to domicile a corporation. The company owned your contracts?"

"Yes."

"So far, so good. Apparently Konig was no fool."

"Of course, he didn't tell me much about it, you see. I didn't even know I *had* a company until just before his death. David simply gave me some papers to sign. I didn't think they were important."

"It's a great mistake to sign something without reading it, darling. Even from your husband."

"I know that now. Anyway, one of the things I signed was a piece of paper which made my company the owner of David's stock in Empire Pictures. I never even looked at it. I didn't find out I owned the stock until some time after he died. I suppose one could say that I was lucky to have signed, but I'd still rather have known. . . ."

Charles's expression did not change. He was silent for a moment, obviously turning this piece of news over in his mind—or *not* obviously, for if Dawn had known him less well, she would have been unable to guess that he was interested. "Then you own a sizable piece of Empire?" he said, in a tone that implied she might just as well have told him that she owned a dog or a collection of English antique silver.

"As it turns out—yes."

"If only it were Alcoa or Dupont or IBM! Empire stock is . . ." Charles made a fluttery motion with his hand to signify instability, then arced the hand down like a diving airplane.

"So I was told."

"Still, looking on the brighter side, it's not without interest."

He blew a plume of cigarette smoke into the still evening air and watched it float away. "A motion picture company," he mused. "One could do a *lot* with a motion picture company."

"Kraus thinks I should sell my shares to Braverman. Diamond does, too."

"Do they? Personally, I wouldn't, darling. If you wanted what the Americans call 'a quick buck,' perhaps it would be the smart move— and the least trouble. . . . But you don't need a quick buck, not now that you're married to me. What you have in your beautiful hands is an opening wedge. I've been thinking of going back to America for some time, you know. . . . Capital is pouring into South America from Europe, but it doesn't want to *stay* in South America, you see. Nobody trusts the governments there—there is greed, corruption, the fear of revolution or expropriation. A banker who could promise his European clients their money would find its way to New York would make a fortune. Are you following me?"

"Yes, I think so. What kind of clients, Charles?"

He shrugged. "A banker never wants to know too much about his depositors, darling. We don't have a confessional booth in our banks. Perhaps the Church. Perhaps some of the more farsighted Nazis and the Fascists—those smart enough to guess Hitler will lose. Perhaps a few of the rich Jews who still hope to escape from Central Europe . . . Oh, the money is there, all right, just looking for a way to flow, like water that's been dammed up." He picked up her hand and kissed it. "Will you let me advise you?"

She thought about it for a moment—a moment too long for Corsini, who squeezed her fingers gently. "You can trust me," he said. "I love you."

"I do trust you, Charles. But I don't want there to be any secrets between us."

"Secrets?" Corsini stared at some invisible point just over her head. He seemed to be looking for his next words, as if they were about to appear on the garden wall behind them in writing. When he finally spoke, his voice was flat and matter-of-fact.

"I have no secrets from you. Your friend Kraus has told you that I was in trouble in America? It's true. The government accused me of breaking the banking laws. Mistakes were made. I put too much trust in my associate—an American called Luckman. It's all in the record. I can get you the press clippings. I admit, it's not a creditable episode. But it's not an unusual one, either, in the financial world."

"I believe you, Charles. I don't want to see the clippings."

"So? What else is there?"

"Tell me about the woman in the photographs."

"Alana? She was my wife," he said quietly. His voice was so flat that either he felt no emotion or he was making a heroic effort to conceal it. "She died. . . ."

"She was very beautiful."

"Yes. Not as beautiful as you."

"What did she die of?"

"Life. She had a very sensitive nature. Small things upset her greatly—out of all proportion. An unstable temperament . . . We wanted children. You understand, when my father was still alive there was a certain dynastic pressure—he wanted to see the beginnings of a new generation before he died. But Alana for some reason couldn't have children. She miscarried, and every time she blamed herself. And perhaps I wasn't sympathetic enough. I was younger then, less patient. There were other things, too—no marriage is without its problems."

"But how did she die, Charles?"

He did not answer for a moment. "A swimming accident," he said quickly, obviously unwilling to go into detail. "The body was never found. That somehow made it worse. I don't know why."

"She looked very much like me."

"Yes? There *is* a certain resemblance, I suppose," he admitted reluctantly.

"More than that—we might have been twins! Was that why you wanted to meet me?"

Charles stood up. "We should have discussed this earlier," he said. He clenched his hand firmly around her wrist. "No, no, don't be afraid. I'm not going to hurt you, Dawn. If I'm angry, it's at myself, not you."

He dragged Dawn into the house, pulling her after him at a quick pace, led the way upstairs, two stairs at a time, and pulled a key out of his pocket. "You may as well see for yourself," he said. "After that you can decide as you please. But before that, let me say that none of this means anything to me anymore. It's part of the past. I haven't been here since we married."

Corsini unlocked the door and pushed it open. "Go in, go in," he said impatiently. "I'll turn on the lights."

He stepped over to the big double window, pulled the curtains apart and opened it. From outside came the sounds of birds. There was nothing particularly horrible in the room, to Dawn's relief. Then she looked more closely, and realized that it was virtually a museum. On the makeup table were rows of cosmetics and perfumes, silver-backed brushes, an antique jar with eyebrow pencils, all of it perfectly ordinary, but somehow sinister because it was obviously untouched.

Facing the bed was a portrait of the young woman in the photographs downstairs, holding a bunch of flowers in her hands, the dark, luminous eyes already reflecting, though it must have been painted long before her death, a certain sadness that the painter had recognized in his subject.

Corsini flung open one of the closets. Inside were rows of dresses, neatly hung, and row after row of shoes, each with its own monogrammed shoe-tree neatly in place.

"I couldn't bear to throw any of this away," Charles said. He seemed, for the first time since Dawn had met him, exposed and vulnerable. "She hated the painting. I don't know why I had it put here. It was the one thing she wouldn't have wanted to see."

"You still love her."

"Watch!" Charles took the silver-handled brushes off the table and with a sportsman's precise, effortless accuracy, hurled them out the window.

He moved quickly, gathering the nightgown, the clothes from the stool, a few of the dresses from the closet, and threw them out the window, too. Dawn watched as the mild afternoon breeze caught them, holding them suspended in midair for a moment, as if they were reluctant to leave. Then they floated gently down to the garden, where the servants were already appearing silently to gather them up. The flat Mexican faces expressed nothing, not even curiosity.

Charles pushed the cosmetics into the wastepaper basket, then walked over and removed the painting from the wall. He put it in the closet, the face against the wall, and slammed the door on it. He came back to the center of the room, where Dawn was standing, put his arms around her, kissed her and pulled her down with him onto the bed.

She shuddered as she reached a climax, faster than she remembered doing before, faster than she had ever thought possible, then she guided his hand to her and pulled one of the lace-edged satin pillows under the small of her back, and came again and again as he moved to her rhythm, holding himself back until she heard herself crying "Come, oh, come, please," and came again herself with him, in a burst of pleasure that seemed to go on and on forever.

He lay in her arms as the sun moved toward the horizon, causing the shadows to lengthen in the room. It was the closest Dawn had ever come to the kind of sexual passion she had felt with Lucien when they first met—in some ways, in fact, it was better and stronger, for she was no longer an innocent who needed to be taught about pleasure. She pressed herself harder against Charles. He kissed her neck, then her breasts, and turning her over made love to her again, this time more gently and for a longer, much longer time.

"I love you," he whispered. Dawn wanted desperately to believe him—she did believe him. Still, she wanted assurance. "And it is really *me* you love? Not Alana?" she asked sleepily.

"You, and only you. We shall have wonderful lives together! You'll see. And many children—all of them beautiful, it goes without saying. . . ."

Dawn felt a sudden chill. It scarcely seemed the right moment to tell Charles that in one crucial respect she was like Alana, if not even worse off. The one thing she could *not* give Charles was children, not without an operation, which she had no intention of having. What Charles didn't know, she decided, wouldn't hurt him. She hoped so anyway. It occurred to her, as he pulled her closer to him in the darkening room, that perhaps it was truly the one thing he wanted, the one failure he couldn't forgive in a woman.

It was not a subject she wanted to pursue, and in any case she had a grievance of her own. "I can't spend the rest of my life here, you know," she said cautiously. "I have a career. I don't want to give it up."

"Of course," Charles said pleasantly, his arms around her. "I'm guilty of monopolizing you."

"I have to get back—soon."

"I've been thinking much the same thing. We'll go back to America together. I've had enough of this house—enough of thinking about the past, too."

As the room grew dark, he fell asleep in the silence. Dawn lay beside him, listening to his breathing and the gentle whispering of the jacaranda trees outside. She closed her eyes and tried to sleep, too, but in her mind she saw images of Morgan, of Lucien, of Cynthia's shoe on the windowsill of the bathroom in New York, of a rough, angry sea, with the waves swept into spray by the wind, and a woman who looked exactly like her swimming through them to her death.

She wondered if there was something in Alana's ambiguous death and that of poor Morgan that provided a common bond between herself and Charles.

She knew it was something they could never discuss, but for one moment she believed it with all her heart. The she fell asleep, curled up against his body.

Dawn was surprised that it was necessary for her to appear in person at the consulate to prove her citizenship before Charles could obtain a visa—and even more surprised at the reaction of the consular officials. She was used to the fact that people like that were in awe of a movie star, but there was something else in their attitude that puzzled her.

When she explained that she was there to obtain a visa for her husband, everybody was all smiles—but when the man behind the visa desk saw Charles and realized who her husband was, he turned pale, rose and went off to find the consul general himself. It took most of the day to accomplish what Dawn had assumed would be a routine piece of business, though Charles himself did not seem surprised by the delays, the officials whispering to each other as they examined the documents over and over again, the furtive telephone calls to Washington.

She had assumed that her stardom and his wealth would speed the process up, but instead they seemed to be creating something like a diplomatic crisis. When the consul finally put down the receiver late in the afternoon after the last telephone call, he was less than gracious. "I guess we have to give it to you," he said—and with every indication of reluctance and even disgust, he stamped Charles's blue diplomatic passport and handed it back to him as if it were contaminated.

"Civil servants," Charles said, with his usual easy smile, "they're all the same the world over."

But from the look in the consul's eyes, Dawn knew there was more to it than that.

. . .

"Where's Corsini?" Aaron growled.

"In the bungalow. The telephone never stops ringing. I thought I was the star, but Charles gets more calls than I do."

"Is the chicken salad chunks, or a whole bunch of crap in mayonnaise?" Diamond asked the captain, peering at the menu through a tinted monocle.

"Chunks."

"That's what you always say. I want white-meat chicken, cut up in chunks, not shredded. No goddamned dark meat. Got it?"

"Got it, Mr. Diamond."

"You can't trust anyone," Diamond said, turning back to Dawn, though whether he was referring to Corsini, the staff of the Polo Lounge or the world at large was unclear.

Aaron Diamond took out his monocle, dipped it in his glass of water and wiped it clean. He cleared his throat. "You were up shit creek before, frankly," he said. "Now you're further up it. Without a goddamned paddle! First you hit the headlines in an adultery-and-suicide scandal. Now you've married a guy who's a crook. Or worse."

Dawn glared at him. "I won't have you say that, Aaron."

"Okay, okay. Maybe I put it too strongly. But talk about bad publicity . . . You wanted to kill your career, you couldn't have made a better move—that's all I'm saying." He waved a breadstick at her. "Have I ever criticized you?" he asked. "I've never criticized you," he answered before Dawn could. "You want to get married? Fine! God bless. You should live and be happy. But I ask you: Why Charles Corsini? You should have talked to me first."

"Aaron, it all happened so quickly. Besides, I love him."

"It was love at first sight?" Diamond asked. "Okay, I'll buy that. But now you got yourself real problems."

"What kinds of problems?"

Diamond paused to examine the chicken salad through his monocle, searching for evidence of dark meat. The captain stood over him like an attending surgeon, holding a silver sauceboat full of mayonnaise. "That looks dark to me," Diamond said triumphantly, holding one piece up on his fork. The captain clicked his fingers at a waiter, and the offending piece was removed on a plate. Diamond polished his fork on the tablecloth. "Stars married to rich guys never made it," he said. "Look at Marion Davies. Look at Gloria Swanson—the moment she became Joe Kennedy's mistress, her career went *pfut*. The guys who run studios don't like stars whose husbands have more clout than they do. You ought to try the chicken salad. It's pretty good."

"I'm not hungry," Dawn said, picking at her fruit cup.

Diamond paid no attention. He clicked his fingers at the captain and ordered a chicken salad for Dawn. He turned back to her again. "You want my opinion, forget about the movies for a while. I've tried all over town, but all I get is zip. People are scared. What you ought to do is sell your stock. We can get your contract renegotiated as part of the deal."

"Charles doesn't want me to sell."

"It's your stock, not his."

"He *is* my husband, Aaron. Besides, maybe he's right. Why sell to Braverman?"

"Let me guess. Corsini wants to get control of the studio himself?"

She nodded.

"The SEC will never let him get away with it. Is that why he's going to New York?"

"He has business there."

"That's where the money is. Is he setting up the bank again?"

"He's a banker."

"You wouldn't find too many bankers who'd agree with you. Well, what's done is done—I think you've made a mistake."

"I don't want to lose your friendship, Aaron."

Diamond shook his head. "You can count on me. Just be careful, that's all I ask."

"Careful about what?"

"Careful about Corsini. He had a bad press," Diamond said. "A bad press is always a problem," he added pointedly, glaring at Dawn through his monocle. "He was front page news there for a while."

"When?"

"Two, three years ago. You ever hear of a guy called Luckman?"

"No," she lied. She wished she hadn't asked Diamond any questions. She tried to look as if she wasn't interested, but there was no stopping Diamond.

"Big financial guy. A real *macher*. Gave terrific parties. I used to go to them. And where is he now? In the slammer. He got ten to fifteen, I think."

"For what? And what does this have to do with Charles?"

"He was Corsini's partner. Luckman was the owner of record for most of Corsini's American companies. I guess Corsini needed an American citizen, and Luckman was happy to oblige. What the hell— Corsini made him a rich man. The only trouble was, when the Feds moved in, the companies were Luckman's, not Corsini's. On paper, of course. Corsini got deported. I think, or almost, but Luckman went to the slammer. The poor son of a bitch never knew what hit him." He turned to the waiter. "Is the goddamned canteloupe ripe?"

"The cranshaw is perfect, Mr. Diamond."

"I wanted cranshaw, I'd have asked for cranshaw, chrissake!" He focused his attention on Dawn again. "Corsini's smart, I'll give you that, but bad things seem to happen to people around him. That's all I'm saying. He ever talk to you about his wife—what was her name?"

"Alana."

"Alana. Right. I *knew* that, chrissake." Diamond was always irritable when his memory failed him, and even more so when somebody helped him out. "That was a bad story. Lousy press."

"Charles has told me all about it, Aaron."

He signaled for the check. "Did he? It was a hell of a thing. Big headlines. Did he tell you there were rumors she was having an affair with Luckman?"

Dawn shook her head.

"Well, who the hell knows? Since we talked I've been asking a few questions. Some guys I know in New York knew about what happened. They didn't like Corsini much—he cost them a few mil, so you can't blame them. *They* said she and Corsini went out sailing together, in a small boat. It's just the kind of crazy thing he'd do—he likes danger. Anyway, the boat capsized and she started to swim back to shore. She never made it. He did."

"I know all about that," she said calmly, though she was beginning to realize that she didn't. She hoped it didn't show.

"Yeah," Diamond said. "There's only one little detail these guys told me that maybe you don't know."

"What's that?"

"She was an Olympic swimmer, kiddo! She could swim like a fish."

Though Dawn wanted to know more, she suddenly saw, in the mirror in front of her, Charles entering the Polo Lounge. At the sight of her, his face lit up. He smiled and opened his arms wide.

And despite her fears, Dawn knew, deep in her heart, that Diamond must be—*was!*—mistaken, that she had nothing to fear.

Dawn had never crossed the country by train, but Charles was not a man who liked to hurry. He had no fear of airplanes—he flew his own—

but he preferred to move at his own pace, like a chess player weighing his moves.

As always, he had made his plans with meticulous, though unobtrusive, attention to detail. He had insisted that Dawn hire a maid to accompany her, and arranged for an employment service in Beverly Hills to present a dozen applicants for the job. His own valet, a dapper, silver-haired Englishman named Quayle, accompanied Charles everywhere, though so unobtrusively that he seemed to have acquired, along with his dark suits and his mournful expression, the gift of invisibility.

When she and Charles boarded the Super Chief at Pasadena to avoid reporters, their two compartments had already been opened to make a suite, Dawn's toilet things and makeup were laid out neatly on freshly pressed, scented linen napkins in her small bathroom, and a silver pot of Charles's own brand of coffee was waiting on the table, together with a bottle of Krug 1934 champagne from Aaron Diamond—Charles had succeeded in winning him over, at least halfway, but not without effort. A fresh pack of Charles's brand of cigarettes—Pall Malls—was on the folding table, with the silver-paper top neatly torn and folded back and one cigarette pushed out halfway, as well as Dawn's jewel case and Charles's briefcase.

It had not escaped Dawn's attention that Charles kept his briefcase close to him when he was traveling, nor that it contained a bulky, blue-black automatic pistol. In Mexico he had kept the gun close to him at all times—on the night-table in the bedroom, or on his desk, when he was working. "It's still a violent country," he had explained casually, when she asked him about it. Apparently, he felt the same about America.

Somewhere on the train were Dawn's three white wardrobe trunks, each of them nearly six feet high so that her evening dresses could be hung without being folded. Each trunk had a domed top—that way they could not be stood upside-down by careless porters—and a brass plaque with Dawn's initials and a number. Marie-Claire, the maid, had a master list of everything that was packed, each item marked 1, 2, or 3, so she knew which trunk it was in, all of it written out on lined paper in Marie-Claire's fine French penmanship.

Charles put his feet up and lit a cigarette. "I look forward to seeing New York again," he said.

"It's never been one of my favorite cities."

"Oh, all cities are the same. But just at this moment, with the war in Europe, New York is the center of things. Berlin is finished, Paris is occupied, London is blitzed, you can't get to Rome or Geneva or Zurich. So the action is in New York."

He watched the desert slip by in the bright morning sun. Outside it was probably one hundred degrees, but here in the silver-and-pale-green compartment of the Super Chief, it was cool and comfortable, though a little like being in a moving aquarium. "You'll see, it has a wonderful social life—so many *layers:* old money, new money, Jewish money, emigré money, refugees with money—it's like Rome before the Goths sacked it. I've rented the Wildners' apartment. They're mostly in Palm Beach now. So we will have a good view of the park—and a superb collection of pictures. Then we'll see—"

There was a knock on the door and Quayle's lugubrious face appeared. He whispered an apology and handed Charles a note. Charles read it, tore it up with considerable violence and nodded to Quayle, who quietly closed the door again. "Did you see two men in dark suits get on the train with us?" he asked Dawn.

"No. I wasn't looking."

"Quayle noticed. They took the compartment in front of ours. What a waste of taxpayers' money!"

"Who are they, Charles?"

"FBI, I suppose. Or Treasury Agents." The fact that he was being followed did not seem to surprise him, she noticed.

"You don't seem to mind."

Charles shrugged. "Why should I mind? Here the government exists to get in the way of business. Luckily it's not too efficient."

Nor did Charles seem affected by the presence of the two agents sitting at the table next to his at dinner, eating their meal silently, like two members of some lay monastic order, in the hope of overhearing a fragment of conversation.

As for Charles, he talked volubly, but not about business. His social plans were ambitious—in part, Dawn guessed, because he still resented the way he had been forced out of the country, and perhaps even more, though he did not say it, the way he had been dropped by many people when the scandal broke. It was as if he were returning from exile, which was in fact the case, with even bigger plans and, this time, a famous movie star for a wife.

There was something conducive to sex about being on a train. In the long night, as the Super Chief roared through small prairie towns with a long, low, mournful whistle, they made slow, passionate love.

On the second evening, when they sat down in the observation lounge for a drink and a game of gin rummy—which Charles had insisted on teaching her, horrified by the fact that she knew no card games at all—a small, plump man with false teeth and wire-rimmed glasses sitting near them stared at them for so long that Dawn finally put her cards down and spoke to him.

She was used to fans, but there was something about this man's concentration that was disturbing, an intensity that went beyond the usual interest in movie stars, which this man, with his unnaturally white teeth and his dark-blue suit, didn't seem the type to feel.

"I'm Dawn Avalon," she said, hoping to get rid of him. "You weren't mistaken." She wondered if he wanted her autograph.

But the man did not seem to have heard of her. He simply inclined his head, baring his square porcelain teeth in a mirthless, apologetic smile. He had the face of a prosperous small-town dentist or merchant, the kind of man who prides himself on his good manners and wears a straw hat in the summer. His black-and-white wingtip shoes were planted firmly on the carpet. Doubtless nobody had told him they had gone out of style a decade ago in the rest of the world, nor would he probably have cared. There were two spots of red on his cheeks, and Dawn assumed that they were a sign of his embarrassment. The eyes behind the thick spectacles, however, were bright with anger.

"Are you Charles Corsini?" he asked quietly. His voice had a strong Midwestern twang, a nasal quality that almost covered the tension in his voice.

Charles looked up from his cards, then glanced at the far end of the lounge, where Quayle was sitting watchfully, as unobtrusive as ever. Did Quayle carry a pistol, Dawn wondered? In any case, he stood up, moving quickly for such a calm man.

"I am," Charles said. His eyes were watchful, focused intently on the man's hands.

But the man's hands did not move. He kept them on his knees, the thumbs dug firmly into the cloth of his trousers. "I thought you were," he said.

"Do I know you?" Charles asked cautiously, signaling Quayle to stand back. Charles did not seem afraid, Dawn thought. He was in control of the situation, whatever it was, and the man seemed to sense it.

"No," he said. "You don't know me. No reason why you should. My brother had his life savings in your investment fund. He used to tell me I was crazy not to join him. Double your money in a year or two, that's what he used to say."

"And did he?"

"Yup." The man's Adam's apple bobbed as he spoke. Either his glasses were misting over or he was beginning to cry.

Corsini's expression was distantly pleasant, but his face was rigid, as if he already knew what was coming next. He waited for the man to speak again.

There was a moment of silence, then the man continued: "When you pulled the plug, he lost everything. Every cent he ever made or owned."

Corsini shrugged, not so much a gesture of indifference as one to indicate that the story was familiar to him, that he had heard it a hundred times before. "And then?" he asked gently.

"And then he killed himself. Couldn't bear to tell his wife, I guess. Or maybe me." He paused. "He put his Winchester twelve-gauge into his mouth and pulled the trigger," he added, as if the details were important. "He liked bird shooting. Never missed a season."

"I see," Charles said. "What do you want me to do?"

The man stood up. Now that he was on his feet, some of his sad dignity seemed to fade away. He stood unsteadily, supporting himself with one hand on the back of his chair. It had not occurred to Dawn that he might be drunk, but it was now clear that he was, if only slightly. Perhaps it had taken him a drink or two to work up his courage.

He held himself stiffly erect, still staring at Charles. "Nothing," he said. "I just wanted to meet the son of a bitch who killed my brother."

"He killed *himself*," Charles whispered, almost to himself, pale as a ghost, but the man had already turned away to stumble down past the two lines of revolving club chairs and vanish into the next car.

Dawn sat rigid, staring at Charles. But Charles did not apologize or explain. He picked up his cards, his blue eyes as expressionless as ever. "My card, I believe," he said, but his hands were trembling and there were beads of sweat on his face. He smiled grimly, as if he were determined to master his emotions by sheer willpower. His hands stopped trembling obediently. She picked up a card and discarded. He took it. "Gin," he said cheerfully and put his cards on the table. "My luck seems to be holding."

That night Charles lay awake, staring at the blue night-light, while Dawn listened to the click of the wheels on the rails. It was the first night since they had been married that they did not make love.

Part Five

THE KINGDOM OF LIES

CHAPTER 20

Yes, Virginia, there *is* such a thing as Cafe Society!—and all of it gathered to ooh and aah the glamorous DAWN AVALON, star of *Flames of Passions*, the hit of the year, at the little clambake "Bunny" and Maggie WINTERHALTER threw for 200 of the *haute-polloi* at The Colony to welcome Prince Charles Corsini and his movie star bride back to New York. THE DUKE AND DUCHESS OF WINDSOR flew in from Bermuda (Bo-Bo Esterhazy sent his private amphibian for them)—and the Duke danced two dances with the formerly British star, who seems to have survived front-page scandal and an accident very nicely, thank you. . . . Also present were man-about-town Hamilton THRUSH; designer Billy SOFKIN; Felix and Happy WILDNER (of Palm Beach and Newport); yours truly, and *everybody* who's *anybody*. . . .

—Cholly Knickerbocker
New York *Journal-American*
November 10, 1941

. . . These ears *only* have heard that Wall Street is buzzing with rumors about Charles Corsini. Maybe it's because Charles is now married to beautiful Dawn (*Flames of Passion*) Avalon, but I hear he's paying *close* attention to movie stocks. You read it here first!

—Walter Winchell
New York *Daily News*
November 20, 1941

Is it true that beautiful Dawn Avalon is giving up her career as a star to play wife to new hubby Charles Corsini? Miss Avalon says "No Comment," but friends deny she's taking cooking classes or learning to sew. . . . Industry insiders say the stories about her role in Cynthia Beaumont's suicide may make her unemployable, but stranger things have happened in Tinseltown. . . .

—*Variety*, November 25, 1941

Prince Charles Corsini, Chairman of the Rio de Plata Bank and the Bank
of Europe and the Americans of Buenos Aires, announced today the
formation of Pacifica Investments, Inc., in partnership with Winterhalter and Felix Wildner. Interviewed in his new offices at Rockefeller
Center, Prince Corsini stressed that Pacifica would have as its goal the
acquisition of "significant" investments in growth companies, but denied
that his intention was to take over any company against the wishes of its
management. . . . Much of Corsini's capital is rumored to be from
Europe, and the Justice Department is said to be working overtime to
trace the sources—a subject Corsini refuses to discuss. In any event, the
only thing that could clip Corsini's wings this time would be America's
entering the war in the near future. . . .

—*Wall Street Journal*
December 1, 1941

"Charles," Felix Wildner said prissily as they danced, his plump
little cheek pressed against hers, the neat little white mustache tickling
her ear, "has learned his lesson!"

"What lesson?" she wanted to ask, but she knew it was pointless.
Wildner was a fool—a pompous, vain, wealthy bottom-pincher, who
was doubtless only passing on something he had heard elsewhere, since
he never had an original thought of his own. Besides, she already knew
the answer. Three weeks in New York were more than enough to learn
that here, at any rate, Charles was affectionately regarded as a fallen
angel.

Here he moved in a society in which people had been born to wealth
and looked down their noses on anyone who had made it himself. Few
of them "did" anything—for somebody like Felix Wildner, looking
after his fortune was a full-time job. She found it strange to spend
every evening, dressed to the nines, among people who had no shoptalk and apparently no reason to get up before noon.

It was one of Charles's talents to fit into this world, but Dawn recognized the cold, hard calculation behind his busy social schedule. The
kind of people whose money he was after were accessible only at parties
and dinners. Nothing seemed real to them unless they heard it over
brandy and cigars, from someone they knew.

At first she found the round of party-going amusing, but it did not
take more than a few days for her enthusiasm to wane. Her stardom
meant little to these people, who judged everybody by the size of his
fortune and his place in society, and who thought the movie business
was "vulgar." Besides, she was restless. She had not subjected herself
to months of loneliness and pain in Mexico merely in order to sit at

dinner parties every night. She was willing to give Charles a chance to reestablish himself, but when he suggested buying an apartment at River House, she firmly discouraged him. While she was willing to contemplate a pied-à-terre in New York, since Charles would always have business here, she made it clear that this was not where she wanted to live.

If Charles was annoyed, he did not show it. Dawn suspected that he was in the habit of agreeing to everything, then going ahead, in his own time, to do whatever he wanted anyway. He wanted to know everything about her financial affairs, without revealing much about his own. He had been astonished to find out that she owned almost nothing except her shares in Empire and the house in Malibu—on which she still owed a small fortune to the bank, the builder and Billy Sofkin.

"But you're a star!" he said. "One reads of enormous salaries. . . . I remember seeing in the papers that your contract was for millions."

She sighed. People outside the movie business always thought that stars were rich. "Two million, yes. Spread over three pictures, or four years. But I'm on suspension, remember. Cantor suspended me just before my—accident. Suspension means no pay. If I *were* getting paid, Aaron gets ten percent. That would leave me about nine thousand dollars a week gross before taxes. Say, six thousand or so, after taxes. It's a lot, I agree—almost top dollar. Gable gets ten or twelve, for example. . . . But if you're going to be a star, you have to *live* like a star. It isn't so much if you're keeping a house in Bel Air, half a dozen servants, a place in Palm Springs . . ."

"I see . . ." Charles cracked his knuckles. The mention of Cantor's name always made him angry. "But *Flames of Passion* made a fortune?"

"For Empire, yes. I don't share in that. Stars are hired help. High-priced help, but help all the same."

"And before?"

"Before, I was under contract to David. Since we were married, there didn't seem any reason to him why he should pay me a high salary. He paid all my bills, after all. The fact is, between the house, David's debts and my medical bills, I've got nothing in the bank, and no income. Echeverría isn't cheap, you know."

"I can imagine. . . . I had no idea. You must give me all the details—the mortgage payments on the house, the bills and so on. What's mine is yours, of course. You know that."

Dawn stared at him. "That's exactly what David used to say, Charles."

"I'm a good deal richer than David Konig was."

"That's not the point. I'm an actress. I want to work again. And I own a piece of Empire. I want to *use* it. I don't ever want to be in the position of having a man like Cantor tell me what to do again."

"I understand," Charles said gravely, but she wasn't sure he did.

In the meantime he kept her busy with a breathless schedule, as if he was determined to be seen everywhere. Charles could sit for hours listening to the Duke of Windsor or Manolo Guzman or Bo-Bo Ester-hazy without the slightest sign of boredom—and keep up his end of the conversation as well. But Dawn detected—or thought she detected—an occasional flicker of hatred and contempt in his eyes, as if buried somewhere behind his smiling facade was a vengeful, angry, coldly cal-culating man.

Late one evening, after a dinner party at the Winterhalters', Bunny Winterhalter, whose notoriously roving eye had been attracted to Dawn from her first day in New York, took her to one side for a chat on the subject. Unlike most of his fellow rich men, Bunny was intelli-gent—too intelligent for comfort, Dawn thought. He was so rich that he could easily have afforded to live in complete idleness, but some basic predatory instinct kept him in business. Like a lazy lion, he occa-sionally emerged from his round of pleasure to snap up a company or seize a majority in some unwary corporation. "I like the smell of fresh blood," he had once told a reporter from *The Wall Street Journal* in an unguarded moment.

Not surprisingly, he seemed to genuinely like Charles and though Winterhalter was older, the two men clearly enjoyed each other's com-pany and shared a certain well-concealed contempt for the rest of the world.

The library of his Manhattan town house contained so many tusks, snarling heads, horns and skins that one wit remarked, "It looks like the waiting room of an unsuccessful vet," but when Dawn commented on it (it was a room that more or less demanded some kind of com-ment), Winterhalter merely shrugged. "It's simply the only socially acceptable reason for going off by yourself in the woods."

He stared at the head of a grizzly bear, which rather resembled his own. "Men need solitude," he said after a moment of silent commu-nion with the bear. "It's our ancestral memory of Adam. There Adam was, all alone in the wilderness with the animals. No woman. No other man. It's at the core of things, you see. Charles has the same need. Most men who are worth a damn do. He's a rogue elephant, like me. A dangerous man. That's why I like him."

"*Is* he dangerous, Bunny?"

Winterhalter nodded. "Oh, yes," he said. "The good ones always are. He loves you, you know."

"I know."

"Of course love is a very unstable emotion. I've been spared it, thank God. I'd rather face a charging Cape Buffalo, like that old fellow there, with only one cartridge left and no place to run."

"That sounds more dangerous than love to me, Bunny."

"Oh, don't you believe it! Love is the most dangerous game of all. The death rate's far higher than in hunting."

Winterhalter gazed around his collection of trophies, as if he expected the animals to join in the conversation. "I knew a gal in India once who kept a pet leopard. Handsome beast. She used to go in and play with it as if it was a large cat. . . . Well it *was*, of course. Fed the damned beast by hand. Wonderful thing to see. She *loved* it, you know, the way some women do love cats. . . . Fond of cats, are you?"

"Not particularly. What happened?"

Bunny looked at her ingenuously. His expression was innocent to the point of naiveté. He liked to play the fool when it suited his purposes, but there was a hint of malice—more than a hint, in fact—behind the bland smile. "What *happened*?" he asked. "Why, my dear girl, one day the leopard killed her." He paused. "What else do you *think* would happen?"

Charles was as unpredictable, in his own charming way, as he was evasive. He loved to surprise Dawn, usually by hiding small gifts for her to find in the most improbable places. She found a diamond ring in her grapefruit one morning, and hardly a day went by when he did not manage to startle her in some way.

The small, charming duplicities that he introduced into their domestic life were—as Dawn was beginning to realize—merely a reflection of Charles's attitude toward the world at large. He was a man who operated in the shadows, not out of necessity, but because conspiracy and double-dealing amused him.

Most of the rich men Dawn had known—Konig and his friends—had goals in mind they could justify or explain, at least to themselves, but Charles, she strongly suspected, liked action for its own sake. He was a man in flight from the horrors of boredom. Manipulating people, building a financial empire, taking over companies, they were all games for him, just like polo—and as in polo, if some of the players got hurt, that too was part of the game.

No sooner was he settled in New York than he was busy acquiring real estate in Florida and California. In one day he bought a controlling interest in a hotel in Boca Raton and traded it to Meyer J. Schine for a piece of the Roney Plaza in Miami Beach, then used his piece of the Roney Plaza to raise a loan from Clarence Davis's Florida Bank to put down a $5 million option on a mile of waterfront property in Fort Lauderdale.

He had the ability to keep the details of the most complex transactions in his head, and an instinct for the moment to sell or cut his losses. No matter how big the numbers were, he never seemed worried. Somewhere along the line, perhaps in school, he had learned not to give anything away.

As she sat down to breakfast—they had both risen late on a winter Sunday—Dawn was therefore surprised to see that for once Charles actually looked worried. He was reading the front page of *The New York Times* with such attention that he didn't rise as she sat down—which was even more unusual, since his manners were impeccable as a rule. Unlike most married men, Charles did not consider intimacy a substitute for courtesy. Even when they had made love in the morning, Charles would get up before she did, shave, shower, dress and appear at breakfast to pull Dawn's chair back for her with the same formality he would have employed if they had just met at a dinner party.

"Not another story about you in the business section?" she asked. She sipped her orange juice. Charles had oranges sent up from his own orange groves in Florida.

"The Japanese have broken off their talks with the Americans."

Dawn thought about that. It meant nothing much to her. "Surely the Japanese wouldn't attack the United States?" she asked.

Charles looked somber. "Oh, they might, they might. . . . Mind you, I don't expect they'll bomb New York—or even Los Angeles. Still, if it happens, there will be all sorts of problems."

"Surely the Japanese are a long way away?"

"The Japanese? Yes, of course. The problems won't come from *them*, darling. Eventually the Americans will beat them, of course. The problems will come from Washington. If there's war, we'll have wage and price controls, excess-profits tax—all sorts of government interference and regulation. War is bad for business."

"I thought people made enormous profits in wartime."

"Some people, admittedly. In my case, I'm not so sure. I'm a foreigner, after all. As *The Times* so rightly points out, not all my affairs would bear close scrutiny. People with financial ties to Germany or Italy aren't going to be popular with the FBI and the SEC. Many of my clients are on the 'other' side. I don't ask them what their politics are, you understand, or why they want to get their capital out of Europe. Some are Jews who are afraid the Nazis will win the war. No doubt some are Nazis who are afraid they'll lose it. . . . Hell, the Trading with the Enemy Act means I could go to jail if America joins the war. . . . It may not come to that, but feelings will run very high, I'm afraid."

"Isn't there anything you can do?"

Charles frowned. Dawn could tell he was about to give up one of his secrets, and knew how much he hated doing so. "The truth is so complicated that I can't even tell you about it," he said. "I've been providing a certain amount of—information, let us say—for the Americans for years. They're miles behind Germany and England in intelligence, but there *is* a small group . . . well, the less you know about them, the better, I think. They're very interested in knowing as much as possible about German purchases in neutral countries. Certain radioactive minerals . . . well, the less said about that, also the better. Even more so!"

"Won't they protect you if there's a problem? Whoever 'they' are?"

She had never seen Charles quite so nervous. He, who never sweated, even in the heat of Mexico, wiped his brow with a napkin, then shook his head.

"Not a chance, I think. The more I'm suspected of being a Nazi agent, the better—from their point of view. And of course I *do* have close contacts in Germany. Otherwise I'd be no use to them. No, I'm afraid I'm going to have to face the Justice Department and the FBI on my own, if it comes to that. I'm not the only one at risk, you understand, but the bureaucrats in Washington will naturally be looking for a scapegoat to set an example. And you may be sure they won't pick a Rockefeller, or Sosthenes Behn of ITT. In any case, whatever happens, you mustn't ever mention this to anyone."

"I promise." The notion of Charles in jail was ridiculous, but still Dawn felt obliged to ask in a gesture of sympathy, "What can I do to help?"

Charles took her hand and kissed it. He picked up a thin red leather portfolio from the floor, unlocked it with a small key and produced a set of typed documents. His manner was businesslike and brisk. "I knew I could count on you. These have been back-dated a bit," he said. "Just to be on the safe side."

"What are they?"

"You remember how Konig set up a corporation for you, then assigned some of his shares to it?"

"Of course."

"In principle, what I'm proposing here is very much the same. I set up the Pacifica Corporation, as you know, to control my various interests in America. I own the majority of the shares—for all practical purposes, it belongs to me, much as Avalon Pictures belongs to you. What I'm proposing is to assign my shares in Pacifica to you. *You* will have control over my American investments—on paper, anyway."

"Isn't that risky?"

Charles studied the roses on the breakfast table, carefully avoiding her eyes. "Risky? I don't see why. I trust you. We love each other. If you suddenly decided to leave me, I would find it difficult to get my shares back, I suppose—but I don't think that's likely, do you?"

"No, but . . ."

"We love each other. Sometimes in an emergency you have to put your fate in someone else's hands. At such times it's foolish to be cautious. Besides, if I can't trust you, whom *can* I trust? If it makes you feel easier, we can have an exchange of letters in which you promise to sell the shares back to me after the war for some token amount . . . but that would have to be between us, you understand—strictly private. The SEC will be looking for loopholes in these documents—with a magnifying glass, I assure you. If I transfer the shares to you, it has to be done without reservations or qualifications, or the whole strategy falls apart."

"That wasn't the risk I had in mind, Charles, dear."

"Ah? What risk *were* you thinking of, then?"

"You once told me never to sign anything I hadn't read—even if my husband asked me to. Is there anything in Pacifica that can get me into real trouble?"

"No, no, you're right to be cautious," he said, though he did not seem pleased. "Of course you should read them."

"What will they tell me?"

"Not all that much. Listen, there's nothing in Pacifica that can get you into trouble. That's the truth. It owns things, that's all. The capital comes from me—and a few eminently respectable investors like Winterhalter and Wildner. Where *my* capital comes from is a question they won't ask *you*."

"I see. I'd feel better about it if I could show all this to somebody like Aaron Diamond."

"By all means. I don't object. You're perfectly right. But there's a problem. I hadn't anticipated things would move so swiftly with the Japanese. Speed may be essential. There may not be time."

"I would like to think it over. And talk about it a little more."

"As you please," Charles said. His smile was as affectionate as ever, but there was, for a brief moment, a flash of anger, or irritation, in his eyes, which vanished so quickly that Dawn was not altogether sure she had seen it. She loved Charles—she was sure of it—and it seemed wrong not to trust him, particularly since he was proposing to place a fortune in her keeping.

She got up, put her arms around him and kissed him. "I'll read the documents, darling," she said. "And think about them. If the United States gets into the war, I promise to sign them immediately. How's that?"

He pulled her down on his lap. "More than fair. Think of it this way—we'd be partners as well as lovers."

"It's an attractive proposition." She stood up. He rose, put his arms around her, and drew her in the direction of the bedroom.

"What will Quayle think when he sees we haven't finished breakfast?" she asked as Charles closed the bedroom door behind them.

"The obvious, I suppose. Never mind. No man is a hero to his valet. Or a saint!"

She ran her hands over his hard, muscular body. Like many rich men, Charles had the gift of remaining in shape without exercise, perhaps because so much of his youth had been spent in violent sport. "Is it true that a wife can't testify against her husband?" she asked with a laugh as he drew her near to him.

She was too close to him to be able to see his expression, but she felt his body stiffen, and hoped he had understood she was merely teasing him.

"Not exactly," he said, very quietly. "She can't be *compelled* to testify against him. If she wants to, she can."

Then he made love to her, and it seemed to Dawn that good as Charles always was in bed, he was just a bit better this time—as if he were determined to give her a demonstration of how much he loved her.

When she woke, Charles was lying back on the pillows, looking at the Wildner Caravaggio. She moved closer to him sleepily, and he put his arm around her shoulders. He smelled faintly of sweat and her own scent. It was a mixture that seemed to Dawn so sensual that she wanted to make love again. She rubbed her foot against his.

But Charles's thoughts were now elsewhere. "There was another painting just like it in Ernst von Saloman's collection in Munich," he said. "Identical, in fact. Old Wildner didn't know that, when he bought this one. He paid half a million dollars for it, then discovered there were two paintings and nobody knew which was real and which was the copy. Even Berenson couldn't decide."

"What did Wildner do?" Dawn slid over onto her side so Charles could rub her back. Like a cat, she loved having her back rubbed gently with a slow, fingertip stroke. Charles had the patience to do this for hours while he talked or thought, or sometimes smoked a cigarette.

"What did he do? He bought von Saloman's Caravaggio, too, of course. For something like seven hundred and fifty thousand dollars! Then he destroyed it—cut the canvas up in little pieces and burned them in the fireplace. 'Now mine is the real one,' he said—and since it was the *only* one, he was right. This is probably worth several million dollars now. Perhaps more. A lot of money for a painting . . ." Charles lit a cigarette and narrowed his eyes to look at the Caravaggio through the smoke. "Words like 'fake' and 'fraud' are meaningless when you're talking about value. Take your shares in Empire, for example. They are of very little value to you now, yes? On the open market, the shares would fetch next to nothing."

"That's what Kraus said to me."

"The Central European with the worried expression? I liked him. A man of considerable intelligence. I'll be frank with you: I think it's time we did something with your piece of Empire."

"You're not thinking of going into the movie business, Charles, are you?"

"I've been giving it some thought. Oh, don't misunderstand me—I don't see myself as a producer. But it's a good business to be in. And it would be convenient to control a big American corporation. A company like Pacifica is merely a legal convenience. It has an address, a telephone number, a secretary—and millions of dollars. The government is always suspicious of that kind of thing. They prefer a company that produces something tangible—one that has real estate, a product, a company cafeteria, a sales force, shareholders. . . . And besides, nobody looks too closely at the movie business. Even the government recognizes that it's crazy—that you can't run it like the steel business, for instance. Besides, Empire is badly run. In the right hands it could be worth a fortune."

"I've been through all this before, with David."

"Yes. But with respect, the situation is a little different now. He was a brilliant showman, but not so good at this kind of thing. And Sigsbee Wolff was basically a thug. I'll tell you how we'll play it. The first thing we do is to sue. After all, Cantor put you on suspension without cause and tried to destroy your career. Then—we shall demand representation on the board. Then—we sue for malfeasance. We'll tie them up with litigation. Your friend Kraus shouldn't find it hard to dig up some facts on the way Braverman and his cronies have been stealing from Empire. After that, we bring in some Wall Street heavies, people like Wildner and Winterhalter—the kind of names the banks like."

Dawn rubbed her foot against his, but this time it was not from any desire for sex. "Who would you put on the board?" she asked, trying to make the question sound casual.

Charles shrugged. "Certainly not me, at first—for obvious reasons. Perhaps Winterhalter. I wonder if there's anything he can shoot in California?"

"They're *my* shares, Charles."

"Yes, to be sure . . ."

"I want the pleasure of taking over Empire myself, darling. I want to see Cantor's face."

Charles stubbed out his cigarette and lit another. The click of his lighter was the only sound in the room. Usually he was quick to answer, but this time he was silent, his face expressionless as he blew smoke rings out toward the Caravaggio.

He sighed. "I'm not sure that's such a good idea," he began.

"Why not? If you can trust me with Pacifica, you can trust me with Empire."

"The transfer of Pacifica is a paper transaction. You won't be *running* it. You know that."

"I know that. But that doesn't mean I can't hold my own in the movie business, Charles. I'm a fast learner. And David was a good teacher. I'm certainly not going to have my shares used just to put Bunny Winterhalter on the board."

It was the first time she had ever confronted Charles about anything that involved business, and she waited for him to lose his temper. She wondered if he would back down. But he did not lose his temper. He turned and looked at her, saw that she meant business and smiled.

"There could be advantages," he said quietly. "A woman. A beautiful woman—a star. The publicity would be extraordinary. And the beauty of it is that nobody has anything against you."

But before Dawn could explain that this was not exactly true, or congratulate herself for having won against Charles's initial reluctance, there was a knock at the door.

Charles slipped on his dressing gown and went out to see what Quayle wanted. When he came back, his expression was somber. He was carrying the leather portfolio he had produced at the breakfast table. He opened it, spread the papers on the bed and took a fountain pen from his pocket. "I'm sorry," he said. "The Japanese have bombed the American fleet in Pearl Harbor."

Dawn took the pen. It felt cold in her fingers. She did not recall having ever signed anything that made her happy or was to her advantage. When a man presented you with something to sign, it was usually bad news.

Still, a promise was a promise. She signed.

"So you're going back to California?" Winterhalter said to her.

She nodded. "Charles told you?"

"He told me some things. Probably not everything, if I know him. You prefer it there?"

"Yes. It's where I belong. I'm an actress."

"Is he going out there, too?"

"He's talking about buying a house. He'd spend some time there, some here."

"I don't think he can run his affairs from there, you know. I can't see Charles settling down to spend the rest of his life in Beverly Hills. The big money is here."

"We'll see, Bunny."

"No doubt about that. Myself, I think most marriages work better when there's an occasional separation between husband and wife—but I'm not sure that you and Charles are cut out for a transcontinental marriage. If I were married to you, my girl, I'd never let you out of my sight."

"I trust *him*," she said.

"Funnily enough, I trust him, too—as much as I'd trust any man I liked."

She glanced at Charles, who stood a little farther off, next to Felix Wildner. Wildner was one of those rich men who had reached the age of fifty without growing up, an adolescent with a neat little gray mustache jutting out over the pouting, self-indulgent lips of a spoiled mama's boy. He had been married five or six times—nobody seemed to know for sure—possibly even those who knew him well had lost count, and interest.

At some time in his life, marriage must have seemed to him a truly adult act, a way of affirming to himself and his formidable father that he was grown-up. The fine tracery of small red lines on Wildner's plump cheeks were like the battle map of a life devoted chiefly to pleasure. He wore velvet slippers, embroidered in gold with his initials, for he suffered from gout, and because of some defect in his eyes, he seemed always to be looking in two directions at the same time, like a flounder or a sole. For the moment, his eyes—one of them, at any rate—were more or less focused on Dawn.

"I was just telling Charles he was a lucky fella," Wildner said, in a surprisingly high, squeaky voice.

Dawn slipped her arm under Charles's to indicate that she too felt he was a lucky fellow, then gave him a small kiss on the cheek to show that she was lucky, too.

"None of *my* wives ever brought me a good investment," Wildner said.

"I didn't marry her for her stock in Empire, Felix," Charles said.

"No, no, it's a bonus." Most of Wildner's wives had stepped right out of the chorus line.

"Of course those *people* out there have to be watched all the goddamned time," Wildner said, pursing his fat little lips in distaste. "They'll steal you blind if you give them a chance," he continued in a whisper.

Dawn had no difficulty in guessing who Wildner meant by "people," and it only increased her dislike of him. She had never understood anti-Semitism, and given the racial prejudices she had suffered from in her own youth, she found it distasteful. She, too, if the truth were known, was an outsider.

She stared at him coldly. He ignored her and went on speaking to Charles, who listened gravely, lifting an eyebrow to show that while he was willing to hear Wildner out, he reserved judgment. Charles seldom disagreed openly with people. He listened to everyone with the same slightly preoccupied polite indifference, which you mistook for agreement at your own risk. Eventually Wildner paused for breath. "Don't know why I'm telling you all this," he said, puffing out his cheeks. "You're a lone wolf, so you'll probably do it your own goddamned way."

"He's not *quite* a lone wolf," Dawn said.

Wildner stared at her with his right eye, while the left one tried to find her and focused on Charles instead. "What?" Wildner asked. He was not used to being interrupted by women, however famous and beautiful.

"What I mean, Felix, is that I plan to be very much involved."

"Involved?"

"I have some ideas of my own about what ought to be done."

"Dawn knows the cast of characters," Charles said lightly. "And the business."

"She's an actress," Wildner said, focusing one eye on Charles and the other on Winterhalter, as if for support.

Winterhalter shrugged. He seemed to be enjoying himself. "Joe Kennedy never made a move at R-K-O without asking for Gloria Swanson's advice," he said.

"Joe Kennedy's a traitor to his class."

"He's a crook," Winterhalter said pensively. "I'll give you that. But I don't think he's a traitor to his class, Felix—and he isn't *in* mine, so he can't betray it."

"He accepted an ambassadorship from Roosevelt. That says it all." Wildner turned a darker shade as he spoke the President's name. He leaned forward as if he were about to say something confidential and sang in a falsetto whisper, "You kiss the niggers, I'll kiss the Jews—and we'll stay in The White House as long as we choose!" He laughed, snuffled a bit, then winked at Dawn. "Eleanor and Franklin," he explained. "Of course *she* runs the President. And we know who runs her. . . ."

"I'm afraid I know nothing about politics," Charles said tactfully, his face completely devoid of expression. "I'm not a citizen, you understand . . ."

"I am," Dawn said firmly, with a cold glare in Wildner's direction.

Wildner seemed to realize he had gone too far. "I'm just saying that finance and corporate politics aren't a woman's business," he said. "It's one thing to own stock. It's another to use it. My mother owned plenty of stock—but she let my father make the business decisions for her. That was his end of things."

"I think I can hold up my end, Felix."

"She's a good negotiator," Charles said quietly. "She out-negotiated me."

"She'll be wanting to run the studio next," Wildner said mournfully, accepting defeat with his usual petulance.

And before Dawn could say anything, Bunny Winterhalter laughed—a great booming laugh that brought all conversation in the room to a stop—and, slapping Wildner on the shoulder with a force that nearly drove the smaller man to his knees, he said, "I wouldn't be surprised."

Charles, Dawn couldn't help noticing, didn't join in the laughter. Neither did she.

The Esterhazys' party at the Colony followed the new social conventions, in which gate-crashers were as welcome as invited guests, with the added attraction of the Duke and Duchess of Windsor as a draw. Graziela Esterhazy (one of the numerous former Mrs. Wildners) was throwing it to celebrate Bo-Bo Esterhazy's birthday, and since the Duke and Duchess were deeply in Esterhazy's debt for many small and large favors, they had consented to appear.

The Duchess, in a pale-gray silk evening gown, sat petulantly at one table, while the Duke, looking like a patient who has just received full anesthesia, was placed between Dawn and Graziela at another, his pale eyes reflecting something that was beyond mere boredom. Those of the women guests who knew how curtsied to him, but they might as well have stood on their heads for all the attention he paid. His mind was elsewhere—perhaps on the crown he had given up or, more likely, on nothing at all. Except for the fact that he chain-smoked and sipped Scotch, he might easily have been mistaken for a man in a coma.

When they were finally seated, Dawn tried several subjects of conversation, but none of them seemed to animate His Royal Highness. After about half an hour a waiter arrived with a small note on a silver platter. The Duke ignored it and the waiter both, until the latter cleared his throat and said, "It's from the Duchess, Sir."

The Duke sprang into life, ripped the note open and read it with a careful slowness that suggested he was uncomfortable with the written word or that he needed glasses and was too vain to wear them. He put the note down on the table quickly, but not before Dawn had seen that it consisted of four words, in the Duchess's firm, spiky handwriting: "Look *alive*, goddamn it!"

His animation was fearful to behold as he hurried to obey the Duchess's order, the washed-out eyes swiveling in their sockets in the Duchess's direction to see if she was satisfied. Her expression from the distance, Dawn thought, would have done credit to Medea.

"How's your husband?" he asked, desperately convivial.

"Very well, Sir. He's sitting opposite you."

The Duke smiled at Charles, then his expression wavered and a look of hesitation crept into his eyes. "He looked older last time I saw him," H.R.H. said.

Dawn was nonplused.

"I like his pictures. The ones you were in."

"I think you mean my *previous* husband, Sir. Sir David Konig."

"Of course I do. So sorry. What happened to Konig? Divorced him? I can't keep up with things." The Duke frowned petulantly. "Bermuda's a bloody backwater."

"Sir David died, Sir."

"Did he? I remember now. Of course he did. I liked him. Daresay you did, too. Who's the new one?"

"Charles Corsini, Sir."

"Is he? I *knew* that, damn it. I used to play polo with him. In the days when I played polo. Don't do it anymore. The Duchess doesn't like me to play dangerous sports." He reached across the table, knocking over his wineglass, and shook Charles's hand limply. The effort seemed to exhaust him. "I could do with a spot of advice from you about my investments," he said to Charles. "Fellow who handles that kind of thing for me is too damned cautious. Manolo Guzman tells me I could be making twice what I'm getting."

"He's probably right, Sir. Naturally, I'm at your service."

"Good chap. Come around and see me for a chat. Bo-Bo's put us up at the Ritz Towers."

"Is Your Royal Highness staying long?" Dawn asked.

"Don't know. Depends on the Duchess's shopping plans. We came up with quite a party. Billy Sofkin. Manolo and Nanette Guzman. Pempy Daventry . . ."

Dawn felt an irrational stab of fear, then suppressed it by sheer will-power. She had been so busy trying to make conversation with the Duke that she had scarcely noticed who the other guests were.

The dinner party was beginning to dissolve as the guests moved from one table to another. Husbands who had been placed near their wives were free to wander now, wives were able to move closer to their lovers—she could almost hear a collective sigh of relief as the party loosened up. Dinner was a formality. The real fun began when it was over and the after-dinner guests began to arrive, like exotic birds with their noisy chatter and bright plumage.

The Duke turned, noticing that Dawn was still at his side. "You know Mrs. Daventry, of course?" he asked, as she appeared from the crowd.

"We met," Dawn said, "years ago. Crossing the Atlantic." She felt her stomach lurch, as if in memory of that awful voyage.

Mrs. Daventry's tan was darker than ever, but overexposure to the sun, and the aging process, had given her skin the appearance of crisp bacon, Dawn was glad to observe, along with the first signs of age freckles.

Mrs. Daventry shook Dawn's hand. The green eyes were as hard as ever and seemed to Dawn to reflect the same smoldering hostility she had seen in them years ago in the ladies' room at Firpo's. The Duke sat down again heavily, indicating with a languid wave of his right hand that the ladies could, or perhaps *should*, do the same. He disliked standing. It reminded him of the endless hours of ceremony when he had been king.

"Mrs. Daventry's been staying with us," the Duke said. "She's a friend of the Duchess's," he added, as if the distinction was important to him. Dawn guessed that he meant no disrespect for Mrs. Daventry— he simply liked to make it clear, when introducing an attractive woman, that there was nothing between them. The Duchess's jealousy was well known, and she was vigilant about the slightest sign that her husband might be interested in another woman.

The Duchess had been known to seat attractive women friends next to her husband at dinner parties with instructions to flirt with him and report back on his reaction. Early on, the Duke had been burned once or twice by these *agentes provocateuses,* and now treated attractive women as if they were time bombs. The Duke did not know Dawn well enough to trust her, and certainly he did not appear to trust Mrs. Daventry.

"Wallis and I are old friends," Mrs. Daventry said, putting a cigarette in her holder. She held it between her sharp little teeth for a moment, but the Duke made no move to light it, either because he was afraid Dawn might think it was a gesture of intimacy or because, as a former king, he did not feel himself obliged to do so.

"You were with my sister when she killed herself?" Mrs. Daventry asked, leaning forward to talk to Dawn as if the Duke were merely an obstacle to conversation.

Dawn tried to convince herself that she had nothing to fear from Mrs. Daventry, and momentarily failed. Her throat went dry at the crisp snap of authority in Mrs. Daventry's voice. She took a sip of water and told herself not to be silly. She was a star, a princess, more famous than Mrs. Daventry would ever be. There was hardly a man in the room who didn't stare at her out of the corner of his eye with desire.

There was not a woman here who didn't envy her. And what had Mrs. Daventry done with her life and her beauty? She had married a fat oaf in a backwater of the Empire.

"I didn't see it happen, if that's what you mean," she said sharply.

Mrs. Daventry raised an eyebrow at the tone of Dawn's voice. "Perhaps so," she said, conceding the point grudgingly. "I always thought it was a great mistake for Cynthia to marry Richard Beaumont. I said so at the time, but she wouldn't listen. Neither would Papa."

"It was a difficult marriage," Dawn agreed, hoping to end the conversation quickly.

"All marriages are difficult. Hers was irresponsible. For one thing, people should never marry out of their class." Mrs. Daventry focused her eyes on Dawn with briskly renewed hostility. "Cynthia was a fool," she said. "Still, she was my half sister. I can forgive her for jumping out the window—though I can't understand it. I *can't* forgive Beaumont. Or her so-called friends."

Dawn looked her right in the eye. "I was her closest friend. As it happens."

"Exactly so," Mrs. Daventry said unpleasantly. "And what did she see that made her jump, I wonder?"

"Does it matter? She'd been drinking, you know. She wasn't supposed to, but nobody could stop her."

"Perhaps nobody tried very hard. Anyway, people don't jump out of windows because they're drunk. Not even Cynthia." She took a cigarette, gave the Duke a quick glance of annoyance and lit it herself. "Mind you," she continued, "I don't say I can't understand. Beaumont's an attractive man. But Cynthia thought you were her friend. She trusted you. You knew she'd already tried to kill herself once before. Was that because she'd found out about you and Beaumont? I suppose so."

"Mrs. Daventry, I don't have to put up with this . . ."

"True enough. You're a princess now, of all things! Cynthia told me that the first time she saw you, you were a dancer in some grubby little Soho nightclub. . . ."

Dawn went white with rage, but the older woman was smiling triumphantly at her, her green eyes gleaming. "I don't think you'll want to create a scene, *Princess.* I shouldn't imagine Corsini would like that much, either, would he? We'll just keep this little chat to ourselves, shall we? Just so you know that it doesn't matter to me whether you're a princess or a film star. I hold you responsible for Cynthia's death."

"I was not! And I *am* not. Whoever was in bed with Dickie Beaumont, it wasn't me—not that it's any of your damned business!"

"If it wasn't you, then who the hell was it? You were there."

Dawn stood up, trembling with anger. "If you must know," she said, "it was another man."

Mrs. Daventry laughed. "You'll have to do better than that, Princess. I'm not fond of Dickie Beaumont, not by a long shot, but there's never been the slightest rumor that he's a queer. Cynthia would have guessed that, and she never mentioned it once. . . . Ah, here comes your latest husband, the dashing prince." Mrs. Daventry looked up as Charles approached the table. She smiled at him as if she and Dawn had been having a pleasant chat, then nudged the Duke in the ribs to wake him up. "Do you know," she said to Dawn, "whenever I see you, I can't help feeling we've met before."

"We did," Dawn replied coldly. There was no point in continuing a scene in front of Charles. "Before the war, on the *Mauretania*."

"*Before* that, I mean. Where did you say you lived in India?"

"I didn't. It was a long time ago. . . ."

Mrs. Daventry held out her hand for Charles to kiss, as he sat down. "Your wife and I were just chatting about India, Prince," Mrs. Daventry said.

"I've never been there."

"It used to be a marvelous place. Of course, that's all over now. They've been promised self-government. That will be the end of everything—you'll see." She sighed and took a long sip of her drink. Her bracelet clinked against the rim.

"A handsome piece," Charles said politely, to change the subject. He had his own opinions about the British Empire and guessed they would hardly dovetail with Mrs. Daventry's.

"Isn't it?" She held up her wrist. "There's quite a story attached to it, as a matter of fact. It was stolen from me. The chap who stole it ran off to England with some little chee-chee tramp."

"What's a chee-chee?" Charles asked.

"A Eurasian. Or Anglo-Indian, as they like to call themselves."

Charles nodded. He was only half listening, as if his mind was on other things. "Fascinating," he said, with patently false enthusiasm.

"Liked India myself," the Duke interrupted. "Hyderabad gave me a terrific tiger hunt. Suppose it's very different now, of course. Most things are. Damned shame, the war." He fell silent.

"Are you on your way home?" Dawn asked Mrs. Daventry, praying she was.

"Home?" Mrs. Daventry asked with a laugh. "There's no room on the convoys for civilians. Even if there *were*, I don't fancy sharing a cabin with four strangers, or traveling without my maid. I think I'll stay here for a while—one has so many friends in America."

She finished her drink and rose. "I'm sure we'll meet again, Miss Avalon." She gave Dawn a smile that contained all the warmth of an ice cube. "Forgive me. *Princess*, of course. One quite forgets these quick changes of—title."

She curtsied to the Duke, who nodded back glumly, then turned and made her way off through the crowd, her exposed back as slim and muscular as ever.

"Are you all right?" Charles whispered.

Dawn nodded.

"You look as if you've seen a ghost."

"I have a headache, that's all. That dreadful woman . . ."

"She didn't seem to me *that* dreadful. A little boring, perhaps . . ."

"Take me home, Charles, *please*. I'm not feeling well."

A look of concern crossed his face. "Of course," he said, quickly making excuses to the Duke. "Shall I get a doctor?"

"No, no . . ."

"It's always best to be on the safe side," Charles said, as he led her through the crowded room on his arm. "At certain times, rest is very important."

"Charles," she said, "it's not that. I'm not pregnant."

"That's all right," he said smoothly.

But it was *not* all right—Dawn knew that. She could hear the disappointment in his voice, however politely he tried to conceal it. Once a month, just before her period, Charles became even more solicitous than ever, and once a month he was obliged to conceal his disappointment when it arrived on schedule.

Sooner or later, she would have to tell him the truth.

That night, for the first time in months, she dreamed about Morgan's death and woke up drenched in sweat, with the image of the poker in her mind.

Charles lay sleeping beside her. From the wall facing the bed, the figure in the Wildner Caravaggio looked down at her, dimly illuminated by the night-light. A young, androgynous face with huge, dark eyes stared out from the canvas in horror. On the table was a bowl of fruit, glowing even in the half-darkness, and an overturned glass of wine.

The hair framing the face was long, dark, disheveled and wreathed with wildflowers, but there was nothing pastoral about the expression. One hand was pressed against the chest, the gold rings gleaming dully. The other was extended gracefully. From it, the scales shining like molten metal, hung a snake, its fangs sunk into the soft white flesh of the hand, just at the wrist. A trickle of blood ran down across the pale-blue veins.

It was a masterly painting, real or fake. There was so much fear in the eyes that Dawn almost expected to hear the figure in the painting scream.

Dawn tried to remember the name of the painting. For some reason, it seemed important to know. She got up quietly and leaned over to look at the small brass plaque on the frame. Engraved on it was the title "Bacchante Punished for a Lie."

She turned off the picture light and went back to bed, but she couldn't put the eyes out of her mind.

They looked exactly like her own.

CHAPTER 21

"This is war!" Myron Cantor had cried, when he heard that Charles Corsini was mobilizing his troops in the East, on Wall Street.

At night the studio was so quiet that it seemed like a deserted kingdom—one of those ghostly cities in India, like Fatehpur Sikri, which the Mogul conquerors had built on a massive scale, then abandoned, because they had neglected to ask the defeated natives whether the water supply was sufficient. The studio was closed off from the outside world, and from reality, too—a kingdom of dreams.

Kraus wandered through it, trying to relieve the cramp in his legs and the pain in his head. Day after day, night after night, he had sat through interminable meetings while Marty Braverman and Myron Cantor looked for ways to protect themselves against Corsini.

A few weeks after Pearl Harbor, Cantor had given a luncheon for the Empire Pictures executives on Sound Stage Number One to rally them for the fight ahead. He did not disguise from them the fact that Dawn's stock made Corsini a formidable opponent. He rose on his feet in front of a huge American flag and lifted his glass. "At this critical hour in our history," he called out, "I ask you to join with me in drinking a toast to our great president"—he paused for effect—"Martin B. Braverman!"

It took the Empire executives, most of whom had been expecting to toast President Roosevelt, a few moments to get over the shock, but Cantor knew what he was doing. He was warning them that the enemy wasn't Hitler or Tojo, but Corsini.

Corsini fired the first shots, but Cantor, who liked to think of himself as a street fighter, was quick to counterattack. Newspaper stories began to appear about Corsini's past, with photographs of poor Luckman in handcuffs at the time of his trial. Charles shrugged these off. He had made errors in the past, he acknowledged with dignity. Who had not? He had learned from them, and he pointed to the undeniable respectability of his new associates. He hinted that even the Duke of Windsor was behind him.

Within a few days there were other, more disturbing stories, this time about the source of funds in his South American banks. There were rumors that these banks served as the repository for large amounts of money from "certain people" in Europe who wanted to keep their money in a safe place, just in case Hitler lost the war. One newspaper managed to discover a photograph of Charles at the Berlin Olympic Games, shaking hands with General Göring. Another showed Charles on horseback with Baldur von Schirach, the leader of the Hitler Youth. He had been in Rome, it was alleged, in 1939, and met with some of the leading Fascists—a story Charles was able to blunt by producing a photograph of himself emerging from an audience with the Pope, to whom he had brought a gift from Colonel and Mrs. Perón.

He had done no more than Colonel Lindbergh, he claimed—he had merely been polite to his hosts. Whatever his personal sympathies were (and he carefully refrained from making them clear), as a businessman he felt free to deal with anybody. Perhaps he had been naive about the Nazi threat, but surely he was not alone?

Besides, Charles pointed out in a rare interview to *The New York Times*, he was not an American citizen—he was merely mobilizing financial support on behalf of his wife, who would soon be returning to California to confront the management of Empire.

Charles leveled countercharges against the directors of Empire. Cantor had refused to employ the studio's leading female star, Dawn Avalon, for purely personal reasons. As for Braverman, Corsini produced evidence that he had charged his personal expenses to the studio for years, including his monthly payment to his mistress, Ina Blaze, and the cost of his daughter's wedding.

These charges were not taken seriously on the West Coast, where it was widely assumed that studio executives had a license to steal—but in the East, where such things were done more subtly, they produced a certain sensation among bankers and financial reporters.

In Kraus they produced acute indigestion, since he had been the one obliged to dig up the evidence. He felt no particular loyalty to Cantor, and certainly none to Braverman, but he could hardly expect any mercy if they won—and discovered he had been working for the other side.

He walked down the dimly lit street of Empire's "Western" town, with its hitching posts and wooden sidewalks, pushed open the swinging doors of the saloon, stepped through the bar and gambling room and out the other side, which was open, into a medieval alleyway, with cobblestones and houses that jutted out so that the upper stories almost touched each other.

He shivered involuntarily. It reminded him of Europe and of the ghettos. At the end of the street, incongruously, a black limousine was parked. He walked over to it, opened the door, kissed Dawn's hand and stepped in.

"You look tired," she said.

He shrugged. "It's like working in an asylum. Well, what can you expect? These people are fighting for their lives. Ever since the revelations about Braverman's financial affairs, the banks have withdrawn their support. They didn't mind Braverman's stealing when he did it quietly—and made a profit. Now they're pretending to be shocked."

"That's a good sign."

"Yes. On the other hand, we're talking about desperate men."

"How desperate?"

"Cantor has been talking to your old friend Dominick Vale. I'd call that pretty desperate."

"What on earth could Dominick do?"

"He has some Empire stock. He's been buying like crazy. He has plenty of money, and access to more. His company controls hotels, casinos, movie theaters. . . . If they bring him in, they might be able to fight off Corsini. Of course, the problem is that Vale's partners will creep in behind him, and they're not exactly conventional businessmen. . . ."

"Gangsters?"

"I believe the phrase is 'mob-connected.' If *they* come in, they'll carve up Empire to the bones and leave the carcass to rot."

"Can they be stopped?"

"Stopped? Not once they have their hooks into Cantor and Braverman, no. But Vale could probably be bought off, I think. At this stage."

"With what?"

"Promise him a seat on the board of directors, for a start, and he'll be perfectly happy for a while. He's not going to get into a war with your husband if he doesn't have to."

"Vale's no friend of mine."

"Who's talking about friendship? He's a realist. Offer him something he doesn't have to share with his partners and he'll eat out of your hand."

"All right, I'll see him. Tell him I'm at the Beverly Hills. Bungalow One."

Kraus cleared his throat. "He won't come there."

"Why on earth not?"

"Vale's changed. You'll see. He's become a little—eccentric. Los Angeles does that to people, of course. You'll have to go to him."

"Oh, all right," Dawn said. Her own nerves were a little frayed. She understood perfectly well why it was necessary for Charles to stay in New York, but it meant that she had to make decisions on her own much of the time, and though he was always supportive when they talked on the telephone, as they did several times a day, she could tell that he was worried. He tried not to second-guess her, but it was difficult for him not to. He was not used to trusting anyone, let alone a woman, where big money was involved. The fact that he didn't have a choice made him all the more unhappy.

She knew it was easier for her. Her goal was revenge—and security. Once she and Charles controlled the studio, she could resume her career on her own terms. There were pressures on Charles, however, which she only half understood, for he was, as always, reticent on the subject. She knew he was afraid the government might take action against him, and the more publicity he received, the more likely it was. She could hardly imagine they would put somebody like Charles in jail, but it was clearly a possibility that *he* took seriously—and who knew better than he what kind of money might have found its way into the Bank of the Rio de la Plata?

One thing she knew: Having begun the fight, she would have to win it, for Charles's sake as well as her own.

"I've got to be going," Kraus said. "There's another meeting. I'll be missed."

"Where do I meet Dominick?"

"I'll be in touch."

It took Dawn an hour to find the address, and when she did, she thought Kraus must have made a mistake for once, since it was that of a costume-rental company on West Pico, on the second floor of a rundown fake adobe building shabbily repainted in various shades of fading pink. The dingy entrance was set between a health-food store with a display of plaster of paris carrots in the dusty window and a wholesale medical-supply store with a window full of trusses and canes. A discreet sign in the stairwell read "Star Dust Cinema Club—Members Only."

It was the least prepossessing of neighborhoods—a wide, empty street, the pavement cracked like the discarded skin of a lizard, with low buildings on either side, most of them devoted to anonymous small-time commerce—bankrupt fender-repair shops, secondhand furniture stores, a fortuneteller, used magazines. Dawn wondered who in Los Angeles would want to buy used magazines? When she parked the car, she noticed her picture on the cover of one of the magazines tied up in a bundle and left outside on the pavement. She hoped it was not an omen.

She climbed the narrow, filthy stairs, knocked on a frosted-glass door and was asked to enter by someone with a deep, rasping voice. In the tiny reception room a heavyset man who looked like a wrestler run to seed stared at her from behind a battered metal desk.

"I've come to see Mr. Vale," she said.

"In back."

She pushed open the door and stepped into a dark, dusty, cavernous room, dimly lit from above. Dominick Vale was sitting at the far end—even from a distance the smell of peppermint lozenges reminded her sharply of their shared past. She guessed instantly why he disliked being seen in public—for Vale had grown fat. His thighs had swollen until they stretched the fabric of his trousers when he sat down, and he had a pair of distinct double chins, as well as the beginning of a ridge of fat around the back of his neck just above the shirt collar.

His hair had always been thin, and he had devoted much effort to combing it various ways that attempted to disguise the fact, but he now had the beginnings of an obvious tonsure. His head was distinctly pear-shaped. He had a fat man's plump cheeks, like a sinister and unjolly version of Friar Tuck.

He was as scrupulous about his clothes as ever, but the picture he presented was no longer one of elegance, but rather that of a painful, almost comic, attempt to hide his bulk. In his beautifully tailored cream silk double-breasted suit Vale resembled a man wearing an expensively cut tent. From time to time he fanned himself with a panama hat, the band of which matched his tie. His eyes, Dawn noticed, were as menacing as ever under the heavy brows.

All around were rows of dresses, a forest of dusty velvet, tattered lace, moth-eaten fur, tarnished gold and bedraggled feathers, moldering in the dim light from the dingy windows. Against the far wall, down a long, narrow corridor of doublets, knee breeches, capes and fur-trimmed robes, stood a cracked pier glass for fittings and a rusty, old-fashioned sewing machine. Above the clothes were hundreds of improbable hats of every historical period. Several suits of armor hung from the ceiling on chains, giving the place an eerie resemblance to a medieval torture chamber or place of execution.

A sign above Vale's head read: "If you burn or damage costumes, you pay for repair or replacement. You have been warned." Another, above the door, announced: "Rental for nontheatrical purposes—costume parties, fancy dress, etc.—requires minimum deposit of $50. No exceptions."

Below that, a prominent notice appeared, in red capitals, underlined: "*Los Angeles County criminal code prohibits us from renting costumes for the purpose of men dressing up as women.*"

"What on earth *is* this place?" Dawn asked, more crossly than she had intended. The dust had given her a headache.

"I own it."

"It doesn't look particularly profitable, Dominick."

"You're quite mistaken. Just before the weekend, it's a hive of activity. A perfect little gold mine!"

Vale seemed to feel the need for a peace offering and held out a silver box of peppermint lozenges. Much as she hated them, she took one. He popped one into his mouth, and rolled it around with satisfaction.

"You can't judge by appearances," he said. "There's always money to be made by giving people what they want. You give them glamour, darling. I appeal to their shadier tastes. Downstairs there's a cozy little screening room, with films for a very select audience. Ten dollars a ticket, plus a thousand dollars a year as a membership fee. Small change, to be sure, but if you multiply this by a hundred, it all adds up. Besides, respectability bores me. The spectacle of human behavior is my hobby." He waved his hat toward a rack of beaded evening dresses, most of them in sizes far too big for even the tallest of women, each with a beaded evening bag and a pair of long white kid gloves in a cellophane bag attached to the hanger. "Like golf," he added. "Or stamp collecting." He closed his eyes in thought. "To what do I owe this pleasure—after so many years?"

"I thought it would be a good idea if we had a chat. So did Charles."

"May I ask why Corsini didn't come himself? Or is he too busy covering his tracks from the good old days in Nazi Germany?"

"The shares in Empire are *mine*, Dominick. I'm here on my own."

"I've already given my word to Cantor and Braverman. They're a pair of clowns. But they're *my* clowns."

"You'll have to fight Charles—and me. You know that. They'd sit back and let you do the fighting."

"I don't mind a little rough stuff. You know that. There was a chap in San Francisco who didn't want to sell me his hotel. I sent some people I know around to talk to him and he signed like a lamb, right on the dotted line."

"Kraus told me all about it. A couple of men held the owner by the ankles in the elevator shaft, from the twentieth floor." She dismissed the story with a wave of her hand. "Cheap melodrama."

"We tried to blackmail him first," Vale said reasonably. "Almost everyone has something to hide, after all. You know that, better than anybody." He gave her a puffy wink, which she ignored.

"If you come in with us, you'll have a seat on the board. No fuss, no fighting—no wasting good money buying up shares in a rising market."

"Is that an offer from Corsini?"

"It's an offer from *me*."

Vale glowered at her. "Who would have thought it?" he asked. "To think I used to know you when you were one of Goldner's dancers! You were too sharp for your own good, even then. . . . Braverman and Cantor would put me on the board, too, you know."

"It would cost you money. They're looking to you for financial support. And you'd end up with a bankrupt studio. Why join losers?"

"Oh, my dear! You *have* learned a thing or two from your husbands. But what makes you think I want to be on the board of Empire in the first place?"

"Oh, I think you do. I don't think you're quite as indifferent to respectability as you pretend. You always did know the value of a good front. 'An image,' as they call it over here."

Vale puffed out his cheeks and blew out a burst of peppermint-scented breath. The suave, sly manner still failed to conceal the essential ruthlessness of the man, which was not lessened by his bulk or his foppish clothes.

"Let's suppose you're right, dear," he said. "What else do you have to offer?"

"What do you want?"

"Ah, no. Show me some cards. I'll pick up the ones I can use."

Dawn guessed that he was testing her. Vale wanted to see how much she knew about the business—and about him. She was grateful that Kraus, invaluable as always, had briefed her.

"Your friends control certain unions, I believe. We can sweeten their contracts."

"Sweetheart deals, I believe they are called, rather charmingly . . . yes, I'll pick up that card, thank you."

"We'd want to be sure we didn't have any unexpected labor trouble, in return."

"Of course. That's understood. What else?"

"We're thinking of setting up a 'young talent' program, like MGM. Empire needs some new faces. We could make room for some of your—protégés."

"Very good. And tactfully phrased. Of course you'll need a good publicity man for something like that."

"Did you have one in mind?"

"As a matter of fact—Basil Goulandris may be available."

"Basil?"

"I need someone to be my eyes and ears in the studio. You have Kraus—no, no, don't deny it, I've guessed that. I would want Basil to do the same for me."

"I haven't seen Basil since David's death."

"Loyalty is not his strong point, I agree. Still, he's good. And his loyalty *can* be bought. He's been very useful to me."

"Oh, all right. We'll take Basil. Anything else?"

"Nothing major. A production contract—that goes without saying. And first call on Empire's stars for live entertainment bookings. I don't suppose you'd like a week's singing engagement at my place in Lake Tahoe, would you? But I'm forgetting—you don't sing; you only undress."

"I don't have to undress for a living anymore, Dominick," Dawn said coldly.

"No, though you *could*, you know. You're quite as beautiful as ever—haven't changed a bit. And what extraordinary willpower you have. You always did, though. I shall have to watch my step. And I'd suggest you watch yours where I'm concerned. I have a good memory—don't forget it. It's amazing what the police can do these days with just a few bones. Whether Corsini killed his wife or not, I don't think he'd be happy to find out he's married a murderess *en deuxièmes noces.*"

"Don't talk nonsense. You'd never dare!"

"Just so long as we understand each other."

"Then we have a deal, I take it?"

"Absolutely." He rose to his feet. He was always, Dawn recalled, courteous to women—it was his way of showing contempt for them. "By the way," he added. "An old friend of yours is coming to stay with me."

Dawn stared at him warily. Vale seemed dangerously pleased with himself.

He chuckled. "It's rather a bore, actually—but in wartime, one can't say no. Pempy Daventry. You know her, I think? Poor Cynthia's half sister? Ah, well, I'm sure we'll have a lot to gossip about. You knew her in India, didn't you?"

"No," she said coldly.

"I could have sworn you did. We must all get together one evening. Now that we're *partners.*" He gave her a sinister wink.

At the thought of Dominick Vale and Mrs. Daventry sitting down for a chat together about her, Dawn felt herself break into a sweat. For a moment she regretted having brought Vale into her plans, but then she reminded herself that there wasn't a choice. "I must be going," she said.

He opened the door for her. "Do be careful, dear," he said with a smile.

She wondered what exactly she was to be careful *of*, as she groped her way downstairs. Outside, the street was baking in the sun, so empty of life and traffic that it seemed suddenly sinister, like walking across a no-man's-land. She walked quickly toward her car, then stopped for a moment as she noticed a dark, hulking figure concealed in the doorway of the magazine shop.

She took in the deep-set eyes, the heavy jaw, the powerful shoulders. The man was built like a wrestler, and while he was certainly fat, there was nothing soft about him. He was chewing a toothpick and doing his best to pretend that he wasn't looking in her direction. He exuded menace and a certain nervous determination, as if he were getting himself ready for an assault.

Momentarily unnerved, Dawn fumbled for her car keys and dropped them. She leaned over to snatch them from the pavement, felt one of her stockings tear, rushed to the car and struggled to unlock the door, cursing herself for not having used a limousine.

In the polished chrome of the window trim, she saw his reflection. For a man his size, he moved fast. He was approaching almost at a run. She guessed he would reach her long before she could open the door, so she swung around to face him, holding her handbag by its strap.

With that last-second clarity that renders every detail visible, she noticed that he had discarded his toothpick. The man's right hand was in his breast pocket, and his face was flushed and sweaty, the rat-trap mouth set in an expression of grim determination.

All around her, the windows of the rundown buildings were empty, the doors shut. The big man had picked the perfect time and place. He stopped in front of her, breathing heavily, and moved his right hand. Dawn took a deep breath, ready to scream—though she could hardly imagine it would do any good. She waited for a weapon to appear, but instead the big man withdrew a pen from his pocket—a black Waterman with an old-fashioned gold clip.

She saw now that he had a magazine rolled up in his pocket, the one she had seen with her photograph on the cover. With a nervous smile the man uncapped his pen and offered it to her, and through the pounding in her ears, she heard him say, "Miss Avalon, I hope you won't mind signing this for me."

For a moment, she thought her knees were going to buckle, but she signed the magazine with an unsteady hand, handed the man back his pen, opened the car door and realized as she did that it had not been locked after all.

She sat in the car for five minutes, her eyes closed, feeling the hot, sticky leather burning against her back and legs. Her head was throbbing and she scarcely trusted herself to drive.

She drove all the way back to Aaron Diamond's office at a crawl, with the windows and the top down, before she stopped sweating. She wished she had never agreed to see Vale, but there was no going back now.

"Jesus, you look a mess!" Aaron Diamond said. "You have an accident or something?"

"No. I got a fright, that's all. I thought I was going to be assaulted, but it turned out to be a fan asking for my autograph."

"In Beverly *Hills*, for chrissake?"

"On West Pico."

"West Pico? I'm not even going to *ask* what you were doing there.

You want to wash up? I can send one of the girls out to buy you stockings."

"It doesn't matter."

"Jesus, you *must* have had a shock! You got another one coming."

Dawn looked at Diamond. He didn't seem like a man who had bad news to give.

"I had a call from Myron Cantor. I think they're looking for a deal."

"A deal?"

"Cantor's willing to talk. He's smart. You can't beat him—not with this guy Vale on his side. So why go on fighting? You want me to talk to him?"

"No."

"No? You mind telling me why?"

"He doesn't have Vale on his side anymore."

Diamond closed his eyes and placed his hands together on his desk blotter like a man about to meditate. "Let me guess. You made a deal with Vale. Right?"

"Right, Aaron."

"Some friends you got. Listen, be careful, will you? First you marry Corsini. Now you're making deals with Dominick Vale. You know who's behind Vale?"

"Frankly, no. I have a terrible headache, Aaron."

Diamond punched the button on his intercom. "Get us two glasses of water, four aspirins. Make it six, come to think of it. And go buy Princess Corsini a pair of stockings . . . I don't know what size, chrissake. The right size for a five-foot-four movie star." He turned his attention back to Dawn. "You ever hear of Harry Faust?"

"Never."

"I used to know him, from my old days in Chicago. He's what the papers call a 'mob figure.' When the families decided to grab themselves a piece of the action out here, they figured they needed a Jew—so they sent Harry out. He and Vale own a hotel in Tahoe, they're buying up land in Nevada, spending money all over the place. The only trouble is Harry's gone native, you know what I mean? He dates starlets, drives a bright-red La Salle convertible, bought himself a big house in Beverly Hills . . . the *padrones* back East don't understand that kind of thing. They sit there in the back of some goddamn Sicilian social club on Mulberry Street and read about Harry's parties and girlfriends, they figure maybe he's getting out of control. They don't like Vale much, either. They got no use for faggots."

"I don't know about Harry Faust, but I imagine Dominick can look after himself."

"You could be right. He's smart. Faust's problem is that he's a god-damned psycho—a twenty-four-karat egomaniac. I told them that, right back at the beginning."

There was a knock at the door and his secretary appeared, holding a silver tray. He divided the aspirins up and toasted Dawn in a glass of ice water as he swallowed his. "Cantor and Braverman will need more than aspirins," he said. "They hear about this, they'll be shitting bricks. I'd like to see their faces when Corsini walks in and gives them the news."

"So would I, Aaron," Dawn said—and suddenly her headache was gone.

Myron Cantor sat at a table surrounded by a dozen men, and felt alone. He could see his own reflection shining back at him from the polished surface of the boardroom table—which was a lot better, he thought, than looking at the angry faces of the rest of the board. His own father-in-law, Marty Braverman, had set the tone of the meeting, referring to Cantor as "our ex-fucking boy genius." Things had gone downhill from there.

Even Adolph Kiss, the founder of Empire Pictures, Chairman of the Board Emeritus, over ninety years old, maybe even over a hundred—who the hell knew?—had been wheeled in for the occasion, a hearing aid in each ear. It was Kiss who had been the first to see the wisdom of making movies in a climate where the long hours of sunshine made it possible to shoot ten hours a day, even in the winter. He founded Empire Pictures when the main business of Los Angeles was still oranges and Beverly Hills consisted of citrus groves and cattle ranches.

Over the years, Kiss had fought Wolff, Fox, Ince, Harry and Jack Warner, Zukor—stubbornly, duplicitously, defending his company. Erich von Stroheim had been a stunt rider on Kiss's payroll at two dollars a day, plus a dollar for each fall; Kiss was said to have discovered Douglas Fairbanks, Senior; Theda Bara had been Kiss's mistress when she was still an extra.

He made no concessions to the California climate. Until his stroke, he appeared at the studio every day in spats, a homburg and a double-breasted suit, carrying a gold-headed cane. Only age could weaken his grasp on the company he had built—for now he was past senility, a comatose figure who was wheeled out for board meetings and ceremonial occasions.

Cantor looked up from his own image and stared at Kiss, upright in his wheelchair like an Egyptian mummy, but there was no comfort to be found there. From farther down the table, Bernie Grieff, Corporate Vice President of Finance, was giving the board the bad news in his monotonous voice. Perhaps out of some atavistic memory of his ancestry, Cantor noticed, Grieff rocked back and forth as he talked, like a shorn *yeshiva bucher* in a four-hundred-dollar gray sharskin suit.

He summed up the figures and paused, as if he were about to give a blessing. He cleared his throat. He was a heavyset, mournful-looking man, whose chief asset was that he looked too dumb to be dishonest. Most people dozed off when Grieff had something to say—which was a mistake, because he was shrewd. He was so boring that even the most skilled negotiators sometimes gave up a few points just to get away from him, and in budget discussions he simply wore people down. He hated everybody who spent the company's money.

Grieff put his pudgy fingertips together and searched for the right words to sum up the situation. "In other words, gentlemen," he said at last, then paused—"a fucking disaster."

From around the long table there was a collective sigh, then silence. Cantor looked at the man from the Bank of America and raised an eyebrow.

The banker studied his notepad. He did not look up. "No," he said, after a moment's silence. "No more. You guys have been to the well too often."

"Suspend production," Grieff said. "That's my advice. Cut costs to the bone."

Cantor shook his head. "We might as well cut our own throats. We got twelve pictures in production. We don't have product, we're dead. What we need is money. We have to finish these pictures fast. We get one hit, just *one*—and we're home free!"

Braverman looked at the production list in the folder in front of him and shook his head. "Not a prayer," he said. "Forget it. You got no stars here. No Ina Blaze. No Ingrid Astar." He lit a fresh cigar, savoring his son-in-law's humiliation. "No Dawn Avalon," he added, letting the name hang in the air heavily, like the smoke that wreathed around his head.

Harry Warmfleisch studied his fingernails. He was married to Braverman's wife's sister, which explained his seat on the board, but he had not worked his way up from landscape contracting to a fortune in real estate without learning that money was thicker—and more important—than blood. "You want my opinion, Corsini's got you by the balls," he said.

Braverman glared at him. "Nobody *asked* your opinion, Harry."

"I'm a director, chrissake! I got a right to say what I think. What are we fighting Corsini for? Tell me that. The company needs money, the banks have pulled the plug. What's wrong with Corsini's fucking money?"

Braverman's face was flushed. He looked at Adolph Kiss as if for inspiration, but apart from a small trickle of saliva at the corner of his lips, there was no sign that Kiss was alive. "Harry—" Braverman pleaded, struggling to control himself—"if Corsini comes in, we're out. We don't want that, do we?"

Warmfleisch shrugged. It was not a prospect that gave *him* any problems. He had never wanted to be a director of Empire in the first place, and he had a self-made man's contempt for Braverman and Cantor, who were merely corporate executives, however highly paid.

Braverman tried again, with what was, for him, superhuman patience. "What would Sylvia say, Harry? Her own sister's husband booted out into the goddamn street?"

Warmfleisch thought it over. Where her sister was concerned, Sylvia had the persistence of a jackhammer. He would never hear the end of it. "I guess you got a point," he said. "I just don't see how you can fight him off, that's all. Not without finding somebody who'll back you and Myron."

Cantor cleared his throat. "I think we have that sewed up, as a matter of fact."

"Yeah? Who's the dummy?"

"Let's not use words like that, Harry. As a matter of fact, this is a very shrewd guy. We'll have to give up quite a few feathers to bring him on board—but at least he doesn't want to run the company. He wants to be behind the scenes, not out front. He'll agree to long-term contracts for Marty and myself as part of the deal."

"No kidding?" Grieff said unpleasantly.

"And for you, too, Bernie," Cantor added quickly. "That goes without saying."

Grieff nodded. He hated Cantor, who in his view knew only how to spend the company's money. "Who is it?" he asked.

"Dominick Vale," Cantor said. There was a long silence. "Jesus!" Grieff said, not even trying to hide the fear in his voice. "Why not Harry Faust?"

"Vale's not as bad as *that*," Cantor argued. "With him on the board, we can fight off Corsini easy. If Marty and I had a choice, okay, but we don't have a choice. It's fish or cut bait."

"I'd cut bait, myself," Warmfleisch said.

Cantor wiped his forehead. "Vale's outside. I invited him to join us. I suggest we call him in and hear what he has to say. I'm not asking you guys to go to bed with him. Just bear in mind, he joins us, we can forget about Corsini; he *doesn't*, there are going to be a lot of people—some of them at this goddamn table—out on their asses."

He waited for any further objections, but there were none. He pressed a button on the table and the big wooden door to the boardroom clicked open. But it was not Vale who appeared. It was Kraus, looking white as a sheet.

"What the hell are you doing here? Bring Vale in," Cantor shouted.

Kraus's manner had none of its usual humility—he seemed suddenly to have acquired an air of authority. "He isn't here," he said briskly.

"I told him noon, chrissake! Where is he?"

Kraus produced a piece of paper from his pocket. "He sent a telegram."

"So read it," Grieff said with satisfaction, having already guessed that whatever was in it would be no comfort to Cantor.

Kraus held it close to his eyes. " 'Regrets, but am joining Corsini, fondly, Dominick Vale.' It was delivered five minutes ago. Collect."

"Maybe we'd better adjourn until we can talk to him again," Cantor began desperately, but he was interrupted by a curious wheezing sound. Kiss's mouth was moving and his eyes were open. His gnarled bony hands were trembling with agitation. For a moment, Cantor thought the old man was about to die—perhaps was going through his death throes at this very moment—and he felt a sudden panic, as if perhaps he would be blamed for this, too.

Then Kiss managed to get control of his tongue. It was clear that he wanted to speak—for the first time in many years. The other members of the board leaned forward expectantly.

Kiss opened one eye and fixed it balefully on Cantor. "Sonny," he said, "you should have been born a woman." His voice sounded like a piece of rusty machinery badly in need of oiling, as he tried to laugh.

Cantor opened his mouth to ask why.

Kiss smiled, a few of his remaining fangs showing long and yellow. "Because you're going to get fucked," he croaked. His eyes closed and he fell silent again.

There was a long pause. Grieff cleared his throat. "Should I put that in the minutes?" he asked.

CHAPTER 22

THE TEMPLE OF DENDUR rose high into the dark. The sand at the massive base had been swept away, exposing hieroglyphics chiseled into the weathered stone. On either side of the entrance two huge seated figures, carved in stone, brooded silently in the dim light. Two men sat huddled on the steps. They might have been waiting for admittance to the underworld, or perhaps tomb robbers nerving themselves to break in.

There was the clink of a bottle against glass, echoing in the hot night air, then silence. The older of the two stretched his legs with a groan. "You think *Braverman* is crazy? You should have been here when Burton Glass was running the studio. Five million bucks on *Helen of Troy*—in 1920 dollars, for chrissake. Straight to the bottom, like the fuckin' *Titanic*. Kiss was busy fighting off that *gonif* Sigsbee Wolff. Marty Braverman was still a fuckin' bookkeeper. Burton Glass—who even remembers him now?"

"Not me, Pop."

"That's what I'm saying. They come and they go. Glass was a big name, a giant. Then Braverman took over, and now *he's* out."

"Not yet, he isn't."

"The hell he ain't, Danny. Dawn Avalon's husband takes control—you think he's going to keep Braverman or Cantor? No way. What do you think they're talking about right now?" Pop Deigh poured himself another drink. Thirty years ago, Adolph Kiss had made him studio manager. He hated the executives and producers who interfered with the orderly running of his sprawling empire; he hated the directors and stars, who took him for granted; he hated Danny Zegrin—young, ambitious, an asthmatic hypochondriac—whom Braverman had pushed into Deigh's department to "learn the ropes," and whom Deigh suspected of being a fink and a spy.

"Who do you think it's going to be, Pop?" Zegrin asked. He was short, sleek, shifty, with doelike dark eyes that failed to conceal ambition and lines around his mouth that suggested he had come out of the womb already aged by cynicism.

"It's hard to figure, Danny. Corsini don't know shit about movies. Of course that never stops guys like him from thinking they know how to run a studio . . . Look at Howard Hughes, or Joe Kennedy. But maybe Corsini's smarter than that. I hope so."

"I hear Dore Schary's not happy at MGM. Corsini might go for him."

"Jesus, I hope not. Schary's pinko. We don't want an outsider in here, anyway." Deigh regarded the rival studios as enemy powers against which Empire waged perpetual warfare.

Zegrin shrugged. All he wanted was to get into the stratosphere where deals were made, away from Deigh and his bullshit. Zegrin wondered how he could get close to Corsini. He had a talent for ingratiating himself with older, more powerful men. "I guess now Corsini has control, he'll put Dawn Avalon back to work," he said.

"I wouldn't be surprised, kid. I knew her first husband—Konig. Now *there* was a man who loved movies! He made a couple of pictures for Empire, just after sound came in. Glass hated Konig—he hated anybody who could read. I remember once we went to Konig's house for a story conference. Glass is walking around the library and sees all these shelves full of leather-bound books. Well, you know, everybody has leather books but they're fake—you buy them by the yard, just the bindings. People used to hide their booze behind them, in those days. So Glass puts his hands on one of the shelves—feeling the goods, you know, it's in the blood with Jews—and he comes away with a book, with pages and all! He takes out another, then another. . . . 'Holy shit!' he says, 'the son of a bitch has real books.' He never trusted Konig after that."

"She's a great-looking woman, Dawn Avalon."

"She's hard to light. Her skin photographs too dark." Deigh saw all stars in terms of the problems they presented, or the peculiarities of their appeal. If you asked him about Gary Cooper, he would say, "His movies only made money when he was wearing a cowboy hat." About Dietrich: "You got to watch the Kraut don't smile—she's got bad teeth."

"Avalon's a good-looking broad," he conceded, sipping his drink. "I'll give you that." He offered the bottle to Zegrin, who shook his head. Zegrin took a small bottle out of his pocket and sprayed his throat. He suffered from chronic asthma and hay fever, which his psychoanalyst had diagnosed as psychosomatic, though his internist leaned toward the theory that Zegrin was allergic to the dust in the sound stages. Either way, Zegrin was convinced he would only be cured by a promotion to the executive wing of the Adolph I. Kiss Building, where the board meeting was taking place now, while the whole studio waited for the outcome.

"It's nearly midnight," Zegrin said. "They've been talking for hours."

"Lawyers! They're paid to talk."

A telephone rang in the dark. Deigh rose to his feet, his joints creaking, and shuffled off in search of it. He listened for a few minutes, then he too began to wheeze alarmingly. Zegrin, who had followed him, thought for a moment the old man was having a heart attack. In the faint blue light from the standby lamps, he could see Deigh's eyes bulging, his mouth open as if he were gasping for breath. He was clutching his chest with one hand, while the other held the receiver so tightly that the knuckles were white.

"They've picked Braverman's replacement!" he shouted.

"Who is it, chrissake?"

Deigh hung up the receiver and laughed maniacally, the noise echoing in the huge sound stage. He stared over Zegrin's head at the temple, as if a miracle had just occurred at its summit. He choked for a moment, trying to catch his breath, while Zegrin—who didn't want to be blamed for letting the old fart die right here in the middle of Stage One, on company property—pounded hard on Deigh's back.

Deigh pushed Zegrin away as the color came back to his sallow cheeks. "Lay off," he moaned, "you're breaking my fuckin' back. They picked . . . a broad!"

Zegrin stared at the old man as if he were crazy. He could feel an asthma attack coming on. "You've got to be kidding," he gasped.

Deigh had recovered his composure and his breath. "Dawn Avalon!" he said. "You hear that noise?"

Zegrin shook his head. He could hear nothing but his own bronchial tubes rattling. He felt panic rising higher in him with each cough. He had been Braverman's man. With what he knew, he figured any guy who took over the studio would find a place for him. He knew how to make himself useful to the kind of men who ran studios. The one possibility he had never imagined was a *woman* taking Braverman's place.

Deigh refilled his glass and drained it in one gulp. "It's Burton Glass—rolling over in his grave," he said.

Charles paced the boardroom restlessly. He had flown in from New York for the meeting, pulling every string he could to get a priority seat on the plane. He had been obliged to leave Quayle behind, and as a result his clothes were not up to his usual standards of perfection. That alone was not sufficient, however, to account for his inability to sit down or the fact that he was, for the first time since Dawn had known him, lighting one cigarette from another.

Dawn did not dislike cigarette smoke as much as she disliked cigars, but tobacco in all its forms annoyed her—a fact of which Charles was aware. He usually did his best to smoke as little as possible in her presence. Tonight he no longer seemed to care. She waved away the smoke with a gesture of annoyance that he failed to notice—or chose to ignore.

It was not just the cigarette smoke that annoyed her. Charles, it was true, had engineered the vote that left the direction of Empire in her hands, but he had done it by arguing that it was the only way he could possibly run the company in the face of all the publicity surrounding his other affairs. Dawn, he promised, would be his alter ego. She would symbolize his presence and his concern, even though he himself might be in New York or Washington. It was unusual, but by no means unheard of, for a wife to sit in for her husband this way, and all the directors accepted the argument with varying degrees of enthusiasm.

More annoying even than that, to Dawn, was the fact that Charles was unapologetic about his explanation of having put her forward as a substitute for himself. He did not believe it himself—he was perfectly willing to admit between the two of them that she could probably run Empire as well as he could—but he made sure most people believed he was operating behind the scenes.

Tired and anxious as he was, he had laughed with satisfaction at his own cleverness as soon as they were alone together. From his point of view, he had gained what he wanted, and given Dawn what she wanted at the same time—while pulling a fast one on the directors and shareholders of Empire.

Dawn was well aware of Charles's belief that only the results mattered, and from that point of view, his tactics had been eminently satisfactory—but she nevertheless felt humiliated, even in victory, and resented it.

Nor was she happy, though she recognized the necessity, to learn that Charles expected her to hold the fort here alone, starting the very next day. He had arrived at the last minute, so she learned the news along with the rest of the board, and couldn't help wondering whether he had broken it that way on purpose. She knew how difficult it was for him to confide in her, and it would certainly be in character for him to avoid bringing up a subject she would find painful, or might object to. He was a master of the *fait accompli*, even when it concerned her.

"Do you *really* have to go back so soon?" she asked, swallowing her pride.

He gave a weary shrug. "Things are very tricky. All this publicity has stirred up all sorts of trouble. Some old trouble—and unfortunately some new trouble, too. My affairs abroad are also at a very delicate stage. There is pressure on me from both sides."

"How serious is the trouble here?"

"That remains to be seen. I've been subpoenaed by at least two congressional committees. We can thank Braverman and Cantor for that. I'm not a Nazi, for God's sake! I did business in Germany and Italy. Well, who didn't? I wish I could tell them the truth about what I've been doing, but that's out of the question. I'm in the same boat as Lindbergh. Still, none of that frightens me. There's only one thing that really worries me."

"What's that?"

He paused. "You remember Luckman?"

She nodded.

"I gather he's hoping for parole. If he were called as a witness, he'd say anything to get out of prison."

"Does Luckman know anything that could be *really* damaging to you?"

Charles shrugged. "Stale stuff, mostly. That's not to say I'd like to hear it dredged up before a congressional subcommittee. However, in the meantime I think I'd better stay well in the background, at least so far as the public is concerned. . . . You're going to give Kraus Cantor's job?"

Dawn nodded. What, she wondered, *did* Luckman have on Charles? What were the "facts"?

"A sound choice. You'll need to surround yourself with good people. That's the most important thing."

"I know," she said, with just a touch of impatience. Now that Charles had put her in a position to control things, he seemed to be getting cold feet. She knew his problems went far beyond those of Empire Pictures. He had many other irons in the fire, many of them no doubt hotter—and more important—than this one, which he had grasped mainly because it seemed the right thing to do with her shares. However, like everything else to do with the movies, the acquisition of Empire had taken on a life of its own. It was not a steel company or a bank, after all. Larger corporations worth far more could be taken over, bought or sold with little or no publicity. Movies were different— as she had warned him.

"I'm not sure this wasn't a mistake, for me," he said. "All this damned publicity! At just the wrong time. Ah, well—there's never a right time for a financier to make headlines, is there? Tell me, do you trust this fellow Vale, now that you've got him on our side?"

"Not really, no. It was necessary, that's all."

"There's nothing more dangerous than the doctrine of necessity. Far from making good bedfellows, it usually makes the worst kind. Still, he delivered his shares. Perhaps he can deliver something else—who knows?"

"He's a troublemaker. We go back a long way."

"The latter I knew. And the former is obvious. The sooner we can get rid of him, then, the better." He rubbed his eyes, then came over and put his arms around her. "My God," he said, "we should be celebrating your victory. Instead I've been complaining like an old woman about my troubles." He kissed her. "How does it feel to have won?"

"I'm numb." It was true, she thought. She had expected to feel elation, but victory had only brought her more worries. She wished that Charles's affairs were not so complicated—and that he could be more open about them. She had her triumph, but for him it was merely one small battle won in a bigger war.

"There's not even any champagne in this godforsaken place," he said. "Let's go back to the hotel. What time is it?"

"Nearly two."

"My God! No wonder there's nobody here. Which way do we go?"

She had no idea. She knew the studio, but she had never been in the boardroom before. She remembered that it was on the third floor and that there was a private elevator, built for Kiss's wheelchair. In one wall of the hallway they found a polished bronze door. Charles pushed the button, and they stepped into a paneled elevator. It descended silently, the door opened, and they found themselves in the basement. The door closed behind them.

Dawn said, "Push the button and we'll go back up and find the stairs."

Charles examined the door. "I think you need a key. There's no call button, just a lock. Come. There's got to be a way out."

They walked through the basement, past rooms full of boilers and humming machinery, and down a long, dim corridor lined with garbage cans and bins full of wastepaper.

At the other end of the corridor was a fire exit. It was unlocked. "Thank God," Charles said. They climbed a short flight of metal stairs and found themselves in a parking lot. The car was nowhere in sight, and the way back to the front entrance of the building was closed off by a wire fence.

The lot was empty and dark except for one car, which a short young man with slicked-back hair was unlocking. Even from a distance, Dawn could hear him wheezing.

"Which way out?" Charles shouted.

The young man looked up, startled. He walked toward them quickly, and Charles, who had suddenly realized he had put himself at the mercy of a total stranger, slipped his hand inside his jacket. Dawn heard the sharp click as he disengaged the safety catch of his pistol.

The young man didn't hear it—or perhaps he simply didn't live in the kind of world where a well-dressed man with a beautiful woman on his arm carries a pistol. "Miss Avalon!" he said with awe.

"We're looking for our car," she explained.

"It's out front, Miss Avalon. I have a key to the gate."

"Then kindly open it," Charles said.

"Pleased to meet you, Prince." The young man held out his right hand, obliging Charles to slip his pistol back in its shoulder holster before he could shake hands. "Danny Zegrin. Assistant Studio Manager."

Charles nodded. "The gate, please," he said, in no mood for polite conversation.

Zegrin stood his ground. Luck had put him in the right place. "I wouldn't go out there," he said with authority. "There's at least a dozen reporters waiting. And photographers."

"Damn. Can you go and ask the chauffeur to drive the car in here for us?"

"Sure. But they'll follow the car. I've got a better idea. Get in the back of my car and scrunch down until we're past the gates. The press will be watching your limousine all night."

"It's a long drive back to the Beverly Hills Hotel, Mr.—ah . . ."

"Zegrin. Danny Zegrin. No sweat. My pleasure."

Corsini gave the young man an encouraging smile. He always appreciated resourcefulness. "I'll remember your name next time," he said. "So will Miss Avalon, I'm sure."

They stepped into Zegrin's Chevrolet convertible and doubled over in the back seat as he started up.

Dawn noticed that Zegrin had stopped wheezing.

It was past noon the next day when Dawn and Charles woke up and made love.

"I've missed you," he said as they lay in the big bed, their limbs still entwined. She had missed him, too, Dawn realized, with a longing that was simple and physical, during the week they had been separated. It was as if her body were addicted to him; withdrawal when he left would be as painful as it would be from a narcotic.

She kissed him for an answer. He sighed. "I shall have to go back tonight," he said. "There are things happening I can't tell you about. I may need to go to Europe. Nothing too dangerous, don't be alarmed. Madrid and Lisbon, perhaps Stockholm for a day or two. The first thing you'd better do is to buy a house. There's nothing more depressing than living in a hotel."

"It's better than living alone in a big house. Charles, will you be all right? Please be careful. For my sake."

"As soon as things have settled down I shall join you. And believe me, I'm always careful. I think this has to be the last trip, thank God. The Gestapo is beginning to ask questions. A neutral's passport won't help me much if Heydrich wants to put me in a concentration camp. Luckily, even the Nazis have a touching faith in millionaires."

He got up, then lit a cigarette, saw the look on her face and stubbed it out. "I shall have a smoking room in the new house," he said. "Like my father. Perhaps I shall wear a velvet smoking jacket!"

"I can't help minding it. Besides, it's bad for you."

"No, no, you're quite right. However, all the men in my family live to great old age, so don't worry. My grandfather was still drinking espresso and smoking six cigars a day when he was ninety."

"And your father?"

"Well, he lived until he was nearly eighty, which isn't bad. There's nothing like an interest in money for keeping you young. He would have liked you. He loved beautiful women—though he was always completely faithful to my mother, you understand. He was very much a one-woman man. Faithful, devoted, jealous. But not suspicious." He paused, as if the comparison to his parents' marriage was painful to him. "Suspicion is a terrible thing. It grows and grows—eventually it extinguishes love. . . ."

It was not a subject she wanted to pursue. "Come back to bed, darling," she said, but his mind was elsewhere. He poured himself a cup of coffee from the Thermos but didn't drink it. Then he poured a glass of orange juice, tasted it and put it down. He did not seem to know what he wanted, which was unlike him.

"Were you suspicious of Alana?"

"Yes. And as it turned out, I was right. That's the worst of being suspicious. It's a self-fulfilling prophecy. . . ." He paused, then gave a grim smile, as if he had decided, against his will, to reveal some part of the truth to her. "She had an affair with Luckman; I think she did it mostly to prove to me that my suspicions were right. I watched her like a hawk, you see. I always wanted to know where she'd been, who she was having lunch with, where she went in the afternoons. . . . Eventually, I suppose, she simply decided to give me something to be suspicious about. I remember what she said to me when I found out. 'You always made me feel guilty,' she said, 'so I decided I might as well *be* guilty.' "

He shook his head. "But she didn't feel guilty at all. I did."

"Did she love Luckman?" Dawn was astonished that Charles had been so frank with her—was that, too, a symptom of his anxiety and fatigue?

"Who can say? I doubt it. It's more likely that she simply picked the one man who could make the most trouble for me. Or perhaps he was simply the most easily available. Poor Luckman! He wasn't good at picking women, I'm afraid, or handling business, either—it's cost him five years in prison, so far. He had a wife and children, too. Still does, I suppose. You can imagine how much he hates me."

"Isn't there anything you can do about it?"

"Perhaps. It won't be easy to reach him. Not if he becomes a damned 'protected witness.' He'll be in solitary—no visitors except his lawyer. . . ."

"Surely there must be something Luckman wants?"

"Buy him off, you mean? I've tried. You can buy off most people, it's true—but seldom the ones who hate you. Hate is a powerful emotion, you see. It can't be bought off. If you try, it merely surfaces again, stronger than ever. This man Vale—does he hate you?"

"What makes you ask?"

"The way he looked at you at the board meeting."

"I hadn't noticed."

"No? Pure hatred, I thought. But the question is, Why?"

"I used to work for him."

"Yes? But that's hardly a reason for him to hate you, is it? I'm not prying into your past, you understand. My interest is purely a business concern. After all, we're married to Vale, as it were."

Dawn slipped on her robe, with a sigh. She didn't like being pumped for information by Charles, and besides, she had to think carefully. There were things about her relationship with Vale that Charles must never know. "That's putting it a little strongly," she said.

"I don't think so. Mind you, I'm not complaining. In some ways he can be very useful. What exactly has he got against you?"

"Years ago, I had a contract with Vale and a man called Goldner."

"Sir Solomon Goldner?"

"Is he Sir Solomon? I didn't know."

"Oh, yes. Fat chap, with a face like an intelligent toad. Owns theaters, cinemas, real estate, a book-publishing house, magazines, God knows what else. . . . I've met him."

She was unpleasantly surprised to hear it. She had hoped to keep her past—as much of it as possible—separate from Charles. Obviously she was failing. "Well, since you know him, you can easily imagine that he wanted to get rid of Vale. I think he probably arranged to have Vale set up. . . ."

"Set up?"

"Vale was caught with a young boy—in compromising circumstances. It was a nasty scandal. He had to leave England. He blamed me for it."

"I see. *Why* did he blame you for it?"

"Oh, it's all so complicated, Charles."

"I have time. And I love complications. Only the simple things are boring to hear."

"Very well. Vale was having an affair with Dickie Beaumont . . ."

"The actor?"

She nodded. "I was living then with a photographer—Lucien Chambrun, I mentioned him. He threw Cynthia Daintry over for me, and she married Dickie Beaumont on the rebound. Vale blamed me for that, too. Then she committed suicide, and Beaumont had to leave the United States. I'm sure Dominick holds me responsible for that, too. Every time our paths cross, something happens to make him unhappy, you see—but it isn't my fault."

"Of course not. Yet one sees his point. Some relationships between people *are* like that . . . a series of misunderstandings, bad luck, mistakes. . . ." His expression was easy, as if this were the kind of problem he was all too familiar with. He kissed her, but his eyes revealed that his mind was on something else. He became briskly practical again: "He isn't in a position to blackmail you over anything, is he?"

"What on earth makes you think that?"

"You seem frightened of him. And I've never seen you frightened of anyone."

"I'm *not* frightened of him," Dawn said with some indignation.

"Good. I didn't mean to annoy you, by the way. There's hardly anybody worth knowing or loving who doesn't have something to hide—and very often it's not all that important in the first place. The truth seldom is. In any case, do your best to accommodate Mister Vale for the moment, if you can. I may need to ask him for a couple of small favors. As for the house, see if Billy Sofkin knows of anything in Bel Air."

"How much do you want to spend?"

"I don't care. I'll have half a million dollars transferred to your account as soon as I get back to New York. The main thing is that it should be secluded. Apart from that, whatever you like." He took her hand in his. "A nice, big house," he said, "with plenty of room for children, and nice grounds."

"Children?" It was the last subject in the world she wanted to discuss.

"Of course, children. Life is so much easier if there's a separate wing for them—a nice nursery, room for a nanny, and so on. . . ."

Charles gave her another gentle kiss. "They'll be beautiful children, that goes without saying, but still one doesn't want them underfoot all the time. . . . I must dress. I have a couple of people to see before I go back to New York."

Dawn wondered if this might not be a good moment to tell him about her miscarriage—but what would he say if he found she couldn't have children? He would certainly suggest that she should see a doctor—and the problem with *that* was that her condition was curable with an operation, as any good doctor would point out.

He rose and slipped on his robe. She hated to break his good mood, but she knew that if there was to be any understanding between them, she must ask him about Alana. Admittedly, she had not told Charles the whole truth about herself—she could never do that—but she had told him enough to insist on some answer to the one story that frightened her. "Charles," she said, "what happened to Alana, at the end?"

He did not seem surprised at the question. "You've heard all the stories?"

She nodded.

"We should have talked about this before. Naturally, it's not a pleasant subject. There are people who believe I killed her. You know that?"

She nodded.

"And you didn't ask me about it? That's quite a proof of your love, I must say. Not that I need it. And trust. Listen to me. I'm not perfect—who the hell is? But I'm not a murderer, either, even in passion. I don't say I'm not capable of it—that in the right circumstances, I might not do it—but I didn't kill Alana. She persuaded me to go boating. A bloody silly thing to do with a storm coming up, but she loved danger and the sea. She was a kind of mermaid." He smiled, as if at the memory. "I suppose I halfway believed she was going to ask me to forgive her, that we'd have a big reconciliation scene, with the waves crashing around us. . . . Instead, as you know, the bloody boat capsized."

He stopped for a moment, trying to decide whether or not to go on; then he closed his eyes and continued. "She was twice the swimmer I am—an Olympic champion! I saw her drift away from the boat, and I thought she was going to swim back to shore on her own. Then it occurred to me that she wasn't swimming. That she was unconscious. Probably the boom hit her head, when we went over. . . ."

He opened his eyes. "Perhaps I could have saved her—who knows? Anyway, I didn't. As things turned out it was the sensible decision—I don't say the *right* decision, you'll notice. If I'd let go of the boat I'd have drowned as well. It was a sin of omission. I could have swum after her. I didn't."

He paused. "That's the whole truth. I've never told anyone before."

"*Did* she ask you to forgive her?"

He shook his head and smiled. "No. She told me to go to hell, as a matter of fact. We had a very unpleasant little scene. No doubt that partly explains why I didn't swim after her. It doesn't justify my failure, however."

"Nobody could possibly blame you, darling."

"For a long time I blamed myself. I still do—it merely seems irrelevant now, that's all. Before I met you it seemed important. Not anymore."

She got up and kissed him, pressing her naked body against the silk of his robe. He put his arms around her. "Now you know the worst," he said. He laughed. "The rest is just business." He went into the bathroom, leaving Dawn to wonder just what he meant by that.

He had a maddening habit of leaving an ambiguous sentence behind him, like the Cheshire cat's smile, to puzzle her just when she thought he'd told her everything. Did he mean that what he did as part of his business didn't count, that morality didn't apply to anything that had to do with money? No sooner had he put her mind to rest about one thing than he set it afire with another. She could hear him showering. She thought of his pale skin. She closed her eyes and tried to imagine what he would say if he found her holding a dark baby in her arms. She thought of Alana drowning. She tried to think of something—anything—else.

Over the noise of the shower she heard Charles's voice. At first she thought he was singing in the shower, as he sometimes did—he was an opera lover, with a good, though untrained, voice, and a preference for the showier arias of Verdi—but then she realized he was talking to someone. She remembered there was a telephone in the bathroom.

Gently, carefully, she picked up the receiver of the telephone by the bed and held her breath.

"It's on very short notice," she heard Dominick Vale say petulantly.

"I'm aware of that."

"I could give him a message."

"I want to speak to him directly—face to face."

"That's not easy to arrange, old boy. He's followed everywhere, you know. They take a photograph of anybody he talks to—telephoto lens, an agent behind every bloody palm tree, all that sort of rot. He doesn't like that, as you can imagine. I daresay you're not all that keen on having them take snaps of you with him yourself, are you?"

"No. Definitely."

"There you are. Hold on, I'll tell you what I'll do. I'll give you the address of a place on West Pico. Come in the back way. It's a costume-rental shop, on the second floor. Shall we say two o'clock?"

"Three. I'm having lunch with Dawn."

"Do give her my best. Perhaps the less said about this on the home front the better, by the way. If you don't mind."

"I don't mind. You'll make sure he's there?"

"My dear Corsini, he's dying to meet you. Harry Faust's a snob, to tell the truth. He'd go a lot further than West Pico for the pleasure of doing business with a prince. And he has a great admiration for legitimate businessmen. He thinks he'd be a Rockefeller himself if he hadn't been born a thug. Mind you, not everyone would regard *you* as a legitimate businessman, but from Harry's point of view, you're as pure as the driven snow . . ."

"Quite," Charles said abruptly, cutting Vale off. He listened to the address, then hung up without saying goodbye. However much he needed Vale, he was not prepared to be snubbed by him.

Dawn heard him turn the shower down a little and begin to sing. She was no opera lover, but she had learned something from Charles.

He was singing Rhadames' part from the tomb scene in *Aida.*

"There are a few people you can trust. The old hands. The senior executives? I would say: *Out.* They are mostly Braverman's cronies. They've been stealing for so long they wouldn't know how to stop."

"Charles said it's worse in the New York office."

"Let him worry about that," Kraus said. "He's there. Here they steal directly. Grieff has a brother-in-law in the accounting department who fills a paper bag with cash for him once a month. They don't count it. They *weigh* it."

"Surely not?" Dawn said. Apart from the theft of Mrs. Daventry's jewels so long ago, she was fanatically honest about money, and careful with her own—what there had been of it.

Kraus shrugged wearily. He was Central European, an instinctive pessimist—he worked on the assumption that even if you imagined the very worst about everyone, most people would still find a way to shock you when you discovered the full truth. "You don't believe me?" he said. "Ask Zegrin."

He nodded toward Zegrin, who had been sitting silently on the edge of his chair, as if he were afraid he would be sent out of the room the moment someone noticed he was there.

He was still astonished by his good luck. He had been in the right place at the right time; Corsini's snap judgment had been enough to get him out of Pop Deigh's office and into the circle of power, where he had always wanted to be. He did not know Kraus well—from Zegrin's point of view, Kraus had always been a remote, powerful figure, Cantor's shadow—but he had no difficulty understanding that if Kraus was going to replace Cantor, he would also need someone to replace himself, a shadow of his own.

Dawn stared at Zegrin, who blushed. "It's true," he said. "Grieff even charged his son's Bar Mitzvah to the company."

"How could he get away with that?" Kraus asked.

"His cousin audits expense accounts."

"He goes," she said firmly. "So do his brother-in-law and his cousin. Draw up a list."

"You're going to make a lot of enemies," Diamond objected.

"I'd rather do it all at once than spread it out, Aaron."

Kraus nodded. She was right. Her instincts were good, he thought. He ticked a point off on his agenda.

"Word has gone round that we're in trouble," he said. "RKO is offering to buy some of our library."

"Why? What are they going to do with our old films?"

"They'd be buying a tax writeoff. And the rentals are worth something. Besides, Howard Hughes is a great believer in television. He thinks one day people are going to be watching old movies at home."

"David thought the same thing," Dawn said. "Don't sell."

"MGM wants to buy a piece of our back lot. They need a bigger tank than the one they've got."

"Rent out ours to them. Don't sell anything."

"You'll have to sell *something*, honey," Diamond said. "You've got nothing coming in and a lot going out. There are assets here you don't need."

"There's one asset we haven't even made plans for yet," Dawn said. "Me. We need a big hit. The first priority is to find the right story and make the right movie. David taught me that. In the meantime, get rid of the scoundrels and thieves, cut to the bone and hold on to anything that's valuable. What's next?"

"Nothing important," Kraus said, putting his agenda away. "A few things to sign, that's all." He handed her a thick leather folder.

Dawn flicked through the papers. They were mostly routine—the kind of thing she was determined to leave to Kraus and Zegrin in the future. She made a mental note to talk to Kraus about it. He was not the kind of man who would seize authority, which was good, but once it was given to him, he would handle it scrupulously. Zegrin, though he was an ugly little man, would do very well as Kraus's watchdog.

At the bottom of the pile was the next day's menu for the studio commissary, a legacy of Cantor's infinite capacity for unnecessary detail. She was about to throw it away when a dish caught her eye. Picking up a pen, she firmly crossed out "Deli Platter à la Myron Cantor" and scrawled her initials beside the change.

It was not much, but it was a start.

Dawn's table in the executive dining room had sliding panels around it to give her privacy, but she ordered them opened, so people could see her, and so those who were important enough to approach her could offer their congratulations. Actresses, by tradition, usually ate in their dressing rooms in seclusion, guarded by hairdressers, makeup men and elderly ladies from the costume department. Dawn's position, however, was unique. She was a star, but she was also a major stockholder. She could not afford to remain secluded, and in any case, she was eager to break with the tradition that kept women apart from those who held power in the studio, like the purdah ladies of her youth.

A studio commissary was a kind of court, and her presence here was as necessary as it was precedent-breaking. Indeed, her new status was confirmed by an overnight addition to the menu—Shrimp Salad à la Dawn Avalon, which she ordered more out of loyalty than because she liked it.

Dawn knew that her ability to control the company would come from the simple fact that nobody knew exactly what her role was to be. She would assume no title and would let Kraus speak for her as much as possible. Kraus was ideally suited for the job. He had none of the flamboyance usually associated with motion picture executives. He was quiet, calm, understated, hardly even visible, and therefore feared. "He doesn't even *shtup* starlets," Aaron Diamond complained to Danny Zegrin. "He gives me the creeps."

"That's his job," Zegrin said with the wisdom of a studio employee.

Kraus gave a lot of people the creeps. He had a way of appearing silently in the most unlikely places. One moment there was nobody there; the next, there he was, the light reflecting off the thick lenses of his spectacles so you couldn't see his eyes, the thin face set in an expression of such impenetrable neutrality that it was impossible to guess whether he was pleased, angry or simply shy. When you talked to him,

it was difficult to tell whether he agreed with you or not. He would
nod, shrug or simply stare at you, with a patience and courtesy that
were unusual for Hollywood, but once he had made a decision, it was
irrevocable. He did not argue or persuade. Roger Aptgeld wanted to
reshoot several scenes of his new picture, as he explained at length to
Kraus, who nodded agreeably. When the director came back from
lunch, he found the set had been struck. It was Kraus's way of saying
no.

Dawn trusted Kraus—as much, at any rate, as she was able to trust
anyone. He was her one indispensable ally at Empire. When Basil
Goulandris suggested it might be a good idea to "build up" Kraus's
image, Kraus immediately turned the idea down. He preferred to remain in the shadows—that was his strength.

Kraus sat down next to Dawn, so quietly that she hardly noticed his
arrival, nodded to Goulandris, took a piece of bread and carefully cut
it up into small, equal squares. A waitress brought him a bowl and two
soft-boiled eggs. Kraus dropped the pieces of bread into the bowl, emptied the eggs on top and stirred the mixture up with a spoon. Goulandris
closed his eyes, then pushed away his own plate of smoked salmon.
Kraus's lunches always made him lose his appetite.

"The story department's no good," Dawn complained, pushing her
shrimp away.

Kraus stared out the plate-glass window gloomily. Dawn was right.
Braverman and Cantor had staffed it with old literary hacks to whom
they owed favors, and with young women they had slept with once
too often. He doubted there was a need for a story department anyway. After all the books, plays and synopses were read and reported
on, the producers always wanted to do something nobody had even
heard of, and most of the reports went unread.

"You're right," he said. "We need new blood there. And most of the
dreck they bought under Cantor should be written off."

"Have you read Irving Kane's *A Woman's Place?*" Goulandris asked.
"It's not bad."

Kraus rubbed his hands together and stared into the distance. He
himself had liked the book, and even suggested that Dawn would be
good in the role, but Cantor had vetoed it. He had been determined
not to use Dawn, and anyway had disliked the idea of a story about a
"strong" woman. Besides, Cantor had thought there would be trouble
with the Hays Office, and perhaps he had been right about that.

"It's good," Kraus agreed. "We had some readings on it, but Cantor
was nervous. There's a part in it for you, Dawn."

"I know. I've read it."

"You ought to talk to your friend Aaron Diamond. He's handling it, so it won't come cheap."

"I've already talked to him. He wants a fortune. He'll come down. I'm supposed to meet Kane tonight, at Aaron's party."

Goulandris and Kraus, though they did not much like each other, exchanged glances. Charles Corsini had urged them both to "look after Dawn," which, for different reasons, they were both happy to do, but in certain matters it was becoming obvious that Dawn needed no "looking after." There were whole areas of the business she knew nothing about, and there she was willing to delegate responsibility, though not until matters had been fully explained to her—but in the areas she knew, she made up her own mind and acted independently.

"Aptgeld is behind schedule," she said.

Kraus nodded wearily. "He wants to reshoot a couple of crowd scenes. He wasn't happy with the footage. Would you like to see it this afternoon, Dawn?"

"I'm house-hunting this afternoon. Tell Aptgeld he can have two more days."

"He won't be happy."

"Would Louie Mayer care about his happiness? Or Myron Cantor?"

"No, admittedly . . ."

"Well then. Run his footage first thing tomorrow morning, and let me know how it is."

Both men rose as Dawn left the table and watched her as she passed through the crowded commissary. Everybody stared at her, even the other stars. She was not only the most beautiful woman in the room— she was also the richest and now the most powerful.

"Of course it's a little *baroque*," Mr. Snayde said, fluttering his hands, "but I thought the Prince would like the loggia. It's Italianate."

"It's as gloomy as a crypt," Dawn said. "My husband has full confidence in my judgment, Mr. Snayde. I want something bright, airy and light."

Snayde stared at the Gothic bulk of the old Huntington mansion sadly. The opportunity of unloading a house like this one, with its own campanile and a Spanish Colonial ballroom, came along only once in a blue moon. "It was once owned by Rudolph Valentino," he said wistfully.

"I don't care."

"There's the old Theda Bara place. It has lovely Moorish tiling. Some of the rooms are very Eastern—just like the Taj Mahal."

"That won't do at all. In fact, that *particularly* won't do."

Mr. Snayde followed Dawn into the car with a sigh. He had vaguely supposed that Dawn might like something exotic, but she was stubbornly resistant. Most of the people Snayde dealt with had no taste of their own and were easily persuaded to buy even the most bizarre of white elephants. Dawn, however, seemed to be that rare woman with a mind of her own, and an impatience that was almost masculine.

Before it, Mr. Snayde wilted. "There's the Bitzer house," he said. "He was D. W. Griffith's cameraman."

"I know. What's it like?"

"A beautiful setting. Very secluded. Marion Davies lived in it for a while. Inside, it's a little like the White House."

Dawn lifted an eyebrow.

"William Randolph Hearst had it rebuilt," he explained. "He wanted the bathrooms and light switches in the same place as the ones in the White House so he'd feel at home if he was ever elected President. . . ."

He turned into a driveway, unlocked a massive wrought-iron gate, then got back in and drove up the long, curving driveway to a big white house with stately columns and the air of a displaced Southern mansion.

It was big—easily big enough to satisfy Charles—but it had a certain elegance, the solidity of a palace rather than the high-flown fantasy of most Hollywood houses. "It's got class," Mr. Snayde said, and for once he was right. Gleaming white, it bore a resemblance to the Daventry mansion in Calcutta—another example of English eighteenth-century elegance transplanted to a tropical climate.

"I'll take it," Dawn said, without even getting out of the car.

No woman in Mr. Snayde's experience had ever done *that* before.

By the next day the story was part of the growing Dawn Avalon legend.

Twice a year, Diamond threw a party. It was always strictly "A-list," the aristocracy of the industry, including even stars so old and eminent that most people had long since assumed they were dead.

Diamond usually told so many people he was giving the party for them that each of at least a dozen men and women spent the evening under the impression that he or she was the guest of honor—but in reality the only guest of honor at Diamond's parties was the host himself, and the evening always included a few speeches by famous actors, directors and writers who rose to their feet from their tables, and explained with varying degrees of emotion and sincerity that they owed everything—Oscars, yachts, fame, fortune—to Aaron Diamond, who sat nodding his agreement happily at the center table.

"You're looking terrific, kid," Diamond said. Dawn did not argue the point. She did look terrific, in a daring white evening dress that raised eyebrows even here, where the spectacle of female flesh on display was part of the business—all of it, in some people's opinion.

"I bought a house today, Aaron. It's the first time I've ever done that!"

"I heard. On the grapevine. Without looking inside. The Bitzer house—I used to go there, but I got tired of Hearst following Marion Davies around in case she talked to another man for more than two minutes. I once walked down to the pool with her, and there was Hearst, following us across the lawn in a goddamned golf cart to make sure we weren't holding hands. . . . You wanna meet Kane?"

"I don't know, Aaron. Do I? I liked the book. How did you know that, by the way?"

"Same grapevine, kiddo. Listen, if you want the book, *buy* it. And do yourself a favor, pass on meeting Kane. Frankly, I'm ashamed of myself. I made a rule years ago—never have a writer in the house, except for Moss Hart. Kane hit the bar the moment he arrived, and he's already made a pass at two perfectly respectable married women. I want two hundred thousand for the book, and he gets to write the screenplay for an additional fifty."

"No deal, Aaron. One hundred thousand. And I don't *want* him to write the screenplay."

"Come on, kid. His heart is set on it."

"No. I'll give him a contract for a thousand dollars a week for one year as a writer—on the condition that he doesn't work on this one."

Diamond nodded. "You got yourself a deal. You're a smart cookie. No writer is any good at adapting his own book. Of course, a year in Hollywood will probably kill the poor son of a bitch's talent—he'll never go back to a cold-water apartment in Greenwich Village to write the Great American Novel, but what the hell, we've all gotta grow up someday, right?"

"Right, Aaron."

"And in the meantime, he can't complain to the press that you're screwing up his book—because he's going to be working for you. Smart! Where's your goddamned husband?"

She could tell him nothing. She had no idea where Charles was, or even if he was alive, she thought, telling herself not to overdramatize her fears. "He's away on business, Aaron."

"He should be *here*. If I were married to a pretty girl like you, I'd at least stay at home, I can tell you that."

"He's got a lot of business problems just at the moment."

"I hear Luckman is one of them. That's a big, *big* problem, honey. I'll tell you one thing I've learned in this business. Never make an enemy. Something doesn't work out—what the hell, there's always another deal tomorrow. . . . Charles should have known that. Luckman's going to go for his balls, and you can't blame him for that. Listen, you ought to relax, have some fun, forget about Charles." Diamond waved a diminutive hand at his glittering guests. "Go dancing, go out more, know what I mean?"

"I don't like to go alone, Aaron. I miss Charles."

"So *don't* go alone—there are plenty of guys who'll take you out."

"I'm not sure how Charles would feel about that."

"This is the twentieth century, kiddo. It's okay to have fun, even if you're married."

Dawn shrugged. She didn't disagree, but with Charles away, she usually went home after work, took a bath, put Nivea cream on her face, ordered a light supper and went to bed early. Her life, when she was not working, had always been shaped by a man. She had never resented it—she still did not altogether resent it—but it was a fact, though not one she cared to explain to Aaron Diamond, who was already getting restless.

Diamond always displayed a certain nervous hysteria, which he struggled manfully to control, in a roomful of celebrities—like a child faced with so many presents beneath the Christmas tree that he cannot decide which to open first. His eyes flickered back and forth as he tried to decide whom he wanted to talk to next. "There's Mrs. Adolph Kiss! You know her?"

"Well, no."

"You oughta get round more, Dawn. There's Clark and Carole coming in!"

Dawn looked up. Even in a room crowded with celebrities, the arrival of Clark Gable and Carole Lombard caused a momentary hush, or at any rate a drop in the level of conversation. Their affair was as close as Hollywood could come to an open, acknowledged scandal, in an industry which refused to admit that people who weren't married ever went to bed with each other, and where marriage, however brief, was held to be as sacred as the flag or motherhood.

"I thought they were hiding out on his ranch," Dawn said. She thought Gable looked glum. He hated the notoriety he had earned for himself, and he seldom smiled—though that, Dawn knew, was more because he had bad teeth.

At parties, Diamond often left a conversation in mid-sentence, so quickly that it sometimes took a few seconds before you realized you were talking to yourself. Dawn was used to it, but this time Diamond did her the honor of completing the conversation, before he turned away to greet his new guests. "Clark didn't want to come," he explained. "He says he's keeping a low profile because of Rhea Gable, and the press. But I told him not to hand me any of that crap. 'I made you, kid, and I can break you,' that's what I said to him—and here he is!"

Dawn laughed. Diamond had known most of the greats of Hollywood while they were still nobodies, and dealt with them accordingly. "You're a goddamned *star*, Dawn," he said. "Go enjoy yourself, chrissake!" Rising on tiptoe, he gave Dawn a kiss and vanished, to reappear, as if by magic, standing between Gable and Lombard.

She glanced at her reflection in Diamond's mirror.

The eyes were as dark and luminous as ever, the cheekbones as sharply defined. She had been in her teens when the perfection of her face caught David Konig's attention. That perfection was still there, even allowing for the scars, but to her critical eye it was ever so slightly flawed, like a perfect piece of china with one fine hairline crack beneath the glaze, still beautiful, but not as beautiful as it had been. Sometimes, for a collector, that single flaw was enough to spoil his pleasure in an object he had once treasured. It was not that the damage need be all that serious, or even noticeable. There was simply no way the object could be the same as it had once been.

She stared critically at the face in the spotless glass. There were no age lines yet, but she had a sense of lines to come, forming beneath the smooth skin even as she looked at herself. Was it a mistake to play a young woman of eighteen, at the beginning of the picture? Was it sensible to attempt a role in which she would have to age? Many actresses thought that was asking for trouble. Most of them were right.

She took a glass of champagne from a passing waiter and walked out onto the terrace with its long row of naked women in bronze and marble. A star was considered by most people to be unapproachable, like a goddess, particularly when she was married to a rich and powerful man. Even on Aaron Diamond's terrace she was treated like royalty. She did not regret it. She did not want company. Men and women made way for her. They did not ask her to join them.

She chatted with a few of those who passed for nobility, here—the Selznicks, Louis Mayer, Mervyn LeRoy—until she found herself at the dark end of the terrace, suddenly alone and lonely. When would Charles come back? She missed him so much that her nights were like a jail sentence.

She heard a noise behind her, turned and saw Aaron Diamond standing on the marble flagstones alone, dwarfed by the statues. He took a silk handkerchief out of the pocket of his white dinner jacket, removed his glasses and polished them. Without the tinted lenses, his eyes seemed smaller and weary. For a second, Dawn was aware of his age, and startled by how old he looked.

"They said you were out here, kid." His voice was low and without a hint of his usual brashness.

Diamond stared at her myopically, still wiping the lenses of his glasses with the same obsessive attention that he gave to cutlery and china in restaurants. He held them up to the moonlight, and, still not satisfied, he breathed on them and began polishing again. "I got some news just came over the ticker tape in my study."

Dawn clutched her arms against her sides. "It's not Charles, is it?" she asked. "He hasn't—had an accident?" She had been about to say "been arrested," but thought the better of it.

Diamond put his glasses back on. "I like being kissed as much as the next man, but my glasses always get smeared. . . . Ina Blaze was just about to kiss me, but I told her 'No dice.' I heard she has a cold. You can't be too careful about germs."

"What *is* it, Aaron?"

"Well, you might think it was good news, I suppose. It looks like Luckman isn't going to testify against Charles, honey."

"How on earth did Charles manage *that?*"

Diamond cleared his throat. He leaned closer to Dawn, his face serious. "Luckman's dead," he said.

"Dead? Of what?"

"Somebody put a knife in his back, right there in the federal holding pen in Washington, the day before he was supposed to testify. One of the inmates must have done it."

Dawn shivered. "He must have had a lot of enemies," she whispered, more to herself than to Diamond.

"Not that I ever heard of. He only had one who mattered, anyway. . . . Of course, it's not easy to have a guy hit when he's surrounded by feds—or cheap. But there are people who can fix that kind of thing. I've known a few."

"Harry Faust?"

Diamond looked surprised. "Harry is one of them, sure. What made you think of him?"

"It was just a thought. People are going to jump to the conclusion that Charles arranged it, aren't they?"

"Yes. That's exactly what they're going to think. And say. Mind you, if he did, it was probably the smart thing to do. Not that it's going to win him the Man of the Year award."

"He's not competing for it."

She turned away from Diamond and the bright lights of his house. She felt a dreadful fear. She was not sorry for the wretched Luckman, whom she did not even know, but now she knew not only that Charles was capable of anything but that he had given Vale another hold over both of them—and Harry Faust too, who was, presumably, even worse. She walked down the steps of the terrace into the garden, holding back her tears.

Before her, on Diamond's lawn, was a pool, lit by underwater floodlights buried in the sides. A beautiful girl appeared from the pool house in a skintight black bathing suit, climbed the ladder to the high diving board and dived in gracefully, her head appearing a moment later among the floating gardenias.

She might be a guest acting on a whim, or perhaps she was somebody hired for the evening, Dawn thought, to provide a water spectacle. Nobody else seemed to have noticed her, but she paid no attention, her long legs carrying her from one end of the pool to the other in a fluid, perfect motion. Her blond hair fanned out behind her, glittering in the beam from the lights below, her body outlined in a silver-blue halo of light.

Dawn sighed. It was one of those rare moments when Hollywood seems as romantic as people who lived outside its narrow confines liked to believe it was, a sudden, haunting vision of glamour and wealth that seemed to justify all the tawdry hustling.

She looked back at the terrace behind her, where dozens of familiar, greedy faces glowed red in the light from the flaming torches and candles, as though at some kind of satanic ball, at once elegant and frightening, and then again at the girl cleaving the water in her lonely, obsessive crawl—who knew why, or for whose pleasure?—and felt a slight chill.

She envied the girl, who could not be more than twenty. She had no responsibilities except her own beauty. Did she have a past to hide? She did not look as if she had a care in the world.

For a moment Dawn would have willingly given up everything she had to have Charles back—and to have a life as simple as that of the girl in the pool.

Then she dabbed her eyes, drained her glass of champagne and started back up the steps. If ever there was a moment to put a good face on things, this was it.

CHAPTER 23

THE WAR NEWS was so bad that it quickly pushed Charles's story off the front pages, then out of the papers altogether. Across the Pacific, outposts Americans never even knew they had were falling to the Japanese one after another, and there seemed no very good reason why the Japanese should not eventually reach Australia. To the east, in Russia, the Germans were entrenched around Leningrad, while in North Africa they were approaching the Suez Canal. In America, the stock market was up and movie attendance had never been higher.

Dawn seldom read the newspapers, though she could see the gloomy headlines in the pile of papers and magazines on Diamond's Chippendale coffee table. Richard Beaumont stared back at her from the cover of *Life,* an annoying reminder that her own career was on ice. Beaumont had rehabilitated himself in the eyes of the public by ferrying trainers for the RAF, then had returned to the stage in triumph to resume his work as a Shakespearean actor. He soon had his own company—and his own theater—despite the vociferous objections of Lord Arlington, now a member of the War Cabinet, who held Beaumont responsible for his younger daughter's death and devoted his spare time to a smear campaign against Beaumont that only increased the actor's swiftly growing popularity.

Dawn had read of Beaumont's triumphs and was, she had to admit to herself, jealous. People thought of her as a star but not as a great actress. And a lot depended on the new picture. Being a star was a precarious business. It sometimes surprised her to realize how much *being* a star meant to her, even now that she had money and power. The script for A *Woman's Place* had already been revised twice to expand her role—Kraus had locked the writers in a bungalow at the Beverly Hills Hotel to work on it day and night and had placed an assistant outside to ensure that they received neither food nor drink until they slid their daily quota of pages under the door.

"Have you got a director yet?" Diamond asked.

Dawn shook her head. Kraus had recommended at least half a dozen directors who were under studio contract, but Dawn was impressed with none of them. One of Cantor's weaknesses had been his preference for hacks. His idea of a good director was a man who could shoot three or four pages of script a day and stay on schedule.

"Try Cukor," Diamond suggested.

"He's on my list."

"He's good."

"I know. I'm more worried about the cameraman, actually. I did a few tests. I wasn't happy."

Diamond shrugged. "There are plenty of good cameramen around, chrissake. Don't worry about details."

But it was the one thing, above all, that she *did* worry about. Kraus, who had a high regard for her common sense, found her concern on the subject of cameramen just as foolish as Diamond did, but then Kraus and Diamond, she told herself, weren't going to have their faces projected onto movie screens all over the world. Under the harsh lights her scars were visible—the camera picked up the fine tracing of Echeverría's handiwork, just as Dawn's own harsh makeup lights did in her dressing room. Other people might not notice, but *she* did. And magnified on the screen, other people would notice. It was the kind of thing that makeup could mask, but the perfection of Dawn's skin, on film as in life, had always been her own, and owed nothing to Max Factor.

She sighed. It was too late to back out now, with the whole industry talking about her. She lifted her chin.

"Billy Sofkin tells me the bills on the house are astronomical," Diamond said.

"Well, speed is expensive. Billy says it's hard to find workmen—they're all in Burbank making airplanes at God-knows-how-much an hour."

"Use the studio workmen."

"I do. But I have to reimburse the studio."

"You're an honest woman. Braverman didn't. Neither did Cantor. But you're right."

"I can't stop other people from stealing from the studio if I do it myself. . . . Anyway, I'm not worried about the money. I want the house ready for Charles."

"Is he going to hole up here for a while?"

"I wouldn't describe living in Bel Air as 'holing up,' Aaron," Dawn said with irritation. She was willing to make allowances for the fact that Aaron didn't altogether trust Charles, but only up to a point. She wished she could tell him the truth about Charles—but he would never forgive her for revealing his secrets to Diamond.

Diamond realized he had passed that point. He sat silently for a moment, working his jaw muscles. Dawn could see her reflection on his bald scalp. She wondered if he polished it daily. "I just meant he's going to have to stay out of the limelight for a while," he added, by way of apology.

"I don't think that's Charles's style."

"It would be the prudent thing to do."

"Prudence isn't exactly his style, either."

"So I notice. All right, all right . . . keep your shirt on. Listen, you want to help him, get yourself some good press. Take some of the bite out of the headlines. Polly Hammer's a friend of mine. She's dying to meet you."

"I hate interviews, Aaron. So does Charles."

"Forget Charles. Polly's syndicated in a hundred papers, chrissake. You make friends with her, she'll make Charles sound like a fucking cub scout. You get on the right side of Polly and she'll back you one hundred percent whatever you do. Trust me on this one. You need a friend in the press, and so does Charles. Give her a call. Ask her around to see the house. She loves to help people decorate."

"I don't need help."

"What does that have to do with it? Take her shopping. Tell her about your plans. Give her a couple of items. You'll have a friend for life, kiddo—a friend who has about ten million readers. Besides, she gets fantastic discounts."

"I'll call her, Aaron. I promise."

"Take your mind off things, right? And Dawn"—Diamond leaned forward, his expression serious—"you love Charles, I understand that, but be careful."

"Careful of *what*, Aaron?"

"Just careful, that's all. Maybe he's only unlucky, but bad things seem to happen to people who get close to Charles Corsini . . ."

"Aaron, he's my husband. Most of the stories they write about him aren't true."

"You could be right. But he has bad luck with people. Charles has left a lot of wreckage behind him, Dawn."

She shook her head, slapped one glove against the other and walked to the door. "I'll phone Polly," she said, cutting off the discussion.

He rose from behind his desk. "You want *my* opinion, Charles is a lucky man. He's got a beautiful, talented wife, with a head for business, who's a lady. That kind of thing counts for something out here. Background, class—people respect that. Don't you forget it. Most people out here come from Nowhere, U.S.A., but you're different and people know it."

"Aaron, Charles is a prince, you know."

"Yeah, yeah, an *Italian* prince. This town is full of princes, chrissake—Polish, Russian, Italian, you name it. What I'm trying to say is that you got the right kind of background that counts, that people look up to: England, the Raj, a father in the Indian Army, growing up in a maharajah's palace. . . . People respect that kind of thing."

Diamond waved at his sporting prints and antique furniture, as if they belonged to Dawn. "It's *solid*. Corsini knows that. He's no dummy. He'd probably give his right arm to have the kind of background you do. You can't buy that kind of class, baby. I know you never talk about it—and that's good, it shows you're no snob. But it *counts*, Dawn, don't you ever forget it. Or let Charles forget it."

Dawn looked at Diamond, standing behind his eighteenth-century partner's desk in his cream silk suit and his black-and-white correspondent's shoes, another Anglophile in a town where an English butler was still the ultimate status symbol, and realized how impossible it would be to tell him the truth about herself. Besides, he was right. The background that she had invented, had pieced together like a patchwork quilt over the years, was now a seamless garment, enshrined in legend. She almost believed it herself.

It was not something which Dawn herself thought about often. How much attention could you pay to a story that was a total fabrication? At least two maharajahs now claimed it was in *their* palace that Dawn Avalon had grown up. One of them had even shown a journalist the pony she had ridden as a child. Scores of English residents in India— sahibs and their mems—wrote to Dawn or to the newspapers, apparently convinced that they had known her as a child, and were well acquainted with her parents. One young woman even wrote an account of her childhood friendship with Dawn, which was published in the Sunday *Express* and the Hearst papers in America, full of descriptions of moonlit rides under the supervision of Akbar, the turbaned, faithful *khidmatgar,* of picnics, of summers spent in the Simla Hills and al fresco lessons under a sacred baobab tree. All agreed that Dawn had been a child of singular beauty, and that she had shown early promise of a great career as an actress.

For a moment she wished there had been at some point an opportunity to detach herself from the legend, but the sight of Diamond staring at her with admiration and envy in his glassy eyes made it more obvious than ever that it was too late.

Twenty years as a Hollywood gossip columnist had made Polly Hammer impervious to the truth, and in fact unable to recognize it. She preferred myth and fantasy. The more improbable a story or a press release was, the more likely she was to believe it. Like her readers, she was a hopeless romantic. She wanted to believe in Dawn's "fabulous" childhood, and in Charles as "a fairy-tale prince." At the same time, she was shrewd about the movie business. She knew everybody's secrets, but only gave away those of the people she didn't like. Dawn liked her instantly, and Polly responded by treating her like an adopted daughter.

"You ought to go to more parties. You ought to *give* some parties, too. There's more to life than the studio, you know."

"I used to go to parties when David was alive. . . ."

"But since then, you've been a recluse. Okay, honey, I understand. There was that dreadful business with Myron Cantor over poor Cynthia Beaumont's death—then you ran away to Mexico and married Charles. It wouldn't do you any harm to settle down and live a normal life for a while."

Dawn wondered if Polly's conception of a "normal life" was anything like her own. Dawn had never run a household or done any of the things most women seemed to concern themselves with. Until recently she had never even *shopped* for herself.

Polly insisted on taking her on a whirlwind tour of the best stores in Beverly Hills. "You're missing one of the great pleasures of life, honey," she told Dawn, and before the morning was out, Dawn had to agree that Polly was right. There was a simple pleasure to buying things without a man standing around to make the final decisions.

Lunch was another of those things that Dawn seldom thought about. At the studio, when she was working, she ate a quick meal. Polly, however, insisted on taking her to lunch at the Beverly Wilshire Hotel, where Dawn was treated with the kind of reverence reserved elsewhere for visiting royalty.

Even here it was possible to shop. Models walked from table to table displaying the hats and dresses of Armand Silk. Silk had dressed Polly for years. He had even made dresses for Dawn once or twice, despite the fact that he usually disliked designing for stars, because people looked at them instead of his clothes. He came over to their table, his bracelets jangling like wind chimes, and sat down unasked, being one of those people who always assume they are welcome. For ten years he had lived with Billy Sofkin, the decorator, and as a couple they had become known from the flats of Beverly Hills to the heights of Bel Air as the "soft trades." He helped himself to a maraschino cherry from Dawn's fruit salad. "A dull house," he complained.

"Not much trade?" Polly asked.

"Forget the trade, dear. If I do a thousand dollars today, I'll be lucky. It hardly even pays for the *models*. No, but I mean *look* at them! Dowdy matrons and their cowlike daughters from Pasadena, in for a day's shopping. . . . And the usual men hoping to pick up a model, or one of the matrons, God forbid. . . . There's Harry Warmfleisch, behind the palm tree. He pays the captain to leave one of his cards on every table with his private telephone number on it, right under the basket of melba toast."

"I didn't get one," Dawn said.

"Oh, my dear—you're a *star*. He wouldn't dare. He's married. Stars live in glass houses. People who have affairs with them get seen."

"Even stars have secrets, surely?"

"Not for long," Silk said. "Look what happened to Chaplin. The bigger you are, the harder it is to keep a secret from the press. Remember Grace Darling?"

"I've never heard of her."

"That's *just* my point. She was very big, long before your time— then one day her sister turned up, complaining that Grace wasn't sending her family any money. . . ."

"*That* killed her career?"

"My dear, Grace's sister was from Alabama. She was *colored*. . . . You *must* let me design some dresses for you," Silk said. "I'm very busy, but for *you* . . ."

"I'd love that," Dawn lied, desperate to get away from him. "We must be going," she added firmly, giving Polly a look that made her finish her coffee in one gulp.

Silk winked at her.

She felt a sudden wave of panic wash over her. It wasn't until she was outside on Wilshire Boulevard that she came to her senses and told herself she was a star, a princess and a major shareholder of Empire Pictures.

She told herself firmly that she had nothing to be afraid of.

But as she stepped into Polly's car, she had to grip her handbag hard with both gloved hands.

They were still trembling.

"I thought you didn't *like* Armand's dresses," Polly said, once they were in the car. "Are you all right?"

"I'm fine."

"You're very pale. Worried about Charles?"

"No, no, he'll be back soon."

"I thought maybe that's what you were worried about. You haven't been playing around while he's away, have you?"

"No, Polly, I have *not*."

"No need to get on your high horse, honey. I've always taken the view that what a woman does when her husband is out of town is just as much her business as what *he* does when he's away." Polly braked sharply, narrowly missing a terrified pedestrian, who took a running jump back to the curb. Dawn closed her eyes at the sight of a limousine bearing down on them. She opened them a moment too soon, just in time to see Marty Braverman cowering in the back seat as Polly's car missed his by an inch or two.

Polly waved at him cheerfully. "He's on his way to see Howard Hughes, I bet," she said. "I hear Marty and Myron Cantor are trying to take over Republic."

"Will they, do you think?"

"Probably. The rumor is that Hughes is financing them." As inaccurate as Polly was about the private lives of the stars, she usually knew her stuff when it came to business. "Listen, it's the best thing that could happen to you. So long as they don't have a studio to run, they'll spend all their time trying to get even with you for kicking them out of Empire. Once they're back at work, they'll forget it. In a year's time they'll be making co-production deals with you and trying to get a loan out of your stars. There are no permanent enemies in this business, honey."

She paused, running a red light with the horn blaring. "And no permanent friends, either . . . Is Charles the jealous type?" she asked, quickly changing subjects. It was a habit of hers, partly because like everyone else in Hollywood she had a short attention span, but also because it was a technique, developed over the years—a sudden, unexpected question often caught the subject off guard. As a result, a conversation with Polly was a series of zigzags at high speed, much like her driving.

"I haven't given him any cause to be jealous, so I don't know," Dawn said impatiently.

"He's got a reputation for being jealous. *And* he's Latin. I like jealous men myself. What's the poop on his first wife?"

"Oh for God's sake, Polly, none of those rumors is true."

"You're not afraid of him, then?"

"There's nothing to be afraid of, Polly. We love each other. And stop pumping me."

"Okay, okay. You're afraid of *something*, honey. You can't hide that kind of thing from Polly. . . . Listen, I can be discreet. If you've got problems, *talk* to me about them. That's what friends are for. We've all got secrets and we can't bottle them up forever, know what I mean? It's bad for you. Me, I always poured my heart out to my hairdresser, until I found out my secrets were the talk of every queer bar in L.A. Armand Silk probably knew more about my life than I did, for God's sake. You're looking pale again. . . . Wait a minute, I have to stop here."

Polly always drove as if hers were the only car on the road. Before Dawn could ask where "here" was, Polly swerved into a parking space without diminishing speed and jammed on the brakes, leaving the tail of the La Salle sticking out into the street at an acute angle. A man who had been backing into the vacant spot leaned out the window of his car and shouted at her. Polly waved at him cheerfully as she got out, exposing a length of thigh that reduced him to silence. "It never fails," she said.

Dawn hurried after her. This time Polly did not seem to have shopping on her mind. The place she had to visit was a storefront on West Pico with a dusty flowered curtain and a bowl of faded flowers in the window. A discreet hand-lettered sign hung in the doorway. It read: "Madame Vera—by appointment only."

Polly banged against the glass with the flat of her diamond ring. The door was unlocked. "You'll love her," she said, pushing it open.

"Love who?"

"Vera. I don't make a move without her."

"Surely you don't believe in fortunetelling?" Dawn asked. The small room was entirely draped in some kind of dark cloth, in the center of which stood a small cloth-covered round table with a bowl of flowers on it and four folding chairs. The light was subdued, even aqueous, and several candles burning in old glass jars raised the temperature in the stuffy room to that of a steam bath. There was something familiar about the smell of the place, something that gave Dawn a sudden and altogether unwelcome feeling of *déjà vu*—a combination of the scented candles, the smell of herbs and spices, the rich scent of the decaying flowers, a suggestion of some heavy, musky perfume.

From behind a flowered curtain at the back of the room there was the sound of someone coughing—a harsh, racking cough that went on for at least a minute. Then whoever was behind the curtain lit a cigarette, coughed again and turned the lights down even lower, so the room was lit only by the flickering candles.

"How are you feeling today, Vera?" Polly asked. Her cheerful voice sounded out of place in this dismal and slightly sinister room, and Madame Vera seemed to feel so too, for she remained silent for a long time. "How should I feel?" she said eventually. "I'm an old woman." The voice was guttural, throaty, foreign in some hard-to-define way. Dawn felt a sudden chill, as if she were standing in a draft. She crossed her bare arms and was surprised to find how cold her skin was, despite the warmth of the room.

The curtain parted, but Madame Vera remained invisible. One moment there was nobody sitting at the table. The next, without any perceptible movement, the place in front of the curtain was occupied by a shadowy figure, wearing a long robe without a hood, a costume similar to that of a medieval monk in one of the more sinister and reclusive orders, except that Vera's was made out of dark flowered silk.

The lights were arranged so as to cast her side of the table in almost total darkness. The only visible part of her was her hands, which she placed neatly on the table, palms down, the fingers spread. The fingers were long, thin and slightly swollen at the joints by arthritis. The nails were pointed and lacquered a fierce red, though chipped at the edges. The lacquer had been applied unevenly, in heavy layers, as if by someone who was farsighted and too restless to keep her hands still while it dried, or who clung to the forms of vanity without really believing that they mattered anymore. "Sit," she said, and they both sat.

"Vera," Polly said, with a nervous edge to her voice that was very unlike her usual breezy, self-confident self, "this is Dawn Avalon."

"Is it?" Madame Vera's voice was harsh, but there was something in the way she asked the question—a flat, gruff challenge—that caught Dawn's attention. She did not seem to be unaware of who Dawn Avalon was, but she was not impressed, either—not that Dawn cared about that, for after all, this was Hollywood, where it was possible to meet Joan Crawford in a drugstore or see Clark Gable shopping at the Farmers' Market. The question seemed somehow to have a deeper significance that made her feel uncomfortable. Dawn had no taste for the occult and no interest in fortunetelling. She wanted to leave, but apparently it was one of the disadvantages of friendship with Polly that she carried you along with her on her whims.

"Vera's the fortuneteller to the stars," Polly said. "Ina Blaze doesn't make a move without her."

"A Pisces. We drew the Seven of Pentacles reversed in the Twelfth House last week. Secret enemies."

"Everybody knows Ina's finished at Metro," Polly said. "Even Ina."

Madame Vera laughed—a brief, throaty laugh that was almost a bark and might have conveyed almost anything except humor. She reached into a drawer and produced a packet wrapped in yellow silk which she placed on the table. "The cards don't tell us anything we don't already know," she said. "We know the future, all of us. We pretend we don't, because we are afraid. The cards draw it out of us, that's all, Miss Avalon."

"I'm not sure I want to know mine," Dawn said lightly. She had an uncomfortable feeling that the old woman was hostile just from the way she had pronounced her name. She wished Polly hadn't brought her here and wondered if there was any way to cut the visit short. But Polly had noticed her fear once already today—there was no point in giving her another glimpse of it.

The old woman unwrapped the package and placed a pack of tarot cards precisely in the center of the table. She folded the square of silk neatly and put it back into the drawer. "They must be wrapped in silk," she explained for Dawn's benefit, "to protect them from discordant vibrations. That's what they say, anyway. The truth is—they're only cards."

She shuffled them quickly, as deftly as a croupier, and placed the deck back on the table. "Just as in life, we have choices to make here. Left, right. Stop, go. Stay, leave. You can't run away from the future any more than you can from the past. Is it the past that frightens you? I think so."

Dawn stared at her—or rather, stared into the darkness—wondering what the old woman meant. She put her hands on the table. Her palms were moist. More than ever, she wanted to go, but it was too late to leave without being rude. Besides, she felt a certain numb inertia, as if part of her wanted to stay.

"You have beautiful hands," Madame Vera said. "I had beautiful hands, too, once upon a time." She paused and coughed. "Not as beautiful as yours, of course, but not bad. . . . So, Mrs. Hammer? A reading? You haven't come here to listen to me talk about myself."

"Do Dawn, Vera. I had a reading last week."

"I remember. The Tree of Life. It's not the best way to start with a beginner. And it takes a long time. Perhaps a quick reading, Miss Avalon? A demonstration, as it were?" She removed one card and handed the rest of the pack to Dawn. "Shuffle!" Her voice was commanding.

"I've forgotten how. I'm not really a card player."

"So? You've missed one of life's great pleasures, then. Cards fill out the empty spaces in a life—the periods of loneliness and boredom. Perhaps you haven't been lonely and bored yet? Believe me, it's not too late to learn solitaire. Sooner or later you'll be glad you know how. Please hold the cards in your hands, then ask a question in your mind—silently."

"What question?"

"Why, the question you want answered, of course."

Dawn held the deck of cards between her crossed hands. They felt strangely warm. She wondered if that too was part of the illusion, or whether it was her own hands that had warmed them. Then she realized that her hands were ice-cold, and she shivered. She thought about the question, but it seemed to her there was no one question to ask. There were many questions, like the facets on a diamond, and each question led to another.

"Can I trust Charles?" she asked herself, and put the cards down.

"You have the question?"

She nodded.

Vera turned the single card face up. "The Queen of Wands." She handed it to Dawn, who looked at it, trying to guess its significance. A forceful-looking woman sat on a throne, holding a staff of living wood in her right hand and a sunflower in her left. A black cat sat before her. At each corner of the throne was a lion's head, and behind her was a tapestry of lions and flowers. There were three pyramids in the background, or possibly hills. "What am I supposed to see here?" she asked.

"Nothing. It is what *I* see. The Queen of Wands, of course, is *you*. A woman of great power, practical with money, highly sexed, determined to have things her own way . . . Usually she is blond, but that doesn't matter. The wands are the signs of life, creativity, action. . . . Cut the deck in three, please."

Vera placed the Queen of Wands in the center of the table, picked up the pile of cards to Dawn's left with her left hand and swiftly dealt the cards, face up. The first two she placed crossed over the Queen of Wands, then four more to form a cross around the center cards, then another four in line, to the right of the cross. The cards were brightly colored and crudely drawn.

Polly gave a startled cry.

"The Ten of Swords covers the Queen of Wands," Vera said. "There is a possibility your life will shortly be ruled by despair. There may be tears. If your question had to do with a business matter, someone may be ruined. It is crossed by the Tower."

"Bankruptcy," Polly whispered.

"Not necessarily. Ruin, or violent death for someone else? This is also possible. Certainly a period of confusion and change will follow the answer to the question. Note the profusion of Court cards—a great many people will be influenced by the outcome. The tenth card is interesting, too. The Four of Wands in the Final Outcome . . . A long life? Prosperity? But at some cost, I think . . . And look at the third card: Justice reversed! There is something in the past, something troubling you, a deed for which you were punished—or perhaps for which you were *never* punished. . . ."

Dawn felt her throat go dry. The voice seemed familiar to her now. She stared at the old woman's hands and realized that they were almost as familiar to her as her own. The brown age spots were new, or perhaps simply more pronounced—it had been eight years after all—but otherwise, they were unchanged. Dawn watched mesmerized as the old woman placed another card between them.

"The moon," the old lady whispered. "You see the twin towers? The road goes past them. We cannot build a fortress strong enough to hold back the changes of life. Isn't that so? We have to continue our journey, on and on, over the mountains we see in the distance, and into the unknown. You see the wolf, the dog, the crayfish in the foreground? We can run away from dangers, but there will be new ones, perhaps even the same ones, waiting for us on the other side of the mountain. . . . Of course, the card's real meaning is bad luck for someone who loves you," the old woman added briskly, tapping it for emphasis.

Dawn hadn't the strength to look at her face. "Someone who loved me in the past, or someone who loves me now?" she asked, her throat dry.

"I think you would know that better than I would—Queenie," the old woman said.

"Who the hell is Queenie?" Polly asked.

"It's nice of you to come back and see me. You may as well sit down."

"I had a hell of a time explaining to Polly why I had to leave in a hurry," Dawn said. She had spent the afternoon trying to decide what to do, sitting in her bungalow in the Beverly Hills Hotel, refusing all telephone calls. She had pleaded a headache as an excuse for being left alone—and in fact she swiftly developed one, so intense that she decided the only way to end it was to come back and have it out with Magda in the privacy of the night. Her head still throbbed. She sat down and pressed her hands over her eyes.

"Your head hurts, darling? You've taken aspirin?"

Dawn nodded. Taking the aspirin had been, for her, an extreme measure, and she was not surprised to find that she felt even worse after swallowing them.

"Aspirin does nothing," Magda said. "I'll make you a cup of tea and give you something that will help." She rose stiffly and shuffled over to turn on the hot plate. "Tea bags," she muttered, as the kettle started to whistle, the sound piercing Dawn's skull, "it's the one thing about this country I can't stand. . . ."

She filled a chipped mug, then carefully squeezed several drops of purple medicine into it.

"What's that?" Dawn asked, with a certain degree of suspicion.

"A harmless vegetable substance," Magda answered. "Drink it like a good girl, Queenie."

The phrase produced—to Dawn's own surprise—instant obedience. For a moment, she *was* Queenie, sitting on the veranda, doing as she was told. She sipped the tea, cautiously at first. She wondered if Magda knew that you could buy tea in bulk here? Dawn never allowed tea bags to be used in her house—not even in the hotel—but she didn't want to say so. Perhaps the packets of tea she used were a luxury? Were tea bags cheaper? She had no idea. She never went shopping for food, and therefore had no idea what things cost.

Her headache vanished as she drank the tea, and so did the indigestion caused by the aspirin. She smiled at Magda.

"You see? I knew what I was talking about, eh? You can trust Magda, darling."

Dawn put her mug down. She would have liked another cup of tea, but it didn't seem the right moment to ask Magda for anything. "*Can I trust you, Magda?* That's the question. That's why I'm here."

"Not for old times' sake, Queenie? What a pity! But you're right." Magda lit a cigarette and studied Dawn through the smoke. "I'll make you another cup of tea," she said. "Don't worry. It won't cost you anything."

"How long have you been in America, Magda?"

"A year. Perhaps a little more." Magda returned with two mugs of tea this time. One she put in front of Dawn. Into the other she poured a couple of fingers of Scotch.

"Why did you leave India?"

"Why did I *go* there? To survive. I was getting too old to be—what shall I say?—a bar girl. Besides, living with your mother was a little depressing after you and Morgan left. Your mother took *un coup de vieux.* How does one say it? She became suddenly old. Of course, that happens anyway in India, as you know. It's not like here, where women the same age as your mother sit by their pools in the afternoon playing cards. A good dentist, a blond rinse, a face lift perhaps, a strict diet, and they can pass for fifty, or maybe forty, at a distance—though unfortunately they can't keep their husband at the right distance . . . but in India it's different, no? There one is young and beautiful, briefly—then suddenly old and wrinkled, with no teeth. There is nothing in between. Perhaps it's the climate. In any case, in your mother's world there is no equivalent of somebody like Mrs. Daventry. . . ."

"You know her?"

"Her, no. But I was her husband's mistress for a time, you know. Oh, one of many. A singularly unimaginative lover, by the way—and not at all generous, either. Generosity is so important, don't you think?" Magda gave a dry snicker, like a branch breaking. "Well, well . . . it seems like only yesterday when we used to sit on the veranda together. You've been very fortunate since then." She looked at Dawn's dress.

"Pink! What would your mother say, I wonder? You made her very unhappy, you know."

"I know. I used to write all the time, but then life got so complicated that I didn't know what to say anymore."

"All the time! Ha!" Magda's expression was disagreeable enough to put Dawn on guard.

"I've been meaning to write . . . so much has been going on. . . ."

"I know. I read the papers. Still, a letter doesn't take that much time. After all, you only have one mother."

Guilt swept away Dawn's caution for an instant—that and surprise. There was no reason why she should have to justify herself to Magda, but she was unable to prevent herself from trying. It was as if she were a small girl again, trying to please the grown-ups. "Once the war is over," she heard herself saying, "I thought of bringing her over here— if she'd come. . . ."

Magda nodded. "Wouldn't that be a little embarrassing, *chérie*? For you? And for your husband? One hardly sees how you would explain—the difference in color. . . ."

"I'd buy her a house somewhere. I wasn't thinking of having her live with us. I don't suppose she'd want to anyway."

"You're probably right. Who knows? You might have gotten away with it without too many questions asked. You were always good at getting away with things, as I remember. It wasn't very pleasant for her when the police arrived, looking for you and Morgan."

"I can imagine."

"Can you?" Magda asked coldly. "I doubt it. Your mother became an outcast. Nobody would talk to her, visit her. . . . Of course, it's different now. People saw your pictures. They knew Ma's little Queenie had become a film star. Your poor mother used to show everybody the little clippings you sent. Then, when they stopped, she invented letters from you, and when it became obvious there were no more letters, she invented reasons why you couldn't write. . . ."

"They know I'm Queenie?"

"What do you think? Of course they do. Every chee-chee in India goes to the movies and says, 'Look at Dawn Avalon, she's one of us.' Without bitterness, I must say. You're a *heroine*, darling. You've done what they all want to do: lied and gotten away with it. You've proved it's possible to escape—even if you did have to steal a bracelet to do it. Your mother, needless to say, wouldn't agree. Her heart was broken. A painful situation—still, it's one that her marriage must have prepared her for, don't you think? She knew *you* wouldn't come back. Why should you? Morgan, on the other hand—that's a different story."

The mention of Morgan's name was enough of a threat to restore Dawn's courage. "I haven't seen Morgan in years," she said briskly. "And I can do without your criticism, Magda. I left home and made a life for myself. I'm not ashamed of that. I don't say there aren't things I'd do differently, if I had it all to do again, but you're not in any position to insult *me*. Not even about Ma."

Magda lifted an eyebrow. "You're right, of course."

"I didn't come here to be lectured."

"Why did you come here, I wonder—curiosity? I don't think so. Or only partly. Fear? But what harm can an old woman like me do to a famous star with all the money in the world?" She lit a cigarette and coughed, the same hacking cough that Dawn had heard so often in the old bungalow in Calcutta when she was a child.

She took up the second pile of cards and dealt them in the same curious pattern. "The Keltic Cross," she said. "It's the easiest pattern. Look at the card in the Fourth Position. Death!" She stubbed out her cigarette in the upturned lid of a jam jar. She put her finger on the card, just below the figure of a skeleton in armor on a white horse.

"In the background, look—there is a ship! So: a journey that ends in death. But then look to the right. There is a woman, you see her? Kneeling. She looks away from the corpse, which is under the hooves of Death's horse. Above her is the rising sun. Life goes on, for her—as it must for everybody. A strange reading, isn't it? A journey that ends in death. But it's in the past. You say Morgan is well?"

"I didn't say that at all. I said I haven't heard from him in years. I expect he's still in England."

Magda nodded. "It's possible," she said. "The cards say otherwise. . . ." She shuffled them again, spreading them out in a new pattern. "The future now—interesting. You see the third card? The Devil. It's unusual to have so many Major Arcana in one reading. Look—there are two naked figures, a young man and a beautiful young woman. The Devil has them chained to a black cube, on which he sits. But observe: The chains are loose around their necks. They could take them off if they chose to. One can read a lot in the card—the wrong use of force, that is the card's secret meaning. And you see, the couple is bound by chains. Does that indicate greed and dependency, or a great love, I wonder? You are in love now?"

Dawn nodded. Her headache was gone, replaced with a warm sense of well-being that she recognized as inappropriate to the circumstances but was unable to shake off.

"With Corsini?"

"Yes."

"Well, that's good. It's not every husband lucky enough to be the man his wife loves. You see, I read the gossip columns, too. I have followed your career, your marriages. I'm—what do they call them?— a fan. After all, I knew you way back when, as they say here." She looked at the last two cards and poured herself another Scotch, stirring it into the tea with a hairpin which she straightened with her fingers.

Dawn stared at her. Magda's face still bore traces of beauty, but they were faint now. She always had pale, beautiful skin—that rare combination of pallor and blond hair that seems to survive aging better than any other—but the wrinkles had at last cut deeply into her face, like erosion in a landscape. The lines of the skull beneath were sharply defined under the skin.

She gathered up the cards briskly and wrapped them in the piece of cloth, folding the edges neatly over with her long fingers. "Lately the readings have had a certain pessimistic tendency. Perhaps it's the war. Or age. You are thinking, Magda drinks too much, yes?"

"Not at all," Dawn said, though she had been thinking exactly that.

"Please don't lie. Unfortunately for me, I've always been able to read people's faces—much better than cards. I *do* drink too much. It's a fact. At my age one begins to worry. My tastes are not extravagant, but I wouldn't like to spend my old age penniless, not in Los Angeles."

"I'm sure you won't, Magda."

"So am I, darling. Of course, I have my circle of clients. I try to keep it small and exclusive, you understand. Some of them have to see me every day—they don't take a step without consulting me first. I used to do your mother's reading sometimes. At first she didn't like it much, but she became quite a believer, eventually. Poor woman, I used to invent happy readings for her, even though it's wrong to lie about the cards. But I could see it all there, of course. Pain, loneliness, death."

"Death?" Dawn asked, feeling her throat turn dry.

Magda grinned triumphantly. "Of course," she said. "*Death!* Oh, no, my dear Queenie, you won't be bringing her over here, not at all. It's too late for that."

"Ma's *dead?*" Dawn's throat tightened. She felt grief, but also anger at having been tricked.

"I'm afraid so."

"How?"

"Does it matter? Age, sadness, a bad heart. Or a sad life."

"Why didn't you tell me before?"

"I wanted to see what you had to say, darling. And as usual, you lied. Oh, white lies, I agree, but still lies. You were going to bring her over here—not in a million years! I can read you, Queenie, just the way I read the cards. I don't imagine you're telling the truth about Morgan, either, but don't worry—I don't want to know what happened."

Dawn wanted to cry. She felt grief, guilt, loss, but no tears came. She had always tried to put Ma out of her mind, something she would solve one day in the future, and now there was no solution. She wanted somebody to tell her it was not her fault—but Magda was not about to do it.

Magda opened a drawer. She took out an envelope and put it on the table. "I brought with me a few mementos of your childhood," she said. "I thought you'd like to see them if we ever met." She opened it and examined the contents. A photograph of your birth certificate. Some snapshots of you with your schoolmates—it's hard to make out their faces, poor dears, because they're so dark, but yours is perfectly recognizable. . . . You were beautiful even then, Queenie. A picture of you with Ma and Morgan . . . I wonder if anybody would recognize him in England? Of course, if you don't want them, darling, I can always find someone to sell them to. A newspaper would love to have them, I'm sure."

Dawn was too numb to fight—besides, she recognized a clearcut piece of blackmail when she heard it. Charles had once advised her casually, or so it had seemed at the time, that the best tactic with blackmail was to pay up, if you could afford to. Her head was throbbing again, and she would have paid almost any price to be out of here. "For old time's sake," she said, "I'd be happy to help you out . . ."

"For old time's sake?" Magda laughed. "*Help?* Dear girl, I don't want to sound mercenary, but I'm not interested in a few dollars a week. I want a house of my own—not in Beverly Hills, I'm not that greedy."

"You're talking about a lot of money. At least fifty thousand dollars!"

"I had in mind a hundred thousand. I would like a pool—there's no point in being uncomfortable, is there?"

"What guarantees do I have?" Dawn asked.

"Absolutely none, darling. My word, of course. For what that's worth. But I'm practically an old woman. My needs aren't excessive. And you'll outlive me. You're getting off cheaply."

"Why didn't you come to me before this?"

"The cards told me to wait. Let me write out the name of my bank for you. You'll have the money deposited there by the beginning of next week, won't you?"

"I haven't agreed to pay it yet, Magda."

Magda laughed. "Oh, yes you have. You did when you came back here tonight—Queenie. It was only the price that was in question."

She rose and slipped a small bottle into Dawn's hand. "A bonus," she said. "It's the best thing for headaches. Almost as good as money— or a clear conscience. And be careful driving home, please."

"What is it?"

"Opium drops. You'll sleep like a top, darling. *That* I can promise you."

Magda kissed her on both cheeks, her breath smelling strongly of cigarettes and whiskey. And as Dawn listened to the click as Magda locked the door, she realized, despite a feeling of dull, heavy fatigue she was still unable to shake off, that Magda was a problem that wouldn't go away. She would be back for more, sooner or later.

She fought to keep awake, started the car and drove slowly down the dark, shabby street—from which Magda would soon be escaping, on *her* money. At the corner she reached into her handbag, took the bottle and threw it out onto the pavement. The noise of the glass shattering woke her up enough so that she was able to drive back to the hotel and fall into bed.

Magda was right: she fell asleep instantly. But her dreams were full of terrors for the first time in years, and when morning came she found herself lying on the rumpled bedcover fully dressed. The pillows were wet with perspiration.

Wearily she rose to clean up the mess and wipe off what remained of her makeup before the maid saw it. There was no point in Marie-Claire's asking questions—and anyway, Dawn believed in neatness. It was one lesson Ma had taught her that she had never forgotten. And at the thought of Ma, quite suddenly the tears she had been holding back started to flow. There was so much to tell her—and now it was too late.

She cried for a time. Then she went into the bathroom, examined her face, sighed and turned on the shower.

When Marie-Claire came in with her breakfast tray, she was lying in bed, on clean sheets and pillowcases, her face showing no trace of her tears. "You're five minutes late," she said as Marie-Claire put the tray down.

It was always a good idea to keep servants on their toes. Ma had believed in that, too.

"A *dream* nest," Billy Sofkin lisped, clapping his plump little hands softly to applaud his own handiwork.

In different circumstances Dawn would have shared his excitement, but the fact that she had just deposited one hundred thousand dollars in Magda's bank account made her feel at once angry and vulnerable. She was all too well aware that it was probably a down payment.

"Cozy and elegant, if I *do* say so myself," Billy added crossly, miffed that she hadn't praised the living room.

Elegant it certainly was, Dawn thought, but "cozy" was not a word that anybody but Billy would have used to describe a living room over sixty feet long and fifteen feet high, with French windows looking out over a sweeping lawn. The paneling was white—a delicate, glossy, slightly pearly white that Dawn had chosen—highlighted with gold leaf. The floor was white marble, flawless and unveined. The furniture was upholstered in flowered chintzes of extraordinary delicacy, so that at first glance the sunny white room seemed to contain not furniture, but glowing masses of flowers. The white curtains billowed slightly in the open windows like sails in a gentle breeze.

Billy had found a dozen gilded candelabra—marvels of sculpture and crystal—that lined the walls. Each was in the form of an arm holding a flaming torch, the legacy of some long-forgotten Empire costume drama that he had discovered in the studio prop room and refurbished. Two immense chandeliers hung from the ceiling, which was covered in pale fabric to look like the most glamorous of tents. The Persian rugs, startlingly framed by the white marble, were like deep pools of dark color, so beautiful that Dawn hesitated to walk on them and instinctively slipped off her shoes, obliging Billy to follow her example.

"You'll *love* the bedroom. Pink everywhere . . . it's so beautiful you could *die!* Charles's bedroom is all tobacco brown—very masculine."

"He'll sleep in mine."

"Well, I hope he likes pink, darling. There aren't many husbands and wives who share the same bed in Hollywood, you know. The stars are up before dawn, and their husbands are up reading scripts until two in the morning. This is Sleep-Mask City! It's a wonder there are any children born here at all . . . speaking of which—I haven't *touched* the nursery, except for a coat of white paint. Do you want me to do anything there?"

"No," Dawn said firmly. "Leave it alone."

"Well, you'd know best, of course. I suppose it makes sense to wait before deciding whether the theme color will be pink or blue. . . . You won't *believe* your dressing room!"

Dawn opened the door and found herself in a room that was entirely mirrored, including the ceiling. She was not surprised, of course—after all, she had commissioned the room and seen the sketches—but still, the reality was startling. She opened the mirrored doors, behind which there were walk-in closets, rows of shelves, closets for shoes, a cedar-lined humidified closet for furs. There were banked rows of thin drawers reaching to the ceiling, since Dawn hated having her things put away in piles. She pulled out a drawer. It moved effortlessly on rollers. She nodded with satisfaction. She opened the door of the shoe closet—the racks were made of polished mahogany, floor to ceiling.

She closed the doors and saw herself reflected from every angle. She was wearing a suit of pale-gray silk with squared shoulders. She wore no hat. Even without shoes, the legs below the mid-calf length of the straight skirt were finely turned and slim. She inspected the seams of her stockings. They were perfectly straight.

She put her hand out to touch the cold, gleaming glass, the long, slim fingers reaching out to brush their own reflection. Her nails were so long now that it was difficult for her to perform even the most ordinary domestic task—even buttoning a blouse or attaching her stockings to the suspenders of her garter belt required the help of her maid. The nails had been lacquered a faint, pearly silver, to match her suit—Max Factor himself had mixed a silver tint into her faint, rose-colored lipstick to produce a color that other women sometimes imitated, but never with the same effect.

"Beautiful!" Billy Sofkin whispered, though whether he was referring to Dawn or her dressing room was unclear.

She looked around the dressing room, imagining where her things would go, impatient to move in. She would have Marie-Claire start moving her belongings tomorrow, she decided, perhaps even today.

No matter how many possessions Dawn had, she had a complete inventory of them in her head, right down to the last delicate lace-edged handkerchief. She did not, in fact, have that many clothes by the standards of most stars, but what she had was the best—and taken care of with an attention to detail that most people would have judged excessive, or even obsessive.

Her shoes were polished with clear wax after each wearing, then placed at the end of the row, so that each pair was worn in order. The rows were arranged by color, each shoe with its own tiny handmade tree in its own soft glove-leather shoe bag, with a label tied to it describing the shoe and the clothes it was to be worn with.

Her routines were as well established as those of a soldier, and she had a good soldier's natural discipline. It was as if she needed to compensate for the chaos of her private life by imposing order on the objects around her, and she made no apology for what most people regarded as a waste of time and energy, since it gave her a sense of peace that life did not. Now that she had the power and the money to do things her way, she was determined that everything should be done right.

Dawn walked into the bathroom with its huge pink walk-in bathtub. Rose marble steps led down to the tub so Dawn could descend into the water as if it were a miniature swimming pool. The house was everything she had ever wanted.

There was only one thing missing—Charles. And suddenly, standing there surrounded by the gleaming bathroom walls, she felt an empty loneliness that even Billy noticed, a slight paling of the famous skin, a momentary blue shadow beneath the huge dark oval eyes that seemed, just for a fraction of a second, to be tearing over.

It was a change that gave Billy Sofkin goose bumps. Then it passed. "Show me Charles's rooms now," she said. And with a flash of intuition, Sofkin realized what the matter was.

It was on the tip of his tongue to ask when Corsini was coming home to his new house, but before he could, Dawn was already on her way, walking with that strange purposeful stride that contrasted so strongly with the graceful languor with which she moved in her movies, leaving Billy to hurry after her breathlessly in his stockinged feet.

He telephoned at last, but in his own charming and evasive way he put off from week to week the date of his return, nor did he say where he was. His voice across the long-distance wires was cautious, as if somebody else was listening to the conversation—which was, of course, altogether possible, Dawn guessed, given the government's continuing interest in his affairs. Luckman's death had been too convenient for comfort, and while the congressional committees and the FBI had reluctantly given up their investigations in the permanent absence of the star witness against Charles, they retaliated by harassing him.

If he *was* back in the United States, Charles didn't seem to be in any hurry to join her. There were days when her whole body seemed to ache, and nights when she could think of nothing but Charles, and she almost wished she *were* promiscuous. She longed for easy release, for the touch of another body; but she wanted it to be Charles's. The strength of her passion for him frightened her, most of all because she was no longer sure that Charles felt the same way about her. If he did, how could he stay away so long? And if he didn't, then what was she doing here, sleeping alone while every nerve in her body seemed to throb with sexual tension?

That Charles loved her, she had no doubt—but could he ever feel for her the kind of intense, single-minded passion that gripped her in the long, lonely hours of the night? Did he know what she felt? Like the spoiled, wealthy child he was, behind that calm, man-of-the-world facade, did he accept it as no more than his due? Dawn wished she were able to express her emotions more openly to him, but there was some reserve, an inner caution, that held her back. She longed for his return so she could try again.

She felt as if she were merely marking time. She went to dinners, parties and openings, often escorted by Aaron Diamond, who was more than happy to appear in public with the most beautiful woman in Hollywood on his arm, and with whom there was no feeling of strain since it was well known that he never slept with a client. When Diamond was busy, she went out with either Kraus or Goulandris. "A queer, a guy who looks like he's impotent and your agent," Polly Hammer said to her, as they sat together at Diamond's party for Harry and Sylvia Warmfleisch. "You might as well wear a sign that says 'Please don't touch the merchandise.'"

"Perhaps I don't *want* it touched, Polly."

"Don't give me that. You've got dark circles under your eyes. I know what you need. You know what you need. I could kill that goddamned Charles!"

"Please don't say that, Polly. What makes you think Kraus is impotent?"

"He looks that way. He's got the eyes of a Jesuit priest."

"How many Jesuit priests do you know, Polly?"

"Plenty. I wasn't *born* here, you know. You're looking at the former Pauline Buszkowski, of Bethlehem, Pennsylvania, honey. Brought up by the nuns, Mass once a day, and a father who came home every night from the steel mill to get drunk and beat the shit out of my mother—or us kids. . . . Look, there are the Colemans. I'd better get to work."

Polly rose and vanished into the crowd. The former pupil of the Bethlehem nuns was wearing a dress with a neckline that swooped down in front so deeply that it was only a miracle her ample breasts didn't pop out. Even in a tent full of far more beautiful women, she attracted attention.

Dawn heard a noise beside her and turned around. It was Kraus, who had been in the house making telephone calls, as he always did at parties. She looked at him closely and decided there was indeed something priestlike about him. If there was a lighter side to Kraus's character, she had not yet discovered it, nor, to her knowledge, had anyone else. No doubt even as a baby he had had worry lines.

"A problem?" she asked.

He cracked his knuckles. "Vale," he said.

"Vale is making problems? What about now?"

"He wants us to sell off the back lot for some kind of real estate development he and his friends have in mind."

"That's ridiculous."

"Not really," Kraus said, giving his knuckles a final crack that made Dawn wince. "It's potentially a valuable site. The frontage on Wilshire Boulevard will be worth a fortune one day. One could build a hotel there—shops, office buildings. Not now, of course, with the war on, but one day. . . ."

"I mean, it's ridiculous for Vale to think we'd sell it."

"Well, unfortunately, *that's* not so ridiculous either. Your husband talked to him about it, apparently. Or so Vale says."

"Charles? I can't believe that."

"Vale says they even discussed price. He mentioned it to me, but it sounded like a steal."

"I'll speak to Charles the next time he calls."

"Please do." Kraus cleared his throat nervously. "Vale also mentioned that Charles talked to him about selling off Empire's library."

"The *library*? Whatever for? We've been all over that!"

"Well, it's not worth so much now—but one day, after the war, when television starts, all those old pictures could be worth a lot of money. What else will they show on television, after all? If it happens . . ."

"I know all about that," Dawn said impatiently. "David talked about it all the time. Of course we should hold on to the library."

"Empire needs capital. We both know that. But stripping its assets isn't the way to raise it, in my opinion. Particularly if Vale gets the assets at a bargain price."

Dawn felt the beginnings—like a faint tremor—of panic. She had assumed that Charles's absence and his increasing reticence on the subject of his affairs were merely a question of his problems with the government, or his work for some secret part of it. It had not occurred to her that he might be undermining her own position, or that the duplicity for which he was famous in business matters might be exercised against her. He was behaving as if her shares in Empire belonged to *him*, she reflected—with a flash of anger that Kraus wrongly interpreted as a blush, and which made him, if anything, more nervous. There were beads of sweat around his thinning blond hair.

"Of course he probably knows what he's doing," he said, hoping he hadn't gone too far in criticizing Corsini.

"Perhaps," she snapped.

"He hasn't talked to you about it at all?"

"Not a word."

"I find that odd. Naturally, there would have to be a board meeting about any such changes. There are others involved. It wouldn't be easy selling this to the other members—or even to the shareholders."

"It's all a misunderstanding, I'm sure."

"Should I talk to Vale?"

Dawn shook her head. The last thing she wanted was Kraus going off on his own to talk to Vale before she had had it out with Charles. She closed her eyes against the insistent throb of a headache. She had once asked herself if it was possible to love someone you didn't trust. Now she knew the answer.

It wasn't a comfortable feeling.

"I can't discuss it on the telephone. Not now."

"I don't understand why not," she said angrily. "I know you called Dominick."

"No names, for God's sake. You have to take my word that I know what I'm doing."

"It doesn't make any *sense*, Charles. I won't be treated like this!

Besides . . ." There was a buzz and a schoolmarmish voice came on the line. "Your three minutes are up," the operator said, cutting in.

"We're still talking," Dawn shouted.

"There's a war on. Transcontinental calls are limited to three minutes."

"This is Dawn *Avalon*! From Hollywood! This is a very important call."

There was a hush, but the operator remained adamant. "I'm sorry, Miss Avalon. Your time is up."

"I'm talking to my *husband*, operator."

"You'll have to hang up and book another call, Miss Avalon," the operator said, with a hint of satisfaction in her voice. No doubt, Dawn thought, it was not every day—or night—that she got the opportunity to put a movie star in her place.

". . . Don't do anything," she heard Charles say, his voice faint and garbled by static and the background of other people's conversation. "In a few days, I will . . ." Then the line went dead, leaving her alone with her anger, and no wiser about Charles's motives.

Dawn put on a robe and went downstairs to make herself a cup of tea. A houseful of servants, and she was making tea for herself! But making tea was a ritual, and rituals calmed her nerves. She wished Charles had been able to explain what he was doing. Was he worried about the possibility that someone was listening to his calls, or was he simply reluctant to tell her? She could not tell. She wished there had been time for him to say he loved her. She wished she could have told him about Ma, but how could she?

She sat in the kitchen, waiting for the kettle to boil. The secret to making tea, Ma had always said, was boiling water. In America the water was never hot enough to make good tea; most people, including the servants, neglected to heat the teapot first with boiling water. It was amazing how many of the little daily things that were important to her came from Ma, Dawn thought. It was too late to thank her now. . . .

Dawn hated living here alone in this big house, with servants who were still strangers. She hardly even knew their names, except for Marie-Claire, who was annoyingly moody. It was difficult to keep the rest of them busy—already the cook was complaining that she wasn't giving any dinner parties, and the butler stood around all day with nothing to do. When *was* Charles coming? she asked herself.

There was a noise outside, and she went to the window. A car stopped on the gravel, a man got out and opened the passenger door for Marie-Claire, then put his arms around her and kissed her. Dawn had no wish to play the peeping tom, and still less to be caught in the act. She pulled the curtain shut, took her tea and went back upstairs.

There was no reason, she thought, why Marie-Claire should not have a man in her life—or even many men—but somehow the notion had never occurred to her. It made her feel more lonely than ever. There was a certain irony in the fact that she was sleeping alone while her maid was in the arms of a man.

What Marie-Claire did on her own time was her own business, but bringing her boyfriends back to the house was another matter, Dawn decided. She would have a chat with her tomorrow. It never hurt to show servants one knew what was going on, she told herself.

She set her alarm clock for five—she had an early call at the studio— and tried to will herself to sleep, but images of Charles ran through her mind, and she lay awake listening to the dry rustle of the eucalyptus trees.

For the first time she understood why Morgan had taken to drink. To be deprived of what you most wanted—of what you thought was yours by right—was a kind of torture, even when you were surrounded by luxury. All she wanted was Charles, here beside her; the strength of that passion, the utter simplicity of it, terrified her. She had never committed her emotions completely to anyone. Now they were in bondage to Charles.

The knowledge of that need scared her more than anything—more even than the thought that Charles was dealing behind her back with her enemy.

"I'm still not happy with the rushes."

"Well, neither is Lacey," Kraus said, in his most conciliatory tone, "though he won't admit it."

"I wish we had gotten Cukor."

"Lacey is just as good. Maybe better. Two Academy Awards. He's a top director."

"If he's such a good director, why do I look so awful in the rushes?"

"We've been through all that. The rushes are getting better. Osman is a first-rate cameraman. Lacey has a lot of confidence in him."

"He isn't photographing Lacey."

Kraus rolled his eyes—a habit that his thick spectacles magnified into something truly horrible to see. He had been instrumental in choosing Robert Rowland Lacey to direct *A Woman's Place*. Lacey had class. To be more exact, Lacey *was* class, a gentleman in a profession full of flamboyant artistic misfits.

Lacey had come to Hollywood from the "legitimate" theater, and was much admired for his high tone and intellectual reputation. Even in Hollywood he wore dark suits, white shirts, a Churchillian bow tie. He had directed two award-winning, commercially successful pictures while at the same time opening an experimental repertory theater on Santa Monica Boulevard. At Lacey's Malibu beach house Kraus had met the most interesting of Hollywood's European intellectual exiles—Isherwood, Mann, Brecht, Remarque. He was impressed, and had sold Lacey to Dawn, despite her doubts.

There was no gainsaying Lacey's talent or the originality of his ideas, but it was his fatal flaw that he wanted both artistic success and money, which was what had brought him to Hollywood at last, where he had sold his soul for what most people, with the exception of Lacey himself, agreed was a pretty good price.

He was cautiously respectful of Dawn. He had never made a movie with a major female star, and he understood perfectly well that he would never be taken seriously in Hollywood until he had. He treated her with the kind of care a prudent man might show toward a package of explosives that had been left in his charge.

Lacey understood story, dialogue, pace, but he had not realized that for Dawn—and for the studio—what mattered most was how she *looked*. Everything else was secondary to that. Once he did realize it, Lacey did his best to comply, but he had no natural gift for the task, and he left the details in the hands of the cameraman, whom he was obliged to replace at frequent intervals. Osman was his latest find, but he, too, had proved unsatisfactory from Dawn's point of view, despite his daring camera angles and use of shadows. "He's not a woman's cameraman," she told Kraus. "Give him a street scene full of shadows, and he'll win an Oscar every time, I grant you that."

"Lacey feels the latest rushes are much better."

"He isn't a woman's director. I should have known better than to hire an intellectual."

"There's some first-rate footage . . ."

"Oh, the hell with the first-rate footage, Kraus!"

"Osman won an Academy Award for . . ."

"Damn his Academy Award, Kraus!" There was a long silence. Dawn seldom swore, and never to Kraus. She looked in the mirror. The face was there, almost as beautiful as ever. All they had to do was *photograph* it!

They were all satisfied with what they saw on the screen, but she knew better. *She* could see the faint traces of her scars, even if they couldn't. *She* could tell that they weren't making use of her beauty, didn't have a feel for her best angles. She had been taught by masters. Nobody knew her own face better than she did, after all. . . . She looked at Kraus, who seemed close to tears. "I'm sorry," she said.

He shrugged mournfully. "No, no, you're right. It's my fault."

"It's not your fault. Lacey had all the right credentials. He just doesn't have the touch, that's all. I should have followed my first instinct."

"I'll talk to him."

"We'll both talk to him." She sighed. It was another confrontation—one that she would have preferred to avoid, if possible, having more than enough problems to face as it was. She had begun the day with an unpleasant scene—for Marie-Claire had been furious that Dawn should have seen her with her boyfriend (who was, in fact, a mature married man) and accused Dawn hysterically of spying on her. Dawn had threatened to fire her. In some ways, she reflected, it would be easier to get rid of Lacey than Marie-Claire. "He'll have to go," she told Kraus.

"Lacey? It's out of the question. We'll never get a director to take over one of his pictures in midstream. Besides, he's good. You know that."

"Then the cameraman."

"Osman? He's the third one we've had. . . ."

"Whose side are you on?"

Kraus blinked myopically. "Yours," he said. Then he paused to think about it. "Also the studio's. There's a lot riding on this picture. We have to prove we can make a big box-office success—on time and on budget—or people are going to start saying that Empire was better off when Braverman and his crew were running it. And don't forget: they're waiting in the wings, hoping to see us fail. You're not the *only* stockholder, you know. . . . Listen, Lacey is waiting for us in the big screening room."

"He can wait."

"He won't like waiting. Listen to me again: You need him. *We* need him! He's a hot director. If we get rid of him, people like Cukor or Wyler or the Huston boy will never work here. We'll be stuck with the kind of second-raters Braverman and Cantor surrounded themselves with. You want to get rid of Osman, okay—but don't screw around with Lacey."

Dawn stared at Kraus. "I've never heard you use language like that before," she said. She clapped her hands together with delight.

He blushed. "I apologize. One gets so used to it out here . . ."

"No, no, it was very impressive. You sounded just like a studio boss for a moment there. And of course, you're right. Lacey stays—but he has to find some way of dealing with the close-ups. I'm not going to have a picture that makes me look ugly, even if it makes a fortune for Empire."

"Lacey knows his own weaknesses as a director, believe me, Dawn. He's been thinking about it. He's got his own brain trust."

"Is that why we're using the big screening room? He's brought his arty Malibu cronies?"

"Cronies, I don't know. He asked if he could bring some people, that's all."

"I don't like the idea that we're outnumbered."

"Forget it. It's not a board meeting," Kraus said, reminding Dawn inadvertently of her larger problem with Charles—not, now that she thought of it, that Kraus would ever be likely to say anything inadvertent.

Kraus walked beside her to the cutting-room block. Behind the cutting rooms themselves were a number of small projection rooms, though most of the studio executives had their own, and the more important directors, producers and executives naturally had a projection room at home as well. The big screening room, which was seldom used, was in fact the size of a small-town movie theater, but more luxurious, with such amenities as a bar and several rows of leather armchairs at the back.

It was already dark in the screening room, and Dawn slipped into one of the chairs at the front, just in time to see a close-up of herself on the screen. Most people would have said it was good, but Dawn knew better. The angle was wrong, the lighting not quite right. There was a slight shadow to one side of her nose—worst of all, a faint suggestion of lines or blemishes on her skin. Osman, she thought, had used a lens of the wrong focal length—there was a suggestion of wide-angle distortion at the edges, as well as the typical flatness that a wide-angle lens conveyed, which made her face seem wider than it really was and emphasized the broadness of her forehead.

She wished she knew more about the technicalities of cinematography. David Konig would have put his finger on the problem after watching half a dozen frames. Dawn could almost hear him muttering, in his guttural voice, between puffs on his cigar, "Use a longer lens, stop it down a bit . . . try a Wrattan density filter, maybe a number two, with a little Vaseline on the edges to diffuse the light; maybe two baby spots on the eyes."

Lacey saw Dawn take her seat and moved closer to her. Like his silver hair, which he wore affectedly long in the back, his voice was richly theatrical, the accent neither English nor American, but that of the professional stage actor. Lacey's voice had a pseudo-Shakespearean ring to it, even in normal conversation—his whisper seemed designed to fill the house, each syllable trembling just a shade too richly in the smoky air. "*Mar*velous, isn't it?" he asked.

Dawn coughed. "Do you think you could ask everyone to stop smoking? I can't breathe."

"Certainly, certainly, *dear* lady," Lacey said, hastily putting out his own cigarette.

Around the darkened room, people put out their cigars and cigarettes obediently. In the corner Dawn saw a single, defiant red glow, marking somebody who was not about to defer to her wishes.

She decided to ignore it. She had nothing to gain from throwing what Lacey would no doubt regard as a fit of female hysterics over a single cigarette.

She looked at the footage on the screen. "I don't like it," she said firmly.

Lacey looked pained. "It's really very good, you know. Osman has a genius for mood. What I'm trying to establish here . . ."

"There's a shadow on my face, on one side of my nose."

"But that's the whole *point*, don't you see? Light and shadow . . ."

"I don't think the public is paying to see shadows," she said, loudly enough so that everyone could hear her.

"No, no, of *course* not . . . but it's beautiful footage, Dawn, believe me. It reminds me of Murnau—a kind of tragic chiaroscuro . . ."

"Like Buñuel's work, in some of the early films," a guttural Central European voice said from the dark. " '*Der Lichtkegel das Bild*,' Reinhardt used to call it."

Dawn looked at her face on the screen. "I don't care. The public isn't paying to see Buñuel. They're paying to see *me*. They want to see me looking beautiful. And Osman is being paid to make me beautiful."

"You *are* beautiful, dear lady," Lacey intoned automatically, as if a quick compliment was the best way of dealing with any objection from a woman.

"Thank you, Mr. Lacey. I know that. But then why am I not beautiful in this shot?"

"Let me explain. What Osman is aiming for here is something—beyond, ah, *conventional* glamour. . . ."

"I'm not talking about conventional glamour myself, Mr. Lacey."

Dawn always kept a certain distance between herself and Lacey by addressing him formally—which he normally preferred—but with a slight smile that was intended to cut him down to size, and did. "Go back and look at the pictures I did for David Konig," she said. "Just because something is ugly doesn't mean it's clever or original."

"Of course not."

"It's not that I'm vain, you do understand that? Oh, I know, all women are vain, and I'm no exception—but we're not talking here about vanity. We're talking about giving the public what it expects when they see me in a movie."

"Quite. Very well put, if I may say so. But I think this is a very striking image of you."

"She's right, Lacey—it's *ugly!*"

The voice was hardly more than a whisper from the side of the room, where the lone remaining smoker was hidden in the darkness. It was weary and rasping, as if from fatigue, illness, exposure to the elements, or perhaps simply too much smoking. Lacey frowned—he knew the man, and obviously had expected his friends, or at least the members of his coterie, to back him up.

Dawn, whose attention was directed toward the screen, heard—or thought she heard—a thin trace of familiarity, a pitch, a tone, a certain way of speaking that seemed to echo in her mind and made her stomach suddenly tighten. She wanted to turn around. She did not dare.

"A woman's face is not a piece of scenery, Lacey, not at all. The camera lens sees in two dimensions; but the face is a three-dimensional object, so we have to *reinvent* it. What we must put on film is the *essence* of the face, not the face itself—the soul of it, so to speak. Besides, any fool should know from tests that Miss Avalon should be photographed from the left side, always—never from the right. Her left is distinctly more harmonious and better-proportioned. And the camera should be lower, the lens below the tip of her nose—angled up a bit maybe, to emphasize the neck and play down the forehead, which is very sexy in real life, but catches too much light in close-ups. And what the hell are those damned lines on her face?"

The cigarette glowed a bright red as he paused to take a puff. "Of course makeup, camera, lights—they all have to work together. There must be a guiding vision. Isn't it so—*Queenie?*"

There was a long silence. Dawn's face continued to flicker on the screen; then the screen turned white as the footage ended and the overhead lights came on in the screening room.

Dawn, who had been staring at the blank screen as if she were paralyzed, slowly turned her head. She could see Kraus rising to his feet, his face as pale as if he had seen a ghost. Behind him, Dawn saw Lacey's coterie of emigré intellectuals and theater people huddled in their seats whispering to each other, puzzled by the spectacle of a real-life drama.

There was a thin, tall figure, hunched in his seat at the side of the room. She rose to her feet, rushing toward him, pushing clumsily past Lacey's knees, treading on Kraus's toes, tearing her stockings against the seats that blocked her way, her tears flowing now without any artifice. In a rush, as if she were drowning, the past flickered before her, then as he stood up, she threw her arms around him.

"Lucien!" she cried. "I can't believe it's you!"

CHAPTER 24

LUCIEN TIPPED HIS CHAIR BACK and looked across the lawn toward the pool. He estimated the length—at least a quarter of a mile, he told himself, with a photographer's instinct for judging distance. He worked that out in his head in acres, then multiplied that by the value of land in Bel Air. He gave a short, low whistle at the impressive sum.

"You've been lucky, Queenie," he said.

"Lucky? I lost you. David died. I don't put much faith in luck."

"No? I do. I was in the desert, you know, just after Bir el Hakim. We dug ourselves into the sand—with our fingers. You'd be surprised how hard it is to dig sand. You work desperately to make a hole and it fills up as fast as you can dig. . . . The Germans were shelling us. Howitzers. The concussion makes your ears and nose bleed, lifts you up like a piece of dirt, buries you in your own goddamned hole. Some men lost their nerve and ran, but once they were out in the open the shrapnel cut them down."

Lucien stared out at the garden as if he were looking at something beyond its well-cared-for lawns and flower beds, at a faraway horror that was still more real to him than the topiary bushes and flowering cacti.

He shook his head, then wiped the sudden sweat from his eyes with his free hand. "The point is—" he went on—"the point is—luck. Some of us died. Some didn't. In some situations, I grant you, it's the strong, the clever, the ruthless, who survive. I've seen that, too. But at the far extreme, life and death, it's just a question of luck. The man next to me—a Polish painter named Komarowski, for what it matters, quite a decent chap—was hit. A shell landed right in his hole. One moment I could hear him praying in Polish at the top of his voice, then an enormous explosion, and afterward there was nothing left of him."

Lucien closed his eyes. "He was *un*lucky, you see. I was lucky. There's no other satisfactory explanation."

Dawn looked at him, searching for traces of the sleek young man who had swept her out of Goldner's basement and put her on the first rung of the ladder that had brought her here. The eyes were the same— as blue as ever—but the rest of the face was as unfamiliar as a stranger's. He was thinner, so thin that the bones seemed close to the surface, and there was a certain hardness to his mouth that she could not remember having been there before. He had grown a mustache, which Dawn did not find becoming. Just below the right eye was a long, jagged scar.

Lucien was the first person she knew who had been directly touched by the war, and she found the changes it had wrought on him frightening. For five years she had thought of him as he had been the last time she saw him, and here he was, an entirely different person from the one she remembered.

She reached over and patted his hand to catch his attention, for he seemed to have fallen into a trance.

"I'd given you up for dead," she said quietly.

"Frankly, so had I."

"When the French arrested you, David tried to get you out. Did you know that?"

Lucien shrugged. "Even Konig couldn't work miracles against fate."

"I made him try when I heard about your arrest."

"I've been arrested so many times," he said vaguely. "I *was* in prison for a while, in France. Then in the French army. Then in a German P.O.W. camp." He shuddered involuntarily. "Then I escaped to North Africa. That was the worst."

"Prison again?"

"No. The Legion." He laughed. "I was arrested as a deserter. I had a choice between prison and the Legion. I made the wrong choice." He sipped his drink for a moment, touching the ice cube to his lips as if he were kissing a holy relic.

"I was in a punishment battalion in the *bled* for a while," he continued. "We dug trenches in the sand while carrying a pack full of rocks. The next day the trenches had filled up with sand again. Naturally. So we dug again. In the evening, we dug graves for those who died. Some people went mad from the heat and the thirst. Myself, it was the flies I hated most. I can't think why people suppose the desert is clean. In fact, it's filthy."

"But you survived. That's what matters."

"Does it? I suppose so. It's disappointing from a moral point of

view, but that's what it all boils down to. It took the war to teach me
that—but I think you knew it always, didn't you?"

"Being poor helps."

"At least I've been spared that." He stood up stiffly. "*You* haven't
changed at all, Queenie," he said. "Though I can see lines—well, no,
not lines, faint tracks, rather—on your face. One would have to think
how to photograph you so they don't show in the lights." His voice was
dispassionate, rather than inquiring or sympathetic. It was a technical
problem, nothing more.

"I had a car accident. Most people don't notice them."

"Most people don't notice anything. All of photography is the eye—
seeing. The rest is just technology."

He framed her face with his hands. "There's no reason it should
show on film." He sighed. "It's been a long time, Queenie. A lifetime,
in fact. But you're as beautiful as ever, scars and all. . . . You wouldn't
have another drink handy, would you?"

She pointed to the bar.

"A handsome piece!" Lucien appraised it with something of his old
enthusiasm. "Boulle!" He ran his fingers over the marquetry and the
ormolu decorations, nodding his approval. He had always had a taste
for good furniture, and his face lit up with pleasure at the sight of the
cabinet.

For a moment the old Lucien, the man she remembered, reappeared
in his face as he smiled. Then the resemblance faded, as if it were a
trick of light, or an accident, like running up to greet a friend in the
street and realizing, too late, that it was a stranger instead.

"How did you manage to get away? And come here?"

Lucien picked a bronze up from the coffee table, examined it in the
light, then put it back. He ran his fingers over it. "Maillol," he whispered. "Amazing that something so hard and cold can be so sensual,
isn't it?"

"David bought it for me—years ago." She wondered if there was a
double meaning to Lucien's comment. Was he bitter about the past?
He had every right to be. But there was no bitterness in his voice.

"Konig always had good taste, one must give him that. . . . How
did I get here? I stole, I cheated, I lied. I ran and kept on running.
And I did a favor for Allied Intelligence in North Africa. . . ."

"Was it dangerous?"

"When it's a question of saving one's skin, it's easy to be brave."

He did not seem anxious to go into more details. He went back to the bar and poured himself another finger of Scotch from the cut-glass Waterford decanter, more, it seemed, for the pleasure of handling the decanter than from any need for a refill. "Very nice," he said. "So you've married again?"

She nodded.

"You're in love?"

"Yes."

"Good. And he's rich, too, I hear—Charles Corsini?"

"Very."

"Even better." Lucien sat down on the white sofa, next to Dawn, and put his glass down on the lacquered table. Dawn slipped a coaster under it. He lifted an eyebrow—a gesture which reminded her of the old days. Dawn instinctively put her hand on his.

"You didn't used to be so house-proud," he said. "Coasters! Marriage has brought out the domesticity in you. Have you learned to cook?"

"No, my domestic interests don't extend quite that far."

"With so many servants, it would hardly be necessary. . . . How many are there?"

"Four. And all bloody-minded."

"And yet one doesn't see them. However bloody-minded—and all servants are—they must be well trained, to be so unobtrusive."

"It's their night out."

"And Charles? It's his night out, too?"

"He's in New York. He's been very busy lately."

"You don't sound happy about it."

"I'm not. How did you guess?"

"I know you as well as I know myself. . . . I see from the papers that he's in all sorts of trouble?"

"It will blow over."

"Yes? You don't sound altogether convinced of it. There was a lot of talk about him in Algiers, you know."

"What kind of talk?"

"It's odd. People who work in intelligence are supposed to be so secretive, but in fact they're usually the worst kind of gossips. There were rumors that he's working for the Americans. He has first-rate connections in Germany and Italy, so it wouldn't be surprising. And of course, if he *was* doing that, it would make sense to come down hard on him here for his Nazi connections. It would make the Germans trust him, you see. . . . On the other hand, there were also rumors that he's been working for the Nazis for years. I suppose that's possible, too. He'd almost have to be a double agent to be worth anything to either side. . . . Does he love you?"

"Very much."

"You don't seem one hundred percent convinced of that, either."

She was not about to argue the point with Lucien. He knew her well enough to guess what she was thinking. "We've been going through a difficult period," she said, suddenly aware of how easy it was to talk to him. Whatever physical passion she had felt for him had long since burned out, but there remained a sense of intimacy she had not felt in years, not even with Charles. With Lucien she did not need to pretend, or even to worry about the past—*most* of it, anyway. And he could be trusted. She sensed that, and for once was willing to trust her senses.

"Why did you come here, Lucien?"

"I'd had it up to here with the war." He held his hand to his throat. "That ruled out London. The Americans were grateful enough for what I'd done to offer me papers. It seemed like a good idea to take them."

"Those are the only reasons?"

"I wanted to see you again. Ah, no, don't misunderstand me. What we had is behind us. But that's not to say there's nothing. . . . Besides, I want to get to work again. When I heard that you now own a studio, that Kraus is running it, I decided I'd come. Then—I don't know—something held me back from calling . . . until I met Lacey."

"Did he talk to you about the picture?"

"A little. You know what this town is like. It's all shoptalk. He said he was having difficulty photographing you, so I thought to myself, I'd better see what the matter is."

"Could you do it better?"

"Of course. Osman is all right, but he doesn't have the right touch for women. To be frank, I *want* to do it. I need a job."

"Do you need money?"

"No, no. Thank you, but I have enough for the moment. I need *work*. I'll have to build up my reputation from scratch over here."

"You'll need a union card, too."

"Yes, that's true."

"For that you *will* need money—quite a lot of it. I'll take care of that part of it. Then Aaron Diamond can pull a few strings with his friends. I'll ask Kraus to get rid of Osman. You can start making tests tomorrow."

He stood up and kissed her hand. "Thank you," he said. "The first time I kissed your hand was in Goldner's basement."

"It was the first time *anybody* had ever kissed my hand, Lucien."

"I remember. I'll photograph you just the way I used to, don't you worry. It will be just like the old days."

"The old days? Lucien, the old days weren't so wonderful, you know."

"They were better than Bir el Hakim."

She laughed. "Granted, I'm sure." She became serious. "There's something you ought to know. David told Kraus to stop your letters to me. And I'm pretty sure Kraus didn't give you mine."

Lucien did not seem shocked, or even particularly interested. "Konig was a devious man," he said unjudgmentally. "I should have guessed. You should have guessed. It would not have occurred to him to 'fight fair,' as we used to say in school. I doubt that there's an equivalent for 'May the best man win' in Hungarian. . . ."

"You don't seem upset."

"What good would it do? You married him. He died. Then you married this Corsini. I should have flown home to have it out with you. But my career seemed so important to me, then. . . . I have always loved you, you know. I suppose I always shall. But there's no point in repeating the follies of the past. As for the old days, I think you are wrong. I remember them with great fondness. At one time in my life they were the only thing that kept me alive."

She felt herself beginning to cry. She put her arms around him and kissed him gently, like a sister. She was shocked at how thin he was, and even more shocked to realize that he was crying too. For a moment she thought she heard a click, like that of a door closing—but when she turned, there was nothing but the silence of the empty house. She looked at Lucien. He seemed not to have noticed anything unusual.

Dawn felt a sudden flash of guilt, then realized the absurdity of it. "Come on," she said, "I'll drive you home."

It was surprising how much pleasure she felt at the reversal of their roles—for it had always been Lucien who owned and drove the car in the old days, and *she* who was the passenger.

He smiled. He had guessed what she was thinking—had thought the same thing himself.

She only wished that Charles understood her that easily.

"Charles wants a board meeting." Kraus stood at the door of the dressing room, nervously swaying from one foot to another.

Dawn stared at herself in the mirror. It had been two weeks since she had last heard from Charles or learned he was back in the country. She was furious that he had called Kraus, and not her, but then she told herself he must have his reasons.

She had slept badly, and she felt it. The makeup man would have his work cut out for him, she thought grimly. No doubt he would think she had overindulged in sex or booze.

She was in a foul temper and wanted most of all to be left alone until it passed—but of course that wasn't going to happen. Kraus was here; the makeup man was waiting, with his boxes and brushes and jars, as well as his ghastly nonstop chatter; Lacey was prowling around, with overnight script changes, pages of which were already on her dressing table, mimeographed on bright-yellow paper, despite Dawn's orders that her changes should be on pink paper so she would know at a glance exactly which pages concerned her; Danny Zegrin was waiting with papers for her to sign. . . .

She had begun the morning by quarreling bitterly with Marie-Claire, who had been late with the breakfast tray and impertinent about it as well. Dawn had put her in her place again, more sharply than she had meant to. She made a mental note that she would have to find a new maid. With so much going on, it was hard to bother.

"He wants a board meeting? When?"

"Within the next couple of weeks."

"He's coming back? He could have told me. Where the hell *is* he?"

"He's hard to reach, he says. He's going to Miami to buy another parcel of land, then to Houston, and I don't know where else. . . ."

"How did he sound?"

"That's hard to say. Like a man under heavy pressure, perhaps."

"Did he mention me at all?"

"He was in a hurry. I did get the impression that he wasn't pleased by the amount of publicity Polly Hammer is giving you in her column. It's hard to tell with Charles, but I thought I detected a certain—resentment."

"I can't think why. It's for his own benefit."

Kraus considered the matter. Years of experience as a subordinate had given him an insight into other people's reactions that Dawn lacked. He understood vanity, hurt pride, jealousy and ego, having worked at close quarters with all of them over the years without the benefit of being beautiful or a star. "Have you considered," he suggested, "that the better Polly makes *you* look, the worse *he* looks?"

"She does lay it on a bit thick."

"I would say so. Charles just might conclude that you're looking after your own image—putting a little distance, as it were, between yourself and his problems."

"That wasn't the idea at all, Kraus. You know that."

"I know it. Does Charles know it?"

"It was Aaron's idea. I told Charles about it. He sounded enthusiastic."

"Well, he doesn't sound enthusiastic now. Of course one has to make allowances—the man is fighting for his life. It's not surprising that he sounds a little manic."

"*Manic?*"

"He spouts off figures like a machine. I thought he was drunk, at first."

"Charles isn't much of a drinker."

"I know, I know, but he talks about deals like—a wild man. It's as if there was more going on in his head than he could put into words, a kind of insane impatience."

"He *does* get carried away sometimes. . . ."

"Is that it then? I'm relieved. I thought he was angry with me—then I realized he simply didn't want to be interrupted."

"Did you discuss Vale's proposition?"

"There was no discussion. He told me to put it on the agenda. He was in no mood to discuss anything. Speaking of which, have you made up your mind what to do about Lacey? He's been here since before dawn, waiting for a chat with you."

"And Osman?"

"He's sitting by his camera, snarling at his assistants. Zegrin is trying to calm him down. Osman thinks he's going to be replaced."

"He is. Lucien is going to do it."

Kraus cracked his knuckles. He nodded. "If he hasn't lost his touch, he'd be perfect," he said—but Dawn couldn't help noticing a certain wariness in his voice, as if he were trying to decide whether it was worth the trouble of arguing with her.

"Out with it," she said. She trusted Kraus's loyalty enough to allow him to disagree with her decisions.

He seemed faintly embarrassed. "It's not my business," he said. "But try to be careful. From what one hears, Charles is a very—jealous—man. He might not understand."

"Understand what? Lucien is an old friend. And he's the best there is. I'm making a professional decision."

"So long as it's merely professional."

"Of course it's professional!" she snapped impatiently.

"Ah, well, that's all right, then," Kraus said, but Dawn judged from his expression that he didn't think it was all right at all. "I only mention it because Charles seemed so odd when I talked to him. Perhaps it's because he was talking from a telephone booth."

"Charles? In a phone booth?"

"He's afraid people are listening in, apparently. He told me he has his chauffeur carrying a bagful of change so he can make calls from pay phones. . . ."

"That explains why he hasn't called me lately. He probably doesn't want my name on an FBI report." But she was only trying to put up a good front with Kraus. Charles would certainly want to keep her name out of whatever investigations were centered on him, but knowing him as she did, it also seemed to her likely that he simply didn't want to discuss his plans for the studio with her. He wanted to make a quick killing, she knew that. She wanted something more. The same thing, it occurred to her, that David Konig had wanted.

It wasn't Charles's way to argue, least of all with her. If he knew she was likely to oppose what he wanted to do, he would simply avoid the subject until he could present her with a *fait accompli*, then win her over after it was done, with charm, love and heartfelt apologies. Generally speaking, the combination never failed.

This time, she was determined not to give in.

Gradually, like a man entering a swimming pool slowly, Lucien step by step reintroduced himself to his art. He sent for the studio manager, and when Pop Deigh arrived, his cheeks puffed out with self-importance, his eyes flickering toward Danny Zegrin, his former subordinate, in fear and hatred, Lucien set him to work.

Deigh groaned, protested, whined—it was his job to hold down costs, and he knew that Zegrin was trying to make a reputation for himself by cutting everything to the bone—but he recognized in Lucien's requests the voice of a true professional. Besides, one look at Dawn's face was enough to make him jump to.

"The dress is terrible," Lucien said. "Too many bits and pieces. This is a movie, not a fashion show."

Kraus stuck his head around the door. "I hope you know what you're doing," he said. "This is costing a fortune."

"Kraus, I taught you everything you know. You should be ashamed of yourself, letting Queenie be handled by mediocrities."

"They're professionals, Lucien," Kraus said mildly.

"Professionals are the worst. They think they know everything. Give me a talented amateur any day."

Dawn sat calmly in the eye of what was rapidly becoming a hurricane. She had always known what was needed: a man who understood glamour—and she had been right. The frantic activity around her did not bother her or even interest her very much. Her job was to be herself.

She did not look at herself in the mirror. She did not need to. She looked at Lucien's face and saw him smile. That told her everything she needed to know. He examined her through the finder he carried around his neck, framing her face, then he nodded. "Good," he said, "very, very good," with the quiet satisfaction of a man appraising his own handiwork. "Put a couple of drops of water on her lips," he told the makeup man, "so they catch the light. Do you have any eye drops?"

The makeup man produced a bottle—it was part of his kit.

"Put two drops in each eye. I want the pupils to be enlarged to make her eyes even darker."

"They will take a minute or two to work. And Miss Avalon will have to be careful. Things will seem out of focus."

"Only the camera needs to be in focus. Put them in. We'll wait."

Dawn tilted her head back, felt the drops sting her eyes, blinked and held her head back so that the drops wouldn't run out onto her makeup. Lucien tapped his wrist and pointed at the makeup man's watch. Lucien had no watch, Dawn realized. She would have to buy him one. Then as the two minutes passed, Lucien opened the door a crack and shouted "Lights!"

The dark outside exploded in dazzling white brilliance. The makeup man had been right, Dawn thought, as she moved toward it, already feeling the heat—everything *was* out of focus. Blurred and in double image, Lucien looked younger now, almost like his old self.

Then she stepped into the light and saw a crowd of faces staring up at her—Lacey, fat and flushed; Zegrin, obsequious as ever, a step behind his betters, his black hair gleaming; Kraus, his eyes hidden by the reflections from his spectacles, his mouth open in admiration; Pop Deigh, his old, battered fedora pulled low on his head. His small army of men had stopped their work to watch her descend the steps of the trailer, and the huge sound stage was suddenly silent.

High overhead, the grips on their catwalks among the blazing lights stared down. There were perhaps two hundred people looking at her in silence, most of them men for whom beauty was part of their profession, stock-in-trade, men who had stood next to some of the most beautiful women in the world, even if it was only to move a piece of scenery or tape a mark on the floor.

Empire had not had a major star for years. MGM had Garbo; Paramount had Dietrich; Empire had been stuck with Marty Braverman's obsession to raise Ina Blaze to that status, without success, and the lack had come to symbolize the studio's slipping fortunes.

Dawn stood in the silence, for she well knew Empire's history and understood the importance of her entrance—besides, with her vision blurred, she hesitated to step down for fear of stumbling. The moment seemed to go on forever—then, from all over the sound stage there was the sound of clapping.

There were no wolf whistles. It was not that kind of moment, and she knew she was not that kind of star. She was what the industry was about, the heart and soul of it: glamour that ordinary people dreamed about. She only wished that Charles could be here. But would he have understood? Probably not.

She smiled—a smile of triumph—and with Lucien behind her, helping her down the steps, she stepped out onto the floor, out in front of the camera, which by now she could hardly see, and heard Lucien shout at the top of his voice, "All right—now let's get it on film!"

And turning toward him, she blew him a kiss.

Everything, she told herself, was going to be all right now.

"It's a beautiful watch," Lucien said, holding his wrist up to the light.

"Not too showy?"

"Not too showy at all." Dawn had picked it with some care, a little ashamed of the fact that she couldn't remember what kind of watch Lucien had worn. Had she forgotten, or had she simply never noticed? She rather thought he had worn an old-fashioned gold wristwatch, but she wasn't sure, and Van Cleef & Arpels had nothing that resembled it anyway.

Acting on the assumption that Charles always had the best of everything, she bought Lucien a watch like Charles's, which, not surprisingly, turned out to be the most expensive one in the shop.

Years ago, in London, when she had nothing, Lucien had taken her to Bond Street on the first shopping spree of her life. Now she was in a position to do the same for him, and more. She gave orders for Kraus to find him a house near her own, and a car.

A studio's powers were unlimited: within twenty-four hours, Lucien had been moved into a furnished Spanish-style cottage in Bel Air with a pool and a Mexican couple. He had no driver's license? A few calls from Empire and a supervisor from the California Department of Motor Vehicles came out to the studio, gave him a test behind the sound stages and issued him a license on the spot. With the war on, it was almost impossible to buy a car, but Lucien's white Chrysler convertible was delivered in two days, along with an ample supply of gas coupons. The studio lent him money against his salary, opened a bank account for him, made an appointment for him to have a full medical checkup, arranged for one of the best dentists in Beverly Hills to examine his teeth, gave him a parking space with his name painted on it. It was all part of a system so pervasive that nobody in power in Hollywood even thought about it. There was no reason, she thought, not to make use of the system on Lucien's behalf.

For the first time in many weeks—even months—Dawn was enjoying herself. She missed Charles, missed him desperately late at night, alone in bed, but she kept herself busy, forced herself to have a good time, confident that he would want her to.

Occasionally Lucien asked her if she thought Charles would mind their being seen together so much. "Why would he mind?" she said, laughing at the question—but the truth was she *wanted* him to mind, at least a little. She resented his silence, whatever his reasons for it, his interfering in Empire's affairs from afar, the fact that he had left her here alone for so long. A dose of jealousy—a small, mild dose—would do him no harm, she thought, and perhaps even teach him a lesson. She was not about to be taken for granted, least of all by her husband. And after all, she told herself, she had no reason to feel guilty.

"Who *are* the Patsons?" Lucien asked, buckling the watch Dawn had just given him onto his wrist, as she drove her big white convertible through the winding roads above Santa Monica.

"Old money," she said. But of course that didn't begin to do them justice. It was not the age of their fortune that was so impressive as the sheer size of it. Many people were under the impression that the Patsons owned California, but that, Polly Hammer had assured her, was an exaggeration. "They own a quarter of it, at most," Polly said, and her tone was perfectly serious.

Norman Patson went to his office at the Patson Foundation every day—though what he did there was a mystery—while Billie Patson, with an energy that terrified everyone who met her, ran the newspapers, distributed the family charities, made the final decisions about investments and real estate, harassed the president and faculty of the university the Patsons had founded, served as a state senator and had even found time in her youth to pursue a career as a minor Hollywood star when she was not bearing children, playing tennis or golf or overseeing the Patson stud, which boasted two Kentucky Derby winners. Norman was reputed to have a "roving eye," Polly reported, but it was said that Billie watched him like a hawk.

Their dinner parties consisted of people whose families had been rich and powerful before the movie industry had even been invented and who were born with vast wealth. Dawn had been invited not because she was a star, but because she was married to an international banker and owned a significant piece of Empire Pictures.

The guests were for the most part rather more than middle-aged, the women with the tanned, leathery faces that come from living outdoors, the men red-faced from a lifetime of martini drinking and golf.

Leaving Lucien to introduce himself to Norman Patson, who justified his reputation by staring at Dawn's bosom until his eyes seemed about to pop, she made her way around the room, determined to prove that she was not a freak merely because she was a star. Dawn had long since learned that in America most stars didn't know how to behave, insulated as they were in their own narrow world. The studios turned them from ordinary people into goddesses overnight, but most of them began with few of the social graces and seldom picked any up along the way. It was one of the things that made Dawn different from most stars, and she was conscious of the fact. She also knew how to make herself charming, and did so to each of the people Billie Patson presented her to, until at the far end of the living room she felt her smile become rigid as she found herself looking into the familiar green cat's eyes of Penelope Daventry.

"We've met," Mrs. Daventry said coldly.

"It's nice to see you again," Dawn said mechanically, eager to move on, but unable to do so as Billie Patson had her by the arm.

"*Is* it?" Mrs. Daventry asked. The skin drawn over the hard muscles of her body was tanned to an improbable darkness; there still remained about her a sexuality that could hardly fail to attract men. She always managed to convey that she was more than a match for any man. The way she stood, her low, husky voice, the cold eyes, were like a deliberate challenge. She did not seduce, she commanded—and, until Dawn's arrival, she had been the center of attention for every man in the room.

Mrs. Daventry did not relish competition any more than she had ten years ago in the Palm Court of the Grand Hotel in Calcutta.

"I hear you're staying with Dominick Vale," Dawn said.

"For the moment. He's a dear man, but not easy to live with. Too many young men drifting in and out, if you know what I mean. I'm planning to rent a nice little house in Beverly Hills for the time being—while poor Daventry sweats out the war in India. Now that the Americans are fighting, at least the Japs won't get to Calcutta. A pity, really. It would have taught the bloody Indians there are worse people than the English. Of course, there are Yank soldiers everywhere. There isn't a chee-chee girl in Calcutta who isn't trying to marry an American."

Dawn laughed uneasily, and at just that moment Lucien, immaculate in his white dinner jacket, appeared beside her. Taking her by the arm, his voice almost as happy as it was in the days before the war, he said, "Ah, Queenie, I've heard enough about politics to last me the evening—"

Then he noticed Mrs. Daventry. He gave a slight bow, ready to kiss her hand. She did not offer it to him. Instead, her green eyes, sparkling in triumph, were fixed on Dawn. "Queenie," she whispered. She examined Dawn through the smoke from her cigarette. "I should have guessed! Morgan Jones' bloody little niece! You *have* come a long way, haven't you—Queenie?"

"I don't know what you're talking about," Dawn said firmly.

"Oh, I think you do, my girl." Mrs. Daventry gave an unpleasant laugh. "I was just thinking, why does that face always remind me of someone—and then Lucien Chambrun came along to jog my memory. Brought up in a maharajah's palace, my foot!"

"This is ridiculous. I don't need to put up with any more of this!"

"Oh, but I think you *do*," Mrs. Daventry said, keeping her voice low. "You wait and see. For Cynthia's sake, if nothing else, I'm going to make sure everybody hears the truth about Dawn Avalon! *Including* Charles. Oh, I can't have you arrested as a thief, more's the pity. But I don't suppose you'll be all that welcome in society when people know you're half nigger, will you? The Americans don't like that any better than we did in India, do they?"

She stubbed out her cigarette and looked at Lucien. "You look as

if you've had a hard war," she said mockingly. "Still, you've fallen on
your feet, too, haven't you? Be careful, though. You must ask Queenie
what happened to her Uncle Morgan. I'm sure we'd all like to know the
answer to that!"

"I haven't the slightest interest in what happened to Morgan,"
Lucien said firmly. "Or in this fairy story."

"You always were a fool when it came to women," Mrs. Daventry
said. She turned on her heel gracefully and was gone.

"The woman's mad," Lucien said, holding Dawn by the arm.
"Menopausal jealousy." But then he looked at Dawn, who was trembling—with rage, or fear? he wondered—and guessed that at least one
or two of her shafts had hit home.

They sat together in the dark in the garden of Lucien's rented cottage. Dawn had no desire to go back to the big, empty house in Bel
Air; she knew she could not bear to be alone there yet. She had survived the interminable evening, watching Mrs. Daventry chatter and
laugh at the other end of the table, the green eyes darting in her
direction from time to time. Were they laughing about her, Dawn
wondered?

She wore Lucien's camel's-hair overcoat over her shoulders—the
evening had turned cold, but she didn't want to go indoors, as if the
Patsons' dinner party had given her a temporary case of claustrophobia.
The humid night air had disarranged her hair. She didn't care. Lucien
sat beside her, smoking in silence. Every so often he waved his hand
to indicate that he was listening. Eventually he stubbed his cigarette
out. "It would be a minor scandal," he said calmly. "Nothing more."

"I can't even afford a *minor* one, Lucien. Not just now."

"Is it your career you're worried about? All you have to do is deny
the rumors if they spread. Worse things have been said about stars before. For years people whispered that Garbo was a lesbian. It didn't
affect her career."

"Mixed blood is worse."

"Maybe. Though I've heard *that* about stars, too . . . But it's your
word against Mrs. Daventry's. Compared to you, she's a nobody. Polly
Hammer will be on your side. As well as Charles."

"Will he? You don't know him. I sometimes think I don't know
him. He's in a very delicate position himself. He'd hate any kind of
scandal. And who knows how he'd feel about being married to an
Anglo-Indian?"

"Nonsense! He probably doesn't even know what an Anglo-Indian *is*, Queenie."

"You don't understand at all!"

"There's no reason to be snappish with *me*. I'm only trying to be helpful. . . . What was all that about Morgan? You told me he was your guardian, not a relative. I haven't thought about him in years."

"Neither have I." Dawn knew there were limits to how much she could tell Lucien, and judged from his expression that there were limits to how much he wanted to know.

"Well, the hell with him, either way. It's Charles you're worried about, isn't it?"

She nodded. "I don't understand what he's doing. And I don't trust him. I want to. I ought to. But I can't."

"You think he has other women?"

"No, no, nothing like that," she said, with some irritation. "Charles is faithful to a fault, like most people who are jealous. I'm the same way myself, so I understand that. But there's some part of him I just can't reach. I think he's using me—using my involvement in Empire. I don't even think it's even something he can *help*, just like his jealousy. It's simply the way he does business. And I *can't* give in to him. I wish I could. I've tried. But I can't do it."

"Maybe you're wrong about him, you know. He may be trying to protect you by not letting you know too much about what he's doing. Even if he has to use you, his instinct will be to keep you out of things as much as possible."

She shrugged. It was not impossible. "I love him so much. And somehow I don't think he knows that. I don't think I've *let* him know. I don't seem to be able to tell him. It's as if I were afraid of making myself seem vulnerable, or dependent. . . . Damn him." She stared out at the small garden. "He wants children, you know."

"Most Latin men do."

"I can't give him any. Not since my miscarriage . . ."

"I didn't realize . . . Doesn't he know?"

She shook her head.

"That's very bad. After all, you could always adopt children if that's so important. But it's a mistake to hide things from the person you love. That's always been your biggest mistake, from the very beginning. You don't *have* to lie. If you hide things from him, why shouldn't he hide things from you? You don't tell him about your childhood, or the fact that you can't have children—which, in any case, knowing you, you don't want. *He* doesn't tell you about his business, or what he's planning to do with Empire. You're afraid he's pathologically jealous. He's afraid that being a star is more important to you than being his wife. It's a comedy of errors—except that there's nothing funny about it."

"What should I do? Tell me that."

"I haven't acquired any special wisdom in the desert, you know. Just a few scars. But I think it's important to go to him and tell him you love him. Tell him about Mrs. Daventry, while you're at it. He sounds to me like the kind of man who would rather know the truth—and who can probably do something about it. I don't suppose he likes surprises—most bankers are that way."

"*Nobody* likes surprises, Lucien." She tucked her legs up on the garden chair and felt one of her stockings rip. Her dress was already creased from the damp—already the rain was falling steadily beyond the awning of the covered-in porch.

She pulled off her stockings and put them down beside her in a ball, alongside her jewelry, which she had taken off so as not to snag it on Lucien's polo coat.

He lit another cigarette. "True," he said. "But we get them all the same, Queenie. Nobody escapes *that*."

In the gray half-light of the clouded moon, the streets gleamed with water, and the palm trees had a spiky look, like a woman who has washed her hair but not yet brushed and dried it. In places, the streets were flooded; Los Angeles was built in the belief that it never rained— as if drains and gutters would have shown a lack of faith.

The whole scene reminded Dawn of Calcutta in the monsoon, except that here the streets were empty, and the rain was an inconvenience rather than a blessing. In Calcutta, she remembered, millions of people ran out into the streets just to stand and *feel* the rain, howling with joy; here it was regarded as an unwelcome freak of nature, a reminder to people who had fled from New York, or Chicago, or Berlin that even in Southern California, which was as far as you could flee, you couldn't escape from all the realities of life. She needed no such reminder.

She felt grubby. More than anything else, she wanted a cup of tea, a hot bath and clean clothes. She was still in the long, décolleté dress she had worn to the Patsons' dinner party, with Lucien's camel's hair coat thrown over her shoulders. She had not bothered to put her jewelry back on—she had simply slipped the pieces into the coat pocket. Nor had she bothered with her torn stockings, which she balled up and stuffed into the other pocket.

She opened the door of the car and walked up the broad, wet marble steps, thankful that the servants were in bed, unlocked the door and kicked off her shoes.

To her annoyance, there was a light in the living room. She would have to speak to the butler about it, she decided. Of course it was diffi-cult, like everything else. If you spoke to servants too harshly, as she had to Marie-Claire, then they became sullen and insubordinate and took their revenge by pretending not to understand what you wanted or by inflicting minor damage to your possessions. Only the other day, Marie-Claire had singed one of Dawn's silk dresses while ironing it, and while she had been apologetic to the point of tears, Dawn was fairly sure it was deliberate. She would have to go. Sighing, she straightened a pic-ture, walked into the living room to turn off the light and stood rooted to the spot in surprise.

"You're home, at last," Charles said. There was not a trace of anger—or even irritation—in his voice or his face, but it was impossible to read any affection there, either. "A good party?" he asked. There was a sharp edge to the question.

"The Patsons. I wasn't *expecting* you, darling."

He stood up to kiss her, then sat down again behind the Louis XVI desk Billy Sofkin had been in ecstasies about. Dawn had shared his enthusiasm, but now that Charles was seated at it, she realized it was too small and delicate for a man to use comfortably. It would have to go in one of the bedrooms, and Billy would have to find Charles a man-sized desk, a serious piece of furniture appropriate to his size and the quantity of his papers—for the tooled leather and gold surface was already covered with files, papers and envelopes.

To make room for them—and a tray with a whiskey decanter and a glass—Charles had moved the ornaments she had placed there to an-other table and put the vase of flowers on the floor. She felt a quick temptation to restore order, but wisely suppressed it. From the level of the decanter it was evident that Charles had been drinking steadily for some time, which was unlike him. Was he anticipating a difficult inter-view—or possibly imagining her in the arms of somebody else?

There were those who thought Charles Corsini controlled his emo-tions superbly and admired him for it; there were others who doubted that he had any emotions at all. Dawn knew the truth: his emotions were held in check by a deliberate act of will. The thread had snapped, once, no doubt, when Alana had betrayed him, and a second time—with less disastrous consequences—when he had taken her up to Alana's bedroom and thrown his wife's belongings out into the garden; but she suspected that Charles lived in constant terror of losing control. He was close to losing it now, which explained his glacial calm.

"I know the Patsons. Norman is a zero, a perfect argument for inheritance taxes. Billie is the man of the family—fantastic energy, but no real intelligence. Instead of having lovers, she backs politicians and supports causes. One of these days she'll do a great deal of harm. It's not like them to dance until dawn—unless they've changed a good deal. Nor like *you*. Still, I hope you had a good time."

"I'm so glad you're back, Charles." She was furious that he had spoiled the homecoming she had looked forward to for so long by his attitude.

"I've been away too long," he said, as if he were speaking to himself. It was an explanation, for his own benefit, Dawn thought, rather than an apology or a statement. "*Far* too long."

"Why on earth haven't you called? It's been two weeks at least since I've heard from you."

"There have been reasons."

"You seem to be able to call Kraus."

"I'm not married to Kraus. There are things I can't tell you about. Everything I say on the telephone is recorded."

"Even 'I love you'?"

He rubbed his hands over his face with exasperation. "Did you sign papers that put you in charge of Pacifica?" he asked, firing the question at her like a prosecutor. He did not wait for an answer. "You did. For reasons that you're better off not knowing, it's been vitally important that I don't give the slightest impression that I still control those shares. You know damn well I would have telephoned you if I could, but the risk was too great. You should know by now you can trust me."

"What's the problem with Pacifica?" she asked.

He shrugged. "It will work itself out." He was obviously unwilling to discuss it, or perhaps his mind was still on where she had been.

"I'm still responsible for Pacifica, aren't I?"

"On paper," he said grudgingly.

"I don't even know what you've been doing."

"Liquidating certain things. Buying others. I don't want to bore you with the details."

"What makes you think I'd be bored?" Pacifica was a sore subject, now that he had brought it up. Charles saw nothing wrong in meddling with Empire—which was hers—and kept her in the dark about Pacifica's affairs, though she was legally responsible.

He backed off a little. "We can discuss it tomorrow. You must be tired."

"Not particularly," she said, though in fact she was exhausted. She knew he was trying to provoke her into an apology. She remained stubbornly silent.

He raised an eyebrow. "It's two in the morning, or thereabouts. Even I am tired." He paused. "I didn't think you liked such late nights."

"I try to enjoy myself, Charles."

"And apparently, you succeed," he said sharply.

"I'm a star. It's part of the job to be seen. And it's not my fault you haven't been here to go out with me. God knows, I've begged you to come."

"If I could have joined you here sooner, I would have, believe me. I can see it was an error."

He glanced down at his cuff links as if he had just noticed them for the first time. "You're not wearing your diamonds?" he asked, suddenly looking at her more closely.

"I took them off. I went dancing with some people. These new dances are all so—violent. Jitterbugging! Can you imagine it? I'm afraid I'm no good at it. The place was full of young soldiers and sailors, everywhere *is* now. Nice boys, but rough dancers. . . ." She looked down at her legs. "I tore my stockings, too."

"I can see I must prepare myself for a new kind of social life. Dancing until dawn at—where did you say you were dancing?"

"I didn't say." She resented being interrogated, particularly since she had nothing to hide—but most of all she hated the fact that their reunion had been spoiled. She had so often imagined what it would be like; instead they were locked in a foolish battle, which she was losing.

She swallowed her anger. If at all possible, she wanted to make peace with him.

"The film goes well?" he asked.

"It does *now*. We had some problems at the beginning. We had to get a new cameraman."

"So I heard," Charles said, dropping a slight warning of his dissatisfaction, like a fisherman casting his fly onto the still waters of a pool.

He was not about to say how much he had heard, or from whom he had heard it. She would have to find out for herself if the bait concealed a hook. She decided wisdom lay in ignoring it.

"Have your things been taken care of? Did you get something to eat?"

He waved a hand to indicate that he attached little importance to such matters—though Dawn knew how much he did. "Quayle accompanied me," he said. "I arrived late, but your maid was still up. She very kindly prepared a meal for me. A very talkative young woman."

Dawn cursed herself silently for not having patched up her quarrel with Marie-Claire. She wondered what she had told Charles while she served him. While Charles would not normally have paid much attention to Marie-Claire's chatter, he might have listened more carefully than usual, finding Dawn missing—particularly if his suspicions had already been aroused by other people.

"She's been very difficult. I've been thinking of getting rid of her."

"Yes? She seemed quite a competent young woman to me. And observant."

"She can't be trusted."

"Ah? You mean she steals? I wouldn't have thought her the type."

"No, no. But she makes trouble. She invents gossip and stories. And she goes out a lot with men. I'm not sure her mind is on her work half the time."

"Even servants have a private life. Except Quayle, who seems to have none at all, I'm happy to say."

"Do you like the house?" She had at least expected praise for what she had done in his absence.

"I haven't seen it all." He wasn't prepared to give an inch. Was he merely disappointed and upset that she was out so late—or had he deliberately planned to catch her by surprise?

"And what you *have* seen?"

"It's very pleasant. Sofkin has excellent taste." Having made a grudging concession, Charles was determined to return to the attack. "This cameraman of yours, Lucien—Chambrun?—he was dancing too?"

It was obvious that he was well informed about her activities by someone. A lie here, Dawn decided, would be dangerous. Hollywood was full of people for whom gossip was a full-time paid occupation—and well paid, at that. The fact that she had taken Lucien to the Patsons' and had left with him was known to too many people for her to conceal.

"Yes," she said, trying to be as casual as possible.

"Quite. Chambrun—he dances well?"

"As a matter of fact, no. He's not much better at that sort of thing than I am."

"But you used to be quite good, didn't you?" Charles's smile was mocking now. "You were a dancer when you arrived in England, you told me. As a matter of fact, weren't you and Chambrun living together then, before you married Konig? I seem to remember you told me that. I thought he was in a prisoner-of-war camp somewhere?"

"He escaped."

"How fortunate for him. It seems mine is not the only homecoming."

"Charles, it's not at all what you think. . . ."

She had not experienced the full brunt of Charles's jealousy before, and for a moment she understood Alana. She held her temper in check, conscious that there was no point in provoking him further.

"Don't presume to tell me what I think!" He stood up, as if he couldn't stand being confined a moment longer behind the desk, and began to pace the room.

It was a sign that his self-control had worn thin, but Dawn ignored it—or rather, because she was tired, she failed to respond to it. Perhaps if she ran to him, put her arms around him, told him how much she loved him, the situation could still be saved. She could go upstairs with him, get him into bed, and after that, things would be easier to discuss. Sex was usually the most reliable way of ending a marital quarrel, and most husbands assumed they had won when things ended that way, but she was not only tired and, in her own eyes, grubby, she was also *in the right*.

Charles had no reason to spy on her, and no right. When business was at stake, he stayed away and put her at the back of his mind, disappearing for weeks on end without a call. Now, when matters were under control again for him, or when he needed her signature, he turned up unexpectedly, breathing fire in the role of the aggrieved husband.

"I don't *care* what you think," she said. "I'm going to bed."

She stood up and walked toward the door, making an effort to ignore Charles, though she could see him out of the corner of her eye, standing beside the fireplace, glaring at her now with undisguised rage. She had never seen him angry before. His face was pale, and now that he was standing he didn't seem to know what to do with his hands.

He put them into his pockets, then behind his back, then placed them in front of him, lacing the fingers together as if he were about to crack his knuckles—a sound he knew she detested.

Anyone who knew him less well than Dawn might have thought he was merely exasperated, but even from a distance, and at a quick glance, his eyes told the story. Still, she was not about to be intimidated by Charles, Dawn told herself, however easily he frightened other people.

"You don't deny it?" he said.

She turned to face him. "I won't even *discuss* it."

It was, as she instantly realized, a tactical error. She had been ahead on points, always assuming that there was an unseen and impartial judge somewhere who kept score, which was the assumption that most marital quarrels seemed to be based on.

He stepped forward between Dawn and the door. Whatever slim hold he had maintained over his temper, it was gone now. "How dare you tell me what we'll discuss and what we won't!" he said, raising his voice for the first time.

Dawn reacted to Charles's shouting at her with a combination of fear and anger. A man raising his voice, telling her what to do, was Szabothy, Cantor, Morgan—the enemy. She stood her ground. "Get out of my way," she said.

"Not until we've talked."

"Then talk. Talk to me about Alana, for example. You were suspicious of her, too. It doesn't seem to produce happy results, does it? And what about Luckman? If we're going to discuss each other's secrets, there's a good one to begin with."

"Luckman?" Charles asked, taken by surprise. "What about Luckman?"

"Don't take me for a fool, Charles. You had him killed, didn't you?"

Charles's pupils narrowed down until they were merely black dots. Dawn had always thought of anger as a warm emotion, hot in fact, but in Charles's case a chill came over him, a killing frost, as if his features were frozen.

He stood motionless for a moment—it seemed like a long time to Dawn, though it was only a matter of seconds—then he moved so swiftly that she didn't see his hand coming until she felt the impact. She stood in shock for a moment, then the pain hit her, and at the same time the fear that Charles had damaged her face, and without a glance in his direction, she turned and ran out of the room, slamming the door behind her, up the marble stairs, her feet slipping on the polished treads, and down the long corridor to her bedroom.

She locked the door, crying now, as much from anger and humiliation as from fear, but Charles did not come after her. She heard a car door slam.

She wondered where Charles was going, and felt a stab of pain at how much she still cared.

The morning brought Charles no peace. He slept badly for an hour or two, in his bungalow at the Beverly Hills Hotel, then rose to order an elaborate breakfast from room service, which he didn't eat. He had ordered a steak, thinking he was hungry, but the thought of eating it made him sick. His head hurt—he should not have allowed himself to drink, he knew that, not with the pressures that were on him. . . .

He sipped his orange juice and looked at the second bed. His open briefcase was on it, filled with problems. He would have to see Vale. Perhaps matters could be straightened out.

He sighed. He had made mistakes. That was the first thing to face. The biggest one was to have panicked and talked to Vale in the first place. If Vale hadn't put him in touch with Faust, if he hadn't tried to scare off Luckman, if he hadn't tried to dot all the i's and cross all the t's . . . if, if, if . . . he rubbed his forehead. The pain grew worse.

He thought of the papers in his briefcase. There were people he had to call, messages to be returned. He had relied on the young Zegrin to keep him informed of what was happening at Empire, knowing that Kraus was too loyal to Dawn to pass on information.

Was Zegrin to be trusted? Zegrin had passed on the rumors that Dawn was seeing a lot of Chambrun, but were the rumors true? In the cold light of day, he did not think she had showed the slightest sign of guilt. Of course, she was an actress, one had to make allowances for that, but still, he knew her as well as a man could know a woman. How he wished he had not hit her! It was hardly her fault that she believed he had killed Luckman. Everybody else believed it, after all. . . .

Had she slept with this Chambrun fellow? Was she in love with him? He was a sophisticated man, Charles told himself, and understood that the two questions were very different. His father had once told him that a man who ignores his wife for too long has only himself to blame for the consequences—certainly this had been true with Alana.

Had he made the same mistake twice? It was possible, Charles decided. Whatever one learned from experience, it was seldom enough to overcome the basic habits of a lifetime. In the end, everyone made the same mistakes over and over again. He was no exception.

If you placed too many bets on the table at once, you never won—every gambler knew that, it was the mark of the amateur. He had made a mistake in spreading himself so thin, investing in real estate, setting up new companies, taking on too many partners—and at the same time marrying a woman who was a world-famous star, which most men would have regarded as a fulltime occupation in itself. As a result he had not paid sufficient attention to any of these demands—which was the same mistake he had made years ago, when he plunged into banking and left Luckman to look after the details, and, in the end, Alana. Too far, too fast, Charles told himself—that might have been his life motto.

Still, the first job of a survivor, when you came right down to it, he reminded himself grimly, was to survive. He splashed hot water on his face and began to shave. The face in the mirror showed no anxiety. That was as it should be. Self-discipline was vital.

He showered quickly and dressed without ringing for Quayle. He could do without Quayle's polite disapproval this morning. Quayle liked Dawn, and had been upset when he learned that his master walked out of the house in the middle of the night. He had even let it show. Charles took two aspirin, and picked up the telephone to call Dawn.

A lugubrious voice, presumably the butler's, informed him that she had left.

At the studio there was no answer—it was too early.

He felt a sense of panic, as if events were slipping out of his control. Next week the Empire board would meet, and he would have to persuade Dawn to satisfy Vale and Faust. More important, with each minute that went by, her anger and resentment against him would increase, perhaps beyond the point of no return.

He tried the studio again, without results. Was she avoiding him? He stared at the breakfast table with its pink linen, the obligatory vase of flowers and the untouched food, trying to put his thoughts in order. By the time he had circled the table three times, the smell of food nauseated him. He wheeled the table out onto the porch and abandoned the meal to the birds.

He remembered Dawn feeding the birds in Mexico, throwing the crumbs from her toast out onto the lawn and laughing with pleasure in the bright sunlight. The birds had been brilliantly colored, shiny reds and yellows, with eyes of gold and cheerful songs. *These* birds were dark and somehow threatening, dull-brown creatures savagely ripping at the breadbasket with their sharp beaks. They did not sing, and when he approached the table, they stood their ground, glaring at him and puffing out their sooty feathers to make themselves look more threatening. One of them had torn a piece out of his steak and was worrying it back and forth, spilling small drops of blood on the table-cloth. Charles shuddered and went back inside. He did not believe in premonitions, he told himself.

He had to find Dawn, to speak to her, to make peace with her if it was still at all possible. He tried Aaron Diamond, waking him up, but Diamond knew nothing. He spoke to Kraus, who said she was not expected at the studio. At Polly Hammer's home there was no reply.

He went to his briefcase and rummaged through the papers. It had not escaped Zegrin's attention that Dawn had authorized the studio to buy Chambrun a car and rent a house for him—it was, in fact, precisely that which had aroused Charles's suspicion in the first place. He scribbled the address on a piece of paper and called for his car.

If she was there, he would at least know the worst.

He prayed she wouldn't be.

"She's not here, *mon ami*. And if you don't mind my saying so, it's a little early in the morning for a visit."

"I was worried about her, you see." Charles felt foolish. The role of a jealous husband was not one he enjoyed playing, least of all in the presence of the man he suspected of being his wife's lover. Another mistake, he told himself. On top of everything else, he had made himself look ridiculous. Was he losing his touch?

Lucien poured him a cup of coffee. "So far as I know, she went home last night."

"She arrived home safely."

"Ah? Then I fail to see what the problem is. Presumably she's in bed asleep."

Charles tasted his coffee. To his pleasure, it was excellent. Most American coffee was watery and tasteless. He took another sip.

"It's good, isn't it?" Chambrun asked. "A mixture of Colombian and Algerian beans. I grind them myself. The stuff they sell in the shops here is undrinkable."

Charles nodded. From the little he had heard about Lucien, he had expected to find a handsome young Englishman, a dandified lady's man. Lucien was handsome, all right, but he was not at all what Charles would have imagined a photographer of women to be. He looked tough, worldly-wise, worn down to the bare essentials, more like a soldier than a fashion photographer, and though his accent was English, his manner, like his taste in coffee, was altogether European.

Charles cleared his throat. "We had a misunderstanding last night," he explained. "I was hoping to clear it up."

"Ah. These things happen. Generally they pass."

"I'm not sure this one will. That's why I'm looking for her."

Lucien nodded. "And you thought she might be here?"

"It crossed my mind."

"I see. Was I part of the—misunderstanding?"

Charles hesitated. He disliked the idea of exposing his problems to a stranger, but he had already made a fool of himself, so there wasn't much to lose. Besides, he found Lucien rather sympathetic. He did not protest his innocence or put on a show of indignation. "I'm afraid so," Charles admitted.

Lucien shrugged. "I did warn her. She's always been headstrong, of course. If she wasn't, she'd still be dancing in a cabaret. You picked a bad night to quarrel with her, *mon ami*. She had an unpleasant shock at the Patsons' dinner party—which was dreadful, by the way."

"What kind of shock?"

"Some terrible woman raking up old stories from her past. I managed to calm her down, but she was still very upset when she left. . . ."

"She was here?"

"Of course she was. Listen to me, Corsini—if there were anything going on between us besides friendship, she'd be the first to tell you."

Charles was surprised to find himself on the defensive. He bristled. "I thought it was a little extraordinary for her to be coming home in the early hours of the morning. Wearing a man't coat."

"*Merde alors*, Corsini, she's a grown-up woman! If she really wanted to cheat on you, she would, and you'd never know about it. Any woman knows how to do that, even Queenie."

"Queenie? Why do you call her that?"

"My God, what a lot you don't know about her. . . . I told her that was a mistake, too. She's always so busy hiding her past that it never occurs to her it might be easier to let it all out. Queenie was her name before Dawn Avalon. Listen again. She has saved my life—put me back on my feet. Well, that's all right. I took *her* out of a sordid Soho nightclub when she was sixteen or seventeen years old, made her famous, introduced her to David Konig. . . . Oh, I was in love with her, of course. Perhaps I always will be. But you don't even know *who* it is you're married to, Corsini. She's got *guts*, Queenie—more than I have. Probably more than you have. She's the most ambitious human being I've ever met, but she's so busy covering up the past that she's always spoiling the present and the future."

"She hasn't told me much about it."

"Well, of course not. That's her problem—she thinks you wouldn't love her if you knew. You should have guessed that, my friend. She loves you. That's not easy for her to handle. I don't think she ever really loved me—perhaps a sexual excitement, but not real love. I don't think she loved Konig, either. She respected him, certainly, but again— not love. *You*, she loves! And that scares her—she's not used to it. She tried to make you a little jealous. That's stupid, and I told her so, but she wanted you to come back. Besides, she's a woman of the world. You couldn't seriously expect her to go everywhere alone, or take Aaron Diamond along as her escort every night. . . . You should have telephoned her, explained things to her, paid attention. You have nobody to blame but yourself, my dear Corsini. Certainly not me."

Charles paced the room. On the desk was a framed photograph of Dawn. He peered at it. In some way it was different, though it was hard to tell how. "Yours?" he asked.

Lucien nodded. "It's from one of the first sittings she did for me. Almost eight years ago."

"She hasn't changed much. It's beautiful."

"I can see changes. In some ways, she's even more beautiful now. She will always be beautiful. You're a very lucky man to have her, Corsini. Try not to throw your good luck away."

"Have you any idea where she could be?"

"No. If she calls me, I'll tell her to get in touch with you. She might be with Diamond. She's been worried about this stupid board meeting of yours."

"I tried Diamond."

"Try again. What is all this nonsense, anyway? You're both rich. Leave it be. What do you care what happens to Empire? You must have bigger fish to fry. There are more important things than money. Life is all that really matters."

Corsini nodded, then looked at his watch. It would not do to be late for his next appointment.

A lot hung on it.

. . .

High in the hills of Hollywood, behind Sunset, there are roads that snake in and out between high walls so sharply that they seem to have been designed as an obstacle course. The gradients are steep, and signs warn the motorist to turn his front wheels at right angles when parking and to place stones or blocks behind the rear wheels. The signs are unnecessary. Nobody ever parks in the street in this part of Los Angeles.

In the twenties, before Beverly Hills was developed, stars built vast, improbably Moorish castles here, but by the 1930s most of them were abandoned or taken over by rich eccentrics and gangsters—people who, in any case, had a mania for privacy. Here Vilma Banky had commissioned a marble swimming pool on three different levels, with artificial waterfalls; Valentino had built a tiled garage for his collection of Hispano-Suizas and Rolls-Royces; and Mickey Costanzo, the gambling and vice king of Hollywood, had been locked in his own steam room and scalded to death. Here, Rayna Lang had been killed by her own pet cheetah, which escaped from her estate and lived on in the hills for years, preying on people's dogs, coyotes and an occasional Japanese gardener, until it was found dead of old age in Lazslo Spink's swimming pool, the gold-and-diamond-crusted collar with Rayna's initials still around the beast's neck. Those who had lived here in the hills for years swore the animal's ghost still prowled among the creaking palm trees, the eucalyptus groves and the flowering bougainvillaea.

It was the perfect place to hide from the press; so remote and difficult of access that no process server would even attempt to serve a subpoena on somebody who lived in the hills. It was for these reasons that Vale had chosen to live here, though he kept a house in Palm Springs for weekends.

It was here that Charles sought him out, in the midmorning. The sun had come out, and Los Angeles had resumed its usual tropical appearance, as if the storm and the rain had never happened. Charles found Vale seated under a tentlike umbrella next to the pool. At his feet, rather surprisingly, was a handsome woman, lying on a mattress in the briefest of bathing suits, her blond hair tied up in a bun. Her skin was so brown and well-oiled that she reminded Charles of a piece of meat on a spit. Vale wore a broad-brimmed straw hat of vaguely Mexican appearance, a flowing robe of white cotton, sunglasses and Moroccan leather slippers with pointed toes. Apparently he disliked the sun, or perhaps, Charles reflected, he simply felt out of his element in the daylight. He draped his robe to protect his ankles and wrapped a towel tightly around his neck. He did not look comfortable.

Charles sat down beside him, concealing his dislike. He glanced at the woman in front of them, lying on her stomach, and raised an eyebrow. Vale shrugged, pulled his various pieces of clothing more tightly around him, rose and waddled over to the pool house, signaling Charles to follow him. A young man stood behind a rattan bar. He shook a cocktail shaker in Vale's direction, giving it a suggestive rattle as if he were playing a mariachi in a rhumba band.

"Not now, Tony," Vale said. "This gentleman and I have business to discuss."

"I'm sure," Tony pouted. "There's a call for Mrs. Daventry—Norman Patson wants to speak to her."

"You'd think he'd just discovered sex, poor man. He's *seeing* her at two! Well, don't just stand there. Off you go and tell her, like a good boy." Vale watched as the youth minced off toward the pool. "It was a little risky of you to come here, don't you think?" he said to Charles.

"I didn't want to talk on the telephone. You never know who's listening in these days."

"So far as I know there's nothing to talk about. We assume you'll deliver as promised."

"Faust's people went too far."

"These things happen. We kept our side of the bargain. You didn't want Luckman to testify. He didn't."

"I asked Faust to get to him before he talked. I didn't ask him to have Luckman *killed*. That wasn't the deal."

"It was always an option, Corsini. Maybe the people who could get to Luckman went too far. And please don't mention Faust's name again. He never met you. You never met him."

"Have you any idea of the trouble this has caused? Even Dawn accused me of having Luckman murdered."

"I shouldn't think that would shock *her*, old boy. Frankly."

Charles moved quickly, narrowing the gap between them, and seized the towel around Vale's neck. He pulled it tighter, drawing Vale toward him. "What do you mean by that?" he asked.

"You ask *her*, old boy. You ask her about her bloody Uncle Morgan. And make sure she votes the right way next week, if you know what's good for you!"

Charles squeezed the towel tighter, sharply enough so that Vale let out a howl. There was a click behind them, and Charles turned to find the woman who had been sunbathing standing in the doorway, lighting a cigarette. She had slipped a diaphanous silk shirt over her bare breasts, and seemed to be watching the scene with more curiosity than fear.

"I hope I'm not interrupting anything," she said. "I do think, dear Prince, that if you're going to strangle poor Dominick, you might find a more private place to do it."

Charles released the towel, while Vale, wheezing and coughing, slumped back against the bar to catch his breath. "We were just having a little business discussion, Mrs.—"

"Daventry. Pempy Daventry. We met in New York."

"Of course, I remember. At the Esterhazys' party."

"Quite. Dominick, dear, your face is a nasty shade of mauve. Do have a sip of water or something. Did I hear the name Morgan, by the way, just now?"

Vale poured himself a shot of brandy and emptied it in one gulp. "We were talking about Dawn," he said, edging cautiously out of Charles's reach.

"Past or present?" Mrs. Daventry asked pleasantly, and sitting down on a bar stool next to Charles, she took another cigarette out of her case, leaned forward for Charles to light it, and said, "I knew her years ago, in Calcutta. . . ."

"If he *didn't* love you, he wouldn't have slapped you," Polly Hammer said. "He's a Latin. They're all passionate."

Dawn glared at her. Polly thought in romantic clichés: a lovers' quarrel, a slap, tears, a reconciliation—she had spent her life sugar-coating reality for her readership, the doyenne of the Hollywood sob sisters, and the result was that she saw everything, however disagreeable, as if it were a romantic item in one of her columns.

It had been Dawn's first instinct to run to Polly, but it was a mistake. "It just shows how much he *cares* for you," she told Dawn. "I'll bet he's out shopping for a great big diamond necklace right now, to show you he's sorry."

Aaron Diamond, at least, was more practical, when he finally arrived. "Well, at least you've got grounds for divorce."

"I once starred in a movie called that," Dawn said sadly. "*Grounds for Divorce*—David directed it himself. It seems a lifetime ago."

Diamond poured himself a cup of coffee and studied Dawn's face more closely. He was a lawyer—nothing shocked him. Every human act had a price. In a California court, slapping a star would cost Corsini a fortune. "Were there witnesses?"

Dawn shook her head.

"Shit! That's a pity. You should have gone to the cops and made a complaint—then to a doctor, then had yourself photographed. In color. Still, let's look on the bright side. We can claim mental *and* physical cruelty. You should get a landmark settlement." He rubbed his hands together. "No sweat."

"I'm not sure that's what I want."

"You don't know what you want. You're still in shock."

"You wait," Polly said. "He'll call. I'll bet the poor man's heart-broken."

"I'm not taking his calls, Polly."

"Goddamn right!" Diamond said. "Change the locks at the house. We'll get a court order barring him from seeing you. We'll book you into Cedars of Lebanon—shock, exhaustion, X-rays for physical damage. . . ."

The telephone rang. Polly picked it up, nodded and passed the receiver to Dawn. "Kraus," she said.

Kraus's voice had an edge to it. To somebody who didn't know him, he might have sounded calm, but Dawn knew better. "Charles is looking for you," he said. "Do you want to speak to him?"

"Absolutely not." She needed time to know what to say.

"It might be a good idea."

"No. Not yet, anyway."

"He's been on the telephone all morning."

"What did he have to say?"

"He didn't make much sense, frankly. I couldn't get him off the phone. He said he'd spent the morning with Vale and some woman called Daventry, and that they'd told him the most astounding things about you. He said he understood everything now."

Dawn gasped. "*Everything?*"

"That's what he said. He wants to see you as soon as possible."

"I'm sure he does," Dawn said bitterly. She could imagine the scene—Charles in a rage, plunging off to talk to Dominick Vale, of all people. And Mrs. Daventry! She had no difficulty in guessing what they would have told him, and with what glee.

Was Charles gathering up information about her to use against her at the board meeting, or even in a divorce proceeding? Or was he simply intending to put more pressure on her somehow? The thought of Charles sitting down for a chat with the two people she feared most in the world was far more unnerving than being slapped by him.

"If you do see him, for God's sake don't let him talk you into anything."

"I haven't the slightest intention of seeing him."

"Is that wise? When he turns up at the board meeting, we don't want a scene."

"I won't make a scene."

"No, quite . . ."

"If Charles wants to make a scene, that's his problem."

"I only thought it might be a good idea to have a talk with him before the meeting, Dawn. To avoid any—unpleasantness—in public. Perhaps I could arrange a meeting between the two of you in private somewhere. . . ."

"No. I don't know what Charles is up to, but I won't be threatened."

"Listen, if life has taught me anything, it's to compromise. Work out a deal. Keep the back lot, for example, and give up the film library. Or vice versa. Or find out if there's something else we can offer. . . ."

"If life has taught *me* anything, it's not to give in when I'm being bullied! Even if the bully is Charles."

"Whatever you say," Kraus murmured unhappily.

"Exactly so."

"There's another complication, I'm afraid. . . ."

Dawn waited for the inevitable pause while Kraus worked up his courage to break the news, whatever it was. If Charles knew "everything," would he use it to destroy her? Had Vale told him about Morgan's death? How he must be laughing, after all her talk about Luckman, to discover that she had killed her own uncle! Had Vale told Charles about her miscarriage? About the fact that she couldn't have children? "Everything" covered a lot of ground—more than she even wanted to think about. "Out with it," she said grimly.

"The news is out," Kraus said. "The house is surrounded by reporters."

"Charles did *that?*" Dawn was baffled for an instant. She tried to think of any reason why Charles would have called in the press, but she couldn't imagine one. Nor was it his style. He was more subtle than that. He had always preferred to work behind the scenes. Vale? That seemed even less likely.

"I don't think it was Charles," Kraus said. "The story is that he beat you up after a quarrel. That's the last thing he'd want printed. I'm getting the most extraordinary questions from reporters. 'Is she disfigured?' 'What hospital is she in?' 'Is she having plastic surgery?' 'Are you canceling her picture?' I don't think you should go home."

"Don't be an old woman, Kraus," she said. "Have the reporters kept in the street. Hire guards. It's *my* bloody house, after all." But even as she gave the orders, she knew they wouldn't work. The best tactic—the *only* tactic—was to hide. If they couldn't find you in forty-eight hours, they lost interest, and the story died a natural death.

She put the receiver down. "I need to talk to you," she said to Diamond. "Seriously."

"Lawyer to client?"

"Lawyer to client. I think Charles is going to play dirty."

Polly shook her head. "I just *know* you're wrong, honey," she said. "When he sees the papers, he'll come to his senses, you'll see." She gave a beatific smile, as if Charles was about to come through the door bearing roses.

Dawn stared at her. Suddenly it was clear to her who had leaked the story. After all, who else had *known*? As usual, Polly's professional instinct and her taste for matchmaking had coincided. She must have made a quick call to her paper to alert them to the news, while telling herself that it was all for Dawn's own good. Dawn cursed herself for trusting her, but having a fight with Polly now would only make matters worse.

She asked for a couple of aspirin to get Polly out of the way so she could speak to Diamond alone. The sooner she got away from Polly's meddling, the better.

"I don't *know* where she is. She left with Aaron Diamond. Why don't you ask *him*?"

"One might as well talk to a clam. I hate lawyers." Charles brooded sullenly in the back of his limousine. He wore dark glasses, despite the fact that the car's windows were tinted a funereal black. The press was tracking him everywhere—he had caught the maid at the hotel going through his wastepaper basket, and the room-service waiter turned out to be a reporter in disguise. He had only to go to a restaurant and five minutes after his arrival the reporters and photographers had collected like a lynch mob.

For that reason he had chosen to meet Polly Hammer in the parking lot of the Brown Derby, close to her office, insisting that she walk there so he could be sure she was alone.

"My feet hurt," she complained. Like most people who lived in Los Angeles, she never walked anywhere.

He was not interested in her feet. "Surely you're in touch with her?" he asked.

"No. I think she's annoyed with me. Are you going to ask her for a reconciliation?"

"I don't know what I'm going to do yet."

"I want a scoop. You have to promise I'll be the first to know."

"We agreed all this was off the record."

"It *is* off the record. But you don't get something for nothing, Prince. What's in it for Polly? You owe me an exclusive."

"You'll get one. What did she say about me?"

"She told Aaron Diamond you were going to fight dirty. Are you?"

"No, no. I haven't the slightest intention of fighting. There's nothing to fight *about*. I'm trying to clear up a few loose ends, that's all. I'm the one who has a problem, not Dawn."

"What's she so frightened of? That's what I want to know."

"Shadows." Charles lit a cigarette, and opened the window a crack to let the smoke out. "It's all a misunderstanding."

"You still love her, don't you? That's what I told her."

"Yes. If you talk to her, please tell her that. It's important she should hear it. Tell her also the past doesn't matter."

"What past?"

"She'll know what I'm talking about." He drew on his cigarette, hating every moment of the conversation.

He wished Dawn had confided in him more, but he had only himself to blame for that. After all, his own life was as complicated as hers, and like her, he had always kept the most important parts of it to himself. He wondered how much it still mattered to her that she was Anglo-Indian? Obviously it mattered enough to have made her lie about it for years, at great inconvenience and risk to herself.

He could understand easily enough why Dawn had invented a new childhood for herself, but she need not have concealed it from *him*. He had uncles and cousins who had married *mestizos*, Jews, even, in one case, a Brazilian lady of great beauty whose color was several shades too dark to be attributable to the sun.

It was nonsense to worry about such things. Besides, that kind of story was easy enough to deny. The theft of the bracelet was not much worse, however strongly Mrs. Daventry felt about it. Dawn's fans might not like it, but it didn't shock Charles. Her inability to bear children was a misfortune, but adoption was always a possibility. He had considered it with Alana, after all. . . . The death of Morgan was, of course, a more serious matter. Vale had been sketchy about the details, presumably because he himself was implicated, but Charles knew enough about the world to assume that there were probably many reasons for Morgan's death, some of which, at least, must have seemed to Dawn important at the time. And it was not as if she had shot him or poisoned him. They had been fighting. She hit him with a poker. It could be seen as an accident, though whether it could be presented that way to the public was, of course, another matter. . . .

In any event, there were certain things he could do—*must* do, now. Vale, he had no doubt, could be bought off or frightened. It was just a question of putting enough pressure on him. As for Mrs. Daventry, there was nothing simpler than to destroy her reputation—the means to do so was sitting beside him in the car. He leaned closer to Polly Hammer. It was not by any means easy to do, since she wore a broad hat that seemed designed to prevent close contact between them. "Listen," he said, "I might have a story for you—a better one than this."

"Is this one on the record?"

"Absolutely. Without my name entering into it, of course."

"Of course."

"You know Norman Patson?"

Polly nodded. Everyone knew the Patsons. Among other things, they owned the rival paper to hers. Any scandal about the Patsons would delight the Chief, as his employees always referred to William Randolph Hearst.

"Do you know a woman called Penelope Daventry?"

Polly nodded again. Mrs. Daventry appeared in her column regularly. She went to the right parties and always wore what Polly referred to as "fabulous" clothes.

"She's Norman Patson's mistress. Did you know that?"

"I can't believe Norman would take the risk. Billie Patson watches him like a hawk."

"Apparently not closely enough. He has a little pied-à-terre near his office. He owns the building. It's all very discreet. He says he's going to the gym, then walks there, so even the chauffeur doesn't know. . . ."

"How do *you* know?"

"I picked up a little clue by accident, so I had someone make a few inquiries. What do you think would happen if they were found out?"

"Norman would be grounded. That's for sure. As for Mrs. Daventry, Billie would close every door in town to her. How do I know it's true?"

Charles handed her a slip of paper. "Here's the address. Two in the

afternoon seems to be the right time to have a photographer there. . . .
You'll pass my message on to Dawn?"

"If I can. I don't promise anything."

"I don't expect a promise," Charles said easily. "There's almost a
week before the board meeting—plenty of time." Polly had served her
purpose even if she didn't reach Dawn, he told himself. A story about
Norman Patson would drive the story about Dawn and himself off the
papers overnight—and get rid of Mrs. Daventry into the bargain. He had
examined Dawn's checkbook with a banker's eye. The cash withdrawals
told him someone was blackmailing her. He would deal with that person, whoever it was.

He would have to prove to Dawn how much he loved her now.

She was afraid of her past? Very well—he would destroy it for her,
piece by piece.

In his anxiety to avoid "unpleasantness," Kraus arranged to bring
Dawn into the board meeting after everyone else was seated. She had
changed into a black silk suit with a cape jacket with wide shoulders
that was faintly Spanish in cut, and a black velvet hat with a short veil,
almost like a mantilla. Dawn wondered if she had overdone things—
the effect was severe, almost one of mourning, which was not quite
what she had in mind. Without the theatrical makeup, the mark on
her face still showed faintly, a mottled bruise against the pale skin. She
wondered whether or not to cover it up, but in the end she decided to
put truth before beauty. If it embarrassed Charles, so much the better.

For nearly five days she had "holed up," as Aaron Diamond put it,
at the Campbell Ranch in Victorville, watched over by the formidable
Mrs. Campbell, who had sheltered Clark Gable during his divorce from
his first wife, Vivien Leigh during her nervous breakdown and Orson
Welles when he was hiding from the press. Mrs. Campbell had mothered
her like Ma in the old days, and there was a kind of mindless relief in
being fed, amused, protected and treated like a daughter. It was not until
she returned, by private plane, that she saw the newspapers and realized
that Mrs. Daventry had replaced her as the story of the week. There was a
photograph of her wearing a Chanel suit and trying to cover her face
with a handbag, while Norman Patson, a look of terror on his face, like
a rabbit caught in the headlights of a car, ran for cover.

It was reported that Mrs. Daventry was leaving Los Angeles for New
York, with the intention of rejoining her husband in India. Norman

Patson was said to be staying "with friends." Even the Patson newspapers were obliged to carry the story, though in a strongly sanitized
version, since they had been scooped by every other gossip columnist
in town—particularly by Polly Hammer, whose story carried the most
details.

Dawn's relief at being rid of one enemy was short-lived when she saw
Dominick Vale sitting at the boardroom table, a smirk on his face. She
glared at him, then noticed there was an empty seat next to his bulky
figure.

"Charles isn't here?" she asked Kraus.

He shrugged, indicating his helplessness to control or explain
Charles's movements.

She sat down next to Kraus and waited for what seemed an interminable time. Had Charles decided not to come? Was he unable to
face her? Was this his way of showing his anger at her? And yet it was
surely in his interest to be here, she told herself. She looked at the
clock.

"We'll have to begin without him," Kraus whispered. "It's just as
well. The best thing that could happen is that he doesn't turn up."

"Another minute."

But the minute passed and still there was no sign of him.

"Let's get on with it," she said to Kraus, who called the meeting to
order over Vale's objections.

She had counted on seeing Charles before the meeting, if only for a
minute or two. She was still half sure that they could reach an agreement,
patch things up somehow. Now there was no chance. She hardly even
listened as the routine business of the meeting began. Her mind was on
Charles.

Then the door opened and he walked in, as handsome as ever, smiling
as if there had never been an argument between them. That alone was
infuriating—to see him standing before her, relaxed and self-confident,
as if he had already won—and been forgiven. "My apologies," he said
smoothly to the board—*not* to her. "My car was delayed."

He leaned over to kiss her. She turned her head away. "Don't be
silly! We *must* talk," he insisted in a whisper. "It's important."

"After the meeting."

"Before. You have to understand what's at stake. Besides, I know
everything. Vale and Daventry talked to me. . . ."

She ignored him, outraged at what she took to be another threat—and here of all places! Did he intend to tell the members of the board about her past, now that he knew "everything"? She saw Dominick Vale's smile—had Charles made a deal with him about her, too? "You'd better be seated," she told him coldly. "There's no point in making a scene in public."

Charles looked at her for a moment, then shrugged. He had his own concept of dignity, she knew that, and there was no possibility of his making a scene in front of the board. He shook his head and went over to sit down next to Vale, hardly even pretending to pay attention as the board dealt with another half dozen items of business.

Dawn paid no more attention herself, though she put on a pantomime of lively interest as each item was brought up and voted on. She had never taken much interest in the board, which for the most part had been handpicked by Kraus and Charles in happier days. Kraus, she knew, felt the board would vote down any proposal to sell part of the company's assets unless she herself voted in favor, but as she glanced at the vaguely familiar faces, she noticed that several of the members were looking toward Vale. Had he gotten to them? It was possible. She had learned enough about corporate politics to know that a large block of stock was no guarantee you would always get your way.

She had telephoned every member of the board except Vale, but those conversations, for which she had been briefed by Kraus, merely made her all the more uneasy. For the most part the members agreed with her, but it was apparent to her that they were afraid of Charles and of Vale—no doubt for different reasons—and hoped for an easy compromise. She was not about to offer one to them. In any case, it was too late, for Charles was already beginning to explain the ways in which the company would benefit from selling off the back lot and the library. He had done his homework well, she thought—or somebody with inside knowledge had done it for him.

She felt a moment's hesitation. Did it really matter whether or not Vale and his friends got the studio back lot and the library at bargain prices? A week ago, if she had been forced to choose between selling them off and her marriage to Charles, what would she have done? She knew the answer—she would have chosen Charles, if he had asked her, explained to her why it was necessary, come to her out of love. Instead, he had tried to force her hand, had gone behind her back to scum like Vale, threatened her personally.

She hated him for putting her in this position, and yet, at the same time, there was a part of her that *wanted* to give in to him. She fought the impulse down. She could *not* give in. She was determined to win. Perhaps afterward the marriage could be patched up—stranger things had happened, after all. If Charles accepted her as an equal, it was possible.

"It's a windfall," Charles said. He had regained some of his usual sang-froid. He leaned back, handsome, exuding confidence, relaxed. The pose would have fooled anyone but Dawn, who could read in his eyes what she took to be anger.

"For whom?" she asked.

Charles made an impatient gesture, dismissing the question. "The studio needs cash. The banks are playing a waiting game. You have only one major picture in the works—if it flops, the banks will pull the rug out from under you. It's time to buy a little breathing space. In the circumstances, it would be folly to hesitate."

Dawn looked around the table. There were several nods of agreement. After all, Charles was a banker himself, however unorthodox. And he had the gift of persuasion—his tone was reasonable, he let it be understood that his concern was genuine. Given enough time, he would have them eating out of his hand, she thought. Most of the directors still assumed she was only on the board as an accommodation to him, a kind of figurehead, good for public relations, but hardly a serious factor when it came to real business. They were men—they would listen to Charles and take it for granted that any disagreement between Charles and herself was emotional, a consequence of their much-publicized quarrel.

Charles sketched in the figures—he had a gift for numbers which she knew she couldn't match. This was *his* world, not hers—cash flow, return on investment, depreciation, price per share—she watched the faces of the men around the table and saw how these phrases comforted them. It was language they understood—or felt obliged to pretend they understood—a kind of secular religion, of which Charles was a priest. She had common sense on her side, but no command over the language of numbers and finances. If it came to an argument on that ground, she would lose. And Charles knew it.

He paused. "I hope I've made myself clear," he concluded. "Are there any questions?"

Dawn nodded. She waited until everyone at the table was looking at her—if nothing else, she knew how to attract attention. "Don't you think you should tell the board that Harry Faust is the one who's going to benefit from the deal?" she asked quietly.

There was a moment of silence. She saw Vale glance unpleasantly at Charles. No doubt Charles had been warned to keep Faust's name out of it—probably they had told him not to mention Faust even to *her*. It was clear from Vale's expression that he was angry at Charles. "What makes you think Faust is involved?" Vale asked, the quick, dark eyebrows lowered menacingly.

She laughed. "There are no secrets between a husband and wife, Mr. Vale," she said.

Charles turned pale. There was a look about him that she found hard to interpret—was it rage or fear? "A preposterous allegation," he said, but without his usual conviction. "I don't even know Mr. Faust."

She smiled at him bitter-sweetly. She had nothing to lose by striking back—and everything to gain. "Oh, darling, surely you do," she said. "You were talking to Dominick about him, months ago, just after the takeover. Dominick arranged a meeting between the two of you. Don't you remember?"

Vale dabbed at his forehead with a silk handkerchief. "Rubbish!" he said.

"Is it? Are you saying that you *don't* know this man Faust?"

"I didn't say that."

"I'm so glad. And is he behind the deal?"

Vale glared at her venomously. "It's a syndicate," he said. "Several people are involved. I don't know all of them—personally."

"And are all of them people who just *happen* to know Harry Faust?"

"Don't go too far, *Queenie*," Vale spat out. "You know what I can do!"

Dawn knew what he could do all right, but she also knew he was unlikely to do it here. In any case, her anger blotted out her fear, even of Vale. She looked around the table and sensed that she had won a temporary advantage. The name of Harry Faust was enough to chill the blood of most of the people around this table. Faust was trouble. People who did business with him had a way of being subpoenaed by the grand jury.

"May we put it to the vote?" Dawn asked briskly. She knew it was now or never.

Harry Warmfleisch—the only holdover from the Braverman board—seconded the motion, as she knew he would. He was anxious to get back to his golf game and could always be relied on to second anything that would shorten the meeting.

She watched as four hands rose for the "ayes." Vale and Charles, she expected. Obviously, they had gotten to two other directors.

Four hands rose against the proposal. Everyone looked at her for the deciding vote. She saw only Charles. She hesitated, waiting for him to say something, but he simply smiled at her.

Was he laughing at her? she wondered. But there was no humor in the smile that she could see. She put her hand up.

She turned to Kraus, who was trying to tell her something—that she had won, that he was happy for her, that everything would be all right. . . . Vale was glaring at her when she looked back at the table again, but Charles's seat was empty. He had left so quickly, so silently, that she had never even noticed his departure.

"Now you've done it, you bitch!" Dominick Vale said.

He was unreachable. Nobody in New York knew where he was. The servants in the house in Cuernavaca denied he was there. Had he gone back to Argentina? Kraus called the American ambassador, but there was no news of Corsini's presence. He had simply vanished.

"He's angry," Kraus said. "You can't blame him for that."

She didn't blame him for that. But she did at least want to speak to him.

"You pushed him too far," Lucien told her. "I rather liked the man myself."

She was irritated that Lucien quietly echoed her own misgivings. She *had* pushed Charles too far. As she replayed the scene in her mind over and over again, she had not given him a chance. She should have spoken to him before the meeting. Now he had vanished, leaving her to an empty victory.

All around her things were falling into place. Her role in the picture was completed—the rest consisted mostly of exteriors and long shots, which could be left to Lacey and Lucien. Already it was being talked about as a box-office winner, perhaps even a classic. Of course, every movie was touted this way by the studios, but in the case of *A Woman's Place*, she knew there was some substance to it.

Whatever it was going to do for her reputation, it had already made Lucien's. Overnight he was "hot." In this town, a man who knew how to photograph beautiful women—or better yet, *make* them beautiful—would never go hungry.

The studio she could leave to Kraus, now that the crisis had passed. *His* star was rising, too. He still avoided the grosser trappings of studio chiefdom, but he was beginning to be mentioned in the same breath with other, better-known studio heads. He had finally moved into Braverman's old office, with its spotlights and Oscars. He traveled in a studio limousine. He appeared at premieres with a starlet on his arm (never the same one twice, for he had a horror of gossip). There was even a dish named for him in the Empire commissary.

Dawn rose late, did nothing and found herself unable to think of anything but Charles.

"You never gave him a chance," Polly Hammer said. "You got so angry that you shut yourself off." Dawn had invited Polly over for a chat precisely to patch up things between them—for Polly was the wrong person to have as an enemy, and she knew it. Diamond had begged her to see Polly. Kraus had pleaded with her. In the end, Dawn gave in—Polly had merely been doing her job.

"He hit me. And he threatened me."

"Okay, he hit you. That happens, honey. Are you sure he *was* threatening you? It didn't sound that way to me when I talked to him."

"When was that?" Dawn asked, surprised to learn that Charles had talked to Polly.

"Right after you left my house. He asked me to meet him in a parked car, near the Brown Derby."

"What on earth did he want?"

"He wanted me to get you to call him. And he gave me a story—the one about Norman Patson and Mrs. Daventry."

"*Charles* gave you that?"

"That's right. He seemed to think you'd be pleased."

"He must have known what would happen to her once the story was out."

"Sure he did. He knew damn well she'd be run out of town by Billie Patson. What had you got against her, honey?"

"It's an old story, Polly. I'd rather not discuss it."

"The man is crazy about you, you know. I could tell. He'd do anything for you. Now he's vanished. I went to see Madame Vera, you know. I figured the tarot cards would tell me where he went."

"And did they?"

"No. It's funny. She's gone. The place is boarded up—no forwarding address. One of the neighbors told me she'd come into a fortune. It's hard to imagine she had any relatives with a fortune to leave her, isn't it?"

Dawn was silent. If Charles had dealt with Mrs. Daventry, had he also taken care of Magda—bought her off? For a moment it occurred to her that perhaps he hadn't been threatening her at all.

But how had he discovered Magda in the first place? Then she realized that if Charles indeed had an inside informant at the studio, he would have no difficulty in learning anything he wanted to know. Somebody had told him about the money she had spent on Lucien. Somebody had filled him in on details of the studio's financial position, information that only Kraus was supposed to know. Somebody could very easily have gone through her files, or made a photocopy of her checkbook, which was handled by one of the girls in Danny Zegrin's office. . . .

She made a note to talk to Kraus about Zegrin at the earliest opportunity. Then it occurred to her that if Zegrin was the man—and she was quite sure he was—there might be a way to use him.

Zegrin's eyes rolled. He was sweating, even in the cool of Dawn's living room. With his dark suit, his somber tie and his slicked-back black hair, he looked like an undertaker who has lost a body. He seemed about to cry.

"I know what you've been doing," Dawn said.

He swallowed. His Adam's apple bobbed up and down. "I don't know what you're talking about, Princess."

"I think you do. I haven't talked to Kraus yet. He'll be angry."

"I'm an innocent man."

"I doubt that, Danny. There are very few of them about, and I don't think you're one."

"You haven't got a thing against me."

"Maybe. Maybe not. Does it matter? All I have to do is talk to Kraus and he'll fire you on the spot. I think he can make sure you never got a job in this town again, too. I won't even need to suggest it to him— you know how he is about things like this. He *trusted* you, Danny."

Zegrin nodded miserably. He knew she was right. Kraus was implacable. There would be no appeal, no mercy. He would have to go back to New York and start all over again in the mailroom of a talent agency, with kids who were five years younger than he was—and even there, Kraus would pursue him. "What do you want me to do?" he asked.

The whine in his voice irritated her, but she concealed it. The industry was full of people like Zegrin, many of them now running studios. "You were sending information on to my husband, weren't you?"

He nodded.

"From the beginning?"

"Well, yes. . . . At first, he just wanted me to keep an eye on Kraus. I wasn't spying on you."

"Did my husband *ask* you to spy on me?"

"No. At first I just passed on things that I thought would interest him. He didn't tell me to stop."

"Are you still in touch with him?"

"Not exactly. I have an address in New York where I can send him things. And a telephone number. I leave a message. He calls back, sooner or later."

"Write them down for me, Danny." She passed him a pad of paper and a pencil. "Have you heard from him lately? In the past week or two, since the board meeting?"

"A couple of times, sure."

"What about?"

"Small stuff, frankly. He had me make a copy of your checkbook. He was afraid you were being blackmailed, so he wanted to see if there were any large checks, or unusual cash withdrawals. He was very interested in that. He had a detective watching some fortuneteller on West Pico, I overheard that."

"Did you go and see her?"

"No. *He* did. He played that one very close to the chest. He came into town to deal with her himself. I went to see him, in an apartment off Sunset. Kind of a dingy hole-in-the-wall, not the sort of place where you'd expect to find a guy like Corsini."

"How was he?"

"Nervous as hell. He had his valet with him. They were both wearing guns. So was the chauffeur."

"What did he say?"

"Not much. I gave him some papers. 'Thanks,' he said. 'If you know what's good for you, you never saw me.' He took a telephone call from England too, while I was there. I remember *that* because it was from some guy named Goldner—a knight, or a lord, or something. . . ."

"Sir Solomon Goldner?"

"That's it. Corsini was talking to him about some real estate he was buying in London. A block of flats—that's what they call apartments over there, I found out."

"In Shepherd's Market?"

"Right. He was in a big hurry. He told Goldner not to bargain. 'Pay the price,' he said. 'I don't care what it costs.' "

Was Charles covering up every problem of her past? First, Mrs.

Daventry—exiled with a scandal leaked to Polly Hammer. Then Magda, bought off, presumably, or threatened off. Now he was acquiring the house in which Morgan had died.

What did he intend to do with it, she wondered? Tear it down? If the place where Morgan was buried ceased to exist, it would be impossible for anyone ever to prove that the crime had taken place. A clean slate—was that what Charles was offering her?

"What's he hiding *from*, Danny?" she asked.

He stared at her in amazement. "You mean you don't know *that?*" He dabbed at his forehead a couple of times with his damp handkerchief, but the sweat continued to pour down his face. "He didn't deliver, Princess! Harry Faust put out a contract on him the same day."

"A contract?"

"The rumor is it's fifty grand. That's big money. Five is average for a hit."

"A hit?"

"Murder," Zegrin said, with a hint of satisfaction in his voice. "Anybody who kills Charles Corsini collects fifty thousand dollars. When you voted against him, you signed his goddamned death warrant!"

"I can try, kiddo—that's all I can say."

"Can't he be bought off?"

Diamond glanced at his desk-top, a piece of gleaming, gold-tooled leather, devoid, as usual, of papers. "Buy off Faust? Jesus, I don't know . . . I doubt it. Faust's a fucking maniac."

"What if we bought out the contract?"

"This isn't the movie business. It's not that kind of contract."

"Not even if we gave him what he wanted?"

Diamond whistled tunelessly. "Maybe. Maybe not. You'd really do that?"

"Yes."

"How are you going to get it past the board?"

"I'll manage somehow. Make the offer."

"Faust might up the ante. Now that he has you by the—well, you know what I mean."

"I know what you mean. Find out."

Diamond took a small key from his pocket and opened the top drawer of his desk. He put on his reading glasses and leafed through the pages of a small leather-bound notebook. "It's not the kind of number you want to leave lying around," he explained. "Faust doesn't like people to write it down, but I can't remember my own goddamned number, never mind *his*." He dialed. "Aaron Diamond!" he shouted into the receiver. "Of course he knows who the hell I am. Everybody knows who I am, chrissake! Oh . . . Yeah? . . . Shit! . . . Okay."

He hung up. He took his glasses off and wiped them. He examined them closely and wiped them again. He did not look at Dawn. "Harry's in the hospital," he said quietly.

"In the hospital?"

"Cedars of Lebanon. A coronary." He undulated his hand. "They give him a fifty-fifty chance, the bastard."

"Isn't there anyone else you can call? Doesn't he have associates? Assistants?"

"He doesn't run a studio, Dawn, chrissake. He's a gangster. Harry's business is strictly personal. He's the only one who can give orders—or cancel one. I could call some people I know in Chicago, but my guess is that they won't do anything so long as Harry is still breathing. Where *is* Charles?"

"I don't know for sure. Probably in New York, but I'm just guessing."

"That's no good. Tell him to get out of the country."

"I left a message for him. Zegrin gave me a number."

"Leave another. I need a few days to talk to people, see if I can straighten things out. Maybe he should go down to Mexico. He's got clout there, people who'll protect him. . . . Go with him."

"Go with him?"

"You love the guy, don't you? So go with him." Diamond avoided Dawn's eyes. "So long as you're around, he's probably safe. They don't kill wives, honey. You're the best insurance policy he can get, the next few days."

She was frantic. The people who took the messages drove her mad. They were calm, cautious, they could only promise to "try" to reach Charles. She guessed that he was trying to work things out in his own way with Faust's colleagues, that he had decided the only way to survive was to hide. She prayed for Faust's death, for if he died, his people might be willing to "reconsider" the contract, for a price—while, as long as he was alive, however feebly, they were obliged to follow his instructions. But Faust did not die. He hung on, day after day, in the intensive care unit, his bodyguards outside the door, just in case somebody tried to give nature a helping hand.

She even tried to reach Dominick Vale, in the faint hope that he could somehow be turned around, but he too had vanished. "He didn't deliver for Faust, either," Diamond said. "He's probably lying low. Or dead."

Daily she followed her routine, as it was the only way to keep her sanity. She breakfasted on the terrace, throwing the crumbs from her plate to the birds, drove to the studio for fittings, meetings, story conferences, dubbing, retakes—the things she had done all her adult life, which now had the advantage of keeping her busy, taking her mind off Charles.

She dined off a tray at home, waiting for the telephone to ring, afraid that it would, with bad news, or that it wouldn't, because Charles hadn't forgiven her.

She understood why people took to drink—she was almost tempted herself. The evenings were unbearable, and yet she felt no desire to go out or to break the tension. Her anxiety was like a thread that bound her to Charles. At night, for the first time in her life, she took sleeping pills, but even they did not help much.

On the fourth day of her self-imposed vigil, Kraus appeared in her dressing room, carrying a bulky package. It did not stir her curiosity or interest. Fans sent her things all the time, and the studio mailroom had strict orders to make sure these presents were acknowledged and never reached her, for they sometimes contained hidden dangers, fishhooks in fruit cakes, caustic soda in pies, bottles of perfume filled with lye.

"Whatever it is," she said, "I don't want it."

"It's harmless. A painting."

"A painting?" Dawn cut the wrapping paper with a pair of nail scissors. She looked inside. Then she tore the paper off, her heart beating faster. It was the Van Gogh that she had sold after David Konig's death, the one he had given her as a wedding present.

She put it on her dressing table and stared at it for a moment. She did not need to wonder where it had come from. Charles had bought it back as a peace offering. Taped to the frame was a plain envelope.

She opened it. There was a thick document bearing the stamps and seals that the English put on everything official. She looked at the front, where a careful calligrapher had inscribed the sale to Princess Dawn Avalon Corsini of a block of flats in Shepherd's Market.

There was also a note, in Charles's handwriting—a hasty, spiky, scrawl that she found difficult to decipher, since he had so seldom had occasion to write to her.

And for the first time since she had met Kraus, she threw her arms around him, tears running down her cheeks. "He's landing in Palm Springs tomorrow," she said. "He wants me to bring Aaron along so he can talk to him. Then we'll fly from there to Mexico."

Kraus straightened his tie. He was blushing. "I'm delighted," he said. "For your sake. If we have to sell off the back lot and the library while you're away—shall I do it?"

Dawn wiped her cheeks. She would have to get the makeup man back to do her face again. What would he think? She didn't care. "Sell anything you have to," she told Kraus. "Do whatever Aaron says we have to do."

She had been given a second chance. That was all that mattered now.

"How does he get a private plane in the middle of a goddamned war?" Aaron Diamond asked.

Dawn stared into the blazing sky and put on her sunglasses. "It's typical of Charles. He always gets what he wants."

"I hate goddamned private planes, you want to know the truth. I don't even like flying commercial. I won't put *my* life in the hands of some yo-yo who makes ten, fifteen grand a year, know what I mean?"

"That isn't a problem for Charles. He flies himself."

"I wouldn't like that either, frankly. He's got too much on his mind—you, his banks, money. . . . I fly, I want the pilot to be thinking about *me*."

"Oh, for God's sake, Aaron, stop worrying. He was setting speed records in his own plane when he was twenty."

"I guess you're right. I hear his plane. Unless the Japs have decided to bomb Palm Springs."

Diamond was wearing his golf clothes—a tam o'shanter, white trousers and a Hawaiian shirt—and resented every moment away from the golf links. It was only because of his affection for Dawn that he had agreed to inconvenience himself on Charles's behalf. "He'd better land soon," he said. "I've got Bing Crosby waiting for me."

The Palm Beach airport was hardly more than a shack, a sweltering hotbox set in the middle of the desert. Diamond's dark-green Packard convertible shimmered and occasionally disappeared in the heat, like an expensive mirage. By now, Dawn guessed, the seats would be hot enough to give second-degree burns. Diamond always covered his own seat with a towel when he parked the car, but his passengers were left to squirm against the broiling leather. She would have to warn Charles, she told herself, staring into the sky for the sight of his Beechcraft.

Charles's plane appeared in the distance, a dark speck against the white sky. Its shadow crossed the sands, then it was suddenly at the end of the runway, its wheels touching the concrete. Charles flew the way he did everything else, she thought—with elegance, style and more dash than was good for him.

Dawn opened the screen door and ran out to meet him as the aircraft taxied down the runway. Now that it was on the ground, it glittered like molten silver, the sun reflecting off the polished surfaces of the twin tails. She could see Charles in the pilot's seat, grinning at his perfect landing, or perhaps at her. He was in shirtsleeves and wearing aviator's sunglasses. She waved at him, her long chiffon head scarf flashing in the air like a pink flag.

He pushed back the Perspex window on his side, and blew her a kiss. Then he simply vanished, as if by some terrible act of magic. The entire aircraft was engulfed in a ball of glowing fire, white at first, for a fraction of a second, then pink—the colors, Dawn thought to herself, with hideous irrelevance, of her own bathroom.

There was a noise like thunder, only louder and sharper. A searing wind knocked her flat, and she could hear pieces of the airplane whistling past her. Above the roar of the flames and the howl of a siren somewhere in the distance, she could hear someone screaming.

It was only later, when she woke up on a battered, smelly sofa in the waiting room, and saw Aaron Diamond looking down at her, that Dawn realized it was she who had been screaming. She did not ask what had happened, or how Charles was. She already knew. She had known he was dead when the bomb went off in front of her, and she could see the truth on Diamond's face.

She stood up unsteadily and looked out the window. Where Charles's airplane had been, there was only a blackened circle on the white concrete, with a few burnt fragments of aluminum, like the charred bones of the corpses on the burning ghats in Calcutta.

She wanted to cry, but for some reason, tears wouldn't come. Perhaps in the heat, they simply evaporated—invisible tears, as it were.

"The place is surrounded by reporters," Diamond said. "We'll have to get you out past them somehow. Maybe if we put you on a stretcher . . ."

But Dawn shook her head. She would face the world on her own terms. Calmly she examined her face in a mirror. "My pocketbook," she said. She repaired her makeup with quick, economical gestures, like a woman telling her beads, for this too was a form of worship. She snapped her compact shut and put the cap back on her lipstick with a loud click.

"I'm ready now," she whispered. She looked for her dark glasses, but realized they had probably been shattered by her fall. Never mind. She would face the world with her eyes open.

In the years to come, people would say she had been heartless, cold, unmoved, more concerned with the way she looked in the photographs than with the tragedy of Charles's death.

Only Dawn knew the truth. At twenty-five she had lived through as much as most people put into a long lifetime. Just as happiness had been within her reach, she had allowed the past, which had always haunted her, to catch up with her. Even as Charles worked to erase, it had still held her in its grip, formed her actions, influenced her feelings and her decisions. It was her weakness. Guilt and fear were the price she paid to become what she was—rich, famous, a star.

Dawn had always relied on her beauty. Now it was all she had left.

She looked straight ahead as she walked, on Aaron Diamond's arm, into the blaze of flashbulbs.

Part Six

THE
MONA
LISA
SMILE

CHAPTER 25

SHE WAS FABULOUSLY RICH—that much was known. The rest was rumor.

Dawn Avalon's fame increased in direct proportion to her absence from the limelight. She acquired a worldwide reputation as a recluse—wealthy, elegant, beautiful, but apparently determined to avoid the public.

It was "rumored" that she had undergone cosmetic surgery on every part of her body, that she ate only health food, that she spent part of every year in spiritual retreat. There were also rumors that she had many love affairs, but if that was so, her lovers were discreet.

Of her husbands, it was said that even the gossip columnists lost count. Her third marriage, to a wealthy Mexican industrialist in the early 1950s, was so sudden and secret that it caught the press by surprise, and it ended as suddenly and mysteriously a year later. Friends said that he had reminded her of Charles Corsini, and that they had parted "amicably." Two years later, she married Count Philip von Krosig, a wealthy German banker with ties to South America. Krosig was a handsome widower, silver-haired and courtly. There were those who thought Corsini would have resembled him had he lived to be sixty. That marriage, too, "failed" after less than a year.

Dawn Avalon moved among the rich and famous, who respected her privacy, and she avoided the show business world. She gave marvelous parties at her house in Bel Air, at the beach house in the Malibu colony and in Mexico. The house she built in Cuernavaca was said to be a fairy-tale palace, but it was set behind walls so high that it had never been photographed.

It was rumored that she had paid the architect one hundred thousand dollars *not* to include it in a photographic book about his work, and also that he had been one of her lovers. People who visited it merely said it was as beautiful as its owner. When Prince Philip visited Mexico, he stayed with her. So did the Shah, the Aga Khan and the King of Belgium, for she was widely regarded as the doyenne of the Cuernavaca foreign colony, as well as the most famous of Dr. Echeverría's many rich and social devotees.

It was "rumored," again, that Dawn was the power behind the throne at Empire Pictures, but she had never been known to attend a board meeting. It was public knowledge that she controlled all of Charles Corsini's vast assets—enough to make her one of the wealthiest women in the world. Those in the know maintained that E. P. Kraus never made a major movie without consulting her—and it was possible. Certainly *somebody* was doing something right. Empire was the only major studio that had held on to its own film library and reaped a fortune in television rentals as a result, so that by the 1960s it had become an entertainment conglomerate, with its own television stations, amusement parks and hotels. Empire even owned a publishing house, purchased at a bargain basement price from the heirs of Emmett Lincoln Starr, for Kraus believed in what he liked to describe to the press as "synergetic communications," on the rare occasions when he could be persuaded to take a reporter from *Fortune* or *The Wall Street Journal* with him on his private jet from coast to coast.

Only he and Lord Goldner, the British entertainment peer who had merged his companies with Empire, knew the truth about Dawn Avalon's involvement in the corporation's affairs, and neither of them ever revealed it. Certainly Lord Goldner was close to her. He visited Cuernavaca often, and was reputed to be her partner in building a block of modern luxury apartments and offices in Shepherd's Market, on the site of some old tenements.

Invisible as she was behind the scenes, she had always been publicly firm about her refusal to act in another film. So the world was astonished when, in 1975, she agreed to a comeback, starring in a picture in which she played a thirty-year-old woman. Her leading man, an unknown, was only twenty, and breathtakingly handsome, and even the genius of Lucien Chambrun failed to conceal the disparity in age between Dawn Avalon and Timmy Tyrone. Still, she was so beautiful that one critic called her "the last star, a reminder of a forgotten age of elegance and beauty." As for Tyrone, there were people who said he bore an astonishing resemblance to the young Charles Corsini. Her marriage to him brought him far more fame than the film, but if he was disappointed, he never showed it.

She never made another film after that. Nor did Tyrone, whom, some people thought, she treated like a servant. But those who were invited to Dawn's house (it was never referred to as "Tyrone's") said they were a devoted couple, even though her manner toward Timmy was perhaps a little imperious at times.

Indeed, she *was* regal, everybody agreed. She sat quietly, seldom moving, bathed in the soft lighting that Billy Sofkin had placed so that she would always look her best. She had the smile of the Mona Lisa, at once mysterious and provocative, though it was widely rumored that facial surgery had made it permanent. "She probably smiles like the Mona Lisa even when she's asleep," Sofkin said in a whisper after one of her dinner parties.

Dawn Avalon's past remained as mysterious as her present. She turned down an invitation from the Indian government to open the Indian Film Institute, despite the fact that she was known to have grown up there, the daughter of an English officer serving in a maharajah's court. The American ambassador to India was obliged to express his government's deep regrets that she was unable to attend for reasons of health.

Even in her homes there were few hints of her past—none of the ordinary souvenirs and keepsakes that filled the houses of most stars. Among the few were a small Van Gogh that accompanied her everywhere, a wedding present from Sir David Konig, her first husband and "discoverer." Below it, on the mantelpiece, was always a photograph in a silver frame of a handsome, though swarthy-looking, young man, in old-fashioned evening clothes, sporting a gallant mustache that failed to conceal a certain weakness in his mouth. Some people who looked at the photograph noticed that the young man's face, particularly the eyes, looked rather like Dawn's, but of course nobody invited to her house was ever tactless enough to ask who he was.

What, after all, did Dawn Avalon's past matter? She was, finally, her own work of art, who, as the years went by, came to seem timeless, beyond change. It was impossible to believe she was sixty or more; impossible to imagine that she would ever age or die.

She was the inspiration, the moving force, behind the Corsini Foundation—and yet the only picture in the museum which truly seemed to interest her was an undistinguished oil portrait of Corsini himself, which greeted the visitor at the head of the broad marble stairs. Framed in gold, Corsini's likeness had been done from photographs. From certain angles his expression was sardonic; from others it was possible to distinguish a ghostly smile. In the blue-gray eyes the painter had succeeded in capturing life of a kind—Corsini seemed amused.

There were fresh flowers on either side of the painting every day.

When she was awarded a special Oscar for a lifetime of achievement in film, she appeared to accept it in a clinging dress by Armand Silk of shimmering pink and silver beads, with a high neck and long sleeves (she was too clever to allow her arms or neck to be compared to those of women who were forty years younger). She wore a magnificent diamond tiara and a necklace of diamonds and emeralds.

She was so beautiful that the audience in the Chandler Pavilion fell into a hushed silence before bursting into applause, and those who were sitting in the front rows could see her eyes welling with tears—but she did not stay to be interviewed by the press, nor to attend any of the parties that followed the award, not even E. P. Kraus's, which was the party of the evening.

Nobody could know how much the effort had cost Dawn, nor how much pain she was in. She faltered for only one moment, and that was at the very end, when she was getting back into her limousine, moving slowly and with great effort, as if each step was an agony. A pretty young woman broke through the police lines and ran up to the long white car, holding out an autograph book and a pen, pushing past the security guards and studio executives until she was face to face with Dawn.

"Miss Avalon," she shouted, holding the autograph book out. "I wish I were as beautiful as you are."

But for once Dawn Avalon did not smile. She slumped back in the limousine and closed her eyes, ignoring the book. She looked frail and exhausted, as if the sheer willpower by which she remained beautiful had failed her at last.

She was never seen in public again.